sins & secrets

WILLOW WINTERS

you are
my reason

From *USA Today* best-selling author Willow Winters comes an intense
romance with second chances, secrets and a twist.

It's been a long time since I've looked at a man and wanted something more.

Even longer since one has looked at me with a gaze I couldn't tear my eyes from.

No one's perfect, but that's how he felt when I was in his arms.

I started to think everything was going to be all right. That life had finally put
the pieces of my broken heart back together.

Fate brought us close.

It's a pretty little thought my poetic mind had.

But there's no doubt that the sins of his past will tear us apart.

You Are My Reason is book 1 in the You Are Mine duet
and should be read first.

"Love is more than words; my heart can tell you that."

—DLS

To Donna, always an inspiration.

chapter 1

Mason

"YOU SHOULD BE THANKING ME FOR CLEANING UP YOUR MESS," MY father says snidely from where he's seated in his high-back desk chair. His fingers grip the leather arms and his thumbs rub gently back and forth across the brass studs.

Though the blinds are closed, the tall windows behind my father fill the large office with fading light from the evening sunset.

Looking over my shoulder, I narrow my gaze at him, still holding a random law textbook I've taken from the floor-to-ceiling shelves that line the walls of his office. The room smells like old books. With the dark wood, tan leather and deep red Beaumont rug, the decor reeks of old money and that's exactly what this room represents.

That and bullshit.

Lies and corruption are what have kept this room in its current state for generations. I've pretended for so long that it wasn't true. But now that I've learned what my father's done to get this "esteemed" position … I can't turn a blind eye to it anymore. His actions are undeniable and unforgivable.

I huff a small laugh, not letting him see how affected I am. "For the last time," I say as I shut the book and smirk at him, "it wasn't my mess."

I'm not admitting to a damn thing. Not even to my own father. In this city, one slipup could send you tumbling into an early grave like my mother. I'm not responsible for the mess my father's referring to and I refuse to take the blame.

I don't trust him. I don't trust anyone any longer.

My father's face reddens before he picks up a cup of hot coffee. He holds the black mug with both hands, blowing across the top and refusing to back down.

"You would have gone through hell—"

"No, I wouldn't have," I say, cutting him off, although my voice doesn't reflect any emotion whatsoever. This is a turning point in our relationship. Instead of his disappointment creeping under my skin, it's the other way around. I look him in the eye as I add, "I would have been just fine."

A moment passes where the only sound is the ticking of the large clock on the right side of the room. "It wasn't my mess you cleaned up, and we both know it." He's the first to look away but instead of showing remorse, his expression only reflects his anger.

"Did you need anything else?" I ask. I just want to get the hell out of here and back to the construction site. This office reminds me of my grandfather, a man I loved and trusted. But he was a man who turned out to be just like all the other powerful men in this city. Ruled by corruption, driven by greed, imperfect. *Devastated* is the word a former therapist would use to describe my reaction when I found out the truth about my family.

"I'm tired of you getting into trouble," my father says and I scoff. This is the first time in my life I've truly been in control of myself. No more fucking around, starting trouble. These recent events have been sobering. When I was a hormone-filled teenager dealing with grief and anger, it was easy to act out and pick fights. Caused first by the death of my grandfather and then later, my mother.

At thirty-three and on my own, I'm not like that anymore. I finally have my life together … all but the ties to my father. It's a tangled mess of lies and offshore bank accounts. Much like the dealings of the elite who rule this city.

The thought makes my gaze fall to the floor before I look back up to the shelves and mindlessly scan the spines of the antique texts.

Being aware of what my father did makes all those old memories of losing my mother surface. My stomach churns and my blood heats, the adrenaline coursing in my veins pushing me to confront the man I no longer know.

I bring a clenched fist to my mouth as I clear my throat and take a few steps toward him. He's the one who called this meeting, demanded it really. But he hasn't even risen from his chair. Lazy prick.

"I don't know what you're talking about," I answer him easily. "I haven't got a single problem on my mind." I give him a polite smile and keep a charming look on my face. It only makes him angrier and I love every second of his pissed-off expression. He thought I'd feel as if I owed him.

I don't owe him a damn thing.

I may be just like him in looks. Tall, dark and handsome, or so I've been told. I've perfected a brilliant smile with an air of ease that's made to fool and seduce the world at large. It makes sense that he's a lawyer. It's the family business but if it wasn't, it'd still be the profession most apt for my father.

"You need to quit this charade and do what you're told, Mason." He stands from his seat quickly, his chair rolling backward until it hits the wall. It disturbs the blinds and streams of dim light flicker into the room.

"I don't need to do anything but breathe and pay taxes."

He could order me around like that all he wanted back when I was a child or before I knew the truth, but now I have no respect for the man in front of me. I'm disgusted by him and caught on the edge of what's right and wrong. I should turn him in to the authorities and let him rot. I grit my teeth as I stare back at him. It's what's right, but I can't bring myself to send my own father to prison.

A low hum of admonishment deep in his throat makes the smirk on my face widen into a smile.

"I have my own company, my own life—" I start but my father cuts me off. Nothing new there.

"You were born a Thatcher, and you'll die a Thatcher." The words leave a chill across my skin. That's the crux of the problem. I was born into this life and I can't run from it. Plus my company is in debt to him. It was a rookie mistake I made back before I knew what I was doing. When I didn't see him for the man he really is.

"Why do you even care what I do?" I finally ask him. His precious reputation is just fine now that I'm an adult and I've moved on from the fuckup I used to be. "I'm not the one coming to you—"

"*She* did," he answers simply with a spark in his eyes and the corners of his lips upturned as if that's all the ammunition he needs. In some respects, he's right. All the people in this city know where I come from and what it means to be a Thatcher. They know I have money and power behind me. That's all anyone here cares about anyway. New York is all about the bottom dollar.

Nonchalantly shrugging my shoulders, I stride closer to the desk, bracing myself by gripping the back of the chair opposite him. "You decided how to deal with her without vetting what she said." I meet his glare easily, willing him to tell me again how he *saved* me. "She didn't have anything on me. She couldn't have done anything." My voice rises toward the end of my statement and I hate that I've shown him this weak side of me. Even if only for a moment.

Control. I thrive with control.

A heavy breath leaves him as he stares back with pure hate but he doesn't say a word. I knew he wouldn't. He's wrong. Dead wrong and ruined if I open my mouth to anyone. He took the initiative so I'd owe him, but in reality we both know that he owes me now.

"It's your fuckup, not mine." I practically spit out the words and shove the chair forward as I turn to leave him. My body's tense and the anger continues to rise. I try not to let it show. I hate that I can't control myself around this prick. Everyone else I can handle, but my own father, not so much.

"Mason!" he calls after me. His voice turns to white noise as the blood rushing in my ears gets louder and louder, drowning out all the bullshit.

The second I open his office door, he goes silent. He'll never let anyone hear us fighting. *Never.* Secrets are always kept behind closed doors. It's a family rule.

The door shuts with a loud *thunk* and as I walk down the empty hall, the thin carpeting muffles the sound of my black leather oxfords smacking against the ground at an incessant pace.

Miss Geist looks up from her spot at her desk. The wrinkles around her eyes deepen as she tilts her head and gives me that familiar smile she always has for me. It's one that says: *Oh, what have you done now?*

Through the years, even after my mother's death, Miss Theresa Geist has given me that look. She's the only one who showed me any genuine regret and kindness when I had to deal with my mother's passing. She's a good person. I have no idea what she's doing here working for a man like my father.

She clutches the small pendant on her thin silver necklace and her forbearing smile changes to something more reserved when I look back at her. It's instantaneous and makes me halt in my steps. I know I must look pissed; I'm beyond furious. It's been two days since my father told me what he'd done all those months ago and my anger hasn't waned one bit. Deep down I think I knew what he'd done back then, even if he never admitted it until now. I wish he hadn't. The whole situation makes me sick.

"He's being a dick," I mutter, waiting for the old lady to be a little more at ease. She doesn't know a thing that goes on outside of the office and I don't owe her an explanation, but I can't help myself.

"Now, now," she says with a bit of playfulness although I can tell she's still shaken. She's not used to seeing me like this. Not in the last decade, at least.

I give her a gentle smile and wink, putting on the act I use so well. Maybe I have a soft spot for her.

"Have a good night, Mr. Thatcher," she tells me as she shuffles the papers on her desk, seeming somewhat less disturbed.

It's enough that it settles me and I push open the double doors leading to the entrance with both hands and keep moving. The sound of my shoes pacing on the granite and the open air of the lobby filled with chatter soothe me.

But only for a moment.

It's not until I leave the building that my true feelings surface. The mask fades, and fear sets in. I didn't know what my father was capable of.

I had an inkling, but I thought I'd always imagined it. I'd thought my memories weren't quite right. It's not that I expected more from him; I just hate that I was right.

What's done is done and I can't stop what's been set in motion.

chapter 2

BLOODRED LIPS. THE SILVER TUBE IN MY HAND IS LABELED BLACK Honey, my favorite color. I've worn it since my freshman year of college and although I've experimented with other colors at times, it's always been a staple in my beauty bag. Pressing my lips together, I smack them once as I examine myself in the mirror.

My complexion is flawless thanks to the full-coverage foundation I'm wearing. My lashes are thick and long, and I've got just a hint of blush. It's a timeless look, classic and clean. And it hides everything. My reddened skin and the dark circles under my eyes are nowhere to be found.

I don't look like the person I've become. This woman in the reflection, she's who I used to be. A very large part of me wants *this* woman back. I want to smile like I used to and hear the sound of a genuine laugh from my own lips.

My heart pangs and stops that thought in its place.

He'll never laugh again. It's as if any small moment of time that passes where he's forgotten for even a second is a disgrace. My eyes fall and I slip the cap back on the tube of lipstick, tossing it into the pouch on my vanity.

No matter what I do, every little thing reminds me of him.

Trivial things, like the color of the granite he insisted we purchase when we remodeled this place together. The knobs on the bathroom drawers he hated and never failed to complain about. The change he left in the cup holder in the Bentley. The pile of dimes and pennies that clink together when I drive over speed bumps or a pothole. The same small coins I refuse to touch. He put them there, and I can't bring myself to move them.

Freaking pieces of metal render me useless.

It may seem pathetic, but not to me. From my perspective, I'm being as strong as I can. I face the New York City judgment every day, putting on a brave face and going about my life, my new normal.

All the while I shove everything I'm feeling deep down inside. That's healthy, right?

I won't let them see me crumble. There are those who want to. I could practically hear them licking their lips months ago when my world fell apart.

Julia Summers, born into wealth and raised on the Upper East Side. She always did everything by the book and married young to her high school sweetheart, Jace Anderson. With a loving family, a handsome and doting husband and the social life every young woman in Manhattan dreams of, Jules had a picture-perfect life. Until her husband suddenly passed away at the age of twenty-eight, leaving the twenty-seven-year-old woman widowed and alone for the first time in her life.

Twenty-eight now and numerous months since the tragic accident.

They're waiting to see what I'll do next. Pens to the papers and cameras ready. There's nothing better for the gossipmongers. It's to be expected. Being in Page Six is how I've made my life.

They'd love to see me fall and I have, but not in front of their eyes. I'll keep my hair pinned up and my concealer on thick.

I know what they say, though. This town whispers, especially in the circles I run in. They don't need to see the truth to figure it out themselves. There are rumors of leaning too heavily on alcohol for comfort. I don't command enough loyalty for discretion; every member of my household staff has sold out to the tabloids looking for a hint of what goes on behind these walls. Living on the Upper East Side, every single person who struts in front of my home is looking for a crack in my veneer.

What's ironic is that there's no glamour here, nothing noteworthy. Just a woman who cries herself to sleep at least once a week still. A woman who's struggling to move on because she's never been with anyone else. I suppose it's what I get, though. I loved posing for the cameras and practically lived for regular mentions in the gossip columns. This is what I deserve. They wanted in my life and I let them. I can't expect them to be shut out now.

Days have turned to weeks and weeks to months. Now that my husband's been gone for nearly eight months, I have plenty of cracks in this so-called perfect life. I'm still shattered but I'm working on gluing little pieces back into place.

I glance at myself as I tug down my dress just slightly and smooth out the black lace. *It's time to face the music.*

I clear my throat as I turn off the light and grab my phone, checking the text again.

Are you sure you don't need me to pick you up?

Kat's a sweetheart. She's always looking out for me. Of all my friends, she's the one who still texts me religiously, which is insane because she's constantly working and I have no idea how she finds the time.

My fingers *tap, tap, tap* away an answer. *I've got it. Leaving now.*

The Penrose is only twenty minutes away if there's no traffic. Seeing how it's 9:00 p.m. on a Friday night, I'm prepared to sit in the back of a taxi for half the night.

A light sigh slips past my lips as I bend down to pick up my favorite Louboutins. With a row of spikes up the back and red-lacquered soles, they have exactly the touch of color and attitude I would've worn back then. I almost second-guess the simple black dress I've picked out. It's a nod to Audrey Hepburn. But looking over my shoulder at the darkened bathroom mirror, all I see is one of the options I had for Jace's funeral.

I would've worn this dress last year before it all happened. Back when I was happy and everything was how it was supposed to be. And don't I want to be that girl again? I want to find a way to move forward on a new path.

Holding the heels in one hand and the iron banister in the other, I descend the winding staircase.

I'm not that woman any longer; I've changed. I accept that, but I don't love who I am now. The crying and feeling sorry for myself. I need something. A change and some light in all the darkness. Eight months of a pity party and being stuck in a rut is long enough. I'd like to say that Jace wouldn't want to see me like this, but I don't even know what Jace would want for me. I've quit wearing my wedding ring, although it still sits on my nightstand. I'm ready to find out who I am without him beside me.

Before I open the front door, I glimpse out the large stained glass window in the foyer. It's nothing but gray outside, and the hustle and bustle is only a fraction of what it could be.

Heavy rain greets me when I step onto my small porch. I decided not to bother with an umbrella, simply grabbing a stylish trench coat on my way outside. Quickly taking the steps to the street out front, I hail a cab. My heels click as I wrap the belt around me and tie my coat tight when the first taxi comes to a slow stop in front of me.

I could have called for someone to do this, to order me a cab so it would be waiting. I could ask for help with so many things. I'd rather do it myself, though.

The light breeze and rain feel real. The rain is cold to the touch and I'm sure I'll be regretting my decision soon. But it's something different. I don't want anyone's help. I just need time.

Climbing into the taxi, I shake off the gathered rain from my jacket; the inside of the cab is warm and welcoming. I push the hair out of my face and say, "Penrose, please."

"You got it," the cabby says as he glances over his shoulder to look at me. His thinning black hair is oiled over and he's more than a little overweight. The buttons on his striped shirt are straining to keep it shut.

I can see curiosity in his eyes but just as he opens his mouth to ask something, I don't know what, I turn to look out the closed window and thank him.

Everything outside is wet and dreary. The people walking by move quickly and a couple only about ten feet away are fighting over an umbrella. It's a cute little struggle though and the tall man in a navy blue Henley lets the woman win. She's dressed in formal work clothes, while he's in casual attire. But as soon as she takes full control of the umbrella, she walks closer to him and he wraps his arm around her waist.

I rip my eyes away and pick at my nails. It's little things like what I just witnessed that I find unbearable. I bite the inside of my cheek and hold back the bitterness.

Luckily, the driver gets the picture. I'm not in the mood to talk and the cab moves ahead, taking me away from my sanctuary and toward another test.

That's what these things really are. Tests.

It's only in this moment that I realize I'm really doing it. I've put it off so many times over the last eight months. I've given so many excuses for not meeting up with the girls.

Why today? I don't know. My heart sinks thinking that maybe I'm really getting over my husband's death.

As much as I want to be the woman I once was, happy and carefree, I don't want to forget him.

I lay my head back on the headrest and close my eyes, my clutch in my lap. Jace gave it to me last Christmas. I snort at the thought, running my fingers over the smooth, hot pink leather. More like I picked it out and he paid for it.

I close my eyes and take in a deep breath. It's calming riding in a quiet cab at night in the city. The quiet rumble of the engine and the white noise of the rain are a serene mix.

The last day I saw my husband was when we were watching my nephew Everett, so my sister could have a mother-daughter day with Lexi. It's rare I see my family at all; everyone is so busy with their own lives and my sister is much older than I am… so we're not exactly close. I still love them though.

The thought of my nephew brings a smile to my face. With sandy blond hair that just barely covers his big blue eyes and a wide smile, you can't help but smile back at him. He was only a few months old back then. A brand-new life in this world. That's the way it works, isn't it? Life and death go hand in hand.

I glance forward out the windshield and give a slight start when we stop far away from Second Avenue where the bar is located; a bit of traffic is holding us up.

The cabby notices my reaction in the rearview mirror and shrugs as he says, "We should be out of it soon." He's tense at the wheel, probably expecting me to snap at him, maybe blame him for taking this particular route. More guilt washes over me. I hate spreading negativity simply by being so … gloom and doom with the air surrounding me. I'm not an ice queen, or at least I don't mean to be.

I give him a soft smile, placing my clutch in the middle seat. "I figured we'd run into something," I say easily. My voice comes out even and calm. It's the voice I use with my mother. The kind of tone that says: *I'm okay, just tired.*

The cabby shifts, making the leather seat grumble and he tries to make small chat.

I nod my head and answer politely, but keep everything short and to the point. I can be accommodating with others and I truly want to do so. I'm tired of being alone and pushing others away. It's just harder than I thought it would be after how I've been since Jace passed.

After a moment of quiet, I look out the window again. The rain's nearly stopped, and the sidewalks are instantly crowded as a result. The people were always there, waiting under awnings for protection. Not many people like to venture into weather that washes away your makeup and ruins even the best put-together look.

They were waiting and ready to keep moving just the same. All they needed was a small break before setting out again. The only question is if there will be another awning to save them when the brutal downpour comes back.

The cabby stops and my eyes whip up to the sign on my right, my heart beating faster as I watch dozens of people walking in front of me on the sidewalk. Each going wherever it is that life has taken them. I don't know if I'm ready, but at least I'm here.

"Miss?" the cabby asks after I remain where I am in this cozy seat. I shake my head slightly with quick motions and play off my hesitation, paying him and leaving a big tip as well. He deserves it for having to suffer my company.

"Have a good night," I tell him as I slip out, my heels hitting the slick asphalt and the door shutting behind me with a resounding click.

chapter 3

IT FIGURES IT WOULD STOP POURING THE SECOND I GET IN HERE. THE BAR is packed and the cacophony of guests chatting and glasses clinking welcome me. I can get lost in the crowds. I know the people here see me, but they don't know me.

This bar in particular is one of my favorites. It's always full. Its tufted leather seats are constantly filled, and the warm rich tones of the wooden ceiling and brick walls make it feel like home somehow.

My suit is nothing fancy, nothing that will stand out in here. Which is how I want it. I run my fingers through my hair and shake away the rain as I shrug off my jacket and toss it over the barstool at the very end.

It's been a long day and the last thing I need is to go home alone. As soon as my eyes lift, the bartender is on me. I think her name is Patricia. She's in here every weekend.

"Whiskey?" she asks me. She never stops moving, shoveling ice into short glasses and pouring liquor like a pro. Unlike the other women in here, she's not looking for a man with deep pockets. She doesn't do chitchat either, which is another reason I like sitting in this section. The biggest reason is that it's out of the way, somewhere I can simply blend in and watch.

"Double," I answer her with a nod and slip my cell phone out from my jacket pocket. I've only been gone from the office for two hours, but I've got a dozen emails waiting for my attention. A huff of a grunt leaves me as a text from Liam pops up.

You coming out tonight?

Already out, I answer him as the glass hits the polished bar top and Patricia slides it over to me.

My phone pings as I lift the tumbler to my lips and let the cool liquor burn all the way down, warming my chest.

Where at?

I contemplate telling him. I like Liam. A lot. If I had any friends, he'd be one of them. But and after talking to my father today, I don't want to be around a damn soul.

A sarcastic laugh makes me grin as I realize I've come to a crowded bar to be alone. It's the truth, though. You're always surrounded by people in this city; there's never a place to hide unless it's in plain sight.

I down the rest of my drink and tap the heavy glass against the bar top as I consider what to tell him. That's when I hear it. Almost as if daring me to stay alone any longer, it's the gentle sound of a feminine laugh. It's genuine and it rings out clear in the bar even though it's soft.

It's a soothing sound, a calming force in the chaos that surrounds us. Everything around me fades except for the woman who uttered that sweet sound.

The smooth glass stays still as I look down the bar in search of her.

The rest of the crowd doesn't seem to notice as they continue with whatever the hell they're saying and doing, but my eyes are drawn to my left. Through the throng of people, I just barely get a glimpse of her.

Dark brunette hair that's pulled back; pale skin covered in black lace.

A man at the opposite end leans away from the bar, digging in his back pocket for his wallet and giving me a clear view of her.

Those dark red lips attract my gaze first. She licks her bottom lip before picking up a large glass of deep red wine. The color matches her lips perfectly. She smiles at something and her shoulders shake as she laughs, making the dark liquid swirl in her glass and bringing a blush to her high cheekbones.

She tosses her hair to the side and her fingers tease the ends as she brings her tendrils over one shoulder, wrapping them around her finger while she sips her wine.

It's when she looks away from whomever she's been giving her attention to that my curiosity is piqued.

Without their eyes on her, her expression morphs into something else. I finally see her eyes, the lightest of blues, and that's when I really see her. Not just the image of what she's portraying.

Pain is clear as day.

It's the lie though, how fucking good she was at hiding it, that's what really gets me. Even I was fooled.

People can hide behind a smile or a laugh; every soul in here can pretend to be someone and something they're not.

The truth is always there though and I'm damn good at recognizing it. Your eyes can never hide two things: age and emotion. Hers speak to me in a way nothing else can.

But had I never looked just then when she thought no one was watching, she never would have shown me willingly.

She straightens her back and I see her profile, her expression. The corners of my lips turn down. Not only do I know her pain, I know her name. I know everything about her.

Julia Summers.

My blood chills as she turns back to the table, the smile on her face slipping back into position just as the man at the end of the bar steps forward, obscuring her from my vision. As if the moment of clarity and recognition was just for me in that moment. Like fate wanted me to know how close I was to her.

I keep my eyes on the bar, doing my best to listen, but her voice is silent or lost in the mix of chatter throughout the crowded place.

"Another?" Patricia's voice sounds close, closer than she usually is. I lift my head to see her standing right in front of me, both hands on the bar and waiting.

I nod my head with my brows pinched, shaking off the mix of emotions. This city is a small place with worlds always colliding, but I've never seen her in person. Only in a photograph. Only that once. I'm sure it's her, though.

The ice clinks in the glass and I watch as the liquid slips over each cube, cracking them and filling the crevices.

"You okay?" Patricia asks me. It's odd. In the year or so since I've been coming here, she's never bothered to make small talk. It's why I don't mind her.

I give her a tight smile as I reply, "I'm fine." I reach her eyes and widen my smile, relaxing my posture as I lean back slightly.

She eyes me warily as she mutters, "You don't look fine."

It takes me a moment before I shrug it off and say, "I'm all right, just tired."

She nods once and goes back to minding her own business, sliding me the whiskey and moving on to other customers.

I tap my pointer finger against the glass, looking casually down the bar.

She's hidden from view, but I know she's there.

Julia

MY BODY TINGLES WITH ANOTHER SIP OF CABERNET. It's my third glass and it's only tasting sweeter on my lips. The tips of my fingers always feel the turning point first when I drink. That familiar buzz that makes my body feel a bit heavy and my mind light.

"I can't believe your license plate says *Alimony*," Maddie says into her wineglass as she snickers again. She's laughing so hard that the white zinfandel splashes onto her lips, but she doesn't care. She merely smiles and takes a large gulp.

Suzette answers with a shrug and a cocky smirk, "The asshole had it coming to him." Her bright pink lipstick smudges against her glass of Long Island iced tea and she wipes it away with her napkin as Maddie continues to laugh. Sue's given herself a makeover since her divorce is now finalized. Currently she's sporting jet-black hair cut into a blunt bob and bangs to go with her snippy attitude.

"Please tell me he saw it when you left the courthouse today. Please?" Maddie practically begs, still grinning from ear to ear.

Maddie's young and naive and thinks Prince Charming is somewhere out there, so you should always be ready. Sue has a marriage, a divorce, and fifteen years on Maddie, so between the three of us, we have as many opinions on love as we do rounds of drinks.

Sue's plastered-on smile slips and she tries to hide it with a shrug as she takes another sip. Her license plate is just one more way for Sue to make fun of her divorce before anyone else can. Her ex put her through hell and she came out cold as ice to all men. Well, except the ones she likes to sink her claws into after a few Long Islands.

Sue leans back in the white leather booth, keeping the glass in her hand and shrugs again as she says, "What says 'fuck you, motherfucker' better than taking his red Ferrari in the proceedings and getting *that* license plate?"

Kat pipes up from her spot in the booth, rolling her eyes and taking a sip of her Pepsi before she says, "I think it says, 'don't touch this bitch' to every man in the city."

A sly smile slips onto Sue's face. "Thank goodness … that's exactly what I was going for," she says, setting her drink down then stretching her arms over her head. "Maybe all these bastards will finally leave me alone then." The other girls start to howl at that and I join in, although my heart's not in it. My nerves are shot just being out here tonight. Sue's directly across from me and both of us are seated at the ends of the semicircular booth. Kat's to my right, then Maddie.

"Another round?" The waiter startles me and I nearly spill my glass as I gasp and back away. All the poor guy did was offer me another drink and I practically had a heart attack. Several distant gazes turn in our direction as my own table watches me like there's something wrong with me and I do what I do best, I play it off and let out a small laugh. Maybe I'm even more like Sue than I realized.

"Sorry," I say a bit too loud. Exaggerating how tipsy I am, I gently place my hand on the waiter's arm. His starched white shirt feels crisp under my fingers as I lean in and sweetly say, "I'm so sorry, I hope I didn't spill any on you."

That's all it takes for everyone to go about their own business, but my heart's still beating wildly. A few stares linger. I'm aware the people in here recognize me; they probably think I shouldn't be out or that I'm "having a moment." Looking across the room, I'm frozen by a pair of eyes I know all too well.

They belong to a woman in her late sixties, Margo Pierce. She's an heiress and an influential investor in the city. Her large sapphire cocktail rings appear even more over the top as she holds a simple glass of champagne with both hands. For a woman in her sixties, she wears her age well. From her perky breasts to the delicate skin around her eyes, not an inch of her hasn't been through some procedure or another. All the work she's had is very tastefully done, though.

The last time I saw her was at a casino up north, the night I got the phone call. I can still remember the dings and bells of the slot machines and the bright, colorful lights. Still remember the weight of the glass of rosé in my right hand as I sat perched on a barstool in the center of the casino. At the Mohegan Sun, the bar is elevated. I could see nearly a hundred of the other guests playing slots and sitting at the card tables; it was packed that night.

Just like tonight, I was with the girls and we were enjoying ourselves and the atmosphere. We were taking a break from roulette to grab cocktails and Sue was cursing out her soon-to-be ex-husband for prolonging their divorce when my phone rang. I only picked it up because it was odd for my mother to call me so late.

Kat leaned in to order from the bartender as I placed the phone to my ear, turning a bit to my left for a hint of privacy. As much as I could get in such a crowded place, anyway. I didn't show them that anything was unusual, keeping a pleasant smile on my face as I answered.

When I heard my mother's voice on the other end, the smile vanished and the vibrant night life, chatter, and sounds from the machines turned to dead air.

I could barely make out my mother's voice, just a few words here and there, but I knew something was wrong. Very wrong. I needed to hear better, so I stood and started walking. I didn't know where I was going, all I knew was that I needed to find a less noisy location.

My heart raced, and the shock caused my body temperature to drop so low that I was shivering.

He's dead. I heard her words clear as day as I got to the front of the casino. My heels clipped the large rug at the entrance. I stumbled forward, my short dress riding up and one heel nearly falling off. My knees hit the hard granite flooring and the phone fell from my hand.

Jace is dead. That's what she said.

I imagine the people around me at the time thought I was drunk. I would have assumed that if I'd seen someone fall the way I had.

Margo Pierce was there to help me. Those damn cocktail rings were digging painfully into my arm as she helped lift me up. I stood there on wobbly legs just trying to breathe, but when I looked into her eyes, I could tell she knew.

I knew in that moment it was real. I could lie to myself, or I could have hung up and driven home, all the while in denial. But the sympathy in her eyes was damning.

I rip my eyes away from hers at the other side of the bar and return back to the girls, back to tonight, leaving that night in the past right where it belongs. I ignore the way my hand itches to drain the wine and order another cabernet and then another while I push my hair back over my shoulders, trying to relax. Trying to shake off the unwanted memory.

"I think you're flagged," Kat says into her glass even as her eyes meet mine. Her sandy brunette hair is colored with a subtle ombre and she's applied her eyeliner in a cat-eye fashion. I don't know why, but I can't stop looking at it. Like if I can just concentrate on her makeup, everything else will leave me alone.

"No such thing," Sue says, quick to come to my defense, an asymmetric grin gracing her lips. "Drink up, girly." She gives me a wink and it forces a smile to my face. It didn't take long for the girls to come find me that night, crying alone in the back of our limo.

With a burn pricking at the back of my eyes, I blink a few times to keep the tears at bay. It was months and months ago, but sometimes the pain comes back full force. I don't know that it will ever go away and if it does, surely that would be a tragedy. I don't know where grief and mourning end and my life begins again, but I'd like to find it.

Pushing away the nearly empty glass, I watch the dark liquid pool in the bottom and sigh deeply. I can't seem to keep a smile on my face. The once easy mask isn't slipping into place. Progress is all I need, though. I remind myself of my motto: Aim for progress, not perfection.

"Let's talk about something and someone else," I suggest. "Is anyone getting laid? One of us must be getting laid, right? At least Kat?" I arch a brow in her direction but her forehead creases in response and the action is followed by a huff and, "Yeah right." *Shit.* I forgot she and her husband are going through something.

Way to put my foot in my mouth.

My skin pricks at the back of my neck as I feel another set of eyes on me. The anxiousness comes back and I put on my best fake smile, staring straight ahead as Maddie starts listing off what was wrong with her last rendezvous. This one was some guy she met online.

The nagging feeling doesn't quit. I don't know who it is, but someone's watching me. It could be the paparazzi but typically every time I go out, they approach me before I even notice them. I'm a socialite, after all, and I know the intrusion is part of this life.

Debating on taking a casual look over my shoulder, I shake off the paranoia. *It's all in your head,* I tell myself. I thought I felt someone watching me earlier, but maybe I was wrong.

"You know enough time has passed." Sue's comment from across the table gets my attention. I look up to find her dark eyes twinkling with mischievousness.

"Enough time for what?" Maddie questions Sue. Maddie's the quintessential younger sister of our group and I swear most of Sue's comments go right over her head.

Sue motions toward me and it's only then that I take in her words. I clear my throat and look away, feeling a blush rise to my cheeks. "When I said someone else …" I say playfully and pick up the glass, lifting it high in the air and tilting my head back to get the last few drops.

The girls laugh it off, but there's a certain gravitas in Sue's eyes.

She lowers her voice and looks me in the eye as she says, "We just want you to be happy."

"It's 'we' now?" I ask her, suddenly feeling defensive. They've been talking about me behind my back?

Sue shrugs and Kat's quick to put a hand on top of mine. She twists in her spot and the white leather squeaks under her skinny ass. "We were just making conversation earlier." My brow rises as she takes in a breath and tries to find the right words.

"We want you happy again," Maddie says from her seat next to Kat. Her hands make two sharp motions emphasizing *happy again* as she leans back and looks straight ahead, avoiding my eyes on her.

Oh my God … is this some kind of intervention? I imagine my face reflects exactly what I'm thinking. Judging by the guilty expressions Kat and Maddie are wearing on their faces, I'm sure it does. Sue is shameless though, back to nursing her drink.

Of course they'd talk about me. I can't explain why it feels like a betrayal, though. Why my throat seems to go dry and itch as if I'm going to cry. Why wouldn't they? Everyone else is.

"Hey, Jules." Kat's voice is soft, placating even.

I pull my hand away from her and suck in a breath. "It's fine," I whisper, grabbing my clutch.

Sue's quick to sit forward and say, "Don't go. It wasn't—"

"Just headed to the powder room," I blurt out. "I just need to freshen up," I tell them with a tight smile, standing up and tugging down my dress.

"Do you want company?" Kat asks, already sliding out behind me.

"I just need a minute," I say and shake my head, giving her pleading eyes. I love them. They only want what's best for me. But don't they know how hard this is? How much it took just to come out here.

I can handle this. I just need something although I'm not sure what that something is. A breath of fresh air, maybe. Or a drink of water or something stronger. I don't know what, but I know I need at least a minute to myself to figure it out.

chapter 5

Mason

THE ANXIOUS FEELING DEEP IN MY GUT WON'T QUIT. IT ONLY GETS more intense as Julia walks behind me, politely maneuvering her small frame amid the crowd of people. Watching her from my periphery, I listen to the rhythmic sound of her heels and watch how her hips sway gently.

She doesn't notice me, which is by design, but still it aggravates me. She passes so close behind me on her way to the restrooms that I catch a hint of her sweet scent. No doubt it's perfume, a gentle floral mixed with citrus of some sort but as it fills my lungs, I can't help but grip the bar top tighter to keep myself from following her.

Ever since I caught a glimpse of her, I haven't been able to move or get her out of my head. For months, I haven't thought twice about her. Each time her picture swept into my head, I pushed it away.

But she's here now, so close that I could touch her.

I can't approach her, though. How fucked up would that be?

I can't cross that line. She doesn't know a damn bit of the truth.

I down the remainder of my whiskey and slide the empty glass forward, pissed off and frustrated.

As I stand abruptly, the stool slides backward and bumps into someone. I turn to look over my shoulder while reaching into my back pocket for my wallet. "Sorry," I say without thinking only to find myself staring directly at Julia.

Her eyes still aren't on me as she waves off my apology, looking at the bottles lining the back of the bar before finally resting her gorgeous blue eyes on me. This close to her I can see they're pale blue with flecks of silver speckled throughout. They're beautiful.

She shakes her head just slightly, making her hair fall off her shoulder and exposing more of her bare skin. "It's fine." Her voice is soft as she walks forward without missing a beat, stepping up to the bar on my right, coming closer. Like a lamb heading into the lion's den, teasing and taunting unknowingly.

She's so close to me, so damn alluring. The black lacy dress clings to her curves. Her hips are seductive and I can just imagine how they'd feel to hold as I took her from behind. I can feel the bartender's eyes flicker to me questioningly as Julia orders, but I can't take my gaze off Julia.

I swallow thickly, leaning my forearms against the bar and attempting to act casual, getting that much closer to her.

She doesn't know anything about how we're linked and she doesn't have to. She'll never know the truth and this is my chance to learn more about who the pretty face in the picture is.

"Julia, right?" My heart pounds, questioning why the hell would I admit that I know anything at all about her. I don't intend to lie to her, though. Nothing but lies of omission. I've heard her name in social circles. Her family is well known so I doubt she'll be surprised that I recognize her.

"Jules," she corrects me warmly, now looking at me differently than she did a moment ago. She seems to do a double take and a hint of playfulness sparkles in her eyes. It's as if I'm suddenly what she's been looking for. Or maybe *who* she's been waiting for.

"Ah, Jules." I tap my fingers on the bar and glance away for a moment. *What the fuck am I doing?* This isn't just playing with fire, this is worse. It's asking to be burned and shoving my fists into the coals.

Patricia sets two shots of what look like chilled tequila in front of Jules. I watch with interest as she throws the first one back without thinking twice. Her slender fingers slip around the second one, ready to down it as well.

The pain comes off her in waves. She's drowning it in alcohol. She's good at hiding her emotions on the surface, but her actions speak so much louder than words.

"For a moment I thought you got two so you could share with me," I say teasingly with a smirk, more to keep her from drinking it than the desire to have it for myself.

She licks her lips and smiles. "You want it?"

Goddamn, does she know how she's coming off right now? She's already testing me, because just hearing those words slip between her lips has my dick straining against my zipper. *Yes, I fucking want it.* She's forbidden. The one woman in this city I should stay far away from.

"If you're offering," I answer her with a flirtatiousness I don't recognize. She blushes and tucks her hair back behind her ear. As she pulls her eyes away from me, she catches a glimpse of something across the room that rips the happiness from her in an instant.

I throw back the shot but keep my eyes on her. The cold liquid burns. I was right about it being tequila. It's strong too. Stronger than I expected and it takes the breath from me, making my chest feel tight, but then it relaxes me all the way down.

I hold up two fingers for Patricia. "Another two," I say and stand, sliding the stool I'd been sitting on over to Jules. "I took your shot so it's only fair," I say. Instantly, her eyes come back to me.

I watch as they swirl with a mix of questions. Vulnerability is clearly present and that only makes her that much more enticing.

"I'm not sure I should," she says softly. Her honesty is so raw, so genuine.

"You really shouldn't," I say with complete honesty as well. She deserves that much. She's Little Red Riding Hood in fuck-me heels and I'm worse than the Big Bad Wolf. I lean forward, knowing I'm breaking every rule I have as I bring my lips just inches from the shell of her ear.

Her fingers tighten on the edge of the stool as I whisper, "But you want to. And this is so much better than whatever you were going to do." I'm not sure if what I said is meant more for her or for me, but either way, I've convinced myself.

My rough voice and hot breath make goosebumps trail down her shoulder. Her nipples pebble under her dress, just barely becoming noticeable beneath the expensive fabric that graces her skin. I pull away from her, offering her space and an out.

She could leave if she wanted to. She could walk away. Fuck, she could call me an asshole and I'd sit here and do my best to pretend I'll never go after her again.

It takes a moment for Jules to pull herself together. She sits there in what seems like a daze. It's only when Patricia sets down the shot glasses, spilling just a touch of the chilled tequila, that she meets my gaze again.

I take the one closest to Jules and hold it out to her. She keeps her eyes on me but accepts it.

"Here's to things we know we shouldn't do," I say with a smile, lifting my glass and extending it for a toast.

Slowly, so very slowly, that bit of happiness comes back to her. Her eyes keep flickering with uncertainty to the floor and across the room.

"Here's to doing what makes us happy," she says, forcing her shoulders back straight as she clinks her glass against mine and then downs every drop. She slams her glass on the bar while I'm left holding mine and watching her every move.

I toss it back as she picks up her clutch, obviously ready to pay for the shots.

"Don't." There's more strength in my voice than I should have used. I soften my tone as I tell her, "It's on me." I hesitate then add, "I was just getting ready to leave."

She watches me cautiously, but I look toward the bartender as I get out my wallet. All the while paying attention to Jules in my periphery.

"Well, thank you … what's your name?" she asks.

"Mason," I answer her hoping she's never heard of me, but she brightens and nods her head.

"Thatcher. Yes, I thought I recognized you." She bites the inside of her cheek as something occurs to her and her expression falls slightly. "I'm sorry to hear—"

"To happiness, right?" I say, cutting off her apology, then pass my card to Patricia. It hurts me to say the words, but I don't bother to hide it.

That only makes her frown, somehow making her appear even more beautiful and alluring. We're both in pain. Both getting over something. Only this shit I did to myself whereas she's collateral damage.

She turns to the bar again, the playfulness gone.

"To happiness, and to the things we want," I tell her as I sign the receipt and leave the pen on the bar. I spear my fingers through my hair, feeling the heat of the moment and the buzz of the liquor starting to affect me.

I glance at her and watch as she closes her eyes. It's affecting her too. She's easy prey—beautiful, naive, innocent. I'm an asshole for doing this, but I can't help that I want her. Her eyes haunt me, but her body tempts me.

"I'm going to get out of here." I let my hungry gaze roam down her sexy curves, not hiding what I want from her in the least. "You want to come with?"

$$\mathit{chapter}\ 6$$

Julia

To HAPPINESS, AND TO THE THINGS WE WANT.

Mason's words echo in my ears. I know I'm buzzed, but the odd mix of anxiety and relaxation running through me are from something else. It's the realization that I'm at a crossroads. I'm standing in front of an open door and I know that going through will change everything. It would put my world into motion again, moving me forward, shoving me from the stagnant place I've been in these last few months.

There would be no way to go back, but there's no telling who I'd be once I'm on the other side. My body is ringing with desire and adrenaline.

Mason Thatcher. I've heard of the handsome devil. The pictures I've seen don't do his broad shoulders and muscular frame justice. The rough stubble on his jaw begs me to reach up and brush my fingertips against it. He's tall, dark and handsome … and a notorious player. A man I shouldn't be caught dead talking to. My husband would have killed me for having drinks with a man like Mason.

But Jace has left me all alone. And Mason's so much more than I thought I could want in a man.

I rip my eyes from his hard body. Although he's in a suit, I noticed his hands first, rough and callused. It's clear they're from years of hard work, something the men in here know little about. Actual manual labor.

I try to relax and casually lean against the bar, slipping my pointer finger into one of the empty shot glasses and forcing it onto its side. I don't know why and it probably makes me appear drunker than I am, but I don't care.

"Mason, do you like tequila?" I ask him and this time when I speak, there's a bit of flirtatiousness in my voice. Guilt weighs heavily in my chest, but only briefly before the alcohol drifting into my blood numbs the memories. I've been alone for too long. I can have him for a night. Just one night.

Mason's steel gray eyes roam over the curves of my waist and ass. He's bold, licking his lips and then taking a step forward to lean against the bar with me. He's close enough that the heat of his body makes me that much hotter.

I want to know what it would be like for a man like him to pin me beneath him. To take me how he wants me. I close my eyes as a warm flush rises into my cheeks from the intensity of his stare.

"I do," he replies and his voice is low and rough. It does bad things to me. I rest my head in my hand, both loving and hating the way the alcohol soothes the pain.

This isn't me moving on, but I'm ready to feel something else. My brow pinches at his response when I look back at him, but then I realize he's just answering my question about whether or not he likes tequila. I'm a bit more than tipsy but I'm still here and present, and I know what I want.

Even if I'll hate myself in the morning, it's one night of not going back to that large, empty house alone.

The tight pull of two small hands at my waist and Sue's loud voice make my heart skip a beat and I swear to God I almost scream. I feel like a child caught with her hand in the cookie jar.

"Jules, Jasper's out front." Sue talks like she has no idea she just scared the shit out of me.

My heart pounds in my chest as I turn to face her fully, my eyes darting from the man candy on my right and then back to her.

Caught red-handed.

It takes a moment for me to realize what Sue said, and a moment for her to catch on to what I was about to do.

She eyes Mason but before she can say a word, I say, "Jasper?"

Although it comes out like a question, it's more of a curse.

Sue gives me a sympathetic look as she says, "The exhibition at Ruppert Park must've ended." Jasper's with the *New York Post*. Every time he sees me he has a question and I know whatever I say will end up misquoted in the paper the next morning. He's not kind like the others.

I blow out a heavy breath, looking through the crowd and toward the entrance. I don't feel like dealing with this shit.

"And what are you doing here?" Sue's question is directed at Mason who's standing behind me, still leaning against the bar and resembling sin incarnate. He doesn't seem to mind the interruption at all. He gives Sue a lazy smile that brings back the heat between my thighs full force.

"Just leaving, actually." Jesus, his voice is as smooth as silk.

One split second passes and a wide grin spreads across Sue's face, her dark hair swaying, brushing against her cheek as she knowingly looks between the two of us. I lean backward, gripping the stool behind me and wanting an escape. It's one thing to flirt with the idea of bringing someone home; it's another thing entirely for everyone to know I was thinking about it.

Sue looks pointedly at Mason's cock and raises a brow, which only makes me want to bury my face in my hands.

"Are you ready to go?" I ask Sue and step away from Mason. Gripping my clutch tighter, I'm ready to get the hell out of here. There's not enough tequila in the world to cancel out the sobriety that the mention of Jasper brings me.

"You two get out of here," Sue says, stopping me in my tracks. That's the last thing I expected her to say.

"What'd you say your name was?" she asks Mason.

"Mason Thatcher." He extends a hand to Sue and she takes his hand coyly with both of hers.

"Mason," Sue says and her voice drips with sex appeal. It always does. She's a cold-hearted bitch to some but just as vivacious and insatiable as she was ten years ago when I first met her during my freshman year of college.

She leans in slightly and I get a good look down her blouse. Her necklace shifts so that the thin gold chain and glittering emerald jewel rest on her perky breasts, but when I look up, Mason's only looking into her eyes. "You take good care of my girl tonight, Mason." Sue looks back at me and that roguish look in her eyes makes me smile.

"I plan on it," Mason tells her and releases her hands.

"You are wicked," I whisper to Sue, my smile widening.

"Just one minute," Sue says. She holds up her pointer finger at Mason and grips my wrist, moving me away from him and closer to the powder room as if he can't hear us a whopping twelve inches away. I keep myself from rolling my eyes.

"It's nothing serious." The words sound defensive even to me. I don't want her to judge me or to hate me. I just want her to understand. Out of all the girls, I think she will. More than anything, I know I want to get out of here with a stranger. It makes me feel dirty and shameful, but right now it's what I want.

"Nothing serious?" she says. "It is for me," Sue says. My lungs stall at her words. She shifts her weight and looks over her shoulder toward our booth. I can't see either Kat or Maddie, although I'm sure they're still there. "You need this." Sue stares into my eyes, the look so serious I'm caught off guard.

"The question is," she says as she lowers her voice and leans into me, "are we telling the others?" Oh, thank the good Lord. I let out a breath I didn't know I was holding. When she pulls away, gripping my elbows in her hands and winking at me, I know everything's going to be okay.

I hesitate, glancing back at Mason and then I bite the inside of my cheek. "I don't want to lie to them," I tell her honestly.

"Then you two slip out the back. Do it fast before I go tell them and before Jasper can get his scrawny, organic, vegan-eating ass inside."

I snicker at Sue's response, but the reality of what I'm doing is settling in. I lean forward as Sue lets go and I grip her hand before she can turn and leave me alone with my soon-to-be one-night stand.

"Tell me I'm not a bad person." The words slip out before I can think about what I'm saying. I try to keep the smile on my face, but it wavers.

"Getting laid doesn't make anyone a bad person."

I nod my head, willing the emotions to go back to being buried deep inside of me as if they don't deserve to surface in this moment.

"Unless he's married," she adds quickly and I chuckle.

The bit of humor helps me feel a sense of relief, but it's small. Her expression softens. "You just need a little something to kick-start your happiness again."

To happiness.

"I do." I nod my head.

True to her nature, Sue ignores the way my voice cracks as she takes a half step closer to me. "Then get over there already. The sooner you leave, the sooner he can be fucking you with your ankles pinned behind your head—"

A laugh escapes me before she can finish. "Can you even put your legs behind your head?"

"For the right man, I can do a lot of things." She looks at Mason, then to me.

"Just have fun tonight," she says, keeping things light but it's calming.

I nod my head as she turns from me, leaving me alone with Mason.

Alone to do bad things and make bad decisions. But at least I'm doing *something.*

Alcohol helps. I can always blame it on the alcohol.

It's then that I notice a few eyes watching. Including Margo, who's taking covert glances. That's when he wraps his arm around my waist and pulls me into him, bringing my back against his front as he whispers in my ear.

"You ready to go?" he asks, his warm breath traveling down my skin and making my body feel alive for the first time in several months.

I don't care that everyone can see. The city can talk; I'll deny it all.

"Will you hold me afterward?" I whisper my one request before I realize what I've said.

His body stills behind me and I close my eyes, hating that I've ruined this before it's even started. It's a one-night stand, nothing more. No emotions.

"Until the morning?" he asks me. My heart beats again, in rhythm with his.

I nod my head, my hair rubbing against his hard chest and his thumb brushing against the black fabric of my dress.

Just until morning.

chapter 7

Mason

WILL YOU HOLD ME AFTERWARD?

I'm calm on the outside, as if there's not a damn thing wrong with what I'm doing. I don't know what's come over me.

The Mercedes's alarm beeps as I unlock it and open Jules's door for her. Her heels are muted on the wet pavement as she rounds me and slips easily into the luxurious leather seat. Her soft blue eyes look up at me as she tucks her hair behind her ears and settles the clutch in her lap as she murmurs, "Thank you."

I merely smile and close her door, the keys jingling as I walk to the driver side, my pulse racing wildly.

This is a mistake. I don't hold women afterward. Sex is sex and nothing else.

But I'm also a selfish prick, and I'd be a liar if I said I didn't want her. What I want, I get.

I start the car, the purr of the engine and soft classical music filling the cabin.

As I look over my shoulder to back out, Jules clears her throat. "Are we going to …" she starts to ask and then a beautiful blush colors her cheeks.

"Are we going to what?"

With a stronger flush, she shakes her head gently and says, "Never mind … Of course we are."

I can't help the smirk on my face at her shyness or the way my cock jumps in my pants. I peek at her before leaving the tight parking lot and heading down Second Avenue. My fingers itch to rest against her bare thigh as her dress rides up slightly. I place my hand on the gearshift instead, stopping at a red light and looking over to her.

She squirms in her seat under my gaze and I fucking love it. It's easy to forget with her. Maybe that's what it is. Maybe that's why I can't say no and walk away. If I can just have her for tonight, then it'll all be all right. I'm her downfall and she's my savior.

"Where are we headed, sweetheart? My place?" I give her the option but she's free to suggest someplace else. She's quick to nod, glancing at me then looking down at her hands in her lap.

I'm enjoying this way too much. I turn to look out the driver side window and ignore that voice in the back of my head saying I'm a Grade A prick for doing this to her.

"Thank you," she says softly as the light turns green and traffic starts to move. "For heading out the back and away from all that ..." she pauses, waving her hands in the air before falling back against the seat and concluding, "bullshit."

The curse word seems foreign on those sweet lips of hers. I nod my head once, looking back to the windshield and twisting my hand around the leather steering wheel.

"No problem," I say easily but I can feel her need to talk, to tell me everything else that's on her mind. I wait for it, staring straight ahead, but nothing comes. Just silence as we drive to the sounds of Tchaikovsky.

It's only fifteen minutes to my place at this rate, but the time can't pass quickly enough. Every second of silence is a second I consider turning back. There's still time to walk away.

"Do you always do this?" Jules asks, breaking up the quiet.

"What's that?"

"This," she says, her cheek resting against the seat as she looks at me.

"Hmm?" I still don't understand her question.

"Pick up women—" she stops and rolls her eyes. "You know, one-night stands." Tapping my thumbs on the steering wheel, I consider her question. I used to without thinking twice. But that was before Avery. Before my father and this hell I've been thrown into.

"So I'm right, you do this often?" she says and I have to suppress my smile at her brazen demeanor.

"I'm not going to answer that, Jules." My voice comes out a little harder than I wanted and she shrinks back some. *Smooth, real fucking smooth.*

It's tense for a moment and I flick on the turn signal as we head down a deserted street. So close. I can't lose her now. "I don't take women to my place," I tell her simply. "And it's been a while."

Her brows pinch for a moment and then she struggles to hold back a laugh. It catches me off guard but then I remember how much she drank. I'm still feeling a bit of the tequila myself. My tolerance is high as fuck, so if I'm feeling it, she must be wasted. The realization has me rethinking things again.

"How are you feeling?" I ask her.

"Fine," she says and then covers her mouth with her hand.

"Are you drunk?" She doesn't look like it in the least.

She purses her lips and shakes her head as she says, "Nope. Just right." She stretches in the seat, covering another yawn when I stop at my gates.

I eye her for a moment and then brush it off.

I know Jules comes from money and was born into this lifestyle like me, so I'm surprised to see admiration on her face when we arrive. "Your home is beautiful." Her voice is even and sincere. I'm proud of my home. I built it myself. Liam, my business partner, helped design it for engineering purposes, but it was all based on my ideas and plans.

I pull up in the driveway as her phone starts vibrating.

She doesn't pay attention as I approach the front of the house. Judging by the look on her face and the way she shoves the phone back into her clutch, her friends from the bar are probably giving her hell.

"Everything all right?" I ask, more to make sure I'm getting her ass into my bed than anything else.

For only a moment, I think she received a message from someone who knows what happened. Someone who saw what I did, although I don't think anyone could have possibly seen. My muscles coil and my knuckles turn white as I grip the gearshift, putting the car into park and searching her face for answers.

She blows a bit of hair out of her face and looks anywhere but at me.

"It's fine," she says but I know she's lying.

"Tell me what's wrong." The command comes out easily.

Her eyes go wide and I almost second-guess talking to her like that. *Almost.* But then she caves to me.

"My friends just found out."

I cock a brow at her. "Found out?" She parts her lips slightly and I'm guessing from the way she leans into me, my touch is all she needs to loosen up. I rest my hand on her thigh, just beneath the hem of her dress, caressing her lightly with my thumb.

"I don't do this often or… ever—"

I lean in and press my lips to hers, stopping her explanation. I move my hand to her cheek and then behind her head as she deepens the kiss. Her lips part for me and her hot tongue massages mine in swift, strong strokes.

I groan into her open mouth, our breath mingling as my dick hardens to fucking stone.

"Forget about them," I tell her as I break the kiss and pull away. She's left breathless, her eyes still closed when I open my door and start to get out, taking the keys with me.

I almost close the door and miss her whispering, "I'll forget about it all."

But I heard her. I heard the whisper, the raw vulnerability and truth in her statement.

I wish I hadn't.

chapter 8

I'VE NEVER HAD A ONE-NIGHT STAND BEFORE.

Not once.

It's not like I have a thing against them and Lord knows my friends enjoy them, with or without discretion. It's just never happened. My body heats everywhere, one place a bit more than others when Mason touches me, and especially when he cuts through it all with his demanding ways.

My thoughts race as Mason wraps his hand around my waist and leads me to the front door. The chill in the night air is sobering. I can't explain how my nerves are shooting through me. My breathing comes in a little faster now that the alcohol's all but worn off.

I try to focus on how even our footsteps sound but all I can think about is how I've never done this before.

I'm doing it. I'm going to sleep with a stranger. *I'm going to sleep with someone other than Jace.*

Jace and I met as children, paired up in boarding school. I've never been with anyone else. My heel slips on the paved steps at the thought, almost making me fall, but Mason catches me.

He's quick to grab on to my elbow and waist, his hands hot on my body. It's a shock as something inside of me reacts almost violently to his very touch.

Eight months alone … even longer since I've been touched. The idea of moving on has never been such a dominating thought, or so terrifying.

I wrap my arms around myself, fueled by both fear and desire. My pulse quickens as I look back over my shoulder and toward his car. Toward an escape.

Mason straightens his shoulders, squaring them and hitting the keys against his leg once. The jingle catches my attention. It's the only sound in the cold dark night.

I stand frozen as I look into his eyes. I'm a fool for doing this. It's not me. Not the woman I am today and not the woman I was before I lost my husband. Mason's steel gray gaze searches my own and I feel lost all over again.

I part my lips, ready to give an excuse, a lie, or even the truth. Anything to just go back in time and avoid being in this situation.

To run, just like I've been doing for the past eight months. Didn't I say I needed a change? I said I needed something drastic, but that was back when the alcohol was flowing and we were surrounded by a crowd of people.

Mason is so very tempting. He's gorgeous and confident, but I can't handle a man like him. I can't deal with this.

Weak and alone. A low whisper from the self-loathing bitch inside of me resonates in my ears. I slam my lips shut without uttering a word, hating that she's right.

I won't leave. I suck in a breath and force myself to be determined. Whether what I'm doing is right or wrong, it doesn't matter. I need a change.

A moment passes with the two of us standing still in front of his porch. Only a handful of steps are between us and his front door. I just have to get there.

My eyes drift from the deep navy door to Mason. I'm caught in place as he takes a single step closer to me. It's only one step, but with it is something powerful. His height, his scent, and his very dominance overwhelm me when he's this close. He radiates desire and my mind may be questioning things, but my body is pulled to him, magnetized by his presence.

It's soothing. Surprisingly so as I let my body move forward, closing the small space between us. He trails a finger down my collarbone lightly, testing my reaction.

"I want to touch you, Jules," he murmurs, forcing my gaze back to his all-consuming stare. I hadn't imagined it'd be this intense. Not at the bar and not in his Mercedes. He didn't push, and he didn't do anything to make me feel trapped. How odd—now that we're out in the open with no one watching and no enclosed spaces, it's only now that I feel cornered. All because of the way he looks at me.

What's most surprising is that I love it. *I want this.* The way he looks at me is addictive; it's freeing in more ways than one.

I can't wimp out. I won't.

I nod my head once and his fingers trail up my throat. His light touch feels much rougher than he's being with me. I tilt my head as his grip moves to my chin and he just barely brushes his lips against mine. It's a soft kiss that leaves me wanting more. I keep my eyes closed and stay as still as can be when he hovers close and whispers, "I want to kiss you."

"Then kiss me," I whimper, a pathetic plea, or maybe one of strength. My head feels so clouded that it's hard to know what's driving me. Raw, primal instinct or desperation. Perhaps a lethal cocktail of both.

He pulls away just slightly, but I don't let him get far. I take a half step closer to him, my breasts brushing against his shirt and I crash my lips into his. I need him. I need this.

He's quick to wrap his arms around me and pull my body against his. The faint noises of the night surround us and they seem to get louder as my breathing gets heavier. His lips travel down my throat and I throw my head back. I may have been tipsy from the alcohol before but in this moment I'm drunk with lust, and I find it too difficult to care.

"I want to fuck you, Jules," Mason practically growls. He pulls me into him suddenly and forces a gasp from me as he nips my earlobe. "I want to make you cum so hard you forget everything."

I moan as my nipples harden and my back arches. "The only thing you need to worry about is remembering my name," he whispers into my ear, his hands roaming down my waist, stopping at my ass. "Just my name and what I've done to you tonight."

I tilt my head back and everything he's saying is exactly what I need to hear. "Yes," I say into the soft breeze that cools my exposed hot skin.

"Only tonight," he says so low, I nearly miss it. My fingers slip under his shirt so I can feel his bare skin, and it triggers him to pull away from me. Just slightly, only so he can look into my eyes, but I grip him harder. I'm afraid to lose what he's offering me.

I want him. I want his promise.

I want to forget and feel alive again.

"Yes, only tonight," I say in agreement and then press my lips to his, moving a hand to the back of his head. My fingers spear through his thick hair as his tongue strokes mine and he lifts me into his arms by my ass.

I gasp at the sudden movement and wrap my legs around his waist. He takes the opportunity to trail open-mouth kisses down my neck and torture my deprived body.

I'm sure of it now. All I need is to be held by this man. Fucked by him and ruined by him.

With my back against the wall of his porch, he slides a hand up my dress and between my legs. Petting me, testing me until the sudden spike of pleasure hits me harder than I expected. He presses his thumb against me just right and my grip on him tightens.

I come alive for him, every nerve ending on fire, ready to burst into a flame so hot I can't control myself. He doesn't stop, even as I writhe and beg for him to take me inside. My fingers dig into his shoulders, my nails scratching along his shirt and wishing it were skin.

The pleasure is so intense already. It's nearly too much. I want to pull away because the inevitable drop from this high is going to shatter me. I'm all too aware of it, but I can't help myself.

He never stops kissing me as he balances me in one strong arm and unlocks the door. He never sets me down until he has me on his bed.

And he never gives me the chance to think about anything but the desire threatening to destroy me.

He doesn't take his time with my dress, desperate to have me bared to him. I reach behind me, unclasping my bra as he pulls the lace down my body. His fingers loop around my thong and take it along with the black dress.

My heels fall to the floor with a loud thud. I'm given a quick moment to consider what I'm doing as he pulls his shirt over his head. But instead of giving in to self-doubt, I'm mesmerized by the rippling of his muscles and then by the girth and rigidity of his cock as he shoves off his pants.

It happened so fast. Like a whirlwind of chaos that only surrounded the two of us. The mattress groans with his weight as I prop myself up on my elbows. He slides between my legs, spreading my thighs. My body opens up for him as if he was meant to be there all along. As if my movements are controlled by his desires.

My heart feels like it's trying to get away from me. His hard, hot body pushes down against mine and I can barely breathe.

My head turns to one side and then the other, feeling the cool sheet beneath my cheeks as he brushes against my slick folds.

"You're so wet for me," he says and Mason's voice is a mixture of wonder and reverence. He captures my lips with his and suddenly pushes his cock deep inside of me, all the way to the hilt in one swift stroke.

I scream out, my neck arching and my back bowing as he stills and gives me a moment to adjust to his size. My breath halts in my chest, but then he moves.

Not just moves. He fucks me with a punishing force. The bed slams against the wall with each thrust. He kisses me as though he's breathing the air from my lungs. He pins me down and takes everything from me, forcing me higher and higher, all while giving me everything I never knew I needed.

It's not until I'm left panting and recovering from waves of pleasure that I start to question what I've done. But it's late and I'm so exhausted. I forget it all except his name and what he's done to me, and give in to sleep.

Don't leave me alone, I cried and I screamed.

Don't leave me alone, my whole life demeaned.

You left me unguarded. My heart raw and bleeding.

You left me forever. The pain there left seething.

You left me here weak. Just a stone in the ground.

You left a place beside me, my picture-perfect life unbound.

chapter 9

Mason

Last night was stupid. Such a juvenile word but I can't think of anything better. Fucking stupid.

I'll blame it on the alcohol. A low exhale travels up my throat as I walk away from the floor-to-ceiling window in my office. The hustle and bustle of the street below is what drives me to keep moving. This city never sleeps and the work never ends.

Last night was about taking a moment to unwind from the shitshow my life has become. From my father, the arrogant prick and criminal that he is. The awareness of just how ruthless my father is has never hurt me more.

That's what it really is. *Pain.* Coming to the realization that your father's a disgusting excuse for a human being and should be behind bars is … difficult to handle. It's even worse when you're tied to his bullshit.

I sink into my leather desk chair and it protests the movement with a groan until I'm comfortable. Unlike my father's office, traditional and smelling of polished wood and old books, my office is the opposite. It's airy and open, modern and sleek. A model of our newest planned development sits in the very center of the space.

That's what started all this shit. A celebration for my company's first suburban development. No more apartments downtown. We're ready to expand into uncharted territories. I'm an idiot for thinking this would change things between my father and me. I really thought things would be different. I'd attributed the tense relationship with him to my own doing. A rebellious child with pent-up anger over his mother's death. Born into this black-tie bullshit.

I was always supposed to act right. Always supposed to say the right thing, stand the right way, behave and pay attention. Well, I didn't want to. I crack my neck remembering the fights I started. A smile kicks up my lips. Four boarding schools and hefty donations from my father still couldn't keep me in line.

Working in construction was just another way to stick it to my father.

Higher education? Fuck that. I got a job … but it didn't last for long. I'm just not made to work for someone else and I wanted a more physical job. So, I started Gray's Homes with Liam nearly three years ago. He had the schooling and I had the designs. I didn't think it'd be this successful or grow so quickly. So successful, in fact, that I ran out of capital and so did he. I took out loan after loan, investing in myself and I'd do it all over again. It was worth it to keep growing and taking advantage of the momentum we had. I should have known better when my father came to me and offered to invest in me too.

Clients were eager to sign contracts with his name on them. Having him back me made bids easier to attain and everything run smoother. I knew it was too good to be true.

He just wanted to be able to hold it over my head. He wanted to *own* me. I narrow my eyes at the model in the center of the room. It's all because of this one project. Now I'm in debt. I owe more than I'm worth and everything is hanging in the balance as we move forward with this one project that I'd love to trash just to spite my father. I should cancel it all now that I know the truth, but that would mean bankruptcy and more people than just myself being affected. Liam and all our employees and contractors. At the thought, there's a sick feeling in the pit of my stomach. One even a night of whiskey and great sex can't dissolve.

I pull my eyes back to the computer screen, back to reviewing all the invoices that have been paid. Everything's moving accordingly and on schedule, but only because of my father's loan.

I run a hand over my face knowing I'm just as much of a fucking prick. I don't deserve to breathe the same air as someone as sweet as Jules.

The thought of her shy smile and innocent looks … God, it does something to me. The guilt and anger are minimal compared to the desire. I want to feel her again. I want to get lost in her touch and be the one to do the same for her.

I can make it all better.

She has no idea how screwed up this situation is. If my father knew who I'd spent last night with, I imagine I'd never hear the end of it. He may be a piece of shit and deserve to be locked away for the rest of his life, but if the world knew what I'd done, they would think the same of me.

I click the mouse to light up my screen as it goes dim once again. I can't think; I can't focus.

As my temples throb and irritation grows, I think back to last night. Back to Jules.

Out of every possible way for this morning to start, I never guessed she'd sneak out.

I imagined how the morning would go over and over again while I watched her sleep, her long hair a messy halo on the pillow. So peaceful and beautiful.

I couldn't get over how fucked up it was. How selfish. But it was everything I wanted and more. *It was fucking worth it.*

As she slept, exhausted and spent from the raw fuck, my fingers longed to travel along her curves. I was still hard for more.

Staring at her lush lips, the vision of her eyes shut tight, her head thrown back, and her mouth parted with soft, strangled moans spilling between them was etched in my memory. It was the sexiest thing I've ever seen. Jules was utterly in rapture from what I was doing to her. She was completely at my mercy and I know she loved every minute.

I tugged the blankets over myself and lay there watching her, debating how I'd end it in the morning. I could crave her more than anything, but it was over. It should never have started to begin with. As I thought up exactly what to say to ease the sting, I watched her steady breathing and my lungs filled with her sweet scent.

Just once more. I should have woken her up, spread her legs wide and taken her again. Had I known that I'd wake up alone, I would have.

I lean back in my seat, letting out the aggravation in a groan as I watch the security footage again. She slipped out just before dawn, leaving only a note behind. I watch in amusement as she keeps looking up from the pad of small sticky notes she'd found on my kitchen counter. The pen never even touched the paper for a full two minutes as she contemplated what to write.

She's lost and confused. She doesn't even know what she wants.

But I do.

I fidget with the yellow sticky note, passing it from my middle finger to my pointer and back again mindlessly.

Thank you.

If last night was more than just last night …

I trace the delicate, feminine script of the letters. She was made to tempt men. I'm convinced of it. Everything from her soft sighs to the way she carries herself.

It's as if she was designed to lure me in unknowingly.

Even the way she's written her phone number calls to me. Each graceful curve makes my fingers itch to punch in the numbers on my phone.

Weakness. Stupidity.

Last night was a one-time thing. I don't have to call her. I don't owe her anything and I'm sure she doesn't expect a damn thing either.

Why does that bother me even more?

The sticky note moves from finger to finger more rapidly now. I know I shouldn't call her. Nothing good can come from this.

My eyes look back to her message and focus on her phone number.

Selfish. So fucking selfish.

That's the problem, though. I just don't give a damn about anyone else. The thought is what strengthens my resolve. It's all going to come crumbling down around me soon. I deserve to enjoy what little time I have left.

chapter 10

Julia

WATER DRIPS FROM THE SPOUT OF THE IRON FAUCET. I GRIP THE side of the claw-foot porcelain tub, the water splashing slightly in the silent room as I get comfortable. Then I rest my cheek against the cool hard porcelain and watch the water as it continues to drip.

The water's nearly lukewarm by now, but I don't want to get out. My wet hair clings to my skin as I sink in deeper, letting the water climb to my neck. My legs sway from side to side and I listen to the steady rhythm of the dripping water.

Part of me wants to pretend like last night didn't happen. And this morning—I close my eyes and bring my hands up to my face, embarrassed by the memory. There's nothing in etiquette class about how to leave your one-night stand.

My throat feels raw as I take in a breath, remembering how last night felt. His hands on my body, his chest against mine as he rocked in and out of me, mercilessly, ruthlessly.

I've never … I swallow thickly, hating that I'm even comparing last night to what I had with my husband. I feel like I've betrayed Jace but I just let myself fall into the water, as if I can wash it all away.

No amount of time spent in this tub will cleanse the sins of last night.

One good thing's come of it, though. The words are flowing through me so easily now. All I've done since I've been home is write. I shouldn't be happy about that; I shouldn't feel like a weight has been lifted, but I do. Every single thing I've written since my husband's passing has been dark and stunted. It's nothing that I would willingly choose to write. My poetry has always been a happy place and now I have a piece of that back.

The pain in my chest though, the way my heart feels tight and my lungs too crushed to breathe, that's because I don't regret it.

I feel guilty that I don't feel guilty. How does that even make sense?

Ping. I groan at the sound, squeezing my eyes tight. I must've been more than a bit tipsy last night to let Sue act as my conscience. She won't leave me alone. There were way too many texts waiting for me this morning for her to have gone home with anyone last night.

I woke up to a myriad of messages.

Please tell me he didn't kill you.

I'm so sorry if he did, though!

Seriously, are you okay? Text me later!

She thinks she's funny. I thought I was doing a good thing by letting her know I was still alive and unharmed, but all that did was open a floodgate of questions.

She's finding more joy in this than I am, which makes me laugh.

I can't help the way my lips beg me to smile and the way my heart flutters. Sue's having a good time teasing me. *Ping.* I turn my head to the right, to where my towel and phone are sitting on the marble bench.

I can only imagine what she wants to know this time.

"I can't hide in here forever," I say under my breath, finally lifting myself out of the comfort of the tub. I lean down and pull the plug, letting the cool air hit my heated skin.

It was nice while it lasted and after last night, it did my body good to relax in here. As I lean over to grab the towel, the sensitive bits between my thighs ache again with slight pain. It's a good kind of hurt though, the kind that lets you know you've been properly laid. I laugh slightly into the towel and dry off my body, then work on patting my hair dry. My feet pad softly against the black-and-white penny tile floor.

The bathroom matches the estate's classic interior. Every accent and piece of decor reflect the timing of when the house was built. There are a few modern pieces, but they only accentuate the charm of the classic architecture. It's expensive to maintain, but the beauty is unmatched.

I continue towel-drying my long hair as the memories of renovating the house come to me one by one. The bit of happiness I'd claimed only moments ago vanishes.

Jace and I got into so many fights over this tile. I can see him standing in front of the mirror, glaring at me for being stubborn. It's my family's house, though. This isn't an Anderson estate. I inherited it when my parents moved from the city. We both knew I was far more well-off than he ever was. The steamy glass doesn't hide the past. I can hear his voice; I can see it all like it was just yesterday.

But the memories are from years ago, and he's never coming back.

Ping. This time when the phone goes off, I can't help but want to cling to whatever Sue's said. She could ask how big he is and I'd give her every detail including the veins. I'd be eternally grateful for a distraction right now. I take a seat on the bench, wincing as my sore bottom rests against the hard marble and pick up the damn phone.

It's not her.

Well, this last message isn't.

I have three from Sue, all wanting to know details about what I did with Mason last night. I roll my eyes and let out a small snort at her question about size. Of course she would ask me. I knew it.

By the looks of him, he should be packing … but I'm going to guess he's only four inches. Am I right?

She cracks me up. She's been sending me these kinds of messages all day. Anything to get me talking.

Nope, only three, I type back just to give her something to laugh about. She deserves it. Without all these messages and prodding, I'm not sure how I would have handled this on my own.

I click over to the other message and my heart does an odd flip in my chest when I see who it's from. Like it can't function for just a moment. Maybe it's the shock and disbelief, or maybe it's fear? I'm not sure, but either way, I'm struck by the fact that Mason messaged me at all. I was sure that sneaking out would have sealed the deal between the two of us. It was a one-time thing. One I'm grateful for and content with. I knew what I was getting when I went into the arrangement.

I wasn't sure if I should leave my phone number. I imagine he was relieved to find his drunken one-night stand gone and I didn't want him to feel obligated to call me.

At the same time, I hoped he would.

Not because of him. It's not that I'm clinging to having a relationship at all. I just … I liked the way he made me … I don't know what the right word is. The way nothing else mattered when I was with him. How it all slipped away and I didn't have to focus on anything but him. Mostly because he was only focused on me.

There's nothing wrong with wanting more of that, is there? I bite down on my bottom lip and read the message.

It's not a hello or an admonishment for leaving him.

I want to see you again. Blue Hill at 8 p.m. tonight.

My lashes flutter a few times as I reread the message. How very presumptuous. As if I have nothing better to do than meet up with him.

I don't, if I'm being honest with myself. I haven't got a single thing to do other than write, which I fell into earlier and loved every second. I lose a little bit of the fight in me at the thought that I am available tonight, but still. This isn't happening like this. I'm not a booty call or whatever he's used to.

I look down at the message again and the second readthrough only pisses me off.

Maybe I want a good lay too, and by maybe, I mean I really do need it, but

I'm not a call girl and I don't want to be treated like one. Last night was something out of my realm.

Sorry. Busy. I type in the words and hit send without even thinking, letting my high and mighty attitude lead me. But as soon as the message pops up on the screen, I wish I could take it back.

My eyes close and my head falls back as I groan in aggravation. I should have just said yes. I mean after all, aren't I using him too? I'm so busy staring at the ceiling and cursing myself that when my phone pings in my hand, I jump slightly.

Are you busy now?

A second passes and then another. Is he toying with me? I think he is. I can just imagine the teasing way he would say it. Like he knows exactly why I responded how I did. I smirk and bite the inside of my cheek as I text back.

Maybe I am.

His response is immediate. *No you aren't and I want to see you. Blue Hill at 8 p.m.*

My shoulders stiffen and I can't help but feel like this is some kind of battle of wills. And I have no intention of losing.

I said I was busy.

I wait for his response, a deep crease settling in between my brows.

There's no immediate message back and I start to question my position. I don't want to be alone tonight. I know it's pathetic but I'm so tired of being lonely, lying in bed at night, staring at the other half of the bed where my husband used to sleep.

Maybe I need to take a step back and think this through. Dating isn't exactly an expertise of mine. Neither is hooking up. With a heavy heart I reread the messages and try not to overthink it all, but I'm sure that's exactly what I'm doing.

I contemplate messaging the girls in our group text when minutes go by and I don't hear from Mason. A lot of pride lives in me, but not when it comes to this. I'm out of my element.

Tossing my phone down, I decide it's probably for the best that I don't see Mason tonight anyway. I've never been alone before and I'm too tempted to cling to him already and overanalyze it all. Pushing my hair back, I wonder if I should try to convince Sue to go out tonight. I'm sure she would if only I asked. Any of the girls would and I love them for it.

The phone pings against the porcelain and I'm quick to read what he's said.

You win. Just tell me when. I'm available for you.

The smile on my face isn't stopped by my teeth sinking into my lip and I sway slightly as I compose my response. The warmth that spreads through me is addictive. It makes me a little too happy, but I'm too caught in the moment to overthink anything else right now.

chapter 11

Mason

"So, who is she?" Liam asks from his office as I'm on my way out. He leans out the doorway, both hands on the doorframe as he smirks at me.

"Who?" I say, turning my back to him so I can lock up my office. It's a habit I've always had. No one else has a key. I've got fifteen employees working here who come and go throughout the day, but my office is only for me.

"The chick you hooked up with last night." I test the doorknob, making sure it's locked and drop my keys into my pocket. I won't be long since I'm only heading out for lunch, which is good because I want to have all these numbers crunched by the time I need to leave for Blue Hill.

When I turn back around, Liam's got his arms crossed and he's leaning against the door, waiting for me like I owe him some sort of explanation.

"None of your damn business," I say, keeping my tone casual and smirking at him.

"Oh shit," he says then lets out a bark of a laugh with a wide grin. "You really did hook up with someone last night?" he asks me with disbelief. Liam's always been a talker. He doesn't seem to mind my demeanor as much as everyone else does. Give him enough time and he can have an entire conversation by himself, so maybe the two of us were meant to be friends.

Pushing off the doorframe he says, "I was going to give you shit for leaving me hanging last night."

"Just didn't want to be alone last night," I tell him honestly. "Better her company than yours," I joke with a grin, trying to lighten the mood even though I want this conversation to be over.

"So, are we going to go over it tonight then?" he asks me.

"Go over what?"

"What our investor said at the meeting you had without me yesterday." By investor, he means my father.

"It wasn't about Gray's Homes." I take a few steps closer to his office. Mine's the largest and in the very back. Liam's is kitty-corner to mine and the only other office in here. Across from his is the boardroom which is currently empty and only ever used for sales pitches and the end of quarter wrap-ups.

"Oh," Liam says and he seems genuinely taken by surprise. His expression lets me know he wants to ask me a million fucking questions, all of which I'm sure I don't want to hear. *Why was my father so persistent on meeting me? Why did he come in here asking for a conference over and over and demanding I sit down with him?*

"It's been a bit rocky between us for the last few months," I say with my voice low enough that it's just the two of us in this conversation. I know Margaret, our secretary, is right down the hall and close enough to hear if we talk loud enough.

"Few months?"

I stare at him, feeling my expression hardening. It was a necessary evil for me to stop talking to my father a while ago. I'm caught between wanting to do what's right and not knowing for sure that I'd be doing the right thing. So instead of taking action, I avoided him every chance I got.

It worked my entire life up until now. Until he told me what I already knew, confirming it and forcing me to face the truth.

"Don't worry about it." I give him a tight smile. "It's got nothing to do with the business."

"And what about you?" he says, pushing further. "I can't be worried about you?"

The simple answer I give him is bullshit and he knows it. "I'm fine."

"Yeah, you keep saying that," he says then turns like he's going to head back into his office as the phone rings.

"Go get it." I nod toward his office. "I'm just picking up a Reuben from across the street."

"All right." He heads into his office but before I make it another two steps, he's popping his head outside of the door again to ask, "Will you get me a Coke?"

Glancing over my shoulder, I tell him yes as the sounds of everyone else working get louder and louder.

I don't break my stride as I head down the hall. Our company owns this entire floor of the Rising Falls Building; it's a tall office building that's made for businesses just like ours. The second I stepped in here, I knew this was where I wanted to work. There's clear glass everywhere. So much natural light and impressive views of the city to provide constant inspiration.

Even the cubicles have plexiglass walls.

"Out to lunch?" Margaret asks as I stride past her, needing to shake the nagging feelings that wrestle in the pit of my stomach.

"I'll be right back." I nod, again not slowing my pace and head past all my employees to the elevator.

"Yes, sir," Margaret answers with a light-hearted tone. I've never seen that woman not smile. As if being our secretary is the highlight of her day. She's damn good at what she does too. At first, I was opposed to letting someone step in and take control of scheduling and inventory, but as we grew, I just couldn't handle it all.

Pressing the button for the elevator, I try to think about anything other than my father. With the button lighting up, I'm reminded of Jules's text. The irritation and anger nearly vanish.

Just the thought of what was going through her mind when she messaged back makes me smile. She's a testy little thing. I didn't expect that. There's more to Miss Summers than I thought and I'm definitely intrigued.

I check my Rolex as the elevator dings and the doors slowly open. There's no one inside, so I walk right in and hit the button for the ground floor. Only six hours until dinner.

My chest feels tight and the small smile leaves me. It's fucked up in so many ways, but she'll never know. I'll make sure she never finds out.

chapter 12

Julia

THERE ARE PINK MACARONS AND CRYSTAL CHANDELIERS EVERYWHERE I look. I love this place. It's a tiny shop and the treats are far too expensive for what they are, but it's the vibe I truly love. I scoot my silver stool closer to the small round table and unpeel the wrapper on my cupcake as I listen to Suzette.

"I want to know every detail," she says with barely contained joy. Kat glances between the two of us and so far, she hasn't touched a thing on the etched tray in the center of the table. I know there's something there that would make her smile, but she's not interested. I bet she and her husband had another fight. I wish they wouldn't; they love each other. It's been obvious to me since the day she met him.

Clearing my throat, I avoid replying to Sue's comment. I can feel both sets of their eyes on me, but I don't look up. It's too pretty in here to feel this anxious. My eyes settle on the crystal flute of pink champagne and I take a quick sip, tilting my head up to gaze at the carved tin ceiling. Everything in here is pink, silver, shiny and new. So beautiful to look at, but useless in saving me from this conversation.

"How could you not tell us?" Kat's voice is low but not scolding, more surprised than anything. She's still standing with her purse on a stool and I don't think she has any intention of sitting down in the least. Until she does, plopping down with her eyes boring into me. "I want to know who you're seeing," she adds with a pout.

The disappointment in her voice makes my appetite for all things sweet and scrumptious vanish. I knew this was coming. You can't just take off from Katerina Thompson and not have her chew you out later.

"It wasn't meant as an insult," I start to tell her. It's not like I was trying to upset her, she should at least know that for a fact.

"It's because you would have stopped her," Sue interjects before shoving a tiny cupcake into her mouth and biting it right down the middle. She has no shame and gives Kat the answer as if it's obvious. Which it is. If I'm an overthinker, Kat is a second-guesser.

"Of course I would have stopped her." Her wrath is directed at Sue now and to be honest, I'm grateful. Sue can handle it. She stares Kat right in the eye as she pushes the other half of the cupcake into her mouth with her pointer finger.

Kat justifies her stance. "She was drunk and how many one-night stands have we regretted right after?" She has a point, I'll give her that.

"It's not that I was keeping it from you," I say. There's a small plea in my voice for Kat to calm down. "I was …"

"You were keeping it from me," Kat says, finishing my sentence for me.

"Only until it was over," I say as my face scrunches with guilt and I hide behind my drink.

"Oh hush," Sue says easily and then nods at me. "Good for you for going out and dusting off those cobwebs." I snort a small laugh and my shoulders shake from it. "He's cute too."

"He'd better be," Kat says beneath her breath, pulling out a bottle of water from her oversized leather hobo bag.

Sue rolls her eyes and says, "You going to track him down and beat the crap out of him if he isn't?" A smile forces its way onto my face and I try to make it go away, but it's not happening. Kat side-eyes Sue for a moment before returning to her water and taking a sip. With that, the tension vanishes. Kat gets why I didn't tell her, I know she does. And I get why she's upset. It's a simple squabble that's over the moment Kat reaches for her own cupcake.

"So, your first one-night stand. How does it feel?" Sue asks.

I could write a whole book on the effects I'm feeling right now. The guilt, the anxiety. But the other things, the bit of liveliness and … is it pride? Is that what it is? Knowing that I was wanted and desired like *that* by a man like Mason. And that he still wants me. Yeah, that's a bit of pride, which is odd to be feeling over this.

"He texted me this morning." I sway a little in my seat, picking at the hem of the tablecloth. "He wants to go out tonight."

Sue's eyes go wide. "Really?" She grins in slow motion and then makes a face as she wipes her fingertips on her napkin.

"What's that for?" I ask her.

Sue shrugs and says, "Nothing."

"That's not a nothing look," I tell her right back. "That's a something look."

Kat reaches for another cupcake, listening intently.

"You must've been good." Sue pops a piece of macaron into her mouth all the while smiling. The tiered tray was filled with an assortment of sugary treats when Sue arrived, but it's almost empty now except for the large cupcakes.

My mouth opens some and I have to force it back shut. By the heat on my cheeks, I imagine I'm beet red. Yeah, it's definitely pride.

"So, what'd you tell him?" Kat says. "Don't worry, I won't try to stop you," she adds with an asymmetric smile.

I'm embarrassed that I first told him I was busy and then suggested the exact time and location he said originally when he told me it was my call, so I just cut to the chase. "I said yes."

"You said yes to a date for tonight that was asked today?" Kat asks with a raised brow. Yup, she's just like me.

"I did," I answer slowly as Sue claps her hands and leans her head back with laughter. She's so loud that a few customers in line at the counter look back at her.

"I love her. This is just too good to be true." Sue's smile just gets bigger and bigger until she spots the last tiny cupcake.

"I know how it sounds but I told him no at first, and then he said he was available whenever I was ready."

"So then you said yes." Kat nods her head and I nod in return. I can see the wheels spinning.

"I want to go out and see him again. It's that simple."

Kat hums, her eyes narrowing like she's thinking far too hard, biting her tongue, or both. She finally settles on her response, asking, "So you like him?"

She's awarded another nod from me as I say, "I do. At least I like the way he makes me feel."

There's another hum from her and Sue shakes her head, opting to finish her drink rather than contribute to the conversation.

"You have fun tonight," Sue says with a wink. I give her a small smile back and kiss her cheek before she leaves us so she can get to her meeting on time.

Maddie's not coming to this little cupcake brunch so it's just me and Kat now. I don't like the feeling that I need armor to have a quick chat with one of my closest friends. I bite the inside of my cheek as I watch Sue leave, the bells hanging above the door ringing as I shift on the stool.

"Kat, look—"

"Nope," she says and holds up her hand. "It's fine. Last night was fine. Tonight is fine." Her eyes are closed as she speaks. She nods her head as if she's convincing herself, moving the purse from on top of her stool to the one Sue was sitting on. She has to shift in her seat to tug down her black pencil skirt. Her white blouse is nearly see-through, but she still resembles the epitome of professionalism. She's always put together and on top of everything.

"I know last night isn't something you would do," I start to say and Kat nods slightly. "I know it upset you for me to leave and not tell you." I lean forward, putting my hand on the table, closer to her.

"I think I overreacted," Kat blurts out before I can say anything else. She doesn't meet my gaze at first, but then she lifts her eyes to mine. "It really is okay, all of it, and I'm not trying to make you feel bad." Her words come out with sincerity and it surprises me how much I needed that. "Or slut-shame you or anything like that. I'm happy that you're happy. I'm just nervous that he's taking advantage of you, or that you're going to get hurt …" I brace for what I know is coming as she lowers her voice and says, "You know, so soon after everything."

"I know. Thank you." My voice cracks some and I look for my glass, but then find it empty. I run my fingertips down the stem, feeling overwhelmed again with a mix of emotions.

Guilt comes out to play more than the rest. It's not her making me feel guilty. It's the thought that I should still be mourning.

"Am I a bad person?" I ask Kat, finally pulling my eyes from the empty flute to her.

"No," she answers with sad eyes, taking my hand in both of hers. "I didn't mean to make you think that—"

"You didn't," I say and wave her off the path she's going down. "I was just thinking this morning … about …" About Jace. I don't say it out loud.

"Just tell me that he's not going to make you miss your deadline." Kat deflects, sidestepping this conversation and creating an out for me. God, I love her. She's my editor and this manuscript is due in two weeks.

A smile grows on my face, but it's not genuine in the least. Not because of Kat or Mason or any of that. It's the use of the word *deadline*. I know for a fact I'm going to miss that deadline. She doesn't need to know that, though. "He won't get in the way of that." I shake my head cheerfully, my hair swishing against my shoulders.

"Okay then," she says as she raises her brows and finally picks up a cupcake. Not the small ones from the tray of random sweets, nope, Kat goes for the largest cupcake with hot pink icing and an Oreo stuck in the center. "Please tell me you're at least using condoms until you get back on the pill or something."

I know she meant for that to be funny, but when I give her a side-eye and a shrug, she practically chokes on that Oreo.

chapter 13

Mason

So close you can touch her,

Delicate and sweet.

You need her, you crave her,

To hide your deceit.

Be gentle and coaxing,

You can't let her know.

If she finds out the truth,

Out the door she will go.

BLUE HILL DIMS THE LIGHTS IN THE EVENING AT SIX O'CLOCK SHARP. The dinner atmosphere is romantic with lit candles on the tables, combined with the soothing sound of water flowing down the river rock wall next to the kitchen. The chatter from the other guests goes unheard as I sit here alone. The only sound that resonates with me is the clink of silverware and glasses as I wait for Jules to walk through the doors.

My fingertips brush over the silver tines of my salad fork as I stare straight ahead toward the entrance and maître d'. Multiple guests have arrived since I sat down twenty minutes ago, each one catching my attention and disappointing me. I glance down at my watch again. She still has five minutes until she's late.

I make a habit of being early, but I'm regretting it this time. Every minute that passes makes me more eager to leave. Curiosity is the only thing keeping me here in my seat. The door opens and the soft cadence of heels clicking on the slate floor echoes in the large open space.

She's here. Jules slips her gray wool peacoat off her shoulders when she walks in and drapes it in her arms as she strides to the maître d'. I stand and button my suit jacket as I walk toward her. I'm only a few tables away and she sees me as the man asks her if she has a reservation.

"She's with me." My voice comes out deep, confident ... possessive even. As she turns toward my voice, the hem of her plum-colored dress sways around her thighs. It's tighter around her ass and waist, showing off her curves and reminding me how she looked beneath me last night.

"Of course," the maître d' says and nods.

"Thank you," Jules answers sweetly, giving him a soft smile and looking back at me. It's only a quick glance before a blush rises to her cheeks and she takes my hand.

She has a shy elegance about her, but there's more to her than that. I want to dig a little deeper, if for nothing more than curiosity's sake.

I gesture toward the table, pulling out her chair for her like a gentleman. It's not in my nature, but I have enough manners to impress a woman at least.

"I'm surprised you wanted to see me again," Jules says as I take my own seat. The confession sits between the two of us for a moment as I consider a response.

Before I can say anything, she adds, "Thank you, by the way." Her eyes flicker from mine to the candle. I don't miss how she takes a few glances around us as if she's searching for someone.

I nod my head easily, setting my napkin in my lap and giving her a moment to get comfortable. The waiter quickly pours her a glass of water from the pitcher he's holding.

"Good evening. May I start you off with something to drink?" The young man squares his shoulders and waits, holding the pitcher at attention. He's dressed in a crisp white button-down and dark gray slacks that match his thin tie.

"A bourbon for me, please," I say and wait for Jules. Her slender neck and shoulders are on display. The way the thin straps of her dress lay across the very edge of her shoulders taunt me to pull them down. A simple thin silver necklace sits right in the dip of her collarbone with the word *happy* etched in the middle. It's the only piece of jewelry she's wearing. No ring on her finger. I didn't notice one last night either.

"A glass of chardonnay, please."

"Right away," the waiter says and nods, leaving us alone. Once again, Jules squirms uncomfortably. I love her nervousness and how she has a habit of tucking her hair behind her ear. It only adds to her innocence.

"No tequila?" I say, playing around with her to break the ice.

She huffs a small laugh and rolls her eyes. "No," she says as she unfolds her napkin and moves it to her lap, smoothing it out. "No tequila tonight."

I shrug, waiting for those soft baby blue eyes to look back up at me. "I didn't mind the tequila." I murmur the confession across the table. There's not a damn thing dirty that I've said but she still blushes. There's an attraction between us that's undeniable. It's easy and carefree. But the air is tense as she looks to her left again and then back to me.

She hesitates to say something, then changes her mind and clears her throat as she picks up the menu. She talks without looking at me. "I've never done anything like this."

"Like what?"

"Like, seeing someone."

"Is that what we're doing?" I ask her. "Seeing each other?"

Jules puts her menu down and looks at me with a serious expression. "I have no idea." The sincere answer and complete honesty in her voice force a rough laugh from my chest. I was only teasing her, but she's too sweet and sincere to get a rise out of her.

"You can laugh all you want, but I have no clue what's going on." She picks her menu back up and says, "I'm just along for the ride, Mr. Thatcher."

"Is that so?" I ask her playfully and reach for my glass of water when the waiter returns, setting down my drink first and then hers.

"It is," she says, smiling into her glass and taking a sip of the white wine. She closes her eyes and lets out the softest moan of satisfaction that's barely audible. My cock hardens as I remember last night, the same sweet sound slipping from her lips as I thrust into her over and over again.

She's completely oblivious. Even with a shiver of desire running down my spine, she doesn't seem to notice what she does to me.

"So, what changed in your plans?" I ask as she eyes the menu again. I don't bother looking at mine. I know exactly what I'll have.

A short, feminine laugh makes her shoulders shake as she pulls her long dark hair over her shoulder and then brushes it back again. "I thought this would be better than what I had planned."

Bullshit. I can tell she's lying from a mile away.

"And what did you have planned before?" I say and smirk, pushing for more and wanting to see her admit to this little game she played this morning.

She takes a sip of wine and then answers, "Writing."

"Writing?"

"I like to go to Central Park to write," she says easily, slipping her hands into her lap and leaning forward.

"Are you a journalist?"

"No," she says and shakes her head, "I'm an author." She takes a sip of wine again and I watch as she fiddles with the stem and continues. "I'm not well known or anything. Just poetry." She tries to wave off her insecurity then adds, "It doesn't really make much money, but it's the career I chose."

She's already justifying herself and I don't like it. She should be proud.

"I think that's wonderful. It takes a lot of work and diligence to write a novel of poetry."

Her eyes light up and she visibly relaxes as she says in a delicate voice, "Thank you."

"Who's your favorite poet?" I ask her.

"Robert Frost," she answers quickly. "Hands down."

"I've read a bit of Frost." It's true, albeit years and years ago in grade school and I'm pretty sure I hated every minute I was forced to read it. It doesn't matter, though; my remark makes her calm and that sweet smile comes back.

I clear my throat, smoothing the napkin on my lap and trying to remember what Mrs. Harper said. "'Poetry is when an emotion has found its thought,'" I say as I look into her eyes and try to say the second part correctly, "'and the thought has found words.' I believe it was Frost who said that." Her entire demeanor changes to one of surprise and ease. I'm shocked that I remembered it myself.

A surprised grin looks back at me. It's amazing how something so small can make her genuinely happy. She nods and says, "Yes, I do believe you're right."

The moment between us is filled with comfortable silence as we each take a sip of our drinks.

"So you're in construction, I believe?"

"I'm a developer," I say, hoping she won't ask too many questions. I don't think she has any idea of the connections. I don't intend to lie to her, but I don't need to give her anything that would help her put the pieces together.

"In the city, right?"

"Brooklyn mostly, although we're currently under contract with the city to renovate and rebuild some properties in Manhattan."

"What's that like?"

"Being a developer?" I've never had anyone ask me before and I take a moment to consider my reply. "It's challenging at times and it pisses me off most days. A lot goes wrong and hardly anything goes the way it's planned." I smirk at her as she laughs into her glass at my answer. "Isn't that what all jobs are like, though?"

She nods her head, setting the glass down but then her expression changes. "I'm not sure I should be doing this," she tells me with her forehead scrunched.

"Doing what?"

"This," she says and gestures between the two of us.

"We're just having dinner."

Her eyes narrow and I ignore the accusatory stare, picking up my bourbon and taking an easy drink of it. It burns just right on the way down, leaving a trail of heat in its wake.

"I just want to feed you," I say in a tone that I hope comes out somewhat innocent.

"And fuck me," she whispers so softly but with a roughness I haven't heard from that sexy voice of hers. I stare into her gorgeous gaze, daring her to blush, to be embarrassed by it, but she only stares back with desire in her baby blue eyes.

"Yes, and fuck you," I say. It doesn't go unnoticed that she clenches her thighs. "You want that, don't you?"

"I'm not sure I should be sleeping with you," she says simply but with a firm resolve in her voice. My heart beats in a way that makes it feel tight. Like there's not quite enough room for it to beat again.

"Are you seeing someone else?" I ask her. My knuckles brush against the white tablecloth as my hands start to fist. I stop them and try to keep my body from showing what I'm really feeling. She better not be fucking anyone else.

She loses the conviction in her voice when she answers, "No."

"Then why shouldn't we?" I say, glancing at the waiter as he makes his way toward us.

"Because—" Jules stops as soon as she notices him. She plasters on a fake smile that doesn't reach her eyes and waits patiently for him to address her.

"Are you ready for me to take your order?" he asks me but I gesture to Jules, taking another sip to settle my irritation.

"For you, miss?"

"May I have the herb-grilled salmon, please?" She passes the menu to him and rests her hands in her lap, giving him her full attention. Meanwhile, I can't take my eyes off her and wondering why the hell she thinks she shouldn't be seeing me.

"Are the grilled vegetables all right with that?" he asks her.

"Yes, they're perfect."

The waiter scribbles on the notepad in his hand then turns toward me.

"Sirloin, medium rare. Vegetables are fine." I preemptively answer his un-asked question, still staring at Jules. The waiter takes the hint, nodding once and immediately leaving us.

"You were saying?" I say, picking up my bourbon.

"I—" Again she hesitates, sensing the change in my temperament. "I don't know if I should really be seeing *anyone*."

I wait for more, taking another sip.

"I'm not sure how to," she says, waving her hand in the air, at a loss for words. "I'm still—" She can't put a sentence together.

"I want to fuck you, Jules. Give me one good reason why there's a problem with that." I hold her gaze listing all the reasons in my head, but ignoring every last one of them. She needs someone to fuck, to hold her, someone to make her smile. I can do that; I can be that person.

"It's just sex?" she asks and from the look in her eyes, I don't know what answer she wants in return.

Fuck, I wish it were. I can't explain why I want her this badly. It's more than the physical attraction, but I'll never admit the truth to her.

"Just sex," I lie. "If that's what you want."

She licks her lush lips, peering down at her silverware and then up to me. "I'd be using you," she says as if she's confessing a sin.

A bark of a laugh leaves me and my tense muscles relax.

"Use me, Jules." I stare into her blue eyes flecked with silver, feeling the tension between us morph into something sweeter, something darker and depraved. "I want you to."

chapter 14

Julia

> *It starts with a kiss.*
>
> *Then dinners and dates.*
>
> *It starts with a smile.*
>
> *Your evenings run late.*
>
> *It tempts and teases.*
>
> *And makes you want more.*
>
> *But it's not how it starts,*
>
> *When it can only end in war.*

THERE'S SOMETHING ABOUT HIM TONIGHT. SOMETHING DARKER THAT I didn't see before. It's the way he looks at me like I should be running from him. It both scares me and lures me in.

Lifting the glass to my lips, my one and only glass, I finish off the sweet wine.

"Did you write today?" Mason asks. We've made a bit of small talk and light conversation. I'm still feeling him out. I thought I wanted this thing between us but the air changed a bit ago, and the tension is something else now. Like we're at war, although I don't know why.

"I did, yes." Every bit of it was about Jace, though. Something I'd rather not bring up with Mason. I pick up my glass again, finding it empty and cursing internally.

I head off whatever other questions he has for me by saying, "Why dinner tonight and not just drinks after?" My voice is low, nearly accusatory, but unlike what happened earlier, he doesn't seem to mind.

It takes a moment for him to respond, but he does. "Because I had to eat and so did you."

He takes another bite of his steak and then asks, "Would you rather we were just having drinks tonight?"

"Yes." My answer is immediate. He doesn't seem taken aback. He's calm, unmoving and unbothered.

"Why's that?"

I can't look him in the eyes as my fingers nervously move up and down the silverware. I don't know how to put it out there. "How did you know my name?" I ask him.

"From the papers," Mason says and then quickly takes a sip of his drink.

I nod my head. That's how everyone knows me. "The papers?" I say, hoping he'll elaborate.

"I've read a few things."

"Then you may have me at a disadvantage. The papers know far too much about me," I joke, seemingly innocent, but I'm sure he's aware that I'm prodding.

"That's possible, probable even." He smirks at me, his brilliant smile adding to his charm. I try not to let it affect me, but I'm at his mercy whenever he looks at me like that. I consider the facts and list out all the reasons I have to end this. Maybe the conversation with Kat got to me more than I thought.

I'm vulnerable. *Check.*

I've never done this before. *Check.*

I don't know that I'm okay with this. *Check.*

And a man like Mason could crush me. *Check a thousand times.*

"Well, all I know about you is that you're a bit of a player," I say and dare to hold his gaze.

"I used to be, yes."

"Used to?" There's a tension between us. It's hot to the touch and it makes me want to move closer to him, but I know that I need to keep my distance right now.

"Yes, used to. I mean it. I used to be … more unattached, then I met someone."

"Oh." I'm surprised by his confession and also by the immediate reaction I have to him meeting someone who made him want to settle down. Maybe all the thoughts and emotions are playing on my face, because Mason continues.

"She's not in the picture anymore and it wasn't anything serious at all." He answers my questions before I have to ask them and I'm grateful for that. "It just changed things for me."

I wish I could keep my expression neutral but I've never been very good at hiding what I'm feeling, and this mix of curiosity and even jealousy surely isn't becoming. "So now you want someone to fuck and take to dinners?"

A deep rough chuckle vibrates up his chest and the way he smiles at me does something to me that makes me reconsider my list of reasons.

"Someone, no." His eyes heat and he licks his bottom lip as he adds, "You, yes."

I huff out a small breath and peer down at my nearly empty plate before looking back up to him.

"I want to take you out, bring you back home and lay you down in my bed." He holds my gaze as he says the words so calmly. I fight the urge to look around the room filled with families and couples to make sure no one's heard us. My body is on fire with the thought of him doing just that, over and over. But the part where he talks about taking me out … that makes this seem serious. It practically begs for drama, given my history as a socialite. Whatever this is between us … I don't want that out there for all the judging eyes.

"I feel …" I trail off as I realize I don't know how I feel, and with that frustration I lay down my silverware.

"What's wrong?"

"I don't really like going out anymore." I blurt out the confession and feel sick to my stomach.

"You don't like going out?" He frowns.

"It just makes me anxious because of something that happened. Something that maybe you read about?" It would be a blessing if he already knew. If he could understand that privacy is an issue for me and this is something I would greatly prefer to keep private.

He stares at me for a moment, although his eyes flash with a knowing look.

I don't want to say it out loud and I wait for him to answer, but he doesn't.

"It's just," I say as my voice gets tight and I choke on the words, but only for a moment, "my husband passed away and it's hard for me to deal with moving on with someone else." I stumble over my next words for a moment when I say, "Because people …"

"Will read about it in the papers?"

"Yes. It's hard going out and not being with him. That's difficult for me." It feels like a massive weight off my chest to just say it out loud. "I don't know how to handle everyone's expectations. It could go over very poorly."

Mason's next words come out hard, a command if I've ever heard one. "Fuck their expectations."

I'm shocked by how blunt Mason is. I don't think he understands. "I just don't want to be judged—"

"Fuck. Them."

I stare back in disbelief, thinking he can't be serious but he is. His eyes hold an intensity and his hard, muscular arms are corded. He clenches his stubbled jaw and then seems to relax slightly, but I'm still caught off guard. Mostly because

I want to obey him. I want to eat up every word he's saying as if it's law and bow down to him.

"You're entitled to feel and do whatever you want. It's no one else's business. Their perception of you is their responsibility. Not yours."

I take a deep breath, hating that he doesn't understand. "Maybe I'm just shallow." I didn't mean to say it out loud, but I did. My breath leaves me and I pick up the empty glass again. Before I have the chance to let out the exasperated sigh begging to choke me, the waiter comes to my rescue, the bottle of chardonnay in his hand.

"Thank you," I say gratefully.

The second the waiter leaves, taking both our plates with him, Mason says, "We can play this however you'd like."

"I don't really want to go out yet. I'm just not ready." I realize he has a point but he doesn't understand that I welcomed these people into my life, and shutting them out now would be like a slap in the face.

"Is it because you loved him?" Mason asks, his forehead wrinkled and his brow furrowed. He can't even look me in the eye. "You loved him and they think you can't move on? Or that you shouldn't?"

"I loved my husband, but that's not why." I take a sip of wine and staring at the glass I answer, "I just don't know how to not feel guilty about being okay and I'm worried because I don't know how it will be taken."

The words came out easier than I thought they would.

"So you're all right?" Mason asks me and he's so genuine with his concern that I could practically cry.

"Some days are better than others, but it's hard because I wasn't much without him."

Mason takes my hand in his at my comment, squeezing it and opening his mouth to say something, but nothing comes out. I'm surprised at how deep our conversation has gotten.

"I'm sorry," I say, shaking my head and pulling my hand away. "I didn't mean to—"

"Stop apologizing," he tells me in a tone that makes all my worries vanish. "I asked you, remember?"

I nod my head and utter a small response, although I don't remember how the conversation started.

"Tell me something that will make me smile," he says.

A grin plays on my lips at the thought of him smiling and I say, "You're a very handsome man. Very charming. Obviously successful." I lean in slightly and let the tips of my fingers play along his large knuckles as I add, "And I really, really liked last night."

I accomplish my task and sit back in my seat, staring at his handsome face.

"I'm glad you enjoyed it." He keeps his eyes on me as we both sip our drinks. "I would have liked to have had you this morning as well."

I almost choke on my wine but luckily I save myself, swallowing it down and taking a moment to get myself together.

"About that …"

"I imagine you'll make up for it tomorrow morning." He says it like it's a statement but I hear the question.

Another night with Mason Thatcher.

"I did say I was just along for the ride," I say, reminding him and myself.

chapter 15

Mason

Pretend it didn't happen.

Don't let the truth show.

Curiosity will lead you.

Just where you should go.

She'll lure you and tempt you.

And bid you farewell.

It's only then you'll realize,

You've wound up in hell.

I COULD BLAME THE FIRST NIGHT ON SHOCK AND ALCOHOL. THE SECOND on curiosity. But this pattern of behavior, this deep-seated need to watch her, to touch her, to have her … there's no fucking excuse for it.

I stare at the computer screen mindlessly. The office is empty; even Liam's gone home, leaving me here alone with simple tasks that should have already been done.

My to-do list consists of analyzing this inventory and comparing the replacement materials Liam thinks will be suitable. It's crucial to our budget that this works and I need to make the decision today. Every penny is accounted for and spent, all except for this last purchase. All of it for one massive project. And all of it I owe to my father.

It's been hours and I'm purposely dragging my feet. I want all this to stop so I can hit pause. Instead I'm falling down a black pit, forced to make a choice of what will happen when I crash at the bottom.

Sitting forward in my chair, elbows on the desk, I nudge the mouse to my computer and it lights up the screen once again. Two gorgeous blue eyes stare back at me. Her long, thick lashes frame them perfectly. Her skin is flawless, with only a hint of color in her cheeks. But it's her expression that had me staring at her picture all morning. Her lips are parted as if she's about to smile. So close to happiness, but the photo caught her before she could have it.

It's only been two days since I've last seen her, but each night I've felt compelled to message her and make sure I knew where she was. The insecure side of me wanted to ensure she wasn't with someone else. That's the truth of the matter. I trust her when she says she's not involved with anyone. However, I know all too well what loneliness can do to a person and I want her completely to myself.

If I pretend like the events that led to meeting Jules didn't happen, then there isn't a damn thing wrong with what's between us. If only it was that easy to forget.

Knock. Knock.

My gaze lifts to the clock and then moves to the door to my office. It's past 8:00 p.m. and almost time to meet Jules.

"Who is it?" I call out, not knowing who the hell it could be. Maintenance, maybe?

"Your partner in crime." Liam's voice comes from the other side of the door and I relax slightly.

"Come in," I yell out to him, checking my cell phone and seeing a text from Jules. She's waiting for me. The very thought spreads a feeling of warmth through my chest.

I set the phone down, giving Liam my full attention although I have no idea why the fuck he's here.

"You seem preoccupied." Although it's meant as a statement, it comes out as a question. Before I can even think about it, Liam's eyes are on my computer screen.

It's an innocent glance, but he doesn't need to see her. More importantly, he doesn't need to know about my new obsession. I'm quick to exit out of the article about Jules. It was about her husband's passing. How she was dealing with the loss, although the picture they used of her was from years before.

I've read dozens of articles about her over the last few days. They're all the same. Every single one of them ooh and ahh over her. Some articles gush about her charity work. Others are less substantial and concern themselves with her opinion of an event or what clothes she's wearing. They put her on a pedestal and in such a precarious place that it's far too easy for her to crash and burn. And that's just what she did according to the articles that came out after her husband's death.

The sole fucking image I can't get out of my head is one of her crying at her husband's funeral. Maybe they showed mercy by using an older photo for the article I spent the day looking at because on the day she buried him she looked as if she'd died herself.

Inhaling deeply, I will the memory to go away. Wishing I'd never seen that grief on her beautiful face. Wishing I didn't have a hand in causing it.

"Well now," Liam says, ignoring my irritation. "Is this—"

"What are you doing here?" I ask him, cutting him off and leaning back in my chair with my shoulders squared. He's still standing and leaning against the desk casually, but my tone has that arrogant smile on his face vanishing instantly.

He rubs the back of his neck, raising his brow and looking past me out the window as he takes a step back. "I was just wondering if you'd put the final numbers in."

I clear my throat, feeling like an absolute prick. "Sorry, it's been a long day." I rub my shoulders and click on the spreadsheet. "I was just getting ready to put them in."

"So it's all finalized?" Liam asks me with a chipper smile, seeming to forget that I'm an asshole just like that.

"So far, so good." I force a smile and try to shake off the unease flowing through me. I can't explain the dichotomy of how I think of Jules. I want to take her out, impress her and please her in every way, including showing her off and showing off for her. But I also want this thing between us to be my secret. I don't want anyone close to me to have an idea of what's going on.

It's a design for failure. I can't help what I want, though.

Liam claps once and says, "Perfect." He starts to walk away but then looks back at me with an expression asking if he can pry. Curiosity is evident in his eyes. "That's all I wanted to know."

"You don't need anything else?" I ask him, the beating of my heart raging loudly in my chest. I don't know if I should refuse to answer whatever questions he has about Jules. Everything in me is screaming to deny it all. I can never let anyone know.

"So … Julia Summers?" the prick has the balls to ask me.

Not hiding the irritation by audibly exhaling, I nod in confession. I can't help that I feel a sense of pride as his cocky smile widens.

"It all makes sense now. I guess I can forgive you for being such an irritable fuck lately."

"Watch it," I say under my breath but the smile on my face only encourages him.

"Good for you," he says as he looks back at the screen, but it's only a spreadsheet. "Is it serious?" he asks me and I don't know why. He's never asked me before about who I'm fucking, or dating for that matter.

When I don't answer, he adds, "You just seem unusually preoccupied recently."

I move my seat closer to the desk, stretching my back and then shrug, doing my best to come off casual. "I've had a lot on my mind."

He waits for a moment, expecting more, but I return to the spreadsheet and open the folder of options on my desk. "I'll have it done before I leave," I tell him, giving him a tight smile and ending the conversation.

He leaves quietly, merely waving a goodbye on his way out and letting the door shut with a loud click that fills the empty room.

I look up when he's gone and tap the pen against the desk. I don't know what to deny and what to keep a secret. Confusing the two could be fatal, but the lines are already blurred.

chapter 16

Julia

> *This is not a date.*
>
> *This is not serious.*
>
> *This isn't something that needs to be more.*
>
> *This is for fun.*
>
> *This is pretend.*

MY PEN STOPS ON THE LAST LINE. I STARE AT THE WORDS I'VE scribbled into the notepad, but my mind is blank. I don't know what I intended for this poem to be. Inspirational maybe?

It all just looks like lies to me.

I click the end of my pen over and over. *Click. Click. Click. Click.* Debating ripping this sheet out of the notebook and balling it up for the round cabinet … a.k.a. the wastebasket.

The clink of several ceramic mugs being stacked together makes me turn to look over my shoulder. I inhale the rich smell of coffee in the small shop. The floors are checkered and the walls painted plain white, but this place serves the best coffee downtown. It's also right across from Mason's office and I told him I'd meet him here. My eyes drift up, my thumb still on the end of my pen.

The Rising Falls Building is sleek and modern. It looks like a polished black sheet of glass all the way up with a thick steel frame outlining everything in matte black, separating the panels. It's tall and dominating, dwarfing the small buildings across from it.

It's everything Mason is. The clicking stops when I drop the pen.

With both hands wrapped around the mug, I pick up my coffee and take a sip. It's not hot anymore, but it's not room temperature either. The smooth ceramic feels just right in my hand as I take in a deep breath.

I keep telling myself I shouldn't be with him; I don't do casual and never have, but this doesn't feel casual. It's been days of seeing him and I'm already catching feelings. Feelings I'm certain are one sided.

Maybe I'm reading into things too much. It's only been a week and a half. It's just sex … or so I keep telling myself. *Maybe I should add that to the list of lies in my notepad.* I huff at the snide thought.

Luckily, not many people have seemed to notice, other than Kat checking up on me and gently prodding. That's not atypical for her.

We aren't seeing each other in public, mostly. Not for events anyway.

There are whispers that I'm dating, but nothing that seems malicious or judgmental. Which is better than I'd hoped.

My heart pounds painfully in my chest at the thought and the small air of confidence leaves me. I would care if they said I was a bitch for moving on too soon. Or that I'm no longer the good girl they thought I was. That Jace's death was in some ways my death too. They wouldn't be wrong about that last one.

Most importantly though, I don't want Jace's father seeing that I've moved on. Or my mother. I close my eyes and try to rid myself of the image of her reading about me in the paper as she sips her morning tea. Drunk at a bar with a known player holding me. Yeah, I don't need my mother seeing that.

The bells above the front door jingle and my eyes instinctively open at the sound.

There he is, Mason, taking the breath in my lungs as he strides toward me. I'm stuck as I sit there, pinned to my seat and captivated by the air of confidence he gives off. His steel gray eyes look darker than ever as he grabs the back of the chair across from me and pulls it out. The legs scrape on the floor, announcing to the world that he's going to sit with me. He claims his seat and fixes those eyes on me.

"Jules," he says, my name falling from his gorgeous lips in a rough baritone and I finally breathe.

"Mason." I say then smile, although I don't know why. I simply can't help it. He makes me feel like a little girl caught in a fantasy. It's the way he wears his suits, the way he walks into buildings, the way he looks at me. As if he owns them all.

A small smile plays on his lips as well. I did that. I made him smile. These feelings, this bubbly laugh that erupts from my lips as I take a sip of my coffee … this is where the real problem hides.

He gestures to my cup and asks, "Should I get one as well?"

I sit up straighter and look over my shoulder again at the counter with the one lonely register and stacks and stacks of mugs behind it. It's late but this coffee shop never closes, because this city never sleeps.

"If you'd like to." I don't expect him to reach across the table and tuck a strand of hair behind my ear. His eyes and hands linger on the exposed part of my neck. The tips of his fingers trail down my skin slowly, with purpose. I feel the heat race through me, the desire creeping slowly down my chest and lower … and lower. He confuses me when I'm near him. I can't think of anything but what I want him to do to me and that's a dangerous thing.

I'm mesmerized by the way he looks at me. The steel gray seems softer, the harsh lines of his jaw less intimidating, more vulnerable. Maybe my poetic mind is getting the best of me.

"I think if I do," he finally answers, leaning back in the chair he's claimed as a throne, "I'd like to get it to go."

Nodding vigorously, I make it obvious that I agree and then feel foolish as he lets out a rough laugh. The bells jingle again in the doorway just as he leans across the table for a kiss.

Anxiety shoots through me, and I pull back just as his scorching hot lips touch mine. My back hits the hard plastic of the chair and my eyes whip over to an old man in a tweed suit. His white hair looks ruffled from the wind, but he doesn't seem to care. His light blue eyes gaze through horn-rimmed glasses and up at the menu behind me.

I'm slightly relieved that it wasn't anyone who would recognize us, but that doesn't last long. My heart drops when I see the expression on his face.

It's more than disappointment; this is something else.

"I don't know …" I say but trail off, clearing my throat. I'm still trying to catch my breath and explain when Mason speaks before I can continue.

"If you're with me," he says and the tone Mason gives me is authoritative as his eyes pierce me, pinning me to my seat and stealing my excuses from the tip of my tongue, "then you're *with me*." He finishes his thought and I can't look away, I can't shake off this guilt.

"You know I prefer discretion," I say and the excuse leaves me in a single breath.

He rises from his seat and buttons his suit jacket. The hold he has on me is finally broken although he doesn't look at me as he walks past me and up to the counter. I stare at the door, wondering if I should just leave. My body feels hot and I don't think I can do this. I still don't even know what *this* is.

It's definitely not "just sex." Going out on dates and coffee meetups aren't in the fuck buddy handbook. Not according to Sue, anyway.

My body stands on its own. Although my legs feel wobbly, my body weak and my head clouded with frustration and confusion, something inside me pushes me forward. It's only four steps, four strides toward him, all the while my heart beats faster.

"I don't know what *this* is." My voice comes out strong, clear and full of a confidence I don't possess.

A shaky breath comes and goes as he faces me, his shoulders squared, to give me his full attention. I try to come up with the right words. "I don't know what I want." The words are so true. "I am not *with* anyone. I'm alone and that's—" I stop midsentence.

I almost say that's how I want it. I almost lie to both him and myself.

From the corner of my eye, I notice the barista who looks away casually as if she wasn't listening. My cheeks flame with embarrassment.

"If you want me to leave you alone, it's done." His statement lacks both conviction and emotion.

"I want you," I whisper, my eyes pleading with his. "I just don't," I say then swallow and force my eyes to meet his. "I don't want people to know."

I feel like an asshole. "I'm not ashamed of you … I'm ashamed of me …" Oh God, even I cringe at my words. It's the truth, but it's so shitty of me. I swallow thickly, searching Mason's face for something. For understanding or anger. For something, anything. Instead there's a coldness that greets me and it hurts. "I don't mean it to come out in a way that is offensive. I've just been thinking a lot about it since the other night and I don't want my family to find out." My voice breaks at the last statement and that's when the barista decides to set down Mason's coffee.

"It's because of your husband?" he finally asks me and I don't waste a second to answer yes. The word is barely a breath. It's more than just publicity and articles that paint me however they want. It all cuts deeper than that.

"I want to take you home," he says then licks his lips, and instinctively my eyes are drawn toward them. He lets his eyes roam down my body. "We can talk about this in bed."

My lips part and I struggle not to look back at the barista who's no doubt watching us.

"Do you want that, Jules?"

I do. I want him to touch me and hold me and make me feel alive.

Why is this so hard? It's emotions, that's why. Luring me in and then snapping me out of it.

"Jules?" he asks, pushing me and I cave to what I really want, because if I deny him, I may lose this chance at an escape forever.

"Yes." I whisper my response and I hope the tone reflects my gratitude.

I think it does because he places his hand on the small of my back, as if he knows I need support in this, leading me away from the counter and toward my jacket and coffee that I've left on the table.

As I pick up the white jean jacket, focused on calming down and ignoring my overactive brain, Mason leans forward and whispers in the crook of my neck,

"I don't know what I want, other than I want you in my bed every night." *Every night.* There's a pang of both fear and desire from his confession. A small wave of relief and arousal flood through my veins. He lifts the jacket over my shoulders, helping me slip it in place and then looks me in the eyes.

"Is that something you want?"

That's what I want, but this seems like more. I choke on the answer, the words colliding together in a jumble and refusing to come out.

It's because I don't know how to separate the two. A relationship versus someone to sleep with at night.

It's going to be a problem for me, I already know it is, but telling Mason that in this moment is something I can't do. If I do, I've lost him.

Silence sits between us for a moment, growing more tense by the second and as though it slows the clock in the room, time stalling and my mind whirling with how this is all going to end.

He's going to crush me. He'll leave me shattered when he's done.

He's not the first though and there's not much of me that can break any more than I already have.

I put a small smile on my face and nod, feeling as though I'm making a death wish. "Yes," I answer, holding his gray eyes, "I want that too."

He doesn't know the truth and I'm too much of a coward to tell him.

I've sealed my own fate in this moment. I know I have.

If only I hadn't said it. If only I could walk away.

chapter 17

What's right and what's wrong are overrated.
The lines are blurred; consequences negated.
I'm left with no truth, only lies that I've built.
I'm left all alone, consumed by the guilt.

S HE'S FIDGETY, QUIET TOO. MY PARKING SPOT IS THE LAST ONE ON THIS level in the garage; it's the largest and away from everyone else's. We walk in unison, my hand still on the small of her back. I'm not letting go until I have her in my car. She's running, we both know it, and I won't fucking allow it.

She needs to know that she belongs to me. She wants to hide this and that's fine with me. But only to the extent that she knows not to be ashamed for going after what she wants. Discretion is one thing but I won't be denied.

I'll give her everything she desires; I want to. I want to see her smile, to hear that laugh that drew me to her. I'll do everything I can to make it up to her.

And she'll give me all of her in return. There's no exception to this compromise.

The passenger side door clicks loudly in the empty garage as I open it but then I stop, shutting it before she has a chance to slip in.

My dick is hard; my blood is hot. Glancing at a confused Jules, her doe eyes stare back at me. The same eyes I've been looking at all day. But there's no hint of a smile, only concern and rejection mixed in those soft blue hues.

There's a large cement post to the right of my car. It's square in shape and maybe three feet wide. If someone drove up, it would block us for the moment. Only a moment, but the odds of anyone coming to a commercial parking garage this late at night are slim. Fixing what's between us right now is worth taking the risk of being caught.

My shoulders are tense as I slip off my jacket and lead her to the front of the car, where we'll be blocked from view. Her heels click and her eyes flicker with a knowing want. Although her steps are hesitant, she follows my lead, looking over her shoulder and no doubt wondering what exactly I have planned for her.

"Mason?" The hesitation in her voice comes out as a gasp as her lush ass presses against the car.

My only answer is to grip her hips and back her up to the hood of my car, pinning her down and crushing my lips against hers. Her hands fly to my chest pushing me away at first, caught off guard by the sudden change of plans. But then they travel up my neck ever so slowly, giving in to me and then move to the back of my head, pulling me in for more.

That's a good girl. My good girl. The woman who needs me and I damn well need to show her I need her too.

I break our heated kiss to breathe, her chest touching mine as I look down at her. "Be good for me and be quiet." I murmur the command and she can only nod in response, her warm breath trailing down my neck.

I crush my lips to hers again and she moans into my mouth, but before she can deepen it, I fist her hair in my hands. Pulling her away, I grab her hip and flip her over so her breasts are pressed against the metal.

"Stick your ass out for me," I command her in a rough voice as I palm my dick through my pants and look around the pillar. There's no one in sight and I fucking need her tight pussy coming on my dick.

Her lust-filled whimpers encourage me as I pull her head back by her hair and kiss her neck. She rocks her hips and that small space between her thighs brushes against my dick. Teasing me.

I'm quick to unzip my pants, my pulse racing from the very thought that someone could see us or hear us. I finally let her go to stroke myself once and wait for her reaction now that she's fully aware of what I plan to do. She lets out a gasp, bracing herself and looking over her slender shoulder at me with those gorgeous blue eyes so full of lust ... and trust.

Slipping her lacy panties to the side, I kiss her neck once more before shoving myself deep inside her tight cunt. *Fuck.* She feels too good. With my eyes closed, I give her a moment to adjust. Only for a moment. This has to be quick, no time for playing.

Her back arches and her fingers scrape along the car, but she doesn't scream out. Nothing leaves her lips but a small gasp as her mouth forms a perfect *O*. Her pussy spasms and feels like heaven as I hold in a groan and place my hand on the small of her back, pressing her down and keeping her in place.

Her eyes are closed tight and her teeth sunk into her bottom lip. I rock out slightly and push back in, forcing the sweetest sound from those beautiful bloodred lips. A moan of pleasure.

I grip her chin in my hand and force her to look at me. I want her to watch me. I want her eyes on mine as I take her just how she needs.

Her eyes slowly open as she lets out a breath and that's when I slam into her again. She bucks forward, a small cry uttering from her lips and I wait again for her to look back at me.

"You need to watch me, sweetheart," I say with an even voice even though it's really a demand.

I'll show her who she belongs to and how good I'll be to her. But she has to watch me, she needs to see it all and know this is exactly what she wanted. *That she wanted me.*

She rests her cheek against the car and keeps her eyes on me as I thrust into her again and again, pulling all the way out and then slamming all the way back in. It's difficult to keep the groans low but I do, and she does what she's told, staying quiet and watching me as I fuck her like she deserves to be fucked.

The sound of tires squealing above us makes her squirm beneath me, but I hush her and lower myself closer to her. Leaning down, I push my chest against her back and kiss her gently on the lips. "They won't see." My hand slips between us and lifts up the front of her dress, lightly running along her clit.

I play with her, teasing and rubbing while watching her writhe under me. "Look at me," I command her and she's quick to turn her eyes to me. They reflect nothing but torturous pleasure and the need to cry out her release. She's gorgeous and I could make this easy for her. I really could. I could fuck her quickly and take her over the edge so she doesn't have to fight the urge for long. I could let her close her eyes and look away.

But I'm not interested in that.

Jules is going to see. I won't let her think this is all pretend and something that it's not.

I'm going to give her everything she needs. I'm going to make it all right again and she's going to love me for it. I couldn't care less if that makes me a prick.

It doesn't matter how it's going to end, just that it happens this way. Right here and right now.

"Mason." She whispers my name as her release takes her gently, her soft folds taking me deeper into her. I have to wait for her to stop trembling, a cold sweat breaking out along my skin before moving my fingers to her lips. I wish she were naked so I could see every inch of her. So I could see the flush that's creeping up her chest.

"Turn around." I give her the simple command and she obeys, her chest rising and falling unsteadily and her legs still trembling slightly.

"This is going to be quick," I tell her and then grab her hips in both my hands and angle her how I want her. I glance up to make sure she's still watching and just like the good girl she is, those gorgeous pale blue eyes are on me. I piston my hips, surprising her as she braces her limp body against the car. The intensity of the raw fuck makes her bottom lip drop with a silent scream as her body tightens. I fist her hair again and pull her head back.

"Mason." My name is a twisted word of desperation on her lips.

"Come for me," I tell her, moving my other hand to her clit again to strum her swollen nub.

She screams out for the first time and I'm quick to bite her neck. Hard. It's a punishment for not obeying me and it only makes her struggle against me harder. And only makes her impending release that much more intense.

I fucking love it. I love what I do to her and how much pleasure it gives her. How she makes me forget everything when we're together like this.

Her body goes rigid and her pussy tightens around my cock. She struggles to breathe and her head falls back as she looks at the cement ceiling, her climax threatening to crash through her.

I nip her chin and move the hand that was gripping her hair to her face. I stare into her eyes as her body shudders and her neck arches, her hair draping over my shoulder. Her face is the epitome of sinful ecstasy. It's the most beautiful thing I've ever seen.

"Fuck," I groan as she finds her release. It only takes four more thrusts, riding through her orgasm and taking her that much higher until I find my own release. My balls draw up and my spine tingles. I bury my head in her neck as my cock pulses deep inside of her.

The sounds of our heavy breathing surround us for a long moment.

I kiss the side of her neck right where she's marked from my bite, running my nose along her soft skin and breathing in her scent. Her legs are still shaking and a shudder runs down her body as I pull my lips away from her. She's perfectly sated, just as she should be.

"You're mine, Jules," I murmur but make sure it's loud enough for her to hear and watch for her reaction. Her long lashes flutter as she opens her eyes and looks back at me. I pull her panties back into place and fix her dress.

"Mason," she says, whispering my name as her forehead creases and her eyes beg me to take it back.

"No, you want me and I want you. You're mine."

She bites down on her bottom lip and says, "I'm not okay." Her voice hitches and her words crack. She closes her eyes and speaks as if it truly pains her to say the words. "I don't know if I can be good for you."

I rest my forehead against hers and ask her, "Why are you so afraid?"

"I don't think this can just be sex for me," she says. I cup her jaw in my hand and brush my thumb across her cheek. "I think I'm going to want more. I think I already—" she stops as her voice cracks again.

My body feels unbearably tense, each breath hurting my chest. *Why am I doing this to her? Why can't I just let her go?* Because I'm a selfish prick and I can't help myself. "I can give you more," I whisper in the air between us, knowing it's what she wants to hear. "We can see how it works between us in private, and keep things quiet in public?"

I'm giving her exactly what she wants, just to keep her.

I'm an asshole for doing it, knowing I can never be what she really needs and wants.

Her eyes light up and that soft smile reappears on her face. She brightens with hope and my shy girl comes back to me. "Are you sure?" she says, still panting, barely recovered from what I've already done to her. "You aren't going to break my heart?"

She has no idea that she should be running from me. I'm well aware that I should turn her away regardless. Instead I smile down at her and kiss the tip of her nose. "I'm sure," I tell her and hate myself that much more.

chapter 18

Julia

THERE'S NO RHYME OR REASON FOR WHEN THE MEMORIES COME BACK. There's nothing I can pinpoint that triggers it. Nothing that I can blame. Lying in Mason's arms, naked and warm, the two of us each working on our laptops in comfortable silence, there's not a damn reason that I should be thinking of Jace, but I am.

I don't want to. Even as I scoot my back close to the sofa, I try to rid myself of the images of him smiling at me. When I'd wake up in the morning, Jace would push the hair from my face and give me a quick kiss. Always on the lips, no matter how much I tried to dodge them. He thought it was cute how I didn't want him to smell my morning breath.

Moments like that, moments we shared together that were easy and fun, where we fit beautifully together, those hurt the most when I remember. I let out an uneasy sigh and try to relax, ignoring Mason's eyes on me.

You'd think I'd be happy that I had that at one point in time. That I had a man who loved me and whom I loved too. It's easy to say: *I'll be glad because it happened and not sad because it's over.* But the truth is I can't say that, because I don't mean it.

"What's wrong?" Mason's deep voice cutting through the silent evening makes me feel even worse. I'm trying to move on, but it's not that easy.

I swallow the lump in my throat and pull the dark gray throw over my legs and up to my shoulders. "Just having a moment," I answer honestly, although I can't look him in the eye. I hope he'll just let it go.

His warm breath surrounds me as he pulls me closer to him and kisses my hair. I don't expect the gentle touch from him. He whispers, "I get it."

He splays his hand on my hip and runs his thumb back and forth over my bare skin. I wait for more, but he doesn't say anything else. Only that he gets it and my treacherous heart thumps in recognition.

My laptop jostles across my legs as I try to get closer to him, loving the warmth, needing more of it. I wonder if it's wrong to be upset over the passing of your husband while in the arms of your lover.

"Sometimes—" Mason starts to speak just as my eyes glaze over and the words on the screen start to blur. I take in a steadying breath and stop that shit. Crying never helped me. It doesn't do any good at all.

Mason clears his throat while I wipe under my eyes.

"When my mom died, sometimes it was the oddest things that set me off." I'm surprised by Mason's confession and grateful to be talking about him and not me.

"I'm sorry about your mom." My condolence is softly spoken; my voice a bit scratchier than I'd like. I stare up into his eyes which appear so much lighter than usual, maybe because it's dark all around us. Only the glow of our laptops and the city lights beyond the large living room window to paint the room in a soft glow.

He tilts his head to the side, tucking my hair behind my ear and I push my cheek into his palm. He has such large hands, rough but warm. They're the perfect size for this.

A coarse hum comes from deep in his chest. It's short, but a sound of approval.

"It's okay to hurt still." His words are comforting. "It's okay to cry and let it out, even if you're already spent."

My heart beats harder and my breathing becomes more difficult with every passing second that I absorb his statement. I search his eyes for something and he must see the panic in mine.

"Or we can do something else?" he says.

"Like what?" I ask him.

He clicks his tongue, his gaze on my face, but not my eyes. Finally, he takes his hand away and types something into the search bar on his computer.

He pulls up a book of poetry. Robert Frost.

I eye him curiously and he pets my hair before pulling my head closer to rest on his shoulder. I get comfortable as he says, "I can read to you?"

My heart hurts so much in this moment. Not the pain of what I've lost, but the pain that I have something so beautiful and something I'm so grateful for, and yet I still have these moments.

I nod against his shoulder and say, "Please."

I could listen to his deep, rugged voice read poetry to me in the dark for hours.

I could rest in his warm embrace for days.

I could stay here with this man forever.

chapter 19

Mason

It wasn't supposed to be like this. It wasn't supposed to be this much more. Two weeks have passed and it's all become more and more normal. More and more it feels like I've finally won her over.

I watch Jules as she licks ice cream from her spoon, her tongue flat against the bottom and mindlessly watches the news. Her notepad is in her lap with the pen on top although she was writing when I walked in here. It's 4:00 a.m. and she can't sleep.

My mother used to feed me ice cream every night before bed. I had to be in my room and under the sheets as soon as I was finished, but I got ice cream every night. She made sure to keep a variety of flavors on hand; I wanted something different every night. Mom always ate strawberry, though. It was her favorite.

Jules glances over at me, a flirtatious look in her eyes. "Do you want some?" she asks, maneuvering her body in catlike motions to crawl over to me.

Even though I shake my head, there's a small smile on my lips as I wrap my arm around her and place my hand on her thigh to scoot her closer to me.

She moans softly as she scoops up a bit of cherry ice cream from the bowl. That move has to be intentional but her gaze stays on the television as if it's not. Maneuvering on the sofa, I readjust myself in my pajama pants.

She peeks at me, blushing and then brushes her arm against my bare chest.

"You're sweet to get me this," she says with that look in her eyes. The look that tells me I've made her happier than she thought she would be. "Thank you," she adds and plants a small kiss on my shoulder.

Staying up to distract her wasn't my intention when I came out here, but I don't mind. Truthfully, I couldn't sleep either. I felt the absence of her warmth the moment she got up. For such a graceful woman, she's not very quiet getting out of bed.

I gave her a few minutes to see what she would do, peeking in the doorway to the living room as she got lost in her words. Watching as she sat cross-legged on the sofa, leaning over her notepad and scribbling like mad. It wasn't until she started to cry that I came into the room. I thought she needed me; I thought it was about him.

But she said they were happy tears, like the kind you cry when you've gotten closure. I don't know why that hurts me more.

"No problem, I wanted to get out anyway."

"Did you go for a run?" she asks me, eating the last of the ice cream and facing me. I shake my head no. I don't have time for that right now. Usually she's in bed when I run early in the morning and then shower before she's gotten up. It's been a week of her staying at my place and that being the routine.

"My fault?" she asks and scrunches her nose, not liking that she's thrown off my schedule.

"It doesn't matter," I tell her. It truly doesn't. "I'll make it up later tonight."

She hums a small sound and then adjusts on the sofa. "Will you come by my place tonight? Instead of here?"

I answer easily, not thinking twice, "Of course. I may be late; I have a lot of things to wrap up at the office."

She straddles me then, a leg on either side of my hips until she settles into my lap. I let my hands rest on her ass as she drops the empty bowl and spoon beside us on the sofa, the spoon clinking as she shoves them farther away.

"Mr. Thatcher," she says as she wraps her arms around my neck and squares her shoulders. "You're going to be late. I need you to stay at the office … and help me …" Her long lashes flutter as she bites down on her lip and continues, "… to file the paperwork."

An asymmetric grin finds its way to my lips as she laughs at her own attempt to be a sultry secretary. I can tell she's holding it in, not taking it too seriously at all. Her straddling me though, that has nothing to do with role play.

Glancing at the clock behind her, I note that I have another hour at least before I need to get going. "I think you may be mistaken, sweetheart," I tell her.

She rocks herself against me and gives me a smoldering look. It's one I don't get often, one full of confidence and determination. But damn, when she does give it to me, it drives me wild. If anything, this woman knows what she wants and with the tension gone between us, she wants me.

"You need your exercise, Mr. Thatcher." She drops her voice low and slides the straps to her silk nightgown off her creamy shoulders, exposing her breasts. They're small but fit perfectly in my hand.

With a groan and another rock of her hips, my dick stirs in my pants and I sit back on the sofa, thrusting my hips once and making her gasp as she reaches out to steady herself by clinging to me.

My hands wrap around her small waist as she kisses my jaw. I don't know when it happened, but my control has waned with Jules. I love it.

This is such a fucking mess. A beautiful mess.

chapter 20

Julia

Happy is relative.

An emotion in time.

Guilt waits in shadows,

Makes you pay for your crime.

When push comes to shove,

And the two have to meet.

You'll be judged, never loved.

It's all bittersweet.

I BREATHE IN THE STEAM OF THE HOT COFFEE IN MY HANDS. IT'S THE MOST amazing smell this early in the morning. That or Mason's pillow. I don't know what it is about the masculine way he smells that drives me crazy. Each morning I pull his pillow out from under him and take it as his alarm goes off.

I can't stop the smile that spreads across my face remembering this morning how he flipped me over and "punished" me for it. Maybe things are moving along too fast, but for the first time in a long time, I'm happy. Genuinely happy.

"Stop smiling like that," Maddie playfully scolds from across the table as she blows on her latte. She lifts the cup to her lips and eyes me before taking a sip. The smile doesn't fade; her next comment only makes it grow larger. "You're making me jealous."

"That is the power of sex," Sue says as she takes her seat across from me. Her coffee is in a to-go cup in her hand, so I imagine she'll be leaving shortly. She sets her bag on the floor and slips onto the stool easily. "It's about time you girls caught on and decided to get some." A coy smile lifts up the corners of her lips as she adds, "Well, except for Kat since she's married."

Maddie laughs into her cup and Kat gives Sue a cold look for a moment then shrugs. "He's good at what he does," Kat says but we all know there have been some complaints recently in that department. Not the bedroom per se but the lack of anything happening in the bedroom.

Whenever Kat looks at me, it takes me down from this high. She represents what I once had and what I should really be striving for. She has a loving husband, a stable and growing career. Children are in her future. I know they'll get over this hump. She loves him and he loves her. Every marriage goes through ups and downs. That's what everyone told me when Jace and I were working out our problems.

I set the cup down on the table and try to stop being … whatever it is that's come over me.

"Is it different?" Maddie asks me as she crumples the wrapper from Kat's straw. She has both hands on it, balling up the small white paper into a perfect circle. "Like since you were only with Jace before this new guy?" she adds and then peers up at me. Gauging my reaction.

The mention of his name … It still affects me. I think it always will. Maddie has horrible timing, though.

"At first." I take a sip of coffee and try not to let the overthinking and insecurity rule this conversation. Baby steps. "It felt like I was cheating on him," I croak out, my chest feeling tight. "But that was in the beginning and it's been a few weeks now, so …"

"Cheating?" Sue's reaction is complete with a huff. "Um no, that's what he did to you," Sue says with a firm voice that grabs my attention. She rests a hand on my forearm. "Moving on is *not* cheating … But you know you two …" she trails off then purses her lips with her eyes on me as if she doesn't know if she should say what's on her mind.

"Say it." My voice is strong as I speak. I just want to get it out there, like ripping off a bandage. Even if it hurts, I need to hear it. I didn't expect her next statement, though.

"I worry about you and Mason." It's like being thrown into ice water. I thought she had something to say about Jace. She didn't really care for him. She didn't hide it either. I wasn't prepared for her to talk about Mason, though. "It doesn't have anything to do with Jace." She waves her hand through the air as if to thoroughly drive home that message and then continues. "You know I never liked Jace much, especially after he hurt you." *Cheating. After cheating on me.* That's what she means. We'd only ever been with each other, so he said he'd been curious and he swore it was a mistake. I forgave him. We moved past that together. Sue never did but it wasn't her marriage and it wasn't her decision.

"Why are you worried?" I ask cautiously, tapping my nails along the side of the cup and removing the thoughts of that infidelity from my mind. "It's nothing serious." I bite the inside of my cheek; even to me, that sounded like a lie.

"That right there," Sue says as she leans back and points her finger at me. "I worry that you don't know what casual dating is or how to act with a fuck buddy, or whatever this is for Mason."

If they could hear the way my heart protests, she'd be doubly worried.

I clear my throat and spit out my next words. "He said he could give me more so it's not exactly just for fun." The tips of my fingers tingle and then go numb as both Sue and Maddie stare at me for a moment. *Say something.*

"What?" Maddie interjects, scooting her stool closer to the table. Her pink dress is pulled tight across her breasts as she leans forward and says, "What did he mean by 'more?'" She's as giddy as a schoolgirl.

"Yeah, what the fuck did he mean by more?" Sue asks, her skepticism obvious. Even Kat looks up from her phone to listen. She's barely said a word since sitting down other than to apologize for having to work and that she swears she's listening. I suppose now she really is.

"I don't know. I just …" I stop and focus on Sue, my former cheerleader and the one I know I need to convince. "I was worried too," I say, making sure I'm careful with my words, "and I told him that I didn't know if I could handle 'just sex' because I would probably want more, and he said he could give me that." I think back to that night just two weeks ago, or has it been more now? I'm fairly certain that's what I said and how he answered. "It makes me feel secure, that I can be open about how I'm feeling and that he's receptive to it."

Maddie lets out a small sigh of satisfaction, like a young girl in puppy love. She's the only one obviously happy about what I've said. Sue taps her nails rhythmically on the table and Kat hasn't moved, still watching me like a hawk. Like I'm prey and she's just circling in the skies above, waiting to strike.

"Can I just ask a question?" Kat says, setting down her phone and turning her full attention to me. "Why him? Are you sure you want more … and with him?"

"Okay … I didn't expect that as the follow-up question." It takes a moment for me to put my thoughts into words. "Mason is nothing like the man I *should* be with. But that man is gone and I'm not interested in replacing him."

I take another sip of coffee, feeling defensive and like I'm not sure that I really want to even have this conversation.

"Are you wanting to settle down with him?" Kat asks and waits for me to look at her. "Like are you dating, dating?"

"I'm not settling down or replacing—" Jace's name gets caught in my throat.

"Oh no, oh no." Kat's quick to correct herself, reaching out for me even though my hands are now clasped in my lap. "I didn't mean … I don't know what I mean."

"Maybe he's a rebound," Sue chimes in with a shrug and then looks up at the menu on the other side of the room. The text is fairly large, but she's not reading it. All four of us have that menu memorized. "It doesn't have to be serious," she says and the other two women all nod in agreement, but I'm certain it's to placate me.

"Yeah," I say noncommittally, holding up my coffee and looking back at Kat for her response. "What if he's just a rebound?"

Kat picks up her phone again but she doesn't look at it. She bites her lip and asks, "Can we meet him?"

"For fuck's sake, Kat," Sue says from across the table, practically glaring at her. "You don't introduce a rebound to your friends."

"Is that a rule?" Kat bites back. "He likes drinks, we like drinks, let's all just have drinks."

"It's weird!" Sue's brow is comically raised as she stares back at Kat like she can't be serious. "Just let her do what she wants to do," she says and Sue's last sentence is hushed.

"I'd like to meet him," Maddie says with a sweet, innocent tone. Staring at each one of my friends in turn, I know they're all looking out for me. All nervous like I was weeks ago.

"I've got this," I say to all three of them at once. "It's just sex, but there's a level of respect and understanding." I nod my head. "That's what the *more* is."

A soft sigh leaves me and I feel like I've fixed my nonexistent problem. That's exactly what this is. "It's just a mutually beneficial arrangement with respect, and sex of course."

Both Kat and Sue are silent, each nodding and probably not convinced with my words. Each for their own reason, and I love them for their concern.

"I have a meeting with my CPA," I say as I glance down at my phone. I was going to walk there but there's no way in hell I'm going to make it on time now. "I have to go," I huff out as I reach down to grab my leather tote off the floor.

"Hey," Kat says. "You're happy?" she asks with all seriousness.

I stand up, slinging the purse over my shoulder and pushing the stool back. "Yeah," I say and that smile comes back. "I'm happy."

I expect some kind of guilt or feeling of inevitable doom, but the girls all smile and Maddie squeals with delight. My chest feels empty, as if I'm lying to myself and afraid that someone will expose it. But I am happy. This is what happiness feels like, isn't it?

"That's what matters," Kat says with finality.

"Damn right," Sue says, adding her two cents as she grabs her purse to join me.

"Want to share a cab?" she asks, the conversation of Mason and whatever the hell I'm doing with him long gone. At least for now.

THIS OFFICE SUCKS. EVEN AS A WRITER, THERE ISN'T A BETTER WORD to describe it that comes to mind. For starters, it's always dark. Crossing my ankles and shifting in the chair, I don't understand why Mr. Allen Walker never opens the curtains. I used to joke with Kat that he's really a vampire. The plain white shades aren't thick but they're very good at blocking out what little sunlight would shine through the windows to my right. The office practically brushes against the neighboring building. Through the small gap where the fabric panels meet, I can see the old brick from Parks Towers next door. I'd rather look at that and have some sunlight than stare at closed curtains.

I scoot back on the chair with my purse in my lap, feeling more and more uncomfortable.

"Miss Summers." Allen addresses me as he always has since I was a little girl and even after I was married, but it feels different now. He shuts the door behind him, a smile on his face as he shoves his wire-rimmed glasses up the bridge of his nose. Fine lines and wrinkles crease around his eyes as he holds out a hand for me. I stand up, the lightweight chair scooting back on the thin carpet as I shake his hand.

"It's been too long," he says warmly. I nod my head and smile politely although I disagree.

The last time I was here was a few days after Jace passed away. That day, Allen made sure to call me by my legal name and not the name I grew up with. The memory makes the tiny hairs on the back of my neck stand on edge as I clear my throat and retake my seat. Uncomfortable as it may be, it's the only one I've got.

It seems he's forgotten that Summers still isn't my legal name. I look down at my barren hand and think that's my fault. I took my ring off months ago. That was easy, all things considered, but changing my name is something else entirely. It would be like erasing Jace, and I won't do that.

"It has," I say lightheartedly, pulling down my light gray pencil skirt and re-adjusting in my seat as he takes his on the other side of the desk.

My chair is small and uncomfortable, while his is large and practically molds to his body.

I shake off the anxiety running through me as I straighten my back and ask, "What is it that you needed me to sign?"

A rough laugh fills the room as he shakes his head then says, "Not just yet. I need decisions, Miss Summers."

My body tenses at hearing my name but I bite my tongue. "Of course. What kind of decisions?"

"As acting advisor to your estate and investments, I need you to look these over," he says as he pulls out several folders and sets them in front of me. My brow furrows as I open the first and then the second. I don't know a thing about any of these. I've never been involved with investments and stocks.

"I—" I start to say and then let out an uneasy breath as I continue, "Is there a way that I could take your advisement, Mr. Walker?"

He turns his head to the side and raises his brow as if to say I should have done that a long time ago. "I advised your husband when he made these transactions. Unfortunately, the choices now are to stay and keep your money in a losing bet or to withdraw and lose a substantial amount."

My body goes cold as I take in his words. "I don't understand."

"Mr. Anderson was adamant about buying these properties and he assured me that it would be worth the risk, but I've waited over nine months now and there's still no growth since the drop."

"The drop?" I ask him, feeling the blood drain from my face. Jace never mentioned buying any properties. "This was with our personal assets? Not the business?"

He nods at my question, taking in a deep inhale. "They were on the decline when he purchased them. He was a bit surprised that they continued to drop, yes." Mr. Walker leans back, waiting for my reaction.

"How much of a decline?"

"Fourteen million."

I close my eyes, gripping the edge of the seat for a moment. Fourteen million. That's ... I can barely think straight. When we married, I know my assets were around twenty million. How could he take such a large chunk and not disclose any of this to me?

"There's still nearly six million invested so you can withdraw if you'd like. I like to say you've never lost money until you sell, but the fact is that I still believe you're not going to see the return your deceased husband was banking on."

My entire body is tense and on edge. Fourteen fucking million dollars. Fourteen million! I want to scream and curse, I want to throw up. It takes me a moment to gather myself to be able to respond.

"Why am I just learning about this now?" I ask him in a voice that's more filled with anger than full of shock and grief. I flip through a few pages with shaking hands, reading through them, but not actually reading a word.

Fourteen million and now I can only sell for six? I'm going to be sick.

"Well, it was stable but it's recently gone up just a touch, and I'm of the opinion that you should take advantage of the current climate."

My mouth hangs open just a bit as I look back at Mr. Walker, eyeing his blue suit and thin red tie. I blink a few times, then fall back into my chair and shut the folder.

"Is this all of the investments?" I ask, realizing how little I knew of Jace's dealings. For the first time in my life, I'm worried. I've never had to concern myself with income. I've been blessed and grateful, but I wasn't careless. This right here, this feels like careless to a maximum degree and I'm embarrassed. I'm sick to my stomach and mortified.

I swallow thickly and cross my legs, not able to stop my foot from rocking back and forth in the air. It's only as I sit here, my mouth feeling dry and my body like ice, that I realize I know nothing about my current financial situation. I trusted Jace to handle all this.

"Allen," I say as I pick at the clutch in my lap and look up at the man I grew up with. He's an old friend of my father and I do trust him, but right now I feel unsettled.

"Yes, Julia?" he asks.

"Financially speaking," I say then pause, taking in a steadying breath before I continue, "is everything all right?"

He takes a moment to answer me and the time ticks by slowly while I wait for his reply.

He opens his mouth, looking down at the desk but doesn't say a word and dread hits me. "You're going to be fine, Miss Summers. You will be." He puts strength behind his words and looks straight into my eyes as he speaks.

I should be relieved, but he didn't exactly answer my question.

"It's going to be difficult getting this money back, especially considering the amount of debt you went into when remodeling your home."

"What?" I feel struck by his last statement. "We didn't go into debt." I got everything I wanted on that remodel because it was funded by the money I'd made with my first publishing contract. It was my personal reward to myself. "I know how every penny was spent and I know it was paid for with the money I brought in."

I can't help that my voice is full of panic and my tone is accusatory. I sit there on the edge of my seat, waiting for a response from Allen. I swallow the lump in my throat as he clicks on his mouse and takes off his glasses, scrolling through a row of spreadsheets.

"The remodel put you in quite a bit of debt, I'm sorry to say." I shake my head in disbelief as he adds, "If you were to sell the apartment, it could potentially make its money back."

Chills travel down every inch of my body as I take one breath, then two. "What apartment?" I ask him, my voice deathly low.

"The one downtown on Pacific Street. The one that was remodeled this past year."

My world spins on its axis and I grip the arms of the chair. "Mr. Walker? I don't own an apartment on Pacific." I lick my dry lips, my body coiled, my muscles feeling tense and tight.

There's a pause, filled with more ticks of the clock. "Well, your husband did and that was left to you. As was everything else in his will. So you do own an apartment on Pacific."

"Why wasn't I told about this sooner?" I ask, focusing my attention on something other than the fact that my husband bought and remodeled an apartment without me knowing. Betrayal consumes me but oddly, I feel numb to it. As if I'd known all along. As if I'd turned a blind eye. It's not naivety or trustworthiness. It's me being stupid. All the late nights at the office, all the weekend trips … My skin pricks and a numbing tingle goes through me. He told me it was just once when I found him in bed with another woman. I try to breathe in easier, but my throat is closing.

Disbelief is outrageous. He didn't. He wasn't cheating on me. There's no way.

"You were given the paperwork, Julia. You signed everything after the funeral."

I look up at Allen, feeling betrayed by him just as much as my husband. I want to question him, scream at him. But at the same time, I don't care. I had this coming to me.

I didn't know about this debt. I didn't know about the apartment. I didn't know about a damn thing because I trusted them.

"I was mourning," I say and I can barely get out the words. They're cold and stagnant. Just a lame excuse for my ignorance.

"I'm sorry, Mrs. Anderson." He starts to say something else but I rise from my chair, a bitter taste in my mouth as I bite out, "Don't call me that."

He cocks a brow at me as I start to leave. "You need to sign these, Julia," he says matter-of-factly, speaking to me like my father does. Ignoring my emotions and simply telling me what I need to do.

My shoulders shudder as I open the door with my back to him and grip the cold brass knob for dear life.

"Email them to me," I tell him. "Email *everything* to me."

"I suggest you read them quickly," he says to my back as I walk through the door.

I nod my head but I don't verbally respond; I don't trust myself to speak. I don't look back at him and I don't even breathe until I'm in the elevator. I can't relax though, even in the empty, closed-off space. I want to sag against the wall, gripping the steel handles. I want to hit the emergency button and give in to the pathetic emotions of sadness and betrayal.

More than any of that, I want to see this apartment and I want to see how the hell my money was spent. I need to get myself together and figure out how deep of a hole I'm in and more importantly, how to get out.

Mason

KNOCK. KNOCK. KNOCK. MY KNUCKLES RAP AGAINST JULES'S DOOR quickly. A second passes and I take a look around, shoving my hands into my suit pockets. The Upper East Side screams old money and is far more traditional compared to downtown where I live.

My father's home is only a few blocks from here.

Jules's street is different from where I grew up, though. The cream stone and intricate carvings have history to them. Real history. I glance back at the small iron picket fence and gate in front of her house. The city sidewalk is just beyond it, littered with people walking by.

I rock on my heels and knock again, wondering what they think of this house.

It looks like wealth and with the well-maintained garden, it only adds to the beauty of the old house.

I've been inside Julia's home a handful of times now, and it's odd that I feel nervous about being here now. It's because I'm coming through the front door in daylight. I smirk at the thought, but it's true. My forehead pinches as I knock again, using the large iron door knocker this time.

The door swings open and there's my Jules, but she doesn't stay there long. She leaves the door hanging open and disappears inside, claiming that she has to get something, but I didn't hear what.

"Jules?" I call out after her, placing a hand on the heavy red door and peeking inside after her. The door creaks and I second-guess going inside after her, but she doesn't answer me.

Taking a few steps inside, I flick on the light switch to my right before shutting the front door. A large crystal chandelier lights up the large hallway. The ceilings are taller than they seem at night. Paisley wallpaper in shades of pale blue and cream covers the upper half of the walls with a deeper blue painted below the chair rail.

It's modern and updated with a feminine and elegant touch, definitely not my taste, but it still holds the classic beauty of the home. A mix of modern and traditional. It's all Jules.

"Jules," I call out again, pocketing my keys and wiping my shoes on the mat before stepping onto the plush area rug in the foyer.

"I'm sorry," I hear Jules say through the hall before I see her. She rounds the corner of what looks like the dining room, both hands on her left ear as she slips an earring into place. She's barefoot, wearing a navy blue dress with white polka dots and a skinny white leather belt at her waist. She's gorgeous as always, but something's off. Something's wrong although I can't tell what.

"Everything okay?" I ask carefully, staying right where I am as she bends down to slip on a pair of navy blue heels.

"Fine, just fine." She shakes out her hair and stands upright, taking a step toward me before turning on her heel and heading back the way she came.

I follow her into the dark dining room. It doesn't look a damn thing like a dining room, though. The furniture is all here, but stacks of papers cover the table, along with a laptop. On top of the buffet is a printer. She's using the room as an office.

"Sorry about the mess." Her voice is dampened as she turns around. "I just need my purse." She starts to walk past me, making her way to the door, but I put my arm out, my palm against the doorway and wait for her to look at me.

When she does, my heart drops. Her eyes are rimmed in red. Although her makeup is flawless, she can't hide that she was crying. Not from me.

"What's wrong?" It comes out as a question, but it's more of a command.

Her lips are the same dark red shade they were when I first met her and as she parts them, my eyes are drawn to them. She doesn't say anything though, she merely licks them and turns away from me. For the first time since we met, she's deliberately disobeying me. Hiding from me.

"I don't want to talk about it." She pushes my arm away, to leave me and deny me again, but I'm not letting this go. I grip her hip tight enough that she stops and looks at me.

"That's not how this works. I told you, if you're with me, you're with me." Her hard expression vanishes as I speak to her, replaced by nothing but hurt.

"You don't own me." She bites out the words meant to make me mad, meant to destroy the ease between us.

"It's not about that, Jules." My voice is low as I release her. She doesn't walk off; she stands there waiting for my next move. She has to know how good this is between us. She knows whatever the hell it is, I'll take the burden from her.

"I don't like seeing you upset." I bring my lips closer to hers. "Tell me what's wrong, so I can fix it." I open my mouth to give her a reason not to push me away, to tell her that she can trust me. That I care for her, to tell her everything I know she wants to hear, but I can't bring myself to do it. Luckily, I don't have to.

She moves her hands to her face for only a moment, her expression crumpling before she falls into my chest. She gives in to me so easily. It's addictive. I wrap my arms around her, feeling her shoulders shake and shudder with a soft sob.

"I didn't want to cry again," she says into my chest, muffled by the suit jacket and her hands still covering her face. She inhales deeply as I bend down, running my hand up and down her back in soothing strokes and kiss her hair repeatedly.

"It's all right, whatever it is, I'll take care of it." I don't know why I promise her something I know I may not be able to accommodate. It's stupid of me to say it and it gets the reaction it should from an independent woman like Jules. She pushes away from me, wiping under her eyes and taking a shuddering breath.

"It's nothing you—" she stops to close her eyes and calm herself. "It can't be fixed." She glances at a photograph in a silver frame behind her on the wall and then wipes under her eyes again, walking to a large mirror on the far side of the dining room.

I only catch a glimpse of the photograph before turning my back to it. It's from her wedding day and he's in it. Obviously. He was her husband after all.

Panic races through me and a sick feeling churns my stomach. "It's about your husband?"

She peeks over her shoulder, looking guilty. The fucking irony. "I'm sorry."

"Don't be." My steps are just as careful as my words as I walk over to her, placing a hand on her delicate shoulder and watching her in the mirror. "Is everything okay?"

"No," she answers quickly and sniffles once. She's already fixed her makeup and looking as though she's back to pretending nothing's wrong, but then her eyes meet mine in the mirror. Her baby blues are filled with anger and an unforgiving chill. "He had an apartment," she says with certainty. "A place for his mistresses or one-night stands or whatever they were."

I attempt a look that expresses shock, but none of that is news to me. I wasn't sure if she knew. For the first time since meeting her, I feel guilty for not telling her. As if somehow I could have saved her this heartache if I'd given her a piece of the truth. Only a piece.

She laughs something wicked and sad, a mix of both as she shakes her head and says, "You think I'm pathetic, don't you? A housewife who had no idea what her husband was doing behind her back." Her voice is strained toward the end of the statement and the strength leaves her with each word. I hate how she does this. How she blames herself, belittles herself. She's stronger than she knows. And worth so much more.

"What he did is a reflection of himself, not you." Taking another step closer to her, I stand behind her with her back touching my chest, just barely. "You aren't pathetic, Jules." I kiss the side of her neck, my eyes on hers in the mirror as I say, "I'd never think that."

"I do," she says. "He cheated once. He was so upset. He cried and swore up and down he'd never do it again. And I believed him."

My heart beats erratically and I'm desperate to ask who he cheated with. To see if Jules knows her name. I keep my mouth closed and wait for more from her.

"I believed him." The pain comes through in her words as she turns in my arms, placing her small hands on the lapels of my jacket. Her eyes travel along the buttons of my shirt, her fingers soon following. "I really thought he was good to me."

I pull away slightly, taking her wrists gently in my hands and getting her attention. "I'm sorry," I tell her with true sympathy but it comes out rough and short, shocking her.

She pulls away from me. "I am too," she says to the ground, turning around and brushing the hair out of her face. "I think maybe tonight—"

I can hear the excuse already, I can see her pushing me away and I'm not going to let it happen. There's no way I'm leaving until I know she's still mine.

Each time she questions me or what's going on between us, I feel the need to hold her tighter.

"Come here," I command her. She stops in her tracks, peeking up at me through thick lashes with a question in her eyes. She doesn't ask whatever it is though, she obeys me, taking two small steps back to me in those heels.

"He was a fool to cheat on you." As I speak, I brush my thumb along her delicate jaw.

She huffs a small laugh at me and I didn't expect that. I narrow my eyes as she says, "You're a well-known player, Mason." The humor vanishes and her smile fades to nothing as she adds, "You don't have to pretend to care. I'll be fine."

My chest tightens with anger. She can have an attitude about him all she wants. But there are boundaries when it comes to us. I won't allow her to demean our relationship. "Bend over the table." I grit the words out between my teeth. I don't even think twice about it.

She merely blinks at me, shocked. She should have known better.

"Now, Jules." My voice comes out hard and I almost take it back. But this is the man I am and this is what she's going to get. There's a war brewing between us, causing the air to suffocate me. I need Jules for the woman she truly is, not this version that the memory of her husband brought back.

She holds my gaze for a moment and my pulse flickers, thinking I'm going to lose her, but she caves before I even blink, submitting just like she wants to. *Good girl.*

She presses her hips against the table, slowly leaning down to lay her upper body against the tabletop. That's the beauty of our relationship—she wants to give in. She desperately wants to trust someone and not be hurt.

"Lift up your dress."

I hear her breathing pick up. "Mason—" she starts to say.

"No, no talking. No excuses." I palm my dick but I have no intention of fucking her. This is all about pleasing her and showing her what she means to me. Showing her what I can give her. "Lift up your dress and show me your pussy." I crouch down behind her as she slowly pulls the cotton fabric up her thighs and exposes her black panties.

My fingers trail up her thighs slowly to her ass, then up to the small of her back, pressing her down flat. I carefully push the panties out of my way, taking a languid lick of her pussy. My tongue brushes along the lacy material and I almost rip them as I pull them farther away, but decide to put my fingers to better use.

I play at her clit first, gently running my nail across the swollen nub and then back to her entrance. Goosebumps travel along her body. It doesn't take long before she's glistening for me, her wet folds begging for my attention.

She hums as she relaxes on the table. It's going to be a slow build for her. I don't care about our dinner reservations. She'll have to deal with being late.

I slide my middle finger deep inside her as I stand up behind her, keeping my other hand on her hip. Her eyes are closed as I fuck my finger in and out of her, loosening her up and testing her readiness. Remembering my anger, I pick up my pace and slip another finger into her.

"Come on, Jules," I say and kiss the back of her neck. "Tell me again how I don't care." A strangled cry leaves her as I press against her clit and she whimpers an apology, still struggling to get away from the intense pleasure.

I push three fingers deep inside of her tight pussy, stroking against her front wall right where that sensitive bundle of nerves is and I don't let up as she moans. Her body writhes in an attempt to get away, pulling at the tablecloth and kicking one leg out, but I've got her pinned down to the table with my hip. One hand continues to rub her hard nub ruthlessly, while the other is inside of her dripping wet cunt.

"I would never cheat on you." And then I tell her, "I'd never take advantage of you." She has no idea how true those words are.

"Mason." She cries out my name as she tightens around my fingers. *My. Name.* I want her to come undone screaming my name. To find her release with what I do to her all because she let me. All she has to do is give in to me.

"Tell me you understand, Jules." I'm not letting her get off until I hear her say it. I swear to God I'll stop it all if she doesn't give me that.

I may be holding back the truth, but I'm not lying.

"Yes," she moans out as she thrashes her head.

"Yes what?"

"Yes, Mason."

I smile into her hair, slowing my pace and making her whimper as she desperately rocks her pussy into my hand.

"Yes, Mason what?"

My heart thrums in my chest, but I need to hear her say it. I don't want that shit with her husband having anything to do with what we have with each other.

"You wouldn't do that." She bites her lip looking back at me with a plea for mercy. "You wouldn't hurt me."

I crash my lips into hers and fuck her cunt with my fingers, relentlessly pressing against her swollen nub. She cries into my mouth as her release hits her hard, her head banging on the table as she tries to pull away from the intensity. I don't let up, coaxing out every single bit of her orgasm from her.

Her back bows with tremors still rocking through her. This is how I want her, always.

No worries in her soft blue eyes, only a look of pleasure on her face.

A look that I put there.

My dick's hard as a fucking rock, but this isn't for me. She looks over her shoulder, still panting with her fingers gripping the cream tablecloth. She's waiting for me to take from her. To fuck her right here and now. But that picture of her husband is right there.

Part of me wants to do it. To force that beautiful cunt to spasm on my dick in front of him. To show him how a real man would treat her. But I can't. I need to get the fuck out of here.

I pull her hips back, her ass pressed against my hard cock.

Her lashes flutter and her wide eyes look back at me, waiting for whatever I have to say. "Dinner first, sweetheart." I kiss her gently then brush her clit through her panties and smile as a tremor runs through her body and forces her head back against my shoulder.

I kiss the dip in her neck and whisper in her ear, "Tonight."

Chapter 25

Julia

> *Naive and stupid, this shit has to end.*
>
> *What did I think? I can't comprehend.*
>
> *Mistakes belong where they're made, in the past.*
>
> *I knew better, I knew this wouldn't last.*
>
> *It left me numb, dead in the ditch.*
>
> *Love is wrong and my heart's a bitch.*

I STARE OUT THE WINDOW OF MASON'S CAR AS THE CITY LIGHTS FLICKER on, although it's not even dark yet. Classical music fills the cabin and my body is still humming from the rush of pleasure he gave me moments ago.

But nothing is okay.

I need to end this. What's the saying? Get over one man by getting under another? I'm not interested for two reasons:

1. I'm not over what Jace did to me.
2. I'm not ready for another man to do the same.

That's what I've been telling myself all day ever since I left Mr. Walker's office. I don't have time for fooling around and I'm not ready for anything serious. And that's what this has become; it's staring me right in the eyes.

This is serious. It's too serious. I'm suffocating and what's worse is that the minute I'm with Mason, the very second that he looks at me just right, says all the right things, the moment his lips press against mine and his skin touches mine, I'm done for.

I'm head over heels for Mason. I didn't even hesitate when he told me to bend over my dining room table for him. I didn't hesitate in the parking garage either. He's had me from the very night we met.

There's something about him that makes me weak, and I'm so very tired of being weak.

I can't do this. I need to end it. Just the very thought … it hurts.

"I—" I start to give him the honest truth, my whole truth. I don't know how to be okay on my own and that's my priority right now. That's the bottom line. Pressing my back against the smooth leather and glancing at him in the driver's seat, the words are right there on the tip of my tongue. *I can't do this anymore.* I don't know what's real and where I stand with anything, and I need space to figure it all out, but my phone goes off in my purse, the ringtone loud and obnoxious.

I let out a frustrated sigh, pulling it out and just missing a call from my mother. I almost call her back, but then I see the text messages. Dozens of them.

I hit the first one from Kat.

The last message makes me sick to my stomach. *It's going to be okay.*

What's going to be okay? What now? I scroll up to read the messages starting from the top.

OMG I just saw, are you okay?

Minutes later:

I can't believe he did that to you!

Everything is all right, we're going to get it taken down.

A chill slips like ice down my skin.

I don't have to ask her what she's talking about. Maddie sent me a link to the online article. It's already been taken down, but she screenshotted it.

My heart sinks as I skim it, but my eyes keep flickering to the picture. It shows me and Jace, and right next to it, Jace and some beautiful woman. It's obvious what the article was about and it makes me sick. My throat goes dry and tears prick my eyes.

Really? They posted this now? I think back to who I told and who would have heard about the apartment. It's up for sale as of 4:00 p.m. today, so that was only five hours for someone to dig up the dirt. I can barely breathe.

"Jules?" Mason's voice doesn't stop me from reading. It's not the worst thing that's been said about me but it's not kind, and it's not true. I wasn't turning a blind eye. There's a difference. I truly didn't know.

My anger only increases when I see what they're saying about me now. I'm not running around town. I'm not spreading my legs … I can't even finish this article. The last paragraph I read is:

Now that her husband is gone, she's letting loose but choosing the same kind of man. The socialite doesn't seem to care about her reputation anymore.

Whoever gave the details to the *Daily Word* knows that I'm seeing Mason but they don't know how often, since they claim he cheated on me two nights ago. I've been with him every single night for weeks now.

Every insecurity in me is replaced by raw rage.

Heat dances along my skin. I'm not this person that they're painting me to be. I'm on the edge of breaking into a million pieces. I told Mason this is why I didn't want us to be public. I knew something like this would happen. *I knew it!*

Is that a stage of grief? Wanting to murder everyone?

I just want to be left alone.

I bite the inside of my cheek and place the phone in my lap as Mason's hand lands on my thigh.

"What's wrong?" he asks, his eyes darting from me to the road.

"Take me home," I say. I don't bother to answer his question and I lick my dry lips. My heart hurts too much.

"What's wrong?" This time his voice is harder. The one he uses right before he turns me into a damn rag doll for his will and then magically fixes everything.

I'm done listening to men and I'm done rolling over for them.

"What's wrong is that this isn't working for me anymore," I finally tell him, although I don't know how, in an even tone that splits my heart right down the center. Guilt consumes the anger immediately. It slices through every emotion with the sharpest knife, the cut clean and quick, but the blood is pouring out and I know it's not going to stop anytime soon.

I lean my head back against the headrest. "I want to go home."

Mason's quiet although his pissed-off expression reads loud and clear as he pushes down his turn signal.

The silence stretches between us and this awkward, horrific dread makes me squirm. I find myself going back to the screenshots. What's really and truly messed up is that I feel safe and happy with Mason. If it were a different time, I could easily fall for him. I *am* easily falling for him. It's as if I'm tumbling down a well in slow motion, giving me enough time as I fall to look up and admire the stonework before crashing to the black bottom of the abyss.

"I can't do this anymore," I say, reaffirming myself and him. "I need to be on my own."

He doesn't look at me and a long moment passes before he says anything at all. Mason's voice is low when he asks, "Because of an article?" He grips the leather steering wheel until his knuckles are white. "I'll take care of it," he says. I'm sure he could fix all my problems. He's so good at that.

But I need to fix myself. I need to be whole before I can give myself so completely to someone.

"It's not the article." The words drop one by one and my eyes burn.

"Is it your prick of a former husband?" he asks with disgust so apparent, I hate him in this moment. I confided in him about my deceased husband and yes, he may have hurt me, cheated on me and lied to me, but that's not for Mason to judge. I still don't even know how to feel about it all. How dare he speak about him like that?

"That's exactly why this needs to stop." My heart rages in my chest, hating me for being so raw, but I can't stop.

"I'm not okay," I say, feeling a burn in my eyes dampened from tears, but I don't care, let them fall. Let everyone see and call me whatever they want. "I haven't been okay and I've been running from it. You can't just fix me. I can't fall into another man's arms and forget about everything I'm going through."

With shaking hands, I almost throw my phone when it pings again. The absurdity of my entire world crashing down around me feels too overwhelming. I'm too hot, too angry, too miserable.

"I just want to go home." There's a finality in the statement and it feels like razors at the back of my throat.

"Stop," Mason commands me as he slows down at a crosswalk. "Just take it easy." His entire demeanor changes to something placating, as if he's talking to a wounded animal. It only makes me angrier.

"No, I won't stop. What do you want from me, Mason?"

A part of me is hoping he really is my knight in shining armor. Part of me wants to be weak. I want him to solve all my problems and just crawl into his bed every night, moving on to a new life and leaving the old one in shattered pieces behind me.

I know it's wrong. It's giving in and denying my responsibilities. But God, I want it. My heart is suffocating, hoping for him to say just the right things to convince me to be his, to forget everything else. Just like he has from the first night I met him. "What is it that you want from me?" My voice shakes.

"Jules." He says my name and looks at me with a gaze I don't understand.

"Just tell me right now, what do you want?" I swallow the spikes growing in my throat, but they don't move. They only grow larger and sharper and make the words scrape as they leave me. "I can't give myself to you right now unless—"

"Unless what?" Mason asks so quickly he cuts me off. His reaction makes the pain that much deeper because I don't have an answer.

I can't give myself to him unless this is forever. Unless I can trust him but right now I can't trust anyone. The harsh reality is what truly does me in. I don't trust anyone anymore. I don't want to love anyone anymore.

I can't breathe as I take off my seat belt. My townhome is only a few blocks away. My shelter. My sanctuary and my grave. My hands shake as the seat belt pulls back, hissing and hating me just as much as I hate myself.

"I can't," I say. "I'm sorry," I whisper.

I unlock the door and push it open. A car drives by close, but I shut the door quickly, avoiding Mason's reach for me. His fingers brush against my back as I get out.

"Jules!" Mason calls after me. I cross the lane, the other driver beeping and holding down his horn. Go ahead, hate me too.

The sound of a door opening alerts me to the fact that Mason is out of his car, leaving it parked in the middle of the road and already holding up traffic. "Jules!" he screams but I keep running. The horns don't stop and it's not lost on me that what I did was wrong.

I rush past the onlookers and ignore the dirty looks and stares. My shoulders rise with a heavy breath. I need to go home. Tears stream down my face. I need to take care of myself and figure out what the hell I'm doing with my life.

Tires screech and make my head throb as Mason drives alongside me now, slow and causing more traffic to build up.

I ignore Mason as I whip open the iron gate. I don't stop until I'm safe inside my house, my back to the hard door, my body shaking and my heart hammering.

I hate myself for running from Mason.

But this is a reckless distraction.

I cover my mouth as another sob leaves me, slowly falling to my knees on the floor.

He's a good man and he deserves someone better than me.

Someone who doesn't have all these problems.

Someone who can fall for him freely and be with him openly.

I sag against the door, letting it all out, still hoping he'll come bang on the door and plead with me to explain. I can't be this person, though. It's better that he doesn't.

It's the way we both knew it would end. I envisioned it would be him leaving me though, not the other way around. I take a shuddering breath, feeling exactly how I should, like shit. Not that any of it matters.

It was never meant to be. That's all there is to it.

chapter 24

Mason

SEVENTEEN. I CALLED HER SEVENTEEN FUCKING TIMES. IT HURTS WORSE knowing she left me for something other than the one reason she should. Knowing that I couldn't keep her on my own. I held on too tight. It's my own fucking mistake.

But I saw what I could do for her.

What I could do *to* her.

And that made me feel … something other than this. This fucking hate that I have brewing inside of me.

What the hell did I expect? I expected to keep her. For her to learn to love me. For that to cancel out what I'd done.

The ice clinks in my glass as I grab a bottle of Macallan single malt.

No reasoning or any amount of logic justifies why I feel betrayed and alone. Not a damn explanation can leave me feeling as though this is something that doesn't need to be mended. The liquor sloshes in the bottle as I read the label, my fingers playing with the seal.

My father gave me this bottle as a gift when I started the company with Liam. When I told him I was going into business for myself, but still doing what I loved. I felt so much pride that day. My breathing quickens and my grip on the bottle tightens.

Relax. I grit my teeth, feeling an uneasy tightness settle through my body.

Jules was a sweet distraction; how fucking ironic. She pulled me away from reality. She made me feel like I had time. Like I had a choice.

I toss the seal onto my sideboard buffet, opening the bottle and not bothering to appreciate the rich scent before pouring it into the glass.

If my father were here, he'd give me hell for drinking it over ice.

"But that bastard's not here," I sneer under my breath. "No one is." The last thought leaves my chest feeling hollow. I take a long drink of the whisky that flows so easily. Burning and traveling through my chest, down deeper and stirring in the pit of my stomach. My head still tipped back I take another and finish the damn thing, the ice frigid against my lips. I slam the glass down a little harder than I should and let the liquor hit me.

It takes too long and I find myself gazing straight ahead to the family portrait sitting on top of the buffet. This room, the dining room, is the only room in the whole place where there's a picture of anyone.

The rest of the house is devoid of anything truly personal. But what do I really have that's personal anyway? My lacrosse stick and all those fucking uniforms stayed at my parents' where they belonged. I'm sure they were thrown away long ago.

I pour more of the whisky into the glass, feeling my breathing slow as my body sways and I remember the first day I walked in here.

I'd just gotten all new clothes, all new furniture, all new everything. This home was the start of the professional version of me. All that was in the cardboard box I was holding were a handful of old tee shirts and a few postcards from a friend of mine in Germany I'd met after I graduated high school and got my first job in construction. We've lost touch since then.

I take a sip, listening to the ice rattle against the glass. The whisky sits on my tongue and I press it against my teeth before swallowing. All the awards I've won are in my office. Framed and arranged just so on the wall.

My gaze drifts back to the portrait of the three of us. I'm standing between the two of them in it. I don't look a damn thing like her, like my mother. I'm the spitting image of my father. Mom's smile is soft, but her eyes are what sparkle. She was so expressive. Soft spoken, but she made what she said count.

She could make an entire room laugh by only speaking once the whole night. I let out a breath, looking at the firm hand my father has on my shoulder in the photograph.

He liked that about her. He told me once she was the perfect example of what a wife should be. That was before he caught her cheating.

I wonder if that man, the one she risked her marriage to sleep with, loved to hear her talk. I wonder if that's why she did it. Because she had more to say than just a single sentence.

I down the whisky, dragging out the chair at the head of the table and taking a seat. I sag and let my head lean back against the crest rail of the antique chair.

This room is so dark. With black textured wallpaper on the longest wall and the other three painted a soft gray, I wanted it to feel masculine. I remember telling the designer that. I told her I wanted it to feel like me.

On the right, centered in the room and next to the dark mahogany buffet, is a long gas fireplace. It's surrounded by a sleek marble hearth. More black. Even the light fixture in the room, a circular pendulum that holds the light inside, is black.

I huff a breath into the short glass and suck an ice cube into my mouth.

This is me.

A heart of fire that's never lit. A dark past that only holds a single moment of time in significance.

I wonder if that bitch designer knew what she was doing.

I kick the leg of the antique chair next to me. It's carved wood that's been stained. The deep brown leather of the chairs has a worn look to it.

What's ironic is how much I loved this room. I loved everything about it when I first laid eyes on it. The only addition I made was that fucking silver picture frame and then I filled that buffet with liquor.

Thank fuck I did that. I raise my glass even though it's empty, save for ice. "To you, you fucking prick," I toast the picture and take another ice cube into my mouth.

I crunch down, wondering if the last three words were for my father or for me.

Pushing the glass across the slick table that I've never sat at for more than a drink or two, I pull out my cell phone from my back pocket.

I fucking want Jules.

She's pure and sweet. Even if she overthinks every last detail, there's so much about her that I want to keep. I really shouldn't have her. I've already been given more than I deserve.

I can't do this anymore.

The screen lights up as I hear her words in my head. She shouldn't get to decide when it's over. Not by herself and not like that. Not because of something so fucking unimportant.

We work together. We make each other happy. I'm tired of living this life with nothing to fight for. I want her back.

My phone rings in my hand, startling me and I drop it on the table. It vibrates, moving slightly as the ringtone goes off again.

Groaning and rubbing my eyes, I feel the heat of the drunken night start to take me in before answering the call.

"Hello?" I think my voice is even. I'm fairly certain it comes out strong.

"Mason, we need to talk." I recognize Liam's voice immediately.

I brace my elbow on the table and rest my head in my hand before pinching the bridge of my nose. We do need to talk; we need to have a long talk about how I can't go through with this.

All the money is spent.

But I can't keep pushing forward.

I need to return it all to my father and cut ties. I need to turn him in.

Every bit of breath in my lungs leaves me, making my body feel light and my stomach sick. We're going to go fucking bankrupt, but I can't be under his thumb any longer.

"We need that investment from your father's firm." A sad, pathetic laugh leaves me as I register what Liam's said.

"We already have it." I stagger to the buffet, placing the phone on speaker, leaving it on the dining room table as I pour another glass. The bottle's already halfway gone. "We've already spent it," I say loud and clear as I bring the amber liquor to my lips.

This time I inhale the sweet scent. Fuck, it smells as good as it tastes.

"We need more." I gulp down the drink, staring at the phone on the table as Liam continues. "We got the estates on the Upper East Side and the committee approved the demolition plans."

As I take a step forward, I start to regret having the last two drinks. My head feels groggy and my body hot. "No, they didn't."

"I got it overturned. We've got everything approved, Mason." I can hear the glee in Liam's voice. Pride even. He claps on the other end of the phone, a rough laugh filling the room as it spins around me. "We just need that last check from your father."

Setting both of my elbows on the table to steady myself, I tell him, "We don't need shit from him."

It takes a moment for Liam to respond, "What?" He took so long I almost forgot he was on the phone.

"Are you drunk?" Liam asks, his annoyance only thinly veiled.

"No." I'm quick to deny it, but I know I am.

"What the hell's wrong with you?" he asks. "What's going on between the two of you?"

I shake my head, not wanting to answer. "We aren't taking shit from my father." It's all I can say.

"We are. We need those funds by Monday." Liam's voice is hard but also panicked.

"We'll find someone else." My eyes narrow as I steady my breathing and steel my resolve. I refuse to owe a man like him. I refuse to play by his rules.

"By Monday?" he says, raising his voice and the disbelief rings through. "Mason, we can't. We'll lose the deal. It's not like no one else was waiting for this property. It took almost a year to get it."

Liam's voice drones on as he lists off every reason why this plan is fucked. How we'll be ruined. How everything will fall around us.

I already knew it, though.

I stand, leaving the glass where it is and the bottle of whisky open, taking the phone and leaving the dining room.

"I don't give a fuck." I take a deep breath, listening to the silence on the other end of the phone. "I'm not taking another cent from him."

I have to face reality. Even if it fucking kills me.

chapter 25

Nothing is suffocating.
It cuts off the air.
Nothing is drowning,
But nothing is fair.
Nothing to hold and nothing to thrill.
When left with nothing, nothing can kill.

THE AIR IS CRISP ON THE IRON BALCONY. THE THICK CANOPY OF OAK trees just barely blocks the sounds of the city traffic. I've always loved the colors of autumn and the way the dark green leaves thin out and shift to gorgeous reds and burnt oranges.

They'll fall and wither away to nothing. Yet every spring they come back, good as new.

I've always loved their majestic natural beauty in the middle of this concrete jungle. Not today, though.

It's not fair that they come back untarnished. It's not right that life continues after death … only for those deserving.

Bundled in my favorite cashmere throw and sipping tea, I let out a deep breath, calming myself. I twist the cap to my flask and pour a bit of tincture into my tea. A small, faint chuckle leaves me as the liquid mixes with the now lukewarm tea. *Tincture.* Really, it's just vodka.

It used to be a tincture. It used to be just enough to take the pain away.

But sips turned to bottles as I preferred to feel numb.

Today is one of those days.

If I can roll out of bed and have the strength to tuck the sheets in and fluff the pillows, the day will be okay. That's what I'd tell myself over and over again when Jace first died. Sometimes it's true. All you need to do is make your bed and somehow the day is possible. As if simply pulling the sheets tight and smoothing out all the wrinkles is enough to hide the past and put the daily routine into motion.

Some days, it's all a lie.

All the time I spent with Mason … all that time feels like a lie. Some fantasy I forced to convince myself that life could be okay again. That it could somehow mend itself.

I take a sip of the tea, but it only makes my throat feel more parched. Instead of gulping it down like I've been doing, it finds its place on the saucer and I press my palms against my sore eyes.

It's been so long since I've felt this empty. Since my heart has felt as though it's been torn open.

It doesn't make sense in the least. I was over him. I was making progress. True progress in healing by being okay with Jace being gone.

I was okay.

For the first time since his death, I felt like I had a reason to be happy. More importantly, like it was okay to be happy.

Glancing over my shoulder, I rub my tired eyes with the sleeve of my silk blouse. I thought I heard someone. Just for a second, I thought I heard someone behind me.

My first thought is Mason. That he's come back and he isn't taking no for an answer. I roll my eyes feeling my heart squeeze violently in my chest.

I can't make that situation more than what it was. A hookup, a fuck buddy, I don't have a clue. I know what it is now, though. It's over.

Settling back down in the iron chair, I snatch up my notepad. I haven't written like this in so long, but there are scribbles everywhere. It's all loose poetry, lazy I suppose. It tells the story of how Jace and I met when we were young. How we fit so well together and everyone told us we were meant to be.

My eyes close as I remember the day we first got together. I can still hear how the school bells went off as we walked on the sidewalk to get to class. I brushed my knuckles against his, waiting and hoping. It had to have been obvious to him. Maybe I was the one to make the first move, but he chose me. He threaded his fingers through mine and he didn't let go. He was a good man, not a perfect man. He was good to me. Or so I thought.

"I hate this." I utter the words beneath my breath and it comes out shaky. They say when someone dies, you remember the good times more than the bad. Rose-colored glasses or something like that. I have to keep reminding myself that there were bad times too. With all these articles, I'm not having a difficult time remembering.

There's guilt too, which is something that I don't want. I don't want to be angry at someone who will never again have the chance to defend himself.

How can I move forward when I'm too busy hating everything as I scribble down scenes of our fights in this notepad? I let the words flow and pour out all of it, but mostly his infidelity.

Creak. The creak of the floorboards behind me sends chills sweeping down my body. I stand abruptly from the chair and the iron scrapes on the balcony.

Every emotion that's made me a wreck washes away, quickly cleansed by fear. I turn slowly, my mouth parted but words refuse to come out.

I don't have the strength or courage to ask who's behind me.

But I don't have to.

I let out a breath as a bushy tail comes into view.

"Boots," I say, greeting the neighbor's tabby cat and add, "You scared me," with my hand over my heart.

She must've snuck in while the balcony door was open and I was busy mulling over my wretched married life. There's an archway between my house and the neighbor's, and Boots used to be a regular on this balcony. Taking a few steps inside the bedroom, I scoop up the small cat. Her fur is soft and she purrs with contentment the moment I pet her. I only have a moment, though. She gets fed up with attention quickly and I've been on the wrong end of her claws before.

"You know you're not supposed to be in here," I scold her. Suddenly feeling exhausted, my conviction wanes. I escort Boots back outside, setting her down and move to shut the door just as my phone rings behind me on the bed.

The balcony is at the end of the bedroom so I have to walk quickly to answer in time, but I do on the last ring.

"Hello?"

"Jules, how are you?" Kat's voice asks. "I was just calling to check in."

"A mess," I say and my throat is tight. Is this what a breakup feels like? Or is this what regret feels like? I'm not sure which is which anymore. I suppose the two are one and the same.

"God, I know … it has to be rough." I nod my head but my lips are pressed into a thin line without any words wanting to come and contribute to the conversation.

"Do you want to talk about it?"

Closing my eyes, I shake my head even though I know she can't see; a moment later I'm able to tell her no.

"Hey, it's all going to be okay," Kat says as if it's a fact. "You know that, don't you?"

A small breath of disbelief leaves me. "No, Kat." I lay back on the bed and add, "No, I don't know it's going to be all right. It doesn't feel like it will."

"Stop it. Stop it right now." Although her tone is harsh, the pain behind her words is undeniable. "Not everything in life is good, but that doesn't mean you don't have a good life."

I lick my dry lips and close my eyes, lying back farther on the bed and trying to absorb my friend's advice.

"You have a great life, Jules. You really do."

"I thought I was okay. I thought I'd be able to move on. I thought I *was* moving on."

"You're going to, Jules."

My exhausted eyes stay shut tight, refusing to feel anymore and I hold my breath. "One day, probably sooner than you know it, it's going to feel normal without him. It's going to feel good without him. And there's not a single thing wrong with that."

"It doesn't feel like it's okay, though. It doesn't feel like it's all right to not be upset."

"It doesn't have to right now. You don't have to do anything right now, except tell me you're going to come to my house tomorrow night."

A sniff is what she gets in response until I'm able to compose myself.

"Of course."

"Good, now … are you all right?"

I answer her honestly. "I'm not, but I think I will be."

"You *definitely* will be," she says with such conviction, I believe her. My body feels lighter as I scoot closer to the edge of the bed, ready to do something.

"Do you want to go out for dinner?" I ask Kat.

Kat takes a deep breath on the other end of the line and I know she's busy and can't. That's her *I wish I could* sigh. She's always busy with work. "I can't—"

"It's fine," I say, cutting her off. "I've got to get out of this house." I speak while looking up at the coffered ceilings in the bedroom. This house has too many memories in it.

"You go out and get some fresh air, maybe get some shopping in and I'll see you tomorrow night."

Nodding in agreement, I answer, "See you tomorrow."

"Love you, Jules." Kat's voice is soft when she tells me she loves me.

"I love you too." It's so true. I'd crumble into a complete mess without her.

As I rise from the bed, it groans slightly and I look back to find it in disarray. I take the time to pull the sheets tight and lay the comforter just right. I even fluff the pillows and place them where they're supposed to be.

As my feet pad against the old wooden floor, it creaks right where I know it should and that chill from earlier comes back to me. I look up at the balcony door and find it unlocked, which is odd. I swear I locked it.

Click. The sound is loud as I stare at the lock, my fingers still on the cold hard metal.

I never did like having a balcony in the bedroom. Jace told me it was a silly fear. I cross my arms, feeling unsteady and colder by the second. I tuck a strand of hair behind my ear, grabbing my phone and clutch then throw on a pair of faded blue jeans.

Unsteady is the feeling that's most recognizable. I'm not sure where I go from here. Worse, I don't know where I want to go.

All I know in this moment, with everything in me, is that I just want to get out of this house.

chapter 26

Mason

I STAND FACING THE WINDOW IN MY FATHER'S OFFICE WITH MY HANDS behind my back and don't bother turning around to greet him as the door opens. I watch as my cold gray eyes narrow in the reflection. The city traffic below is stirring with life, but it's silent up here. So many people surround us, but not one of them can save me. Not one of them would even give a fuck.

Julia would. *My sweetheart.* Or at least she would have days ago before she realized she needed to get away from me.

"Mason," my father says and I turn around, finally facing him and knowing I need to confront him along with everything else I've been running from. As much as I want to hold Jules close and pretend just being with her will make this right, I know it won't.

"Father," I say, greeting him with an icy tone in my voice, hating that I'm even related to this man. I stare into his eyes and see my own. Everything about him reminds me of what I'm becoming. I fucking hate it.

"We need to get over this," my father says and gestures between the two of us.

"We do." I clench my jaw, my pulse rushing faster. I rip my gaze away from his, staring down at my hands. "I don't think there should be any more ties." It pains me to tell him that. Even after all these years and everything he's done, I still feel a gaping hole in my chest at the thought of severing this relationship.

"Ties to what?" he asks.

"Between the two of us."

My father flinches as if I've struck him. But what did he expect?

"Watch your mouth," he says. I'm surprised he has the nerve to admonish me as if what I'm saying is unspeakable.

"I want to walk away. I don't want to be tied to this anymore. I don't want to be associated with you."

"I'm your father, Mason. You can't walk away from that."

The fuck I can't. I bite down on my tongue to stop from blurting out that answer, gritting my teeth as he walks closer to the left side of the desk. I walk to the right, matching his pace, a careful dance of power that escalates the conversation.

"You need to just forgive—"

"I'll never forgive you for what you did to Avery," I say, looking my father in the eye as I say her name for the first time in months. Every muscle in me is wound tightly, waiting for his next move so I can destroy him and let out this rage.

His eyes flash with something—anger, maybe betrayal, I don't know what.

"I did what I had to do to protect you," he says, pushing out the words from between clenched teeth, but his nerve is shaken, unlike mine.

"She didn't deserve to be murdered." My hands ball into fists. Avery was a mistake. A fiery redhead with long legs and a smile that could kill. She had *mistake* written all over her.

I met her late one night at an event and I knew she was trouble. I knew it from the start but I needed a quick fuck. She tempted me and I took the bait. But I could never have imagined how it would all end.

"That's what happens when you blackmail a Thatcher." My father practically spits. "She decided to roll the dice. She's the one who came to me with demands and tried to back us into a corner."

"You could have sent her to me." My muscles twitch with the need to pound my fist into his face as I take a step forward. "I would have told her the baby couldn't have been mine."

"If I'd known then—"

"You didn't have to know!" I shout, unable to control myself any longer. My throat feels raw as the words are ripped from me, screaming up my chest. "She wasn't innocent." I take a step toward my father and grab the edge of the desk to keep from gripping his collar and say, "But she didn't deserve to die."

"She did." My father's voice is hard, his back straight and his gaze full of confidence.

"She was pregnant!" I tell him. Hating how he could so easily dismiss her existence. He had her murdered. He didn't even think twice about ending her life.

"With a married man's child!" my father sneers, his face turning red as he leans in closer to me and I can't take it any longer.

I can't take the arrogance and justification of ending a person's life so easily. I clench my fist until my knuckles are white and punch my father in the jaw. His teeth crack from the weight of the blow. His head whips to the side as he falls to the floor, limp and shocked. My arm stings with the pain of impact.

It feels so fucking good to finally give him a piece of what he deserves.

He lays there for a moment, his hand over his mouth as a trickle of blood leaks from the corner of his lips. I shake out my hand, adrenaline rushing through my veins. I just barely restrain myself from kicking him in the ribs, from letting all this anger and pent-up guilt out on him.

"You ungrateful prick." He spits blood onto the floor and looks up at me with a menacing glare. "You chose some whore over your own family."

No, I'm choosing what's right. I'm choosing to be better than this life I was born into.

My father doesn't quit with his justification. "Anderson didn't want that kid. Think about what she would have done to him!"

The mention of Jace Anderson makes my gaze break from my father's. The memories come back and make my tense muscles spasm. I can't hear whatever my father's yelling at me. It's all white noise.

I may have been born a Thatcher and I'll die a Thatcher, but I refuse to be anything like my father. Not today, not ever.

"I won't forgive you." I force my body to relax. I've said what I came to say. This ends now. "I never will." I start to walk out, accompanied by the sound of my heart racing.

Just as my hand grips the doorknob, I finally get the balls to ask him.

One last thing to say. One final question.

Walking back to his desk with confident steps, I imagine his answer as if I already know it. He turns slightly from facing the window, still curled up on the floor behind his desk, looking at me as if he doesn't trust me. He shouldn't. Not with how I'm feeling at this moment.

I stop on the opposite side of the desk, my mind racing as I go back years and years. Back to only a boy who lost his mother. Scared, confused … and angry.

"Mom didn't die from an overdose." The statement comes out accusatory and it's meant to. He wipes the blood from his mouth with the bright white sleeve of his dress shirt. He doesn't look me in the eye, doesn't acknowledge what I said in the least.

I take one step toward him, a large step that gets his attention. His gaze whips up to me. "Did you have her killed too?"

"How dare you!" His nostrils flare as he pins me with his gaze. "How dare you, you fucking …" he trails off and doesn't finish. His shoulders are hunched forward as he grips his desk chair for balance to stand.

I'm struck by the powerful way he's affected. I've wondered for so long, months now. If he had Avery killed, maybe he did the same with my mother.

I flex my hand and swallow thickly, feeling the need to explain. My question was prompted by a gut feeling more than anything else. I don't remember much from around the time she died, but I remember how I felt. How the air between them was tense. How scared my mother was that he would find out her dirty little secret. "I know she was cheating—"

"Get out!" My father shouts at me, not holding anything back as he throws his chair to the side, putting all of his weight into it. It crashes against the bookshelf, several of the books tumbling to the floor as he slams his fists against his desk.

I turn my back on him, my fist pulsing in agony from the punch and my chest hurting with a pain I can't explain.

He pounds his fists again and again on the maple desk as I force myself to walk away from him.

Leaving my father alone in his office and promising myself never to see him again, never to speak to him, never to trust him. And never to be like him.

Never again.

chapter 27

Julia

I STARE DOWN AT THE NEAT PILES OF PAPERS TO MY RIGHT IN THE DINING room. My back is killing me and my shoulders are screaming in pain. It's so wrong that now that these contracts and files are sorted out, my first thought is to call Mason, to see if he's free and tell him that I miss him.

God, do I miss him.

He could ease my physical pains, but also that sick lonely feeling I have after going through three years of finances.

Three years of hard evidence of Jace cheating. Three long years compiled in black ink on white pages.

I glance at the email still open on my laptop. Mr. Walker will have more for me tomorrow. It makes my stomach lurch because I know I'll see more credit card statements for hotel charges during the day when he was supposed to be working, along with charges for jewelry and everything else he bought the women he kept on the side. I don't need to see it. That's the messed-up part of it all.

Selling the apartment and being done with it is the last of all the problems and loose ends Jace left.

I'll be fine financially; everything is going to be okay on that front. But I want to know how long it went on. I want to know at what point in my life I wasn't good enough for him anymore.

The wine in the glass is almost gone and it's late, but I pour myself another. We all have our vices and it turns out mine are cabernet and Mason Thatcher. My lips curl into a pathetic weak smile and then I take a sip of the sweet wine.

I stare at the open newspaper on the table. The one with a photograph of Mason and someone else. Someone *new*. It's not hard to admit that it hurts to see it, to think that he's moved on already. It hasn't even been two weeks since I saw him last. It has their picture but the accompanying article is about me being used by the playboy bachelor and left brokenhearted. They know nothing and I couldn't care less about what they think happened. What matters is that I am heartbroken.

Mason. I've stared at that photo for far too long praying it isn't true. Mostly because I'm selfish. I'm not ready to commit to him, or to anyone, but I want him all the same.

Sue has assured me it's all made up and the woman in the photo is someone he dated long ago.

I take another gulp of wine and only look up from the same paragraph I've read five times when I hear my phone go off.

It's a text from Kat wanting my manuscript. Oh God.

It's a good thing I have an apartment up for sale, I suppose. Maybe I should thank my cheating deceased husband for that.

It takes a small sip before I have the courage to text her back, asking for an extension and then open my laptop to write. To let the words flow. If anything, I expect it to be about anger, grief, betrayal. But all that comes are thoughts of Mason's touch. How powerful his physical presence can be. How he can soothe my every pain. How he wants to do just that, and about how much I want it even more.

I let my head fall to the side when I remember him kissing me as he played my body right at this very spot that I'm sitting. My fingers never stop tapping on the keys as I relive the moment. I open my eyes and stare at the grain woven into the wooden table where I bent over for him. I confessed something so real, so painful and he made me feel alive and as though nothing else mattered.

I suck in a deep breath, hating that I left him the way that I did. I'm so damn broken. I don't understand why he wants me when it's obvious that I'm a wreck.

Biting down on my lip, I stare at the phone and think of texting him.

I miss you. I type in the words and then delete them.

I'm sorry. I stare at the two words that are so simple, yet mean so much.

I think I love you. That's what I should send him. Scare him away for good.

I delete the text as Kat messages me back. She's usually hard on me. Guilting me if I miss a deadline and reminding me about everyone else's schedules involved. It lights a fire under my bottom.

But all she's written this time is that it's okay and to take care of myself.

"Take care of myself," I whisper beneath my breath and let my fingers trail down the stem of the wineglass.

I wish Mason were here, but that's just an easy out.

This is supposed to hurt. It's supposed to be hard.

I want to crawl back to him and beg for forgiveness. Beg him to take away the pain again. It's selfish and I won't do that to him, but I'd be a liar if I said I didn't want to.

chapter 28

"I JUST GOT AN EMAIL." I HEAR LIAM'S IRRITATION AS THE DOOR OPENS. His light gray suit is sharp and crisp, but he looks like shit himself. His dirty blond hair is a mess on top of his head and the dark circles under his eyes prove he hasn't gotten much sleep.

"About what?" I ask. I don't let on that I already know what the email was about as I rest my elbows on the desk. Waiting for him to speak, I make a steeple with my pointer fingers. I know what this is about. My father's pulled the funds.

We're fucked. And I don't have a way out of this.

"What happened, Mason?" His question is drenched with desperation.

I swallow hard, hating that I owe Liam anything. I know I do. At the very least I owe him an explanation, but what can I tell him? My jaw clenches and I look down at my desk as I pick at my hands where a small cut mars my knuckles. I can't turn in my father. I don't have any hard evidence of his misdeeds but more than that, I can't bring myself to do it to my own father. That last part causes me more shame than I'm willing to admit.

I clear my throat and lean forward to face Liam.

"We have to back down or find new investors."

"Back down?" His wide eyes stare at me as though I'm the insane one here. Maybe I am. "We can't fucking back down. We've sunk millions into this!" I can practically see his heart racing out of his chest.

"I'm sorry, but—"

"What the fuck happened?" he shouts as he stands up, throwing the papers on the desk behind him. My blood heats as I glare at Liam.

"Sit down." The words come out harsh and as a demand. It gets his attention, like a child who's been scolded. I'll own up to failing him but I have my limits, and when it comes to business, I demand respect. He's still, almost frozen for a long moment and then he places both his hands flat on the desk and leans over, getting closer to my face. He's still a foot away, but it's too fucking close for my liking.

"Don't tell me what to do, Thatcher," he says low in his throat. "This is going to ruin us. Ruin *me*," he hisses.

"We'll recover." I don't have the confidence my voice reflects. But I'll do whatever I have to in order to make this work. I have no intention of going anywhere. If I have to start from the bottom again and claw my way back up to the top, so be it.

"You need to get over whatever it is that's going on between you and your father. Whatever the fuck it is, just let it go."

He glares at me long and hard. Waiting for me to comply, but it's not going to happen. I may not be sending my father away to prison for life, but I'm through with him for good. I'm sure as fuck not going to take his money.

"I have a few meetings tomorrow with Marcus Jennings and Austin Hook." I lean back in my seat, daring him to come closer. His body tenses as he turns his head in disbelief, still leaning over my desk.

He shakes his head, looking bewildered. "How could you do this to me?" He barely gets out the words. He pushes off the desk, shaking his head again and walking a few feet away before looking back at me.

I can see each emotion as they flow through him and finally he settles on anger. "Is it because of Anderson?" he asks and my heart stops in my chest.

I stand up straight out of instinct. Out of the need to figure out how much he knows.

"What the fuck does he have to do with this?" My voice is deathly low as my eyes narrow; my muscles are coiled and ready for a fight. *What does he know?*

He gives me a confused look in return. "'He?'" Liam tilts his head and it's then that I realize he was talking about Jules and using her married name. My heart sinks lower and a cold sweat breaks out over my body. *Fuck!*

"I'm talking about the bitch you've been fucking." My body turns to stone, stuck in place by an anger I can't control. Everything goes red as he keeps talking, oblivious to my reaction. "Everything's changed since she's come around."

I crack my neck to the side, deciding to ignore it. To give him one chance. That's all he'll get. "It has nothing to do with her."

"Oh yeah? She didn't convince you not to make amends with your father? Or fuck him over or fuck me over?" With each question, his voice gets louder and louder.

"She doesn't know shit about my father and she has no place here or in any of this."

He flashes me a cocky grin. "Really gets you worked up, doesn't it?" He rounds the desk as he talks. "Is it because she dumped your ass on Madison Avenue?" The question comes with a laugh and he closes the space between us. I already know this is going to end badly; I'm only waiting for the right moment to strike at this point. "What'd you do that had her running out of that car, Mason? You fuck her over too? Just like you fucked—"

I can't stop what's started. He shouldn't have brought up Jules. I can't control myself when it comes to her.

My fist comes out of nowhere, hitting him square on the jaw and sending him flying backward. Twice in one week I've hit a man. And for the second time, I don't give a shit.

My knuckle flares where the cut from the last punch is still healing and my shoulder screams with pain from the impact. My vision clouds, anger making it redder by the second. Everything rages inside. The anger of her leaving me, the disappointment of my father, the regret of what I've done all mix into a deadly concoction. I take two steps forward with my hands up, ready to beat the piss out of him, ready for the fight he obviously wants, but he's limp on the floor, blood leaking from his nose.

Crouching down, I grip the lapels of his jacket, pulling harder than I should but I can't stop myself, panic warring against everything else. He's motionless and unresponsive. I fist his jacket in my hands, shaking him. "Liam!" Dread courses through me. What the hell did I do? I slap him lightly across the face, but he doesn't respond.

I hold a hand over his nose just to make sure he's breathing. The warm air confirms that he is. *Thank fuck.* My body aches as I stand, running my hands through my hair and then down my face as I pace the floor.

I look up to the clock and I only have five, maybe ten minutes before everyone arrives at the office. I lean my forearm against the wall of windows, feeling defeated and like a fucking idiot. This isn't who I am now. This isn't the man I wanted to be. I lean all of my weight into the glass. I'm spiraling, all from the mention of her name.

The realization that I just knocked out Liam weighs heavily on my shoulders. The one man I could occasionally refer to as a friend.

I stare at my own reflection as I realize how badly I've fucked up.

It doesn't take long before I decide I need to call an ambulance and I'm very much aware they'll call the police. I clench my jaw and swallow my pride. *It'll be a fucking spectacle.*

He shouldn't have talked about Jules, though.

He had to know this was going to happen.

chapter 29

Why do you haunt me so?
You take control of my thoughts,
You consume my sleep.
How do you wound me still?
You need to leave me alone,
I'm not yours to keep.

"IT CAN'T BE TRUE." I ONLY PARTED MY LIPS, BUT THE WORDS TUMBLED out without thinking. Sitting around the same small table in the coffee shop feels surreal as I read the article. We were just here not even a month ago and it's unreal how everything has changed.

"You broke him," Maddie says somewhat jokingly to try to lighten the mood.

His company, his friendships, his father. I know the tabloids make up a good portion of their content, but the mug shot is something that can't be denied.

"It's all dropped and he'll be fine," Sue says airily as if it's no big deal.

The newspaper falls to the table and the faint sound of the paper rustling is all I can hear.

"I don't understand what happened," I say, thinking out loud. "He never said anything to me about his father or about the business."

Sue shrugs. "Sometimes people don't talk about the things that bother them. He'll be fine." How can I not know, though? I shared so much of myself with Mason. I was raw and open and giving of so much of me. I know he did the same. I could feel it between us. It wasn't one sided. I hid the darkest secrets from him … and he did the same with me. A new form of regret wraps itself around my throat. *I should make sure he's all right like he did for me.* That's an excuse I can use to run back to him.

"Coffee?" Kat asks as she sits down and places a hot ceramic mug in front of me. It's been mixed with an almost offensive amount of creamer and the color matches my cream accent pillows at home… just the way I like it.

With a grateful smile, I accept it and blow over the top, inhaling the smell and trying to feel normal. Or as normal as I can, all things considered. Kat's busy reading over the manuscript on her phone, but whether or not it will do is nowhere on my mind. All I can think about is the fact that Mason was there for me, so many times. He needs someone right now. The only question is whether or not he'd let me in.

She murmurs the lines as she opens the book.

Sweet lies you told me, beautiful forever.
A dream or a terror, I craved it, whichever.
A taste so sweet, too much to say no,
I couldn't resist and you couldn't let go.
Your healing touch and comforting kiss—
But I never thought it would end like this.

Kat tilts her head, her lips stopping mid-poem and she gives me a questioning look as she says, "Is this one about Jace?"

The book was supposed to be about mourning and loss. It is, but it's a deceptive cocktail of the two men. I loved and lost both of them.

All I can do is take a sip of coffee and try not to choke on the lie as I say, "I don't remember."

"So have you heard from him?" Maddie asks me, thankfully saving me from Kat's interrogation.

My ponytail swishes along the crook of my neck as I shake my head no. He got the message that we were over after I repeatedly refused his calls. I don't think he'll ever reach out to me again.

"Have you called him?" Maddie asks.

"Not yet," I tell her. "Or, no. No, I haven't." *Thump, thump, thump,* my poor little heart won't stay where it's supposed to and I hide in my coffee cup again.

Her voice is hopeful as she scoots forward, the sound of the stool scratching against the floor making an annoying screech. "You should."

"I don't know … I want to. He was …" I trail off as I run my fingers up and down the cup and stare at a lone muffin in front of me. I haven't eaten since I heard about Mason this morning.

"I think you should," Maddie says softly.

"I think you should shut your mouth and let things happen as they should," Sue bites out and Maddie merely gives her a look of defiance.

"She breaks up with him and he falls apart—" Maddie looks like she's about to go off on Sue, but she doesn't get much out.

"Stop it," Sue says. "That's not her fault." Sue points at the paper and adds, "This has nothing to do with Jules."

"You don't know that." Maddie's response is soft as she looks down to her own blueberry muffin and picks at the top of it. "Everyone's saying he's heartbroken."

"Jesus, Maddie!" Sue snaps. "Jules, this is not your fault and you don't owe him anything. Don't go back to a man because of guilt." Her voice cracks and her eyes hold a warning. "Please. If you want to reach out to him, do it for any other reason than feeling guilty or like you owe him." There's a tear at my chest, an open wound knowing Sue is speaking from experience.

"I wasn't trying to hurt him, Maddie." I can't respond to Sue right now, my throat feels tight. "I didn't think he'd care, to be honest …" I don't know if that's true. I wasn't thinking of him when I ended it. I was only thinking of me. Of my anger. "It just happened so fast and it was too much."

"There's nothing wrong with fast," Kat says, surprising the three of us. It's then that I notice she hasn't moved past the first page. "Evan and I got engaged in three months."

Their story was a whirlwind romance. Everyone's story is different. Maybe this is regret or guilt pushing me toward Mason, but it's different from what Sue went through. I swear our story has to be different.

My heart begs me to stop, but I have to ask them a question that's kept me up the last three nights I've dreamed of Mason. It's killing me slowly and carefully, destroying everything I thought I knew. "Isn't it wrong to fall for someone *else* so quickly after Jace?"

"No," Kat says and shakes her head. "It's wrong to throw something away because you're afraid of it, though." Her voice is full of regret, but it didn't stop her from telling me exactly what she thinks.

"You guys are giving me whiplash." I swallow thickly and brush the loose locks out of my face, resting my elbows on the table and burying my face in my hands. "I shouldn't be with him, I should be with him. I hurt him by breaking up with him, but I shouldn't be with him if I feel regret. I don't know what to think!" I say, my voice raw and the words tearing their way up my throat.

"What do you want, Jules?" Sue asks me, not missing a beat although my other two friends only stare at me with questions and guilt of their own. "Love isn't about thinking, it's only about what you feel." Of all the women in this group, I'm not sure I should take her advice on love, but she says it with such conviction that I believe it. And I trust her.

"I feel like I've been sad for too long," I say. "I feel like I deserve to be punished for moving on. I feel like I miss Mason. Like really miss him. And I know I hurt him." I brush my fingers under my eyes and suck in a breath to keep myself from falling to pieces. "I didn't know it would be like this. I feel like life was spinning out of control and he was the one steady thing and I was taking advantage of that." My fingers tremble as I press my palms against my eyes, finally finishing my thoughts. "I don't know if I'm running away from all this hurt or running to him." I swallow and whisper, "Maybe some of both? And it scares me."

It's too much to take in and process, but I need all this mayhem to stop.

"You don't have to know. You don't have to do anything," Kat says. Her phone's flipped over on the table and as soon as I notice that, I also notice all three women staring at me with sympathy. Waiting for me. I don't deserve this. I don't know how I ended up so close with these women but without them, I'd be so lost.

"You can take as much time as you need," Maddie says with a small nod.

That's the problem, though. I wanted things to be slow, but he was a force I couldn't control. My body bowed down to his and I would have been swallowed whole if I gave any more of myself to him.

It doesn't stop me from wanting him and the way I feel when I'm with him. He was right that first night when he said he'd make me forget everything but his name and what he'd done to me.

"Are you sure it's not wrong? Because it feels like the worst kind of wrong." I glance at each of the girls, feeling like whatever they tell me will propel me in the direction I need to go.

"It's scary," Maddie says, shifting in her seat and breaking eye contact.

"Love is terrifying," Kat adds.

"It's not wrong. You haven't done anything wrong and you should do what you want to do. Even if that's breaking every bachelor's heart in New York City." A soft, playful smile greets me as I look at Sue. She nudges me and reaches for the paper. "This wasn't your fault, but I can't say I'm not curious about the gossip … and that I don't think there was something good about you two being together."

chapter 30

Mason

Anger management. The paper crinkles in my hand as I crumple it.

No charges were pressed, but I'm sure Liam's getting a kick out of the anger management classes the judge ordered me to attend. *Prick.* I know the asshole would have pushed the issue further if it wasn't for the company. He wants to save face and hold this over me so I can do his bidding.

That's not going to fucking happen. I'll take on all the debt if I have to and do it myself. The project is canceled; I'm taking the hit and dissolving the company. It's better that I'm alone. It's as simple as that.

I drop the empty bottle of whisky in the trash can as well as the notice regarding the anger management course. The glass bottle clinks against the metal frame of the photograph. I stare down into the bin, the shattered glass marring the photo of the picture-perfect family. It's destroyed … but really, it's always been that way.

I'm tired and angry, and tired of being angry too. This isn't what I wanted or planned. I wanted more. For me, that meant Jules. With my fingers pinching the bridge of my nose, I lean back against the kitchen wall.

Call it what you want. Out of everything in life, she's the only thing I know I truly want. That should mean something.

I make my way upstairs, walking slowly and dreading another night alone in this empty house. It never bothered me much before, but I can't fucking stand the silence now.

Someone knocks three times at the front door and I still with my hand on the banister.

I wait a moment, wondering who the fuck would be here this late at night, even though only one name comes to mind. I steel myself for the worst, thinking it's my father. I can't face him right now. Not after what he's done and what I accused him of. It's only after another three knocks that I force myself to face the consequences. I open the door with a swift pull, prepared to turn him away, but my voice is caught in my throat.

Jules's baby blue eyes look at me with a mix of emotions. Fear, sorrow ... hope. The chill of the wind spreads goosebumps along her arms and blows her long brunette hair off her shoulders. She looks to her left and then right, pulling her leather jacket tighter around her and taking a small step toward me.

"Mason," she says and licks her lush lips, painted with that same color I've grown to expect from her. "I—" She stops to clear her throat and looks away again as I stand numb in the doorway.

Fate's delivered her to me. I can't let her go this time. I won't.

"I was hoping we could talk?" Her voice is timid and her heels click on the cement porch as she shifts in place. Her tight blue jeans hug her curves, although the loose cream blouse beneath her jacket leaves much to the imagination. I know what's under there, though.

I don't say a word, too afraid of scaring her off. Instead I take a step to the side and open the door wider, waiting for her to walk in.

Her cheeks and the tip of her nose are a beautiful rosy red from the bite of the night air.

She hesitantly steps inside and looks around as if she hasn't been here enough times to have the place memorized. I close the door and stare at the lock a moment too long before turning it.

"Mason, I'm sorry." Jules's voice calls to me as I turn around to face her. I watch her swallow and then bite down on her bottom lip. She's worried and apologetic, but I don't give a fuck about the past. I never did. I care about what she wants now.

"Why are you here, Jules?" I ask her in a deep voice. It's rougher than I intended, but it's all I can manage.

"I heard about what happened," she says. She fidgets as she waits for my response, but I don't give her one. I'm not interested in talking about anything but us. I don't want to taint her with the bullshit. "I just wanted to say I'm sorry for hurting you," she says in a tight voice full of agony.

"Is that all?" I say and it takes all the air I have in my lungs. Taking a step forward and closing the space between us, my heart thumps chaotically in my chest.

She twists her fingers around one another nervously. "I also," she starts to say and then swallows. "I was wondering if you still ... if you were interested ..."

"In what?" My eagerness gets the best of me. *Make this easy for me, Jules, and I'll make everything right. I promise you, sweetheart, I'll make it up to you.*

"If you'd like to maybe go out again? If that's what we were doing?" A nervous huff of a laugh accompanies her proposition. I stare at her a moment, thinking it's just too good to be true. She came back to me. There's a saying about that, but it's not meant for real life. It's not meant for men like me.

"If you still want me," Jules adds, the raw vulnerability so thick in her voice.

"I never stopped wanting you," I say, my voice barely a murmur. Her doe eyes never leave mine as I gently push her jacket off her shoulders. If she thinks I don't want her, she'll know better soon enough.

"Mason," she says and gasps as I lean down and kiss her neck. Maybe it's the alcohol or maybe it's just that my body knows hers. But I'm not waiting for apologies or excuses or explanations.

I need to *feel* her.

"Mason, stop." She pushes her hands against my chest, shrugging her jacket back on as I take a step back. "I need you to know that I'm worried we're going too fast. I'm worried that this isn't going to last."

A deep breath steadies me as I stare down at my sweetheart. "I told you, Jules. If you're with me, then you're with me and that's all there is to it." I take her hand in mine and kiss one knuckle, then another.

"Mason," she whimpers as if I've broken her heart. She has no idea. I turn her hand over and kiss her pulse, my heart beating faster.

"No more of this running from me or from us, Jules. Are you with me?" I ask her, feeling more vulnerable than I ever have in my entire life. I whisper, "Are you mine?"

"I don't know that my heart is mine to give, Mason. It's broken and I don't know if it will heal the right way." Jules sniffs and looks ashamed, but she has no idea how much I understand. I truly do.

Grief is a journey and she doesn't have to go it all alone.

I wrap my arm around her waist and pull her into me. "You don't have to be perfect, Jules, in order to be perfect for me." I kiss her hair and hope that she can understand. "I want you how you are today, and tomorrow I'll want you how you are then."

Jules buries her head into my chest, her hair brushing against my chin and I kiss the top of her head. "Why are you so perfect, Mason?" she says and relaxes in my embrace. "How do you know just the right words to say?" Her voice is soft and relaxed as she molds her body to mine and that's when I know I've won her over.

"I'm not perfect, Jules." My heart aches in my chest, knowing just how imperfect I am. And how imperfect I am *for her*. She has no idea. We aren't meant to fit together, but I'll force the pieces to line up and pretend it's meant to be.

For her. Because I owe her that much.

"I can't tell you how happy I am that you came back," I whisper and run my hand in soothing circles along her back.

chapter 31

Julia

I asked you to leave.

I need to be alone.

But you stayed in my head.

My heart and my home.

I asked you to leave me,

But you won't go away.

When I go to find you tomorrow,

I only hope that you'll stay.

MASON'S BEDROOM IS SO MUCH DARKER THAN MINE. FULL OF DEEP grays and dark wood. It matches the rest of his home, I suppose. His curtains are thick velvet and shut tight. Even with hardly any light, I can see him, all of him. His muscles ripple in the faint light. It makes Mason seem so much more dominating, which is criminal.

He already owns me, consuming me with his presence. But right now, at this very moment as he towers over me, skimming his fingers over my sensitized skin, I'm weaker for him than I've ever been in my entire life.

"Mason." I murmur his name as he lays me down on his bed. I turn my head to the side and arch my back as he leaves open-mouth kisses down my neck. We're both naked, but it's more than that. So much more. We've been here before plenty of times, but this is different. We're bared to each other.

"If we do this, can you promise me one thing?" My heart is pounding in my chest as I lay back on the bed, because I feel like this is the end. It's putting so much to rest and moving on toward the unknown. I'm terrified that I'll fall and he'll let me shatter when he's done with me.

"What?" He whispers the question between kisses.

"Please don't hurt me," I beg him. "I want you and I want what we have …" I trail off, barely able to breathe. "But promise if you want me to go, you'll do it easy and as soon as you know." He braces his forearms on either side of my head and looks down at me with an intense look in his gray eyes that pierces my lungs, stopping me from breathing.

"You need to stop this." His voice is hard, but it always is when I say something he doesn't like. "Do you understand?"

I nod my head and say, "Yes." I really do. I want this to stop and for *us* to begin.

"Don't hide from me, Jules. Don't run from me," Mason tells me with an authority that can't be denied.

I nod my head in complete agreement. I'm tired of running and denying myself what I really want. "No more secrets," I say into the hot air between us.

Mason pulls away, looking at me as if he's going to tell me something. The silence and tension grow, but no words come. Instead he crashes his lips to mine and pushes his body against me, forcing me to spread my legs for him.

And I do, I let him have all of me.

His fingers trail down between my legs as my core heats. He doesn't stop nipping and kissing all over my heated body, his hands roaming freely, taking in every inch of me. I'm helpless beneath him. Falling deeper and deeper into the darkness and loving how overwhelming it all is.

I missed this. God, how I missed this.

He groans in the crook of my neck, a sexy deep sound that makes my body arch toward him as if drawn even closer to him by an undeniable pull. His heated skin brushes against mine as he pushes himself inside of me.

My mouth opens and I stare up at him, his steel gray eyes holding my gaze as he enters me, slowly stretching me and not stopping until he's fully inside of me.

My heart beats faster, my body numb and on edge, waiting for him to move and take me how he wants me. Rough, raw, and making me his.

His fingers dig into my hips, pinning me down as he pulls out slightly and then slams back in, forcing a whimper from me. My body bucks instinctively, but I never break eye contact. I can't. He holds me captive beneath his gaze.

He does it over and over again until I'm so wet and hot for him that he easily slips in and out, each time forcefully smacking against my clit.

My body writhes and begs me to move away; it's too much, too intense. But that's just how Mason is. I knew it when I met him. More than that, I need him. I need this.

I love you, my heart whispers but I don't say it aloud. Small whimpers of pleasure spill from my lips with each thrust and I swear I'm close to admitting it. So close.

He groans low in his throat as he speeds up his relentless thrusts, resting his forehead against mine and kissing me mercilessly. Our lips barely touch, but they do, kiss after kiss after kiss. A series of slow kisses with our hearts racing fast beg me to confess.

He steals the breath from my lungs. His hot body makes mine burn with desire. I cling to him, wrapping my legs around him and digging my nails into his shoulder.

Higher and higher he pushes me.

The pleasure comes in small waves, dim at first but growing stronger and stronger. They threaten to overwhelm me as my fingers and toes tingle. The crash will shatter me, I know it. I don't beg him to stop. I don't try to pull away. I want it, I crave it, I'm desperate for him to ruin me.

"Mason!" I cry out as the wave consumes me, pulling me under in an intense orgasm that paralyzes my body. It's Mason's cue to devour me and he does, fucking me with no regard for the state I'm in. He's chasing his own release, pounding into me recklessly and extending my pleasure that much longer.

I scream out as he whispers, "Mine," in the crook of my neck again and again. His throaty voice gets louder as he fucks me harder. I can't do a damn thing but take everything he's giving me. And I do, with my nails digging into his skin and his masculine scent surrounding me. His large body suffocating me in the most delicious way.

It's only when he stills deep inside of me as I pant under him, desperately trying to breathe, that I'm able to moan out my pleasure. His thick cock pulses and the wetness between my thighs leaks between us.

He doesn't stop holding me.

He doesn't stop kissing me.

I almost don't tell him. I almost hide from him, but I promised him I wouldn't.

"I love you," I whisper and give that piece of me to him too. He doesn't say it back, but I know he heard it.

He kisses me without mercy, soothing my pain and taking everything I have.

chapter 32

Mason

How long is long enough? I keep thinking it with every second that passes. As if I'm not a complete fraud for asking Jules to marry me. It's been two weeks of things falling perfectly into place. She's still waiting for the other shoe to drop. For this fantasy we're living in together to crumble into pieces. I won't let it, though. I'll give her everything she wants and that includes a ring, a sense of security that will seal us together and truly put our respective pasts behind us.

Financially, with my business in shambles and the money tied up in contracts I'm obligated to fulfill but can't, I'm fucked. I was smart enough to incorporate the business as an LLC, though. Personally, all I have is my house and stocks. It's nothing compared to her bank account. But I'm stable and when the contracts are finalized and the business assets are split, I'll be able to give her even more. I'm surprised she hasn't asked, but I'm prepared if that's a concern for her.

My eyes focus on the deep red petals scattered on every surface. I want her. I don't care about anything else anymore.

The only thing I give a damn about is making Jules mine in every way.

I don't want her to tell me no. I can't stand the thought of her turning me down or worse, if simply asking her to be my wife could push her away.

It doesn't matter how fast she is if she runs though, how quickly she'll turn me down and try to hide. I'll find her, I'll catch her and I'll wait for her. Always.

I close the small black velvet box, making the vision of the four-carat, cushion-cut diamond vanish and shove it into my pocket. Letting a heavy breath leave me, I turn and look at the living room. It's obvious. So damn obvious that I'm going to propose.

The second she walks in here and sees the crystal vases of deep red roses on every surface, she's going to know what I have planned.

I can see her now, standing in the doorway, gripping onto the frame while her beautiful blue eyes go wide and she breathes in the floral scent. The lights are low and the tea lights are scattered.

I'm not a romantic man by nature, but for her and for this … Hopefully for the start of our lives together, I can do romance. *All for her.* I'll pretend to be someone else until both of us believe it.

At the sound of the doorknob turning, my heart skips in my chest, hammering harder than I anticipated. I take a step back, pulling the box from my pocket and preparing to get down on my knee. My blood heats and anxiety suddenly washes through me. It's really happening. I'm really going to ask her to marry me. The thought itself calms me.

Of course I am. *I love her.*

I run my hand through my hair as she steps forward enough to come through the doors. I thought she'd be astonished by the sight of the room. I imagined her taking it all in, but she's only looking at me.

"Julianna Lynn Summers, I would be honored—" I start and already I've fucked up. I had this damn thing rehearsed. I thought I had it all memorized but having to look up at her, and not knowing what she's going to say … I stumbled over my words.

Jules covers her mouth with a gasp, letting the front door shut slowly behind her. Her shoulders hunch forward some as her purse falls to the ground. I knew she'd be emotional; I just wish the shock would wane so I could see which side of her was winning out. The side that loves me and wants to live in the moment, or the side stuck in the past and afraid to move on.

Jules takes a few steps forward when I don't continue, her thin heels clicking on the polished wood floors as she places her hands on my shoulders and starts to lower herself to the ground, but that's not how I want her. I don't know how I'm able to wrap an arm around her long legs and look up at her, still holding the ring out although she's staring into my eyes. Her skin is soft beneath my touch.

"Jules, I love you and I want to spend every day of my life with you." I hesitate to say the words but I have to, even if she says she can't. "I want you as my wife," I tell her and watch her facial expression crumple with a hint of pain reflected in her eyes as I say the words.

"I love you too, Mason." She barely gets out the words as she covers her face with both her hands and then wipes under her eyes. Her eyes are glossy with tears and her voice is choked as she says it again. "I love you and I didn't know if I could …" Hearing her start her confession breaks my heart and I rise just enough to hold her. She wraps her arms around my shoulders, gripping onto me as though she needs me to stand. And in so many ways, she does. She needs someone there and I'll always be that person for her.

So long as she'll let me.

She pulls away slightly, trying to pull herself together as she brushes her hair out of her face and looks away, taking a calming breath.

"I want all of you, Jules," I tell her as I cup her chin in my hand and force her to look at me. "When you're upset, I want to know so I can make you smile. When you're angry, just tell me. I'll let you take it out on me however you need, then make you come so hard you'll forget you ever felt anything other than bliss. I want the real you. Always. I never want you to hide from me."

Those lush lips part and a soft breath escapes her as she stares into my eyes. She's searching for something. She better not fucking wonder if everything I've just said is true or not.

"I want the same from you, Mason." I'm surprised at her response. I stay still on the ground, wondering how she could think for a second I wouldn't share all of me with her. Not my past, though. She doesn't know shit about that and she never will. None of it. I'm going to fix it all and keep it hidden in the shadows and buried nine feet deep where it all belongs.

She kneels on the floor in front of me and takes my jaw in both her hands, planting a soft sweet kiss on my lips. Her touch calms all my worries. It dispels the demons threatening to surface. She does this to me. She makes me a better person and I desperately want to be that man for her.

She speaks with her eyes closed, her lips close to mine and her hot breath filling the air between us. Her long, thick lashes are damp with her tears as she tells me, "I love you for you. The good and the bad. And I do want to be with you, Mason." Her voice is pained and I can't help but reach out and hold her, pulling her closer to me. "I need you," she whispers.

I kiss the crook of her neck. "All I need is your love."

"You have it, Mason."

She has yet to answer; I need to hear her tell me yes. I want to be good enough to be her husband and if I'm not today, then tomorrow I'll be better. I'm determined and she needs to know that. I put my hands on her shoulders.

"I love you, Jules. Will you marry me?" I ask her, looking deep into her eyes.

She gives me a sweet smile, almost a shy one as she sniffles and finally gives me everything I need by saying, "I love you too. Yes." Her words come out as if it's obvious. As if it's only natural.

I finally breathe a deep sigh of relief, heaving in the air and holding her close to me. I stand up, still carrying her and swing her in my arms as I rise.

I kiss up her neck and every inch of her exposed skin, making her let out a small, feminine laugh and push away from me slightly. This is the only kind of pushing I ever want her to do again. From this day forward, she's mine.

I only set her down so I can take out the ring from the box. I watch as Jules's eyes widen once again. "Oh my gosh," she says softly, eyeing the ring as though it's the most beautiful thing she's ever seen.

"Do you like it?" I ask her as I slip the box into my pocket and hold the ring out for her.

She bites her bottom lip as she nods vigorously and says, "Mason, it's beautiful." Finally, she looks up at me as I slip the ring onto her finger. "I love it," she whispers.

A small breath leaves her as she rubs her fingers over my five o'clock shadow and gently kisses me. I've never felt anything like what I feel for her. Seeing my ring on her finger makes it seem as though it's all going to be all right.

As long as the past will stay buried where it belongs.

Lies lies go away,

The sins are all from yesterday.

We tried to run, you tried to beat us.

Now we're ruined, left defeated.

THE FRAME CLICKS INTO PLACE AND I TURN IT OVER IN MY HANDS and smile. I straighten my back and hold up the heavy silver frame. This isn't for hanging out here where everyone can see. It's silly really, but I wanted it framed.

My engagement ring clinks against the silver frame as I hold it up, the sunlight from the large bay window in Mason's house, well our house now, reflecting off the glass as I read the words.

A New Love and New Beginning.

It's a picture of us from the first article about us that was run in the papers. Back when I didn't know how to feel about the two of us. When I was riddled with guilt and pain and not seeing things clearly, I hated that we were in the papers at all. But I loved the candid photo.

I happened to come across it online the other day and when I read it, I lost it. Mason had to come in and find out why I was crying. He's always worried that I'm going to break down. I wish he wasn't so concerned for me. Yes, I'm emotional, but I know what I want. *I want him.* Something as simple as this article shouldn't get me so emotional, especially since half the facts aren't even true. But I love that our story has a beginning that was captured. I love that everyone around us knew.

I would never have thought that this article would give me a sense of pride and bring back a memory I want to be reminded of. A night when two lost souls knew they needed each other, even if we were too blind or stubborn to see it, we felt it.

"Finally," I say. It's framed and perfect. Just how I wanted it.

I hear Mason's rough chuckle as he walks into the kitchen and wraps his hands around my hips then plants a kiss on my shoulder.

I have to close my eyes as he hums and places his hand on my lower belly. He wants a baby. The very thought warms my heart and makes my head fall back against his broad chest. Wedding first, though. I want it all with him.

"Soon," I say softly with my eyes closed.

"What's this?" Mason asks, picking up the frame and reading the article left on the counter from where I cut out the photo. I watch his eyebrows raise as he reads the first few lines and he looks at me questioningly.

"I was going to put it on *my* nightstand," I tell him softly, waiting for his reaction. I'm still adjusting to moving in. I'll never sell my family home but I'm happier here, away from all the reminders of what used to be.

With no response, he sets the frame down and kisses me again. It's soft and sweet, but it lasts. My heart swells each time he kisses me like this. When he pulls away, he grins at me. It's a cocky one that lets me know he thinks he's got me all tied up in knots. And he does.

"Why this one?" he asks me.

Truthfully, I'm not sure I can vocalize why I want this particular one on my nightstand, so I just shrug.

"I just want it," I tell him simply and my easy response makes him smile.

"Well if you want it, then it's all yours."

That right there is why it was so easy to fall for this man. It's simple and natural. No rhyme or reason. It just feels right.

I set the frame down on the counter. It's not at all a lazy weekend; I have to write like crazy to get this manuscript in before the deadline, but I'm doing everything I can to procrastinate.

"You want a drink?" Mason offers, his voice dripping with sex appeal. He has a sexy grin on his lips and I know he wants to stay in and do bad things tonight.

I can't resist him, so I nod my head and his smile widens, filling me with warmth. I'll never get enough of him and how he makes me feel.

I pick up the envelope on top of the pile of mail sitting to my right as he heads to the fridge. The envelope tears easily and a handwritten letter slips out.

I feel my forehead crease as I unfold the thick cream parchment. Who sends a letter like this in a plain envelope? Before I read it, I check the envelope again. My name is there, but there's no return address.

Dear Julia,

It pains me to tell you this, but I can't stand to watch from a distance as you fall into a trap. Your husband was murdered. I know this is going to shock you, but I have proof. You may not believe me but I pray that you do.

Mason Thatcher murdered him. Don't trust him. Don't let him know that you know. If he finds out, you won't be safe.

My blood runs cold as I stand at the counter, my heart racing out of my chest. There's more written, but I can't read it. A shiver rolls through my body and everything seems to blur.

There's no way this is true. There's no way, yet my fingers tremble and my gaze shifts from the letter to the man accused, standing only feet from me.

My eyes dart from Mason's back as he rummages in the fridge, then back to the paper.

My heart thumps.

Murdered. Jace wasn't murdered. I deny it all, swallowing thickly.

I reread the letter, blinking and taking it in. My lips move with the words, but I can't breathe. I can't focus.

The handwritten letters seem to swirl together into a cloud of distrust. My vision fades and I feel so fucking dizzy. I back up slowly, pushing from the island and letting the feet of the stool scrape against the tile. Mason looks up at the noise and my weak legs barely hold me up as I grip the stool, the paper crinkling in my hand, my bare feet padding against the cold floor.

My head shakes on its own. That's not true. It's not true. It can't be true.

"Jules?" Mason's voice is riddled with concern and something else. Something I never registered before, but I can hear it now. I can see it on his face as I barely breathe and look up at him.

"The—" I can't bring myself to confess what I've just read. It's a lie. It has to be a lie. What a cruel lie it is. But Mason's response is throwing me off.

He's careful as he sets a bottle of beer on the counter, squaring his shoulders, all humor gone from his face and something else, *someone* else, stands in his place.

"Mason?" I barely get out his name.

"What is it?" he asks me in a voice so menacing, fear lights a fire deep in the marrow of my bones. No. I shake my head. "Mason, no," I say as my throat goes dry and my words crack. *He didn't do anything. He didn't even know Jace.*

This isn't real. My fist grips the stool tighter and I struggle to react. This is a nightmare. It has to be.

I'm caught between my need to run to somewhere I can think and the need to know the truth. I need the truth. No more lies; no more secrets.

He promised.

He loves me.

There's just no way.

"Did you do it?" The question leaves me in a single weak breath and in an instant, something snaps into place. As if he's very aware of what I'm saying. As if he's been waiting for this.

No. My body turns to ice; my blood and lungs freeze and I can't believe this is reality. It can't be true.

Mason takes a step forward, around the island and it breaks me from my denial.

It's my cue to run, a natural instinct that takes over. The stool falls hard, crashing to the tiled floor as I take off, but Mason's faster, gripping my waist and making me jerk backward. I cry out from fear and he releases me, only for me to fall onto the floor. His large frame towers over me, his hands up as if he's approaching a wild animal. I feel as if I am just that. My eyes wide, my heart pounds in my chest. *Thump, thump, thump.*

"Did I do what?" he asks, his eyes narrowed and with a coldness I haven't seen before. This isn't the man I know.

My bottom lip wobbles, the small bit of strength vanishing as I take in the raw truth. "Did you kill my husband?"

you are

my hope

Mason gave me chills when I first laid eyes on him. The good kind. The kind
that make your body ache, and your heart hammer.

It's not fair that his touch eased my pain.
That his lips on mine made my worries vanish.
That his love gave me a reason to breathe again.

With him I felt complete, as if fate had given me a second chance.

Then I learned the truth—the sins and secrets of what had
really brought us together.
I only hope we can go back. I never could have imagined this.

This is book 2 in the You Are Mine duet.
You Are My Reason should be read first.

Kintsukuroi,
Means to repair with gold.
The once destroyed and shattered,
Repaired with binds to hold.

The bits are mended over time,
The piece stronger than before.
It's more beautiful for being broken.
Different? Yes, but ruined no more.

Prologue

Mason

One month ago

DON'T LET THEM SEE.

Her words echo in my head as I stalk toward the quiet bedroom. She whispered them against my lips last night. The cool air slipped between us as she broke our heated kiss and slowly opened her eyes in the dark of night.

The streetlamp shined down around us like a spotlight on the back porch of her place on the Upper East Side. The city life slept quietly so late at night—or early in the morning, depending on how you look at it. Only the sinners like us were left awake.

Don't let them see. She left me with the parting plea and here I am… complying with her wish.

I've never crept through anyone's back door before. Not once in my life have I had to sneak around like this.

I don't want to keep this up, but here I am. What the hell has this woman done to me? *I'm wrapped around her little finger.*

She doesn't want anyone to notice me walking through her door because she's ashamed. I know that's why she doesn't want people to know we're together.

This isn't a fling; this isn't a rebound fuck. There's something more to us now, but she still doesn't want the world to know.

The floorboards creak under my weight and I hesitate in the doorway, the dim lamp from the hall filling the dark room with a hint of light. I'm being careful so her neighbors won't be able to hear anything. I just don't want to disturb her.

It's obvious she's sleeping, but then she stirs beneath the silk duvet until finally she opens her eyes and sees me. She tilts her head to the side as she looks at me, burying her cheek into the pillow, a soft smile playing on her lips as she utters a pleasant feminine hum.

"I missed you," she whispers and her voice is laced with an equal mix of sleep and lust.

If only she knew the real reason I crave her touch. The reason I'm so tempted to break all my rules.

"I'm sorry I'm late," I tell her in a deep, rough voice as I start unbuttoning my shirt. A smirk lifts up the corners of my lips as her eyes sparkle with humor. She doesn't care when I come and go, so long as I lie in her bed at night, or she in mine.

Her doe eyes peer back at me while I slip off my button-up and let it pool into a puddle at my feet. I yank my tight white undershirt over my head and look back to see those lush lips parted.

My muscles ripple as I let the tank drop to the floor, the moonlight bathing the room and the two of us in a faint glow.

She may want to keep this a secret but she wants me nonetheless, and she can't hide it. I've become addicted to the way she looks at me like she needs my touch to stay grounded, just as she needs to breathe air to survive. I'm conditioned to crave the faint sounds of her quickened breath as she waits for me to come to her. *As if she'd die without me.*

I'm slow to unbuckle my belt as my eyes roam down her luscious curves. She's mine to take. Mine to touch. *Mine to keep.*

I don't want to sneak around anymore and I don't give a shit who knows. I'm tired of all the secrets and politics, all the gossip in this town.

The anger boils in my blood as I grip my leather belt tighter, making it sing in the air as I pull it through the loops. The buckle drops to the floor with a *thunk*. All the while my gaze is on her gorgeous eyes, and she stares back at me with the same desire I have for her.

The past is over and done. No one else will ever know what really happened— not her, not anyone. *So why can't I truly have her?*

"Mason." She practically whimpers my name and it pulls the beast in me closer to her. My knee dips into the bed, making it groan with my weight as I crawl over to her.

Her soft blue eyes pierce through me, cutting through the dark room. More of the soft lighting from the city slips between us as the heat kicks on and the curtains sway. The way the light kisses her skin as she pushes away the blush silk duvet makes her all the more beautiful.

She's laid out for me. *All for me.* She needs me.

I crush my lips to hers and dig my fingers into the flesh of her hips as she spreads her thighs for me. Her soft moans fill the hot air between us.

She's ashamed to be moving on so quickly. Especially with a man like me. I wasn't made for a woman like her. I'm someone who could tarnish her sterling reputation and make the cracks in her picture-perfect life even deeper. To say I'm rough around the edges is putting it lightly, but I have what it takes to keep her.

She thinks she's ruined, but she's perfect. It's my sins and secrets that could destroy us both. I'll never let them come to light. Not now that I have something worth fighting for.

chapter 1

Julia

Present day

I'M CAUGHT BETWEEN MY NEED TO RUN AWAY AND THE NEED TO KNOW the truth. I need the truth from him. No more secrets; no more lies.

He promised.

He loves me.

There's just no way.

"Did you do it?" The question leaves me in a single weak breath and in an instant, something snaps into place. It's as if he's not at all shocked by what I'm saying. As if he's been waiting for this.

No. My body turns to ice; my blood freezes in my veins and I can't believe this is reality. It can't be true.

Mason takes a step forward, starting to move around the island and it breaks me from my denial.

It's my cue to run, a natural instinct that takes over. The stool falls hard, crashing to the floor as I take off, but Mason's faster, grabbing my waist and jerking me backward. I cry out from fear and he releases me, only for me to fall onto the tiles at my feet. His large frame towers over me, and he puts his hands up as though he's approaching a wild animal. I feel like I am just that. Eyes wide as I stare up at him, my heart pounds painfully in my chest. *Thump, thump, thump.*

"Did I do what?" he asks with a coldness I haven't seen before and his eyes narrowed. This isn't the man I know.

My bottom lip trembles, the small bit of strength I had vanishing as I take in the raw truth. "Did you kill my husband?"

The words leave me in agony as they hover in the tense air between us.

I can't believe I even asked him that. *Deny it. Please deny it. Tell me I'm a fool. And this, whatever this is, it's something that's already over and never happened.*

Mason stands up straight, giving me enough space so that my breath can come back to me, but my lungs refuse to fill until he answers me.

"They think they can do whatever they want," Mason says, still standing over me as he snatches the paper from where it lays on the floor. I didn't even realize I'd dropped it.

No. That's not what he should be saying right now.

"Your husband wasn't a good man," Mason adds lowly, his eyes piercing me before flicking back to the paper. He crumples it in his fist as a cold sweat spreads across my skin.

"No." It's all I can say. "You didn't." I try to say more but it's in vain as my throat dries up and constricts. I don't know if it's the shock or if I'm just that pathetic. I didn't fall for a murderer. Mason couldn't—

"I did." Mason's confession makes me light-headed, and a sickness churns in my gut.

My heart twists with a pain that's unbearable as I crawl away quickly, trying to escape. I slip against the ground, crashing hard to the cold, unforgiving floor.

"No!" I scream at him, leaving a strangled cry to linger between us. It's only then that I even register I'm crying.

I try again to run, managing to get to my feet this time and the foyer is so close as I stumble out of the kitchen. I call out for help, although I doubt anyone could hear us. Not here inside Mason's home. I practically slam into the front door, but Mason's right behind me.

With one hand on the door and one on the knob, his hard body presses against mine, trapping me between him and my only escape.

His large body cages me in. I'm left facing the door, barely able to stand or breathe. "You were never supposed to know," he whispers. I shrink beneath him, the weight of the reality crashing down on me. "I'm sorry."

I've fallen in love with my husband's killer. I've slept with him and given him everything.

"I'm not going to hurt you, Jules." His warm breath sends shivers down my back as he adds, "But I can't let you leave."

chapter 2

Julia

THE ONLY THING YOU NEED TO WORRY ABOUT IS REMEMBERING MY *name. Just my name and what I've done to you tonight.*

Mason whispered those words so close to my ear, sending a shiver of want through my body. It was everything I desired when I met him. He made that promise to me the first night, and I so easily fell into his bed.

I'd been so desperate to feel *anything* but the heartache and misery I'd succumbed to.

If only I could take it back.

If only I'd known this man was the cause of my pain.

Anger seethes inside me as I stare at him across the other side of his bedroom, where he's sitting in the corner. His elbows rest on his thighs as he hunches over the edge of the reading chair with his head in his hands. His fingers run back and forth along the back of his head as if there's a thought inside his mind he can't quite reach.

He won't look at me; he merely stares at the ground in complete silence. All the while I'm shattered, and with every minute that passes I feel the broken pieces more and more.

My body is restless and my eyes burn with a desperate need to cry, but I have nothing left.

I try to scoot my exhausted body up the bed to soothe my sore arms, but the rope tied around my wrists tightens with the sudden pull, chafing me. I wince and suck in a breath through clenched teeth; my shoulders are screaming in pain.

Hours have passed since I found out the truth. Hours spent restrained to this bed. When I wouldn't stop screaming and fighting him, clawing at him and trying to escape his strong grip, he tied me up.

It's been only minutes since he's come back into the room, though. Minutes since he's opened that door and let his eyes rest on me. I'm pathetic, weak and completely at his mercy. Captive to a man I loved who hid a secret so dark and corrupt it's ruined me. I'll never be the same. There's no way to recover.

Ticktock. Ticktock.

It's only been minutes since he lowered himself into the chair without speaking a word to me, I remind myself. He sits in a chair I brought from my home to his. A chair I'd cried countless tears in after my husband died.

And yet he says nothing. It's the silence that kills me.

"I hate you." The words slowly scrape their way up my sore throat. They're barely audible, since my voice is so raspy and weak from all the screaming.

He slowly lifts his head, his corded muscles rippling. For the first time since I've been with Mason, after months spent falling in love with him, I feel real agony. The small involuntary shudder my body makes proves there's a bit of fear present too.

The sharp lines of his jaw look more intense in the dim light, the shadows only making them seem more severe. His steel gray eyes are like daggers as he captures my gaze.

I can't breathe; I can't look away. I hate him for what he did then and I hate him for how he's making me feel now.

"You don't," he says and his voice is rough and deep. He sounds stronger than before. But it's a lie. All lies.

I do. I hate him more than I could ever express.

Finally, I gasp for air rather than crying any more tears, breaking his gaze to stare up at the ceiling. Even that minor movement makes the raw wounds at my wrists hurt. I try to hide it, though.

I gave this man everything. How could I have been so foolish? "I hate you more than you'll ever know," I murmur to the ceiling in an eerily calm voice although my heart is anything but.

The creaking of the floorboards grabs my attention, and my gaze whips to Mason as he stands. Goosebumps spread slowly over every inch of my skin as he rises.

His muscular frame seems so much larger in this moment, and a hint of a lethal concoction gives a low stir in the pit of my stomach. He's always been dominating and intimidating, but this is something darker… something more.

I have nothing to protect me, not even a sheet. He stripped the linens off the bed before tying me up and I was left in only the underwear and baggy, thin cotton T-shirt I slipped on this morning. The chill is getting to me.

The bed dips and groans as he places a knee on it only inches away from me. I would struggle to pull away, but I'm stuck here. Both of us know that.

"I love you, Jules," he murmurs and his words are a mix of strangled pain and determination. He's a broken man with a tortured soul.

I don't know how I could possibly look at a man who's done this to me and feel any kind of sorrow for him, but I do.

I've met men before who've been wound tight, waiting to go off like a bomb. They were always constantly on edge and ready for a fight at a moment's notice. Mason's not like that. Instead he's like thread loosely wrapped around a spindle, nothing but a mess of tangles. It's not soft string; this thread's sharp to the touch and there's no hope at unraveling it without cutting yourself.

I never knew how deeply he'd wounded me. I had no idea that while I was busy mending myself and leaning on him for support, he was watching me bleed out, saying nothing. The closer he got, the deeper the inevitable betrayal, but that didn't stop him. He had so many chances to tell me what he'd done.

I let my head drop to look him in the eyes. It makes my heart swell with an unbearable pain to have him so close to me. To see how injured he is, but knowing it's nothing compared to what he's done to me.

I truly loved him. I thought fate had given me a second chance at love and happiness. I knew it was too good to be true.

"How could you do that?" The aching question isn't what I'd planned to say when I narrowed my eyes. "You're sick," I add and the words are gritted out somehow, bearing the strength I was aiming for and I wait for him to strike back with the same venom I've given him.

His steady breathing is somehow calming and it irritates me as I watch his chest rise and fall. "Maybe," he says before rising off the bed and turning away from me. My heart plummets at the sight of his back to me and my expression crumples. It physically hurts me to know he's hurting too. I thought I knew agony before. My God.

Why did this happen? How could it happen?

Tears threaten and I shove them back, hating all of this and praying to just wake up and find it's merely a bad dream. *Please! Please, I would give anything for this to only be a nightmare.* My silent prayers are disrupted by the wood floors creaking as Mason heads toward the door, leaving me here and not giving me any indication of what's to come.

"Aren't you going to say you're sorry?" I whisper the ragged question. Maybe that's what's most shocking; he hasn't said he's sorry. Not for tying me up and keeping me here… not for murdering my husband almost a year ago.

His tall frame pauses in the partially opened doorway, stopping in his tracks as he registers what I've said. He turns his head slowly to look back at me over his shoulder, his hand still on the carved glass doorknob.

"I already told you that I'm sorry. You were never supposed to know the truth."

"You're only sorry that I found out?" I ask with equal amounts of disbelief and hurt.

His eyes dart to the floor and the bedroom door groans as it opens slightly wider.

He glances up at me hesitantly, as if debating on telling me something. It would be the truth; I can see it, can feel the intensity. Instead he says nothing, walking out of the bedroom with even strides before slamming the door shut behind him.

chapter 3

Mason

The past is dark,
And filled with pain.
Mistakes were made,
And nothing gained.

If I had known,
I'd have found a way.
But what's done is done,
The past never goes away.

SOMEONE KNOWS. THE KNOWLEDGE BRINGS A CHILL THAT PRICKLES down my shoulders to the base of my spine. Someone knows what I've done. It's been nearly a year. So much time has passed and yet they've said and done nothing until now. All the possibilities of who it could possibly be are jumbled in the forefront of my mind. For hours I've been focused on this rather than what I've done to Jules. My poor Jules.

I didn't think anyone knew until Jules received that letter.

It destroys me that I couldn't lie to her. I couldn't hide what I'd done. Some sick, twisted part of me is relieved that now she knows.

But then I see the way she looks at me. I deserve the hate… I knew it would come to this and still I want to fix it. I don't have any other choice but to make this right. I can't let her go.

I won't.

They say if you love someone, you should let them go.

That's bullshit.

I didn't know it until I lost her, but I had nothing to live for without Jules. There's no possibility in this life that I'm going back to what I was before her.

The idea that she could turn me in has barely even registered. It's merely a passing thought that intrudes upon the images replaying in my head of seeing her walk away from me. The memories of her pushing against my chest, violently scratching and kicking me. Her screams that she hates me echo in my ears over and over.

She doesn't mean it. She can't hate me. Not for that.

I swallow thickly as I descend the stairs, gripping the railing and matching the pounding of my heart with the heavy thud of my bare feet.

I can make it right. I can and I will. My palm is clammy as I hold the railing tighter.

It's a priority to figure out how to make her forget the past and remember her future is with me. I nod, envisioning how this was *supposed* to be. How it could have ended so beautifully.

I check to make sure the front door's locked as I pass the foyer, still completely trashed from our earlier struggle and head for the dining room, ignoring the mess.

More importantly, I need to find out who the fuck knows what I did and if they have any evidence. That's first. Jules needs time to cool off and while she does, I need to work out who sent that letter and why.

Jules is angry, and I get that. Saying it was a shock is obviously an understatement. I flick on the light and my eyes are instantly drawn to the bar. To a vice I desperately need to lean on while I process my lack of grace at what I did to her.

She was never meant to find out what happened. I was a different man then. If I'd known her at the time, I would have handled it differently. I would have ripped her away from that piece of shit and taken her for myself. In another life, perhaps it happened that way.

But that's not our reality.

Picking up a glass from the rack on the edge of the bar, I remember the haunting look in her eyes; the glass clinks as the adrenaline in my blood begins to wane for the first time since seeing her face as she read the letter.

I don't know how to fix this. Every other trouble Jules has had has been easy to remedy. This… I know it's unforgivable, but what she wants isn't an option for us. I can't go back to what I once had and who I used to be.

I need her and she may not want to admit it right now, but she needs me. Deep down, she knows it's true. This doesn't change anything.

She just needs time and so do I. I'll figure out a way to keep her and make her happy again. *It's not the first time I've destroyed her,* I think as the bottom of the heavy glass hits the bar top.

I crack my neck to the side as I hear her cry out again, sharp profanity echoing down the stairway and hall. Her voice is raw and hoarse, and I know the regret plagues her.

A smirk lifts up my lips. She's right, I must be sick. The thought that lingers is that she has to regret moving in with me. My house is on the edges of the city and in a secluded, remote location. If we were at her place, the neighbors would have heard everything, and the cops would have already been called. I'd be fucked.

I give a small grin as I twist off the cap to the whiskey and slowly pour it into the tumbler. No one can hear her but me while we're in here.

I'm the only knight in shining armor she's going to get.

I bring the glass to my lips and the smile vanishes, my eyes drifting to the lit fireplace. She turned it on earlier, claiming it brings a warmth to the darkness in the dining room.

Downing my whiskey and then raking my fingers through my hair, I let out a frustrated sigh over the sound of her screaming.

She's going to be sore and angry, and the marks on her wrists will need time to fade, but she'll survive. She'll get over it.

Whoever wrote that note though, whoever tried to tear my sweetheart from me, that fucker won't survive this. I grit my teeth as I slam the glass down and feel the burn of the liquor spread through my chest.

The thought prompts me to head to the entryway. The rug is crooked from when I dragged Jules up the stairs, and the lamp on the hall table is on its side, but at least it's not broken. My keys and wallet are still on the floor from when she knocked them off the table in her frantic attempt to hold on to something, anything to keep her from being taken upstairs.

My eyes dart up to the wall behind the iron banister. A low hum of admonishment leaves me as I bend down to pick up the scattered items.

The dents and scrapes on the walls are going to be a bit more difficult to fix. Recalling the feel of her struggling against me stirs an unrecognizable emotion inside my gut. I close my eyes and picture how I held her tight against me, forcing her still and pushing her against the wall, trapping her. She never stopped fighting, though. I count every little mark. Her nails scratched against the drywall, desperate for something to save her. It's *evidence* that's not so easy to clean up.

I did what I had to do, I think although the justification sounds hollow in the back of my mind.

The keys jingle as I toss them onto the table, scooting it back into place and then I snatch up the crumpled piece of thick cream parchment.

The note that destroyed what I had.

I clear my throat, willing the images and memories to go away as my chest tightens with unbearable pain. I had her. I had my sweetheart and she loved me, I know she did.

The letter crinkles as I focus my eyes on it and turn my back to the staircase, resting my shoulder against the doorframe of the dining room and listening to the crackling of the fire.

It's handwritten and leans more toward feminine penmanship. My eyes narrow as I look over every inch of the paper attempting to recognize the curve of a letter, something, anything. Not a damn memory comes to mind. There's no name. No way to identify who it came from.

Dear Julia,

It pains me to tell you this, but I can't stand to watch from a distance as you fall into a trap. Your husband was murdered. I know this is going to shock you, but I have proof. You may not believe me, but I pray that you do.

Mason Thatcher murdered him. Don't trust him. Don't let him know that you know. If he finds out, you won't be safe.

All I can tell you is that you need to run. Stay far away.

I can't say any more. I hope this letter finds you safe and you take every word for what it is, the truth.

Truly yours,

X

Proof. My narrowed gaze focuses on the single word, my heart racing faster and faster. There's not a single possibility that someone has proof.

There were no cameras around. There's no fucking way anyone saw. Her prick of a husband was leaving his apartment after screwing his mistress, and on his way back home. Back to Jules, his wife he didn't deserve. My chest rumbles with a low murmur of anger at the memory. His arrogance was one of the things I hated most about him.

My eyes whip to the stairs as I hear Jules call out again. Her voice is cracked and so uneven I can't make out a damn word she's saying. I grit my teeth and resist the urge to burn the note. I need it and the envelope it came in.

This is a fucking mess. But I make a solemn promise to Jules: I'll fix this.

Gripping the banister, I wait a moment for her cries to cease and then slowly ascend the staircase. A tic in my jaw starts to twitch as I formulate a plan. I need to explain why I did it and calm her down. I need time or a fucking miracle. It's too late to deny any of it. I was too rash, too caught up in the moment when she confronted me. All I could see was red.

The door opens with a gentle push. I didn't bother to lock it since she's tied to the bed.

My eyes latch onto her the second I step into our bedroom. She's barely clothed, her gorgeous pale skin on full display, although most of it is flushed from her struggling and screaming.

"What do you need, sweetheart?" I ask her calmly, completely ignoring the current situation.

Her eyes narrow as she sucks in a breath, and I can feel the anger rolling off of her in waves. I nearly let out a sigh of relief. *Anger I can deal with.* The thought almost makes me smile.

"Let me out," she says although her eyes flicker down and her voice wavers with the demand.

"I can't do that if you're going to run."

"Just let me go, Mason," she pleads with a soft whimper. She licks her lips and attempts to push herself upright. Jules winces from the binds cutting into her wrists, and I can't fucking stand it.

My hands ball into fists, but I stay put. I can't risk her trying to escape.

"You need to stay here, with me, until we figure this out," I say to her in a placating tone as I step forward, rounding the bed to get closer to her. Her breathing quickens and I'm not sure if it's due to anger or fear from me getting closer to her. My blood runs cold at the second possibility.

"We need to talk about this," I tell her gently as I sit down carefully and attempt to ease whatever worry I can. I don't want to tell her anything, and everything in me is screaming to lie and let it all be forgotten. But she's mine, and I won't do that to her. It was one thing to withhold the truth about the past, but it's another to outright lie about it.

She should know the truth, even if she doesn't like it.

"Ask me anything." My gaze is struck by hers as I speak. Her baby blues are rimmed in red, and her cheeks tearstained. She's gorgeous even like this, but not when she misbehaves. She presses her lips into a thin line, even though the bottom one trembles, and shakes her head. It seems fear is the dominant emotion. A vise tightens over my chest.

I look past her as the thick gray velvet curtain sways slightly when the heater turns on with a click. I watch it for a moment, steadying my breath and quickly come up with a solution.

"For every question," I start to say and then pause to look back at her. She's wary and when she realizes I'm offering her something, her entire body noticeably stiffens. "Every question you ask, I'll answer you honestly and untie you a bit."

It's not the best solution, seeing as how there are only four knots total keeping the rope in place. One on each wrist, and two tying her to the bed.

"You can't fight me, Jules." I harden my voice just before she can answer. "I'll let you go, but I won't let you run. Do you understand?"

She swallows and then licks her lips. "Yes," she says, the answer just above a murmur. I can tell it hurts her to speak at all, because she withdraws the moment the word slips into the tense air between us, a look of pain evident on her face.

She needs tea and to be held. She needs a gentle hand.

The bed groans as I sit, resting my hand on her bare thigh. Like a good girl she doesn't move, but she does close her eyes as if she can't stand my touch. I gently rub my thumb in soothing circles and I stare down at where our skin meets as I wait for her.

She'll forgive me, I know she will. It's only a matter of time and I'll let her lead. But only if she moves in the right direction. Closer to the two of us regaining what we had only hours ago. I just need time and given the fact my development company is now dissolved, I have plenty of it.

"Why did you do it?" she asks.

My head lifts at her question, and I meet her gaze head-on. There's nothing but sadness in those gorgeous doe eyes. "He was responsible for a woman's death."

Before I've even finished saying the words, she's already shaking her head. Already in denial. "No, I don't believe you." Her voice cracks, a telltale sign of her refusal to accept the truth as she rips her gaze from me and stares straight ahead at the door.

"I'm not lying to you, Jules." It's a struggle to keep my voice tender, thinking back on what came over me when I decided Jace Anderson deserved to die.

"You lied," she practically hisses at me, taking me by surprise. She screams with outrage, "You're a liar!"

"I never lied to you," I answer evenly, correcting her and ignoring her outburst while I tighten my grip on the edge of the bed. I have to wait a moment for her to calm down before reaching up and slowly untying the knot on her left wrist. A deal is a deal. Even if I fucking hate her response. Her tender skin is bright pink, and it makes my chest feel tight with guilt. I never wanted to hurt her. Never. I retake my seat as she whispers, "You didn't tell the truth."

My throat dries and a rawness takes over, dampening every nerve ending along my skin. I don't have many memories of my mother, but the ones I do, the ones that are clear, are the ones where she calls my father a liar. The images flash in front of me, and my body goes cold. "I'm not a liar. I did what I had to do."

"I could never do what you did," she says.

Everyone can kill. I keep the thought to myself, hating how true it is. It's only a matter of what would push someone to do it.

"Do you have any other questions?"

"Are you going to kill me?" she asks as if it's a real possibility. Her breathing is hesitant and then hitches when she closes her eyes tight.

Waiting for those doe eyes to look back at me, desperate for an answer, the one word I give her is filled with a promise. "Never." It makes my heart hurt that she thinks it's even an option. "I told you I'd never hurt you." Of all the things today that have me on edge, that right there is the most distressing. The thought in her head that I'm someone who would hurt her is unacceptable.

My hand rests gently against her thigh and she's quick to pull away, as if I've scorched her skin. I still at the sobering sight of her.

Her blue eyes have never looked so cold as she looks up at me and says, "No." Her next words carry so much conviction, so much hate. "Don't touch me… please."

I clench my jaw and hesitate. This is too much. Too far, and too much. I'm quick to untie all the remaining binds, blood rushing in my ears and my fingers seemingly going numb. I drop the thin rope and it pools into a puddle around her, but she doesn't move to get up. She doesn't do anything but lean farther away from me.

Her mouth opens as I push off the bed and stand to leave, but she doesn't say anything. There's only silence.

"You may hate me now, Jules, but I still love you, and you're not going anywhere until you know that and until you understand why it had to happen."

The door closes behind me with a loud click and I don't stop walking until I get to the office to retrieve the house keys. I'll lock the door. I'll keep her here until she understands.

There's no fucking way I'm letting her leave. She'll figure it out eventually; she's always been mine. It was only a matter of me finding her.

chapter 4

Julia

ALTHOUGH MY EYES ARE TIRED AND MY HEAD AND LIMBS ACHE, I DON'T move. Not an inch. Not since I took the engagement ring off my finger and flung it across the room.

I'm far too aware of every event that led to this. It's as if I've lived my life under the warm silk sheets of the most welcoming bed, only to be kicked out, landing face-first on the cold, cracked concrete floor.

More than anything, one word keeps coming to mind. *Unprepared.* I have no idea what to do, or even what to think. It's all a mess. My life is a jumbled mess of chaos and tragedy. It's hard enough to grasp the fact that Jace was murdered. Much harder still to think that I fell in love with his murderer.

I need to get away. Far away from Mason just so I can think straight.

I can't focus on anything else other than that one truth: I need to get the hell out of this room.

The bedroom door's locked from the outside; the telltale jingle of keys and then the loud click of the lock a few moments ago alerted me to that. I already know it's the case without even trying to turn the knob. I suppose that's better than having to face him. To my left, the curtain sways and draws my eyes.

My throat closes at the thought of seeing him again. I loved him. My heart feels like a vise is clamped around it, squeezing tighter each time I think about who Mason really is and what I've done. I fell in love with my husband's killer.

The shock is still there, but it's not enough to keep the sickness of my reality at bay.

My head feels dizzy—from exhaustion maybe, I'm not sure, but I don't have time to think. I don't have time for anything until I'm far away from here.

I stare at the lone window in this room. I know it's an idiotic notion to think

I can climb down from the second story and land safely below, but I have no other choice and I refuse not to try.

If there's one thing the recollection of the events leading up to this have screamed at me, it's that I need to take action and stop allowing life to railroad me.

I don't have my keys, my phone or wallet. With the groan of the bed seemingly chiding me as I stand up and make my way to the window, I peek outside to see there's already a thin layer of snow on the ground. Given its late November in New York, I'm not shocked but it's still frustrating. If I make it down there alive without breaking my neck, he'll be able to see where I've gone. A part of me huffs at the thought, knowing this is foolish, trying to escape.

But I only need to flag someone down on the road or bang on a neighbor's door. *I have to try, and I'm not waiting another second.*

The floor in the bedroom is creaky and every little sound forces me to check that the door is still closed. I know he'll be able to hear me from downstairs if he's listening. I'm careful with each step and do my best to limit the noise as I move around. I inhale deeply through clenched teeth as I open the dresser as quietly as I can but it's loud just the same as I slowly pull on the drawer. I've never noticed it before, but right now every single noise is far too loud.

My heart rampages in protest at each squeak and groan from the wooden floors. *I'm only getting dressed,* I tell myself over and over. If he comes up now, if he hears me and storms into the room to check on me, I'm only getting dressed. Surely that's what he must think.

My eyes burn with unshed tears thinking about Mason coming up here. Realizing the fear I now have for a man I once loved makes my chest feel unbearably tight.

What if he catches me?

What will he do when he's realized I've left?

Even worse: *What would he do to me?*

I swallow down the insecurity and fear; I can't be paralyzed by them. I can't wait here in this damn room for him to decide what to do with me. I'm stronger than that.

The first shirt and pair of leggings I pull out are good enough and then from the drawer below, I grab a pair of jeans to pull over top of the leggings. It's freezing outside. I don't have a coat because they're all downstairs in the hall closet, but I layer a sweater and then another one over my long-sleeved shirt. It's hard to tell if the burning heat is from the fabrics or from the anxiety that rages through me.

My fingers shake as I pull down the long cashmere sleeves. If he came up now, he'd know for sure that this is more than me just getting dressed. I'm dressed to leave. The thoughts don't slow me, they only push me to be faster; I'm fueled by nerves and the desperation to save myself.

I can barely breathe as I kneel and tie the shoelaces on a pair of sneakers I grabbed from the walk-in closet. My hands don't stop trembling and my vision keeps going in and out as the dull pain behind my eyes gets worse. I sway as my light-headedness becomes too much, and I have to close my eyes and breathe. Just breathe.

I stand on wobbly legs and walk as quietly as I can to the window, which is just as unhelpful as it was a moment ago. Staring over my shoulder at the closed door, I lick my dry, cracked lips as I unlock the window. The lock on the left turns easily but the one on the right is tight, and I need both hands and all my focus to loosen it. Each second that passes seems too long, as if this small moment is enough time for him to stop me.

Tick, tick, tick.

The sound of my heavy breathing and the blood rushing in my ears are all I hear as I push the window up as high as I can. I manage to lift the heavy thing about two feet, and I hope it'll be enough. I know there's a way to somehow angle the window and get the screen out, but in my haste and nervousness, I can't figure it out.

The heater clicks on again and I nearly have a heart attack, my scream barely contained as it tries to escape from my throat.

Tick, tick, tick.

I can't wait any longer. As the heat drifts up from the vent and mixes with the frigid November air that blows across my face, I panic.

My only thought is to rip out the screen. Without wasting another tick of the internal clock, I snatch a shirt from the hamper to my right and wrap it around my hand. My footsteps were far too loud, but time is more important.

I take one more look back at the door before punching through the screen. It breaks surprisingly easily and I nearly fall forward, the torn mesh scraping against my forearm. I contain my gasp and ignore how my heart seems to leap up my throat as I look down two stories to the cold hard ground below. It's a sobering sight.

There's a thin layer of white snow coating the grass and although the weather has let up, the air is sharp from the biting wind. I take a deep breath, pulling the ripped screen back and tearing it open more, protecting my hand with the clothing. Somehow ripping it wider is more difficult than making the initial tear.

My breathing comes in faster, and the light-headed sensation returns when the hole is large enough for me to climb through.

All the spiked edges of the broken screen are going to catch on my sweater, I already know. Once I get footing out on the sill, I'll have to try to grip onto the pillar to my right and slowly climb down while balancing myself on the stones that line the house. It's practically impossible. My head shakes of its own accord at the thought, refusing to feel defeated. I have to do this. I have no other choice.

The threads of my sweater snag like I knew they would the moment I climb through the window and brush against the screen, but I press forward. As my left foot finds purchase on the windowsill, the wind blows so forcefully that I cling to the frame with my right hand and consider abandoning the idea completely. *I've gone absolutely mad.* My nose and cheeks burn from the biting cold, and I have to close my eyes.

Breathe. Just breathe.

I refuse to go back in there. The second the wind stops, I finish crawling out and balance on the ledge, my knuckles bright white from holding on so tightly. Each time I have to readjust my grip, I'm filled with a renewed sense of terror. Only the balls of my feet are balanced on the thin ledge, and my hands already ache from clutching the window in the bitter cold.

I make the mistake of looking down and seeing how far I'd drop and how there's nothing to break my fall if the wind were to blow too hard. Or if my grip gives out, or if something else happens and I fail. *I don't want to die.*

A few moments pass and I simply can't move. The wind whips my hair around my face and I shut my eyes tight, frozen by the vision of me plummeting to my death.

This is taking too much time. I need to get going. My left foot moves first, all the way to the edge of the sill and as far as I can get with both of my hands still gripping the window frame.

I have to let go in order to lean over, and I do it so quickly and with so much force that I nearly push myself off. My head spins from the height, but I keep moving. My right hand grips the window and my left reaches for the brick closest to the pillar. My nails scratch at the rough stone, but my grip is solid.

I feel stuck for the longest time. The cold makes my hands numb and the wind is coming and going so frequently that I'm afraid the second I move, it will violently rip me away from the pillar, but I manage the motion in a single leap.

A scream is torn from my throat as I fall an inch or two until my sneaker hits the decorative carving on the pillar and I'm able to wrap my arms around it. Adrenaline roars inside of me and I pray Mason didn't hear. And then I make another silent prayer: that this foolish plan will work.

Slowly, ever so slowly, I climb down inch by inch. The only places I dare to look are directly in front of me and up to the open window. I watch the curtains sway inside of the bedroom as I slip down the pillar at a snail's pace, relying on the tread of my sneakers against the carved marble pillar for purchase.

I don't even realize I've made it safely until I try to slide farther down and can't. There's ground beneath my feet.

Astonished and still very much consumed by fear, I note my sweater is torn with pulls everywhere, and I'm so cold I can hardly move my limbs. I look up once more at the open window and realize it's only a matter of time before he realizes I'm gone.

Run. I don't hesitate one more second. My sore limbs come to life as I take off down Mason's driveway and I don't look back.

chapter 5

Mason

I NEED TO MAKE TWO THINGS CLEAR TO HER.
1. I love her, and I always will.
2. She's not leaving me.

We're going to work through this one way or another. Even if I have to drug her. I know the chances of a roofie working at this point are slim to none, but depending on her reaction, it's the only thing I can think of and the only easy out to make things right again. If only she would forget.

As I draw closer to the top of the stairs, a cold draft wraps itself around me. At first, I'm confused, then furious. She didn't. She wouldn't… my denial is pointless. I already know she did.

My pace picks up and I bang on the bedroom door. My knuckles slam against the hard wood door and I yell out, "Jules!"

How long has it been, maybe a half hour at most since I locked her in there? My heart hammers in my chest. She's gone. *She's left me.*

It's no use. I can already feel the cold air seeping into the hall from under the door. The keys are already in my hand as I pound my fist against the door again like a fucking fool, nearly breaking down the door. They rattle as I find the right one and shove it into the lock before throwing open the door. I'm greeted with an empty bed and the biting cold blowing in through a torn window screen.

I stare at the window for only a second before taking long strides across the room, pulling the curtain back to look down at the ground outside. I half expect to see her lying dead on the grass.

She'd rather risk this than deal with me.

My throat closes at the bitter thought, and the harsh wind whispers, taunting me that she simply jumped to end it all. Relief is unexpected but welcome when I peer out and trace the footsteps in the snow. She hasn't been gone long judging by how clean and clear the prints are.

My lungs threaten to fail me as I take off out the room and down the stairs, and I don't stop moving as I snatch my car keys and phone off the front hall table. She's out there with a head start and I only have so much time to catch her. My coat's in the living room, but I don't bother with it. I don't bother with anything other than climbing into my Mercedes and reversing out of the driveway as quickly as I can.

A thin layer of sweat covers my skin and only adds to the freezing effect of the air.

If she tells anyone… I'm fucked.

"She can't," I say under my breath and curse, the vision of her testifying against me flashing in front of my eyes. There's hardly any snow on the asphalt, and her footprints disappear in less than a quarter mile. With my hands gripping and twisting the leather steering wheel, I continue to drive ahead. I glance down every small gap I pass, although the main road is vacant. It's early morning and I know there are plenty of cars that drive by here on their way to work. She could have flagged someone down.

She's gone. My throat tightens with the realization and I pound my fist against the window.

She doesn't have any evidence. My thoughts take over. She has no proof, and there's nothing the police would ever find. She couldn't possibly go to them. There's no fucking way. But if not to the police, then where?

My heart's racing as I pull over, and I don't know what the hell she's thinking. *That you're a murderer. That you'll hurt her.*

I ignore the damning truth and keep pushing down the ache that takes over.

It doesn't take long before I decide my next move should be to search her home. If not there, then I need to find her friend's addresses. My tires squeal as I pull back onto the road, intent on finding her and bringing her back here. I don't need anyone else trying to keep her away from me.

I lean over and click the radio off, only just now realizing it's on and then turn the heat all the way up. I'm numb from the combination of the wintry air and the thoughts that won't quit yelling in my head that I'm fucked. Turning on my blinker to head onto a busier street, I struggle to take in an easy breath.

Act normal. Come up with a plan.

There was a nasty rumor going around that Jules has had issues with alcohol ever since Jace's death. I'd never talk about her as if she were a drunk, but I have to use something that would make people question why she'd accuse me of murder.

I tap my thumb against the steering wheel.

I don't know if it would work. It'd be her word against mine. And there's no real evidence.

But if I went down that route, I'd definitely lose her and everyone in this city would question if there was any truth to what she claimed.

My family name would be called into question.

My business reputation would be ruined.

More than that, the only person I ever loved would be my downfall.

A bitter huff of a humorless laugh leaves me as I look to my left and turn down the street.

I could go away for life if the police do believe her and look into it. If they find something, or if the person who sent that note comes forward with their proof. I don't give a fuck about that, though. I haven't known what love is since my mother died. But I know it's what I feel for Jules.

I've given her the power to ruin me. That's what true love is.

If I let her get away, she'll do it.

She'll destroy every piece of me.

As I struggle to come to terms with the realization, my phone rings from the passenger seat where I'd thrown it earlier. I lean over and pick it up, answering without looking to see who it is while I drive down Jules's street.

"Hello," I answer, hoping it's her. Hoping she's only asking for time or space. I won't give her either, but at least then I'll know we have a chance.

"Mason," my father says.

"Father," I say, feeling disappointment that it's not her, followed by distrust. We haven't spoken since I knocked him out in his office. What the hell does he want?

His voice is full of confidence but more than that, imperiousness. "I have a little something I think you want." I pull up alongside Jules's street but the only parking space available is a few doors down from her place, and I slow down to lean forward and look out the windshield. It's starting to get light outside, but not so much that I wouldn't see lights on inside her house. I scan the windows as I absently say, "And what would that be?"

"I got a call from Commissioner Haynes." My body stills as my father continues.

His words snap my attention to him. *Commissioner.* "It seems your recent love interest has something urgent to confess."

If my father thinks she's a threat, that's a much more concerning issue.

"She doesn't know anything." I'm quick to respond. I speed down the street, cutting someone off and they lean on their horn. I have to weave through the few cars out this early in the morning to get down to Fourth Street. I need to get to her. "Don't touch her," I say.

"I wouldn't dare," my father says, and I can practically see the smug smile on his face. *Jules.* I grit my teeth in anger.

"I imagine you'll be here soon?" he asks with a thin veil of arrogance.

"I'm ten minutes from the station," I answer grudgingly. I hate that he's involved and interfering, but if he wasn't, she would have talked. She has no idea what she's done. She's put herself in danger.

My foot presses down harder on the gas pedal with each passing thought. I need to get to Jules before she says a fucking word.

chapter 6

Julia

I'VE BEEN PICKING AT THE SAME SNARLED THREAD ON MY SWEATER FOR nearly fifteen minutes now.

My sneaker taps nervously against the leg of the simple wooden table; they're still damp from the snow. Something feels off and wrong. Crossing my arms, I look away from the mirror. Anywhere but the mirror.

The stranger in the car kept asking me over and over what was wrong, but I could barely speak. I was so cold, and nothing would come out except that I needed the police. I was lucky he pulled over and offered me a ride. The concern in his pale blue eyes was comforting but only so much that it allowed me to get in the car. His checkered sweater slid down his bony arms as he drove, and he kept looking over at me in the passenger seat. He had to be in his fifties, or maybe sixties. The wrinkles around his eyes told me he was at least my father's age.

That comfort is long gone and a different sensation took over the second he stopped in front of the station. I have no proof, no evidence. I don't know if anyone is going to believe me. I need to tell someone, though. I swallow thickly, realizing I don't know where to begin or if a soul will believe me or do anything at all.

The old man stayed with me while a young officer gave me a blanket and told me it was all right. *Whatever it is, you're safe now.* Dressed in his blues, the man was maybe in his mid-twenties and didn't have a clue what I was there for. It was such a spectacle, but even though they were kind and open I still couldn't spit out the words.

Then I was handed over to Detective Myer.

He's much too young for someone in his position, clean-shaven and tall with dark brown eyes. He has to be around the same age as the officer who greeted me warmly. There's no warmth to Myer, though; he's all corded muscle, although he doesn't have the broad shoulders or height to him to balance out his body. Even with his badge and prying stare, he doesn't have an air around him that commands authority.

There's something else as well, something about the way he looks at me that makes me feel as though I'm not safe. Like I should have changed my mind and headed back out into the snow and never stopped running. I don't trust the detective. I didn't when he told me to sit in here and twenty minutes later, what little hope and faith I had has faded.

Maybe I'm being paranoid and it's all in my head, but it seems wrong he never asked any questions. He simply told me to follow him back here and sat me down while he went to talk to the commissioner. I'm alone and left wondering what the hell I'm doing here at all.

Guilt worms its way through every bone in my body. Every tick of the clock tempts me to get up from this table. I'm going to choke on my words. I can't do this. They'll never believe me and I can't say the truth out loud.

Just as the notion hits me, the door opens and I stand mostly out of instinct, but also possibly fear. The need to run is overwhelming, but when my eyes catch sight of the imposing man walking in behind Detective Myer and another man who I assume is the commissioner, my knees go weak.

I don't need to be told he's Mason's father. I don't need to be introduced. His gray eyes and sharp cheekbones give it away. He even clears his throat like Mason as he unbuttons his suit jacket and sits in the empty chair across from me.

My eyes flicker to Detective Myer's, who simply crosses his arms and leans against the wall in the far left corner. His dark eyes bore into me and send a chill down my spine. The commissioner makes a show of closing the door and then taking a seat at the far end of the table.

"Sit, sit," Mason's father insists. "Jules, isn't it?" he says with a smile that doesn't reach his eyes.

My knees are so weak that I obey him, falling into my seat and staring at the commissioner who isn't looking at me at all. He casually picks at his nails instead. I glance back to the mirror and pray there's a camera recording or someone behind it watching this. Someone else. God, please help me.

I'm not safe here. That's the only thing I'm sure of. *What have I gotten myself into?*

"Good girl," Mason's father says approvingly, and it sickens me to my core. There's something about the air of ownership he projects. Something about the way his words roll off his tongue. The fear is only partially brushed aside by my disgust, but I'm at least able to look him in the eye.

"Where's Mason?" I ask evenly, although I don't know how I got the courage to speak.

His father's eyes twinkle with something that brightens the gray. Something that makes my stomach churn.

"Don't worry, he's coming shortly." Mr. Thatcher looks over his shoulder at the detective. As his mouth parts to say something his straight white teeth peek out from behind his thin lips, but he's interrupted by the door banging open.

"I'm sorry, Detective Myer," a young woman says from the hallway as Mason stands in the doorway, hovering in the opening with an authority that's incomparable.

And he's pissed.

The way his steel gray eyes seem to turn a sharp silver and pierce through me makes every tiny hair on my body stand on end. Every inch of my skin chills and then heats so quickly I can't move. All I can do is stare into his eyes, caught in his gaze.

He breaks it before I can relax, and only then can I breathe.

My eyes drop to the floor as the shock withdraws, and my reality strikes me across the face. The emotions that swarm me are confusing to say the least. I'm relieved to see the very man I fled from only hours ago.

"Jules," he says and Mason's voice isn't cold like I imagined it would be. I lift my eyes to his, and my heart beats in rhythm with the seconds that tick by ever so slowly. *Tick, tick, tick.* The room is silent as the other men wait for my reaction. I can't give them anything, though. I'm numb and useless with exhaustion and a thread of fear so easily broken. My throat is dry, and I can barely manage to make eye contact with Mason. I pick at my sleeve and look back at the table, feeling defeated, foolish and guilty.

How is it possible that guilt is what consumes me most?

"Sweetheart, what are you doing here?" Mason asks me with sympathy in his voice as he pulls out the chair next to me. The legs scrape on the floor and Mason wraps his arm around the back of my chair as he sits close to me, but not an inch of him touches me. Not his arm, not his knee to mine. He's so close I can feel the heat of his body, but he's distant all the same.

"Is something wrong?" he asks me, and I immediately shake my head no.

I'm retreating like a coward. "I want to go home," I say, whispering the plea just above a murmur, still not looking any of the men in the eye.

"What's that?" Detective Myer says from the corner of the room, pushing off the wall and uncrossing his arms for the first time since he's been in here. He starts to walk over.

I clear my throat and ignore how scratchy my voice is as I repeat myself. "I want to go home."

The detective leans against the table, his palms flat as he waits for me to look up at him. His voice is strong and hard, filled with contempt as he says, "Issuing a false report and taking up the time—"

"What false report?" Mason asks at the same time that I refute the detective.

"No one has taken a statement from me. I haven't said anything," I say and my voice is stronger than I imagined it would be.

Mason rises from his chair abruptly, leaning over the table and bracing his forearms in front of me as he gets in Myer's face. "Don't you dare," Mason says, speaking with a tone of malice that makes me flinch. "Don't you dare threaten her."

Mason's chiseled jaw is covered with stubble and the way it clenches while his hands fist on the table takes the commissioner by surprise. He visibly balks, and it's then that Mason's father pipes up.

"Now, now. Miss Summers had something she wanted to say, Mason." Mason's head tilts slowly, daring his father to speak again and the old man does just that, the glint in his eye ever present.

He looks past Mason and asks me, "What was it that brought you here, Julia?"

"Nothing," I say and my voice croaks.

"Oh, come now," he says. Mr. Thatcher's voice is lighthearted, but it's never been more apparent how dark the situation has become. Do they already know? *They must.*

And now they know that I know.

My throat tightens instantly, as if a strong hand has gripped it to choke me. "You can come to me with anything, Miss Summers," Mason's father says, staring me straight in the eyes as he continues, "I know everyone, Jules, and I'll be sure you're taken care of—"

"Enough," Mason practically growls at his father.

His father finally takes his assessing stare from me to give Mason his attention. "Just out of curiosity, Mason, what little secret did you tell our Jules?"

Mason ignores his father, taking my hand in his with a bruising force and leading me to the door. My legs are weak but I keep up with him. He rips the door open so violently I swear he nearly pulls it off the hinges.

"Go," Mason commands me, sweeping his arm forward and I listen immediately, grateful to be getting the fuck out of here mostly unscathed.

"Bye for now, Jules," Mr. Thatcher says to my back as I leave, and I'm grateful Mason is between us. I can't breathe or do anything other than follow Mason's lead until we've left the station. I can feel everyone watching us and my face blazes with the awareness, but fear is what keeps me moving and my eyes staring straight ahead.

"Mason," I whimper as he braces his hand against the small of my back and leads me across the street to where he's parked. I stare at his car, feeling as though I'm so close to safety, but knowing I'm going back to a cell.

Mason doesn't respond but he pulls me in close, wrapping his arm around my waist as we cross the street to the parking lot. Without knowing what to think or feel, my head spins. I have to walk quickly to keep up with his purposeful strides, but I feel comforted just from his arm wrapped around me, needing his embrace.

For a moment, as Mason opens my door and waits for me to get in his car, I think there's hope. I think I can repair the damage I've caused even though I'm not sure why I'm even considering it.

I'm so confused, so conflicted. The only thing I'm certain of is that if Mason hadn't come to get me, something bad would have happened. Something to make sure I was silenced.

Foolish. I'm so damn foolish. At the thought, I struggle to breathe and I lay my head back against the seat, feeling the weight of what just happened flow through every limb. Heat flows around my skin, uncomfortably and unbearably so.

Mason shuts his door with a loud thud as he gets in and starts the car, all without sparing me a glance while he backs out and merges into traffic.

With tension pulled through every inch of me, I wait for something, for a moment to speak or for him to say something, but I'm given nothing.

"Mason?" I take a chance and say his name as the car stops at a red light. His fingers flex on the steering wheel and then his knuckles turn white as he grips it and slowly turns to look at me.

His eyes are cold, ice cold, and I instantly regret speaking at all.

"We'll talk when we get home," he says beneath his breath. I nod once, feeling alone and abandoned and utterly hopeless.

chapter 7

Mason

Forever doesn't end,
But it also doesn't last.
What you feel right now,
Will soon be the past.

Left only with the memories,
And the desire to hold.
But time doesn't wait,
And even love grows old.

I WOULD HAVE KILLED THEM. BOTH THE DETECTIVE AND THE commissioner. Possibly even my father. I've never been so close to snapping, never. I've never come close to feeling that pull. Pure anger and hatred are fueling my thoughts. I'm barely contained, on the edge of something dangerous, something so dark I've never confronted it before. Not even that fateful day I destroyed Jules's life. Even that wasn't like this.

Dragging my hand down my face, I listen as my shoes smack against the hardwood floors, but then the sound is muted on the rug in front of the gray suede sofa in my living room.

"What were you going to tell them?" I ask as I pace in front of her, my gaze still focused downward.

It's never felt colder or darker in this house before. Not to me. Even with the bright white snow reflecting light through the large modern windows on the back wall, there's not an ounce of warmth in the room.

Ice courses through my blood, but even that's not cold enough to take the heat from my anger.

I can't stop moving; every muscle is coiled and ready to fight. She doesn't know what she does to me. She has no fucking idea what she's done. What kind of danger she's put herself in.

"How could you?" I say. The question is menacing and it stops me in my tracks. It holds a vicious tone I can't contain. I take a single glance up and regret it. With her beautiful blue eyes widened, Jules looks as though I've slapped her, flinching and her mouth dropping open, but she doesn't answer.

"I—" she tries to speak, but can't finish her sentence. It's fucking infuriating. I don't know what's worse, how she's impulsively made everything worse for us, or the fact that she left to turn me in. My jaw clenches so hard I nearly crack my teeth. I have to stare past her at the blanket of snow as she squirms on the sofa. "Mason, I—"

"You what?" My voice booms from my chest as my heart pounds. She would be dead if my father hadn't called me. He could have killed her. Or have had her killed rather, so he wouldn't have blood on his own hands. He'd have done it too, if he hadn't wanted to toy with me. If he hadn't wanted something to hold over my head. If he hadn't wanted me to know that I owe him now. "You have no idea what you've done."

I can only imagine my father is under the impression that she knows about his involvement with Avery's death. That I told her. That she was there to rat *him* out and not me.

"Fuck." The curse lays under my breath as my pacing continues. It takes every ounce of self-control not to destroy this place.

He doesn't know a damn thing about Jace's murder. No one does but the anonymous stranger who sent Jules that note.

My father won't let Jules live. I take in a ragged breath, but it doesn't calm me.

There's no fucking way I'll let him touch her. She's mine, and she'll be my wife and mother to my children. If he dares try any of that shit with her again, I'll destroy him. I'll end his life so fucking miserably that he'll be thankful when I finally slide the edge of a knife across his throat.

"Mason," she says and fear clings to the single whispered word.

"They would have killed you, Jules." I swallow the ball of spikes in my throat and finally look down at her glassed-over eyes. Her baby blues are full of so much emotion. "They would have killed you," I repeat in a whisper and it's that sickening thought that breaks the rage. It shatters into something else. Something that feels like weakness.

Jules holds my gaze, but she doesn't answer me. Tears leak from the corner of her eyes, but Jules doesn't acknowledge them. Her face displays an expression of sincerity. "I'm scared," she says. She gently shakes her head and looks past me, down the hallway and avoiding eye contact. My heart clenches in my chest.

"I didn't want any of this," she says and her voice is raw with emotion.

I swallow thickly and tell her the simple truth, "You never should have left."

She looks up at me with daggers in her eyes as she hisses at me without a second passing between us, "You never should have killed my husband."

It catches me off guard for a moment, but the pure venom and hate she had only hours ago is dimmed, the stark reality of the situation taking its toll on her. I keep my eyes on hers as I tell her, "Your husband deserved to die for what he did."

Jules's lips part as she takes in a heavy breath, looking as if she's going to respond, but no words come out. After a moment she looks away, finally wiping the tears from her reddened cheeks with the sleeve of her ruined sweater and sniffling.

"I don't want to die, Mason," she says weakly. Her chest rises and falls with her steady breathing. "I just want to go home and I'll never say a word."

"You can't go home." My voice is hard and leaves no room for negotiation. I won't risk putting her in danger. I don't know what my father's told the commissioner. I need to make it clear to him that she knows nothing about what happened. I'll lie. I'll tell him I hit her.

He's always seen through my lies, though. He's a damn good liar, and the challenge of outsmarting him has never seemed so daunting.

I could tell him the truth. I'll tell him anything I need to in order to make him believe she's not a threat.

"If you leave me, you're putting yourself at risk—" I can't finish because it's at that moment that Jules finally breaks down. Her always composed demeanor cracks and her shoulders hunch forward as a sob wracks her body.

Any explanation dies at the back of my throat. All of my anger dissipates. She's broken because of me. This happened because of me. I fucking hate myself.

"I'll protect you," I tell her. I only hesitate for a moment before taking the seat next to her. My weight causes her small body to lean into mine, and I'm surprised when she doesn't resist. She lets me hold her for a moment as her cries get softer and she wipes the tears from beneath her eyes. I've craved this warmth since she found out the truth. "I promise."

I lean forward and kiss her hair, taking in her sweet scent but it makes her withdraw. She doesn't look at me, and the moment she has her composure back she pulls away from me.

"Is it really that bad to stay with me?"

Her body stiffens at the question, and she doesn't answer.

"You have no other options but to stay where I tell you and do what I say. You need to convince everyone in this city that you're mine, that everything between us is better than it's ever been."

"I just want to go home." She'll never know how much that desire damages me in the worst way. How empty and hollow her confession leaves me. "I won't tell anyone," she adds, peeking up through her thick lashes.

"You don't have a choice," I tell her as I cup her cheek in my hand. I run the rough pad of my thumb along her lush lips, and they beg me to kiss her. Her pale skin is flushed a beautiful shade of pink and everything in me wants to hold her close. I want to take her pain away; I want to remind her who she belongs to.

"You're mine, Jules. There's no changing that."

chapter 8

Julia

Pressed against a hard wall,
No choices, no way out.
Without the air to breathe,
And only left with doubt.

There's no way to move forward,
No will to make amends.
Nothing but what he gives me,
Trapped and at dead ends.

I'M DESPERATE FOR MY MOTHER, OF ALL THINGS. DESPERATE TO CALL HER, to confess what's happened, to plead with her to protect me. As if something so simple could save me.

I pick at the comforter on the bed and wish I had my computer or my phone. Or any way at all to contact someone.

Not a single soul has come up Mason's driveway since he brought me back here. There are no neighbors close enough to just drop by, not that Mason's the neighborly type. Even the mailbox is all the way at the end of the long driveway. I'm trapped in this house that's practically a gilded cage without a damn thing to do other than write down every forsaken emotion and thought that comes to me. Time is moving slowly; the past three days have felt like a year, and all I can do is be consumed by the thoughts of how I got here. *How did this become my life?*

The moment I look out a window or walk toward a door, Mason's there. Watching me, waiting to see what I'll do. He went from being my lover and my hope, to a prison warden. Every time he enters the room, I can *feel* him.

Yet he's pretending he's not monitoring me, that he trusts I'll behave because

I'm afraid. Part of that's true, but mostly I'm waiting, simply biding my time. I'll be quiet and listen until I have a chance to leave him. He can't keep me here forever.

The bathroom door opens with a soft creak, stealing me away from my thoughts as Mason steps into the bedroom from the en suite. He's bare-chested, his tanned skin on display as he strides toward the dresser with only a towel wrapped around his waist. His demeanor is casual, as if nothing happened. As if I can live with the fact that he's a murderer, and my life is in danger because of him and his father. If I'd known he was tied to anything at all like this, I'd never have gone home with him that first night. I'd never have flirted, I'd never have touched him, let alone fallen in love with him.

I have to bite my cheek to keep from screaming, to keep from doing something stupid as Mason turns his back to me, letting the towel drop as he selects a pair of boxers from the top drawer of his dresser. Between the multiple heartaches and chaos, loss is there. Loss of someone I thought I loved who didn't exist. Loss of the independence I was so sure I had.

"I bought you a dress for Saturday," he informs me matter-of-factly as he unzips a garment bag with his back to me.

My eyes flicker to the beautiful evening gown hanging on the back of the closet door. Its jewels sparkle as the light hits it; they're sparser on top, just a faint pattern that forms the outline of an hourglass, overlaying the darker gray on the sides and absent on the light gray inlay. From the hips down, the gown is completely covered in the dazzling Swarovski crystals.

It's stunning. I'm sure it would impress everyone at the charity event. I don't remember which one this is; I only know that Mason wants to attend to discuss business with a number of investors and it's an annual charity gala I've gone to without fail for years.

For a moment, I can only watch Mason continue with the business of getting dressed, wondering how he could even consider the two of us attending an event together. "I don't see how I could possibly go." I can't imagine standing in a room smiling and playing nice when I feel like this. When I'm trapped and cornered. When I'm literally scared for my life.

Mason's steel gray eyes pierce through me as if he heard every one of my thoughts when I look at his reflection in the cheval mirror.

"You've had a couple of nights to think about things. You'll have another handful of days to come around," he says confidently and breaks my gaze to shut a drawer, holding a pair of socks in his right hand.

"Where are you going?" I ask him, feeling a touch of hope rise in my chest at the prospect of him leaving. *I just want to go home.* The thought plays in my head on a loop like a broken record.

His lips press into a thin line and he turns slowly to face me, leaning back against the dresser. "Do you think it would be wise?" he asks. He hasn't moved but somehow he seems much closer than he was a moment ago.

I feel the blood drain from my face. "What do you mean?"

"Jules, my sweetheart," he says as he sets the clothes on top of the dresser and strides toward me. The bed dips as he sits on the edge, my heart racing from the proximity even though he doesn't touch me. "I'm still the man I was," he says calmly; his voice is soft and it breaks something inside of me. The smile he gives me is sad and doesn't reach his eyes. Leaning forward, he adds, "I can practically hear what you're thinking."

Thud, my heart pauses, caught in a trap that snaps shut around it. I swallow and focus on calming down to pry it free from the steel bars, attempting to pretend I don't know what he's talking about.

My head shakes to deny the truth but he reaches out, grabbing me by the nape of the neck and my hip, holding me in place and forcing me to look at him. It's possessive, it's dominating and it steals my breath. He hasn't been this close to me in days. His lips are so very close to mine. Just like my heart, I'm trapped.

"I'm not going to lose you, Jules." He speaks with an intensity that makes the world blur around him.

"I'm not leaving," I whisper with a shaky breath, although even I can tell it's a lie. My words are just as weak as I am when it comes to him. The corner of his lips twitch as if he wants to smile and pretend I'm telling the truth, but he doesn't.

"I'm the same man you fell in love with." The steel gray gaze softens, begging me to understand and believe him, but I can't. The tension is thick between us, but how can he expect me to simply forget? When I look at him, I see it all play out, over and over again.

I refuse to believe I ever knew this man, but the very thought splits my heart down the center.

I could never love a murderer. I could never be with the person who killed Jace. Pain lances through my chest, and I have to look away. As much as I wish I could turn it off and stop loving him entirely, I know that's not a possibility either. A piece of my heart is his forever, but that only makes me hate him more.

A question begs to be asked. One I've thought every night since he confessed. "You knew when you saw me that first night?" I ask him with a raw voice. That's what I simply can't wrap my head around. He knew who I was. He knew how much he'd hurt me and ruined me. Yet it didn't stop him.

"Knew what?" he asks, sitting easily across from me and I look him in the eyes to confront him as I say, "You knew who I was? Jace's widow."

He nods once.

"How could you?" I ask as my blood races and whatever took over a moment ago vanishes. It's yet again another betrayal. "Was I a prize to you? A reward for getting away with it?" I say out of spite.

His expression changes to one I'm growing familiar with. To distaste and anger. Apparently we both feel it. "Don't you dare." His nostrils flare as he adds, "Don't you dare do that to us. To what we have."

"Had," I say and my throat hurts as the word leaves my lips. I don't see how I could ever forgive him or how he can expect that I would. He may be the only thing keeping me alive and standing in the way of his father silencing me, but he'll forever be my husband's murderer. A liar, a sinner, and ultimately someone who used me.

"You were only Jules to me. Only a woman who was hurt and broken." His words hang in the air between us and my conviction sways. Mason hesitates then adds, "I knew your pain was because of what I'd done. I knew it was my fault, and I wanted to make it better."

My lips part with disbelief. "Make it better?"

"I don't know what to say, Jules." He lets his hands fall to the bed beside me, his fingers resting against my thigh. "I don't know what to tell you."

"There's nothing to say." I'm certain of that at least. I stare at the comforter and avoid the hurt look in his eyes. He has no right to be saddened or angered. He has no right to expect anything from me. He's the one who put all of this into motion. He could have stopped it.

"There is more to say. And in time you'll want to know more."

My shoulders rise with a heavy breath. I know it's true. I need to know if my husband did have a woman murdered. How could he? Mason must be wrong.

I just can't imagine it. I can't believe I was married to a man who would have someone killed. He was living with me, sharing my bed and kissing me every morning. I can't see it. What's worse, I don't want to see it. Just like I didn't want to see the other lies that came out after he died. *I didn't know the man I once loved.* I look up into Mason's gray eyes and I don't know which man that thought was for. Jace or Mason.

I suppose both.

"I just want to go home," I tell Mason one last time. One last plea.

"No, you're staying here. Don't try to run, Jules," he tells me and his voice is so low. He leans forward, resting his forehead against mine. "I would kill for you. I'd die for you. I love you."

His words send a chill through me, not because of the intensity, but because I feel with everything in me that each word is utterly and completely true.

chapter 9

Mason

I CAN'T FUCKING STAND THIS. EVERY TIME SHE PASSES ME, EVERY TIME I look at her there's a look in her eyes that warns me to stay away. To not touch her, to not approach her, to not say a damn word to her.

I'm the same man I was when I slipped that ring around her finger. The one that lays in the drawer of my nightstand now. The one I picked up off the floor when she left me. I figured it'd be better to hide it from her than give it back and risk her flushing it.

With the ring between two of my fingers, I twist it back and forth, the cushion-cut diamond moving from side to side with moonlight glinting off it as it pours in through the gap in the curtains. I turn my gaze to the window, knowing just beyond the thick velvet fabric is a ripped screen that still needs to be replaced.

This bedroom has become a cage. A prison of her own making. I've given her time. I've been gentle, given her space, but it's only pissing me off when she glares at me. She's a stubborn woman and I understand her needs, but it feels like I'm slowly snapping, not bending.

It's time for a change. I don't know how long it takes to mourn or forgive, but I also don't give a fuck. There's too much on my mind for me to be worried about where we are with each other. I need her. More importantly, I need to know she won't run so I can keep her safe.

I can't have anyone else questioning it either. They need to be very aware that we're still in love. Every. Single. Person.

With a particular person in mind, I glance at the phone on my nightstand. My father isn't answering my calls.

I'm tempted to go to his office to make sure he backs off, but that means either leaving Jules alone or taking her with me. Between those two options of course I'd be bringing her along, but I don't want him anywhere near her. Just walking into the station, knowing he was with her, toying with her, and hearing him threaten her was almost too much for me. I take in a heavy breath, staring at the diamond to calm myself again.

He has one more chance. One meeting on Saturday to treat her the way she deserves and apologize for what happened at the station. She's everything to me, and I won't let him frighten her. It's bad enough as it is. Otherwise… I'll have no choice but to kill him. My plan at this charity, the only plan I have, is to make that promise very clear to my father.

We're in the eye of the storm, I know it. Chaos is lurking in the shadows surrounding us, and I need my sweetheart by my side. I need her clinging to me and letting me protect her.

Right now, with her on the other side of the bed, she's hardly speaking to me let alone capable of trusting me. I can't sleep at night until she does, because I don't trust her either, and it's a battle of wills. Neither of us sleeping, neither of us giving an inch. And that's exactly what will happen tonight if I don't do something.

The diamond sparkles brilliantly, the light shining from one facet to the other.

This belongs on her fucking finger.

I stand abruptly, wanting nothing more than to tell her it's never parting from her again. But the moment I see her, she's running her fingers along her wrists. At the faint bruises and small cuts left from when I tied her up days ago.

My anger leaves slowly, like a leak, leaving me empty and hollow with regret.

"I can't take it back." I clear my throat and give her the words as they come to me. "You need to stop this, Jules. We can't continue like this."

Her posture changes, the bed creaking along with the slow movements as she grips the comforter and pulls it closer to her. Her expression shifts, and she's not pretending anymore. She's not hiding her anger; she glares at me, leaning forward. It thrills me. *Give me that anger, sweetheart. Fight me, slam your fists into my chest, take it out on me. I'll show you I can take it. I can let you get it all out and then soothe it away and fuck you so hard and so thoroughly you won't remember a damn thing except for how much you love my cock inside of you.*

"Did you like it?" I ask her as my dick twitches with the need to push her and make her angrier.

A moment passes and she simply stares at me, refusing to answer.

"Did you like it when I tied you up?" I ask and this time, she can't ignore my question.

"Fuck you," she says, jumping off the bed and making her way toward the door to leave me again. She's not fucking leaving me, though. I'm quicker than her and she knows it. I slam the door shut before she can walk through. With both my palms above her pressed firmly against the door, I cage her in with my arms as she spins to face me with a gasp of shock. My arms are long and her body's small, so there's still nearly a foot of space between us, but it feels as if we're closer than we've been in so long.

Because it's real. This tension and this moment are more real than the lifeless days we've spent together living like ghosts of ourselves since I told her she wasn't leaving.

She slowly takes an inch forward, waiting for me to stop her from leaving, but I don't. By this point, she should know I'm not going to hurt her. I meant what I said. I will never hurt her.

"Just forget it all, Jules." She tries to walk around me and under my arm, ignoring me and I can't stand it. My forearms press against the door and close the space between us, trapping her there and forcing her to talk to me.

"What do you want from me?" she screams out, her lips close to mine and her anger tangible.

"Forgiveness," I answer lowly, but with a rawness I pray she can feel.

"I can't forgive you."

"I had to do it."

Her brow pinches and she looks like she's going to argue, but she stays silent, biting her tongue and attempting to go back to the version of her I've dealt with for days. She stares at anything except me, as if ignoring me will free her from this moment.

I'm not going to let her get off that easy. She has to say something; I need to force her to confront me, because I know she won't say something on her own. "You have to get over it."

"Never," she says, finally looking back at me and staring me in the eyes. "You're a monster."

"Is that what you want?" I ask her as I take a half step forward to force her back against the door, both of my hands pinning her hips in place. "For me to turn into some kind of monster so you can justify hating me?" My grip's not so strong that it hurts her, but it's forceful enough to get her attention. Her head comes forward and I crash my lips against hers, stealing a quick kiss before she can move away. I move my lips to her ear, pinning her whole body against the wall as my right hand travels up her side while my left grips the hair at the nape of her neck. She's trapped.

"There's a difference between what you've been thinking I'd do and what I've really been doing, sweetheart." I speak just above a murmur. My breathing picks up along with hers, and her nails dig into the shirt on my chest. She's not pushing me away; she's holding me right where I am. I'm just as close to her as I wanted to be.

"You think I'm a bad man in that pretty little head of yours, but you fell in love with me. With the real me and there's no hiding from that." I run the tip of my nose from her cheek to her temple, breathing in her scent. Her small body is so hot against mine. Her rapid pants only aid in making me hard as fuck for her.

"I'll never stop loving you." I speak so low, I'm not sure she hears. I open my eyes and stare at the wall, realizing how fucked up this is, aching over it, but unable to let her go. I'm too afraid of losing her forever. I won't let it happen.

"Just do it, Mason." Jules nearly chokes on her words, and I have to look down into her eyes to see the defiance there. She's pushing me. She knows I'll never hurt her. It's so fucking obvious, and the realization makes me smile slightly.

"Do what?" I ask.

"Whatever you want with me," she says, although her gaze drops to my chest with nothing but defeat in her eyes. "Or let your father kill me."

"Is that what you want?"

"You won't let me leave," is the only answer she gives me.

"That doesn't answer my question." My heart pounds in protest at the question: Would she really rather die than love me again?

Jules looks away, turning her head to the side even as I grip her nape tighter. I pull back slightly, forcing her to look at me.

"That would make it easy for you, wouldn't it?" I ask, hearing my own voice crack. I nip her earlobe with my teeth and wait a moment for her to answer, but all I can hear is the combined sound of our heavy breathing. "It would be so easy to hate me if I were the monster you want to believe I am." I struggle with how true my words are. "If I wasn't the man you fell in love with, but I am."

I kiss the side of her neck, my fingers trailing along her skin and pulling her sleep shirt up slowly. My body's so close to hers but I don't touch her, because I want her to feel my absence. I want her to crave how I make her feel.

I trail the words down her neck, whispering against her skin. "All I want is for you to remember how much I love you and how much you love me."

I want her to beg for my touch again, just like she did when we first met. I know she will. She needs me just as much as I need her. "Give me one month." I speak without thinking, desperate for a change between us. "One month of just pretending. Of trying to forget or forgive and going back to what we once had."

She peers up at me with a brightness in her eyes, but they narrow with distrust. I add, "If you hate me still at the end of the month, I'll let you go." I can barely speak the pained words, but I push out the offering.

My heart beats hard in my chest, knowing it's a lie. But it's something she can hold on to. It's a deal with the devil for her, and I'm sure she knows it.

She doesn't reply, and I couldn't give a fuck so long as tomorrow things have changed for us.

My strides are heavy as I leave her to grab the ring from where it lays, once again on the floor. She stares at it rather than at me when I take her hand. "I'm the same man I was when I first put this ring on your finger." I slide the diamond on her ring finger and hold it there, waiting for her eyes to reach mine.

I lean in and breathe in her scent, closing my eyes and forcing myself to let go of her. "Don't take it off, Jules. That ring will stay on your finger." I watch as her eyes close and her chest rises. "I'll make sure of it."

chapter 10

Julia

The mind plays tricks,
It likes to deceive.
What once brought you joy,
Will now make you grieve.
What to think, what to do,
When there's no easy way out.
When your heart's torn and broken,
And all you know is doubt.

I WISH A HOT SHOWER COULD WASH IT ALL AWAY. AS IF THE STEAM AND heat could cleanse the burden of knowing what Mason did nearly a year ago. So long ago, when we were both two different people. When we were both strangers to each other.

I don't know what to think, and I don't know how to react or which emotion is coming through the strongest. It makes me feel crazy. It's like the sway of the ocean. As soon as one wave comes and crashes over me, another is already waiting to drown me. It's making me weak.

It's late, but I don't want to sleep.

I move to my dresser and sift through the nightgowns mindlessly, remembering how even last night, I questioned if I should refuse him. When Mason laid his arm across my belly, turning on his side to be closer to me, I hesitated before asking him to move and let me be like I have been. It comes down to one truth: I wanted him to take the pain away. The pain he caused. Only him. He's responsible for it all. *Just the same, only he could take it away.*

Glancing down in the drawer I trail my fingers across a nightgown; it's all silk and fine lace. Tempting, luxurious and expensive. I bought new lingerie a few weeks back, for Mason of course. The shine of the navy blue silk catches my eye, but I can't bring myself to pick it up.

I don't want to tempt him anymore. I don't want to try to look beautiful for him. My heart aches with a pain that feels as if it will strangle the life from me. I wish Mason were done with me, because I already feel myself needing his touch again.

It makes me feel pathetic, but what choice do I have? I have no one and nothing, and I've been forced into a corner I can't escape.

I shut my mouth tightly, gritting my teeth as I ball up the silk gown's matching thong in my hand and slam the drawer closed.

He's not a good man. He planned my husband's murder in cold blood.

But he's damn good to me in ways my husband wasn't. If what he said was true... I take in a ragged breath before sitting on the edge of the bed, still only covered by the towel from my shower. The mattress groans as my eyes close and I lean back, collapsing on the bed.

A thought has taken over, one I least expected. I'm still angry with Jace and the more I want to believe Mason, the more I think Jace really did it. He had a woman killed.

How could I not have known what kind of man Jace was? I already know he lied to me, that he stole from me. I have evidence of that from bank account statements and the deed to the apartment he took his mistress to. *Or mistresses.* I'll never know.

If you'll lie, you'll cheat. If you'll cheat, you'll steal. If you'll steal, you'll kill.

I know for a fact Jace did two of those things. Three, technically, since he used my money and not his to buy that property.

I'm disgusted in every way possible. What's worse is that if Jace hadn't passed, maybe I never would have known. We'd still be together and I'd still be living a lie, completely blind to it all. Utterly naïve.

The reality is sickening. I do believe Mason. I believe my husband had a woman killed. But that doesn't mean moving forward I choose to be with a murderer. How could I ever trust Mason again? How could I ever look at him the same?

If only the shower could rinse it all away. Or a pill could erase my memory.

But then I'd be back to the life I once had, not knowing a thing about the lies and corruption, all the sins I've been blind to.

Defeated but still moving forward, I mumble, "To hell with going back to that." I stretch my back as I stand up, knowing I need to get dressed for bed before Mason barges in here. I don't have the luxury of being lost in my thoughts.

One month, and then what? It's pointless to truly consider the question because I don't believe Mason will let me go. Besides, what would I do if in one month he lets me walk out the door?

I pretend that I don't know how that scenario plays out. I go back to being alone, but never trust anyone again? That's really what hurts the most, the lies and secrets make me feel as though no one is truthful. The two men I gave everything I ever had to turned out to be liars and murderers. I huff a pathetic and humorless laugh.

My girlfriends were right, I really do pick winners.

I'm only able to take two steps to the bathroom door before hearing the door at the end of the hall open. I stare at my closed door, waiting for Mason to enter, but then I hear another door open and shut only a moment later with a click that echoes down the hall.

My forehead pinches with confusion as I hear it again. It's as if someone is checking inside of each room in the hallway. I almost call out to tell Mason that I'm in here and I'm not hiding, but something eerie stops me. A chill I've never felt before, like a grave warning from someone or something watching over me, runs down every inch of my skin and my heart races with sudden fear.

Another door opens, then closes. And this last one was closer.

All I can hear is my heart pounding in my chest as I get down on my knees as quietly as I can and crawl under the bed. *Something's wrong.* I hear the door next to the master bedroom close as I try to turn onto my side, but I can't. I'm stuck, wedged between the floor and the bed frame, but it's enough. My heart beats wildly and I try to convince myself it's just Mason and I'm being stupidly foolish again. Keeping as still as possible, I watch the door only six feet or so away, the light from the hallway faintly pouring in through the crack and shining against the gleaming hardwood.

Click. It opens softly, and two shiny black shoes walk in softly. *It's not Mason.* I know it's not. Fear fills my veins. Violently and with a chill that's paralyzing.

I can't stop the adrenaline from pumping through my blood as the shoes leave my periphery. The footsteps thud to my right, but I can't see him. I hear the bathroom door open and terror runs through me, wondering if I've left the light on. If whoever it is that's come up here will know I'm in this room.

Steam will still be on the bathroom mirror and he's going to see where I've messed the bed up from lying there just a moment ago. My heart rages so hard that I swear it's trying to leave my body. If he touches the comforter, he'll feel that it's warm. He'll know I was here only moments ago.

"Jules?" My eyes widen and flash to the open doorway as I hear Mason call for me from downstairs. I can faintly hear him walking to the bottom of the staircase, and I can practically see him standing down there. Given his casual tone, he's completely unaware there's someone else in the house.

God help me; I want to scream.

The black shoes quickly leave the bedroom but not so quick that the man ran.

His steps were silent. He gently closes the door and the click is barely heard. I'm caught between wanting to scream out to warn Mason and saving myself.

Whoever it is that was in this room a moment ago doesn't answer Mason and he doesn't go down the stairs; instead he goes to the left, farther into the house.

I didn't think it possible, but my heart slams harder as I hear Mason start to climb the stairs.

Move! my inner voice begs me. My palms are clammy against the wooden floors as I drag myself across the floor. *Do something!* I don't know who's here, I don't know what they've come for. But I can't stay here and let Mason walk into what could be his death sentence.

I crawl out as quickly as I can, the rug beside the bed burning against my forearms and the metal from the bed frame scraping against my back, but I'm out with time enough to open the door just as Mason reaches the top of the stairs. I swing the door open prepared to scream and when I do, the man is standing right there, staring at the stairwell with a gun in his hand. The thin silencer on the end is pointed straight ahead, right at where Mason should be in only a moment.

"Mason!" I yell out his name, or at least I think I do. I can't hear anything but a loud ringing and my body is so numb from fear and the heat coursing through my body that I can barely feel a thing. As if I'm not even here. As if I've left my body, yet I'm still standing where I was.

The end of the gun points straight at me, only feet away with nothing in between us.

My head spins, and my vision nearly goes black from fear. I never imagined what it would be like to know that you're dying. That you only have a precious second or two left to live.

How time would slow and my body would sway, yet be utterly still.

As I stare at the man's cold dark eyes, it feels as if I don't even exist anymore. They're so brown, they're nearly black. His skin is a beautiful tan, but it looks pale against the black turtleneck and leather jacket he's wearing.

He doesn't look like a killer; he's too handsome, his clothes too expensive.

But that's just what he is.

I'd think this was all a nightmare, if it wasn't for the way Mason screams out and snaps me from this moment, bringing me right back as my own scream pierces my ears.

But the man doesn't shoot, and instead he turns and runs.

chapter 11

Mason

"No!" The word is ripped from my throat as my body moves forward purely out of instinct. My muscles scream as I move as fast as I can, watching the end of the silencer swing toward Jules.

Not my Jules. Not my sweetheart. *Take me instead.*

I lunge forward to block her, but I already know it's too late. The strike of a bullet doesn't hit me and I can barely stand to open my eyes, my body pressed to Jules, expecting the bullet to have already found her. It's her wide eyes and heavy breathing that hammer the message into my thick skull that she's all right. I search her body for any sign of an injury, but she pushes my hands away. "He's running!" she screams in my face.

He could have killed her. I saw it happen. In that split second, she was dead. It takes more than a moment to come to grips with the fact that she's still here. She's alive. She's okay. And the prick who pointed a gun at her is getting away. With his back to us, he sprints toward the end of the hall and into the last bedroom.

My muscles coil as I stand up, hell-bent on killing the bastard. "Stay there!" I scream at Jules as I chase after him, my heart pounding.

He slams the door behind him, but the palms of my hands smack against it and my shoulder shoves the door open.

It all happens so fast, I can't think, I can't control what I do. With my hands still on the door, a fist crashes into my face, catching me off guard.

My jaw cracks as my head snaps back and he lands another blow before I've recovered from the first.

I bring my fists up, ready to fight, but he shoves me back, even as I strike him hard in the shoulder. He yells out in agony but doesn't stop. The push gives him enough room to get by me. I can't let him go. He's fucking dead.

Fisting his jacket, I grab him with everything I've got, ripping at it and ignoring the shit that falls from his pocket. My nails scratch at his slacks, ripping down the fabric but I get ahold of him, tripping up his right leg and the man falls hard to the ground.

Adrenaline courses through my veins and all I can see is my fist pounding into him over and over. But then I hear her scream.

Jules cries out, terrified, and I stop to look at her, my heart leaping up my throat. I stare at her and search for the threat, the danger that's scared her. There's no threat that I can place. She stands there in the doorway, her hands over her mouth, pale with fright and looking so frail. It's only when I feel the man beneath me buck his hips, lunging with all of his strength and moving so fucking fast I can't pin him down that my attention leaves her.

"Stay in the room!" I shout at her, hating that I can't be in two places at once. Torn between protecting her by staying close, and eliminating the danger. I launch myself forward, grabbing at him once again but failing to find purchase. My muscles scream in pain as I lunge at full speed after the man I don't recognize. He swings around the banister and gets ahead of me, but I take the stairs two at a time, feeling my blood get colder and colder as I leave her behind.

Someone else could be here.

The thought makes my foot slip on the last stair. My heel catches the edge and I fall forward. I'm so close to him though that when I reach out for him, I pull him back by closing my fist around his sweater. I reach up with my other hand, ready to wrap my arm around his throat, ready to pull his body to my chest and hold him there until the struggling stops.

I'll strangle him until he has no life left.

But he's quicker and has better balance than I do, slipping the thin leather jacket off and tearing for the door.

It's unlocked. It's never unlocked. It wasn't earlier. Not a damn soul has a key other than me.

The door stays wide open as he disappears from view. The jacket flies behind me as I follow after him. The harsh and brutal wind wraps around every inch of my heated skin.

I'm only a few feet behind him, but he's running faster and with every step I'm reminded that I'm leaving her farther and farther behind.

Someone else could be there. You can't leave her alone.

The man darts to the right, gaining ground and slipping from my vision behind the row of trees. *Fuck!* I can't think straight with thoughts of her.

Closer to the street, the sound of cars passing parallel to us surround me as I sprint after him, but it's useless. I can't see a damn thing through the pine trees. I keep running even though I don't see him. I don't stop even when the cars flying by lay on their horns.

Where the fuck did he go? There's nowhere to hide. I stand on the curb, listening to the cars whizzing by only feet away and searching everywhere. I spin around to my right and left trying to find the man, but he's vanished.

Another car beeps several times as the cold sinks in, and I realize I'm not even wearing shoes. My bare feet sink into the thin layer of snow and my heavy breath fogs in front of my face.

Jules.

Her name echoes in my head as I race back to the house, breathing in the cold air and letting it soothe my tired lungs.

The vision of her staring down the silencer of the gun is the only thing I can see as I ignore the harsh weather, and the screaming of my aching muscles as I run with everything I have back to the house.

The warmth of the house is anything but calming. It's too eerie. Too quiet. I barely hold onto the banister as I fly up the stairs, terrified I've played into this fucker's hand. That he outsmarted me. That he came back for her. I don't know who he is. I don't know how he got in here. All I know is that he was here, and he was going to kill her.

I don't stop moving until I'm upstairs. I just need her here, I need her to be safe.

"Jules!" I cry out before I shove the bedroom door open.

"Mason," she whimpers. She's worried and terrified, but she runs straight to me, burying her head in my chest and clinging to me.

"Thank fuck," I whisper into her hair, holding on to her just as tight. Her chest meets mine and she's pressed against me like she can't get close enough. I stroke her damp hair with my cheek, leaving soft kisses and rubbing her back over and over.

She's okay. Thank fuck she's here. I close my eyes, but the moment I do, the fucker's face flashes into my mind.

Who is he? And why the fuck was he here?

The answers come easily, making my grip on Jules tighten.

A hitman. Here to kill. Because he was hired to do just that.

"My father is a dead man." It's all I can say. "I'll kill him for this." My throat scratches with a rawness of pain that touches the very marrow of my bones. Jules pulls away from me, sniffling and looking up at me with a look I can't make out in her eyes.

She doesn't answer for the longest time, just staring back at me as I slowly catch my breath. *I'm so sorry, Jules.* The apology is trapped at the back of my throat.

"He had this." Jules breaks the moment with her weakly spoken words. She holds out what she found and a chill sweeps over me. A syringe. "It fell on the floor when," she says and pauses, clearing her throat, then tucks her hair behind her ears, looking past me to the last bedroom. She swallows, wrapping her arms around her shoulders and taking a step away before finishing her statement. "When you were on him."

She doesn't look at me, she continues to back away, moving farther into the master bedroom and I follow until the back of her knees hit the bed and she sits on the edge. Is she angry with me? I miss her warmth immediately, my knuckles pulsing with pain at the memory of beating the piss out of the man who would have killed her.

"I had to, Jules."

Her eyes rip away from the ground and she stares into my own. "I know," she whispers, but the pain and sadness in her eyes won't go away. My chest rises with a heavy breath. I don't understand her reaction.

I close my fist around the syringe as I take a step closer to her. She doesn't pull away, not even when I cup her chin in my hand. "Are you okay?" I ask, staring deep into her eyes.

She nods her head and pushes her cheek into my palm. My worry leaves me when she leans into me, covering my hand with her own and closing her eyes.

"Mason," she whispers in a pained voice and it breaks my heart.

I bend down to hold her, to embrace her and tell her that everything's going to be all right. It'll never happen again.

As I get closer to her, my cell phone goes off in my back pocket.

She bites down on her lip as I rest my forehead against hers, hating that I'm being pulled away from her. I take it out from my back pocket only to silence it, to give her my full attention and make sure she knows she's safe, but I see it's my father.

"Stay here," I tell her softly.

"Where are you going?" she asks as she reaches out for me, grabbing my hand as if I'm leaving her alone in hell.

"Just downstairs," I say, letting go of her hand but not before kissing her knuckles. They're soft and undamaged, unlike my own. I look over my shoulder at her as I answer the phone and pass through the bedroom door.

"Hello," I say coldly as I shut the door and take each step of the stairs carefully. The thuds of my feet are in time with the beating of my heart, slow and meticulous.

"Mason, I have the numbers and it's going to be rough," my father says and doesn't wait for me to reply. He's in full-on business mode. As if I would buy that and this isn't damage control.

The click is loud as I lock the front door. I'm barely listening to the man ramble on the other end. He's an idiot if he thinks for one moment this call will fool me.

Dragging out the chair at the head of my dining room table, I stare at the front door, my eyes focused on the lock before flicking over to the stairs.

I can't fucking calm down being so far away from her.

She's safe, I tell myself repeatedly.

"Stop," I say into the phone, halting my father midsentence. "Do you think I don't know it was you?" My tone is menacing.

"What was me? Are you still on about the… incident?"

Rage pushes down the accusations.

"You have something and I have something. I'll be damned if you're going to screw me on this deal, Mason. Think with your fucking head for once!" He scolds me like he used to, his anger on full display. "I thought we had a deal after I let her walk out with you. Was the understanding not clear?" There's silence after the unspoken threat.

"Attempting to have her murdered is a part of your deal?" I ask him evenly, although my pulse betrays any calmness I attempt to maintain.

"Jesus Christ, Mason! Why won't you get over it?"

"So you wouldn't hurt her? You wouldn't threaten her life?" The recent events play in my vision as the syringe in my hand taps back and forth on the table.

He snuck in. He had a syringe. He had a gun but didn't use it.

"I meant to scare her. But I…" he trails off and the strength leaves my father's voice. "I made a mistake before and maybe I am a little heavy handed, but whatever she was going to say, she didn't. You can't be angry with me for that."

"The hell I can't. And if you ever hurt her, I'll kill you." I don't bother mincing my words; we're well past thinly veiled threats. "If anything happens to her," I say as my blood runs cold as I swallow thickly before continuing, "I'll kill you myself."

All I can hear on the other line is a long exhale. "You control her, Mason," my father says and continues with business. He carries on like this conversation didn't include a threat to his life. All the while, I stare at the sharp silver needle of the syringe.

If my father didn't do this, who did?

"Something happened." My throat dries up and I lean forward, hating that I'm relying on him. Hating that I'm in such deep shit I can't get out myself. I take in a heavy breath before saying, "Someone came here."

There's a pause on the other end of the line. "Where's here? Your home?"

"Yes, someone broke in; I don't know how. Someone with a gun and he tried—"

"Are you all right?" my father asks, not letting me finish, and he sounds genuinely concerned.

"I'll be all right when he's dead," I answer him coldly, and it's the truth. "And if I find out you had anything to do with it—"

"I didn't," he says, his sharp tone meant to assure me.

I don't respond, not knowing any longer what to believe.

"Are you sure you want to discuss this over the phone?" he asks after a moment of quiet, and I already know I shouldn't. I pause, and he continues.

"Do you know who it was?" my father asks, but there's something in his voice that's off. Something that makes my blood turn cold. "Was there anything on him?" he asks me with a hint of desperation. The line is silent as I look at the syringe on the table.

"No," I say, my voice falling flat.

"Where is he?" he asks me.

I clear my throat and say, "There wasn't anything on him."

"Tell me his location, I'll take care of this. You don't have to worry—"

"He's gone!" I scream into the phone, feeling increasingly angrier.

A hitman. I only know one man who's ever hired a hitman, and he's on the other end of the phone.

The front door was locked. Someone made that bastard a key. I was only downstairs in the office to talk to my lawyers about the separation of the business. I was preoccupied as he crept up the stairs.

My father knew about the call. He knew. My vision turns to red and even though, for a small moment, I questioned if it could be him, it has to be.

It was my father. All the logical pieces click together, fitting nice and pretty as my father's voice comes through the phone. He just happens to call when the bastard got away? I don't fucking believe in coincidences.

I stare at the syringe on my desk. An overdose of something. That's why there was no gunshot. Too messy. The gun was for protection only.

He was here to murder Jules in a clean way so that no one would know, not even me.

My father set me up. I grip the phone tighter. He tried to kill her. A dark whisper deep in the back of my head hisses, *Just like he killed your mother.*

"It was you." The words come out of my mouth as an accusation. "You're fucking dead."

"Me?" My father's voice echoes with disbelief. "You can't be serious, Mason!"

My skin feels like it's on fire; I try to contain my rage, but it's useless.

"Never," he says on the other end. "I would never hurt her. She's yours, Mason. I'm very aware of that," he tells me, and he sounds so sincere.

I don't respond, thinking. Trying to think who would want to hurt her. Or maybe me. Maybe the asshole was after me. He didn't shoot her. He could have, but he didn't. Maybe the syringe was meant for me. Maybe the man was hired by whomever left the note. For all I know, that man is the one who left the note.

"Scare her, yes. Yes I would and if she ever did anything to hurt you, she'd be there on my list, Mason. But I would tell you. It would be your call."

My father disgusts me. Just the thought of what he's done and what he's willing to do is sickening. But he's saying this wasn't his doing. If it wasn't him, I have no clue where to look next. Nothing but a note with no name and this syringe.

"Who then?" I finally say and as I do, I hear Jules's faint steps as she comes down the stairs. I turn in my seat in the dining room to watch as she walks down slowly and then freezes when she sees me.

Her large eyes plead with me, and I instantly rise to meet her.

"Upstairs, sweetheart," I tell her as my father speaks.

"Has she upset anyone? What was she at the station for? You need to be honest with me."

I place my hand on the small of her back and lead her up the stairs. Her eyes dart to the phone as my father talks, and I know she can hear.

"No, she hasn't upset anyone," I tell him. "Her going to the station was a mistake."

"Well, someone knows something, Mason." He says it like it's obvious. "What about Liam?" he asks me. "He knew we'd be having the conference about the division of the assets. He has a motive." Jules nearly trips on the stairs. She shouldn't be listening to this shit.

I grab her hip to keep her from falling and almost drop the phone.

"I have to call you back," I tell him, content with the fact that it wasn't my father.

Someone knows what I did, and they're after me. They may also be after Jules. Especially now that she's seen this. We both saw his face. She's woven so deeply into my mess.

My father continues speaking into the phone but his words turn to white noise, and I simply end the call. My focus is entirely on Jules.

Her grip on me is tight, and she lets me hold her as I drop the phone to the ground and simply pull her into my lap to sit on the stairs.

Maybe it's the shock, maybe it's something else.

But I don't want to let go of her.

I don't want her to let go of me either.

"I'll find out who did this, Jules," I whisper. "I'll find them, and I'll kill them."

The stars are always present,
Even though we cannot see.
The clouds will block them out,
And leave us with a plea.

Sometimes it takes the darkness,
And the coldest, purest lights.
To see what's always been there,
And cherish those stars at night.

"MASON."

He's silent as he sits on the chair in the corner of the bedroom. It's a reading chair that I bought a while back and tucked into the corner of the master when I moved in with Mason. He seems to prefer it now when he's thinking about what to do. Or maybe it's when life is breaking him down to the point where he can't stand on his own any longer.

"Mason?" I call out his name, my voice soft and again he doesn't seem to hear it. There's a comfortable groove and warmth that surrounds me since I haven't moved from my spot on the bed since we came back in here after he talked with his father. Silence sits between us, with both of us letting our thoughts run wild. His chin rests in his hand and his eyes are staring straight ahead at the armoire, unblinking.

Someone attempted to kill one of us. Or at the very least, inject whatever is in that syringe… Closing my eyes, I calmly breathe out, my fingers tightening on the blanket huddled in my lap.

"Mason, please talk to me," I say, raising my voice even louder. I want to know what he knows. I can't be left in the dark. This time his gray eyes look back at me, smoldering the moment he sees me. As if I've lit a fire, and the intensity of it stops me right where I am.

The only thing I can think in this moment is that he's going to eliminate the distance between us, to push me back on the bed, to take me like he used to with that look. My breath halts and my body stays frozen, but not with fear or denial. *This is lust.* I want him to take me, to feel my body and for me to feel his. Right now I need to be held. Just like I did all those months ago when Mason first took me home.

I want to forget it all.

Mason doesn't do any of that. The chair scoots back against the hardwood floor as he rises from the corner. He walks past me leaving a trail of coldness in his wake as he stands in front of his dresser, his back to me for a long moment.

Leaning back on the bed, I attempt to push down the wave of rejection that flows through every inch of my body. A hollowness presses against my chest. Does he no longer want me?

Isn't this what I wanted not so long ago? Why does it hurt so much, why does it hurt even worse?

Mason drops to a crouch in front of the dresser, pulling out the third drawer down and not stopping until it's completely removed from the dresser.

"What are you doing?"

"You need protection when I can't be here." It takes a moment to register what he said, but only until he reaches inside the dresser where the drawer was and pulls out a case. It's thin and silver, obviously a gun case. My gaze never leaves the brushed satin metal as he carries it to the bed.

A numbness pricks its way to my fingers at the very thought of touching it. I've never shot a gun before. I haven't ever even seen one in person until today. Until the sight of one was trained on me.

I scoot back slightly and keep my eyes on Mason, ridding myself of the thoughts of the gun that was here only hours ago.

"If someone ever comes in here again, you're going to shoot them. Do you understand me?" Mason asks.

My heart races and my body heats with an anxiety that's nearly paralyzing. I don't know if I can kill someone.

"Who was that man?" I ask Mason rather than answer, but he merely flicks his eyes to mine before turning the case around and ignoring my question.

"The combination is my mother's birthday: ten, fifteen, fifty-seven." I blink up at him, waiting for more, but he simply pushes the box closer to me, rattling it to get my attention until my fingertips slide to the cold silver metal of the combination lock.

Ten. Fifteen. Fifty-seven. *Click.* The loud noise of the case opening doesn't startle me as much as I thought it would; I'm still waiting to learn who the man was and why he was here. I need to know what he was searching for and what was in that syringe.

Mason swallows thickly, opening the case and revealing a shiny handgun.

"It's a nine millimeter. It—"

"Mason," I say, cutting him off, waiting for his eyes to meet mine. "Who was that?" I ask him when I have his full attention.

"I don't know," he answers lowly, holding my gaze.

"Why..." I can't finish my sentence, my blood rushing in my ears and my body heating.

My throat goes dry as Mason gives me nothing. His expression is unchanging, and I know right then he's not going to tell me a damn thing.

I lick my lips and push the case away from me. I didn't choose this, and I don't want it.

"You need to know how to use this, Jules," Mason says, grabbing the gun by the barrel and passing it to me handle out, insisting I take it. I stare at it, but I don't really see it. Everything's a blur.

"I can't describe how absolutely terrified I was," I say, swallowing down every fear as I rush to get it all out. "Not for my own life or what was going to happen to me, or what could have happened..." Chancing a look in his eyes, I know he hears me. I know he understands what I'm saying.

I was worried he'd never come back. I was worried Mason was going to die.

"I need you to talk to me," I tell him as my eyes burn with the emotions finally surfacing. Scooting closer to him on the bed, I lean closer and plead, "I need to know what's going on." I take a steadying breath, surprised at how even my cadence is. At how strong my voice sounds although I feel as if I'm on the verge of collapsing with hopelessness.

"I don't want to tell you more than you need to know, Jules," Mason says and looks up at me with sympathy, his strength and dominance ever present. He reaches out to cup my jaw but I flinch and move away, scooting backward slightly as I shake my head.

"No, you don't get to decide that," I tell him with a voice much louder than I anticipated. A small bit of anger seeps into the firm statement.

Mason's gaze narrows, but he doesn't respond.

"I need to know." My voice cracks, and I hate that it does, but I am truly desperate and there's no way to hide that. "You need to tell me." Without a response, I lick my dry lips and shamefully look away, down at the patterned rug on the floor. I wish my voice held the strength I feel. I wish I were stronger overall. I'm trying, I'm truly giving everything I can not to be the meek woman I was raised to be and praised for being.

"You don't need to know." His answer is short but he keeps my gaze as if he's ready to cave to me, to give me what I want. I know that look well. I only need to ask.

"I want to know, Mason," I tell him honestly. "Please," I add as I lean forward slightly, almost reaching for his hand. Almost.

With a heavy sigh, he puts the gun back into the case. He shoves it to the side and finally tells me, "I think he was a hitman. I think there's a hit out—"

"A hit?" I blurt out, not quite picking up what he's saying at first, but then the realization floods through me, along with a coldness that cracks my composure. "Someone wants to kill you?" How I have any voice at all is beyond me.

His expression softens as he shakes his head once. "It could be either of us. But I would think that the killer knew I was downstairs in the office."

"Someone tried to kill me?" I manage to get out, but then immediately have to fight back the need to vomit. The shock is just too much. "Why?" My hands shake without my conscious consent. *Someone's trying to kill me.*

"Your father?" I can only surmise it's him. "He warned me. He... he—"

"I don't think so. I think he'd rather use you to get to me than kill you."

"Then who?" The question is torn from me. "Who the hell would try to kill me if not him?"

Mason doesn't answer me.

"Mason." I whisper his name, my face crumpling with pain as I beg him, "I don't want to die." I've thought about death so much this past year, ever since Jace died. It often occurred to me that it would be so easy to just end the pain. But I don't want that. I want to live. I want to be happy. Like I was with Mason, before I found out all the lies.

"No one's going to hurt you," Mason states with finality in a voice so full of confidence, I believe him. His white T-shirt is pulled snug across his broad shoulders and as he leans forward, looking me deep in my eyes, my heart flips and everything else but him blurs around me. "I'll always protect you, Jules. I promise," he tells me. I think he's going to reach out and touch me, that he's going to kiss me and hold me in that comforting way I've grown used to. But he doesn't. He's only inches away, so close I could touch him, but the distance between us is still there and I know I only need to give my consent to let him in. To let his touch soothe the pain that's suffocating me.

"Please hold me." I hate myself in this moment for needing Mason, for forgiving him enough to give in to my own weakness and desires. I close my eyes tight, willing my conscience to go away so he can comfort me. It's not the first time I've had to do this. And the last time sent me spiraling into a darkness I couldn't control.

"I need more than that, Jules." Mason's voice is full of raw emotion for the first time since coming back in here. My eyes open slowly, feeling the sting of tears subside and something else forcing its way through me. His cold gray eyes soften and fill with vulnerability.

Mason reaches across the bed and grips the back of my head in his hand. It's large and strong and his fingers spear through my hair with a strength that forces my lips up to his. He crashes his own against mine and pushes my body back.

I don't know how to describe the rush of desire that sparks to life between us. It's like thunder and lightning all at once, right before a downpour in the middle of an open field with no shelter in sight. It's hot and drenched between us. That's what his kiss does to me. It's a natural storm that I can't stay away from.

"Mason." I moan his name as he breaks our kiss, resting his forehead against mine and breathing heavily. His warm breath fills the small space between us, but when I look up there's nothing but pain etched on his face. Does he not feel it like I do? If I could have anything right now, I'd have him in the field with me, letting the rain soak our skin.

Wordlessly, I reach up and trail my fingers along the stubble of his strong jaw.

"I thought I'd lost you," he whispers and his voice is low and carries the same agony I'm feeling. I almost tell him I know what it feels like, I almost let the tears come back, but then his lips meet mine in a soft, slow kiss that makes my heart race.

I thought I'd lost him. I thought I was going to die before that. "Just hold me," I whimper, my voice a strangled plea.

"Always," Mason murmurs before kissing me long and deep. My back hits the bed and my legs part for him. The tension blisters between us with a passion I thought was long gone. Its intensity refuses to be denied as I cling to him, every bit of me wanting to be pressed against him. He breaks the kiss and I have to tilt my head back to breathe in the cool air as he kisses down my body. Each one takes time, leaving a cool sensation behind as his hot kisses move on to the next spot. It's too slow, yet it's just right.

He takes off my clothes as he goes, slowly stripping me for him. With every moment I'm conscious of what I'm allowing him to do. Watching myself give in to baser needs and allow a man I despised to crawl down my body, holding me as if he owns me, but he does it so gently, as if I'm precious to him. I love every second of it and I know I still love him. The swarm of emotions rages, but only one wins out.

My head digs into the mattress as my neck arches and I lift my hips for him.

I may be a fool, but I know what I want and need.

He kisses just below my belly, sending goosebumps to flow across my bare skin before moving lower. I'm hot for him; my body aches for him. His heated breath causes a sweet sensation of desire to travel up my body and harden my nipples.

I let my hands slowly travel from my breasts to his hair, running my fingernails down his scalp as he pulls off the rest of my clothes and lets them drop to the floor. They fall into a crumpled heap and make the only sound that fills the room besides our breathing and the pounding of my heart.

Mason places his hands on my inner thighs and he doesn't have to push; I immediately spread them wider for him. He stares between my legs and even though my cheeks heat with a violent blush, I can't tear my eyes away from his as he leans forward and gently sucks on my clit.

I cry out my pleasure. It's instant and forceful, just as Mason is.

My legs try to close together to force him away, my fingers gripping onto his muscular shoulders and nails digging into his skin, but he doesn't let up until a wave of my orgasm rises slowly through my toes and fingers. It moves higher and higher and then crashes hard, rocking through my body without any mercy. My head thrashes to the side as I cry out, and I'm only vaguely aware as Mason kisses back up my body with purpose and need this time. He buries his head in the crook of my neck, biting down slightly as he slams himself deep inside of me. He doesn't wait for me to adjust. He only takes his pleasure from me as easily as he gave me my own, ruthlessly riding through my release.

He groans deep and low as he pounds into me over and over again. My body begs me to move, but I'm paralyzed by pleasure. By Mason.

It's fitting really. I'm held beneath him with a passion I can't fight. With a love I can't deny. I can try to fight it, but it's useless.

He braces himself on his forearms to look down at me, never relenting his powerful thrusts. My arousal leaks between us as he lowers his lips to mine.

The dim waves rise again through me, making my body shiver and the rest of me tense. It's coming fast and strong and it's inevitable, I know it is. I hold on to Mason for dear life, letting him take from me and crashing my lips into his.

chapter 13

> *She's broken,*
> *Shattered,*
> *Ruined beyond repair.*
> *The truth has destroyed her,*
> *And left her*
> *Choking on the air.*

MY MOTHER DIED OF AN OVERDOSE.

This can't be a coincidence. It's all I keep thinking as I remember the syringe. I threw it into the fireplace and watched it burn, the thick plastic slowly melting and the liquid boiling into nothing, leaving only a thin needle in the ashes.

I couldn't take it to the police. It only took an opioid test to prove what I thought. It was heroin. It's been two days and I only have one answer to all the questions. The syringe was filled with an opioid and I imagine if the killer had done his job, I would have gone upstairs to find Jules dead of an overdose.

I readjust in my seat in the corner of the bedroom, my laptop on the night-stand I've pulled over to the chair. The dim light from the screen provides the only illumination in the dark room. My tumbler of whiskey sits next to it, but I can't drink. I can't do anything but read the report of my mother's death and let the doubt and anxiety wash through me.

For years I blamed my father.

The therapist he sent me to was under the impression she took her own life because all they did was fight and there were concerns about my mother's sudden erratic behavior. Concerns that wound themselves around whispers of drug use.

I blamed my father because I thought he did it.

He wasn't home when it happened, but that was nothing new. He was never around on the weekends. I was in my bed, but the house was so cold. The air conditioner was turned down far too low.

I remember thinking it was odd that the heat had been turned off. Our house became an icebox.

The moment I clicked it on, I heard the shower upstairs. Maybe I was waiting for the telltale sound of the heater, but until then I hadn't realized I could hear the shower.

I remember how I knocked on the bathroom door, but didn't go in at first. I waited and waited, wondering why she'd be in there so late. Wondering if she was crying again.

I only opened the door an hour later because I'd convinced myself she couldn't still be in there. Not after so long. The water had to be cold by then.

My parents' bathroom door wasn't locked. The knob turned easily and when the door opened and I didn't see a shadow behind the curtain, I was confused but relieved to discover the water had just been left on. Everything felt so off that night, like something was horribly wrong. I was genuinely relieved.

It wasn't until I pulled back the curtain that I saw her.

I slam the computer shut, willing the memory to leave me.

The vision of my mother dead, her body at an unnatural angle. The water was freezing, and it'd turned her lips blue. It didn't stop me from shaking her. From trying to make her wake up.

I screamed and cried out helplessly even though I knew we were alone. There was no one to help. I had to leave her to call the police. I couldn't though, not for a long time. I was shivering in my wet clothes by the time I ran down the stairs to call the cops. I couldn't believe she was gone, but she was limp and heavy and so cold.

It didn't take long for the police to come. Commissioner Haynes was there first.

My father took hours to arrive, though. Hours of sitting on my bed, being questioned over and over until I wasn't sure anymore what had happened.

I only knew I felt completely alone in the world.

The first thing my father said to me was, "I thought you were staying over at your friend's this weekend." No sorrow was evident. No sympathy that I'd found my mother dead in the shower.

His tone carried an accusation even. I remember staring up at him. The police moved around the house, blurring my vision as my father came into focus and the pieces clicked into place.

For years I've felt he was responsible and even now, even after he'd managed to convince me on the phone that it wasn't him, I imagine he's somehow involved.

I can't shake my gut feeling.

I want to murder him.

The thought makes me close my eyes, trying to rein in the anger from today and from all the years of second-guessing what happened to my mother.

When I open them, they've adjusted to the darkness and I stare at my phone. I've asked him, but he's a liar. I already know he's capable of murder.

Everything in me is telling me it's my father who hired that man and possibly left the note to scare Jules off before deciding to kill her. I have no other leads.

The person who left a note had different handwriting than his though, more feminine. Perhaps he has a partner or maybe he hired someone but who would he trust?

The only other enemy I have is Liam. He's married, but I can't see it being him and having his wife involved. And Liam wasn't around when my mother died.

I run my hand down my face, feeling exhaustion weighing down on me, but not wanting to sleep. I can't. I'm too afraid to take my eyes away from Jules. My guard refuses to go down for even a second.

I know she hasn't forgotten everything and that maybe the other night, the moment we shared, was a mistake in her eyes. It kills me just to imagine her thinking of it as if that's all it was. A mistake.

The sound of her stirring on the bed and the accompanying slow movements catch my attention. A soft sound of pain carries through the air, and I rise to see if she's all right.

She turns on her side, pulling the sheet between her legs and letting it fall off her gorgeous curves. I brush her hair from her face, leaning down to kiss her gently on the cheek, loving how she can't fight me in her sleep.

When I pull back, her long lashes flutter open and she looks up at me. At first there's a softness to her expression, like the way she used to look at me. But it quickly changes, the trace of a smile dimming as her memories come back to her.

Her shoulders tense and she turns her head, but she doesn't push me away, even as I run my hand down to her waist and sit next to her on the bed.

The bed protests as I climb in under the sheet, still in my white undershirt and flannel pajama pants. I sigh heavily, feeling exhaustion desperately try to force me to sleep as I rest my head on the pillow and pull Jules close to me.

Just like earlier this week, she lets me hold her. She doesn't hold me back, though. Her hand merely rests against my chest, her head on my shoulder. Still, I'll take it. The feel of her small body pressed to mine, the faint sounds of her breathing and the way she nestles her head down against me, brushing the hair from her face is everything to me.

"Talk to me, Jules," I say softly. I miss her. I miss the banter and her optimistic energy. I miss her stories and the sweet sound of her laughter. "I miss you," I confess.

"I'm not sure if we're okay," she says quietly, as if it's a reminder to herself. "There are parts of you that scare me."

I tell her, "But not all of me."

Her eyes are wide open but staring across the room. I readjust my shoulders on the pillow, keeping my arm around her and debating what to tell her. She's quiet for a long time but then she asks, "You said Jace had a woman killed?"

I can only nod.

She's silent, obviously waiting for me to continue.

"I didn't know him well, but he was…" I pause to take a deep breath and stare at the mirror across the room. In the reflection I can see the top of Jules's head resting on my chest. Her eyes are vacant, as if she's broken. Not the woman I once knew, not the Jules I fell in love with. She's not running from me, as if this new woman has become resigned to her fate.

"I saw him for a meeting, and it was the only time I met him," I tell her. I want to explain and I pray she understands.

She shifts on my chest and I splay my hand on her back to keep her close to me, to keep her from moving away, but I don't have to. She's only readjusting and she stays with her cheek pressed against my chest as she pulls the sheet up higher.

"I did it," I say, feeling the words dying to come out of me. To tell her the truth. To tell her how angry he made me. How Jace was so sure of himself, so happy with what he'd done. "Her life was meaningless to him."

"Whose? Whose life?" Jules brings her hand back toward herself, retreating slightly but I reach out to grab it. I bring her fingers to my lips and slowly kiss each knuckle. She doesn't look at me while I do, but when I set her hand back down, she leaves it there.

I don't know what to make of her in this moment. Maybe she's numb, but she's receptive. She's lost her fight to deny it all.

"Her name was Avery."

Jules shifts uncomfortably as she says the words before I can. "She was his mistress?"

I nod my head as I say, "I knew her as well." It's the gentlest way I can put it.

"You *knew* her?" Jules asks in a tight voice. It's the loudest she's spoken for this conversation.

"I did," I answer honestly. "Obviously it was before we met. Before I knew you."

She nods her head into my chest and whispers, "Why?"

"Why did he want to kill her?"

My question forces her expression to fall even farther, but she nods.

"She was pregnant," I tell her and that's the last straw for Jules's composure. I hold her close as she tries to turn away. I kiss her shoulder as she hunches over and tries to hide her face from me.

"It's okay," I whisper into the tense air between us. The hurt and betrayal are echoed in her ragged breaths. I can only imagine how much it shredded her to hear the words, because it killed me to say them to her.

She pushes her hands against my chest slightly, and I let her go for a moment.

Sitting up as if searching for more air, she pushes the thick sheet off of her and pulls her long brunette hair over her shoulder as she scoots up the bed and readjusts herself to lean against the headboard. All the while I can see her reining in the emotions, hiding it all and shoving it down. But she's swallowed the truth of it all: her husband wanted his mistress dead because she was pregnant. It will stay with her forever.

"Was the baby…" she starts to ask in a choked voice as she lies back next to me and instantly places her head on my chest. "Whose was it?" she asks.

My heart clenches in my chest, hating that I have to answer her and knowing it's going to torture her. "His," I finally answer.

She nods once, letting me know she acknowledges what I've just told her, but she's silent. A long time passes with neither of us saying anything. My fingers trail up and down her arm, moving to the dip in her waist and back up her body again. Her breathing becomes steadier, deeper and so does mine. Slowly, she gets comfortable alongside me again, resting down in bed, but neither of us sleeping.

"Did you love her?" she asks just as my eyelids feel so heavy I could fall asleep, her fingers gripping onto my shirt but still she doesn't look at me.

"No. I've never loved anyone like I love you," I tell her and then realize she may not believe me. It's true, though. I'd never planned on spending my life with someone. I didn't think it possible for someone who carries the demons that drag me down. But now I can't see my life without Jules in it. She's a bright light to my darkness. The only hope I've ever had is in her hands.

Again, she acknowledges me with only a small nod.

"Can you forgive me?" I ask her quietly, almost too afraid of her answer to even utter the word *forgiveness*.

Time passes and I think she may have fallen asleep, but then her shoulders shake with a small sob.

"No," she says and my chest sinks from her admission but also from the raw pain in her voice. "You didn't have to murder him." She adds, nearly choking on her words, "But I believe you." She sniffles once and it's then I feel her tears soaking into my shirt. She brushes her cheek against my shirt and settles back down against me.

She believes me, and that's a start.

She needs me, and she's clinging to me because she has nowhere else to go.

At least I can hold her for a little while, but even with her so close to me, even with this progress, I feel farther away from her than I've ever been.

Julia

It's absurd to move through life,
When there's nothing left inside.
When you're hollow and unfeeling,
When all you know has died.

Numb to touch, numb to move,
And silent with no voice.
But strength comes in the darkest times,
When you no longer have a choice.

FRAUD. I KEEP HEARING THE WORD OVER AND OVER IN MY HEAD. THERE'S no way I can do this. No way I can stand in front of a room full of people, this hollow shell of a woman, and smile as if nothing has changed. There's no way I can laugh and play along with the façade of a happy couple deeply in love.

They'll see through me; I know they will.

I've always been acutely aware of my public persona. My mother used to tell me it was important for the family name. All my life I've known how to hide behind a beautiful face and stay polite even when offended. I know just what to say, and how to act.

But right now? This moment? No. I can't go through with it. I can't pretend anymore. Pretending's what got me into this mess.

"You look beautiful." Mason's deep baritone voice sends a thrill through my body. His approval always has, and my natural instinct is to cling to him right now. I want to hide behind him. He could make everything all right or at least that's the way it would feel.

Even more than that, I so desperately care for him despite everything that's happened, and that's what's breaking me.

"Thank you," I whisper and then clear my throat, turning my gaze back to the entrance of the Regency Auditorium as the limo stops in front of the building, my fingertips haphazardly grazing the crystals on my dress with nerves that won't be tamed.

I used to live for this. All the gorgeous gowns and flowing champagne, the photographs and mingling. Now instead of desire and excitement and anticipation, all I feel is dread.

I turn back to Mason just as he places his large hand over mine, and in that moment I remember who he is and what he's done and why everything has changed. I want to pull away. My body and mind are confused. I feel attacked and cornered, but I don't know who to blame other than myself.

"It's going to be all right. You're fine," Mason tells me. His voice is a soothing balm, but it's a lie. A sweet, pretty lie meant to calm me down so I can do as I'm told and act appropriately.

Pulling my hand away from him, I watch his face fall and the divider rolls down slowly; it's the only sound in the cabin.

"Is this all right, Mr. Thatcher?" Marcus, the driver, asks. I can't look him in the eye. I swallow thickly, watching the sparkling gowns flow by as women walk past. I know many of them, or at least recognize their faces. Tonight is a fundraiser for diabetic children. Nearly three hundred people will be in the grand ballroom, bidding on donations lined with spotlights and making small talk while sipping champagne and gossiping or bragging.

It's how these functions run. Who you know and who you talk to can be different, so long as you're seen with each group of individuals accordingly.

My role has changed from socialite sweetheart who brings the press to that of devoted arm candy. The to-do list hasn't changed, though: look pretty, smile and be charming. It didn't seem so bad all these years I've been doing this. Even my father used to bring me to events like this as a teen. I loved it. I was proud to come and be a part of the social scene especially when they involved causes like this one.

"This is fine," Mason answers Marcus and I grip my Chanel clutch as if it will protect me and save me from having to walk out there. "I'll open her door; thank you."

"I don't know that I'm ready," I whisper to Mason, turning to him and leaning in, acutely aware that Marcus is watching. I don't have to look up to see his eyes in the rearview mirror assessing the situation to know he's taking it all in. Everyone is always watching.

Mason searches my face for something, and then the corners of his lips twitch as he reaches his arm around my waist and pulls me in closer to him.

His strength and heat and proximity all make my blood temperature rise, and the anxiety and fear are replaced with something else entirely.

"You're definitely ready," Mason says before leaning into me for a kiss. A split second passes before I even question it. It feels so natural, as if I'm the one who intended for it to happen.

As if nothing ever happened. As if the envelope had never been opened and this part of the tale ceased to exist.

I pull away suddenly, sucking in the hot air and pushing back against the leather seat. My eyes flicker to the mirror as I regain my composure, to Marcus's ever-prying view and immediately the divider begins to move back into place, granting us privacy.

Mason's hand splays on my back before I can move any farther. "Please stop," I say. He must know what he's doing to me.

"Stop what?" he asks as if he doesn't know that his kindness is worse than anything else. That craving his affection only makes me hate myself more.

I look up through my lashes, not bothering to face him as I hold the clutch tighter with both hands.

"I can't do this, Mason," I blurt out with my voice low and pleading. "I can't pretend."

He rests his hand on the back of my neck, gripping my nape but running his thumb back and forth ever so gently. Each action sends mixed signals, and that's the very crux of my position.

"You could ignore me all night," he suggests with a sad smile. "It would be better if you did that… if we were to split in a month anyway. Wouldn't it?"

His words are accompanied by a shadow, the night already darkening. Three weeks. I don't correct him, but it's three weeks that are left, not a month. Swallowing thickly, I glance at the entrance rather than entertaining his suggestion.

"Either way," he continues, "we have to attend. We can't appear to be hiding and no one is going to hurt you here."

The lights from the massive crystal chandelier just inside the auditorium's foyer sparkle and blur in a beautiful dance as two more couples enter. I ignore it and stare at the shrubbery that's barely visible.

It hurts to hear him plan a split between us. I didn't think his compromise, promise, whatever it was, was even a real possibility. Yet here he is, speaking it into existence.

Mason opens his door and leaves me without another word. I simultaneously fear him and love him, but worse, I hate myself for having any emotion toward him other than revulsion knowing he's a murderer. That's what I can't get past. It's easy to put a smile on your face and be what everyone else wants you to be when you know who you are and you're happy as that person. When you have faith in yourself.

I've lost that. It's a new low that's left me shattered and scattered into small pieces on the floor. I don't even know where to start picking them up. I only know the sharp edges will leave me bleeding out as I do.

Cool air drifts into the limo and the light shines just a bit brighter as Mason opens my door. With the wind comes his scent, a natural masculine scent mixed with a clean fragrance from his cologne.

"Don't deny me, sweetheart," Mason says just under his breath as I stare at his outstretched hand. His statement makes my eyes lift to his and I get lost in his swirls of gray and silver. I never had a chance with this man. A tortured soul lies behind those eyes that makes me weak for him. He needs love so desperately; he needs someone, and my very soul craves his.

He was my downfall. Created to destroy me. I slip my hand into his, comforted by the warmth as he wraps his fingers slowly around mine and supports me as I rise from the limo. I keep my eyes down and don't look forward. I can hardly focus on breathing as my heels click on the pavement and Mason leads me forward.

I pull my black bolero shrug tighter around my shoulders and attempt to hide from the harsh weather while ignoring everyone around me.

The doors open and the mix of chatter and the soft melody of an orchestra carry through the air and envelop me as though it's home, as though it's safe. But I'm very much aware that I'm in danger. I scan every face for the one I saw only days ago. The man holding a gun.

At the thought I grip Mason's hand tighter and he pulls me in closer to him, walking in time with me, our steps in unison as the lights get brighter and the air warmer. A small smile slips onto my face, although inside I'm screaming.

I'm dying from the hypocrisy, but intensely aware it's my only chance of survival.

"Mason," I hear a man call out and my smile falters only slightly as my steps are halted. We're to be seen. Unwaveringly present.

"Father," Mason says tightly and I stand there with a sweetness in my composure, tilting my head slightly as the breeze from the doors being opened again sends a chill up my back. My shoulders shudder and Mason wraps his hand around my hip, pulling me in closer.

I don't flinch when his father looks at me. In a crisp suit complete with a charming smile, he appears to be an entirely different man than the one I met before.

"Miss Summers, you look utterly breathtaking this evening," his father says and naturally my smile widens. It's a shame a man like him can possess such poise and charm. I suppose everyone needs some way to survive and thrive.

My heart beats faster and my limbs scream at me to run, or worse, slap the bastard across the face for what he did only days ago, but instead I part my lips and respond sweetly, "I'm so sorry for the other day. I'm afraid I wasn't well."

He falters, the real emotions showing through and just when I think he's going to hide it, when I think the mask that slipped will be forced back into place, he leans in slightly and says, "I do apologize as well," and I swear it seems sincere. "I had no right to come between you two."

Mason stiffens beside me, and my own composure threatens to dissolve. I've never faced this kind of mastery of manipulation before. I don't know whether to react sincerely or how to play this game.

"I only want what's best for my son."

It's only then that I realize our games are different. I'm no match for him, but in the same vein, he's no match for me.

"Champagne?" a server asks on my right, breaking the moment and I instantly turn to her.

"No, thank you," spills from my mouth easily and she's quick to move on after the men each shake their heads.

I watch from my periphery as she leaves, walking easily without a care and holding the tray just so. The champagne doesn't even seem to move; she's learned to do her job well.

"Excuse me a moment, Mason," I tell him, patting his forearm and waiting for him to release my hand. He doesn't, though.

He holds me a moment longer than he should, quietly watching me and waiting for a reason. "I need to use the restroom," I whisper to him as softly and flirtatiously as I can, feeling the number of eyes on us grow. It may all be in my head, because for all I know I'm losing it, and with every second my anxiety grows.

"Of course," he says although the reflection in his eyes is something else. Something far more vulnerable and unwilling. He kisses my hand, bringing it to his lips and then releasing me without another word.

I force a smile to stay in place although it begs to fall. Everything in me is screaming that something is wrong. I walk as quickly as I can to the back of the room, deeper and deeper through the crowd of beautiful guests. I turn my body slightly when needed and ignore the conversations around me as I head to the restrooms.

I could just run. I could run away.

Away from all of this, and never stop.

I'll find myself again, but not here. Not when I know I want the very thing that will bury me.

chapter 15

So close to having everything,
So close to nothing at all.
The teeter-totter rocks back and forth,
While knowing you will fall.

It's all there within your grasp,
But the life has turned to stone.
You should have known, you foolish man,
You were meant to live alone.

"I APPRECIATE THE APOLOGY," I TELL MY FATHER, ALTHOUGH MY GAZE isn't on him at all. My eyes are on Jules's back as her hips sway and she leaves me.

When I first laid eyes on her, she blended in so easily. Each small motion was seemingly genuine. Not tonight.

My sweetheart is obviously full of hurt and pain and insecurity. In a room full of fake assholes brimming with confidence and arrogance, my Jules doesn't belong.

I wonder if everyone else in this room can see it as clearly as I do. I was wrong to bring her. I could have found another way. My father's voice interrupts my thoughts. "Miss Harrington will be there, and she made it clear she's interested."

Marcy Harrington's an investor who likes to get close with her clients and "know" them before writing a check with her family inheritance. Promiscuous would be a kind word to use. In addition, she's practically untouchable, and always gets what and who she wants.

"This is about appearances, not business. I couldn't give two shits about business right now."

"Appearances?" my father asks, and I feel my hands clench at my sides. He knows damn well what the papers are saying.

"I'd like the world to know that I'm not beating her behind closed doors."

My father shrugs as if the rumor swirling around the city isn't a concern in the least. "I'd like to know what you are doing behind closed doors. Or more importantly… what's being said between you two," he says, turning his body to follow my gaze. She's vanished though, wherever she's gone.

As my eyes drift back to him, I feel the accusations rise. *Now's not the time or place*, I think over and over as my forehead furrows and I shove my hands into my pockets to keep from grabbing him. My muscles are tense, and the words are on the tip of my tongue.

There's no use in letting them out though, because I know he'll just lie. He's damn good at it and so used to it, I doubt he knows the truth from a lie anymore.

"We should have a meeting soon," I say easily, completely at odds with my true feelings. "Business and otherwise."

My father's brows raise slightly, and he looks genuinely surprised. "Of course," he says, patting me on the back. "I trust it's about the matter from the other night?" he asks although it's said as a statement.

"It is," I say, feeling the ball of rage grow larger, getting harder to contain. I clear my throat and glance back to where Jules disappeared, only to see her good friend and editor Katerina striding toward me.

My face stays neutral, with no emotions expressed whatsoever as she approaches.

"I'll talk to you soon," my father says beneath his breath, turning his back to Kat and walking away without waiting for me to acknowledge him.

Kat approaches me with an expression of distrust, an air about her that makes it obvious she's here because she hasn't heard from Jules. I thought about responding to her messages myself. Jules received texts from so many people feigning concern, but really wanting gossip. And then her friends, who seem genuinely worried.

Before she stops in front of me, I force a small smile to my lips, one that's welcoming. I'm already losing my sweetheart; I need to play this right.

"Mason." Kat states my name as if she's ready for a fight, but that's not how this is going to go down. She just doesn't know it yet.

"I'm so happy you're here, Kat," I say and nod my head slightly. "Have you seen Jules already?" I play up the concern in my own voice and expression, and watch as her anger slips and her forehead pinches. She finally looks behind her for only a moment before turning her attention back to me.

"We just got here. She's here?"

"You came with Evan?" I ask her. Her husband is well known in the public relations industry, although he travels with an entirely different sort of social circle.

The industry has treated him well, but he's rarely home. That's the angle I have. Two couples; the men friends, the women friends. She'll trust me. She'll help me. At least I pray she will.

"I did," she says and peers to her right, closer to the entrance before clearing her throat and adding, "He's here somewhere." She licks her lips and squares her shoulders, remembering what she's come here to yell at me about.

I cut her off before she can begin by saying, "I'd really like it if you could talk to Jules." Jules's name on my lips and the thought of someone talking to her privately makes apprehension creep into my veins at the possibility of her spilling the truth. I shrug it off and use the intensity of the truth to help create the lie. "She's taking the wedding situation a little bit hard."

Kat watches me for a moment, her eyes narrowing as she assesses my words. I lean forward, dropping my voice and letting the insecurity that is all too real show. "She's not okay," I tell her. "She could really use a friend right now."

"I haven't spoken to her in over a week," Kat says, confiding in me and I don't let on that I know it's uncommon for Jules not to return a call. I play my emotions as I should.

"I'm not sure she *wants* to talk about it"—I can see Kat's objection on the tip of her tongue and I say it before she can—"but she needs to."

Kat's mouth stays parted and she tilts her head, still judging my request as her husband walks up behind her.

"Evan." I pull back from Kat and press my lips into an acceptable smile. One that reflects my unease for what Jules is going through. At least that's what it shows Kat. A part of me feels like a prick, like the manipulative asshole I am, undeserving of Jules. But I already knew I wasn't good enough for her, and this show, this front, is all to save us. To save what we have.

"Thatcher, how are you, man?"

A huff of a grunt leaves me as I rock back on my heels and shove my hands in my suit pockets. "That's my father's name," I say jokingly and Evan laughs deep from his chest, raising a tumbler of amber liquid to his lips. The ice clinks in his glass as he wraps his arm around his wife's waist.

"You two make quite the couple," I say, complimenting them. They have definitely been the talk of the city on more than one occasion.

"Speaking of couples," Evan says, and his cuff slips back over his wrist as he lowers the whiskey, hiding the sleeve tattoo. His left arm is covered in tattoos. His background is perfect for his profession. He's from Brooklyn with the reputation of a man who grew up on the wrong side of the law. He made a name for himself, but only in the best of ways for his job.

He never got caught. Never had a conviction, and he knows the ins and outs of the press.

That's the kind of man the industry wants representing their clients when they're out of the spotlight. Someone to party with and respect and be genuine friends with. But someone who knows when to leave the scene before it gets too rough, what to tell the press and who to go to when shit goes down.

He's damn good at what he does, but how the two of them have stayed married, I have no idea.

"Where did Jules go?" Kat interjects before her husband can finish his thought. He glances at her from the corner of his eye and then releases her, taking a sip of whiskey and looking past me as Kat steps forward. She has no idea how she's affected him.

"Just to the restroom," I say and motion to the back with my chin.

"How's she been?"

"I think she's really taking this transition hard… moving on and getting married again." I could choke on the words.

"I'm sorry to hear that." Evan's condolences are sincere, but I'm more than certain he doesn't want a part in this conversation.

"You better be good to her," Kat says, the declaration sounding like a threat.

I turn my attention back to her. "I'll take care of her, I promise," I assure her, meeting her prying gaze. I can see the moment my lies slip into place and Kat reaches up to give me a quick hug.

"I'll talk to her," she says firmly, nodding her head and giving me a sympathetic look.

"Thank you," I say and hide the fact that dread is slowly consuming me. Jules was willing to tell the police before. Her dear friend who's concerned for her well-being… I'm certain she'll tell her something.

chapter 16

Julia

MY BODY GETS HOTTER AND HOTTER WITH EACH STEP I TAKE. Leaning against the counter, I listen to the water rushing from the faucet; it fills the empty restroom with white noise. *Just breathe. Just breathe.* I've never wanted to run so badly. That's all I can think about.

My heels click as I walk casually out of the side exit, smiling as best as I can although I'm not meeting the eyes of any of the guests who are having quiet conversations in the hall. As they sip on their cocktails and throw their heads back in jovial laughter, I want to walk faster; my body begs me to run. It takes great effort to keep my pace easy and pretend that nothing's wrong as I tuck my hair back and say thank you to the doorman when I head outside.

Goosebumps prickle along my skin as the bitter cold greets me. I pull the shrug tighter and maintain my composure when the look from the young man holding the door is riddled with questions.

It's too cold for me to be outside without a coat; I'm certain that's what he's thinking. But I cling to my clutch, the beaded fabric nearly slipping from the sweat on my hands.

My heart races and all I can hear is the blood rushing in my ears as the door closes behind me. The dark night lays before me, the busy street only a block away and through a small alley.

This exit isn't meant for departing guests. It's meant for smoking and the faint smell gets stronger as I take a few steps farther out into the night. Away from the gala, from the spotlight and from Mason.

Glancing to my left purely out of instinct from knowing someone's there incites shock and fear both. Liam Olsen stares back at me. He pushes off of the wall, exhaling a puff of smoke that mixes with the fog of his breath. The bright red and orange embers of the cigarette travel through the air as he walks toward me. His oxford shoes crunch the snow beneath his heavy steps.

I turn to face him, my eyes flitting between him and the exit I've just left. I'm not sure anyone can see me from here. There's no light, only darkness where I've gone.

The moonlight makes Liam's skin look pale and his eyes dark as he walks closer to me. I swallow the dread in my throat and greet him accordingly. "How are you, Mr. Olsen?" My skin feels numb with the cold, yet alive with fear. I've never actually met the man, but I know the business he had with Mason dissolving has left its mark on him.

"Where's Mason?" Liam asks harshly, tossing his cigarette to the side where it's instantly extinguished by the wet snow. Smoke billows from his nostrils as he comes closer, close enough to get a glimpse of his eyes. They're nearly blood-shot and his walk uneven, but his question is forceful. I'm not sure if he's drunk or angry. Maybe both.

"Whatever happened between you two…" I can't finish the thought.

My voice is caught in my throat for a moment, my eyes going back to the exit where I can clearly see the guests. My heart pounds once then twice as time seems to pass in slow motion and I have to think quick. Liam takes a large step forward, closing the distance between us and I instantly take one back, although it's on the edge of the sidewalk and my heel slips. I almost fall backward, and he catches me.

He chuckles and reeks of liquor. I push my hands against his chest as I find purchase on the sidewalk, turning my body so he's no longer between me and the exit.

He's drunk and he's angry, so I'm careful as I pry his hands off me as respect-fully as possible and desperately try to put more space between us.

"He's coming," I tell Liam breathlessly. I have to clear my throat and repeat myself to sound surer of what I'm saying, but it doesn't fool Liam. Either that, or he doesn't care.

"You really want a man like that?" he asks me. "After what he's done?" he says and squints his eyes, and my throat closes with fear with the tone he takes. *What does he know?*

"What?" I say, licking my lips although in the cold air it only makes them feel chapped. "What exactly did he do?" I ask Liam, taking another step back. I watch as he looks toward the door and then takes another step closer to me, his hands slipping into the pockets of his slacks. "Business partnerships don't always—"

"I'm going to make him pay," he says, cutting me off and raising his brow as he reaches in his pocket for something. I involuntarily tense up, but it's only a pack of cigarettes. He takes one out, then offers the pack to me as he slips a cig between his lips and tilts his head back.

"No thank you," I tell him, "I was just heading inside."

"No you weren't," he says as he lights the cigarette, the tiny flame illuminating his face. He takes the cigarette out of his mouth, pinching it between his forefinger and thumb as he says, "You just came out here."

"I made a mistake." I'm quick to answer and it only makes him smile.

"Yeah you did," he says and the smile morphs from cocky to something else. Something sinister.

"I have to go," I say and turn my back to him, heading for the door. But I only take a single step before his hand is wrapped around my hip, pulling me backward and into his hard chest.

"Get off me!" I yell out and drop my clutch as I try to pry his fingers away from me. He's holding me with a bruising force, the tips of his fingers digging into the flesh at my hips.

"Hey now," Liam says, nearly laughing the words as he spits out the cigarette and covers my mouth with his other hand. "Hush, hush, it's okay," he whispers against the shell of my ear. The cocktail of smoke and lingering alcohol mixes and fills my lungs as I heave in a breath. This is not happening.

I yank my elbow back with everything I have and shove it into Liam's gut. He releases me and I don't waste a second, I run for the door straight in front of me. My shrug falls off and I've already lost my clutch, but as far as I'm concerned, it can stay wherever it is forever.

My palms slap against the glass door, forcing my body to come to a halt and the doorman looks at me with complete surprise as I stand there doubled over and desperate for air.

I'm shaking and completely wrecked. I've dealt with drunken men and roaming hands before. But never from a man angry with my supposed fiancé. I can barely wrap my head around what happened. He grabbed me. He held his hand over my mouth.

The door opens and even though I feel like I'm going to be sick, I walk in, trying to hide what's happened, but completely unable to compose myself. My legs are shaky and I still struggle to come to terms with being grabbed like that. I don't know what to do. I grip onto the man's arm and try to clear my head from the fog of shock, but I'm not given long before a strong grip pulls me away from him.

I yell out in surprise and fear until I realize it's Mason. He holds my forearms and forces me to look at him, and I lose it.

"Jules?" He says my name, compassion and worry evident. I shake my head, and say the only thing I can think of. "Liam—" I say but then my voice croaks, unable to get out the rest of the words. Unable to express what just happened moments ago.

Tears leak from the corners of my eyes, and his concern turns to anger. I can't say for certain what he was going to do, but there's not a chance he didn't know I was scared. He knew he crossed a boundary. "He… he—"

Mason releases me quickly, slamming his arm into the door and forcing it to fly open as I nearly fall to the gleaming marble floor.

"Jules!" I hear Kat call my name from behind me. I hear the commotion around us. I can see from the reflection in the glass a crowd's come to watch.

I can't respond, I can't even turn to her or form a single thought concerning all of them.

Even as she pulls me to stand straighter and puts her face close to mine, grabbing onto me and trying to get my attention, I can't give it to her. All I can do is watch Mason disappear and wish he'd just come back. *I need him.*

Kat grips my face with both her hands and forces me to look at her. I stare into her worried eyes and confess in a ragged breath, "I'm not okay."

chapter 17

Mason

Anger cannot be denied,
It cannot be contained.
Carnal sins and violent ways,
Its brutality cannot be chained.

It's passion that drives the fist,
It's fear that leaves the cage.
Every movement desperate,
Pain seeping through the rage.

EVERY HOT BREATH TURNS TO WHITE FOG IN FRONT OF MY FACE, AND it pisses me off. It obstructs my view of the bastard standing right in front of me. His back is to me as he taps a carton of cigarettes against his palm. He should have run while he had the chance.

"Liam," I call out, my chest rising and falling, my lungs filling with ice-cold air.

Knowing him, he'd fucking love for me to make a scene. I'm sure I'm playing right into his hand, and I don't give a damn.

He's drunk and looks high. His suit's disheveled as he turns to me with a half-cocked smile on his lips.

"Don't you ever fucking touch her!" I say as I walk forward and get closer to him. I have no intention of talking. I don't need to find out what happened or why. All I know is that she was terrified. And the only thing she could say was his name.

He's a dead man.

"How do you know what she came out here for?" he asks with a smirk, and I swing my fist as hard as I can into his pretty-boy smile.

I grab his collar, using it to hold him still as I hammer my fist into his face over and over again.

I smash my knuckles against his cheekbones, his nose, his mouth, the skin splitting open on contact. At first he shoved against me, a pathetic attempt to push me away. He doesn't stand a chance.

I can feel her slipping away, and I'm so fucking desperate to hold on to her. I clutch his throat, forcing him still.

My teeth grit against one another as adrenaline pumps in my blood. *Crack!* His nose breaks as my knuckles collide with his face and I lose my hold on him. The back of his head slams into the ground. I don't stop, I can't. All I can see is red. I lower myself to the ground but he gets in a punch, surprising me. His fist crashes against my cheek and whips my head to the side.

I barely feel it. The taste of metallic hot blood fills my mouth, but that doesn't stop me either. All it does is fuel me.

"She's mine!" I scream out and Liam's eyes widen with fear. I must sound crazy. Even to my own ears, the words I yell out are those of a madman. The worst part, the most sickening, is that I don't care. Maybe I have lost it. Maybe I am crazy when it comes to Jules. I'm perfectly fucking fine with that.

I yank him up by the collar, my knees sinking into the freezing snow and the thick silk fabric of my suit pants slowly absorbing the melting snow. He slams another fist into my face, so low on my chin he nearly catches my throat, and I return the blow by headbutting his nose.

He screams out in pain and I drop him to the ground.

My breathing is erratic, my vision blurred. I know I've won, but I can't stop because never in my life has it been more apparent than seeing Jules quaking with fear that I'm losing. I'm losing it all.

I pull back to smash my fist against his jaw again. To hear the satisfying crack, but two arms wrap around my chest and pull my back into a hard wall of muscle.

"It's just me. Just calm down," someone says from behind me. An angry growl rumbles through my chest as I throw my head back to smash the fucker's nose in. He leans away and I buck him off of me, ready to beat the piss out of him too.

Until I see who it is. It's Evan, and I can hear Kat screaming at him to break us up. They need to stay out of it.

"He tried to hurt her! He put his fucking hands on her!" All the boiling rage rises to the surface and I take it out on Evan. Everyone needs to stay the fuck away.

Liam deserves everything that's coming to him.

I get one more punch in when Liam lurches for me, and his head snaps back from the blow. It lands square on his chin, and my knuckles scream from the sharp impact against his jaw. His lip splits, but it throws him off. As I lunge forward,

Evan's hand grabs my fist and he twists his body to the side, making me fall forward. He pins my arm behind my back and again grabs me, my back to his chest.

My breath comes in heavy pants and I struggle harder when I hear Jules cry out. I can't see her, and I can't see Liam. I shove backward, but Evan's a strong bastard.

"Knock it off," I hear him grit through his teeth as the sound of a car pulling up catches my attention. I lift my eyes and see the headlights, but no one gets out. No sirens. It's not the cops… yet.

"Think about Jules," he tells me, his breath close to the back of my neck as I push back against his grip. "It's only about Jules, all right?" he says as I stop struggling.

I stare down at the ground, at Liam laying in the snow that's speckled with red. He's propped up on an elbow and on his side. In the bright streaks of light from the limo headlights, the blood shines a bright red against the pure white snow.

Liam spits, and another splash of red paints the ground.

"Mason," Jules calls out as she runs over to me, and the second my attention goes to her, Evan releases me.

My muscles are still wound tight and ready to go off. My fists still clenched even as she runs into my chest. I kiss her hair as I hear the limo door open and far too many people—too many witnesses—gather around.

"Leave," Evan tells me in a low voice. "It's mine, I'll take yours." He nods behind me and I glance at the white stretch limo before nodding my head. The rough stubble on my chin brushes against Jules's hair. I meet his crystal blue eyes as he says through clenched teeth, "Go! Just get the fuck out of here."

chapter 18

Julia

Intentions—cruel, helpless, hopeful,
They come in different shades.
They leave the nights with bright light,
And sharpen the dullest blades.

They bend your will and change your plans,
And make you do bad things.
They don't change the outcome,
Nor stop what justice brings.

MY THUMBNAIL NERVOUSLY SCRAPES AGAINST MY FINGERNAILS ONE at a time. I don't have polish on, although I wish I did so I could pick it off. I've always done this. A nervous habit, I suppose.

My eyes drift back to Mason. His head is back against the headrest and it jostles as the limo drives over a speed bump. His hands are clasped in his lap, the knuckles torn and bloodied and his eyes are focused on the roof of the cabin.

His cheek is already bruised. There's a split on the left side of his lips. My fingers itch to touch it. To comfort him.

He hasn't said a word. Silence is the only thing that accompanies us.

I swallow thickly as his head turns to the side and he stares at me. A burning sensation prickles over my skin and begs me to look away, but I can't. It's hopeless.

He licks his lower lip, the tip of his tongue sliding down the cut as he sets his hand on my thigh. I watch as he swallows and then breathes in heavily, all the while holding my gaze. Even blind eyes could see he is a damaged man.

"Are you okay?" he asks in a low voice, deep and heavy and riddled with pain.

"Are you?" I question back with just as much sincerity, but Mason presses on.

"I mean after Liam grabbed you?"

The lump in my throat expands as the memory comes flooding back.

I shake my head immediately, closing my eyes only to recall the unhinged look in Liam's eyes. I shudder and wrap my arms around myself. Mason immediately pulls me into him, holding me. He never fails to comfort me. I breathe easier enveloped in his warmth and resting my head on his chest. I love that he comforts me but just this once, I want to be the one comforting him.

He rocks me softly back and forth for a moment. As I calm down, the guilt weighs heavily on me. Both times now that I've tried to leave Mason, I've come to face regret and remorse for my actions.

"I shouldn't have gone outside," I say, letting the confession drift between us.

"Why were you out there?" Mason asks me, and it only solidifies the offense. I don't answer. Instead I look away, my cheek still resting on his shoulder and his arms still around me.

I hear him swallow and let out a strangled breath before rocking me again ever so slightly. He doesn't let go of me though, and he doesn't question me again. I'm grateful for both.

"I'm sorry," I whisper as I watch the lights of the city slip past us in a blur on our way back to his home.

His deep voice rumbles, "Are you?" There's no animosity there, no curiosity either. Simply a flat question devoid of all the emotion he just gave me a moment ago.

"I am."

A moment passes in silence and the limo rocks us as it passes over another speed bump before Mason kisses my hair and moves me to settle in his lap.

"It's okay," Mason says, running his hand down my hair to my back as he consoles me. He plants a soft kiss on my shoulder and my neck, and then a sweet kiss on my lips before looking me in the eyes. He gives me a sad smile and then kisses me once more before saying, "It's okay, I understand."

His forgiveness is what shatters me. His love and devotion to my happiness are what will ruin me entirely.

"Are you okay?" I ask him genuinely once again, desperate to put the attention and comfort on him. I'll never forget the look in his eyes when he left me. The primal man he became. The way he fought Liam… because of me. My voice catches in my throat as I finally lean toward him and let the tips of my fingers trail over the faint bruise. "I'm sorry," I whisper.

He turns his head, capturing my fingers with his hand and kissing their tips before looking at me. "You have nothing to be sorry for, Jules." His eyes brim with sincerity. "You never did," he says.

Tears prick my eyes, and I don't know which cause is in the forefront. The fear of what happened tonight? The desire to run away from what my life has become?

Or the love I feel for this man.

Maybe it's something instinctual for a woman to want to stay with someone who would fight to protect them. Maybe I feel I owe him for what he's done. All I know is that I can't deny what I feel.

His cold gray eyes stare deep into my own as he cups my chin in his hand and his gaze falls to my lips. He says softly, "I need you, Jules. Even if it's not real…" his voice chokes at the word but he continues with a pained look in his eyes, "Right now, I just need to feel like you love me again."

His hand slips behind my head, holding me still as his fingers tangle in my locks and his hot lips press against mine. I mold my lips to his and part them when he traces the seam with his tongue. My body obeys his and he takes full advantage, pushing against me until my back hits the seat and he settles his hips between my legs. He pins my hips down as he rocks against me, all the while stealing kisses and deepening the intensity. I break away to breathe.

My chest rises as he nibbles along my neck, desire shooting through me and making my nipples pebble.

"I love you, Jules," he whispers into the crook of my neck.

My heart aches. I want to love this man, not because of him, not because of his actions, but because of how I feel about him. A true love-hate relationship. Hot and cold.

I can see myself falling into his arms while simultaneously making plans to sneak out of his bed late at night. I'm ruined beyond repair, and I only blame myself.

chapter 19

Mason

It slips through my fingers,
That which I cannot hold.
I cry for it, would die for it,
This love I can't control.

THE ONLY FRIEND I EVER HAD IS DEAD TO ME.

The woman I love tried again to leave me, and only came back because she was threatened.

My father may be trying to kill the woman I love. If not him, then someone else.

I've run my business into the ground and with my reputation in the shitter, I don't think I'll ever come back from it.

Last, a secret is out there that could destroy me, evidence that I murdered a man, and I haven't a clue who it is that knows or what they have on me. I'm waiting in the dark, and I can feel my sanity slipping away.

I imagine this is what they mean when they say rock bottom. I slip the heavy law textbook back into its place on the bookshelf as I hear my father's office door open and then close. I don't turn around to face him. I don't have to in order to know it's him.

My father's voice bellows from behind me. "You need to relax, Mason. That shit you pulled—"

"What does it matter?" I say, cutting him off and turning to face him as his forehead creases with anger.

"You look like you've lost it," he hisses at me, slapping the newspaper in his hand down onto his desk as he takes his seat.

"I have though, haven't I?" It's the conclusion I come to, knowing Jules was going to leave me. Again. That's what did me in this time. I take in a heavy breath.

It's all the lies too. Keeping track of them has pulled its weight in bringing me down.

I don't even know what's the truth anymore or who to trust. I only know that I hate everyone I'm surrounded by except for the one person who's desperate to leave me.

"I need the truth," I say, getting straight to the point as I stare my father in the eyes. Although I know it doesn't matter, I add, "Don't lie to me."

"I wouldn't lie to you, Ma—" my father starts, intent on saying something else, but I cut him off.

"You lie to everyone; why would I be any different?" I shrug my shoulders and stride closer to his desk, my pace quick and careless.

"What's on your mind then?" he asks, his eyes narrowed and his frustration barely contained. He must see how on edge I am. I can practically smell the fear coming off of him. The fear of not knowing what I'm going to ask, or maybe of what I'm going to do. "You called this meeting," he adds as he sits back in his cognac leather chair. He unbuttons his suit jacket and adopts a casual posture.

"Did you kill her?" I ask him in a whisper.

He cocks a brow at me before answering in a deathly low voice, "I've never killed anyone."

I don't know why his answer makes my lips tip up into a smile. It's sickening that he doesn't take responsibility. I nod my head, and a rough laugh spills from my lips. "I do apologize," I say as I pace in front of his desk, letting my fingers run over the edges of the leather chair opposite his and then the next. "You *had* her killed."

"You'll have to be more specific as to whom you're referring," my father says as he flicks a switch.

"You think I'm wearing a wire?" I ask incredulously. As if the police could help. As if I wouldn't be completely ruined if I turned to them.

"I don't know what to think about you right now."

I stop in my tracks and face him, bracing a hand on each chair. "I don't either," I say barely above a murmur.

"You were saying?" he says before his eyes shift to the door. This time I know why the smile comes. It's because he wants to get rid of me. He's done with me. It's about fucking time.

"You killed my mother," I say, getting the accusation out into the open once and for all.

"I didn't. I can't believe you'd think that." I stare at him, hearing how false his words sound as they ring in my ears. "There's a difference between killing your own and protecting your own." My father's voice turns hard and at first I think he's justifying having her murdered, but then I realize he's talking about Avery. "Your mother hurt me," he says and leans forward, placing his hand against his chest as he adds, "but I loved her. I would have never done that to her. Or to you."

"I don't believe you," I tell him. "I think you murdered her, and I think you want Jules dead too."

"You have her under control, don't you?" my father says although he knows damn well I don't. After last night, the whole city is talking and now Liam is the topic of the day, not her or me. But three people know what really happened last night.

Jules. Myself. And my father. He knows she wants to leave me. He just doesn't know why.

He doesn't wait for an answer, instead he pulls out a desk drawer and reaches in, rifling through paperwork while he talks. "I looked into Liam's books and subsequent finances." A thick stack of papers lands on his desk with a thud and then he slams the drawer closed. "Would you sit down, Mason? You're going to kill me with this," he says and waves his hands in the air. "Just calm down."

"Calm down?" I ask him before swallowing down the pain, pinching the bridge of my nose as I close my eyes. I've never felt quite like this. Only because the harsh reality has never been so clear to me.

"Mason," my father says my name as if it's a plea, "I promise you, I will protect you with everything I have. If that includes protecting her, I will. You're my son. My one and only, and the only thing I have to live for anymore."

"Whatever it is that's gotten into you," my father continues as he breaks eye contact and shakes his head. "I said I'm sorry about Avery," he adds and presses his lips into a thin line. "You weren't here when she came in." He turns in his chair and looks out of the window. "Or Anderson." He runs a hand down his face and stares out at the city skyline.

"There are choices we make that have to be done quickly." He swallows thickly. "I was only trying to protect you."

I finally take the seat opposite him slowly and wait for him to face me. "No. Stop protecting me." I shake my head slowly and hold his gaze. "I don't want your idea of protection."

"Well maybe this will help," he says as he slides the papers over to me. "Liam Olsen is in the hole, and his life is falling apart."

I hesitantly look through the stack, lifting the corner of the top sheet to look at the next and the one after that. They're all copies of bill after bill he's racked up over the last year.

"We need to talk about what happened the other night before the gala."

It takes me a moment before I realize he's talking about the man with the gun.

The intruder with a syringe. An obvious fucking hit. "Someone was hired to kill Jules. I don't know who or why, but it was a hit."

"Are you sure?" my father asks me.

"He could have killed me, he could have turned when I was chasing him and shot me. But then again he could have killed Jules too."

"Then why didn't he?"

I remember the syringe, the heroin. I shift in my seat, staring at my father as I tell him, "He had a syringe on him. He didn't want the hit to be obvious."

My father's expression doesn't change; he doesn't give anything away. "A syringe?"

"Filled with heroin," I tell him and this time he breaks eye contact. He pulls his jacket down and clears his throat, obviously uncomfortable.

"Your mother," he starts to say but doesn't finish. I give him a moment, again remembering the way my mother lay there on the tiled bathroom floor. "So, this is where that shit is coming from?" His question is laced with feigned anger. More than anything, it's a veil over his sadness.

I nod once, not trusting myself to respond verbally.

He nods, although he doesn't look me in the eyes. "Your mother..." he starts to say again and then stops. He waves the thought away, shaking his head and dropping the discussion entirely. I've never seen my father so visibly shaken.

"I don't see why anyone would want you or Jules dead other than Olsen. Even then, it would have to be because of money and I've made it clear to him that the debt owed to me is void. So killing you would most likely be related to some sort of quarrel between the two of you." He finally looks me in the eyes again before adding, "After last night, there must be something between you two... Undoubtedly."

I don't know what possessed Liam to go after Jules last night. I didn't take him for that kind of a man. An arrogant ass, yes. A man who'd hurt a woman? I huff at the thought. Any man who would do something like that isn't a man.

"If not Olsen, who else?"

Every hair stands on end and a chill flows down my skin. I question telling my father about Anderson, the entire truth. I have no one else, my back's against a wall, and this is for Jules. I would do anything for Jules. If that means confessing murder to a murderer, so be it.

I look my father in the eye as I tell him, "I killed Jace Anderson and someone knows."

I wait for a reaction and the only one I get is that his brows raise slightly and he tilts his head to the side, considering.

"I see," he says after a moment and again turns away from his seat. His foot taps against the desk as he thinks. "Over Avery, I assume?" he says.

I nod once. He has the dignity to look ashamed for a split second.

"You didn't love her. You didn't want her. You told me that much."

"That doesn't make it right," I say and grip the armrests, feeling the anger rise, but he holds up his hands in both defense and understanding.

It's quiet for a moment, with only the ticking of the clock counting the seconds to keep us company as my father takes in the truth of what happened.

Finally, he looks up and says, "You could have come to me."

"I was angry at you too," I say and his eyes spark with indignation at my admission.

As if just now putting the pieces together, his expression changes and he asks, "That's why Jules went to the police? She knows?"

"Yes." I swallow the spiked lump in my throat.

"Who is it who knows?" he asks me, thankfully leaving the difficulties with Jules out of the conversation. "And what exactly do they know?"

"I don't know," I say and he clicks his tongue against the roof of his mouth. "Jules received an anonymous letter." The paper lays in my wallet as we speak, but I don't present it to him. "It was a warning to get away from me with no evidence."

"Someone knows you killed Jace, warned her to get away from you… but then tried to kill her?" he asks me with confusion.

I nod my head, fully comprehending the lack of logic.

"I don't think they were planning on doing anything when it came to Anderson. They only told Jules to get back at me. And then tried to kill her to keep the secret silenced."

"Who would do that?" he asks me.

You, I think, but I don't say it. I don't have to, though.

His face contorts with disbelief before he turns completely in his chair and opens a cabinet door. I watch in the reflection of the glass, clearly seeing a safe and what's more, the numbers of the combination to open it.

It's the same combination he had on the garage when I was a child. I rip my eyes away from the reflection when he peers back up, holding a stack of photographs in his hand and shutting the door to the safe and then the cabinet with a kick of his foot.

"I wasn't sure if I should show you this or not," he says and lets out an uneasy breath. "It would have complicated things between you and Liam."

I glance down at the photographs and then immediately back up to my father's gaze. *Jace Anderson and Liam's wife, Cecile?*

"No," I say and the word leaves me without my consent.

"They're getting a divorce, so I imagine Liam found out about the affair somehow," my father says absently.

"Maybe Liam? Maybe his wife?" my father says, shrugging. "Either way, I'm sure now that the hit failed, I doubt they'll attempt it again."

His last statement catches me by surprise, and I tear my eyes away from the evidence of Cecile's affair to gauge my father's reaction.

"I'm keeping my ear to the ground and waiting to hear back from a certain someone," he says then shakes his head slightly, "but no one knows anything according to my source."

I can't imagine how deep my father's depravity goes that he has contacts in such low places.

My father continues without looking at me. "I talked to the commissioner." I've been waiting for this. I know there are consequences to what happened the other night. Liam's gunning for me.

"You may have to go in for questioning. You won't be charged with anything, of course. But they have to make it seem like they've done their due diligence." *Thatchers belong on only one side of the courtroom.* It's a saying the men in my family have carried for years.

"I need to go," my father tells me, rising from his seat and gesturing to the door. "If you need help this time, let me know."

Julia

> *It's not the anger toward him,*
> *It's not the dimming fire.*
> *It's not the love I feel for him,*
> *Or how my heart bleeds with desire.*
> *My soul is broken, torn and bent,*
> *Never to repair.*
> *To truly hate oneself,*
> *The sin leaves me in despair.*

SEVENTEEN DAYS HAVE PASSED SINCE I GOT THE ANONYMOUS LETTER in the mail.

Each day, Mason looks at me differently. It's like he knows I'm leaving. I'm not convinced leaving is the answer; I'm not convinced I should stay though either.

The bedroom door creaks open as I brush my hair, getting ready for bed. There's no doubt in my mind that he'll be sleeping in bed with me tonight. He walks into the room quietly, shutting the door behind him. The left side of his face is bruised and cut, but somehow it only adds to his beauty. A prince, wounded in battle saving his princess.

I almost laugh. A hint of it must have escaped at the thought, because he turns to look at me as the door clicks shut. The only light in the room is from the small lamp on the nightstand and the way the shadows sharpen his features does the worst things to me.

There's an odd dynamic between the two of us. He wants to touch me, he keeps coming close to doing just that, circling me and waiting, but he doesn't.

The part that's truly insane is that it disappoints me, every single time. I'm crazy for feeling any attraction to him at all, but I'm drawn like a moth to a flame.

He picked me up when I fell.

He protected me when I was weak.

And even though I hate him for what he's done, he's the only reason I'm still alive.

"You can't hide in here forever, Jules," Mason comments half-heartedly with a small smile on his lips that doesn't reach his eyes. He closes the space between us easily, and I let him. His lips brush against mine in what I presume will be a gentle kiss, but he deepens it and without my conscious consent, I lean into it. I didn't realize how much I missed his touch.

He moans into my mouth as he kisses me deeply, not holding back a damn thing. I wish I could do the same, but all I find myself doing is forcing myself to stay away, to keep my guard up around him. I can't let myself fall again. I won't. I utterly refuse to give him that chance or else I know he'll keep me forever. And I don't know who exactly I'll be if I let that happen.

I break the kiss before he's finished with me, but he only pushes harder into me, wanting more and letting me know exactly what he needs.

I turn away from him, shame filling every piece of me. Ashamed to be kissing him. Ashamed that I *want* to kiss him.

"Is that how you want it, Jules?" he asks and his deep voice comes out rough as I look into his eyes. The passion is still there. The desire that ignites mine stares back at me.

"You want to hate me." He brings his lips to my ear, making a burning ache flow down every inch of my skin. "Try hating me while you cum on my dick, sweetheart," he tells me and I know I'm done for. My head falls back, hitting the wall as his hands trail over my sides, slowly making their way down my curves.

He rakes his teeth down my collarbone, the sensation directly linked to both my sensitive nipples and needy clit. I'm desperate for more. Aching for him to take me and own my body like I know only he can. His teeth sink into the crook of my neck as his hands pin my hips down, holding me in place as I cry out in sheer frustration.

His large body towers over me, the heat from his body suffocating me as his hard erection digs into my lower belly.

"Fight me, Jules," he says, gripping the hair at the nape of my neck and twisting it around his wrist. "Fight me like you want to."

I slap him, his rough stubble scraping against my hand. A low growl rumbles up his chest; it's just as filthy and perverted as I feel, keenly aware of how much he turns me on. I press both of my hands against his chest, a weak and helpless attempt at pushing him away and he just chuckles at me, his gray eyes flickering to life with a heat I've missed. Nothing but wanting moans escape my lips.

He grabs the nape of my neck, forcing my head to tilt and claiming a cry from me as he steals a kiss along my jaw. I shove my weight forward, attempting to push him away with more vigor, but he merely uses my attempt to push and twist me down onto the bed.

My belly presses against the mattress, my back arching as he stands behind me, leaning against me and pinning me down as his fingertips slide up my outer thighs.

My heart squeezes too tightly without being able to see him and feel him. I don't know why, but I don't want this, not like this.

"Mason," I call out for him, and his name is nothing more than a plea with the frantic need I feel.

He instantly braces his forearms around me, no longer touching me and no longer pinning me to the bed. He breathes heavily, panting as I turn slowly, still caged under him. It's an awkward way to lie, with my bottom barely on the edge of the bed.

His eyes are closed, shut tight and his plump lips parted as I lie beneath him. A caged animal, hurt and tortured and needing a way out is all I see. "Mason," I whisper his name and he opens his eyes.

I gently press my lips to his, taking a sweet kiss before nipping his bottom lip. I brush the tip of my nose against his, and the spark ignites again. He attempts a soft kiss, but it quickly turns into something else. Something primal and filled with lust.

He kisses down my neck, over the small bite marks still red on my skin and aching for attention. He strips my underwear from me and kicks off his own as we slowly climb deeper into the bed. Slowly parting from our clothes and the worries that wait beyond the heavy sheets.

I don't stop whispering his name, I don't stop pushing and pulling against him until he slams into me, filling me and stretching my walls in one swift thrust. My back arches, and a silent scream rips up my throat.

The pleasure he gives me is unmatched, indescribable and something only for us. It's sinful and wrong, but it feels like heaven.

A strangled moan is torn from me and he almost stops when I push against his cheek yet again. I can see the hesitation, the worry in his eyes. I arch my neck and rock my hips, letting him know that I'm his. That I want this and him just the same. My head thrashes from side to side as my throbbing clit brushes against his rough pubic hair as he stills deep inside of me, buried to the hilt and hovering over me, watching my expression. "More," I whimper, desperate for whatever he will give me. I'm deprived without his touch. He should know that; he's done this to me.

Crashing his lips against mine, he moves his hand to my hip, positioning me how he wants me and tilting my ass up just slightly so he can thrust deeper into me. He slams himself harder and deeper into me, unrelenting and unmerciful. "Fuck," I moan, and he's quick to echo my pleasure.

From him, it's a groan of awe filled with gratitude and devotion, fueling him to push me farther and farther as he races for his release. He whispers the word over and over in the crook of my neck, his hot breath sending chills over my body.

From me, it's a strangled cry as my nails scratch down his back and my body pleads for more and also to run from the intensity. It's a mix of pleasure and pain, a cocktail strong enough to kill me and I don't know which one it will be that finally brings me to my death.

<h1 style="text-align:center">chapter 21</h1>

I T'S DIFFICULT TO CONFRONT A PERSON WHEN THEY HAVE A RESTRAINING order against you. Regardless, I consider driving by Liam's house, knocking on the door and beating the fucking piss out of him all over again. A week has passed, and not a damn thing has changed. The air is stagnant and I don't know what to do but I won't sit and wait for the next onslaught.

The once sought-after developer and bachelor has taken a fall.

The excerpt of the news article lays above my mug shot. At least I knew it was coming; the journalist was decent enough to give me a heads-up. Evan could only do so much to hold me back from Liam, but he worked as much magic as he could with the press.

It's only a mug shot. No charges pressed and nothing on my record, but the city has a way of talking. The most shocking thing in the article is the information concerning Liam. Apparently he has a criminal record from college for assault and battery, and attempts at much worse. Divorce papers have already been signed between him and his now ex-wife, and the article compares that to the supposed breakup between Jules and myself.

I'm not sure what is true concerning Liam. I'm grateful the spotlight is on him in the article. The article got my father and Jules all worked up. I can only imagine how they'd react if they knew about the letter that arrived today too.

The paper in my hands rustles in the quiet office as I read it again.

I was mad at you for what you did, and I'm sorry.

It's not what you think.
The gentleman was only there to find something, but I found it elsewhere.

I'm sorry for what I've done.
And I forgive you for what you did; I hope you can forgive me as well.
Sincerely,
X

It's the same feminine writing as the other note. This one sits in my wallet, and it's been here for hours, refusing to allow me to think of anything else.

Whoever it was is damn good at concealing their identity. Not a single fingerprint on the envelope or the paper itself. The security footage shows it was delivered by the mailman, but has no return address. I'm lost, and I have absolutely no leads.

I finally crumple the letter, hating it and the fucker more now than ever. The hopeless feeling weighs down on me. I can't fix it. I can't fix anything without knowing who to blame.

They fucked with me, ruined something so precious and perfect, tearing Jules from my life. And now they're just backing away? They wanted to destroy me. Mission fucking accomplished.

I don't know who to trust anymore or what to live for. My only hope is to pretend it's all right. To move through life like nothing's wrong, and pray that Jules can one day do the same. The rough edges of the letter rub harshly against my skin as I close my eyes and tighten my fist around it. It's never going to happen.

She's never going to forgive me.

She loves me deep down. She has to. I can't feel this strongly about her without her feeling something for me.

Tossing the letter into the small trash can beneath my desk, I rise from my seat and wonder about my father, about Liam's wife and how she plays into this. But this game is so much different than any other I've played before.

Too many pieces and moving parts, but I can't see a damn one of them.

It feels a lot like giving up. A lot like losing. But sometimes you need to keep going through the motions, stay on your guard, and just let them think you've lost.

I flick off the light switch as I open the office door and stand there in the hall, contemplating where Jules is most likely to be in the house. My hand tightens on the doorknob, as I wonder if she'll talk to me like we used to. If she'll let me hold her. If those moments when she forgets and looks at me with those gorgeous blue eyes will last longer than seconds tonight.

I'll leave it be, if only to let them think I've lost and given up. I nod my head as I leave; that's what I tell myself.

As I shut the door behind me, it feels like I truly have lost everything already.

chapter 22

Julia

T'S NEARLY PICTURE PERFECT.

To anyone looking in, we're a couple sitting on the sofa in front of a roaring fire.

There's plenty of lighting for the scene in Mason's living room. The light's brighter and has been all winter with the curtains open and the snow covering the grounds. The white reflects the sunshine into the room, no matter how dim it is. I watch the flames lick along the log. This fireplace is different from the one in the dining room. It's odd they don't match. I would've changed that if it were up to me. But it wasn't. Because this isn't where I belong.

I'm trapped here. I've made up my mind and I'm done.

I swallow thickly, moving more of the blanket over my chest as Mason shifts on the other end of the sofa. I came down here to write and to get this tale out of my head. To put an ending on it and hoping I could get a different perspective, but these words that stare back at me make me want to scream. Scratching out the lines over and over, I attempt to change them and deny it, but it is what it is. There's no changing this ending.

My foot brushes against the pad of paper on the ottoman as I turn to face Mason.

He's working, too, but completely unaffected. If I had to pinpoint what's caused the finality and resentment, it's the way he continues; I hate how easily he can move forward.

I've heard of that psychological condition where the woman falls for her captor. Stockholm syndrome. That's not what this is. I loved this man with my whole heart before. I can feel myself falling, slipping back into that place and I refuse to go there.

He brought me into this hell, and I want out. I need to get out.

I'm scared, and I don't know what to do. But I know I need to be alone. That's what it comes down to. I'm destroyed, and I need to be okay alone.

I'll never stop loving him, but I need to stop hating myself and I can't do that if I'm with him. "This isn't a life," I blurt out and then look up at Mason. "I want to leave, Mason."

He doesn't look at me at first, but he stops typing. The quiet clacking of the keys turns to nothing, leaving the room silent but for the crackling of the fire.

When he turns to look at me, I can see the fight in him is almost gone. He's almost given up as well. It shouldn't crush me the way it does. It shouldn't cause this pain. This hole in my chest, but it does.

Taking a moment to swallow, the cords in his neck tighten before he answers, "You told me that you'd give me a month."

A sadistic laugh leaves me—one that's terrifying and rude, one that I should feel apologetic for letting slip out, but I can't keep up with all the lies like he does. "You and I both know it's never going to happen." The words come out like a knife—knives, really. They cut us both, each in different ways.

"You can't leave," he tells me simply and I can't help but feel enraged.

"I'm not staying," I state with finality and narrow my eyes at him, and I feel a side of me that wants to fight. Not like the other night. I want to fight for my life. For my freedom and for a happiness I don't ever see myself having with Mason. Not ever again.

"There's someone—"

"I don't care," I spit at him. "I can take care of myself."

His voice holds a note of admonishment as he says, "Don't be stupid, Jules."

"Fuck you," I hiss, gripping the sofa as I lean closer to him. "I was fine before I met you." I'm on edge, and violence brews inside of me. "How dare you!" I yell at him. I hold on to the anger. It's the only sane part of me anymore. "How dare you start this when you knew from the very beginning—" My voice gets so tight I can't finish.

Mason stares at me, judging how to handle me. It's what he does, but this is too much for either of us. High and mighty with his tone, he pushes back, "You were lonely, and don't pretend—"

"Because of you!" I scream the interruption, my voice and throat raw and full of pain. "You did this to me!" I yell. "I'm not okay, and it's because I'm fucking you!" All of my pent-up rage, all the boiling anger spills over and I kick out, throwing the blanket off and getting away from him. There's not enough distance between us, only feet from where he sits and where I stand. I can't leave though, not until he lets me go. Our stares are locked, brutalized with both sadness and anger.

It's quiet for a moment, with only the sounds of my heavy breathing and the fire.

"You need me to fix it," Mason says with confidence.

"You can't fix this," I say dully and my heart hurts as I answer him. I wish he could. I so desperately wish he could fix this. Because I want him. I want to love him, and have him forever. But that isn't our ending. I swallow and say, "You can't fix this."

"You need me—"

"I don't need anyone." I cut him off, letting out a deep breath and slowly lifting my head to look him in the eyes. The silver specks pierce through me as I say, "Mason, I'm done with all this. I'm done." The last two words of my confession are only whispers.

His expression softens as he leans back and I take the seat on the far end of the sofa, wanting the tension to leave us both. "Do you hate me?" he asks, his eyes turning glossy but I know he won't cry. That's not the man Mason is. I already know he loves me. I know he wants me. I know I want him too, but that's not in our cards. He decided that long ago, before he even met me.

"No." My voice croaks as I answer him and that hurts so much worse, telling him and confessing. "I don't hate you, it's not you."

He huffs a sarcastic and defensive sound. "It's not you, it's me," he says as he slams his laptop shut and pushes it off of him.

I lick my dry lips, feeling the cracks with the tip of my tongue. "You know it's what you've done, Mason." I wait for him to look at me again and I sniffle, wiping my tears and nose with my sleeve. "It's who you used to be that I can't get over.

"It's not about you, or what you want. It's about me being okay with this, and I never will be. How can I?" I shrug, wiping the tears as they come carelessly.

"Let me hold you," Mason says although it sounds like a demand, reaching out for me, but I move away, taking the throw with me in haste and then letting it fall to the floor.

"I can't," I say with my back to him. I tell him, "If you touch me, I don't think I'll be able to go."

"Then don't," he says with desperation, but he doesn't move.

"I can't forget, I can't pretend. And I hate myself for loving you." It's the hate I can't live with. I turn to face him, pleading with him to understand and accept it. "I hate myself."

I watch as Mason stands and leaves, as the first tear rolls down his cheek and he brushes it away angrily.

I can't let him walk away like this. I reach out to him, gripping onto his arm and he stops but doesn't look at me.

"Mason, please," I say, begging him, but I don't know what for. "I don't want to hurt you."

He shakes his head as he tells me, "It's my fault." That's all he says as I stand there waiting for more. My body wars with me, wanting to cave and let him hold me. I haven't realized it until now, but all this time, holding me has been his only way to be held in return.

"I need to give you your gun," Mason says in a tight voice, looking past me and toward the stairs.

"You're giving me the gun?" I ask him more as a distraction from standing there so numb and full of despair than anything else.

He nods once.

"And you'll leave me alone?" I ask him, both wanting him to tell me yes and give in to my wishes, and also to tell me no and say he'll love me forever.

"Yes," he says and my heart breaks into two. "I'll watch over you," he says as he nods his head and I nod in return, reflexively. "When you're safe," he says and swallows thickly before continuing, "I'll leave you alone. I promise."

Mason

Time be still,
Show me a way.
To turn back what's done,
And change our yesterday.
I'm so damn sorry,
I would repent,
Alas, that time is already spent.

THERE'S NO WAY I'M LEAVING HER ALONE.

In time, she'll forgive me. I'm sure she will. It's easier to ask for forgiveness, isn't it? That's how the saying goes.

A heavy sigh leaves me as I climb back into my car and double-check every window of her place. I've got a security system in place so she can be alone during the day, but at night, I'm slipping in through the back like I used to. I'll be quiet. I won't let anyone see. Not even her if she doesn't want to.

It wouldn't be right to leave her alone, but I can still let her leave.

The leather behind me protests as I close my eyes, leaning my head back with an overwhelmingly pathetic feeling consuming me. Everything I've done is to protect her, yes. But I can't let her go. I'm holding on to the last bit of her that I can. She's slipping, running away from me and I'd be a liar to say it doesn't shred me.

It's been weeks of nothing. Weeks of waiting. I don't believe for a moment whoever wrote that note and sent that man is done with me. Or with her.

I press the button on my phone for the security feed. I have it all here. I'll keep her safe.

I'll know the second anyone enters. The locks are all new. The alarms are set. Every door that opens in that house, I'll be alerted—same with every window.

She doesn't want to stay with me, and I can't force her to love me enough to stay. But I'll protect her and care for her. I have nothing and no one else. I have no choice.

The keys jingle as I start my car and the heater blows out cold air while the radio plays soft music. I turn them both off and listen to the hum of the engine. Taking another look over my shoulder and then another glance at the feed on my phone, I make a promise to let her go one day, just not today. I'll leave her alone like she wants. I'll let her move on and live a normal life.

I can never give her that, I know that. Not with the way our worlds collided. She deserves that with someone else.

My throat feels tight as I gently press the pedal down and pull away from her row of condos on the Upper East Side. There's still a chance if I just hold on… I won't have to let her go. She'll forgive me.

My warring thoughts storm through me. Let her go or hold on to hope.

Even knowing how wrong it is, I'll be back tonight. I can't leave her alone. I can't let her go. That truth always wins out.

Julia

> *When did life become like this?*
> *When did I lose it all?*
> *When did my will to move on,*
> *Become my wish to fall?*
> *When was it that I gave up?*
> *I'm a hollow, empty shell.*
> *There's no answer that I know of,*
> *And no way out of this hell.*

EVERYWHERE I LOOK, I SEE MY DEAD HUSBAND. LYING IN BED, SITTING on a chair. He haunts this house in a way he never has before. It's not fear I'm feeling when the ghost of him appears as distant memories. It's anger. I shouldn't have come back here.

I ran away from a man I love, only to come back to a past I hate.

My reflection is pale in the mirror. The bags under my eyes are back, and I look like shit. I wipe the fog from the shiny surface. The steam of the shower still lingers. It's late and I'm drained, both physically and emotionally, but I can't sleep.

Not without Mason next to me. I'm cold without him and feel weaker than I do when I'm with him. Maybe that's the way I trained myself. To be brave when there's someone to lean on. *What kind of bravery is that?*

I swallow the lump in my throat and close my eyes. I tell myself that I was wrong to love him, and somehow fooled into thinking it was real. If I convince myself it was never real, it will be so much easier to let go.

Opening my eyes only reveals the men of my past surrounding me in the mirror. Mason on my right, and Jace on my left, standing next to me in the reflection.

I blink once, and they're gone.

Leaving me alone, and isn't that what I wanted?

A chill runs through my blood as I focus on just breathing and calming myself. Bottles of perfume are lined up so neatly on the shelf. Chanel Chance is the first one in the row of expensive and elegant bottles. My breathing comes in harsh pants as I stare at it. It's nearly halfway empty. It was a Christmas gift.

I wonder if he gave his mistresses the same kind of gifts? What about the woman he had killed? *The one pregnant with his child?*

The last thought snaps my last bit of control. A wretched cry echoes in the bathroom, burning my throat as I whip my hand across the shelf. The tinkling, crashing and shattering of glass fills the room as I stand there heaving. I grip the edge of the bathroom door, tears blurring my vision and stare back at myself. I fucking hate who I was. Naïve and stupid. "So fucking stupid!" I scream at myself. "I hate you!" I yell out. "I hate what you did to me!"

My body sways as I harshly wipe under my eyes, turning from the mirror before I shatter it as well. The overwhelming scent of the perfumes mix in the air and I slam the door shut behind me, hating how it reeks and how the mess from my outburst, reckless and yet again stupid, will stay there until I clean it up. I'll be the one picking up the tiny pieces of shattered glass. That's how it works when these men storm in, destroying everything and demanding I follow their lead.

Jace's closet is across from the bathroom. It was untouchable before when he passed. I couldn't bear to open it and see all of his clothes. Suits he would never wear again. Shirts that held memories.

I rip the doors open chaotically, but then pause and walk in ever so slowly, flicking on the light. The U-shaped closet is lined with crisp white dress shirts and a myriad of colors on the left. Suits on the right. In the very back is his collection of soccer jerseys. He started buying them all the way back in high school. I remember the first one he ever got. I spot it as the memory comes flooding back.

I told him the red brought out his eyes.

I clench my teeth as I tear the shirt down. The fabric feels like nothing in my fisted hand.

I told him how handsome he looked in it.

A scream I don't recognize as my own joins me when I grab the others, tearing them off the hangers and tossing them onto the floor.

He whispered that he wanted to see me in nothing but the jersey.

I kick the pile of jerseys aside and then dump the suits onto the floor, screaming as the memory washes over me.

I smiled, I wore it just for him and made love to him for the first time in that fucking jersey.

"I hate you!"

I blushed with innocence and handed everything I had right over to him. "I'll never forgive you!"

I don't stop until every last garment is littered on the floor. I take a shaky breath, not knowing if it's him I hate or myself.

My gaze searches the closet for something, anything to validate my rage. I tear open shoeboxes looking for little black books. Ripping through the drawers of a small watch armoire I tear them all out, flinging the cold metal behind me.

Each is a moment I wish I could take back.

Support that I'd given him blindly. The trust. Our marriage vows that meant nothing to him.

There's nothing that overtly makes him a *bad man* in this closet. No evidence that he deserved to die. There's nothing here. Nothing but ghosts of the past and memories I haven't suffered through in a year.

My shoulders rise and fall heavily as I move from one post to the next, focusing on taking it all down. I can't stand to see his things hanging there.

It's all the memories and the details he hid from me. They don't deserve their place anymore. I can't stand it and I want them gone.

I know deep in my gut that everything Mason told me is true. I always go with my gut, and it led me here. Crying in the middle of a trashed closet, with my prick of a dead husband's clothes scattered around me.

I'm searching for anything. Anything at all that would tell me it's okay to hate Jace and be done with him forever. That everything Mason said is true, and therefore it's okay to love him. That it's okay… for him to have murdered Jace.

I use the sleeve of a suit to bury my face. The cool material makes my heated face feel even hotter. I've finally lost it.

"I'll hate you forever, Jace Anderson." Exhaustion makes my legs shaky and I just want to lie down. I want to wake up and forget it all. I push the hair out of my face, taking in a deep breath.

My eyes close, and I see Mason. His gorgeous smile, and those deep gray eyes full of so much emotion.

I wish I could smile. I wish I could go to him and beg him to take me back. That's how far gone I am. I open my eyes, promising myself to be strong, but I can't walk another step.

My body tingles with awareness and fear as I look straight ahead.

The balcony doors are closed, but unlocked.

I know they were locked. My body feels frozen as I look to my left, the gun still in plain sight on my nightstand.

I look back to the balcony, staring at the lock and knowing without a doubt that someone else is in this house.

chapter 25

Dressed in all black, I'm certain I'll slip into the night for most people as I casually stroll along the sidewalk to William Street Towers, my father's office building. It's late and although the building is unlocked, the offices inside are locked up and most of the lights are off.

Opening the main door, my blood heats with anxiety as it swings open. The cameras are on. I don't have to look up at the little red lights to know they're recording.

My posture is relaxed, and I'll act like I belong. I won't appear out of place in the least. It's silent in the building as I rock on my heels and hit the button for the elevator. Someone coughs to my right, and I chance a look at a woman in a pencil skirt walking quickly to the narrow hallway where the restrooms are. A lone soul, working late.

This is how men go to prison for life for crimes they committed, but didn't get caught for.

This is how you fuck up and drown in your past mistakes for something so damn stupid.

An arrest for trespassing, or breaking and entering? They could charge me with that, and it wouldn't be the worst thing to have happened to me.

But they won't stop there. If I get caught, then my father will find out. He'll know what I was doing. He can push, and the powers that be will sentence me harsher than justice would allow.

This is how men are taken down. For doing stupid shit, rather than keeping their noses clean. But I don't give a damn. I need to know what's in that safe. I need answers.

It's been itching at me, an irritating thought in the back of my head, over and over ever since I left. A nagging that won't stop and a whisper that tells me everything is there, right there.

He had information on Liam… what else does he have in that safe?

The elevator dings as it arrives, the doors parting for me and sealing my fate.

Miss Theresa Geist has a bad habit. I'm not sure if anyone else knows, but growing up so close to her, spending so much time with her, I've learned that she sometimes forgets her keys. She takes the subway to work, and it's happened more than a time or two.

Because of this, she leaves the main office key tucked in the drawer of the reception desk in the hallway. It's hidden in a false bottom to the drawer. Or at least she used to hide it there. I swing the large glass door open and my heart races as I commit the first crime tonight, knowing it's being recorded. Knowing it's capturing my face.

It doesn't matter. It won't matter unless the cops or security have to pull up the tapes for a reason.

I swallow thickly, picking up the tray of paper clips and collection of pens and thumbtacks.

A small smile curves my lips up as I find the key. I stare at it a moment, watching it gleam in the lights from the hallway. It'll only get me into his practice's section of the building, but his office lock can be picked now that I'll be completely out of sight.

Open from 7:00 a.m. to 6:00 p.m. The white letters look back at me as I slip in the key and unlock the door.

With the soft click, all I can think is that I should have done this weeks ago. I prop the door open with a desk chair and return the key to where it belongs. No one will be the wiser. I should have come in here the moment I knew about the safe and the combination to its secrets.

But Jules was still with me.

She was still in my house and in my bed. Still a target if something were to happen to me. Everyone knows she's left me, thanks to the article in the morning paper.

Everyone is very aware that she left me after the incident that occurred at the gala. Or at least that's what's being read in black and white.

My heart clenches and I grit my teeth, kicking the chair back as I head straight for my father's door in the back. I slip my hand into my pocket, feeling the bent paper clips there. My fingers travel up and down the thin metal.

She would never do something like this. Jules isn't capable of it. I smile and a rough laugh slips through my lips as I stop at his door and slide the paper clips into the lock. Back in the day, I was damn good at this.

Jules would hate to know all the shit I did years ago. My pulse slows at the thought, turning cold, beating in time with the lock clicking and then the knob turns. I push open the door slowly, ignoring the memories.

The room is brighter than the hall was. The city lights pour through the blinds, creating alternating stripes of light and shadow throughout the room.

I don't waste any time, letting the door shut behind me and moving to his desk, to the cabinet. It swings open easily as if there's no challenge at all presenting itself.

I hesitate only for a moment, realizing whatever's in the safe may tell me more than I ever wanted to know.

There may be evidence of him murdering my mother. It's the first thought that comes to mind, and inwardly I curse myself. It's been twenty years.

Slipping on leather gloves first, I press the buttons slowly, mimicking my father's movements although the safe itself looks typical and ordinary. My lungs still, and my blood rushes in my ears as I wait for the light to flash and the small click that tells me it's unlocked.

It was far too easy.

Piles of paper lay in the safe. Stacks of photographs are the first that I remove, right where he kept the ones of Liam's wife and Jace Anderson. The photos are still on top. I flip through them, still in disbelief. How the hell did she even know him?

The stack directly underneath the one my father showed me makes me do a double take. I grab the photo of Jace and Cecile together and hold it next to a photo of Cecile alone. As I compare the two, my anger rises.

I've always known he was a liar.

It's altered. The photo is faked. My shoulders rise and fall with a tense breath.

Why set her up? They're already getting a divorce. *It's for you,* a soft voice whispers in the back of my head. *It was all to convince you it wasn't him. He'd let anyone else take the fall.*

I slip the photo back into place and scan through the others, searching for shots of Jules or myself, or anything else that proves what a conniving bastard my father is.

The next print is of someone I don't know. I'm confused at first because I have no idea why it was even taken. There's nothing remotely scandalous about it. I stare at the man in question and try to place him. It takes me a moment before I realize it's Jules's CPA, her financial advisor. The prick she went to go see months and months ago. I make it a habit to know who she interacts with. Why him? It doesn't make sense. Maybe he blackmailed him into doing something. I'm not sure.

I stop short at the next stack. It's a letter.

I stare at the photograph of Avery's blackmail letter. Her signature is there. I remember how she used to sign her name. Her handwriting was distinct when she signed documents. All I ever saw was her signature. The curves though, the curves of her writing are so familiar.

My blood runs cold. It's not possible.

It's her handwriting in the notes. I turn to the next photograph and it's another letter from Avery. No it's not. It's just a list of what looks like groceries.

I flip to the next, and that's when I realize what these are. Photographs of her handwriting. My skin pricks with an unforgiving chill. I set the photographs down after searching through several more stacks, but not finding anything at all that makes sense.

I lay them on the seat of the leather chair before looking back into the safe.

There's cash stuffed in the bottom. I take a stack of bound hundred-dollar bills and look behind them, shuffling the money to be sure that's all that's at the bottom. There must be over a million here. Although the safe is small, most of it is stacked with nothing but the bundled hundreds. So much money, it reeks of wealth.

I shove it back into place, not giving two shits about it, and that's when my eyes are drawn up to the top shelf. A thin, brown leather-bound notebook leans against the upper compartment of the safe where the photos were. I take it out, wondering what he'd confess in a bound journal, or if it's even his. I expect to find names and dollar amounts. Or names and account numbers, something of that nature. Information that's irrelevant to what I'm after.

The list of addresses I see first, I recognize immediately. They're ones Anderson bought, the ones my company wanted. But next to them are columns of figures. Dollar amounts of what they sold for at the time of purchase, and what they're projected to be worth after the surrounding properties are developed.

My forehead pinches not understanding why he'd give a shit. He doesn't own them, and they aren't for sale. They never were. Next to the dollar amounts are dates. A word has been repeatedly scribbled in tiny cursive next to some of them, but it's hard to make it out. I squint, my lips moving as I try to figure it out.

Acquired.

He bought them. They're investments. He had a plan, and everyone played a role. But Anderson had no intention of selling. He'd made that clear in the single meeting I had with him. Maybe he knew the properties would go up in value. Or maybe he wanted more money.

I run my fingers over the list of numbers as I try to piece together what corrupt business transaction the two men had together, but that's when I come across something familiar. Something I've become intimately acquainted with these past few weeks.

In the back of the notebook, there are several sheets of paper. Paper I'd consider elegant under other circumstances.

But this paper almost made me lose everything.

The thick cream parchment is unmistakable. My hand clenches into a fist as I fall onto my ass. My back hits the cabinet door as I picture my father writing the letters.

Practicing Avery's handwriting. Planning his next move. I was a target, and so was she.

It was him. It was always him. It's that moment when an alert sounds on my phone. *Jules.*

Julia

Emotions will trap you,
You have no choice.
Those bitter words?
That's not your voice.
They play with your mind,
And take over your will.
Anger is deadly, and
Fear can kill.

THE GUN IS HEAVY AND IT SLIPS IN MY HANDS AS I SLOWLY WALK down the steps, careful not to make too much noise. I cringe each time the stairs creak. So much noise. My hands are sweaty and my heart races as I move down the stairs with my back against the wall.

Thud, thud, thud, my heartbeat is loud in my ears. Too loud; I can barely hear anything else beyond the constant rhythm.

Barely breathing, my gaze flickers to the front door and then back up the staircase as light creeps in through the stained glass. I hold my breath until my feet land on the cold tile of the foyer. The front door is only feet away but as I get there, footsteps sound from the other side. The knob rattles, and my heart attempts to climb up my throat.

Whoever it is doesn't knock or ring the bell. I wait for a moment, trembling as I grip the gun for dear life, praying they'll prove to be someone I know, but there's only silence on the other side.

My heart is pounding harder now as I quietly race down the hallway, looking ahead and checking behind me every few seconds. *I need to escape out the back.*

The closed-in backyard won't do me any good, but I can climb the fence and slip through the thin veil of a forest straight to the crowded sidewalks of the city.

So close to protection, so close to safety. *Just run.*

I pause, my back pressed firmly against the wall as I get to the edge and peek around the corner and into the living room.

It's empty, and only fifteen or so feet to the sliding doors.

I'll run. The moment the thought occurs, I take off. But a sudden clatter in the kitchen startles me and I scream out, fumbling the gun and falling on my ass. I cover my mouth and turn quickly to face whoever's there. My pulse races and my body trembles.

The gun landed behind me and I struggle to reach it, my arms propping me up. I keep my eyes forward, though. I'm shocked to find I'm staring at Liam Olsen.

"Whoa," he says easily, a smile on his face. "There you are," he says like he's been waiting for me. Like he's been expecting me. He takes two steps forward and my fear intensifies as he bends down, picking up a magnet that was on the fridge.

"It fell," he says with a shrug.

"What are you doing here?" I barely get out the question as I stand slowly, bringing the gun up behind my back and placing my finger next to the trigger.

"I was told you wanted to talk about something very important?" Liam's tone is playful, teasing and with a grin, he starts loosening the tie around his neck. "That you wanted—"

I bring the gun out in front of me slowly and steady my hands.

Liam's hands go up instantly, his eyes wide with shock.

"I don't want to talk about anything," I tell him and my voice shakes. My body is on fire, and the only thing pumping in my blood other than adrenaline is fear. The memories of the other night come back full force. His hands on me, his lips so close to my neck. "Stay away from me!" I scream at him, and the force of my emotions makes me tremble.

"All right now, you need to put that down," he says with more authority than he has, although his expression is still riddled with worry. He takes a step forward, arms still raised.

"I said stay away!" I cry out as if I'm scared and powerless, because that's how I feel. "Get the fuck out!"

"I'm going, I'm going," Liam says quickly. "I came in through the front and I'm headed out the front door, okay?" He says the words quickly, his own breathing ragged. "There must've been a misunderstanding," he tells me quickly, rushing out the words. Just then, his gaze rises just a touch higher, his focus no longer on me, but instead trained on something behind me. I didn't hear the back door sliding open until it was too late, and my skin pricks with the realization that I'm trapped. *There's someone behind me.*

I scream and as I do, the gun slips again in my sweaty grip and goes off. My eyes dart to it and it's like I'm watching in slow motion as it happens.

The sound of the bang.

The kick of the gun, making my arms jerk.

Large hands settle on my shoulders as the scream tears up my throat.

The bang still resonates in my ears as my body shakes and I try to push the man behind me away, but he holds me close as he says, "It's okay!"

I can hardly breathe, let alone recognize the voice.

Fear is what guided everything. I swear. I didn't mean for any of it to happen.

I look up and into the eyes of Mason, only it's not him. It's his father, looking down at me with sympathy, with sadness and horror.

Only when I see it's him do I look back at Liam.

The blood drains from my body when I see he's not moving. He's face-down, his arm at an awkward angle. "Liam," I call out, but he doesn't answer.

The gun is hot in my hands. A sickness grows in my stomach.

I shake my head over and over. What happened? I didn't. I swear I didn't shoot him.

Mason's father grips me again and I stumble backward, desperate to get away from him. My legs kick out as I scramble across the floor.

"Leave me alone!" I yell at him, still holding the gun, but pointing it toward the ground. *He isn't dead. I didn't kill him. I didn't mean to pull the trigger.*

He lets me go and says with nothing but compassion, "I saw what happened. It was an accident." He almost whispers the words. His eyes are wide as he nods. "It's okay, I saw it."

His words are comforting.

It was an accident. I swear it was. I look back at the body on the floor, my vision blurred from tears. *It was an accident. How did this happen? Why are they here?*

Too many questions scream in my head. Too many things are so very wrong. I look up at him with desperation and say, "Please, help me." My face crumples as the sobs start. "Save him."

What have I done?

chapter 27

Mason

THE DOOR IS ALREADY OPEN AS I STORM INTO THE HOUSE. EVERYTHING rages inside of me. I drove as fast as I could. But it's not fast enough. I've never prayed so much in my life as I did on my way to her place.

Bang! I swear I heard a gunshot, and I've never felt so cold in my life. The only thing keeping me from dying inside as I race through the first floor of her place, is hearing her cry. It means she's still alive.

"Jules!" I call out her name just as I get to her living room, all the way in the back of the townhouse.

My world spins as I stop short in the room. My father's hands are on Jules's shoulders, and Liam is dead on the floor.

"It was an accident," she whimpers over and over and Jules's hands shake as the gun falls to the floor.

"It's all right," my father whispers into her ear. "I saw it," he says and looks up at me, "it was an accident." His statement is firm. Just like his grip on her. He nods and I can already see the wheels spinning. He set this up. It's the ending he wrote. Liam the villain, and he gets to be the hero. Liam's wife gets his properties, then my father can buy them. Jules and I have our villain and he's in the clear.

Everything clicks into place. Each event, everything he's done and how he's played each piece.

I take a careful step forward, so aware of how close he is to her and the gun. *Too close.*

"Mason," Jules cries out. God I want to go to her, I desperately want to hold her, but as I take another step closer, my only goal is to get between the two of them. To keep him away from her.

This all ends tonight. I won't let him live to breathe the same air as us. His greed is deadly. If he did it once, he'll do it again.

"Stay behind me," I say as I rip Jules away from my father, grabbing her hand and forcing her behind me. I kick the gun behind me as well as I keep my gaze on him. His cold gray eyes darken and narrow at me.

"You can't pin this on me," he huffs. Naturally he'd think I was trying to save her and destroy him. It's all he's ever thought. Everyone's always out to get him. This time I am.

"Stay away from her." I swallow and say, "It was you."

My father's eyes dart to the gun behind me and I take a step to the right, keeping my arms out as Jules grips onto me. "Mason," she whispers desperately, her cries waning as she realizes there's still reason to be afraid. That this isn't over.

"Jules," I say although I stare straight ahead, keeping my eyes right where they belong. "He's the one who wrote the note. The one who set me up to meet your husband. He set Liam up and used all of us. All for a fucking payout."

All over a chunk of property in New York City that Anderson bought out from under him. One corrupt man upping the ante in a game he couldn't afford.

"Now, now, let's not get ahead of ourselves," my father says easily. "It wasn't meant to turn into this, Mason."

Jules releases me, letting out a gasp from behind me. I can't feel her, I can't see her, but I can't turn around. I have to keep my eyes on him. On the liar and murderer and sinner I was born from.

He raises his hands defensively, as if giving up the fight and says, "I swear to you, it wasn't supposed to end like this." All the lies, the spinning of a delicate web woven with manipulation and deceit.

"I don't believe you," I tell him. "I think you didn't care how many people had to be sacrificed."

The corner of his lips twist into a wry smile. "I certainly didn't intend for this, Mason." He shakes his head and adds, "Never."

"And Mom?" I ask, feeling the rage come back to me. Knowing this isn't the first time. I don't know how many lies he's told, or how many people he's killed. "Did you intend for her to die, or was she just a casualty of your games?"

The mention of my mother gets a rise from him, his eyes heating and his expression morphing into a snarl. "Your mother was a whore," he sneers. It's all I can take.

I heave in a breath as my body lunges for him. No punches, no hits. I wrap both of my hands around his throat. The weight of my body makes us topple over, both of us crashing to the ground as my blunt nails dig into the thin skin around his neck. I grip him with everything I have in me. My teeth clench and every muscle in my body is tight as I squeeze the life from him.

He tries to slam his fist into me at first, but he's not the young man he once was. I lean forward, balancing my weight as he tries to buck me off. I have him pinned.

Finally, he reaches up to his throat, desperate to pry away my fingers. His nails scratch at my skin, but I have no intention of letting go. All the desire in me focuses on leaning my weight into his throat. But the victory is stolen from me.

Bang! Bang!

My body tenses with the shock and fear. Two bullets have been fired. The noise rings in my ears as my father stills beneath me. His eyes are wide and lifeless, staring at nothing. His nails no longer digging into my hands.

Jules shot him. Once in the forehead, the other just an inch from his nose on his left cheek.

I stare at his face, the vision distorted by the blood dripping from the bullet holes down his weathered face and onto the carpet. Even knowing he's dead, I can't relax my grip around his throat.

Tell me! I scream in my head as tears prick the back of my eyes. I just want to hear him admit it. I want him to tell me to my face how he plotted my mother's death. How he hired someone to make it look like a suicide. My body trembles as I come to terms with the fact that it will never happen. His secrets will never be told, and my fingers loosen as I take in an unsteady breath.

It takes a long moment for me to glance up at Jules, who's eerily quiet only to see that she has the gun still pointed at him.

"He's dead. It's over, Jules."

Something in her seems to snap at my words, and she drops the gun as if it's burned her hands. She backs away, shaking and covering her mouth with horror.

The blood drains from her as the realization sets in. "Don't scream," I tell her.

"Look at me," I tell her and she does as I command. "It's okay." I swallow down every insecurity. For her, I'll be strong. I'll take care of this. "It's okay," I repeat and hold her gaze until she nods back although she's still on edge and drenched in terror.

I wipe the gun off on my shirt, getting rid of her prints and trying to think straight. The cops will be here soon. There's no doubt in my mind. She needs an alibi. "Run, Jules." I set the gun back down where it fell and rise to take a step closer to her. She's still trembling and can't take her eyes from the bodies on the ground. I reach out, grabbing her shoulders and shaking her slightly to get her attention. "Go to the Westin. You left me last night. Everyone knows that. I came here to get you, but you weren't here. I'll call the owner of the Westin." I nod as I speak, as if reassuring myself and her. I know for a fact the owner was in my father's back pocket and now he'll be in mine since I have my father's little black book. "He'll do what I tell him to if anyone asks. You checked in last night and that's where you've been."

Jules shakes her head, the implication of what I'm saying setting in. "Mason," she says and sucks in a breath. "No. You can't."

"I can and I am," I tell her, staring deep into her eyes. My beautiful Jules, my sweetheart. I should have known it would end like this. It's how it should have started. With me killing my father and letting everything else go.

"I love you," I tell her, "even if you can't be with me. I love you."

She stares deep into my eyes, and I can see how much it tortures her. We were never meant to be. It was my mistake. I deserve this pain. She parts her lips, I'm sure to explain, I know her so well and I'm certain that's what's coming. But I don't need it. She doesn't have to explain it to me; I already know. I press my finger to her lips, silencing her and then giving her one last kiss.

She leans into me as I pull away and it makes the pain in my chest grow that much deeper. I look down at her with the tears soaking her lashes until she finally peeks up at me.

We share a look, but it only makes her cry harder. We both know it's over.

I hold her, wrapping my arms around her and kissing her hair until she's able to calm herself down. The clock is ticking, and the time we have is already up.

She gives me the saddest smile when I pull away again for the last time, and says, "You're always cleaning up my messes, aren't you?"

"It was never your mess, Jules." She can't stop the tears flowing freely down her face as I tell her, "I'm so fucking sorry." I drop her hand and take a step backward as she covers her face with her hand. I say, "Know that I'm sorry. Know that I love you."

She nods once, licking the tears from her lips as I tell her to go, listening to the sirens getting louder and louder.

I watch her disappear, and I don't regret it.

She needed me to let her go. I know that now. I'm only capable of destroying her. She deserves so much more than that.

chapter 28

The truth is, everyone can kill.
Some born to defend, others for thrill.
What would it take? It's not that hard.
Threaten you? Or leave you scarred?
How much can they push you,
How much can they take?
Until you pull the trigger,
And you finally break.

I'VE NEVER HURT LIKE THIS BEFORE. LIKE MY SOUL'S BEEN GUTTED.

I can't get the look in Mason's eyes out of my head. A darkness sets in around me as I close my eyes. The vision of his handsome face displaying nothing but hopelessness is only replaced with something more morbid.

I killed a man. Two.

The first I could convince myself was an accident. I was terrified; I felt threatened. I swear it was an accident.

The second, though… I shot his father out of anger. I wonder if this is what Mason felt like almost a year ago when he killed Jace. If that rage that consumed me was the same for him. I shot his father because I wanted to. That is the only explanation.

I shift on the sofa and pull the chenille throw closer up to my neck. My shoulders brush against the armrest until I get my head right on the pillow. I can't go to the bedroom. I can't go anywhere in this hotel room without feeling like the cops will burst through the doors at any minute. I've only spoken to them on the phone. I can't imagine they believed my lies. Even as I said them, I could tell they sounded nothing like the truth. *Because I'm a liar now. I'm a murderer.*

I'm not the woman people think I am. I don't belong here and I don't deserve to get away without punishment. There's no denying that.

It's one thing to mourn the loss of a loved one. It's only natural, much like a breakup, but you have no way of going back, no way to mend the broken pieces. They simply don't exist anymore except in memories. Consuming your thoughts with no way to recover, other than to move on. Which, in itself, is a tragedy.

It's quite a different thing to mourn the loss of yourself. To realize you're no longer who you once were or who you wanted to be. Your identity has vanished, and staring back at you in the mirror is someone else entirely.

The faint sounds of the TV get louder as a commercial comes on and it makes my skin prick. I turn to face the lights, but I'm not watching it. I don't even know what's showing, it's all blurred. I wanted to turn something on to try to fill the hollowness in me. As if simply hearing something and someone else would make me feel less alone. As if I could somehow ignore my own reality by getting lost in a movie.

When Jace died, this method worked well. I'd turn on a heart-wrenching chick flick just to convince myself that the movie was the reason I was crying. The movie was why I felt the way I did and I could turn it off, if only I wanted to.

It's not working today, though. I'm all too aware of my current state. I bite down on my thumbnail, looking past the television and over at the curtains, hiding the view from the only window in the living room of the hotel penthouse.

I'm not the sweet good girl I was brought up to be.

And I never will be again. My stomach churns and I roll over to my side, trying to ignore the overwhelming guilt.

I try to convince myself that it'll be okay, that it was all a mistake or an accident or someone else's fault, but I've never been a good liar.

My throat dries and seems to close as I try to take a breath of air. It's all too much, this burden, this truth. Mostly the fact that I'm going to get away with it.

I wonder if Jace felt like this back when he sentenced that woman to death? I think back to each morning in his last days with me. But nothing was different. He was the same as any other day. The same smile, the same kiss. The same light-heartedness about him.

He had no remorse. I bite the inside of my cheek wondering how he could go about his days as if everything was all right. Nothing is. And nothing has been for so long.

I can't hide that any longer. I can't run from it.

When did I become this woman? One willing to kill. Eager to, even.

I can't answer that, because I'd never been in this position until Jace died. All of my life, I've been handed everything easily. Even if I was grateful, it wasn't right.

I've never had to fight for a damn thing. I've never felt the need to defend myself. Maybe this woman, the one who kills out of anger, the one who's quick to end what threatens her… maybe I've always been her. I just didn't know it, because she was dormant deep down inside of me, comforted by the fact that she didn't need to act.

Life was kind to her, but not anymore.

My phone goes off by my thigh, making me jump as it rips me from my thoughts. Instinctively, I look to the door first. Where the cops should be coming any minute. They had to know I was the one who really did it. All the evidence is there in my home. *I should confess.*

They'll take me away and force me to pay for my crimes.

I'm expecting it. *I want it.* I want this all-consuming dread to leave me. I want the guilt to wash away. I want to be tried for my sins and sentenced as I should be.

Even if I sat on a jury and heard my story, I don't know how I'd find myself.

I'm guilty of so much, been baptized in the blood of other people's victims.

Maybe at this point, I'm insane. Maybe that will be my plea. It doesn't make me any less guilty.

I'm just as much of a murderer as Mason is.

And even more so than Jace, in a way.

I answer the phone on the last ring.

"Hello." I expect it to be the police, but it's Kat.

"Are you all right?" I close my eyes. It's good to hear her voice.

"How could I be?" I ask her with a pain she can't even imagine. She has no idea.

"It's going to be okay. I just got a call."

"From who?" I ask as I sit up straighter and pull my knees into my chest. "About Mason?" I need to know. "Is he going to be okay? Mason's going to be okay, is that what—"

"Calm down," she says, cutting me off. I sit uneasily, waiting for her to speak. "What did you hear?"

She's quiet a second longer than I can stand. "He's in interrogation," she says. "They can charge him with obstruction now though, but that's it." My throat tightens and makes my words come out in a higher pitch than I intended.

"Obstruction?" I blink over and over, feeling light-headed.

Kat continues, "That's what I've heard. Nothing is set in stone yet."

My heart races erratically.

"It's not… I can't." I struggle to speak, to breathe even. "Kat, you have to help him. You have to help me." It's my chance to confess. To tell her everything. I throw my head back and I rock with the need to let it all out.

"It's okay, he didn't do it."

"I know he didn't. They can't keep him. They can't charge him with anything," I say, pleading with her as if I know how this all works. But I have no idea.

"Kat," I say as my voice cracks again and the words are right there, threatening to come out.

He's taking the fall for me, because he loves me.

And I'm letting him. God, it hurts. It's so wrong. I bury my face between my knees, hating my reality.

He said he loves me; he's taking the fall for me. I didn't even have the balls to tell him how I feel in return. He said I love you, and I said nothing. He must know. He has to. What we have is real and tangible. But I need to tell him.

"Is he going to get off?" I ask her and wait with bated breath. The other line is filled with the sound of her breathing deeply and I find myself hunching forward, my lungs squeezing with the need to breathe.

"Jules, they have some evidence."

Her words make my blood run cold. *Evidence?*

"He didn't do it," I say and the words leave me without my consent. I know they're from me, I know I said it, but I'm somewhere else. Not here, safe in a luxurious hotel penthouse while Mason sits in jail for a crime I committed.

"I know he didn't," she says and I'm not sure if she speaks with certainty for my benefit or if she really believes he didn't. She continues, "But for them to be holding him this long, it means they have something on him, Jules. Evan says they have something. There's something going on."

I swallow thickly, not responding as Kat repeats my name over and over again. The flashes of what happened haunt me. The blood, the heat, the kick of the gun in my hands.

"What can I do?" My voice is eerily calm as I stare straight ahead, although I see nothing but his father's lifeless eyes.

"There's nothing we can do, Jules," Kat says and I shake my head even though she can't see.

I could tell them everything.

"I'm coming over to the hotel," Kat says just as I say, "I'm going to the station."

"Why the hell would you do that?" she says as if it's absurd. "Don't you dare move.

"Trust me, Jules. Mason's going to get out of this. It's just a matter of time before we find out why he's still in holding." I run a hand through my hair, feeling desperate to do something.

"I can't just stay here," I tell her with the desperation apparent in my voice. "I have to do something."

"Not yet," she says. "Don't worry, he's going to be okay. I promise you. You need to stay where you are. Evan is going to keep his ear to the ground. I'll tell you everything as we know it. Right now, they could charge him with obstruction but they aren't… we're waiting to see what they have. Just wait."

My teeth pinch the inside of my cheek as I debate on waiting. It's what Mason told me to do too. I'm so tired of waiting. Waiting to feel again, waiting for the truth, waiting for vengeance, waiting for the guilt to leave.

"I can't—" I start to say but my voice cracks, and I close my eyes. I swallow before firming my resolve to tell Kat, but she cuts me off.

"Just wait one more day. They can't hold him more than that."

The guilt seeps into my veins as I nod my head once as I end the call. One day. One more day.

I learned to live without Jace. And I was better off for it. I was happily living a lie. A false life that was devoid of real meaning.

I don't know that I can live without Mason, and I don't want to find out.

If I confess, we're apart.

If he takes the fall, we're apart.

I have to wait. I have no patience for fate. I don't know what's to come, but I won't let him do this.

As I walk to the large window watching the snow fall from the sky, I listen to the ticking of the clock, waiting to strike.

chapter 29

Mason

"**I** DON'T HAVE ANYTHING ELSE TO SAY," I TELL THE DETECTIVE WHO'S questioning me, the one who refuses to leave. The commissioner is across the room, waiting, eyeing me and probably wondering what his best move to make is. Now that my father's gone, the balance of power has shifted, so it's just a question as to where it's gone and how I play into this game.

Cracking my knuckles one by one, I watch as the skin tightens and turns white before settling into a bright red as I flex my hand.

I don't want anything to do with this shit. I never did, and I never will.

My eyes lift as Commissioner Haynes strides across the room, pulling out his chair slowly and letting the steel drag across the floor.

He leans back, crossing his arms and looking at me as if he's sizing me up. I'm sure this is an act, a game, something that he's done before. I merely look back to my hands. The ones I wrapped around my father's throat right before he died.

It's an odd sense of calm that washes over me at the thought. It shouldn't comfort me. It's not right to be grateful for another's death. I carried the weight and burden of Anderson's death for months. It was only after meeting Jules and knowing I could make her happy that made it all disappear. Maybe if I told her that, it would make it better, but I can't bring myself to do it. I don't want her to know how selfish I was.

I wish I could take it back. I wish I'd murdered my father instead. The rage was meant for him, it always was. I was too much of a coward to do it.

"We have the residue from your shirt, Thatcher." The commissioner finally speaks. I don't look up, I merely pick under my nails, ignoring him and the heat that makes every inch of my skin tingle. He leans across the table, moving closer to me with his hands clasped as he says matter-of-factly, "We know you didn't shoot him, but you're covering for someone. You wiped that gun clean."

Stupid. I grit my teeth, realizing just how stupid I was for doing that shit. I was so desperate to save her, I wasn't thinking. My heart pounds over and over again. But I don't show them a damn thing. I won't give them anything they can use against her.

It doesn't escape me that she could tell them everything. She could speak the truth and knowing my Jules, my sweetheart, I can see her doing it.

I could see her admitting it all, every last detail of the past year that's brought us to this moment. I'd still love her. I'd love her for it.

"I requested my lawyer," I remind them as I lift my head to look him in the eyes.

He clenches his jaw and the cop on my right shifts his stance, gaining my attention. He's pissed. He's young and naïve and thought he was going to break me. He thought that little bit of evidence would do something to scare me into talking.

But my father and grandfather taught me well. When the lies are too big to weave together, you stay silent. You wait for the right story to come along and slowly the pieces will snake in between the crevices. Those around you will create something that will hide them. Silence will kill the evidence. It only needs time.

"Your money can't save you this time," the young detective says. I don't even know his name, nor do I give a fuck. His dark eyes shine with conviction as he squares his shoulders and nods his head. He's clean-shaven, which only makes him appear younger, but of all the men I've met in this building, he's the only one I have respect for. He believes in justice.

"It never could," I speak without thinking, saying the first thing that came to mind.

"What's that mean?" Haynes questions from across the table. He's desperate for me to give him something.

I don't spare him a glance as the young cop responds, "You're going away. There's no negotiating, no lesser sentence for talking." His eyes narrow as he nods his head once and walks closer to the table, bracing himself on it with both of his fists. "We're going to find who really did it. And you're both going down."

My unaffected façade falters at the thought of them learning that Jules did it. My hands flex and ball into fists, and I have to look away. Not Jules. I already ruined her life enough. I destroyed a pure and beautiful soul.

Piece by piece I tore her down before I even knew what I was doing. I can't let her go down for this.

"Not talking is only making it worse for you."

I open my mouth to do what I do best, to be true to my heritage and lie. I have to think of something good, a reason for changing my shirt before cleaning the gun. I lick my lips, trying to come up with the right scenario, something believable. Something the evidence will prove is true. It doesn't have to be factual, only enough that will convince them I'm guilty.

This is what I deserve, even if it's a fucked-up way of going about it. I murdered a man. I tried and convicted him without thinking twice. It's only fair the same is done to me.

"Let's not get ahead of ourselves, Mickey," the commissioner says from across from me. "You already know that's not going to happen."

His last words catch my attention and I turn to him, ignoring how the detective's back straightens and he stalks toward Haynes. "Sir," the cop says and straightens, waiting for the commissioner to explain, maybe? I'm not sure. There's a duel between them with a thick tension that's suffocating.

The commissioner cocks a brow as if not understanding what Mickey is after.

"He's a witness, he tampered with the crime scene—"

"No judge is going to allow charges with that little evidence."

"Bullshit—"

"It's done," he says and the sharp words strike the young man, leaving him standing frozen, staring down the commissioner with his eyes flicking between the two of us. I don't know about legalities. I don't know how much is enough evidence. More importantly, I refuse to believe anything said by a man my father considered a friend.

"Find more evidence or let him go. It's that simple. We're not taking anything to trial unless we can ensure a conviction, get that through your head."

"You're as corrupt as they are," the detective says with contempt before turning his back to the commissioner and storming out of the room.

Before he can slam the door, I see a familiar face in the doorway, eyebrows raised as he's escorted in by a young female cop with a ponytail. She's looking between the cop who's just left and at Commissioner Haynes.

"I trust my client is free to go?" Mr. Millard asks as he shifts the leather handle of his black briefcase from one hand to the other and watches the female cop close the door to the room. "I'm sure you're aware—" Mr. Millard begins, but doesn't finish.

"I've already spoken to the judge," Commissioner Haynes says, once again leaning back in his chair and eyeing me, as if considering who I am and whether or not my existence even matters to him. "He's free to go," he says with finality as my family lawyer nods once and quickly reopens the door to the interrogation room. "We want the murderer and only him. Evidence proves Mason is not our suspect."

I don't need another invitation to leave. Standing abruptly, I take one last look at the commissioner, who's still staring straight ahead, but no longer at me. Only an empty chair, although the same look is in his eyes.

My pulse quickens as I walk through the station, feeling everyone's eyes on me and listening to the sound of our shoes smacking against the floor as we walk out.

"Just like that?" I say beneath my breath as Mr. Millard opens the large front glass door for me. His brow raises as I walk through, still looking at him and waiting for the other shoe to drop. For whatever deal was made and figuring out who I owe now.

He nods his head once, appearing uncomfortable but not adding any more.

This isn't the first time I've gotten away with things. A slap on the wrist for vandalism, shit like that. *But this?*

I stare at my lawyer, wondering what he knows and what he thinks of me as we leave, no charges pressed. The air is bitter cold and the snow on the street is blackened, but on the sidewalks it's still a brilliant white and makes the late evening seem lighter than it should.

"Just like that," Millard says, repeating my words and looking back over his shoulder before walking across the street. I follow him and wait. Always waiting for what's next.

He opens his car's passenger door and says, "Home, Mr. Thatcher?"

I shake my head no. A gust of wind blows by and the air seeps through my clothes, chilling me to the bone. Mr. Millard waits, as if expecting me to change my mind. But I'm not interested. I shake my head again, shoving my hands in my pockets.

My lawyer clears his throat and looks toward the station before shutting the door with a click and walking toward me. His oxford shoes crunch the snow beneath him as he leans in closer to me and says, "Don't tell anyone anything." He lets out a breath and it turns to fog in the air as he looks behind him one last time.

"It's going to take a couple of months for this to die down, of course. But the evidence found on the scene that could tie you to murder has been dismissed already. It's a matter of finding motive and suspects now. The judge is never going to charge a Thatcher, and he doesn't want any digging around the circumstances of your father's death." For the first time, Mr. Millard looks at me as if he thinks I may have done it, but there's no contempt, no disgust, only curiosity behind his eyes.

"For you, it's over. A few months, and it's all buried. Just stay quiet and don't talk to anyone. Don't give them a reason to come back to you. As far as they know, they followed you there, there was an altercation but a fourth unknown individual shot them both. Evidence proves you didn't fire a gun. They can't change that; they can only hunt down a fourth… and you have no idea of that person's identity. If anyone asks, you're only grateful he didn't shoot you too."

I nod my head, feeling the weight of everything and how it all seems heavier for some reason. Knowing how unjust it is. That a select few have already decided the fate of the case.

I'm a hypocrite, because it's what I did when I saw that look in Anderson's eyes. The smile on his face as I left his office. I did the same. His fate was sealed. Even a glance at the photograph on his desk didn't stop me.

I saw her. I knew he was married. I knew she was his. I told myself I didn't care and that it didn't matter. He had to die.

It's that overwhelming feeling of power that made the first domino tip as I turned my back on him, knowing his fate was decided.

"Thank you, Mr. Millard," I say and turn away from the station, away from him and toward the crowded streets of the city.

I didn't know how the other dominoes would fall. And the judge and the lawyers, they have no idea either. So many pieces tumbled over. So many lives affected.

There's only one who matters to me.

Only one I need to keep safe.

Her piece is bound to fall if I touch her. I almost ruined her once. I won't do it again.

I was never any good for her. I should have stayed away if I loved her, and I think I did even all that time ago. I think I loved her before I ever heard that sweet laugh. Before I saw her gorgeous lips and that sadness in her beautiful doe eyes that she hid from everyone but me. I think I loved her even then.

And I should have stayed far away.

chapter 30

Julia

THEY SAY IF YOU LOVE SOMEONE, YOU SHOULD LET THEM GO.

That's all I keep thinking over and over as I stare out the windows of the penthouse, staring blankly at the city skyline. Mason's been out for over twenty-four hours now. I knew the second he walked out, and I waited. And waited. I owe him and all I can think is that if I send him a message, I'm going to beg him for even more. That's not fair and that's not right.

I swallow thickly, and my dry throat sends a spike of pain running through me. Or maybe it's my heart. I'm not sure which. I shake my head, turning abruptly and walk over to the kitchen to fix myself some coffee. If he wanted to speak to me, he would have come or he would have called. The fact is, he doesn't want me. Why did it take me this long to realize that wanting him and loving him wasn't enough?

He hasn't called, hasn't sent a text. I take a steadying breath, balancing myself on a padded barstool at the island counter and then gripping the hot mug of coffee with both hands. The ceramic mug has veins of gold running through the thick cream pottery. I focus on it and drift my finger over the raised texture remembering how he used to trail his fingers down my lips before kissing me.

Everything is a reminder of him and it hurts. I let my head fall back to exhale before taking a slow sip of the coffee. It's worse than death because I could have him. It could be different… He's right there.

I keep thinking he's merely let me go because he loves me. They say if you love someone, you should let them go. Maybe that's what I should do. I should let him go.

But isn't it done with? Isn't it over? The ending is so much different from what I envisioned. I will take this one where there is hope, over anything else. I want a chance.

The truth is, if Mason loved me, he'd be here. If he wanted me, he'd take me. That's the kind of man he is.

"If you want to go to his house…" Maddie says gently from the seat next to me, moving her hand to my thigh. She hasn't left my side since last night when the girls came over. When Kat told me Mason had been released from custody and I had waited for him to show, and he never did. After the first hour, I started to worry. After several hours, it was hard not to assume the worst. I'm glad my friends were here with me instead. I still don't know when I'll be able to return to my condo. The police say it's a crime scene, and that means it's off-limits in the meantime. I should message him… I should message Mason and let him know that. Shouldn't I? He should know that I'm still here in this penthouse when he's the one who's footing the bill.

"Maddie, please." Kat's patience is waning thin with a restless Maddie who won't stop asking questions. I'm grateful for the distraction, though.

Kat's sitting at the dining room table and Sue went to work. She didn't want to, but I insisted.

"There's nothing wrong with going after what you want," Maddie says, finishing her suggestion.

I glance from her to Kat, who's gently nodding her head. "That's true," she whispers. Both of them stare at me as if I'm broken. Like this is the one thing over the last year that has managed to finally destroy me.

I've lost a husband, then fell in love with his murderer. I've been held against my will, killed a man out of anger and another out of fear for my life.

Yet here I sit, worried about the man who brought all of this chaos in my life.

Worried he doesn't want me. Worried I can never have him again. Worried I'll never love anyone or be loved by anyone like him.

The mug clinks as I set it down on the counter, pushing it away to rest my face in my hands. The granite's cold on my elbows, but everything today has been brutally cold. I should be used to it by now.

Shifting on the stool next to me, Maddie gently rubs my back in soothing strokes, making the cotton blouse travel slightly up and down my back as she shushes me.

The padding of Kat's feet are muted by her socks when she gets up to sit by us too. She takes a seat alongside us at the island with me sitting between her and Maddie.

"Hey, it's okay. He didn't do it," Kat says in such a tender voice. It only makes the pain in my chest grow.

I didn't tell them a word, and I never will. They'll never know any of this truth. Not if I can help it.

"I know," I say and my voice cracks as I agree. I clear my throat and stare straight ahead, pushing the hair out of my face and ignoring both sets of their questioning eyes on me.

I can see myself in the reflection of the steel fridge, but it's not quite me, it's something else. Some different version that stares back, distorted. Perception is what's changed my life. It could have gone on and on with me not knowing a damn thing, only seeing what they wanted me to, and then none of this would have ever happened.

"He didn't do it," I say in a stronger voice, swallowing the lump in my throat.

"Why don't you call him maybe?" Maddie offers.

I have to drop my gaze. I can't look them in the eyes and lie. "I don't think he wants me to," I answer honestly, staring fixedly at the granite countertops.

"You're wrong, Jules." Kat's voice comes out harsher than I expected as she speaks, and I grip the edge of the counter to turn my body on the stool and face her. "Of course he loves you. That's more than obvious."

"You don't understand," I tell her even though I already know there's no convincing her. Kat's stubborn. She stares at me, waiting for an explanation. My eyes flicker to Maddie's, both of them waiting impatiently. I settle for a partial truth. "He said he loves me." I clear my throat and look past Kat. "I didn't say it back," I add. "The last time I saw him, I didn't say it back."

"Why?" Maddie sounds horrified, and it only makes me feel worse.

"It's just that he did something," I say haltingly, and my stomach churns as I look back to the gold flecks on the mug in front of me.

"Something like what?" Kat seems hesitant.

"It was something from a while ago, but it hurt me," I say then close my eyes, wishing they could just know. Wishing I didn't have to say it for them to understand.

"Did he mean to hurt you?" Kat asks and there's a pain in her gaze. I know it's because of what she and Evan are going through right now. I wish she'd talk to me about that, rather than feeling like I'm prying when I try to ask how she's holding up.

"I'm sure he didn't," Maddie says softly, but her brow is furrowed with sympathy as she waits for my response.

"It wasn't meant to, no, but it was meant to hurt someone else and it wasn't right." I see Maddie and Kat exchange glances.

"What did he do?" Maddie asks.

"Maybe he's not here because he thinks you want to keep your distance for now since he was arrested?" Kat says, delicately hinting around the fact that I'm very self-conscious of negative publicity.

"I don't care about that," I tell her bluntly. "He's not here now, because when I left…" I can't finish. I can't say the words because I'm ashamed that I didn't answer him. I've known I still love him. I know damn well I do, and I did then. I just didn't want to admit it.

"You upset him?" Kat says, taking a guess.

"I knew I might not see him again… and I still didn't say it back. He said I love you, and I didn't say it back."

"It's just words," Kat says, "Actions are what count. And if you love him, go for him. Fix it. You can always fix it." She's full of so much confidence. So much conviction, I have to believe her although part of me wonders if she's telling me what she's telling herself when it comes to her own relationship.

"Go to him," Maddie says sweetly.

"Don't you want him?" Kat presses when I don't respond, too caught up in my own thoughts.

Had I known the truth, I never would have gotten close, but he didn't give me that chance. He pulled me in and drowned me before I realized I couldn't breathe. I'll forever be his. All the sins and secrets could never tear us apart. We both have them. But if we have each other… they don't matter.

Maddie nods her head in agreement. "Just because you're fighting over something that happened before this doesn't mean anything." Her voice is firm. "He needs you."

And I need him. We always have, both in our own way.

All three of us turn our heads to the door as I hear it open with a loud thud. My heart hammers in my chest, pounding harder and harder as I see him. Mason.

The breath leaves my lungs and I nearly fall off the stool at the sight of him.

He doesn't look at me or even in this direction as he closes the door and tucks the keycard into his pocket. He slips off his boots easily, as if he belongs here and it's only natural.

As if he hadn't kept me waiting here for him for hours.

When he finally looks up, something breaks in me. The walls crumble, and I want to run to him. To climb off the stool and embrace him.

To thank him for taking the fall. For protecting me. For loving me even if he brought all this hell along with him. To check him over and make sure he's okay.

But I'm frozen in place. Paralyzed by the sight of him. He rolls his broad shoulders before tossing the jacket over the sofa and finally looking up at me. His steel gray eyes pierce through me, questioning only for a moment before turning his attention to the other two women.

Kat's hand squeezes mine briefly before she whispers, "Do you want us to get out of here?"

"Yeah," Maddie answers for me. "We'll see you tomorrow?" Maddie asks with wide eyes.

I nod my head, but still I can't speak. I can't answer either of them. He's here. All I can do is be thankful that he's here.

He's standing right there, only inches away from me. I can still feel the coldness from the outdoors around him. But it doesn't belong to him in the least. His tanned skin is pink on his cheeks and the tip of his nose. My fingers itch to reach out to him, to touch him and pass the chill of the air and feel his hot skin.

I'm vaguely aware of Kat and Maddie leaving, the sounds of keys jingling and each saying hello and then goodbye to Mason.

He gives them a tight smile and nods, his deep voice sending a soothing wave through me as he shoves his hands in his pockets and watches them leave.

As soon as the door shuts, he looks back at me, consuming me the way he does with his full attention as comes to the bar, close to me. Close enough to touch.

I lick my lips and scoot forward on the stool, my left knee brushing his right. "Mason," I say, whispering his name with a reverence I'm not sure he hears or recognizes, but his eyes look the same way they did months ago when I first left him. Raw and vulnerable. Emotional.

He can hide a lot of things from me, and I won't deny that because it's the absolute truth. But I can see the pain and love in his gaze when he looks at me like this.

I know that's real. He can't ever hide that from me.

"Jules," he says and Mason's voice is low. Too low. Panic drifts into my veins. It courses through me as he reaches out to run his fingers down my hair before resting his large hand on my thigh. His thumb runs back and forth in soothing strokes, but there's something about the way he's looking at me, something off about his body language. Something I don't like.

"I never should have put you through all this, Jules."

My heart clenches, feeling so constricted that I can't fathom the amount of pain I'm feeling. He's letting me go. He gave me hope, walking through the door. *No! No! Go back to the hope. We have hope. We don't have everything but we have hope, don't we?* The words tangle over themselves in the back of my throat.

"I never should have," he says then swallows before continuing, "I never should have killed him. I'm sorry." All I can do is shake my head slightly as I listen to Mason. It was a mistake, an unforgivable sin. An act that ruined my life. But he had his reasons. I can't deny that it was wrong, but so much was wrong. The pieces fell, and there was blood on everyone's hands.

"I was a different man then. I didn't know you yet, and I can't ever take it back." Mason pulls his hand away, and the warmth and comfort of his touch vanishes, replaced by a sudden chill.

"I fell in love with you and I'd do anything to keep you, but I know you don't want that.

I hate myself as much as you hate me."

He starts to turn away from me. To leave me like I've wanted since I learned the truth, but my body comes to life, my blood a mix of anxiety and depression. I grip Mason's hand as I stumble off the stool, the damn thing nearly toppling over.

"Don't you dare leave me," I say. My voice comes out raw as tears threaten to spill from my eyes. I refuse to take my hands from his to wipe under my eyes.

Never.

He's as much mine as I am his. I refuse to let him go.

His expression changes as he registers my words. "Don't you ever leave me again," I tell him with a strength formed from panic. *Please, please God, don't let him deny me.*

"I need you." The hot tears fall to my lips and I try to swallow, but it hurts too much. Everything hurts as I stand before the man I love, knowing it's wrong. Knowing he broke me, ruined me and then showed me how fucked up love can be. The only cruel thing left for him to do to me would be to leave me like this. To throw me away after everything we've been through.

"There's hope, isn't there?" I say. "I love you," I whisper with complete conviction.

Just as I part my lips to confess every emotion in me to him, he crashes his lips against mine, filling my chest with a warm flow of desire and completion. My lips are hard at first, caught off guard, but I'm quick to mold them to his, spearing my fingers through his hair as his hand splays at the small of my back, both of us deepening the kiss, both of us wanting more.

"Mason." I moan his name as he breaks the kiss, my eyes still closed as our hot breath mingles between us.

"Just hold me. I love you," I tell him and bury my head into his hard chest. He wraps his strong arms around me as his warmth consumes me and kisses my hair over and over. This is where I belong, I know it is.

"I love you," he says and it's all I need.

I love Mason. And he loves me.

Epilogue

Julia

Deceit is pretty,
The truth is better than the lie.
Its beauty lurks in darkness,
It's gorgeous in ways you can't deny.

Although the tale is strange,
Not the ever after for you and me.
It's broken and imperfect,
And the way fate meant it to be.

MY BRUNETTE HAIR LOOKS NEARLY BLACK WHEN IT'S WET. THE BRUSH makes a loud thud as I set it down and reach for my makeup bag. Looks can be so deceiving, can't they?

We have a beautiful home, seemingly the perfect life and many days, that's all I see. It's all I saw with Jace too, but that was a sham and a lie and I realize now that I knew the truth well back then. I was happy with the image, but the truth was something I hid; I wanted it that way.

What I have with Mason is the opposite. Although no one can see the truth, I know what we are. Raw and broken, but together, we're whole.

The world will never know what it took for the two of us to come out of this alive. No one will ever realize how much strength there is between us. We're unbreakable. Shattered to pieces, but healed together with a scar that's so much stronger than what was once there.

It's not a fairytale, but it's a happily ever after suited for us both. It gives me chills when I look back at the past, but I don't do that often. It's much better to look ahead, at the true happiness and comfort we give each other. At the full life of trust and faith that's been forged between us.

My phone pings with another text from Kat. And then another.

She finally told me what's happening with her and Evan.

He's still your Evan, I answer and stare at my phone, waiting for her response.

If anyone ever heard my story, maybe they'd say what I did was wrong. That crawling back to Mason after knowing what he did, is simply unforgivable.

Even my closest friends. I don't think they would understand. No one would.

Love is inexplicable. It makes you do crazy things. Love is blind… that's a saying for a reason, isn't it?

I know, Kat writes back. *He's still the man I married. Dangerous in ways I don't like to think about. I did this to myself. I knew better than to fall for him.*

My heart hurts for her when she messages again before I can respond: *I only wish love were enough to fix this…*

It is. I'm desperate to write that back to her. But there are pieces to their story I'm missing. Pieces that will come out one way or another…

you know 4

love you

I married the bad boy from Brooklyn.

The one with the tattoos and a look in his eyes that told me he was bad news.
The kind of look that comes with all sorts of warnings.

I knew what I was doing.
I knew by the way he first held me that he would be my downfall; how he
owned me with his forceful touch.

I couldn't say no to him, not that I wanted to. That was then,
and it seems like forever ago.

Years later, I've grown up and moved on. But he's still the man I married.
Dangerous in ways I don't like to think about and tried to ignore for so long.
I did this to myself. I knew better than to fall for him.

I only wish love were enough to fix this …

You Know I Love You is book 1 of a duet. It is the second duet in the You Are
Mine series, but it can be read first.

Kat

It only took one night; one moment, and my fate was sealed. He knew I would never tell him   no.

I wonder what would have happened if I'd never met Evan. The thought makes my stomach sink and twist, and a cold chill flows in waves over my body.

It *pains* me to consider such a thing. To have never been with the man I love. Dragging in a lungful of cold air, I steady myself with deep breaths.

It physically hurts to imagine not having him in my life for the last six years.

I didn't know I was setting myself up for heartbreak all those years ago. Yet here I am, and that reality is what keeps me up at night. My eyes burn from both exhaustion and the tears begging to be shed.

That chance encounter set everything into motion, and only months ago I would have said it was a blessing, bestowed upon me by fate, or maybe kismet. But now I know better.

I wish I'd never stopped that night.

I wish I'd never met Evan at that gas station.

Whoever said it's better to have loved and lost than never to have loved at all was a liar and a fool.

This pain isn't worth it.

If only I could go back, because I don't know how we'll get through this.

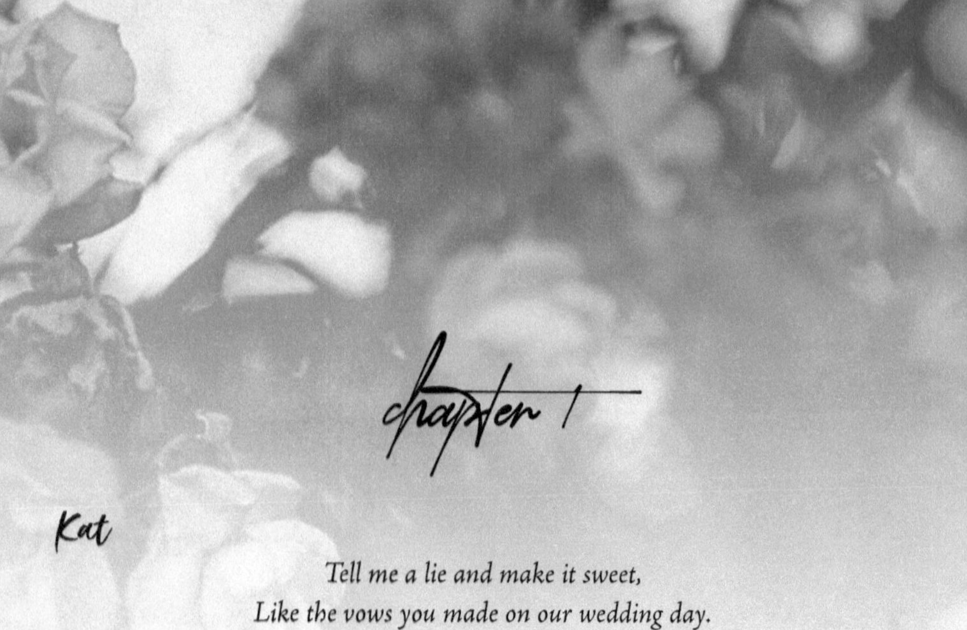

Kat

Tell me a lie and make it sweet,
Like the vows you made on our wedding day.
Tell me a lie, don't make it hurt,
The pain in my chest won't go away.
Don't tell me the truth, I can't face what's to come.
I'll yell and I'll kick, I'll fight it, I'll run.
Don't tell me the truth, I don't want to hear.
Tell me pretty lies with whispers sincere.

T HE CHILL ON MY SKIN LINGERS AND FLOWS DOWN MY SHOULDERS. It's an odd sensation that travels across my arms and I'd like to blame it on the alcohol, but I've felt it all day. From the very start of this morning, before the drinks came easier and easier. For days, really, I've been feeling this strange sensation of not quite being in my own body. As if I'm not really here. This isn't really happening to me.

It's been going on for more than a few days if I'm honest … maybe even weeks, but I've been ignoring the signs and whispers, pretending like they weren't real.

Now that this sickness won't leave me, I can't deny it.

Ever since I let the words slip through my lips.

I hate you.

You're a fucking liar.

I want a divorce.

An ache in my chest prompts me to take a sip of wine. Letting it slide down my throat, I pretend that it soothes me. It's numbing, that's what it is. That's what I need. Tears prick at my eyes, but I don't let them fall. Instead a shuddering breath leaves me and I lift up my glass, downing the remaining wine. It's too sweet for being so dark.

Startled by a sound from the floor above me, the glass nearly tips over as I set it down quickly to wipe under my eyes. I don't want him to see me cry; I won't let him. But the creak I heard was a false alarm. I don't hear the heavy footsteps of him coming down the stairs to our townhouse. I'm still alone in the dining room, waiting for him to leave.

Left only with bittersweet memories and the constant question: *How did this happen?*

The thick, dark drapes behind me are pulled shut but even they can't completely drown out the night sounds of busy New York City. There's always a bit that travels through. It used to bother me when I initially moved here, but now it's soothing. It calms me as my gaze drifts toward the empty stairwell, where it lingers.

I shouldn't be drunk, not when I'm supposed to be preparing to meet with a potential client tomorrow. As one of the top literary agents in New York City, I'm damn good at what I do but tonight, I don't care.

I shouldn't have closed my laptop and logged off all social media when I have promotions and advertisements running around the clock for these launches.

I shouldn't be doing a lot of things.

But here I am, sitting at the head of the dining room table, and I refuse to do anything but watch the stairs and wait for him to leave. The very thought of staring at his back as the front door closes forces me to reach for the bottle.

I listen carefully as I pour the last of the wine into my glass. He's packing at the last minute, like he always does, but this time it's so much different. He's traveling for work, but when he leaves from his rendezvous in London, he's not coming back here. That sudden realization brings a fresh flood of unshed tears to burn my eyes, but I remain very still. As if maybe playing dead will hold back these emotions.

"He better not," I mutter beneath my breath, holding on to my resolve.

I lift the glass to my lips, the dark cabernet tasting sweeter and sweeter with each sip, lulling me into a lethargy where the memory of yesterday fades.

Where the article doesn't exist. Where the denial of an affair can fall on deaf ears. The picture itself was innocent. But Evan doesn't have a single explanation for me. He can't make clear to me why he's lying, why he's stumbling over his words to come up with a justification.

What hurts the most is the look in his eyes when he lies to me. The paparazzi photo is of him with his boss's wife Samantha, who just so happens to be in the middle of a vicious divorce. He was with her at 3:00 in the morning in her hotel lobby. Three fucking a.m. *Nothing good happens past 2:00 a.m.* He used to make that joke all the time when we first met. I used to laugh with him when he said it.

There's only one explanation for that photograph and both of us know it.

Even though he can't come up with a plausible excuse, he still denies it. It's a slap in my face. I'm done pretending like I can forgive him for this. If he can't give me his truth, I'm left with my own, which is that my husband is not the man I fell in love with. Or at the very least, his decisions aren't ones I can live with.

I suck in a long, deep breath, pushing my phone away as it beeps again with a message from a friend and I lean back in my chair. I don't want to read it. With the palms of my hands, I cover my eyes, suddenly feeling hot. Too hot.

They keep asking me the same things, but with different words.

Maddie: *Are you all right?*

Julia: *Is it true? It can't be true.*

Suzette: *So you went through with it? Is there anything I can do?*

Messages from my friends have been hitting my phone one by one, each of them making it vibrate on the table throughout the day.

It takes everything in me to face them, as if they were really here in person asking me all these questions. I don't have answers to give them, none that I want to say out loud anyway. I'm not pushing away my husband because I want to. I'm doing it because I have to and I don't have the resolve to speak that confession.

Even I'm disappointed in myself.

My friends want what's best for me. They only want to help me and I know that's the truth, but it doesn't keep me from being angry at the phone as it goes off again.

Heaving in a deep breath, I wish I wasn't in the big city. I wish I wasn't well known. I wish I could hide under the guise of anonymity and just be no one. More importantly, I wish no one knew. I'd crawl back to him if that were the case. I'd beg him to hold me every time I cried, even if he's the one who brought out this side of me.

I'd beg him to love me. He would, I know it. And then I'd hate myself.

You deserve better than this. Another message from Suzette comes through next and I can only run the pad of my thumb down the screen over her words. It's an attempt to make myself believe it.

Just leave me alone. Everyone get out of my life, my marriage. It wasn't for them to see. It's not for them to judge like every fucking gossip column in New York City. It's not the first time our marriage has been mentioned in the papers, but I pray it'll be the last.

My knuckles turn white as I grip the phone with the intent of throwing it, letting it smack against the wall to silence it, but I don't. It's the sound of Evan's boots rhythmically hitting each step as he walks down the stairs that forces me to compose myself. At the very least I pretend to; he's always seen through it, though. He knows how much this kills me.

I hit the button to turn off my phone and ignore the texts and calls, squaring my shoulders as I attempt to pull myself together.

I haven't answered a single message or email since this morning when Page Six came out with an article about our separation. It's funny how I only uttered the words two nights ago, yet it was already circulating gossip columns before the weekend hit, blasted all over social media. I wonder if he wanted this. If that was Evan's way of finally pushing his workaholic wife to the brink of divorce.

My gaze morphs into a glare as he comes into view, but it doesn't stay long. My skin is suddenly feeling hotter, but in a way that's joined with desire. I can't help but to imagine how his rough stubble would feel against my palm as I caressed his cheek, how his lips would taste as he leaned down to kiss me. A very large part of me wants to savor it. Our last goodbye kiss. It's funny how the goodbye kisses are the ones I value most, but I won't let him kiss me before he leaves this time. Not when the last things that came from his lips were lies.

My deep inhales are silent, although the heavy rise and fall of my chest betrays me. If he notices, he doesn't let on as he places his luggage by the front door. My own hands turn numb watching his.

Even if he is only wearing a pair of faded jeans and a plain white T-shirt, he's still devilishly handsome. It's his muscular physique and tanned, tattooed skin that let you know he's a classic bad boy regardless of what he's wearing. My heart beats slower as the seconds pass between us; it's calming just to look at him. That's how he got me in the beginning. The desire and attraction are undeniable despite what he's done.

He's the first to break our gaze as he runs his fingers through his dark brown hair and lets out an uneasy sigh. In response my lips curl into a sarcastic smile, mocking both me and my thoughts. I'm not the only one to fall for his charm and allure, but I should have learned my lesson by now. My fingers slip down the thin stem of the wineglass as I smile weakly and force back the sting in my eyes, pretending I'm not going to cry, pretending that I've made my decision final. Like I don't already regret it.

"I have to go," Evan states after a moment of uncomfortable silence, apart from the constant background hum of traffic.

My blood rushes and I try to swallow the lump in my throat. I focus on the wine, the dark red liquid pooling in the base of the glass. I try to swirl it, but it doesn't move; there's so little left.

"Is she going to be there?" I ask him, staring straight ahead at a black and white photo of the two of us taken years ago on vacation in Mexico.

Why? Why even bother? Why did I let it slip out? I'd planned to just say goodbye. Just end this suffering already.

As he answers, I continue to stare at the genuine smile on my face and then to where his arm is wrapped possessively around my waist in the photograph.

I hate that I asked. It's my insecurity, my hate. My envy even.

"No, she's not. And I already told you it doesn't matter." Any trace of a smile or even of disinterest leaves me. I can't hide what it does to me, what his lie has done to me.

It doesn't matter. Let it go. They're all non-answers. They're words to hide the truth and we both know it.

My elbow is planted on the table as I rest my chin in my hand and try to cover up how much it hurts. To keep it from him just like he's keeping the truth from me, even if I sniff a little too loud. I speak low as I stare straight ahead at nothing in particular. "You told me it's not true, but you didn't deny it to the press," I tell him and finally look him in the eye. "You didn't deny it to anyone but me, and I know you're lying." My words crack at the end and I have to tear my gaze away. "It's been different since you came home." My last statement is drawn out and practically a whisper. It's been difficult between us over the past year, but the last two weeks … The tension between us changed the second he came home. I knew something bad had happened. I knew it.

Everyone told me to be careful and warned me about Evan six years ago when I first started seeing him. I knew what I was doing when I first said yes to a date with him, when I gave myself to him and let myself fall for someone like him. I'm a fool.

"I told you, Kat, it's not what it looks like," he says and his voice is soft, like he's afraid to say the words louder.

"Then why not tell them?" I ask, staring into his pleading expression. "Why let the world believe you've cheated on me? What could you possibly gain?" Each question gets louder as the words rush out of my mouth. I'm ashamed of how much passion there is in my voice. How much of my pain is on display.

In stark contrast is how little pain he shows and I don't miss how he hasn't budged. He hasn't made a single move to come to me. So I stay planted in my seat as well.

I know why he doesn't deny it, and it's because it's true. Years of just the two of us have shown me who he is and I know he's not a liar, but he's lying to me now. I've never been more sure of anything in my life. "It's been weeks, hasn't it?" I say, forcing out the words from between clenched teeth. This morning I couldn't talk without screaming. Without slamming my fists onto the table, making it shake and causing a glass of water to fall and shatter on the hardwood floor.

I reached my breaking point when he looked me in the eye and told me there was nothing to that picture. I refuse to listen when he lies; not when he does such a horrible job of it.

"Stop it, Kat," Evan commands firmly and his voice is harsh and unforgiving, like I'm the one in the wrong.

"Oh, I see," I respond, raising a brow and feeling a sick smile tug at my lips. "You can cheat, you can lie, but I should be quiet and give you a kiss on the way out to go do whatever you want to do?"

"Don't do this," he says with a rawness that makes my heart clench.

"Then tell me what happened. I know something did." He's been distant, even cold toward me ever since he came home.

A moment passes and I lose my composure again, bared to him in every way as I wait for an answer. But I don't get the one thing I need. The truth. *Or a believable lie.*

"I have to go," is all he says as he gathers his luggage. Slinging a black duffle bag over one shoulder, gripping a suitcase with his other hand, he adds, "I love you."

He says the words without looking at me.

I love you.

It hurts so damn much because he knows I love him. He knows it and he throws the words back at me like it doesn't matter that he's risking it all.

"If you won't tell me the truth," I say lowly as I stare at the table, pushing out the words and feeling each one slice open the cut in my heart that much deeper, "then don't bother coming back." My throat tightens and my lungs refuse to fill as silence is all that answers me.

There's only a slight hesitation, a small creaking sound as he adjusts his grip on the luggage. That's all I get. That's it. The creak of the floorboards that's barely heard over my racing heart.

He leaves without attempting to kiss me or approaching me in the least. His strides don't break in cadence until the heavy walnut front door opens and closes, leaving me with nothing but the tortured sob that's desperate to come up and the faint sounds of the city life filling the empty space once again.

My hands tremble as I close my eyes and try to calm down.

If he really loved me, he wouldn't have let it come to this.

If he loved me, he'd tell me the truth.

Secrets break up marriages.

I keep telling myself that he's to blame, but as a cry rips up my throat and I bring my knees into my chest, my heels resting on the seat of the chair, I replay the last few years and I know I'm at fault too. Deep down, I know. I bury my face in my knees and rock slightly, feeling pathetic as I break down yet again.

If I were him, I'd have cheated on me too.

He says he didn't. He swears it's a lie.

But he doesn't explain it. He can't even look me in the eye.

I did this to myself. I should've known better.

Evan

WHEN DID I TURN INTO THE PIECE OF SHIT I AM RIGHT NOW? *Pathetic.* That's how I feel as the plane rumbles beneath my feet and I shake my head slightly, waving off the flight attendant and whatever small bag of snacks she was offering.

I crack my neck to the left and right as a ding indicates the seatbelt sign is off and everyone can move about the cabin. I have no intention of getting up or doing a damn thing other than sit here and try to figure out exactly where it all went wrong.

The Wi-Fi is available and I take my time setting it up, prolonging the moment when I'll have to face the fact that she most likely hasn't messaged me. She can yell at me, hit me, take it all out on me, but her silence is what kills me. Her shutting me out is like a knife to the heart.

There's no way to make it right, but I'm not letting her go.

Kat's mine. My wife. *My love.* She's everything to me, even if she hates me to the point where I'm nothing to her.

We used to be … Something special. Something other assholes dream about and pray for. And now? I couldn't even kiss her before leaving. The very thought of doing it felt too much like goodbye. Like the kind of goodbye that would kill me.

She's kidding herself if she thinks I'm not coming home to her. I don't care that we're going through this, I don't care how bad our fighting is or that I fucked up beyond repair. She doesn't know what happened and I hope she never will, but that doesn't change the fact that she's mine. Above all else, I love her and she loves me. She can't deny that.

My seat groans as I readjust in first class. I clear my throat and clench my teeth as the plane rumbles again, reminding me that she's miles and miles away. Reminding me that I left her again.

I can't bring myself to feel like I deserve her forgiveness. Or that I deserve her at all. That's always been the case between us. She's always been too good for me. The guilt is all-consuming and now I'm trapped in a corner, desperately looking for a way out of the mess I've gotten myself into.

My computer pings as the plane continues to fly across the ocean taking me farther away from her, and I lean forward to check it. I'm far too quick to do it too, praying it's Kat.

Praying's never helped me before and sure enough, it didn't this time either. It's only a message from James, my boss and Samantha's now ex.

My teeth grind against one another, making my jaw even more tense as I read the message. It's the schedule for the rest of the day and my room number for the hotel.

It feels like a slap in the face. I can't keep up this façade and live each day as if nothing's happened. Pretending like nothing's changed.

The back of my head pushes into the seat as I take a calming breath.

Stuck between a rock and a hard place is an inadequate saying.

I'm fucked. Just waiting for them to pick, pick, pick away at me while I have my hands tied behind my back.

Only years ago, I loved my life. It was a high most would be envious of. This is what I wanted more than anything. On the outside, it's glamorous. I stay at five-star resorts, party with celebrities and have every sinful pleasure at my fingertips. That's what a life of helping the rich and famous avoid prison has afforded me.

I protect the clients from any bad press, keep charges from sticking, and avoid any altercations that could lead to something … unwanted. In return, I'm paid generously and live the high life.

I didn't sign up for *this*, but I sure as fuck cashed every check along the way. My email beeps and it's another message from James, as if confirming that exact thought: this is exactly what I signed up for. It's what I asked for.

Let me know when you land. That's all the email says.

I clear my throat as my hand clenches into a fist and I run the rough pad of my thumb over my knuckles slowly. My reflection in the screen stares back at me and I note the scowl, the dark circles under my eyes. *The anger.*

When I was younger, this was all I wanted. I get paid to party and live in a perpetual state of drunkenness. I lived for the thrill.

Kat used to love it too. Years ago, when we first met and things were different. I glance at the empty seat to my left and picture her sitting beside me. She used to play with the buckle on every flight. Unbuckle, buckle, unbuckle, buckle.

At first I thought it was a nervous habit that had to do with a fear of flying, but it was just due to the excitement.

She loved coming with me to events. It was what we did together. Back when everything was the way it was supposed to be.

Back when life was less complicated.

Back when we were kids and I didn't realize that life was going to catch up to me and her career was going to take off, placing us on two very different paths in life.

A huff of a sigh leaves me as I shift in my seat and look back to my computer.

I click over to the flight tab and see there are four hours remaining until we land in London. Four hours to sit in silence and dwell on each and every moment where I fucked up. Every step I took that led me to this very hour.

I turned thirty-two just four months ago, but I'm living the same life I had when we were in our twenties.

She's the one who changed.

She grew up and I'm the one who screwed up.

I run a hand down my face, trying to get the images out of my head.

She can never know, but I was a fool to think I'd hidden it from her.

There's no way out of this.

How can she love me when she knows I'm lying to her?

How can she forgive me for a sin she has no idea I've committed?

How can I keep her when I don't deserve her?

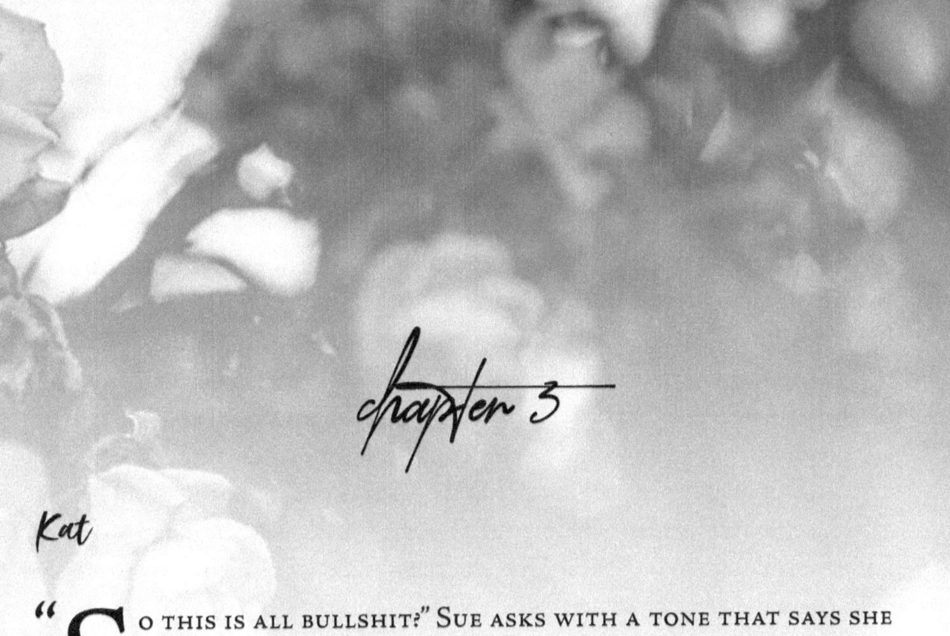

chapter 3

Kat

"**S**O THIS IS ALL BULLSHIT?" SUE ASKS WITH A TONE THAT SAYS SHE believes otherwise as she motions to the newspaper. Her voice is soft, but my nerves make it seem louder than it is here in this small coffee shop. I almost shush her before realizing she's not speaking loudly at all.

"It doesn't look like it's …" I can't finish my thought, my eyes drawn to the same picture I stared at for hours last night, plus the night before.

"Well, she's all over him. There's no denying that."

"Women are always all over him." My answer comes out flat. I'm nothing if not blunt and transparent. It's one of the reasons my clients trust me.

"I used to like it … when they'd try to be all over him," I admit to her but bite my tongue at the urge to voice the additional confession: *I loved it.* "How they'd fawn over him, desperate for Evan's attention. But he only had eyes for me."

"Why is this one any different then?" The paper hits the slick surface of the coffee table as she tosses it down and immediately digs into her large Chanel hobo bag. I know she believes exactly what Evan denied. It's written all over her perfectly red, pursed lips. This is only an attempt to appease me.

It's not the first, the second, or even the third time Evan's had his name in the tabloids for less than angelic reasons. Suzette has her opinions, but she's always refrained from voicing them when it comes to Evan.

His reputation and his livelihood depend on the fact that he's gotten away with things that would send most people to jail for the night.

That was the case before I met him, anyway. Now he gets paid to make sure his clients meet the same fate.

Sue talks as she pulls out a tube of deep red lipstick and a compact mirror.

"Do you think he really did it this time?" she asks as if the weight of our marriage doesn't rest on my answer.

The reason this time is different is because I know there's truth to it.

It's because of how he reacts.

It's how he looks at me as if he's guilty.

"He says it's not what it looks like," I answer and roll my eyes as I do, trying to downplay the pain that coils in my chest. My throat goes tight, but I'm saved by the return of Maddie.

For so many years, since I first moved here really, there's been one constant. It's these women. Jules, my first client and the New York socialite who brought us all together, isn't here. I owe her so much for helping my career take off as quickly as it did, but Jules has everything and all she really wants is companionship. She's getting settled into married life, but she'd be here if I asked. Maddie and Sue were both available and to be honest, I'd prefer them right now. They're not helplessly in love and therefore blind as a bat.

"Pumpkin spice," Maddie says as she sets a hot cup of coffee down in front of me. She doesn't look me in the eyes, like she's afraid doing even that will make me cry.

The strong scent of cinnamon smacks me in the face, but I wrap my hand around the cup, giving her a grateful smile as she takes her seat to my right. I don't like flavored coffee—I don't even like pumpkin, but I'll drink it. I desperately need the caffeine.

My gaze travels to Sue, sitting straight across from me as she returns to the conversation and says, "He says it's not what it looks like?" Her brow quirks as she adds, "… And what does that mean?" It's not a question, it's an accusation and the two of us know it.

"What does what mean?" Maddie asks innocently, the legs of her chair scraping along the floor.

"It means he's lying," Sue answers matter-of-factly and folds the newspaper over, reading the article again. It's only a paragraph, maybe two. It doesn't say much other than the fact that Samantha Lapour and her husband James are now separated, due to an affair she had with my husband, Evan Thompson. Which is a blatant lie. Their marriage has been on the rocks for months and they were separated long before this happened.

Inwardly I cringe at defending my husband at all. An affair is an affair. In an effort to ease the guilt that weighs down my chest, I rub the small spot just below my collarbone.

Maddie's expression turns hard with a look of warning that would normally make me laugh considering how petite and naïve she is. "We're talking about Evan," she says under her breath. Her eyes stay on Sue, who slowly purses her lips and acknowledges Maddie with only a short nod.

The newly divorced Suzette doesn't give men a chance to explain. For good reason, seeing as how she's been through hell and back.

"I'm sorry," Maddie whispers and then clings to her own coffee. French vanilla if I had to guess.

"It's fine," I say lowly, shaking off the emotions rocking through my body and easing the tension at the table. "There's no reason for us to get into this." I don't look at either of them, blowing on the hot coffee and reluctantly drinking it. I don't taste it on the way down, though.

"Well, what do you think?" Maddie asks me and then she puts down her own cup. The coffee shop on Madison Avenue is fairly empty, probably due to the rain and chill of the late fall in the air.

As the shop door opens with a small chime and the busy sounds of the street flood into the small space for a moment, I think of how to answer her.

I don't know what to say.

I think he cheated on me.

I think he's sorry and he regrets it.

I think he loves me. No, I know he loves me.

And I feel like a fool for still loving him and wanting him.

That's what's in my head as I look around the small coffee shop, taking in every detail of the bright white chair rail and cream walls. The framed macro photographs of coffee pots and coffee beans keep my attention a little longer. I've never really noticed them before. This place is so familiar, yet I couldn't have described any of these details if someone had asked me. I've been coming here for years and yet I'd never cared enough to look at what was right here in front of me.

"Why would he lie to you?" Maddie asks, pulling my attention back to her. She huffs, sitting back and causing the chair to grind against the floor as she does. "I just can't imagine Evan doing this." My shoulders rise with a deep intake of breath as I pick at a small square napkin on the table.

I roll the tiny piece I've ripped off between my forefinger and thumb, watching as it crumples into a small ball.

"I don't know why," I answer softly. I can feel all the overwhelming sadness and betrayal rise up and make my throat tighten as I try to come up with a response. "Maybe I'm stupid, but I can't remember him ever lying to me before." I swallow thickly and flick the tiny ball onto the table. "Not like this." Defeat drips from my words.

"Sorry," I tell them and wipe under my tired eyes, hating that I could possibly feel the telltale prick of tears behind them given how much I've already cried. "I tried not to let it …" I can't finish. I watch as the rain batters the large glass window in the front of the shop and I slip my internal armor back on.

"Don't you dare be sorry," Sue says with a strength that pulls my attention back to her. Her jet-black hair cut into a blunt bob sways as she leans forward, moving closer to me while she speaks with an undeniable authority. "If you want to cry, cry. If you want to scream, do it. Whatever you need to do, just let it out."

Maddie nods her head in my periphery, but I can't do the same. Looking at the two of them, the stark contrast between Maddie and Suzette is more than obvious. Maddie's a young brunette with large doe eyes, equally in love with love itself and the big city. Sue's a recent divorcée with a bitter sense of humor she's earned. Even their fashion choices are at odds. Maddie's wearing a maxi dress and has a teal raincoat and clear umbrella hanging off the back of her chair, while Sue's in a black and white tweed dress with a matching jacket, plus a broad-brimmed, black Breton hat she wears to keep people away.

Somewhere in the middle is where I fall.

What if I want to deal with it by falling into his arms and letting him lie to me? I bite my tongue, letting the silence be eaten up by the ticking of the clock. I know it's not okay, yet that's all I want. I want him to fight for me. I want him to love me. I want to forgive him, even if he won't admit what he's done.

And that makes me a coward and a pathetic excuse for a modern-day woman, doesn't it?

The snide thought makes me turn my attention back to the dreary state of affairs outside. The clouds have set in and the sky quickly turns dark.

"This is crap weather for a first meeting," I say out loud, not really meaning to.

"Way to change the topic," Sue half jokes as she picks up her coffee cup and takes a sip, the smirk ever present on her lips. Her light blue eyes stare back at me from over the rim and it almost makes me laugh. Almost.

"So you're meeting your client here?" Maddie asks, gracefully accepting my invitation to talk about anything else. I've never loved her more than in this very moment.

I nod, still not trusting myself to speak and take another gulp of my coffee. I forgot it was pumpkin spice and I nearly spit it out, startled by the flavor, but then I swallow it down. It's not so bad.

Maddie pulls her dark brown, curly hair over her shoulder and scrunches her nose as she takes in my expression. "You don't like pumpkin?" she asks, raising a brow in disbelief.

"It's okay," I say, answering her with a straight face and Sue erupts with a laugh that catches the attention of an elderly couple behind us. Her good humor is infectious and I find myself smiling. This is what I need. To talk and think about something else. Anything else.

"I'll get you something else," Maddie says as Sue starts to speak. "Just regular? Cream and sugar?"

"Thanks, but don't worry about it, Maddie. It's good." I wave off her concern and take another sip. "I just needed some caffeine."

"Well, you look professional," Sue says with a nod. "The rain didn't ruin your hair."

I shake out my hair playfully in response to Sue's attempt at a distraction but Maddie doesn't pick up on the hint, and when I yawn, she goes right back to the conversation I hoped we were done with.

"Trouble sleeping?" Maddie asks and I nod my head once then turn back to the cup, hating that we're back on this again.

"I just wish I had …" I can't finish the sentence and I struggle to come up with something to say as I push the hair from my face while trying to remember what I want. I haven't got a clue. "I wish I had my life together," I practically whisper, but they hear and I know they do.

"You do have your life together. You're an established publisher. An entrepreneur and a hard worker."

I have work. Yes. Maddie happily agrees with Sue, reminding me of how many people in this very city would kill for my job.

But I don't have a damn thing else. Not enough to hold on to a life I somehow strayed from.

The thought makes me miserable and I focus on the coffee again, knocking it back as if it'll save me. When I set it down, I notice how empty it is as I tap the bottom of it against the table and hear a hollow sound. I'm going to need a refill. I'll get it myself, though. I push away from the table slightly. "I'm going to grab another. At this rate it'll be empty before Jacob gets here."

"Oh, Jacob." Sue says his name with a hint of something I can't describe in her voice. A devilish smile grows on her face and it makes me roll my eyes. Of all the girls, Sue's the one who gets over one man by getting under another. And she's given the advice freely to our tight group of friends. I can practically feel her elbow in my ribs.

"Yes, *Jacob*," I echo, mocking the way she said it, feeling irritable and juvenile, but it only makes Sue smile.

"Well I hope he's a good distraction for you," Sue says then winks and slides her bag off her lap, onto her shoulder.

"Work is always a good distraction." My tone destroys the bit of lightness. "I'm good at burying myself in it." The girls are quiet as my words sit stale in the air. It's part of the reason my marriage is tainted. I don't have to say it out loud and they don't have to tell me. Everyone already knows it.

She worked herself to death will be written on my tombstone. It's all I think while I stand at the counter and order another coffee. Regular this time, with a splash of cream and plenty of sugar.

"I read his book you gave me," Maddie says when I retake my seat a moment later, changing the subject back to Jacob Scott. "I looked him up online too," she adds as a smile spreads across her lips and her cheeks brighten with a blush. She scoots to the back of her seat and holds her cup in both hands, gladly taking the attention off of me. "He's cute," she says and smiles in a way I don't see often from her. My left brow raises as I watch her pink cheeks turn brighter. *Little Miss Innocent.*

"Is he now?" Sue comments and the two share a look as Maddie nods.

"Want me to put in a good word for you?" I question—it's meant for either of them really—and reach into my Kate Spade satchel for my laptop and notebook, setting them up on the table as Sue stands and puts on her jacket. There's no way Maddie would actually make a move. She's so sheltered and inexperienced. There's also no way I'd let someone like Jacob near her.

"You can always stay and wait for him to get here?" I say jokingly. "Or maybe leave something behind and have to come back for it?"

She doesn't answer, merely shakes her head and slides off her seat to join Sue in leaving me to my fresh coffee and waiting laptop.

"I wouldn't want to impose," Maddie finally says and then walks over to give me a hug. Even in her heels, I still sit a little higher at the bar-height table as she embraces me.

I half expect her to say something in my ear, to tell me it'll be all right or that Evan's made a mistake. But she doesn't say a word until she lets me go. "I'm just a call away," she says with a chipper tone that wouldn't clue in anyone around us that I'd need to call her because my life is falling apart. Both of her hands grip my shoulders just a second too long.

My heart goes pitter-patter.

"Same here, darling," Sue adds, placing her own hand on Maddie's shoulder as a cue, and then the two walk off. The sound of Sue's heels starts to fade as she opens the door. But the chime sounds just the same as when we first walked in here.

"Later, loves." I force a smile on my face as they leave me here alone.

But my expression doesn't reflect anything I truly feel.

And nothing's changed.

Evan

BERKELEY SQUARE IN LONDON FEELS THE SAME AS IT HAS FOR YEARS. The crisp air and old trees that tower over the park always feel timeless when I'm here. The black iron and white stone that speak to the history of this place never fail to impress. The dark, narrow alleys and the nightlife tucked away in the shadows of this city are what make my blood heat and my foot tap anxiously on the floorboard of the car.

It's always given me a rush to come here. There are a number of cities I'm fond of, cities that are playgrounds for the wealthy and where the best parties are had. Los Angeles, San Francisco, and New York City, of course. But London is one of the best. There's something to be said about being away from your normal life and getting to unwind in a city you don't have any obligations to stay in, yet welcomes you as if it's always been home.

The cabby clears his throat and his accent greets me as he tries to make small talk. I give him a curt nod and as many one-word answers as it takes to make it clear he doesn't need to fill the time with needless conversation. I'm not interested.

Rubbing sleep from my eyes, I lean back in the leather seat, feeling more and more exhausted as we pass the park, the dark green landscape fading from sight and rows of homes taking the place of the public areas.

I've felt comfortable here for years. It's a constant go-to for the PR company and I've been sent here to look after clients multiple times. But as the sky turns gray and the rain starts to beat against the tin roof, the welcoming feeling leaves me, and I'm left empty. Brought back to the present and brooding on how much the past has fucked me over.

The cab takes a left onto Hay Hill and I pass an old townhome where I used to crash. I've had so many close calls here. I was too much of a hothead, always looking for a thrill and pushing my luck further and further.

The cabby comes to a stop before I'm ready. The memories play on a loop in the back of my head of all the years I spent wasted. I can still feel the crunch of bone from the last fight I got into not three blocks from here.

"Here we are," the cabby states, turning in his seat, but before he can say anything else, I jam some cash into his hand and grab my bags on my own.

"Have a good day, sir," I hear him call out as I shut the door, the patter of rain already soaking through my collar at the back of my neck.

I have to walk with my head down to keep the rain from hitting me in the face. The door opens easily and I drag my luggage in, tossing it to the right side where the coatrack and desk are meant to greet clients. This condo's been converted into an office space. It's blocks from the nightlife and blends in with the community. A perfect location for client drop-off.

The high ceilings and intricate crown molding make the already expensive building feel that much wealthier. It's all been done in shades of white and cream, without an actual color in sight. It makes the bright neon sticky note atop a stack of papers sitting on the edge of the welcome desk stand out even more.

Sterile, but rich.

"You were supposed to tell me when you landed." I hear James's voice before I see him, his heavy steps echoing in the expansive room.

"I did," I tell him flatly, not bothering to take out my phone and check. I'm positive I did, as I always do, and he ignored it. That seems to have been his preference for the last two weeks. The air about him has changed; ever since that night, things have been tense between us. As if we're in a silent war, each waiting for the other to show weakness.

I'm not interested in this shit. The only thing I give a damn about is my Kat, keeping her safe from the crossfire. So I'll play nice. I'll do what he says. But I'm not his bitch and I don't play games.

"I didn't get it," he says, stopping in front of me in the foyer. He has to tilt his head back slightly to look me in the eyes since he's a few inches shorter.

I shrug as if it doesn't matter, not bothering to confirm or deny whether a text was sent. "Well, I'm here now," I tell him as I slide off my jacket, soaked from the usual London rain, and hang it on the coatrack.

"You look like shit," he comments and an asymmetric grin tilts up my lips.

"Thanks." Running a hand over my damp hair and wiping it off on my jeans, I respond, "I'd say I feel better than I look, but that'd be a lie."

I've known James a long time, nearly a decade and I expect him to ask why, even though he already knows. I anticipate him starting the conversation, but instead he says nothing. Avoiding the obvious and walking down the hallway of the townhouse.

That's right, how could I forget? We're at war.

My feet move on their own, following him even though adrenaline courses faster in my blood. It makes me feel sick to not talk about it. To not clear the air.

"Whiskey?" he asks me as he pours himself a glass in the converted dining room. It's more of a bar now with a long plank of cedar serving as a makeshift counter in the back of the room. The recessed lighting shines softly on the bottles of clear and amber liquids and creates an intimate feel in the room. The humidor full of Cuban cigars and pair of dark leather wingback chairs on either side of it must have been added after I was here last.

"Kane Buchan," he says, speaking the name and then hands me a manila folder. I'm sure it's filled with the same shit that was emailed to me. I've got Kane's profile memorized already. He was the lead singer in a rock band from the Bronx. They had one smash hit and then he split from the rest of them. He decided to go his own way thinking he was too good for the band. Most said it was his ego, but it turns out he was right. Three number one hits on the top record charts and now he's a client.

They all want the same. To flaunt their wealth, get drunk or high. Fuck whomever they want. Kane Buchan is no different.

"He said something about going to Annabel's tonight," James tells me and I nod my head. I've been there more than a time or two. It's exclusive and ridiculously overpriced, so of course an up-and-coming star wants to be seen there.

I already know exactly how the night's going to play out. I just have to keep it clean enough so there are no problems. Kane's had enough of them from the fallout with his previous drummer.

"Did you even hear what I said?" James asks in a raised voice laced with irritation.

"Annabel's," I answer as I look him in the eyes and hope he was still going on about the club.

"No, I said he's married now so make sure there are no pictures if he does something stupid."

"I know." That's a given.

"He's staying a few days, maybe less depending on what his agent wants. Just keep an eye on him, show him a good time—" He's pissing me off. Treating me like a new hire and nothing more.

"I know what to do," I say, cutting off James deliberately with my retort. "I've been here before."

I've had days to think of how to approach this, but I still hesitate to get everything off my chest.

He huffs a response, sounding something like disbelief and then grabs the tumbler of whiskey from the table. The ice clinks as he takes a sip and holds it in front of him.

"Buchan's agent doesn't need any more press other than what they've arranged."

"I want you to know," I start to say as I stare him in the eyes, forcing him to listen to what I'm telling him. "I think it was a setup." Maybe I'm paranoid, but I don't give a fuck. I have to tell someone. And I'm sure as shit not going to Samantha. "It was an accident, but it just doesn't seem right. Something's off."

He shrugs and says, "It was handled." He takes a sip of his whiskey before adding, "So I don't give a shit if it was."

"I do." My words come out hard and bitter, but James is already walking away from me. I know if I move an inch, if I even breathe, I'll beat the piss out of him for leaving this all on me. And risk losing everything.

chapter 5

Kat

MY BLOODSHOT EYES HATE ME. THEY BURN FROM THE ONSLAUGHT of cool air as I finally sit back down in my office. I'm always here. I never leave this room unless I have to.

When I do decide to perch on the sofa or go to bed, I always bring my laptop with me.

Workaholic is a word for it. I'm not sure even that does it justice. I gave up everything for this. For sitting in this damn office, making deal after deal.

It's why I came to New York.

It's why I spent years in the publishing industry, collecting contacts and building a brand that's recognizable. I do it on my own and it's always been rewarding. Up until recently, this was my dream.

While Evan stayed the same and carried on with a life that was a fun distraction, I buried myself in work. Growing farther and farther apart from my husband. Knowingly creating distance between us. I thought it was worth it and that they'd all understand.

Ignored friends … at least I didn't have family to ignore. Other than Evan.

I rub my eyes again and try to soothe them, but the darkness is all I can see. It begs me to sleep.

I desperately need it. I can't even read an email right, partly from how tired my eyes are and partly from my inability to focus on anything at all. I've reread this pending message about a dozen times and I couldn't tell a soul what the content is to save my life. My meeting with Jacob is *next* week. I spent an entire hour on my own sitting mindlessly in the coffee shop before I bothered to check the time and date.

The errors are piling up and so is my anxiousness.

At least the coffee in the shop was comforting and the little biscuits were delicious. But the rain was coming down in sheets, and any sense of ease was gone by the time I dragged my ass back home to an empty townhouse with soaking wet jeans slick around my ankles.

My shoulders rise and fall as I take another glance at the screen. The contrast of the black and white is too harsh and I almost shut the laptop down and give in to sleep, but my phone goes off, scaring the shit out of me.

Evan.

It's my first thought and I hate how disappointed I am when I see it's not him. It's his father. My heart sinks and I pretend it doesn't hurt.

In my contact list, it still says "Evan's parents' house." It's tied to the number for the landline at the house where he grew up. He said he had the number memorized when he was only six years old.

Marie gave the number to me the night I first saw her, so she could call me about next Sunday's dinner, all those years ago. Every time I see the words *Evan's parents' house*, I'm reminded that only Henry remains.

It brings a number of memories I don't welcome. Just the same as the reminder of my own parents' sudden death in a car crash. Tragedy brought us together. It wasn't love. It was a need for love and that's something else entirely.

That's something Evan and I had in common, both of us losing our loved ones so quickly. He still has his father at least, but I've had no one for most of my life.

The phone rings and rings as I attempt to gather my composure. We'd only been seeing each other for a few months when I got the first call from this number. I was expecting it to be Marie, but it wasn't his mother making the call, it was Evan because his cell phone had died.

He told me he couldn't make it to our date and the first thought I had was that he was breaking up with me, simply because of the tone of his voice. It wasn't until he apologized that I realized it was something else.

He couldn't hold it together on the phone. His voice shook and his sentences were short. I'll never forget that feeling in my chest, like I knew something horrible had happened and there was nothing I could do about it.

There was something in his voice that I recognized. It's how I sound when I'm trying to convince someone else I'm okay, but I'm not. I knew it well.

After my parents died, I got tired of having to convince people there was more to me than tragedy. People who didn't bother to get to know me, because I was just the sad girl at the end of the block. The *poor child* everyone talked about.

It was why I moved to New York. Living in the small town where my family died wasn't a healthy place for someone who just wanted to feel like there's something else in this world other than the past.

For Evan it wasn't a sudden car crash, it was the phrase "two weeks to live" that brought him to his weakest moment.

I insisted on seeing him and meeting him at his parents' place and even though I thought he'd object, he didn't. He'd never been so passive toward anything like he was that night.

Evan's only cried twice since I've known him.

That night after his mother had finally gone to bed and we went back to his childhood bedroom. And nineteen days later, when she was put in the ground.

My hand itches to hold his right now. Instead I hold a ringing cell phone in an empty home.

"Henry," I say, answering the phone as if nothing's wrong although I'm very aware my voice sounds nearly breathless. Clearing my throat, I repeat his name. My voice is peppy and full of life, even though it's nearly 10:00 p.m. and I feel nothing but dead inside.

I squint at the clock on the computer and wonder why he's calling so late. "Is everything all right?" I ask, rushing out the words, my heart beating slower and a deep fear of loss settling in.

"My favorite daughter-in-law," Henry says and his greeting makes a soft smile lift up my lips. I even feel the warmth from it.

"Your *only* daughter-in-law," I correct him, picking at a bit of fuzz on the sleeve of my shirt.

"Still my favorite," he replies and I give him the laugh that he's after, even if it is a little short and quiet.

"What are you calling for?" I ask him and rest my elbow on the desk, chin in my hand. I absently minimize the document on my screen and clear out all my tabs, checking my email yet again as Henry talks.

"I just wanted to check on you, make sure everything's going well."

Again, I get the sense that something's off. "That's sweet of you," I tell him but before I can say everything's fine, he gets right to the real reason he called.

"You two all right?"

"Yeah," I say and instantly feel like shit. The single word is a vicious lie on my lips. I question what I should tell him: I don't know if my marriage to his son will last? That I'm falling apart and I have no idea how to make this better? That his son is a liar and I hate him for the pain he's putting me through?

"I spoke to Evan and he said he's not sure about the holidays coming up," Henry tells me and his tone reflects that he's baiting me. Henry's kind, polite, keeps to himself and doesn't want to be a bother, but he has a way of getting the truth out of people. Evan certainly inherited his charm from his father.

The screen of my laptop dims, ridding the room of any light so I hit the space bar and bring it back to life.

"It's a bit away, but," I say then pause and swallow, not knowing how to articulate the onslaught of thoughts. They all crowd themselves into a jam at the back of my throat, refusing to come out. I don't have family, so it's not as if I can use them as an excuse. "Work may be a little much." I finally say the words and breathe out slowly, giving him a lie I'm sure he knows is exactly that.

"He said you're going through something." There's no bullshit in his voice as he adds, "That you two aren't doing the best."

A pricking numbness dances across my hands as I ask weakly, "Did he?" Staring blankly ahead, the rhetorical question is like a knife in my back. It's a betrayal. That's how I feel hearing that Evan's told his father what we're going through. It makes the crack in my heart that much wider.

We aren't doing the best. I hear it over and over and each time the knife stabs deeper.

It's not fair that he invites so much attention. I don't need the judgment, because I don't want their opinions. I don't want them to know we're flawed. I just want us whole again. I wish no one knew so I could silently be the weak wife I am. The one willing to turn a blind eye for the unfaithful man she loves more than herself.

"I don't want to talk about it, Henry," I say bluntly as my eyes close at the confession. I can tell the computer has gone into sleep mode again and this time I don't hit the keys to bring it back to life. The darkness is too comforting.

"I just want you to know I'm here for you," Henry says clearly into the phone. "You're my daughter," he adds and it breaks my composure.

I push away from the desk, the chair legs catching on the rug and nearly tipping over. With a heavy inhale, I walk slowly to the door and then to my bedroom, the phone still pressed to my ear. I'm just going through the motions and trying to be numb to it all.

"Thank you," I finally say as I lean against the bedroom door, closing it. I almost tell him he's like a father to me.

Almost, but when we do get a divorce, Henry won't be there for me. It doesn't matter what he says. It doesn't matter that I'll be alone, because that's how I've been most of my life anyway.

"I love you and I'm sorry you two are going through this." I let Henry's words echo in my head.

He's not the only one who's sorry.

chapter 6

Evan

THE MUSIC POUNDS AWAY, THE BASS CRANKED UP SO HIGH IT VIBRATES my chest. The interior of the nightclub alternates between dark shadows and bright, colorful lights that flash in time with the beat. Vibrant reds and greens scatter across the slim bodies that come and go from sight with the sudden darkness in between the beats.

"Another!" Kane's friend Mikey yells on my left, a little too loud, a little too close to my ear for comfort. I give him a smile in return and pretend to take another swig of my beer. I'm used to guys like him.

Another time in my life, I'd actually be drinking. The feel that I get on the right side of a heavy buzz is comforting. That light-headedness where you still have control, but not a damn thing matters. That's the place I craved to be for so long, but not anymore.

Not when so much is slipping through my fingers.

It's been a few hours since we got to Annabel's and so far the job's been easy. Kane and his friends are trashed and most importantly, the rock star is having the time of his life. His crew is saddled up to the bar with a few women pressing their bodies against the men who welcome it, letting their hands stray every so often. One in particular for Kane, which has me on edge and keeping an eye out for the telltale glow of a cell phone in the air, ready to capture a snapshot.

She's the woman closest to Kane, Christi is what she said her name was, and the loudest by far. The more she drinks, the louder she gets, and the closer to Kane. Not that Kane seems to notice any of that.

According to his file, the tall, loudmouthed blonde is his type and it wouldn't be the first time he's strayed from his wife. Fame and fortune tend to do it. I've seen it too many times to keep track.

Kat thinks this is the type of shit I do. The thought makes me sick to my stomach, a scowl marring my face. I can't change what my clients do; I learned that all too fast. You can't change people. You accept it and work with what you're given. A prick's a prick. He's never going to be anything but that. So I raise the beer to my lips and take a long swig, nearly draining the bottle.

With the change of music bringing the group a little closer as the lights fade, I watch them each carefully, but all I can think about is Kat. What she'd think of this mess.

She's never questioned me before, but last night she let out shit I had no idea about. Insecurities and accusations that made me feel like less of a man.

I can't blame her, can I? Not when I have secrets. Not when I can't look her in the eyes and tell her I haven't fucked up.

A strong grip on my arm rouses me from my thoughts.

"Can you get me something?" Kane asks, sidling up next to me. The smell of whiskey is heavy on his breath. It takes great effort not to put immediate distance between us.

Just like Mikey, he's a little too close as he slurs his request to the point where I can't tell what he's saying.

"What are you looking for?" I ask him to clarify and stare at the half-empty bottles of liquor lining the top shelf of the bar.

"Something a little stronger," he says as he tilts his head and tries to be subtle, but fails miserably, putting his hand to his nose and sniffing loudly. Cocaine.

I hesitate and waver on my answer. Luckily, I don't have to respond. Instead a loud, high-pitched voice on my right screams out, "We've got absinthe!" Apparently Christi was eavesdropping. *Surprise, surprise.* Her bright red talons are digging tight into Kane and I know she's going to stay within hearing range until we're out of here, just like she's been doing since she recognized him from across the room. She's leaning over a barstool, her breasts on full display and when I look back at Kane, the only thing he's looking at is her chest.

"Never had it," Kane says too low and the blonde screams, practically in my ear, "What?"

Giving them distance and getting out from between the two of them, I wait for him to agree. I know he will. She's got him wrapped around her little finger. I'll do it with a smile on my face and babysit this fucker. I used to think of this differently. This all used to be fun. But it wasn't like *this*, was it?

It doesn't take more than one feminine mewl and a *please* from her to convince Kane that absinthe is good enough and that we should all head to her place.

It's two blocks down and up a set of iron rails to get to the apartment. The sidewalk's still wet and this late at night, there's no one else on the streets. Just a bunch of drunk assholes stumbling on their way home. We fit in perfectly. I keep my eyes ahead, but occasionally look back and in all directions casually. I know the street and the apartment complex well. There aren't any cameras or storefronts for onlookers. Still, I watch and wait for any type of paparazzi.

I follow them as Kane and his friend cling to the group of women. There are three of them, two blond chicks and a dark brunette with curls, each barely covered in skimpy clubwear as they grip the railing to the apartment stairs and laugh as they stumble their way up in heels. It's difficult to tell with the other blonde if it's an act and she's playing up the drunkenness, or if she's really that plastered.

Kane's hands are all over Christi, moving from her hips to her ass as he walks behind her. Mikey's into the other blond chick and the brunette's checked out, only interested in smoking weed and getting trashed.

I tolerated the attention and flirting in the beginning of the night, but after a few minutes of ignoring the women, they lost interest and moved on. I'm certain this brunette is well aware there's nothing happening between us. The number one rule of my job is to not bring down the vibe. So I offer her a smile when she peeks at me, but then go back to scanning the surroundings and blocking the view from the street. One thought gnaws at me as the group travels along: I just want to get back to Kat and make her take it all back. Make her forget what happened and remind her why we're meant to be together. Remind her why she's mine.

I don't want this life anymore. Not when it makes Kat doubt me and what we have. Rightfully so.

I can't take this shit. I'll give it up for her. She'd take that, wouldn't she?

As the girls laugh nearly in unison to something that Mikey yelled out and the door opens, I take my phone out of my pocket, glancing up to make sure none of the girls have theirs out.

The number two rule of my job: no pictures.

That's my second concern. The first is getting Kane and peacing out of here. He's had a good time; he'll remember enough of it at least. I'm not interested in being here any longer than I have to be.

I'm distracted for only a moment. Half a second, but the moment I stop watching these girls, one of them breaks rule number two.

The second Christi's blond friend pulls out her iPhone, flicking her long hair behind her as if she's only taking a selfie, turning and posing with Kane in the background, I snatch it from her. She gasps and tries to grab it back like this is a game and I'm making a move on her. Her smile widens and she lets out a small laugh, again trying to snatch it from me.

Keeping the smile in place, I'm firm. It takes her a minute to realize no matter how much she pulls on my arm and makes that girlish cry, I have no intention of giving it back.

"No pictures," I tell her simply, my voice low and admonishing. I don't have time for this shit or her antics. She knows what she's doing and it's not cute or funny.

The smile drops from her face, her disappointment evident. I force myself to stare into her drunken hazel gaze until she looks down and then holds out her hand. The flirtation is completely gone. "I get it," she snaps.

I place the phone in her palm after I shut it off and she huffs like I'm an asshole, but she'll listen. They always do. It's obvious she's biting her tongue over wanting to tell me off and I can't really blame her. She wouldn't be the first. I've been slapped more times than I know. Mostly by women. Years of doing this have led to plenty of fights and unfortunate events.

I've beaten the shit out of assholes.

Called doctors and paid them in cash to come to hotel rooms.

I've paid off cops, bouncers, bookies. At this point I've seen it all, done it all. And I'm tired of this shit.

This little blonde, though? She'll pout and listen, even if she tries to make a move on me and probably attempt even more pictures throughout the night.

The bright green of the absinthe bottle catches my eye as the blonde I just pissed off brings it to the coffee table. I watch as she sets it in the center and lines up three shot glasses before going back to the small kitchen only ten feet away to grab more.

Kane's in the middle of the sofa with both arms draped across the back as Christi and the brunette cuddle up next to him. The sounds of them laughing and Kane saying something in a low voice as they huddle closer to him are barely on my mind as I turn my focus back to my phone.

I text the driver and let him know I'm going to need the car in about thirty minutes then send him the address.

It takes fifteen minutes for the alcohol to hit their systems. Heavy pours and three shots each will have them all out on their asses. Normally I'd feel bad cutting their party short, but I don't give a shit. All I can think about is Kat.

I need to get back to her.

With an asymmetric grin forced onto my face, I roll up my sleeves, letting the tats show. "Let me get it, doll," I tell the blonde as I make my way to the kitchen. "You sit back and relax," I add, taking the bottle from her hands. I'll pour the second round while they're throwing back the first. She gives me a flirtatious smirk. "I knew you weren't *all* asshole," she teases with a playful peek up at me and then sits on her knees next to the coffee table. Too close, too presumptuous.

"You had it right the first time," I murmur under my breath as I fill all six glasses and pass them out.

"Let's do a couple rounds and get this party started."

chapter 7

Kat

"I'm stronger than this. I deserve so much more."
They're the words I breathe, then collapse on the floor.
My eyes close tight; tears trapped, lungs still.
I can't speak the truth; I can't fight the chill.
"I'm stronger than this." I whisper the words, my face hot.
But I know I'm a liar, and I know that I'm not.

EVAN ALMOST NEVER TEXTS ME WHEN HE'S WORKING BUT HE DID TONIGHT, and I can't take my eyes away from my phone because of that little fact. In all the years we've been together, I can count on one hand when he's messaged me while out on a job. I've never minded it; he's working. I've never needed a message that said he missed me, I always knew he did and that he'd be home soon. I had work to occupy me while he was away. Come morning, there was always a message to greet me, but while he was out, he was simply unavailable.

My body's still and my focus is nonexistent when it comes to work now, though. There's not a damn thing keeping me company but the memories of us and the constant worry of what'll happen when—and if—he comes home.

Staring down at my cell, I swallow thickly. *He messaged me. He reached out to me.* I can't explain why it makes my bruised heart hurt even more. Maybe I wish he'd just be cruel and not try or not care. It hurts so much more to think that he's trying. Hope is an odd little thing. I want to cling to it, but if I do, the inevitable fall will be that much more deadly.

He always messaged in the morning, though, after the late night of whatever the hell he'd been up to. I've always thought it was cute how he'd text me to tell me good morning, even if he was only just then getting into bed.

But it's 2:00 a.m. in London, his prime time, and my phone's lit up on the desk with a message from him.

I was finally getting some work done, the keys clacking and the to-do list shrinking somewhat although for every item crossed off, I feel as if I've added two. Focusing and managing to write up some feedback along with creating a marketing tactic for a client has been a highlight of my night ... Until that message came through.

Half of me doesn't want to answer him. Cue the grinding halt to any progress I'd made. I don't want to read whatever he's sent and go back into the black hole of self-pity. But I can't resist. He is a drug and I am an addict. We could go days without speaking before, but in this moment, every second that I stare at my phone knowing there's an unread message from him feels like an eternity in hell.

My hand inches toward it, the need to see what he has to say overriding the anger and the sadness. The need to be wanted by him and to feel loved winning out over my dignity.

So I click on the damn thing and my heart does a little pitter-patter of acknowledgment. When I swallow, it's as if I'm shoving my heart back down where it belongs.

I hate it when you're mad at me.

I stare at his message, feeling the vise in my chest tighten. My fingers hesitate over the keys as I read it again and again. Before I can respond, another message comes through.

Forgive me.

That's the crux of the situation. The dams break loose.

Forgive you for what exactly? I message him back without even thinking. Whatever he's hiding is bad, I know it is. I can feel it deep down in my core. Just like I knew that night when his mother was diagnosed. Whatever he's done is enough to ruin us.

But we were already ruined, weren't we? It's been a slow burn of destruction. My intuition is hardly ever wrong. We've grown apart. We're different people now. *We don't belong together.* We never did, not really. Admitting that is what hurts the most.

With my body trembling, I force myself to get up and move, even if it's just to walk through the house. I'm only wearing a baggy shirt and a pair of socks. I wore the shirt to bed last night and I should really shower and get dressed. It's a rule I've had since I started working from home.

Every day, I dress as if I'm going into the office. Right now I just don't have the energy.

Evan sends two texts, one right after the other as I walk to the kitchen.

We can work through this.

I love you.

I only glance at them before putting the phone down on the counter and heading straight to the fridge for some wine. Taking in a staggered breath, I focus on ignoring the pain. *Think logically*, I command myself. *Don't fall back into his arms without having a grasp on the problem. Because otherwise it will happen again. That's what happens when you accept a behavior without acknowledgment and a plan to change.*

There's only half a glass left in the dark red bottle, but it'll have to do.

I glance at the clock as I sip it. It's after 9:00 p.m. I've barely slept, barely worked and hours passed before I realized I hadn't brushed my teeth today. At least I'm drinking from a clean glass.

It only takes one sip before I tell him what's on my mind. Communication is key. All the years of therapy taught me that. There is no relationship worth keeping if you don't trust what someone says.

I don't understand why you won't tell me what you did.

Won't tell you what? he texts back and it pisses me off.

"Does he think I'm stupid?" I mutter beneath my breath as my blood boils. The anger is only an ounce stronger than the pain. In the back of my mind I note that only crazy people talk to themselves, but even if that's the case, I accept it. This man makes me crazy. I can admit that much.

Don't treat me like this, I answer him, feeling weak. I'm practically begging him in my head but when I reread the text it sounds strong. *I deserve better.*

I down the remaining wine after sending the last line, the cool red soothing a tiny bit of an ache. I don't know exactly what it is I deserve but I have a rough idea. Him telling me the truth. Him confiding in me. Or a better husband altogether.

As I grab the last bottle of red wine on the rack and bring it back to the kitchen, I realize this is how women feel when they stay in these marriages.

They'd rather be told a sweet little lie and believe it than face the truth. Those are my choices: demand the truth and accept the lie he gives me or … I don't know.

Right now, it's exactly what I want. Just lie to me. Tell me there's nothing that happened. That it's blown out of proportion. *That it was just a kiss.* Yes, that one. That last one. I could forgive it, but better yet, I could believe it. I could allow myself to believe it, even if deep down inside I know it was more.

Lie to me and love me. He knows I'll still love him. It would make everything better.

The barstool legs scratch on the floor as I sit down to uncork the new bottle.

I just want him to come home. Tell me everything is fine and make up something that's easy to forgive. It was only a kiss.

With a bottle of wine and a full glass in front of me, I go back to the beginning. Back to when I was stronger and I actually had self-respect.

Back to when I knew better.

The memory and the wine are the only things to keep me company for the rest of the night, because Evan doesn't text me back with the truth or a lie. He gives me silence.

Six years ago

The wind blows in my face, alleviating some of the stifling summer heat as I pull into the gas station parking lot in Brooklyn. It's late and the hustle and bustle of New York has waned, but the nightlife on this side of the city is only getting started.

Some would say it's the bad part of town, but others say it's the fun part. I guess it depends on what circles you run in. New to New York and struggling to find where I belong, I suppose I'm keeping an open mind. The bright lights and sophistication are what I came here for, but making it here isn't so easily achieved.

I'm slow to step on the brakes and pull into the last spot that lines the front of the small convenience store. I've only been here a few times, either needing to stop for gas or a quick bite to eat on my way to or from work on the west side of the city. It's a clerical job for a newspaper, but beggars can't be choosers and the bills need to be paid while I learn the ropes, snag clients and rub elbows, so to speak.

Several cars are parked in front of the store and a few men head inside as I pull up. They vary from obviously expensive to looking like they're falling apart. The vehicles, that is.

I notice the men, and they notice me. Averting my eyes to avoid making small talk, I turn down my radio and put my car in park.

I mind my business and everyone around me seems to do the same. In the city that never sleeps, there's always something happening. And I'm not interested in a damn one of those somethings. Distractions get a bad rap for a reason.

Grabbing my purse and keys in the same hand, I make haste, opening the car door to step out in a rush, but my eyes glance back to the cars and straight into a man's gaze.

Not just any man, a man exuding power and confidence, along with defiance. Although he's wearing a simple shirt and faded dark jeans, the way he wears them makes me think they were made to be fitted to his muscular body. He's hot as hell, and given the way he looks at me, he could be a temptation the devil made just for me.

My driver's side door shuts with a loud bang as I stand there caught in the heat in his gaze. He leans against the hood of a car, I'm assuming is his, a shiny black Mercedes that reflects the light from the store in its slick exterior. The windows are rolled up and tinted so dark it's hard to see the inside. As my eyes move back to the man, my movements are slowed and I grip my keys tighter.

He doesn't stop looking, taking me in and letting his eyes follow along the curves of my body. Arrogance and sinful thrill dance in his cocky grin. He obviously wants me to know that he's watching me. Something about that small fact forces a blush to rise to my cheeks.

My breathing picks up and I subconsciously pull the hem of my dress down just slightly, smoothing out the cherry red pleats and wishing I hadn't been wearing it all day. I take one step and the click of my heels keeps time with my racing pulse as I walk forward, knowing I have to pass him on my way in.

I can't help that my eyes flicker over to his as I grip my purse strap and settle it in place. His shirt is pulled taut and over his muscular frame and his tanned skin is decorated with ink. Tattoos travel down his chest and arms, peeking out below his collarbone from the crisp white cotton shirt and leaving a trail of intricate designs all the way down to his wrists. I'm too far away to see what they say or what they are. I know if he were in a suit, the tattoos would be hidden, but something tells me he's proud to have them on full display.

"What are you up to?" he asks me and catches me off guard.

"I don't think that's any of your business," I answer him easily, although I don't know how, swaying a little from side to side in a flirtatious way I didn't intend. My body can't help but be attracted to his. Some part of me is eager to know how his tattooed skin would feel against my fingertips.

There's a scar over his left eyebrow and it's subtle, but even from this distance I notice it. As his deep rough chuckle fills the night air and drowns out the other sounds of the city, I find myself wondering how he got it.

"A man can wonder, though," he says, causing a hot blush to creep slowly into my cheeks. I bite down on my lower lip, but that doesn't stop the shy smile from showing. I have to stop and give him the attention he's looking for as he leans forward, holding me captive to whatever's on his mind.

"You're pretty, you know that?" he says and I roll my eyes. Even if I know this flirtation isn't just for me, that he's simply playing with me, I still enjoy it. I crave it even. I'm sure he's already used these lines tonight.

"Sure, and you're not too bad looking either." I enjoy the flirting, the attention. At least coming from him. He makes me feel things I haven't before.

He splays a hand over his heart and cocks his head as he says, "Well thank you, beautiful, I aim for 'not bad.'" This time I'm the one laughing, a short, soft snicker as I kick the bottom of my heels against the ground and stare at them for a moment, readying myself to say goodbye and end his bout of teasing. I don't trust myself not to say anything and instead I just wave and carry on, expecting him to do the same.

"You didn't answer me," he calls out after I take a few steps. "What are you doing out here so late?" he asks. It's forward of him and I usually despise that, but instead I savor the challenge in his voice. Something about it tells me he thinks I'm already his. And that ownership makes my blood that much hotter.

I know I shouldn't give him any information at all, but I find myself telling him *the truth before I can stop myself. "I'm hungry and overworked. So I stopped to grab a bite to eat."*

"You're getting your dinner from here?" he asks, gesturing to the store and I nod. "A woman like you should be taken out, not eating dinner from the gas station."

A woman like you plays over and over in my head. He doesn't know what type of woman I am. "You don't even know my name," I say, the half smile and challenge firm on my expression.

He nods and grins, flashing me a cocky smile as he replies, "Don't make me guess."

I chew on my lip for a moment, rocking from side to side. He's bad news and I'm flirting with fire … but I love the thrill. I can't deny it. "It's Kat," I tell him and a smile is slow to form on his face. One of complete satisfaction, as if hearing my name is the best thing that's happened to him all night.

"I'm Evan," he says and I taste his name on the tip of my tongue, nearly whispering it. "Let me take you to dinner, Kat," he suggests with an easiness I don't like. I wonder how many times that's worked for him before.

"I'm not your type," I respond, intentionally looking past him at the bars that wrap around the glass door to the convenience store. I just need a late-night snack to hold me over till morning. That's all this little errand was supposed to turn into.

"I don't think you should tell me what is and isn't my type." Although it comes out playful, there's a hint of admonishment, and my naïve little heart doesn't like that. "You might be surprised," he adds.

I clear my throat and try to breathe evenly, wanting this flirting session to end so I can get back to work. I have to admit the attention is very much appreciated, though. And the desire in his eyes looks genuine.

"Sorry, Charlie, didn't mean to upset you," I tell him with a playful pout as I walk past him.

"It's Evan," he says, repeating his name and that makes a wicked grin play at my lips, "and you're wrong." The last part is spoken with a seriousness I wasn't expecting. His tone is hard and when I turn around to face him fully, finally taking a step onto the curb, he's no longer leaning on the hood of the Mercedes. He takes a few strides across the asphalt parking lot and stops in front of me as I ask, "Wrong about what?"

Up close he's taller than I first thought, more intimidating too and his shoulders seem broader, stronger. Even his subtle moves as he brushes his jaw with his rough fingers and licks his lower lip again, are dominating. He glances to the left and right before opening his mouth again and letting that deep, rough voice practically ignite the air between us.

"You're wrong that you aren't my type and that I'm not your type."

The compliment makes my body feel hotter than it already is in the hot summer night. Someone behind me exits the store, the telltale jingle of the bells and the whoosh of air-conditioning reminding me that I'm supposed to be in and out of this store. Reminding me that Evan isn't a part of my to-do list tonight.

"I never said you weren't my type," I say and my voice comes out sultry, laced with the desire I feel coursing in my blood. I try to hold his gaze, but the fire and intensity swirling in his dark eyes make me back down.

I can try to be tough all I want, but he's a bad boy through and through and I should know better.

"Good to know," he says with a cocky undertone that makes my eyes whip up to his. I half expect him to blow me off now that his ego's been fed. He licks his lower lip and my eyes are drawn to the motion, imagining how it'd feel to have his lips on every inch of my skin. "Come out with me tonight," he says. As if I don't have anything better to do. As if he can just command me to do what he wants.

"Sorry … Evan. I can't tonight," I tell him and turn back around, hiking my purse up higher on my shoulder, ready to go about my business.

"Tomorrow night then," he says, raising his voice so I can hear him as I wrap my hand around the handle and pull the door open. Again the chill of the store greets me, but this time it's unwanted.

I'm all too aware of what this man could do to me. He's the type to pin you down as he takes you how he wants you and doesn't stop until you're screaming. And I can't lie, just that thought alone makes me desperate to say yes.

He takes another step closer as I stand with the door wide open and hesitate to answer. Shoving his hands into his pockets, he manages a shrug as if it's a casual question.

"Just one date," he adds as he looks at me with a raised brow and his version of puppy dog eyes. It's enough to force a smile on my face.

"And what am I supposed to do? Meet you here at ten?" I ask him.

"How about at Jean-Georges in Central Park?" he asks and I'm taken aback. It's an expensive place and my eyes glance back to his car, to his ripped body and tattooed skin. There's something about the air that follows him that screams he's no good. The danger in the way he looks at me is so tempting, though.

"I just want to feed you," he adds as the time ticks by slowly and a short, older man with salt-and-pepper hair walks out of the exit, stealing our attention and making my hand slip slightly on the handle.

I chew on the inside of my cheek. The answer is an easy one. No. Simple as that. He's a bad boy who only wants one thing, but I can't deny that I want it too.

I said yes.

To the date, and then again a year later to marrying him.

That initial yes, pushed through my lips by an undeniable attraction, was my first mistake on a list of too fucking many.

All because I can't tell him no.

chapter 8

Evan

I TRY TO SHUT THE FRONT DOOR SOFTLY, AS QUIETLY AS I CAN SO I DON'T wake up Kat if she's passed out.

I know she told me not to come back. She says a lot of things and then apologizes and changes her mind. Silence isn't better, though. It still hurts, just in a different way. Our loft is small and the walls are thin so you can hear everything in here. I stop in the foyer, setting down my duffle bag and luggage then toss the bunched-up chenille blanket that's in a puddle on the floor onto the sofa in the living room.

The room is mostly gray, just like the city. There's a paned glass mirror above the long sofa and black and white accents everywhere. I hated that mirror from the moment we got it, but Kat loved it, so I never said a word. It belongs in some farmhouse up north, not in the heart of New York, the devil's playground. But it made her smile. I'll be damned if that isn't reason enough to keep that cheap-ass mirror.

My eyes scan the room in the faint light from the city that's shining through the gap in the curtains.

Five years of marriage, six of creating this place together.

Each piece of furniture is a memory. The wine rack that we purchased was the first thing we bought together. The gray sofa with removable pillows was a fight I lost. I didn't want the cushions to be removable, because they always end up sagging, but Kat insisted the brand was quality.

The plush cushions still look like they did in the store, and I wonder if she was right or if it's just because we don't even sit on the damn thing. Maybe both but I lean toward the latter.

I'm never here and she's always working. What's the point of it?

The bitter thought makes me kick the duffle bag out of my way and head past the living room and dining room, straight to the stairs so I can get to bed and lie down with Kat. It's been almost a week since I've slept in the same room as her and I refuse to let that go on for another night. I pause to look at the photos on the wall, the light streaming in leaving a sunbeam down the glass.

Almost all are in black and white, the way Kat likes her décor. All but one, the largest in the very center. It's also the only one that's not staged.

She's leaning toward me, and her lips look so red as she's mid-laugh, holding a crystal champagne flute and wrapping her fingers around my forearm. Her eyes are on whoever was giving a speech. I don't remember who it was or what they said, but I can still hear her laugh. It's the most beautiful sound.

She was so happy on our wedding day. I thought she'd be stressed and worried, but it was like a weight was lifted and the sweetest version of her was given to me that day. There's nothing but love in the photo. No work, no bullshit, just the two of us telling the world we loved each other enough to stay together forever.

My eyes are on her in that picture, with a smile on my face and pride in my reflection.

I tear my gaze away and keep walking, feeling the weight of everything press down on my shoulders. I'm exhausted and like the childish fool I am, I wish I could just go to sleep and this would all be a dream. A huff of sarcasm accompanies my gentle footsteps up the stairs.

I want to go back to when we first got married. Before we both got caught up in work and started to live separate lives. Before I fucked up.

If only we could start over and go back to that day.

As I pass the open office door, I hear the clacking of the computer keyboard. So many nights I've come home to this, so many mornings I've woken up to it. She's always in her office, which is a shame. There's hardly any light, or anything at all in the room. File cabinets, papers, a shredder and a desk. There's not a hint of the woman Kat is in this room.

I guess it's the same as the living room, but at least a classic elegance is present there. It's nothing but cold in here. If a to-do list could be made into décor, that's what this cramped room resembles.

"Hey, babe," I say softly and Kat ignores me. I clear my throat and speak louder. "I'm home," I tell her and again, I get nothing from Kat, just the steady clicks. There's an empty wineglass and two bottles on the floor by her feet.

Maybe she's a little drunk, maybe she has her earplugs in too, but still, she'd hear me. Was it a long shot that she'd kindly accept me coming home? *Yes.* It's not too much to ask for an acknowledgment, though. Even if she tells me to fuck off. I'd take it.

My teeth grind together as I grip the handle of the door harder. She deserves better. I know she does. This is exactly what I deserve, but I don't want it. I won't go down without fighting for what I want.

The standing floor lamp in the corner of her office is on, but it's not enough to brighten the room. Even the glow of the computer screen is visible.

"Do you want to talk?" I ask her and her only response is that her fingers stop moving across the keys.

She doesn't turn to face me or give any sign that I've spoken to her. She heard it, though, and her gaze drops to the keyboard for a second too long not to give that away.

"I don't want to fight, Kat," I tell her and force every bit of emotion I'm feeling into my words. "I don't want this between us."

She turns slowly in her seat, a baggy T-shirt covering her slim body and ending at her upper thighs. Her exposed skin is pale and the dark room makes her look that much paler. Her viridian eyes give her away the most, though. Nothing but sadness stares back at me.

My body is pulled to her, and I can't help it. I can't stand that look in her eyes. Before I can tell her I love her and I'm sorry, before I can come up with some lame excuse, she cuts me off.

"I wanted to last night," she says and then crosses her arms. She looks uncomfortable and unnatural. Like she's doing what she thinks she should be doing, not what she wants. "When you texted me and then I texted you back. I was ready to talk then."

"I'm here now," I offer and walk closer to her, the floorboards creaking gently. There's a set of chairs in the corner of the room from our first apartment and I almost drag one over, but I'm too afraid to break eye contact with her. It's progress. I'll be damned if I stop progress for a place to sit.

At least she's looking at me, talking to me, receptive to what I have to say.

"Ask me whatever you want." My voice is calm but deep down I'm screaming. Because I know I'll answer her. I'll tell her everything just to take that pain away, even if it's only temporary, even if it fucks her too.

Her doe eyes widen slightly and she cowers back, swallowing before answering me. "Aren't you tired?" she says softly and her eyes flicker to the door and then to the floor.

She doesn't want to know the truth.

"Yeah, I'm exhausted. But I'm not going to bed until you do." I lick my lips and clear my throat, hoping she'll give in to me. For nearly the past year when I'm home, I've tried to stay up with her or brush off the fact that I'd pass out while she was still working and vice versa. Not tonight, not from this point forward. The advice my father gave me on our wedding night was to go to bed together. I should have listened. I'll make it better, I can at least fix that.

"I can stay up for you," I say, offering her the suggestion. It's not what she wants, but it's something.

"Well, this has to get done, and it's going to take hours."

"I can wait," I tell her but the second the words slip out she turns back to the computer and says, "Don't."

With her back to me and her fingers already flying across the keys again, I've never felt more alone and crestfallen.

"I'll go unpack and relax on the bed then," I say as I grip the doorframe to stay upright and keep myself from ripping her out of that chair and bringing her to bed.

"Here?" Shock coats the single word.

It takes me a moment to realize why the hell she's asking me that and when I do, it's like a bullet to the chest.

A mix of emotions swell in my gut and heat my blood. Anger is there, but the dejectedness is what cuts me the most.

"Is that all right?" I ask sarcastically.

She nods, conceding to let me stay in my own damn house, but the look in her eyes doesn't fade. She really wants me out. She wants me to just leave? Did she think I wouldn't fight for her? That I'd let this destroy us? It may ruin me, but I'd rather chew on broken glass than let it ruin *us*.

"I said I don't want a divorce." My words come out hard. I'm sick of this. "I want you," I tell her with conviction and walk closer to her, not leaving any space between us.

"I don't know what I want," Kat responds in a murmur, gripping the armrests of the desk chair as her lips form a painful frown and her eyes gloss over. Like she's on the verge of breaking. The last thread that was holding her together has snapped, leaving her falling. I'm not there to catch her, because I'm the one that pushed her over the edge. I hate myself for it.

It's my fault, and this is all on me, but I'll make it right.

"You don't have to, Kat," I say, softening my voice and moving just a little closer. I need a chance. She's vulnerable; I can feel it coming off of her in waves. *Give in to me, baby.*

I cup her cheek in my hand to lean down and kiss her, but she pushes back, quickly standing and making the chair slam against the desk.

My pride, my ego, whatever it is that makes me a man, is destroyed in this moment. My limbs freeze and the tension makes me feel like I'm breaking. Literally cracking in my very center.

I lick my lips, finally letting out a breath as Kat whispers, "I'm sorry, I'm just …" She doesn't finish, and I have to look up at her before I can stand upright again.

"You just what?"

"I don't know, Evan," she answers with desperation in her voice.

"Don't think," I tell her, grasping for anything to keep her from running. "Just let me make it better," I offer and she stands there, in nothing but that T-shirt, and looks at me as if I'm both her savior and her enemy.

I walk slowly, each step making the floor groan in quiet protest. I don't quicken my pace until I'm close enough to her to feel her heat. And she lets me, standing still and giving me the chance I need.

My lips crash against hers, my body molding to her small frame and forcing her back. For each step she takes, I take one with her.

"Stop," she tells me and pushes me away. My breathing is ragged as my hands clench to keep from holding on to her as she leaves me. I can still taste her, my body ringing with desire to make it up to her.

To ease her pain and remind her how good I make her feel. It's what she needs. It's been weeks and I can't deny I need her even more. I need to bury my-self inside her warmth.

My hands grasp her hips and I push her back against the wall. Her arms wrap around my neck as she comes in for the kiss this time. Taking the passion from me, letting me give her what she needs. Comfort and an escape from reality. A welcome distraction to the fact that our marriage is at risk.

Right now there's nothing but what we feel for each other. Nothing else. No logic or reason. Just the devotion and intense desire.

I'm grateful it still exists. I only wish this moment would last forever. Where we're both weak for each other, desperate and drunk with lust.

"You're mine, Kat," I whisper against the shell of her ear. My breath is hot and it's making the air between us that much hotter.

Her back arches against the wall and she pushes her soft curves into mine. A quiet moan spills from her sweet lips. I stare at her face, the expression of utter rapture with her eyes closed and her lips parted just slightly.

I rock my palm over her again and again, putting pressure on her swollen nub and feeling her cunt get hotter and wetter.

"This is mine," I whisper louder, not holding back the possession in my voice.

A strangled moan fills the air. At first I don't know if it's from me or her, but the sweet cadence of her voice prolongs the sound of pleasure as her body writhes against mine. She's so close.

I tear the thin lace fabric of her panties off in one tug after ripping it with my thumb and watch her face as her eyes pop open. The gorgeous greens stare back at me with a mix of emotions, the overwhelming two being desire and vulnerability.

I don't give her the chance to second-guess this. This is how we're meant to be. Together, raw and bared.

I only release my grip on her to unzip my pants. The sound mixes with Kat's heavy breathing.

"Evan," she says, whispering my name as if it's a question.

She wants me, although she knows we shouldn't do this. Fuck, I know she's going to question this. Maybe even regret it. But she just needs to feel me again; she needs this as much as I do.

I press the head of my dick against her opening and slide myself through her slick folds, teasing her and watching as her eyes close tight. She squirms when I just barely touch her clit.

So close.

"Evan," she whispers again and this time it's a plea. One I can satisfy.

In one swift stroke I slam into her all the way to the hilt, making her scream out.

Her blunt nails dig into my shoulders as her body is forced against the wall and her head falls back.

I kiss her throat ravenously, desperate to taste her, but not willing to mute the sounds of pleasure she's making.

My thrusts are primal, ruthless. I take from her over and over. Each time her back hits the wall, her whimpers get louder and louder.

Her grip tightens as my balls draw up. My spine tingles with the need to release, but I need her to find hers with me. I'm desperate to feel her walls tighten around my cock. Desperate to feel her pulsing and lost in pleasure.

The moment I think I can't take any more, she gives me what I need. Screaming out my name as her orgasm rips through her body.

"Fuck," I groan into the crook of her neck. My dick pulses and I come hard, buried deep inside of her. My heart hammers hard and fast and refuses to stop as she clings to me for dear life. A cold sweat lines my skin. Her eyes are closed and her teeth are digging into her bottom lip when I finally look at her.

"I love you, Kat," I whisper as I pull away from her, finally breathing and starting to come down from the highest high.

"I love …" Kat starts to reply, but she doesn't finish. She doesn't look me in the eyes.

She's so ashamed to love me, she can't even say it back.

Kat

I DON'T KNOW WHAT I'M MORE ASHAMED ABOUT AS I CARELESSLY TOSS the throw blanket over one arm of the sofa and force myself get up, still feeling the ache between my thighs.

The fact that I fucked my husband.

Or the fact that I then refused to go to bed with him.

Not that I told him so much. I hid behind work and then snuck out here to the living room. I didn't sleep on the sofa for more than a few hours. Maybe that's all I'm entitled to for being so weak and falling right into his arms the moment he pulled me in.

It's like our union is a spiraling dark hole and I'm falling deeper and deeper, to the point where what I want and what I'm feeling don't make sense and nothing adds up. Not that I could hold on to anything anyway; I've lost all control.

I couldn't possibly feel more pathetic at this point.

Because I love him and hate myself for it.

I glance at my phone on the dining room table as I make my way to the kitchen, the charging cord is in a tangled heap on the floor.

I already know what Sue would say. She'd feel sorry for me for going back to the man who cheated on me. Her lips would purse in that way where it's obvious she's holding back some snarky remark.

Pity and sorrow for the pathetic girl, clinging to an unfaithful man. Even the bitter thought echoes what I already know she'd say.

The thing about love though is that it's not a light switch. You can't just turn it off. No matter how much you may want to, you can't erase the memories and move on. Sue knows that much, she just chooses to forget that it's not so easy.

My head throbs and I'm not sure if it's from the lack of sleep or the absence of caffeine. Even the faint sounds of city life from stories down are enough to make my temples pulse. I've felt more put together with a hangover than I do now. This is not the unfortunate side effect of too much cabernet last night. I wish it was only that.

I groan as I rest against the wall of the living room and try to calm the headache. I close my eyes and feel the weight of all the stress from the last two weeks.

I need aspirin or coffee. Or both. My heart sputters as I slowly walk up the stairs, knowing Evan's lying in bed alone and that it was my choice.

As I pass the office, I remember last night and my thighs clench; I can still feel him inside of me. His warm lips on my neck, his rough hands on my body … it's more than a memory, the act still lingers on my skin. He took from me. Relentlessly, possessively. Each step brings my body temperature higher and higher, yet my heart hurts more and more.

Why won't the pain just go away? Why can't my head just shut the fuck up so I can pretend I'm okay for a single moment? Jules told me once I overthink everything. She was referring to some edits I gave her but still, the woman had a point.

The bedroom door is open and as I walk through the door, I can't take my eyes off the perfectly made bed. The cream and white comforter printed with black dahlias is pulled tight, looking pristine. A crease forms in the center of my forehead as I walk to the bathroom, listening to my heart beat with each step, but finding the bathroom empty. *Evan wasn't downstairs*, I think as I open the medicine cabinet and silently grab a bottle of aspirin. He wasn't downstairs, and he's not up here.

I swallow the pills without water, staring into the mirror as my heart clenches, the dark bags under my eyes looking significantly worse than yesterday morning. Did he even stay last night? Did he find me asleep on the sofa and decide to leave? *It's what I wanted, wasn't it?*

The cabinet door slams shut; I give the push more force than I meant to, but I ignore it, striding quickly down to the kitchen, the baggy T-shirt flowing around my thighs as one sleeve slips down my shoulder.

I just need coffee. Coffee will wake me, rid me of this headache and give me the energy I need to deal with this mess.

It is such a chaotic mess; I'm not sure how it possibly got worse than it was. A mix of emotions and desires that thrashes me side to side like an unforgiving earthquake. The only thing certain is that I can't stand on my own two feet. At least not without a cup of coffee.

A sarcastic huff of a humorless laugh leaves me as I round the bottom of the stairs and head to the kitchen, a pitiful smile adorning my lips. Ask and you shall receive; I'm a spiteful self-fulfilling prophecy.

All the plans I had are threatening to blow away like the stubborn seeds of a dandelion. Marriage, traveling, success and recognition. Then what? A small bump at my stomach cradled by his hand on top of mine.

Using the wineglass from last night I left next to the sink, I fill it with water and pour it into the back of the coffee maker, remembering the days when having a child was on my mind. Back when my career was only a long shot of a dream, when my time was monopolized by Evan and we owned the world together. We could be and do anything we wanted.

I slip a fresh coffee pod into the machine and turn it on as I remember how he'd hold my belly and plant a kiss there, just below my belly button, telling me what a wonderful mother I would be one day to his son.

With my throat tight I admit one thing: *we were fools.* I knew this would never last. I knew it back then. Just like I know it now.

I bite the inside of my cheek and take in a heavy breath, slipping the ceramic mug with *Rise and Shine* scrolled on the side under the spigot to the coffee machine.

My bare feet pad on the tiled kitchen floor as I open the fridge and search for the creamer, ignoring the old dreams and memories being dredged up. I stare longer than I should at the empty spot on the shelf. *I can't even remember to get creamer.* My teeth grind back and forth and the throbbing comes back with a vengeance to my temples.

I slam the fridge door shut as the coffee maker sputters to life. It's quite something when you've fallen so hard that a mundane task like going to the grocery store is enough to push you over the edge. Maybe I've truly gone crazy.

The creak of the front door opening is the last thing I need right now. The door closes softly, as if Evan didn't want to wake me. I wipe under my eyes and push my hair out of my face as I lean against the wall with my arms crossed, waiting for him to make his way in here.

I can't explain why I feel guilty. It's all I feel, like everything I've done is wrong and I'm the one to blame. Is this normal? I feel like this is what I deserve. Like somehow I've orchestrated all of this just so I could feel lonely and miserable. Maybe I had it too good and I decided I needed to go right back to the mental space where I used to feel like I was drowning.

"Morning." I hear Evan's voice and the sound of a plastic bag crinkling before I see him.

My lips part to tell him good morning, but then I catch sight of him.

He looks tired, his scruff a little too grown out, his dark hair a little too long and a bit of darkness under his eyes. For the first time I've laid eyes on him, he looks older, more mature but still as handsome as ever.

It all brings me to an abrupt halt. His jaw tenses as he rests the bag on the counter and then looks over his shoulder at me. "Did you sleep well?" he asks, barely looking at me before turning his attention to the corner cabinet and grabbing a mug for himself.

"No," I say, forcing out the word. "Evan …" I try to keep talking but my heart slams at the same time that Evan shuts the cabinet and turns around to face me. He leaves the stark white mug on the granite countertop where it clinks in protest, and I stare at it, rather than at him.

I have to spend time away from him. That's what I need. To get used to being alone again and stopping this back and forth.

"I need you to leave," I tell Evan evenly and then peek up at him. It hurts to say the words after last night. I should have said them before, but I was so tired and felt so alone. It was selfish to need him then. I used him in a way, but I won't do it again. I won't keep pretending.

He shakes his head, not once or twice but continuously as if he's in disbelief. Like I didn't actually tell him that. He had to know it was going to come to this.

"Last night—"

"Was a mistake," I say, cutting him off forcefully and my voice cracks. My chest feels tight and it's harder to breathe, but I stand my ground.

"We're different people, Evan." I try to say more but my words are stuck in my throat, threatening to choke me.

"We've always been different, Kat. Always," Evan says and his words come out hard. I can already hear him convincing me. I can already see myself falling right back into his arms because that's where I feel so safe and so loved. But he can't hold me forever.

"I can't do this, Evan," I tell him honestly, feeling my heart break as I voice the words. It's a slow break, one meant to be torturous.

"Do what?" he asks me cautiously and it pisses me off. The plastic bag rustles as he reaches behind him, brushing against it and bracing himself against the counter.

"This. I can't." I look him in the eyes even as mine water. I let the tears fall as my blood turns to ice, yet my skin heats.

Evan takes a step toward me, my name falling from his lips as his arms open and spread wide.

"If you won't tell me the truth about what happened, you need to get out."

With his eyes still widening, he shakes his head, an apology from his subconscious before he has the chance to say the words himself.

"Get out!" I yell at him, feeling the weakness threatening to consume me. Threatening to bring me right back to him. "I don't want this. I don't want you here."

"It's going to be all right," he says, attempting to calm me, that placating tone in his voice making me even angrier.

"Well, it's not now, and you need to get the fuck out," I say and seethe. I fold my arms across my chest as I look him in the eyes and tell him again. "I need space, and that means you're leaving." This townhouse is in both our names, I'm more than aware of that and he could easily bring that up. He has a right to be here and part of me wishes he would fight me on that, but he doesn't. He stares at the ground for a moment, his broad shoulders rising slowly with each heavy breath. My body shakes as he snatches his keys off the counter and leaves, slamming the door behind him.

I try to convince myself as I move to the counter, bracing my hot palms on the cold granite and focusing on breathing. This is the worst it's ever been between us. I know it's the end of us. I can feel it deep down in my bones. Shattering my core.

Out of the need to move, to do something and just go through the motions, I reach for the bag on the counter.

It's a mistake. Inside is a bottle of coffee creamer.

It's so stupid that something like this could shred me. That it can make me fall to the floor. That it can make me feel like I've made the worst decision of my life.

That it makes me feel like I'm alone. And that it's my fault for pushing Evan away.

Evan

IT'S ODD HOW LOVE WAS THERE RIGHT FROM THE START AND I DIDN'T even know it. Hindsight is twenty-twenty; I've made enough mistakes to know that. It doesn't explain how I couldn't see how obvious it was, right from the first night. Everything I did and said was different, everything I wanted changed.

My old bedroom in my father's house reminds me of all the times I spent here, but more than anything it reminds me of the last time I was in here. When I was crying like a bitch on my bed, burying my head into the pillow and refusing to accept that my mother was dying.

The red plaid flannel sheets are tucked in tight. It feels like this room's been frozen in time since I was here last. Kat fixed the sheets the same way when she made the bed the next morning. She held me all night. She let me cry and didn't tell me to stop or tell me to do anything at all. She just loved me. Freely and for no good reason.

I think she loved me from the very beginning, though. Looking back on it all, I know I had to have loved her right from the moment she stepped out of that car. The door shut with a click and my heart was finally in motion.

I remember that first date we had a few days after we met. I could still feel the beat of the heavy music in the club pumping through my veins as I opened the door to my apartment on the edge of Brooklyn. I glanced over my shoulder to take a peek at her, knowing the alcohol was wearing off and what I wanted was more than obvious. Part of me expected her to back out of coming upstairs.

I could tell she was surprised by how nice my place was. Maybe I can credit her curiosity for why she gathered up the nerve to follow my lead. There was a lot of remodeling going on in the city and I spent my money wisely, always have. Investing in properties is what my father did when he had the chance. I learned from him, but did it on a much larger scale.

The second the door closed, my hands were all over her just like they had been in the taxi and in the club. We were drawn toward each other.

That's why I think it was love. Lust is one thing. It comes and goes. The moment you're filled and satisfied, disinterest takes its place. But that's never been the case for us. There was always more. Even as we grew apart, it only made what could be that much more tempting.

I turn the lights off in my bedroom as a distant siren drowns out the silence of the room and headlights from a passing car leave stripes of light moving through the small space.

Again, I remember what we used to have. Who we used to be. The first night we spent together is all I can think about. The day she ruined me forever. And I didn't even know it was happening.

She wrapped those sweet lips of hers around my dick before I could stop her. We'd only just gotten inside and I was planning on moving a little slower. I would've skipped the foreplay and gone straight for what I wanted if I didn't think she'd appreciate taking my time. When she dropped to her knees in front of me, taking me by surprise, I wasn't going to tell her no.

I was paralyzed as she dug her fingers into my thighs and sucked her way down my length. Her cheeks hollowed as she moaned and I swear I almost came just from the sight of her.

My balls tightened as she pulled back, letting my dick pop out of her mouth and then licking the tip. Her tongue slid up my slit as she worked my shaft and then did it again. The sight of her on her knees and practically worshipping my cock is something I can never forget. It was the shock mostly, I think. A woman who was already too good for me. A woman who was probably slumming it, was on her knees devouring me and loving every second of it.

My fingers speared through her hair as I closed my eyes and let myself enjoy it. Only for a moment, though. I wanted more of her and I was sure I only had the night.

Time moved so slowly as I savored each second of her, wanting more and knowing I could have it, but not ready for it to end.

She stared up at me, licking her lips and shaking her head when I tugged on her to come up and stop. Her lips were already swollen as she panted and then leaned forward. Ignoring me and taking what she wanted.

I watched as she closed her eyes and pushed me all the way to the back of her throat, forcing me to groan from deep in my chest. My dick twitches remembering how her mouth felt like heaven. I fisted my hand in her hair and pulled her off of me; it was fucking torture, wanting what she was giving me, but knowing I'd need more.

"Strip down," I groaned out, my head leaned back and my eyes closed. As if I had any control at all over her.

She shook her head again and I couldn't believe the plea that slipped from her lips.

"I want you to come in my mouth." She said it so simply, although breathlessly with her chest rising and falling, but full of truth. Her voice was laced with desire, but it was the way her shoulders rose and fell with her heavy breathing and the way she scooted closer to me, eager and begging for more that convinced me.

I could never say no to Kat. She doesn't ask for a damn thing. Never has, and I've wished she would. I'd give her the world if I could. But that night there was no fucking way I was going to deny her that.

I'm a selfish man, after all.

I slipped my hand around the back of her head as my toes curled. I was almost embarrassed by how quickly she got me off.

She didn't stop swallowing until I was spent and even then, she bobbed lightly on my dick and sucked like she wanted more. My greedy little sex kitten.

After she was done with me, when I'd pulled my pants up and stared down at her, the atmosphere changed.

"I don't have sex on the first date," she stated shyly, wiping her lips. A blush rose to her cheeks as she slowly stood up, trying to keep her balance by gripping onto my arm. She was hesitant, embarrassed maybe. I think it was vulnerability. I think she was afraid I'd be done. *She was afraid it was only lust.*

"Oh yeah?" I responded, still trying to catch my breath and get a sense of who this girl was. "So what's this then?"

When I looked in her eyes, I knew what the real reason was. She thought I'd be done with her if I got her in bed.

More importantly, it meant she wanted to keep me.

The cockiness at that realization has never felt so good.

She wanted more and all the same, she was terrified to have me. Maybe scared she couldn't keep me, or scared to keep me. I still can't tell which was the motivating factor.

The thought made my still-hard dick even harder. And I stroked myself once and then again until she noticed. A smirk lifted up my lips as I saw her eyes widen.

"What if I want you? What if I want to take care of you now?" I asked her, taking a step forward and forcing her back. Her knees hit the bed and she nearly collapsed, the heat growing between us and nearly suffocating me.

I kissed my way down her neck, letting the heat between us climb higher and higher.

"Not just yet," I said as I stroked my dick again, feeling it turn hard as steel again already. "Let me taste you," I whispered.

Her gorgeous eyes peeked up at me through her thick lashes.

"Take it easy on me, will you?" Her words were playful, again feigning a strength that wasn't quite there. She was exposed and weak for me. Both of us knew it, only she was pretending she wasn't.

It's something that made me crave her more.

"Sure," I whispered in her ear as I pushed her onto the bed. But I never had any intention of holding back when it came to her.

I fucked her as hard as I could into that mattress. I buried myself inside her and held off as long as possible, taking her higher and higher each time until she was holding on to me for her life. Her nails scratched and dug into my skin as she screamed out my name.

I destroyed her the best way I could. And I've never been more satisfied of anything else in my life.

Kat's an emotional woman. I didn't see it at first, but that night, our first night, I got my first taste of it. I could practically hear her tell me she loved me. If nothing else, I know she loved what I did to her.

I wanted to hear her tell me those words so badly. More than anything else, I wanted *this* woman to admit it. She fell in love with me that first night.

I was desperate for it.

I didn't realize that night that the look in her eyes was exactly what I felt too. Desperate to keep her, but knowing it was never supposed to happen.

I turn on my heels, facing the door as the sound of someone coming up the stairs brings me back to today. Six years later, that night is just a distant memory.

The door to my bedroom opens wide, creaking as it does and revealing my father. I haven't seen him like this in a long damn time.

His hair's been gray for a while, but it's just a bit too long and thinner. With the deep wrinkles around his eyes and only wearing a T-shirt and flannel pants, he looks older and frailer than I remember. Beaten down. Just a few years can change everything. Has it been that long since I really looked at him?

"You getting comfortable in here?" Pops asks me as he walks in and takes a look at the dresser. He runs a hand along it and then makes a face as he turns his hand over and sees the dust there. As he wipes his hand on the flannel pajamas he adds, "It's about time you came back to clean your room."

A rough chuckle barely makes its way up my chest.

"When are you moving out of this place?" I ask him jokingly.

"When I'm dead and gone," my father answers me the same way he has for years now. Ever since Ma passed, I've wanted him to move. He won't, though, and I can't blame him.

"Good thing I'm not in a nursing home. Don't think you'd like to crash there, would you?"

I give him a tight smile, feeling nothing but shame. I run my hand through my hair searching for some sort of an explanation, but I can't lie to my father and I don't want to tell him the truth. So I don't say anything and stare past him instead.

The silence is thick between us until he speaks, glancing around the room rather than looking at me.

"I messed up before with your mother, you know. She kicked me out. I thought it was over." My father flicks on the light and stalks slowly toward the bed, ignoring the fact that I just wanted to pass out and try to sleep. As if I'd be able to in this room.

"I was younger than you, though. By the time I was your age, we'd had you. I'd settled down and stopped being stupid."

"What'd you do?" I ask my father out of genuine curiosity. I'd never seen anything but love from my parents. They never fought in front of me and the one time I came home early, catching them in the heat of a fight, they stopped immediately.

Later that night, when I was sitting in front of the TV, cross-legged and way too close, all I could hear was him apologizing in the kitchen. It'd been quiet all afternoon and night.

"I don't want you to go to bed mad at me," I heard him tell her.

It was the only fight I'd ever witnessed and I remember being scared that he'd done something that Ma wasn't going to forgive.

But she did. I never asked back then, and I'm sure if I did he wouldn't remember. This fight he's talking about obviously isn't that.

"What do you think I did?" he answers me. "We were young and stupid and had a bad fight over money or something. I got drunk, kissed a girl at a bar … went back to her place. I felt like shit about it and she smacked me right across the face too." He smirks at the memory. "She beat the hell out of me. Kicked me out." The smile falls and he shakes his head as he adds, "I deserved it."

"I can't imagine you ever doing that."

"I loved your mother. I was angry at her over something stupid, I can't even remember what."

The silence stretches between us again as he struggles to come up with what to say next. "I proposed to her a few months after we got back together." A huff of a laugh leaves him and he adds, "God rest her soul," as he twists the wedding band around his ring finger. He's never taken it off. For the same reason he'll never leave this house.

He still needs her. Even if it's just the memory of her.

"The point is, we all make mistakes," he says and then squares his shoulders at me, raising both of his hands and shaking them, "when we're young and allowed to be stupid."

"I'm not that old," I tell him half-heartedly, trying to play it all off. I know what he's getting at, but I don't need to be lectured. I'm well aware of how stupid I've been. He's the one who has no idea how badly I've fucked up. "I'll fix it, Pops."

The silence drags on again and all I can think about is every position I've put myself in where not being faithful to my wife would have been the easy thing to do. I focus on that truth and not the night that still haunts me.

"What are you doing, Evan?" my father asks as I dump my bag on the bed. "You've fucked up more than you should have. You're too old to be carrying on like this."

My initial reaction is to bite back that he's wrong. That he has no idea what's going on. But it wouldn't matter.

I nod my head and let the strap from the bag fall off my shoulder. "Yeah, I know."

"You need to make this right," he tells me, holding my gaze and pointing a finger at me.

I swallow thickly, knowing he's right. But I haven't got a clue how to make this better. I can't take back what's been done.

I'm fucked.

"Yeah, I know."

chapter 11

Kat

Just get it over with,
Tell me that we're done.
Leave me to this madness,
I accept that you have won.

You've broken me to pieces,
Left me numb and blind.
Made me only yours—
I've completely lost my mind.

"I NEED A DISTRACTION, THAT'S WHAT I NEED." I SPEAK THE WORDS ON my mind without realizing it. It gets the attention of both Maddie and Jules and that's when I realize I've said anything at all. Cue swallowing down another sip of wine.

We've been here in Jules's house helping her unpack for at least two hours now, and everyone's been kind enough to not only *not* ask about what's going on between Evan and me, but to not treat me like I'm some wounded animal either.

That's what friends are for, although the girls do seem to be walking on eggshells around me. I'm grateful, but I need to talk and have someone sift through this mess and give me a straight answer as to what I should do.

I roll my eyes at the thought. I'm a grown woman. I should know what to do and make the decision with certainty. But I've never felt so uncertain in my life.

"A distraction?" Jules questions, a little more pep in her tone than she's had all night.

"That makes sense," Maddie says and nods her head as she takes out a picture frame, wrapped in thick brown packing paper. She's careful with it as she removes the wrapping and exposes the pristine silver frame. "Distractions are a good thing," she adds with a small nod. "Sometimes."

I don't know what photo is already nestled inside of the frame, but whatever it is, it makes her smile. I can only imagine it's a wedding photo ... I lift the glass to my lips again.

"I can't go home to the townhouse with all his things and our things and every reminder of everything ..." Pausing to take in a lungful of air, I try to steady myself then add, "Let alone go to sleep in the same bed we've had together for forever."

I stare at the artwork centered over Julia's fireplace as I talk.

The crinkling of the packaging paper is all the response I get from the other side of the expansive room. It's so loud that I'm not sure anyone but Maddie even heard me. We've been working in relative silence save for the soft sound of music flowing from the kitchen behind us.

"We should go on a girls' trip," I offer up and look over my shoulder at Maddie. I shift in my seat and wait for her to meet my gaze.

"Hell yeah," she answers without hesitation. "What does the newlywed think?" Maddie asks and instantly Jules brightens.

She shrugs as if the word *newlywed* didn't make her day and puts the attention back on me as she says, "I'm happy to do whatever you want, Kat." I hate that Jules is holding back. Every response from her tonight seems muted. She's happy and she knows I'm not. She's a newlywed and my marriage is falling apart.

I get it, but she should be happy. She doesn't have to hold back her joy because I'm falling apart.

"You're glowing," I tell her and wait for a response to the compliment, feeling guilty that I haven't said it sooner. My chest feels tight and I shift into a cross-legged position on the plush carpet as I grab a plastic bottle of water, drinking it down slowly even though it's room temperature now. The sweeping room of this new build is ridiculous. The entire house still smells of fresh paint. I can imagine they spent several million on it and the movers did most of the work carrying in all the heavy furniture. Jules didn't trust them with these boxes, though.

Maddie quirks an eyebrow. "You already make a baby?" she asks Jules, her tone devious. I can't help that my brow raises comically.

"Oh my God, Jules, are you pregnant?" I pile on and Maddie snickers as Jules pulls her tawny hair back and rolls her eyes.

"Shut up," Jules says playfully and then goes to the granite counter behind us and makes a show of drinking from her glass of wine. Her simple yet chic rose dress flutters as she waves her glass in the air. She's the epitome of an upper-class socialite.

We exchange amused looks, waiting for her to reply with a straight yes or no.

"Not yet," Jules finally answers.

"Yet!" Maddie practically shrieks. "First comes love, then comes marriage—"

"Then comes a new home and a fresh start," Jules says, cutting her off and Sue laughs from her spot in the corner of the living room where she's been silent all night. Something's definitely gotten to Sue too.

Although maybe it's me, maybe I'm why everyone seems off.

"House first, then the baby," Jules states and then switches the song playing to something more upbeat and less sad. I agree with that decision wholeheartedly.

"Love your house," Sue comments, not bothering to bring up the idea of a child. "Or is it technically a mansion?" she half jokes.

It's grand and spacious and much more like Jules's style than her new husband Mason's previous home. She got a deal on this property and the amount of space is making me regret buying a place so close to the park. It reminds me how tiny our townhouse is. At least compared to this. Location is everything and we paid handsomely for our little place.

This is also a family home, and I live in a townhouse that's not meant for anything more than two people … potentially one child, but it would be cramped. I force my lips to stay in place and swallow down the frown and all the feelings threatening to come up.

Full circle I go, all day long. My thoughts always come back to Evan and what we had and everything we could still have.

With a bitter sigh I hope no one heard, I finish my water and get up to grab another drink, shimmying past the three opened boxes and paper sitting on the floor. I made this decision. I need to own up to it and deal with the consequences.

"I'm not sure I can do this girls' trip," Sue says seemingly out of nowhere. I'd nearly forgotten about the mention of a trip. I guess that's how much it means to me.

"It's just that work …" she adds and then pauses to chew the inside of her cheek. She braces herself on a polished wingback chair before rising and picking up her wineglass. "I've got a new boss and he's a dick with a capital D. There's no way he's going to give me time off."

"It's not really his position to give it to you," Maddie says skeptically. "Like, you *earn* your days. And we haven't even set a date yet." The aggressiveness in Maddie's voice catches me off guard.

Sue stands, an empty glass in hand, meeting me at the small sink filled with ice and bottles of rosé and cabernet. With a glass of wine in her right hand and a ball of packaging paper in her left, she strides past a very young and not at all familiar with the corporate world Maddie, and responds with certainty, "He'll give me shit."

"So fuck him," Maddie says, a little anger coming out. She doesn't usually get worked up, so I'm taken aback. Everyone is off today … there must be something in the air.

"It's fine, it was just a thought," I say and try to smooth the tension flowing between the two of them. "You okay?" I direct my question at Maddie, who doesn't seem to notice it's for her, picking up her wineglass and throwing it back.

"I don't want to set a bad precedent," Sue states staring directly at Maddie, who refuses to look back at Suzette.

My gaze moves between the two of them and I'm only distracted by the loud clap behind me from Jules. "Who wants some charcuterie?" Jules says and we all turn slowly to see her lifting a tray of cut meats and cheese as if it's the peace treaty between us.

Sue has the decency to laugh and the small moment of tension is immediately diffused.

I feel odd sitting in this room all of a sudden. Looking around the room, I'm surrounded by friends, but I feel alone. I take another sip of water. It's all in my head, I'm more than aware of that, but it doesn't change how I feel.

"Have you slept with him?" Jules regards me as she grabs a contraption from one of her drawers that she uses to uncork the wine bottles. The kitchen is all white. White cabinets and a sleek white countertop. The only color is in the ebony floorboards. It's luxurious and would be fitting for an editorial photoshoot. Which I promptly told her the moment I stepped foot in this place. I am her agent after all.

"Who with who?" Maddie asks for clarification with a sly smile on her face. "Is Sue sleeping with her boss?" Her question makes Suzette tense and stare back at Maddie with daggers. But Maddie's oblivious. The two of them should have their own show. If it was up to me, they would and the ratings would be through the roof. Maddie would probably go for it, Sue would never.

"Kat," Jules answers and her tone is casual, not sympathetic or pushy, no motive apparent. "Have you slept with Evan since it all happened?" she asks again, but more directly and pops the cork from the bottle.

It fizzes as my face heats, knowing the other two women are looking at me, but I wait for Jules. The second she raises her eyes to mine, although it was only meant to be a glance, I nod my head.

I anticipate the scoff of disdain from Sue, the tilted head with a sympathetic look from Maddie, but I don't know what to expect from Jules.

She shrugs her shoulders, the soft pink fabric slipping down and making her look that much thinner, that much more beautiful. "Was it any good?" she asks and lifts the glass to her lips. It's dark red wine, the same color she wears on her lips. It's one thing I like about Jules; she's nothing if not consistent.

Rolling my eyes, I wipe my face with my hand. It's always good with Evan. "It was a mistake," I tell her instead. My dismal tone immediately changes the mood and frustration flows through me.

"People make mistakes," Jules says low, so low I almost didn't hear her. And then she looks at me and adds, "It happens." She sounds so sad and I can't help but to wonder what's going on with her. For just a moment, a short glimpse, there's something there other than the perfect façade she always carries. But the moment she registers that I can see it, the crack in her demeanor, she straightens her shoulders and takes in a heavy breath.

Silence passes and the only thing that can be heard is the rustling of paper as Maddie unwraps something. Staring down into the newly poured glass of wine I realize I've never felt so alone and unwelcomed. It's not them, it's me and my head, I know it is. "I just don't know what to do," I say, speaking to all of them or none of them, it doesn't matter, I just needed to say it. "We slept together and I think it was a mistake … Because I kicked him out the next morning." A groan leaves me, nearly comical, as I take a small sip but it's not satisfying. Not nearly large enough either.

"You don't need to decide right now," Jules says easily. "There's a lot to consider and talk about." She nods her head as she talks, almost like she's talking to herself.

"The thing is … I don't know what I want, but I know he'll convince me to stay with him."

"Men have a way with words," Sue chimes in, agreeing with me, and tips her glass in an air-cheers with me. "It's called lying."

I huff in agreement, opting for my water instead of more wine, as I watch Sue saunter over to the tray of cheese.

"I mean … not that he lied … he's just …" Sue says softly and then clears her throat to add with a touch of sympathy, "I keep letting my shitty experience color my opinion. Sorry," she says, looking me in the eyes. The sincerity there kills me.

"It's fine. It's called experience."

"So you're indecisive, and that makes sense. You're married. You love him. But you're hurt." Maddie cuts through all the silence and unease like it's so simple and easy to comprehend. But it's not. There's a raging war of emotions inside of me. I don't know that I can trust my husband, and that alone is enough to end it and what pushed me to kick him out this morning.

Rather than confess about my lack of trust, I offer a partial truth. "I slept with him last night and then kicked him out this morning." I shake my head realizing how awful that sounds, how crazy it seems.

"Sounds like a divorce to me," Sue says and then fills her glass again. "I did it for years, Kat. Years of back and forth. Forgiving but not forgetting." Her slender fingers play on the stem of the glass. "Wish I had those years back."

The need to defend Evan overrides my common sense. "I don't know what I did that pushed him away." Even as I say the words, I know that's not true. I let distance grow between us. I ignored him in favor of my career.

"Nothing, it's not you. It's not your fault." Sue's words are hard, with no negotiation allowed. So I don't correct her.

Maddie adds in, ever comforting, "It's not your fault in the least. Don't let him make you feel that way."

They don't understand. They just don't get it.

"What if—"

Sue cuts me off to say, "If you want to sleep with him, do it. Want to kick him out, do it. Want to hurl something at his head … maybe don't because that's assault." Her joke forces a bark of a laugh from me and a snicker from Jules. Her glass setting down on the counter offers a clink and she adds, "Yes please, for the love of all things holy don't make us come bail you out."

"You would, though," I say and cock a brow, knowing any of the three of these women would bail me out in a heartbeat.

"It's whatever you want," Maddie continues and Jules and Sue both nod. "You can be friends with benefits if that's what you want, fuck buddies, you can use him for revenge sex. I don't think any of us have any answers other than we're here for you." She side-eyes Sue and adds, "Although Sue is cockblocking our girls' trip."

"Oh my Lord, someone … get her," Sue groans and Jules and I laugh while Maddie purses her lips and tosses a balled-up bit of paper at Sue's back. It doesn't reach, but the comic relief helps to calm all the nerves I've been feeling. Most of them, anyway. There's still a little flutter in the pit of my stomach.

"We'll plan a girls' trip," Jules states as if it's a fact. "It just might be a bit difficult, but we will make this happen and it'll be great for you to get out."

"I think it will be fun, and I'll figure out how to make it work," Sue says all the while staring at Maddie who finally smiles.

"Yes. Girls' trip and fuck or dump whomever we want … Except Jules. Because she might be pregnant."

I nearly choke on my wine at that thought.

chapter 12

I TRIED IT. I SWEAR I TRIED TO GIVE HER SPACE.

Kat says that's what she needs, but I know it's not. This plan of hers isn't what she needs and it's sure as hell not what I want.

She needs me. Period. She needs me to be there and that's where I've failed. Not just in the last few weeks. For years, I chose a lifestyle that forced us apart.

I can fix this, but not by running to Pops and leaving her all alone with nothing but this city whispering in her ear.

My arm stiffens as I slide the key into the lock to our townhouse. My heart doesn't beat until it turns, proving she didn't change the locks. I let out a breath I didn't know I was still holding and push it open. I'm prepared with what I need to say. Prepared to hold my ground and not take no for an answer.

But it only takes one step inside of our living room for all of it to slip away from me.

Kat looks so tired, so worn out propped up in the corner of the sofa with her laptop sitting to the left of her, but the screen's black. She has a cup of coffee in her hands as well as bags under her eyes. She turns to me slowly, wiping the sleep from her eyes and adjusting herself slightly. With the gentle protest of the sofa, I shut the door behind me.

"What are you doing here?" she asks me, still seated with her legs tucked underneath her on the sofa. I'm stunned for a moment because she's so fucking beautiful, even in this state. My body's drawn to her. If it were another time, I'd go to the sofa, push the laptop off and lie down, making her take a break. I'd kiss her until her body writhed against mine.

And she'd let me. She'd let me make her relax. At least she would have a year ago.

"This is my house." I try not to say the words too firmly. "Our house," I correct myself and swallow before continuing and taking a single step closer to her. "I worked my ass off—"

"Then I'll move out," Kat quickly states matter-of-factly, but the pain is barely disguised. She seems to snap out of whatever daze had her captive before I came in here.

"I don't want you to move out. We don't need this." I emphasize my words.

"I asked for time and space because I don't know what to do, Evan. You aren't giving me any options without telling me what happened."

"You want to know?" I look her in the eyes, feeling my blood pulse harder in my veins.

"Are you going to tell me the truth?" she asks me in a cracked whisper. "All of it?"

All of it? I have to break her gaze. I can't. I can't confess everything. I'd lose her forever.

The second I break eye contact, she scoffs. "You're so full of shit. Why are you doing this to me?" she asks me, although it's rhetorical. There's a loathing in her tone but more than that it's pain.

Why am I doing this to her? If it was only so easy as *doing* something. There's nothing I can do.

"I didn't come home to fight."

"Neither did I … but here we are," she retorts, taking in a shuddering breath. "I asked for time, Evan."

Tossing my keys on the coffee table, I make my way into the living room and sit across from her in the armchair. I'm not foolish enough to think she'd let me sit close enough to touch her. Even as I sit here, feet away, she bends her legs in closer and pushes the laptop to the side. Like she's ready to run at a moment's notice.

Time slips by as I lean back, letting a long exhale take up some of it. "I just want to be home with you while this blows over."

"Blows over?" I don't know how she can make a whisper seem hysterical. I'm not good with words. I never have been, but I wish I had the wisdom to say the right thing right now.

"Maybe this is the moment," she states with a sad smile on her beautiful face.

"The moment?"

"The moment that changes everything for the rest of my life. I've been wondering exactly what moment it was, but thought maybe it hasn't happened yet."

Her words settle deep in my very core and a tingling runs through my fingers up my arms. Slow, yet all-consuming. Her face changes from the sarcastic disappointment that she had when she said the words. As if only just now realizing the magnitude of them herself.

"We can go back. I promise," I tell her softly, raising my hands just slightly, but the fear of losing her keeps my blood cold and my motions subtle.

"It's called separating for a reason," she says, whispering her response. As if what we had the other night meant nothing. As if there's no reason for us to be together. Maybe she really doesn't love me anymore. The fissure in my chest deepens, feeling like it's cracked wide open.

"We're not separated."

"Yes we are."

"We didn't decide to do that," I answer her. "You were angry."

"Rightfully so," she spits back.

"I told you it's not true," I plead with her as I stare deep into her eyes. I watch as they gloss over and her lower lip trembles. "Just …" I swallow thickly, the lump growing in the back of my throat suffocating any plea I have for her. *Just love me. Just forgive me.*

I turn away from her for a moment, not able to voice what I'm feeling. I lean forward in the chair, and it creaks as I rest my weight in it. Kat starts to get up in response.

"I don't want to fight," I remind her.

"I don't want this, Evan. I didn't ask for this," she says, raising her voice for the second part, the anger coming back. She stops moving, though, and I can tell she's losing the will to fight. It's by the way her lips are parted just so, and her breathing is quicker and she has that little crease in the center of her forehead.

"I don't know what to do or say, or what to think. I feel crazy." She stares at me wide eyed, her voice sounding hoarse. "Do you understand what that's like? To be so stupid? To know I'm being stupid and setting myself up for you to hurt me again."

"I won't hurt you—" The truth rushes out of me in a single breath, but she doesn't let me finish.

"But you did," she says, cutting me off and rocking forward just slightly as she points out the obvious. "And you won't even tell me why." Her shoulders shudder, but she doesn't cry, she holds her ground.

"I don't want to lose you, Kat," I manage to speak and peek up to look at her. I'm such a piece of shit. "I just want you. It's the honest to God truth. I just want you."

"I want you to quit," she tells me and rocks on her feet to stand. She nods her head and visibly swallows. "You need to quit." She stares at me, her emerald eyes pleading. Her body's still, like she's not breathing. Just waiting.

"It's not that easy," I say and God I wish she knew. I want to tell her everything, but I can't risk it. I can't leave right now. I just need time.

"It is that easy; you quit or leave." I stare into her eyes that swirl with nothing but raw vulnerability, and hesitate.

"You're giving me an ultimatum?" Even as I ask her, I know that's what she's doing.

She has no idea.

"I just need time." I need her to just give me time. As soon as I'm out of this, I can do whatever she wants.

But not right now.

I can feel her slipping away. Every second that passes where I don't tell her, she's turning colder toward me. But she can't know. No one can.

My lips part and I can feel my lungs still. The words are right there. Begging me, and desperate for her to hear. I need her more than anything.

"Kat." I say her name but it's so much more. It's me begging for her to love me blindly, to trust that I love her and that I'd never do anything to hurt her.

I can't. I can't risk losing her, and I won't do it.

My mouth closes and I turn away from her, running my hand over my face.

"Get out," Kat states and her voice hitches at the end. I turn to see her cover her face.

The next bit happens so fast. It's a blur as I close the distance between us. It only takes three steps, but by the time my arms wrap around her, she's pushing me away. Her hands slam into my chest. She tries to knock me back, but only manages to throw herself off-balance instead.

I grip her hips to steady her, but she slaps me. Hard across the face and the sting catches me by surprise.

I flex my jaw as she screams at me to get out. Her body's shaking. The sinful mix of hatred and betrayal ring in the air between us.

How the hell did I let this happen?

"Do you really want me out?" I ask her, genuinely not knowing anymore. I don't know at what point I lost her completely. There's only so many times I can ask her to give me everything while I hold back.

I guess I should be more surprised it hasn't happened sooner.

Rubbing my jaw as I take a step back, I give her the only bit of space I'm willing to offer. "I know you still love me," I tell her and watch as she rips her eyes from me. Her face is blotchy and red and her breathing is frantic.

But she calms as she stands there not able to answer me. That's all I needed. Just a little bit. *Please, Kat. Just hold on a little while longer.*

"Just tell me the truth," she begs me and I wish I could. I feel my throat tighten and my body tense. My hands clench as I swallow.

"I didn't sleep with her." I answer without wasting a second and even I don't believe my words. But it's not what she thinks. I wish I could tell her, but the moment she finds out, everything will be at risk.

"Why don't I believe you?" she says and I don't have the decency to answer.

"I swear, Kat."

"So you've never slept with her?" she asks me and I know it's over. Her expression changes and her eyes darken when the silence stretches too long. So many secrets have built up. Too many to hide. She was never supposed to know. "Since we've been married," I start to say, knowing I'm toeing the line of truth, "I've never slept with anyone. Never kissed anyone but you." I look her in the eyes so she can see it's the truth. "The day I put that ring on your finger, it was only you."

"Then why put me through this?" she asks me with tears in her eyes. "And what were you doing?" I struggle to keep my breathing calm as the questions start piling up. "What were you doing with her in that hotel if you weren't sleeping with her."

I lick my dry lips and take a step forward. "Things got out of hand."

"Why were you with her?" Kat presses and I know she wants an answer right now.

"Because it's what I had to do," I say, telling her the truth with my eyes closed.

"What you had to do? You had to go to her hotel at three in the morning?" I can't look at her as I nod my head. "And you couldn't tell me this before?" I nod my head again.

"You tell me everything right now, or you leave."

"Another ultimatum?" The words drip with disdain.

"Don't talk to me like that," she says. Her tone is dismissive and I can hear her resolve harden.

"It's better if you didn't know everything," I answer gently yet firmly just the same.

"Are you serious right now? You're throwing away our marriage over her? Over your job?"

"Kat, just—" I start to say, but she cuts me off.

"Fuck you," she sneers then yells, "I said get out."

"I'm not leaving," I tell her firmly, staring back at her, even as she turns her back to me.

"It doesn't matter, the weekend's coming," she says beneath her breath as she leaves me.

I keep my feet planted as she stomps up the stairs and I wait for more. I wait for her to push me out, to yell at me, to demand more from me. I'm ready to fight, ready for war with her to keep her. But that's not what I get.

She gives me back exactly what I gave her. *Nothing.*

chapter 13

FOUR MANUSCRIPTS TO GO THROUGH THIS WEEKEND.

Four authors waiting to hear back from me.

I doubt I'll be able to focus enough to comprehend a full page. I've been reading the same paragraph over and over and not a damn sentence is staying with me.

It doesn't matter, though. None of this really does.

All that matters is that I stay in this office for as long as Evan's here. He's like a ghost in this house. A ghost of his former self.

So I do what I've always done, I bury myself in work. That was the plan anyway, but now I can't focus on anything but the sounds of him moving through the house.

He walks by the door every few hours, making the floor groan, and I know he wants to open it, wants me to talk to him. All I can hear is him saying it'd be better if I didn't know. To hell with that.

I'm not going to give him all of me when he can't be bothered to do the same. There is nothing more important than us. Not a single thing that should come between us; yet it feels like he's got plenty in the space between my heart and his.

So we're at a standstill, him refusing to leave and me refusing to blindly forgive.

His voice plays in my head over and over again, telling me it's only ever been me. I want to believe it. It's everything I've been praying for him to say.

But then what is he hiding?

My eyes flicker to the screen as my nails tap on the pale blue ceramic mug next to my laptop. *Tick, tick, tick.* I read the line over and over: *Love is a stubborn heart.*

Magdalene, the editor, highlighted the line. She thinks it's beautiful and she wants repetition of the metaphor throughout the book.

Love is a stubborn heart.

Is it, though? My forehead scrunches as I think back to the story in the manuscript. The tale about a modern-day Romeo and Juliet. Two families who hated each other and their children who wanted nothing more than to run away together. It's not a tragedy but it doesn't have a happily ever after either. It's too realistic.

If love really was that stubborn, wouldn't they have been together in the end?

Maybe it wasn't really love.

Or maybe love just wasn't enough.

I don't know that I agree that love is stubborn. I suppose it is, but more than that, it's stealthy and lethal. I nod my head at the thought.

Love is deadly.

Rolling my eyes. I push the laptop away. My comments don't belong on this manuscript right now.

I don't know the very moment I fell in love with Evan. It felt like I was counting the days until it would be over, and then one day, I simply decided on forever. Just like that, a snap of my fingers. Slow, so slow and resistant, and then in an instant, I was his and he was mine. And that's how it was going to be forever.

I smile at the thought and try to focus on the lines staring back at me from the computer. I try to read the words, but I keep glancing at the wall behind me. At a photo of the first night he took me to meet his parents. It was after I'd decided on forever.

I'd never felt that kind of fear before. The fear of rejection. Not like I did that night and I know why: it's because I'd never put my heart out there for anyone to take.

I was very much aware that Evan had every piece of me. Unless he didn't want me. In which case, I'd be broken and I didn't know how I'd recover.

The thought consumed me the night he brought me to his family home. I was sure his family wouldn't like me. It'd been so long since I'd been with a family for dinner. I used to go to my friend Marissa's when I was in high school. But that's not the same. Not at all. It was also a rarity that I accepted Marissa's parents' offer for dinner.

When you lose your parents at fifteen, people tend to look at you as though they've never seen anything sadder. I'd rather be alone than deal with that.

So I was, until Evan. And he didn't come on his own, he had a family that "had to meet me."

My back rests against the desk chair as my gaze lingers on the photograph. I had it printed in black and white. It's the four of us on the sofa in his family home's living room. It's funny how I can see the colors of the sofa so clearly, the faded plaid, even though there isn't any color in the picture that hangs on my wall.

All four of us are smiling. His mother insisted on taking the photo. Just as she'd insisted he bring me that night.

It's only now that I can remember how Evan's father looked at her. I didn't think anything of it at the time, but that's because they hadn't told us that she was sick.

I guess in some ways it was the last photograph. If that isn't accepting someone into your family, I don't know what is.

I have to hold back the prick of tears as I think of her. I only met Marie a handful of times. The dinner was the second. The third was after she'd told Evan; she didn't have a choice, seeing as how she had to be hospitalized. The last time I saw her was at the funeral.

I may not know when I fell in love with him, but I think I know the moment he fell in love with me. The moment a part of his heart died and he needed something, or someone, to fill it. Maybe I got lucky that it was me. Or maybe it was a curse.

I roll my eyes, hating that I'm stuck in the past because I can't move ahead with the future.

Maybe we weren't really meant to be. Maybe it was never the type of love that's meant to keep people together. Just the type of love when you feel compelled to give someone compassion.

Are there types of love? I find myself leaving the question as a comment on the book and then deleting it.

If there are, then maybe Evan's love is the stubborn kind. He's not so stubborn that he'll stay this weekend, though. Come Friday he'll be gone again. Maybe it's a different kind of love then …

It's only when I hear the bedroom door shut that I finally look back at the manuscript and email the editor back. I need more time before I can give feedback on any of these to the author and I'm ready to fall asleep in the corner chair, or any place I can where Evan will leave me alone.

I need more time for so much more. I need time and a clear head to move forward with my own life. I need someone to tell me I'm not walking away from the only man who will ever love me, but there's no email I can write for that unfortunate request.

Evan

If I could focus on the hate and leave her all alone,
I'd be able to move forward, if only I had known.
I can't speak the truth, I don't want to make it real,
I can't stand what I've done or what it makes me feel.
Regret will settle in my chest and suffocate the day.
If only I could make it right, if only there was a way.

"IT'S GOOD TO SEE NEW YORK AGAIN," JAMES SAYS AS I WALK INTO HIS office on Greene Street in lower Manhattan.

Even as he speaks, he stares out the office window. It's an impressive eight-by-eight-foot picture window, making the view seem like it's not quite real.

I don't return his sentiment. I'm fucking miserable regardless of the scenery or location. I want to drop to my knees and confess everything to Kat. The weight of it all is burying me. I think she'd forgive me. I can see it in her eyes that she wants to accept anything I'm willing to divulge. I could tell her almost everything and I think she'd let me stay.

I'm too scared to do it, though, and bring her into this mess. If they find out she knows … she just can't know. Not until I end things here at least. It's step one to getting my Kat back.

"It's crazy how you miss it, isn't it?" he continues as he turns to me. He's more relaxed than he was in London, although his suit is crisp and fresh from the dry cleaner. I close the door as he takes a seat at the desk, unbuttoning his dark gray jacket.

"Sorry you had to wait a minute, I was just getting this paperwork wrapped up." He leans back in his chair, loosening his slim navy tie and unfastening the top button of his crisp white dress shirt.

"Are we going to talk about it?" I ask, needing to get this shit off my chest. I kept quiet in London, but I can't anymore. It's been weeks. That must be enough time.

Is that how long it takes to get away with murder?

"Talk about what?" he questions and his voice is gravelly and low.

"Talk about the fact that the charges against Bruce are dropped?" I say then hold his cold gaze with one I hope informs him I have no time for bullshit and I'm out of patience.

He may have been relaxed before I sat down, but now he's still. And silent. I let my eyes fall to the stack of papers on his desk, then drift to a small picture frame. It's a cube and matte black on all sides, and I have no idea who the woman in the picture is.

I absently pick it up, ignoring how his eyes bore into me, how his icy gaze heats as I let the question hang in the air, forcing him to answer.

The block is lighter than I thought it'd be and I don't recognize the broad with a closer look either. It's not his ex-wife, or his current girlfriend. Not that I thought Luna or whatever her name was, the fling of the month, would have a place in his office.

"My sister," James says, answering the unasked question. "A Christmas gift."

I nod my head once, putting the block back down and waiting for him to answer me.

"Bruce didn't *do* anything, so of course the charges didn't stick," James states in an eerily calm voice. "We knew he was innocent." James pulls out a drawer and shuffles something inside of it, but I can't see what. He doesn't elaborate or give any room to further the conversation that we should have.

"What's done is done, and there's nothing more to say."

"That's not what Sam told me. She told me she's scared." It's the only reason I let her get so close. She's terrified that the truth is going to come out. She helped me, so she'd go down with me.

"Whose fault is that?" James sneers.

"She's your wife," I say, pushing out the words through my clenched teeth.

"I don't have a wife," he answers me with a sly smile, as if he's clean of this mess. As if it's all on me. Deep down in my gut, I know it is.

"Ex then," I concede and add, "I didn't know the divorce had been finalized." He picks up a pen and taps it against the desk but doesn't take his eyes off me. It hasn't gone through yet, according to Samantha. All the money needs to be split one way or the other, and neither him nor Samantha, his ex-partner in this business and future ex-wife, wants to take less than the other.

"Either way, what's done is done and the two of you need to let it die."

"An innocent man—"

"Got off!" He looks me in the eyes as he leans forward and adds, "And a guilty man got away."

"We should have come forward."

"Should have, but you listened to a shady bitch. That's your problem, not mine."

My gaze falls to the desk as my fingers itch to form a fist. I called *him*. The number I dialed that night was to *his* office. I had no idea she'd be the one who answered.

"I panicked—" I start to say, but he cuts me off.

"Because you fucked up. And now I have to clean up your mess and make sure you stay out of trouble."

"Is that what this is? You doing me a favor?" I ask sarcastically, letting the memory of that night fade. I can't quit while there's still an investigation. I can't bring more attention to myself or to the company. One of my clients dies and I get fired or quit shortly after? Yeah, that'll get the police's attention.

I wish I could tell Kat everything, but then she'd know she was married to a murderer. Even if it was just an accident. I'm a coward and I'll never be a man she deserves. But every day that goes by, I want to be more of the man I was the day before it all changed.

"I need time off," I state, fed up with the conversation. I imagine this isn't the first time something like this has happened and I sift through the memories of all the shit that's gone on behind the scenes for years. I never questioned anything, I never suspected a thing. Not until James brought me into the inner circle.

"No," James answers immediately with no negotiation in his voice.

"Then I quit," I tell him as my fingers dig into the chair. The only thing I can think about is Kat. She'll get over the fact I kept this from her. I know she will. It's not the first time I've kept a secret from her. We'll be okay as long as I'm through with this shit.

His thin lips twist into a half smile as he says, "Well, that can't happen." He looks at me with a calculated glint in his eyes. Like he's been waiting for this and he's ready for my rebuttal, eager for it even.

"Why not?" I question as my muscles coil. Even though I'm aware it could cause suspicion, I can do whatever the fuck I want. "I'm not going to work for this company anymore."

"That's not—"

"It's called quitting," I spit back at him. I don't need this job; I've got plenty of money in the bank and my investments, and Kat's career is finally stable. She bled money for years, but it's leveling out. We'll be all right financially and this is what she wants and what I need.

"You can't just quit."

"I can, and I am."

James's smile fades and he tilts his head to the side, an expression of the utmost sympathy on his weathered face. His deep brown eyes look darker as he picks up a folder on the left side of his desk. It wasn't hidden, but it's not labeled and it looks like all the rest.

My eyes follow his movement and my brow furrows until he opens it.

"The hotel had cameras. They're gone now, of course, but a few snapshots were taken. Some I think you'd find particularly interesting. Maybe enough so to stay."

I can imagine what they are before he flips the folder open. The eight-by-ten glossy photo paper shows the one thing that proves I lied. I'm walking into the hotel lobby I claimed I didn't enter. And I'm not alone. Standing right next to me is Tony. Only hours before he was found dead in the rec room of the hotel. The one reserved for our company and the division Bruce is the head of. The photograph of Tony and his bloodshot eyes takes me back to that night. To the moment I found him dead on the floor.

My limbs freeze in waves. Like the betrayal that moves through me.

"It's a security net on my end," James says and then closes the folder, pulling it off the desk and into his lap.

"So if I quit," I start to say, but instead I stop and stare ahead out of the window. I want to kill him. There's never been a time in my life when I've desired someone dead. But right now, it's all I want.

"Then I assume it's for less than moral reasons," James says, spelling it out for me. "I need to protect myself."

"That's bullshit," I tell him and my words are hard. My hands turn to fists as they tremble with the need to get this anger out.

"I know, trust me I know," James says. "And I don't like this any more than you do."

A sarcastic huff of a laugh leaves me. "Fuck off," I sneer at him.

I stand up from the office chair so quickly it nearly falls over. I grip it so tight I think I'll break it. Fuck, I want to break it. I can picture beating the piss out of him with the broken wood.

My body is hot, my mind in a daze of regret and sickness.

"I'm leaving," I barely speak as I turn my back to him and start to walk off.

"The fuck you are," he says.

My body whips around, tense and ready to let it all out. Every day it's been building and building, the tension winding tighter and the need to destroy something climbing higher and higher. I only took a few steps away, and with his words I'm right back across the desk, ready to do something stupid.

My body heats as my fist moves from the chair to the desk and I lean closer. He may not want to show it, but I see the fear in his eyes.

He should be scared. He's fucking with me. Threatening me. No one is going to take my wife from me. I won't allow it.

"I need to get away from this. From you."

I never should have listened to him and tried to cover it up. He set me up. He used that night to his advantage and I played right into his hand.

It takes everything in me not to reach across the desk and haul him up by his collar. To fist the fine cloth in my grip and spit in his face.

Pure rage and adrenaline pump through my blood.

"Careful now, Evan." James smiles as he says it, but I notice how he leans back. Both of us know he's scared. If I throw this punch, if I push, he could bring it all to light.

And then I'll lose her forever.

"I'm going home, and I'll let you know when I'm available again." *Never.* The word is whispered in the back of my head. I'm never returning to this office. I'm never doing another thing for this prick.

"You can't leave me. I'll ruin you," he practically whispers with nothing but hate. He says the words I already know.

"Ruin me then," I respond easily, looking into his dark eyes as I turn the doorknob and leave him behind me. On the surface I'm calm, but brewing just beneath my skin is nothing but chaos. Everything I've feared has finally come.

Proof I was there.

Proof I lied to the police.

I leave the office with the threat echoing in my head. I did this to myself, digging the hole deeper and deeper.

There's no way Kat will stay when it all goes down.

chapter 15

Kat

MY IPHONE LIGHTS UP AS I PUSH THE TOP BUTTON TO CHECK THE time again, and then again to look at the date. I'm anxious for this meeting; unusually so. Then again, I'm anxious all the time now.

Evan hasn't come home; he isn't talking to me. It's been four days and each day I feel like I need to cave more and more. I didn't know how much I wanted him there until he was gone. I just need him back.

A huff leaves me and I shake my head at the thought. Breakups are always hard and that's what this is, so there's only one way to move on and that's to get it over with.

I don't want to be in our townhouse, but I have nowhere else to go.

An easy breath leaves me as I stand behind the only woman in line at Brew Madison and tilt my head to read the sign on the back wall. All the beverages they have to offer are written on a large chalkboard, and large bakery cases house all the treats they have available. From small pastries to toasted breakfast sandwiches, all lined up as if they're plastic replicas, even though I know they're freshly made and just simply that good.

I haven't had much of an appetite, but every sip of my coffee this morning made me nauseated, so a blueberry muffin top it is.

The brunette curls of the woman in front of me swing from side to side as she gives her order. I can't see her face, but I know she's young. From her bright red high heels and black leather jacket paired with white shorts a bit too short for fall, she's definitely a downtown girl.

I smile at the thought as she waits for her coffee: pumpkin spice.

I used to be like her. Stylish and in charge of my destiny. New to the city and ready to tame it.

I thought I had.

A career and reputation in this publishing industry that I reached within only a few years. I'm an agent worth my weight now and everyone knows it. My name and brand have a meaning to them. The clients are coming in and I'm able to hire more reps and editors. It's the business I've always wanted. More than that, I'm married to a man who still drips of sex appeal and has an edge to him that is irresistible. We own our townhouse near Madison Square Garden. Even if it is small, it's the closest we could get. And it's New York, so location is *everything*.

And my closet … the girl in front of me would kill for my closet. Not that she would know it based on how I'm dressed at the moment.

My name has a purpose and strength to it that made me proud. Evan and I were a powerhouse in the social scene. The couple everyone wanted to be. But envy comes with threats and in its nature, ruins. Rumors and gossip created a wedge between the two of us.

In the last few years, the highs of this world have crashed as my marriage slowly dissolved.

I let it. I spent my life not living it, wanting more and more from my work. Running as fast as I could, just to stay still while I ignored every other change in the world around me. How could I not have seen it deteriorating?

As the woman turns and I get a look at her cat eye makeup that's subtle enough to still be businesslike and red lips that match her heels, I remember that feeling that used to flow through me. The one that said I could conquer anything.

Yeah, I used to be like her. I still have the heels and even the stylish clothes, although I lean toward professional these days with my wardrobe and those shorts sure as heck don't lean that way.

"What can I get you?" the young man asks me from behind the counter. He's got to be in his early twenties at most. I catch a glimpse of his sleeve tattoo and it reminds me of Evan's tattoos for only a moment.

More thoughts of Evan. Everything reminds me of him.

"A chai and a blueberry muffin top," I answer him with a tight voice and clear my throat as I reach for my card in my wallet. It's a Kate Spade and the soft pink and white match the purse, but I'm only just now realizing that it looks a bit dingy. Not so much so that it's noticeably dirty. Just enough where it doesn't look so new anymore.

As I wait for my chai, I get a look at my reflection in the glass. I guess the same can be said about me. My fingers tease my hair at the roots, putting a little more volume there and I apply a coat of stain on my lips while I wait.

I wrap the belt around my shirt a little tighter, showing off my waist and lean to my right in the reflection.

I'm not done yet. There's still life in me. There's still that girl who wants more buried deep down inside. But what exactly she wants more of remains a question.

Evan, the silent answer, is obvious.

But instead the voice in my head whispers *love*.

Even if he can't give me everything, I know what I'm desperate for: to love and be loved.

The bells to the door chime as I accept my chai and muffin top. I silently pray that it's not Jacob so I can have a moment to try to shovel this down.

No such luck.

I smile broadly when I see him, hiding everything I was just thinking and focusing on my potential client and his career. I mentally tally up how much work we both need to do to get his branding both going in the right direction and noticed by the right market.

"Jacob," I greet him and his deep green, hazel eyes focus on me.

"Katerina, it's wonderful to finally have a one-on-one," he says as he steps over the welcome mat and slips off his thin, black wool jacket. He has a downtown style that would pair well with the woman who was just here. From his gray shirt that hangs low but is fitted tight across his chest, to the boyish grin and messy dark hair. He's sex on a stick for sure.

"It is wonderful to see you in person, thank you so much for meeting me here," I say as I make my way to the front of the shop, making sure not to spill the hot drink in my hand.

"Finally meeting my maybe new agent," he says with both an asymmetric smile and pride.

"I'm so happy you're thinking of signing with us," I answer sweetly.

"The rain this fall is ridiculous," Jacob states as he runs his hand over his hair and then wipes it off on his worn jeans.

His white Chuck Taylor sneakers squeak on the floor as he takes a step closer to me. His expression is comical. With both hands full, one of chai and the other with the muffin top, I gesture to the table where I already have my laptop set up. "Right over here," I tell him and put both the chai and the pastry to the left side of my computer before turning around to face him.

I have to crane my neck. "You're so much taller in person," I tell him and hold out a hand for a handshake. His right hand engulfs mine and his shake is firm.

The grin on his face grows to a wide smile and his perfect teeth flash back at me.

He's damn good looking and the fact that his face isn't anywhere on his profiles or brand is a mistake. I watch him as I take my seat, keeping the smile where it belongs on my expression.

"You are too good looking for every one of your readers not to see your face. I know this is a meeting to see if you're interested in coming on board and if our goals align, but the way I like to approach things is to treat you like a client from the start so you know what you're getting. There's so much we have to offer at the agency and I'm sure you'll appreciate not wasting time."

"I like to know what I'm getting; let's dive in. What do you want from me, Katerina?" Jacob asks me and for a split second, a thought enters my mind.

It's only a fraction of a second. A glimpse of his mouth on mine, his hands on my body. Pushing me against the wall like Evan did only a few nights ago.

Thankfully, it vanishes before I can show any admission of what I was thinking.

With a deep inhale, I shake off the unwanted thought and I focus on the plan I have laid out for him as I rotate the computer around on the table.

"We're going to start with your strengths. Obviously. your writing is one of them. Let's also work our way into other aspects of marketing and social media that I think you're ignoring. We can come up with a solid plan that you're comfortable with, but more importantly, one that will work to give you momentum before this upcoming release."

The words come out of my mouth smoothly even though my mind's racing.

It's been a while since I've looked at a man and thought the things running through my head. I tell myself it's because I'm looking for comfort. Searching for someone to desire me like Evan does.

So I don't feel trapped and alone.

"Lead the way, Miss Thompson."

I shake my head, ready to correct him, ready to tell him it's *Mrs.* Thompson. Instead I bite my tongue. In fact, I find myself hiding my left hand behind the computer.

It's only because the attention is nice.

A distraction, a sweet voice whispers in the back of my head as I smile at Jacob and hit the right arrow on the keyboard to move to the first point I want to make.

I leave my hand where it's hidden and when he tells me goodbye, again referring to me as "Miss," I still don't correct him.

chapter 16

Evan

B REW MADISON IS MY WIFE'S FAVORITE PLACE IN THIS WHOLE DAMN city. My shoes smack on the wet pavement and rain spits from the sky as I close the door a block down and stride down the sidewalk to the coffee shop.

For years she's come here. She and Jules used to write together in the corner. Jules was her first client here in New York. It's how she met her now close friend. I huff and my breath turns to steam as I peek in through the glass window.

It used to be a habit of mine to stop here before going home when I landed. Nine times out of ten, she'd be in the same back corner, immersed in a book or a contract. Half the time she was in a meeting.

But then things changed. She stopped going out with too much work piling up as her business grew, and I stopped searching for her when I left the airport. I knew she'd be home, stuck in her office and working no matter what time of day it was.

Work will take as much time as you give it. And Kat gives it all her time and then some.

Today is a different day, though. Given I just told my boss to fuck off knowing he has evidence that could get me locked up, I need to find Kat. I have to see her.

Just before I get to the glass door, I spot my wife. But more importantly, I see who she's with.

Some asshole is with her. I'm sure he's only a client, but as they walk toward the exit, Kat's eyes on her purse as she rummages through it, looking for her keys I'd think, his eyes are all over her body.

The bastard licks his lower lip, and his gaze flickers to Kat's breasts and then to her eyes as she peeks up at him.

She smiles so naively and tucks her hair behind her ear, but what lights up the anger and the possessiveness running through me, is the blush that rises to her cheeks. My body goes cold and my feet turn to cement standing outside of the shop, watching the two of them unknowingly walk toward me.

She knows he's looking. She knows he likes what he sees. And she's letting him.

The chill that runs through my body fuels something deep inside of me. Something primal and raw. The rain that crashes down on me as the clouds roll in and the sky turns darker by the second does nothing to calm the rage growing inside of me.

I open the door just as the two of them are leaving. My grip on the handle is tight and unforgiving as I wait for them to look up at me.

Kat doesn't stop talking, her sweet voice rattling off something about a signing and who needs to be called to schedule some event.

The dick with a hard-on for my wife sees me first, his eyes widening slightly as he takes in my expression. His first instinct is to angle his body, putting himself between me and Kat. It pisses me off even more and I force my body to stay still, keeping myself from shoving him away from her.

My teeth grind against one another as I stare at his hand, still on her lower back as if he has any right to touch her.

"Evan." Kat looks up at me surprised at first, without a hint of anything other than shock, but instantly her expression changes. "What are you doing? You're getting soaked!" she admonishes me in front of the fucker still standing far too close.

Pride flows through me as she pulls me into the coffee shop, even if she's doing it out of frustration.

She looks from my wet shoulders and the rain dripping down my hair to my forehead and back and then glances outside the shop. She hasn't even acknowledged the man she's with. The demon inside me is at least appeased by that small fact. Her small hands focus on wiping off as much water as she can as she positions me over the large welcome mat at the front of the store.

"Nice to meet you," I say to the man eyeing the two of us. "I'm Kat's husband."

Kat looks up at me and it's obvious she bites her tongue from how her expression scrunches.

"Didn't know she was married," the fucker says and I read him loud and clear.

I knew there was a crack in my marriage. But this shit isn't something I'm going to let ruin us. It takes everything in me not to be aggressive toward this shithead.

Kat turns a bright shade of red, but instead of defending us and our relationship, instead of taking my side, she says the worst thing she could to me right now.

"I don't know what we are right now," she states more to me than to him as she looks me in the eyes, daring me to say another word. When I'm quiet, she turns to him.

"I'm sorry for the interruption, Jacob."

"Jake, you can call me Jake," he answers and doesn't even bother to look at me. The awkward tension heats. The thumping of blood rushing in my ears is accompanied with an uncomfortable heat. It was between us. Our problem was only between us. And she made it known to him?

"I'll touch base with you after I get the schedule drawn up, and make sure you get me those summaries as soon as you're able to."

Jake nods his head at Kat and then looks at me to say, "Nice to meet you." He takes his time leaving, glancing over his shoulder more than once, with the rain now coming down in sheets.

"You don't know what we are?" I ask her, feeling the rage wane as the door closes and the sound of the rain is muffled again.

"When you make an ass out of yourself in front of a client, what do you expect me to do?" she hisses.

The rain gets harder and louder as we stand off to the side of the entrance. I take a look around and there are only two other people in the entire place. Both of them women who look like they're on a lunch break, dressed for office jobs. One on each side of the room, both of them on their phones and one with headphones in her ears.

"We can wait out the rain. Get a cup of coffee?" I ask her.

At first Kat looks up at me like I'm crazy. Maybe I am.

"And do what?" she asks. "Play let's-keep-a-secret and hide-away-for-days?"

I ignore her brutal tone and take a chance, wrapping my arm around her waist.

She jumps back for a second, but only because I'm soaking wet.

I chuckle at her response, deep and rough and it makes her smile. She's quick to hide it, but it's there.

"I know you're mad at me," I tell her softly. "I don't want to make you angry, Kat. I love you, and I'm trying."

The trace of all humor fades and she peeks up at me and whispers, "I wish you wouldn't."

I brush the hair from her face and smile down at her as I tell her, "I'll never stop fighting for you."

At my words, she pushes away from me and says, "Then let's talk until the rain lets up." She looks over her shoulder and out of the window, as if checking to see if our time is already up.

We head to the back corner of the shop, to her spot and her safe place. I can't count the number of times I've sat here with her while she rambled on and told me about her day. Although that was before. It's been too long.

The rest of the seating in the place is all high-top tables and bar-height seats, but in the corner is an L-shaped booth. The same shiny white tabletop, but the seating is for customers who want to spend a while in here and that's what I need with her right now, more time.

She doesn't look at me as she tosses her purse into the booth and then fishes out her wallet.

"You like him?" I question, feeling small pieces of my heart crumble off. Kat's eyes narrow as she huffs out a breath of frustration.

"Knock it off," she answers and I feel torn. I saw the look in her eyes. She's a natural flirt and so am I, but I know she liked the attention more than she should. She felt comfortable with it.

"I don't like him."

"Good to know," she answers me immediately, crossing her arms as she walks toward the counter to order something.

I follow her like a lost fucking puppy. It's quiet between us and the tension is thick as she orders a coffee or whatever the hell it is. The blood is pounding so hard in my ears, I can't hear a damn thing.

"I mean it. He wants you, Kat," I tell her and then nearly flinch from the look in her eyes. "I don't want anyone else's hands on you."

"It was innocent."

"The hell it was," I bite back instantly, keeping my voice low. I don't give her a chance to speak.

"You can't look me in the eyes and tell me you didn't like it." The air between us turns hot instantly.

"He's a client," she says beneath her breath. My eyes dart from her to the man behind the counter. As soon as I look at him, he averts his eyes, pretending like he didn't just hear the venom in Kat's voice.

"Client or not," I say, standing my ground but all it does is wind Kat up more.

"I'm not the one keeping secrets and lying, I'm not the one who's breaking up this marriage," she says much lower, so much so that it sounds like it was hard for her to even get the words out.

"Stop it," I tell her and grip her hip as she tries to walk past me, back to the booth and undoubtedly to get her stuff and leave.

"I'm sorry," I whisper in her ear and hold her closer to me. I splay my hand on her lower back, feeling the tension in her body slowly leave her. Her body is hot next to mine.

I could fight this, but it's not worth it to upset her. I wait, giving her a moment to calm down and forget about that asshole. For now.

I sit back in the seat, watching the steam rise from her cup as she slips the lid off and grabs a packet of sugar from the center of the table.

The packet makes a flapping sound as she shakes it back and forth between her forefinger and thumb to get the sugar down. The motion is forceful and she stares at it as she does it, before finally ripping it open and dumping the sugar into the cup.

"I don't tell you everything." The words slip out as the need to win her back takes over everything else.

She's still for a moment, waiting for more, but not looking me in the eyes.

"It's not like I do anything that's … that I want to hide from you. You know what it's like when I go to work."

"I know," Kat says with zero trace of a fight in her voice. "I remember."

"I loved it when you came out with me. You know that, right?"

She finally looks up at me, but only for a moment before she nods her head then slips on the cap to her coffee cup. Her voice is full of remorse as she tells me, "I don't have time for that anymore."

I love that her mind immediately went to the thought of me asking her to come with me. At the beginning of this year, that's all I wanted from her. So we could spend more time together and I could show her off. But the answer was always "no, I can't take time off" so I stopped asking. My heart thumps hard in my chest, remembering how we got into a fight over her not wanting to come with me to Rome a few months back.

"I gave my notice," I tell her and her eyes fly to mine, looking accusing more than anything. "Because you wanted me to." I say the words as if they're the truth and for a moment it feels like they are. But then I remember that's not the reason. I remember what happened. I remember everything in a flood and I have to turn away to breathe in deep and focus on keeping Kat. That's the only thing I care about while everything else collapses around me.

"And because I want to quit too."

"When's your last day?" There's a small bit of hope in her voice, and I watch it shatter as I hesitate to answer.

"I don't know. He … umm. James." I run my hand down the back of my head and I hate how Kat sees through it all. Her head shakes with disappointment. "It's not finalized."

I nearly forget everything I planned on telling her, but somehow I hold on to it and continue, "I regret a lot of the things I've done this year and maybe for a while now—"

"For a while?" Kat repeats and her eyes reflect the pain that's in her voice.

"I didn't cheat on you, Kat. It's not what you think," I tell her and feel like a liar. "I told you, you're the only one for me."

Before I can say anything else, she shakes her head and that false smile mars her face. "I don't know what you did. But I don't want to know anymore," she says quietly, staring at the cup in her hands before looking back up at me. "We're different people and I think it was only a matter of time before something like this …," her voice cracks, but she doesn't cry. She simply looks away.

My heartbeat slows. So slow that it's painful.

"Where are you sleeping tonight?" Kat asks me and I have to swallow the spiked lump deep down in my throat before I can answer.

"You still don't want me to come home?"

"It would be easier if you didn't."

"Easier for what?"

"Easier for the breakup, Evan." Her lips part and then she adds, "It's not about love anymore or about what we had. It's about trust and what we've become. I need a fresh start and a life I'm proud of. And I don't think it includes you in it."

"It does," I answer her instantly. "And I want the same."

She stares back at me with an expression that shows how vulnerable she is. How much she wants to believe what I'm telling her.

I take her hand in mine and tell her, "I'll do whatever you want, so long as when it's all said and done I get to keep you."

I stare in her eyes knowing I've never said anything more truthful, but something deep down inside tells me that's not how this story will end.

"It's too little, too late, Evan. I'm sorry."

chapter 17

Kat

THE BED GROANS AND DIPS AS I TURN BACK ONTO MY RIGHT SHOULDER, pushing the pillow between my knees and trying to force myself to sleep. My mind won't stop playing back every minute of the coffee shop. Every little moment. Even sleeping pills aren't working.

I've been alone all my life. Until Evan. When he first started sleeping over, it was hard to fall asleep. Unless he fucked me to the point of exhaustion, which was often.

You'd think it'd be easy going back to being alone. I was a pro at it for years and worse yet, I was proud of it. The train goes by and the sound cuts through the white noise of the city. The windows are closed, but I still hear it. I can even feel the rumble and vibrations as I try to lie still on the bed. And that's when I get a hint of Evan's scent. When I'm alone, missing him, I sleep on his side of the bed. It's easiest the first night he's gone. It smells just like him. Each day it gets a little harder and working late nights gets more appealing. But even the masculine scent that drifts toward me as I inch my head closer to his pillow isn't enough to comfort me. Why would it? I'm losing him and everything we had.

I toss the heavy comforter off my body and sit up, wiping the sleep from my eyes and dangling my feet over the side of the bed. It's nearly 1:00 a.m. and pitch black in the room. I should be sleeping, considering the fatigue plaguing my body and all too conscious it should come easy.

My fingers run through my long hair, separating it and braiding it loosely before I take a sip of water from the glass on the nightstand. If I get up and start working, I know I won't sleep at all tonight. The very thought makes my heart thump harder. Work is killing me, lack of sleep is destroying me. But both are because I'm completely and utterly alone.

Just breathe. I let my head fall back and slowly creep back under the covers. All I need to do is breathe.

But that hope is short lived as I hear Evan climb the stairs. I had one condition to him coming home, and that was leaving me the bedroom. Even if it hurts me, I'd rather feel pain in his absence than a fraction of that pain in his presence.

I close my eyes as I hear the door open. For a moment I think I should pretend to be asleep, but I don't want any more lies in our relationship. Whatever our relationship even is now.

"I thought you were going to sleep on the sofa?" I ask him and then hold my breath. I should want him to leave. That's what a sane woman who's getting a divorce should want. But there isn't an ounce of me that wants to see him walk out that door.

"I was going to," Evan answers and then slips his shirt off over his head. He keeps his eyes on me, daring me to say something, but my eyes focus on his broad chest.

In six years his body has changed, as has mine. But he's still lean and muscular. My body heats and my thighs clench, but I play it off, turning my back to him to lie on my left shoulder.

"Is this all right?" he asks me, his voice carrying through the dark night and cutting me down to my deepest insecurity. It's not all right and nothing about this situation is, but those aren't the words that come out of my mouth.

My eyes squeeze shut tight and I give in to what I want, slowly moving my body toward his. Wouldn't it be a lie to deny it?

"I'm afraid I'll like it too much if you stay," I finally answer with my eyes closed as the bed dips. I stay perfectly still as I lay out the bare truth. "I'm afraid I'll forgive you and I'll forget why we shouldn't be together." All the words pour out from deep down in my soul, leaving my lips in a rush.

A rough sound comes from deep in his throat as the comforter pulls just slightly. "You don't know what you want, Kat," Evan tells me although the confidence is missing. "You want me to leave because you're afraid. You won't fight for me to stay because you know I will regardless of what you say, isn't that right?"

My brow furrows as I take in his assessment. He scoots closer to me, making the bed shift beneath my still body. When I turn to meet him, still under the covers, his dark gaze stares at me as if I'm his prey and that's just how I feel. "No. I want you to leave because we're leading different lives." I have to second-guess my words.

"Then let's get back on track. Let's start over," he whispers and then leans closer to me. As if testing my boundaries, he rests his hand on the pillow above my head. I don't push him away, but I don't move toward him either.

I'm fucked no matter what I do.

I'm empty and hollow. All the sadness and regret has been shed from me, leaving nothing behind but faint memories of what we had and the hint of all the hopes and dreams I had so long ago to make my heart flutter. As I close my eyes and swallow the lump in my throat, Evan lies next to me, gently resting his hand on my hip. He's silent but I can hear his steady breath and smell a hint of his scent. I inhale deeper. God, what that scent does to me. My head dips further into the pillow as I readjust under the covers and when I do, Evan lifts his hand slightly. Waiting to see which way I'll turn.

And I turn toward him.

"You make me a foolish woman," I tell him as my eyes slowly open. His hazel eyes are so clear at this angle. Maybe it's the moon creeping in from the slit between the curtains.

He smirks at me, although there's a sadness in his smile as he brushes my hair from my face.

"Tell me you'll stay with me."

"Tell me why I should," I reply instantly and the soft look of longing in his eyes fades away as the soothing motion of his thumb rubbing along my temple falters. My eyes drop to his chest and my heart plummets to the pit of my stomach. "You said you didn't cheat," I tell him, but mostly I make a promise to myself. "So I believe you."

"Thank you," he says so softly beneath his breath I hardly hear him. His shoulders sag slightly and it makes the bed creak with relief.

I want to say more. I want to make some sort of demand or ultimatum … or ask why he was there in that hotel lobby in the middle of the night. Why he lied to the world. Why he's lying to me. But instead I curl into him.

"Don't leave me," he says, giving me the request and wraps his arms around me, pulling me closer to him. Closer to his scent, his warmth, to the man I've been desperate to be with for so damn long. His heat wraps around me in the most comforting of ways.

"I won't promise you that," I answer with honesty with my eyes open, staring at a small scar on his left shoulder. I lift my hand up and let my fingers play along the silvery indent of it. "You're right that I don't know what I want. So we'll just have to find out."

He's quiet for a long time. And part of my heart, a very large part of it, aches. It's a horrible feeling and it makes my eyes sting. But I won't mourn what I'm not even sure I've lost. It's just the threat of ending something I've valued so dearly and for so long that hurts.

My shoulders shake slightly as I take in a shuddering breath, and that's when he cups my chin and forces me to look at him.

"You know I love you," he says with a ragged breath. "More than anything, anything in the world."

I sniffle and try to ignore how the pain grows. "I do," I tell him and then try to hide my face, but his grip on my chin is too strong and I can only close my eyes, feeling the smallest bit of tears threaten to spill over and soak into my lashes.

"Don't cry, Kat," Evan whispers as he rests his forehead against mine. "I love you, and that's all that matters." For some reason it seems so obvious to me in this moment that those words were more for him than they were for me. My eyes open to find his still closed. To see the pain there. To see how desperate he is.

That's what I can blame it on. And it's my undoing.

It always has been. He needs me, and I crave it.

"Kiss me—" Before the command leaves my lips, his are on mine. Devouring me and taking every little piece I'm willing to give. I crumble underneath him. My hands fly to his hair as he deepens the kiss. The air turns hotter as my skin heats and our breathing quickens.

"Kat." He barely breaks away from me to whisper my name and then presses his lips harder against mine as he grabs my hips and pulls me toward him.

My gasp is muted as his tongue dives into my mouth. My back arches and my breasts push against his hard chest as he climbs on top of me.

Every second I'm acutely aware that I'm falling backward. It pains my heart as I pull away from him, digging my head into the pillow to feel the cool air. But I can't stop this. I never could. He nips along my neck and my body clenches with need as my legs wrap around his waist.

My heels dig into his ass while I close my eyes tight and let my body do what it wants. It's only ever wanted him and I won't deny my own needs.

Not when he worships me like this, kissing his way down my body as he strips the clothes from me. The only sound is our breathing as I cautiously open my eyes to watch.

His fingertips brush against my skin as he takes off the last piece and stares at my glistening sex.

"You're wet for me." He says the words out loud, although I don't think he meant for me to hear. Another time, I'd blush. But there's no shame or embarrassment right now. It's desperation.

He parts from his clothes faster than I can steady my breath. The moonlight casts shadows on his chiseled chest and every sensitive bit of me is on fire and singing with need. My eyes are drawn to his hands as he strokes his length. When he does it again, I can't help how my lips part with desire and my legs spread wider. My body's ready, willing and aching for him to take me.

"I'm the only one who can satisfy you like this, Kat." My gaze shifts to Evan and he captures it with an intensity that pins me down. "Don't ever forget that."

I can't respond, I don't have time. In one swift motion he's buried to the hilt inside of me. Stretching my walls and sending a spike of heat, desire and a bit of pain through me. Every nerve ending screams to life as a strangled moan tears through me.

It's nothing but pleasure as he stills deep inside of me. Waiting for me to adjust to his girth. He takes his time kissing his way up my collarbone to my lips.

The touches are softer now. Small pecks and nips until I open my eyes and he brings them to a halt.

"I love you," he whispers. My legs wrap around his waist and my fingers dig into his strong shoulders as he moves slowly at first. Burying his head into my neck before I can tell him the same.

He rocks his hips, his rough pubic hair rubbing against my clit with each small movement and bringing me higher and higher. My release feels so close but so far away just the same.

I can only make small whimpers as he speeds up, knowing he's going to send me crashing in the end. All the while he rides through my orgasm, fueled by my cries of pleasure. I cling to him for dear life as my body seems paralyzed and he continues to take from me. Pounding into me, harder and harder. Pistoning his hips until the headboard slams against the wall rhythmically in time with his relentless thrusts. He has his way with me, and then he holds me. I would do it all again just for this moment in time. Just to be held by him, as if he'll never let me go.

chapter 18

Evan

IT'S BEEN A LONG DAMN TIME SINCE I'VE MADE BREAKFAST FOR KAT. It's probably been a year or more since we've woken up together, that's how fucked our schedules have become.

Her bare feet pad down the stairs as I set the last plate on the table. It's brimming with fresh diced pineapple and strawberries. Bacon's still the prominent scent, though. Bacon and eggs for breakfast. Plus a platter of hotcakes with fruit in the center and of course, her coffee.

I grab her mug from her spot on the table. It's still burning hot but I make sure to put it handle out as I turn around to face her. Maybe I'm pussywhipped. Maybe I'm sucking up. Either way, I don't give a fuck.

The sight of her messy halo of hair and wide eyes with a bit of mascara still lingering from yesterday makes my heart pump hard in my chest. She's gorgeous even when she's a mess. She's got nothing on but a baggy Henley of mine and it makes her seem even more petite than she already is. My Kat's never been an early riser. Only when she has to, or apparently when the smell of breakfast is in the air.

"You have good timing," I tell her as she hesitantly grabs the coffee. I can see her shoulders sag just a bit and her eyes close as she takes in the smell, though. It gives me a sense of pride. Even if it's just for the moment.

"Good morning," she says with a soft smile, but it's barely hiding her true feelings. I force a smile back and pull out her chair.

"I don't know the last time I had an actual breakfast," she says as she takes the seat and then looks up at me. "Thank you." It's genuine, but with her shoulders hunched and that sad look in her eyes, I don't give her a response.

I wish I could hold on to last night forever. But the sun had to rise, and I need to come clean to her. She deserves that much.

The chair legs scratch on the wooden floor as I pull out my seat. I grimace slightly and then clear my throat as I sit down, noticing how Kat doesn't seem to care. She's not nearly awake enough; sleep still dominates her expression.

With both hands cradling her mug, she leans back in her seat and gives me a small smile but doesn't reach for any food. She doesn't say anything either. All she does is wait. I wish I had something better to offer her than what's going to come out of my mouth.

"I want a fresh start … and the marriage we were supposed to have," I say as I push a fork through the pancake on my plate, but I don't eat it. I'm already sick to my stomach.

A heavy breath leaves me and I rub my forehead to get out some of the tension. I can't tell her everything, but I can give her something that has killed me for years; a truth I wish didn't exist.

My skin's hot and my throat's dry. It's been years, and I never intended on telling Kat. I didn't want her to know and it was before things changed for me. Before my mother told me she was dying. Before Kat came to me and showed me she was the person I needed in my life forever. It happened before I realized she was mine and I was never going to let her go.

"You okay?" Kat asks and there's genuine pain in her voice. Sadness and concern I wish weren't there. She's too good for me. I've made so many mistakes and this is going to crush her and hurt her more than it should. It meant nothing to me back then, but it'll mean everything to her right now. And I hate it.

"There's something I have to tell you." As I say the words I look Kat in the eyes, and her expression changes. The corners of her lips turn down and a deep crease settles between her brows. She has this way of hiding her emotions, but it doesn't last long. She offers me a hard stare with her lips pressed into a thin line. She gives it to me all the time, but I know the second I give her silence, Kat's mouth will open and every emotion she's feeling will show. She can't hide it from me.

"When you asked me about Samantha, if I'd slept with her …" I have to break off from my thought and pause to take in another breath.

The clink of Kat's fork hitting the plate makes my chest feel tight. She lets out a small sound, almost like a sigh but weighted down with a bitter hopelessness.

"I told you the truth, that I haven't been with anyone since we got married," I say and watch her eyes, her expression, everything about her, but she doesn't look back at me. Her shoulders rise like she's holding her breath and waiting for a bomb to go off.

"It was years ago, Kat. Before I knew how much you meant to me." The words come up my throat as if they're scratching and clawing to stay buried down deep inside of me.

Her expression crumples the second I hint at the affair. If you can even call it that. "I felt like I was lying to you. Every. Single. Time." I bang my fist on the table and the plates rattle with each word and make Kat jump, but I can't help it. "I felt like a bastard when I looked you in the eyes and said nothing happened, because you should have already known."

"When?" Kat asks me.

"I swear that night in the papers was about something else. Something that has nothing to do with that woman or sleeping with her. It was—"

"When?" She screams out the question as her eyes gloss over. She doesn't stop staring at me, but the emotion I expect to see isn't there. It's only anger, a furious rage that stares back at me. "When did you sleep with her?"

"The night I got the call from my mother." I swallow thickly and add, "I was with her."

"The night she told you?" she asks me with a morbid tone and I nod, feeling that acidic churning in my stomach as my clammy hands clench. "You were at the company party?" she asks instantly, although it's more of her recalling that night than an actual question.

"You were supposed to take me out that night afterward," Kat says and each word sounds sadder and sadder as she looks away from me. "You were fucking her while at work."

"It was a one-time thing. A mistake. I didn't know who she was and things were getting serious with us, Kat. You don't understand. It wasn't how it seems." I stumble over my words. Leaning closer to her and reaching for her, she abruptly pushes away from the table, slamming her palms against it and scooting the chair back.

My hands fly into the air, keeping them up. As if I'm not a threat. Trying to keep her here with me to give me a chance to explain.

"Look, we were getting serious and I needed … I don't know how to explain it."

"You didn't want to be with me anymore so you went and slept with the first girl to bat her eyelashes at you?" she asks although it's less of a question and more an accusation, a bitter one at that.

I can't explain how pathetic I feel as she looks at me like I'm the devil. It was a game back then. I wish I could change it. If I'd known what Kat would mean to me, I'd have put a ring on her finger the moment I laid eyes on her. I never would have done anything to risk what we had. *Lies. So many lies,* a voice in the back of my mind whispers. If that was the truth, I wouldn't have needed to call Samantha with my eyes on a lifeless body in the corporate hotel room. If she knew everything, she'd hate me.

"I messed up and I made a lot of mistakes," I say and lean toward her, but she's not having it.

"How many women have you fucked since I've been with you?" Her voice is hard and full of nothing but bitterness.

"Just her, just Samantha and just that once. Please, Kat." My voice begs her for mercy as I lean forward but she's quick to stand up, nearly toppling the chair over just so she can get away from me.

Regret consumes me. I wish I hadn't told her. Fuck. I don't know what to wish for anymore.

I swallow thickly and try to remember everything else I was going to say and the point of bringing up the past. "It's why I feel so guilty about these allegations and why I didn't say anything to the press. I needed them to think it'd happened and it kind of did, just years ago."

"Why were you in the hotel lobby with her at three in the morning?" she asks me—for the dozenth time—as she crosses her arms over her chest, bunching the shirt and finally letting her gaze trap mine.

I have to swallow the hard lump in my dry throat before I can answer her. "I needed an alibi."

"Are you fucking serious, Evan?" she says, spitting out her words as she looks at me with more disgust than I've ever seen on her face.

"I'm sorry. It was an accident."

"It's always an accident. Always a mistake. Why do you do this? Why do you put yourself in these situations?" She screams at me with a rage I know she's had pent up inside of her for a while now. I'm too old to be this stupid. I never should have continued working for James once her career took off. But the money and the lifestyle were so addictive. It was a high I couldn't refuse.

"I told you, I quit. I'm not going to put myself in—" As I shake my head, trying to get out the words, I can't remember a damn thing I'd planned on saying.

"It's too little, too late, Evan," Kat says, cutting me off before leaving me alone in the room, whipping around and not bothering to say another word. I stare at her back as she storms up the stairs.

I've never felt this way before in my life. Like I've hurt the one person in the world who would never hurt me. Like I betrayed her. Like I'm not worth a damn thing.

And there's no way to make that right.

I don't know how to make any of this right.

chapter 19

Kat

I CAN'T STOP THINKING ABOUT HOW EVAN FUCKED HER. SAMANTHA IS … the opposite of me. Everything about her is exactly the opposite. Disgust doesn't begin to cover it. All I can imagine is how that night would have played out had his mother not called him. If tragedy hadn't stepped in to intervene. He fucked her, and then what? Was he going to bail on our date or was he still planning on seeing me?

I should be focused on the fact that he told me he needed an alibi. The fact that only weeks ago he was doing shit he knows is wrong and could send him to jail. But that's the man he's always been. I knew better than to turn a blind eye, but that's exactly what I've been doing, isn't it?

It's an odd feeling, like waking up from a long and deep sleep or having a blindfold taken off after wearing it for days. Has it always been this way?

I knew what kind of life he was leading and the risks that came with it. I didn't do a damn thing about it. I should be ashamed, mortified.

And yet all I can think about is him fucking her.

Not to mention how many times I've seen that woman at events and socialized with her. Not once did she make it seem like anything had happened between them. She comes off sweet and innocent. She's slim like me, but taller and she prefers soft, muted colors. Samantha always has perfectly manicured, pale pink nails. She pretties herself up like a little doll, prim and proper. I never would have expected it. I remember how genuinely happy for me she seemed when she gushed over my engagement ring.

That fucking bitch.

The door to my office opens behind me, the telltale creak forcing my eyes to shoot open. They narrow as I see his reflection on the black computer screen. I don't even know if the damn thing is on anymore or how long I've been sitting here. All I've done is stare at a worn spot on my desk and think about how he fucked her, even knowing he was going to see me only hours later.

What would have happened if his mother hadn't chosen that moment to tell him to come home and that she wasn't well? Maybe that would have been the night he chose to break it off with me. After all, every day with him was like ticking off a checkbox. I knew it wasn't going to last. I was waiting for it to end.

Marie screwed me over by telling him.

"Kat." Evan calls my name from behind me. Hearing his voice causes a shudder to run down my spine. It's a slow one that sends a chill over my body.

"I'm going to do everything I can to prove to you how much I love you."

"Do I even know you?" Even as I whip around and sneer at him a sick voice in the back of my head answers me. *Yes. Yes, you knew what you were doing. You knew the man you married.*

"You're the only one who does," he answers, looking me in the eyes as his broad shoulders fill the doorframe to my office. "You know I love you."

I scoff at him, choosing to ignore the truth and how much I blame myself.

Right now, it's all on him. I didn't cheat on him. I didn't continue to live a lifestyle that was obviously going to tear us apart.

He did. And fuck him for that.

"I hate you right now." The words slip out in a breath and he visibly flinches.

"You're angry, and you have every right to be."

"Angry doesn't cut it!" I scream, my throat feeling raw as the salty tears burn my eyes. "I loved you. I would have done anything for you!" I grit out the words through my clenched teeth and try to grip the chair as I stand on shaky legs.

"I loved you so much. And this is how you treat our marriage. With lies and secrets and all this shit I don't even know about."

"I'm sorry I kept that from you, but that was it." He says *that was it* as if it's easily accepted. As if he's never told a lie or done anything else that would ruin us.

"Liar! How many laws have you broken at work?" I let the words tumble from my mouth, all the rage coursing through my blood. "But you kept at it. You were never going to stop until something made you. You didn't care about me or what it did to us!"

"What kind of marriage is that!" As the words tear from my throat and Evan stares back at me a guilty man, the reality hits me like a bullet to the chest.

I was blinded by my lust for him. Maybe even my love. Either way, I've been denying the reality.

"I want more than this. I deserve better."

"I love you," he says like that's the answer to all of this. Like it will save us.

"You keep saying that, but I don't think you know what it means." *Or maybe love just simply isn't enough anymore.*

"What really gets me," I start to say then take in a long, ragged breath, finally taking a step toward him but immediately stop when he does the same.

Standing across from him in the small office I look him in the eyes and get what I've been thinking about out of me. "You saw her all the time. You were with her at every function." My voice lowers as I add, "Even *I* was with her so many times. And you didn't bother to tell me."

"What happened was a mistake for her too."

"Don't talk to me like she didn't know what she was doing. She was married and she knew we were together. How could you? How could you stand to be around her?"

"I was working. If you'll recall, you were broke and we needed money. What was I supposed to do? Quit?"

"Does your boss know?" His expression turns to stone, although he looks more pissed off than anything else. "Does James know?" I ask him again.

"I don't know."

It's silent as I breathe out a huff of disgust.

"I'm sorry. I fucked up but it was years ago."

"It wasn't just years ago. Every day you went back was a mistake. Every day you kept it from me was a mistake!"

"What part of it being my job don't you get?" he asks me in a low voice full of anger as he takes another step forward.

"You could have gotten another job." All I can see is red. The words come out automatically, but my mind is racing. My breathing is heavy.

"Who would hire me?" he asks with sincerity. "You were just starting out and needed every penny I could earn."

"Don't act like you did this for me!" I spit at him with anger. My fist pounds against my chest. "Don't you dare blame this on me!"

Tears prick my eyes as he stares at me without saying a word.

Shame and guilt heat my body. Both of us are raging with emotion. Both of us want to tear the other person apart. That realization is all I can take. Tears spill over and I have to turn away from him. With my back to him, he tries to touch me and I rip my arm away from him. I shake my head and firm my resolve.

"Please leave me alone. I'm begging you, Evan. If you love me, please get away from me."

chapter 20

Evan

The truth I cannot change,
I'm a sinner and I confess.
But I refuse to let her go,
She's my love and nothing less.

I LOVE YOU, KAT, AND I'M SORRY.

I text her again, the cellphone screen lighting up the dark bedroom in Pops's house, my old bedroom. The glossy posters reflect the light that scatters into the room in stripes from the blinds on the window. The sound of the traffic is louder here and everything about it reminds me of the life I used to lead. The one before Kat. The one I'm so damn ashamed of now.

I'll never forget the look of disappointment on his face when I showed up a few hours ago with a duffle bag. It's like even he lost hope in me making it right with Kat.

It's crushing to leave her. But it's different this time. I get exactly why she needs space. This is why I never told her. She needed something to hold on to, though, she needed a solid reason to be pissed at me, so we could get through it and move on.

Still, I didn't expect it to go down like it did. I'm worthless and it's never been more apparent to me that my life is meaningless without Kat in it.

I swallow thickly as I lean back on the bed and fall against the pillow. I've never felt so alone. I wish I could take it all back.

My eyes close as I feel my heart slow and my blood turn cold. Being here like this makes me remember one of the last conversations I had with my mother.

She'd seen me with Kat while we were out one night. Just a coincidence, but she acted like it was more than it was.

Kat was a fling and a good time. She was someone I wanted more and more of and I made damn sure to monopolize her time until I had my fill, but of course that time would never come. I just didn't know it back then or I liked to pretend I didn't anyway.

"She seems sweet," my mother told me when I came home for Sunday dinner. Looking back at that night now, I realize how much slower she was to set the table. How everything was a little off, but to me, Sunday dinner was just an obligation I had to my mother before I would be leaving to go out and have a good time.

"You didn't really talk to her," I said and laughed at my mom, shaking my head and taking a drink from whatever was in my cup. I leaned back and looked at my father, waiting for him to agree with me. When he didn't, I added, "Plus she's the only girl you've seen me with."

"That's true," Ma replied and shrugged. "I like the way you two look together," she stated matter-of-factly and then looked me in the eyes as she smiled. "Is it too much to ask that you pretend to value your mother's opinion?"

I let out a small laugh and shook my head. "I'm glad you approve," I told her. More just to make her happy than anything else, but it only opened the door for Ma to invite her over for the next family dinner. I had already started coming up with reasons to end it that night.

It was too much. I was young and in my prime and working a job that would keep my appetite well-fed.

I was ready to end it too the next night; it was too serious, too soon. But her smile and the way she laughed at me when I pulled up wearing an old rugby shirt caught me off guard in a way I found completely endearing. She thought it was the oddest thing and I'll never forget the way her soft voice hummed with laughter and it carried into the night. Who was I to take that away? I knew she'd end it with me anyway. I didn't know it would be after marriage and six years later.

If I could go back to that night, I would change it all and I'd make sure I told Ma she was right.

"I'm heading to bed." My father's voice catches me by surprise and my body jolts from the memory. I pretend to rub the sleep from my burning eyes and clear my throat to tell my father good night. It's tight with emotion and it takes me a second to sit up in bed.

"You look like hell," Pops says.

Nodding in agreement, I take a moment to set my feet on the floor. My head is still hung low and my shoulders are sagging as I rest my elbows on my knees.

"How did you keep Ma out of it? All the stupid shit you did?" I ask him. I know he led a wild life. He's got the stories and the scars to prove it. I came by my lifestyle honestly.

I lift my head and look him in the eyes, forcing a small smile to my face. "I need to know what to do. I need advice."

"You can't. It's gotta stop." He shrugs his shoulders, the faint light from the hallway casting a long shadow of him into the room, ending at my feet. "That's the advice I can give you. Don't keep a thing from her. You should already know that."

I swallow, or try to, as a ball of spikes grows in my throat. "What if you can't stop? What if I can't quit this job and this life?" The image of Tony dead on the floor remains firm in my sight. Even as I blink it away and look up at my father, I can still see him. Dead from an overdose and staring back at me with glassy, lifeless eyes as if it was my fault.

I brought him to that room. The one reserved for partying in our company.

I gave him the coke, but I didn't know it was laced. And then I left him there to get whiskey and cigarettes.

I brought him to his death.

I can never tell her that. I can barely admit it to myself.

"Did you ever mess up so bad, you thought you could never make it right?" I ask even though his answer doesn't matter. I guess I just don't want to feel so alone.

"We all do; you just find a way. I'm sorry, but it's the best I've got."

"Find a way …" I say the words softly, barely moving my lips as I look at the edge of the comforter, wishing it were that easy.

"I don't know what to tell you, Evan. I did everything for your mom, and I'd do it all again. Maybe that's where you went wrong?"

"What's that?" I'm quick to ask him, my gaze focused on Pops and whatever it is he has to say. I'm desperate for an answer to all this shit. I need to take it all back.

"You weren't thinking about her."

His words sink in slow, but deep.

I shake my head and agree, "No, I wasn't."

"The best thing you ever did was marry that girl." I nod my head, feeling a jagged pain move through my body. "Worse thing you ever did was leave her side."

He doesn't know how true his words are.

chapter 21

Kat

You left a space beside me,
You left me all alone.
You left a space beside me,
I thought my heart would turn to stone.
You left a space beside me,
Desire creeps in the night.
You left a space beside me,
Lust fills the emptiness up just right.

THE EVENING SKYLINE IS GORGEOUS. THE COLORS OF AUTUMN DANCE along the buildings and the beautiful hues of orange and soft reds travel up to the bright full moon.

It's early for the moon to be out, but as I walk away from the townhouse, down the stone steps as the heavy walnut door shuts behind me, I can't help but admire it. There's beauty in nature and having the small bit of it above the city is something I've taken for granted for so long.

With each step, my boots click on the concrete, until my body stumbles forward and I nearly fall down the last two stairs.

"Shoot!" I cry out as I frantically reach for the iron rail and just barely get a grip tight enough to keep me upright. My purse is flung down to the crook of my arm, spilling odds and ends, including my phone, onto the busy street.

I curse beneath my breath as my cheeks heat with embarrassment and I keep my head down. Most people walk around me, and I'm fine with that. Better than fine. I'm happy that they're just ignoring me and my clumsiness.

I crouch down low to grab the fallen items, ignoring the bystanders as they steer clear of me but as I stand up, I realize someone didn't miss my fall and their eyes haven't left me.

"You okay?" Jacob asks as he comes toward me, nearly out of breath. His cheeks are slightly red, the chill of the air getting to him. His hand is cold on my shoulder as he helps me stand upright. His thick black wool jacket brushes against mine and the heavy scent of pine, a masculine fragrance I love, fills my lungs.

"I saw you from across the street," he tells me as I blink away my surprise. Not only from his presence, but from my reaction.

I brush the hair from my face and give him a grateful smile as the crowd continues to walk around us. This city doesn't stop for anything or anyone. Jacob walks with me to move out of the way and stand on the stairs to my townhome.

"Just a clumsy moment," I say in a breathy voice and reluctantly laugh at my-self as I steady the bag back onto my shoulder. This is so embarrassing.

Jacob shrugs and slips his hands into his pockets as he says, "I expected worse." As he speaks, his perfect teeth show, and I can't help but eye his lush lips. "Honestly, that was a nice save."

A warmth flows through me.

"Well thanks," I say, shifting my weight and shaking my head. "What are you doing here?"

"I'm checking out a townhouse down the street. Moving to the city was defi-nitely the right move for me."

"And have you thought of the contract at all?" I ask him and then bite the in-side of my cheek. "I don't mean to be forward. I'm just excited to work together."

I don't miss how his eyes stray slightly to my breasts when I breathe in deep. He turns away, toward the street to try to play it off and licks his lower lip. Maybe it was a subconscious thing on my part. I almost feel the need to apologize.

"I'm thinking I should get to signing it. I just was hoping maybe we could meet up to go over a few minor details?" he asks as he brings his attention back to me.

I smile and nod my head, my hair falling back in front of my shoulders. "I'd be happy to," I answer a little too eagerly. His eyes flash with something they shouldn't, but I ignore it.

"Well, I should get going," I say and the words rush out of my mouth.

"Me too," Jacob says and looks back across the street. "My realtor is over there somewhere waiting on the steps to let me in to 'my dream home,'" he says, mim-icking what must be his realtor's nasally voice, and then he gives me another view of his gorgeous smile.

"If you ever need anything, I'm always home or a call away," I offer and then bite the inside of my cheek. *What the hell was that?*

"Sounds good. Be safe," he says comically and then takes a few steps forward. "I'll text you," he says over his shoulder and I simply nod. Not able to speak, just standing there, gripping my purse strap with both hands and wondering why he gets to me so much.

I won't deny that he does.

That's not the part that bothers me.

It's why. Is it him? The timing?

What is it about Jacob that makes me want him, when I haven't lusted for a man other than my husband in years?

chapter 22

Evan

"**H**AVE YOU TRIED ROSES?"

My gaze moves from the cell phone in my hand to my father. With his arm braced against the wall, he taps his knuckles against the cream wall.

"I'm not sure roses are going to help," I reply and give him a weak smile.

"You'd be surprised. Flowers are a girl's best friend."

A small but genuine smile graces my lips as I toss the phone onto the end table. "It's diamonds, Pops. The saying is diamonds are a girl's best friend."

"Then get her diamonds," he replies with a stern look before making his way to the worn, caramel-colored leather recliner in the corner of the living room. There's a game on the TV. I'm not sure who's playing since the volume is so low I can barely hear it.

"She still hasn't messaged you back?" he asks.

"Nothing yet," I answer lowly, not bothering to hide my disappointment, and then look back at the phone, wishing it would go off.

"You going back home to talk? Or what's the plan?"

"I don't know," I tell him. "I know she wants space; I just don't know if it's what's best."

From my periphery, I watch him nod and then he says, "It's hard to know. Especially when she's not talking to you."

"I wouldn't talk to me either," I say, mostly out of the need to defend her. "I'd have kicked me out too."

"It was a long time ago," my father says, but there's hardly any conviction in his voice.

It's quiet for longer than I'd like. Both of us not knowing where to go in the conversation.

"I remember when you moved in with her," Pops finally says and breaks the silence.

"It feels like forever ago. I hardly even remember what it was like before her."

"Feels like it just happened to me. All the boxes and her wanting to paint first and then wanting everything in a specific order. She sure has a certain way of going about things."

I lean my head back, staring at the ceiling fan as I say, "Yeah she does" with a hint of a smile on my lips. "She's particular."

"That's one word for it," Pops says back with a small laugh, the kind where I can feel his smile in the laugh, not missing a beat.

"You love her, though. Particular and all," I remind him.

He nods his head. "I love her for it too." He clears his throat and says, "I never told you this, but I felt like I'd lost your mother and then lost you."

"Pops, no—" I try to stop that shit, but he's already moved on before I can get a thought out.

"It was a short-lived feeling. Kat came over more than you did after the move, if you remember."

"She's the one who wanted the family dinners. I remember her pushing for that. Probably wouldn't have happened if it wasn't for her. I think she was just trying to make things right."

"I know she was. She's a lot like your mother in that regard. You did good picking her."

I can't respond to my father. He's never talked to me about Kat really. Now of all times, it's just making the pain that much worse.

"You remember that heavy-ass dresser?" Pops asks me and it makes me huff a laugh as I nod. More than anything I'm thankful for the change in topic.

"She had to have it," I say absently. "It was her mother's."

"Oh, I know. I remember her telling me a dozen times."

"She kept talking about the movers." I shake my head. "We didn't need any movers."

"Sure, sure. I remember that squabble."

"Squabble," I repeat and run my hand over my hair. "She knew I could handle it."

Pops laughs at the thought. A deep laugh, and then he leans back in his chair.

"You guys can handle that, then you guys can handle anything."

"It feels different, Pops." I swallow and fight back the swell of emotion. "This isn't just a fight."

"How would you know? You haven't even really had a fight, have you?"

I stare at him blankly, knowing me and Kat haven't ever gone at it before, not really. A little bickering here or there, but this isn't some argument over dishes. This is worse than he can imagine, and I'm ashamed to speak that truth.

"Just get her something shiny. Spoil the woman," he says, throwing his hand up.

I let a trace of a smile linger on my lips as I picture handing Kat a bouquet of roses. I'd pick the dark red ones, but make sure there's some baby's breath in the package too. One of the large bouquets. The ones that make you lean in and smell them. Too good to resist. That's the kind I'd get her.

I can see her soft smile as she peeks up at me, holding it in both her hands.

A warmth settles through me. I wish it were that easy. I'd buy every flower I could if that were the case.

"Whatever you do," Pops says, distracting me from the vision of Kat forgiving me, "just don't give up."

"I won't," I tell him and I damn well mean it.

chapter 23

Kat

MY FINGERS RELENTLESSLY TAP ON MY PHONE AND MY GAZE DRIFTS to the door. He's coming. Soon.

Evan needs to get his things and get out. Mistake after mistake after mistake. That's what this relationship has been. There's undeniable love between us. I won't argue with that. But some people aren't meant to be together and at this point in my life, I should be concerned with having children and not the possibility of having to bail my husband out of jail.

There's a bit of anger that's carried me through the last two days. It's what I focus on. It's what gives me the strength to tell him I don't want to be with him anymore. To tell him it doesn't matter when he says he loves me.

I know it matters, and I'd be a liar if I didn't admit that I'll always want him and have love for him. I'll always want to feel loved like I did when we first got together.

But there's only one way for the story of the two of us to end and that's with him packing his things and getting out. Loving each other simply isn't enough when we're so far apart in other ways.

As if he heard my thought, the front doorknob jiggles and the sound of keys clinking creeps into the room.

Fate hates me. No, that's not strong enough of a word. It must *loathe* me because the sight of my husband standing in our doorway shatters my heart.

I attempt to keep my expression cold, but my body goes numb and the same coldness that swept over my body only weeks ago when I felt my marriage falling apart drifts over my skin now. His eyes are bloodshot. He can't force a look of anything but agony as he turns his gaze from me and walks slowly into the room, closing the door behind him. The shock to my system is crippling and I can't look him in the eyes. He doesn't try to hide the desperation. His disheveled hair and all-around rough appearance make my body itch to touch him. To comfort him. To make the obvious pain go away.

I think that's why I'll never be able to deny that I love him. The image of him in pain destroys me to my core. My soul hurts for his, and I want nothing more than to take his misery away.

I need to love myself more than I could ever love him. I'm trying to. My God, am I trying.

He nods his head as he tosses his keys down on the coffee table and stands awkwardly in front of me.

I have to swallow the tightness in my throat and ignore the heat flowing through my body begging me to give in. "Hi." I'm the first to say anything at all and break the uneasy tension in the living room.

"How are you?" he asks and it feels so odd. Like we're just old friends or acquaintances.

"Not the best," I answer him. I try to find that anger, I remember everything as my eyes shift to the entrance to the dining room, but there's not an ounce of anger that will come to my rescue.

"I miss you," he says as the last word spills from my lips.

"I miss you too," I admit, my voice cracking and I lick my lips.

"Things have gotten rough, but I never stopped loving you. You're the only thing that matters."

"What you say is everything I want to hear, Evan. But it's what you've done that makes it impossible for me to stay with you."

His boots smack on the hardwood floor as he makes his way to me. And I don't move. I don't object. I even lean into him slightly when he sits down next to me. At first he's angled away from me, his elbows on his knees but then he looks at me with a hurt in his eyes that makes me inch closer to him, and he does the same.

I may be angry about what he's done. What I've done as well. But no amount of anger can outweigh the pain we both feel in this moment.

The pain from knowing we're damaged beyond repair.

"Will you ever forgive me?" he questions and then takes a chance, moving his large hand to my thigh and gently rubbing his thumb back and forth.

"I already have," I tell him and feel slightly less strong. Weak for being okay with what's happened. Or at least for accepting it.

"Do you just not love me anymore then?" he asks me, his eyes piercing into mine and holding me captive. His words are raw, coming from a damaged man.

My lungs still and the words hang on the tip of my tongue. They're too afraid to leave me. I'm so weak for him, so bendable and disposable. If I admit such a flaw, he may never give me a fighting chance for something more.

What's worse, I may be content with that.

"Please just tell me you love me," Evan whispers. "I know I fuck up, more than I should. But please don't stop loving me."

"I've never felt so alone." It's one thing to be left alone. It's quite another to choose it. In this moment, I don't want it. I don't want to be alone another day, but I know I have to.

"I don't want to be alone. I don't want to be mad at you," I tell him, wiping from under my eyes and leaning my body into his. He kisses my forehead before enveloping me in his arms. And I let him. My biggest flaw.

"Then don't," he whispers and then pulls away to look down at me, waiting for my eyes to meet his. "Forgive me, please," he says and when I look to him, his dark hazel eyes beg me. His voice is raw and full of nothing but pain and remorse. "For everything. For being so stupid. For putting you through all this shit."

The question is right there, right on the tip of my tongue. I should ask, I should know what he's hiding. But the look in his eyes is so familiar.

"I meant what I said," I tell him. "I need you to leave."

"But you still love me?" he asks me even though it comes out as a statement.

My body heats, my breath stutters and the words get caught in my throat, refusing to come out. I'm on the edge of leaving him, of ruining this man I love so much.

"Yes, I still love you. So much," I admit and the confession is like a weight off my chest, but one that only leaves a gaping, painful hole in its absence.

"I can fix this."

"I need you to leave, Evan," I plead with him weakly.

"Just give me time."

"We're separated, Evan. That's what that means."

"I don't want this. Please, Kat." Evan closes his eyes and buries his face in the crook of my neck. I've never seen him so weak. So desperate for mercy.

I've never wanted to forgive so badly in my life, but it's not forgiveness that I need. It's a different life that I need moving forward and I won't get that with Evan.

"I'm sorry." My lips move but the words aren't audible, and I have to say it again.

His fingers dig into me, holding me closer and tighter, as if the moment he loosens them, I'll leave his grasp forever.

"I'm sorry, but it's what I want," I tell him and I've never heard such a horrible lie in my life. But he nods his head, pulling away slightly although still refusing to let go.

"It's what I deserve," he says beneath his breath. His eyes are glossy and his breathing slower as he looks away from me, still holding on but trying to gather the strength to say something. I don't trust myself to speak. So I just wait, praying for this moment to be over. Praying for something better to come once this has all left me. But how? I have no idea. I've never felt so dead inside.

"One last time. Please, just once more. I love you, Kat. I swear I've never loved anyone like I love you. And maybe it's not enough to keep you, but for tonight?"

Again I don't trust myself to speak. I'm not sure what words would pass through my lips. But I know what I want and I lean forward to take it, spearing my fingers through his hair and pressing my lips to his. It's only when I feel the wetness against our lips that I realize I was crying.

I let him hold me, and I try my best to remember every detail.

The way he smells, masculine like fresh pine and dew.

The way his heart beats just a bit faster than mine as I rest my palm against his hard chest.

I try to remember everything. I pray that I will, because even though he said he can make it right, I know he can't. I know that time will aid in the growing distance between us. I know we're leading two different lives.

I know I need more, and that I deserve someone who won't hide things from me and make me feel like I've lost myself.

So I need to remember this, because I want it to be the last time.

Not for him, not for us, but for me.

chapter 24

Don't throw me away, don't tell me you're through.
Don't stop loving me, I can't live without you.
That ring on your finger, that makes you my wife.
You're my everything, my love and my life.

I DIDN'T MEAN IT WHEN I SAID ONE LAST TIME. IT'S THE SAME WAY AN addict is desperate for more and will say anything to get it. All I have to do is be next to her when she needs a single thing. Anything. Just one small crack in her armor. At least that's what I keep hoping for.

It's what's keeping me from dissolving into the nothingness I feel in my hollow chest.

I wonder if she'll get over me before that time comes. If the few years we had together was enough to make her love me even when she doesn't want to. That's all I keep thinking about as I stare at her sleeping form. There's only a thin sheet over her gorgeous body, hiding it from me. Her back is toward me as she lies on her side, her hair fanned out along the pillow. I've been awake for hours; I'm not even sure I slept at all.

It feels like it's over, but that can't be true. I can't let her go this easily and walk away. But somehow it doesn't feel like letting her go. It feels like I don't have her anymore. Like I don't even have the option to keep her anymore.

A sudden buzz from my phone vibrating on the nightstand strips my thoughts from me and causes Kat to stir next to me.

I keep my eyes on her as I reach for it. She slowly turns to look over her shoulder and then looks away, pulling the sheet tighter around her. Closing herself off from me.

There's a heaviness on my chest as I let it sink in that she doesn't belong to me anymore. The bed dips as Kat pulls the sheet with her and walks quietly to the bathroom.

I would think my life couldn't get any lower than this, but the text from James mocks that thought.

My hands rake over my face as the phone drops and I inhale deeply, grateful Kat left when she did. There's still so much shit that I need to fix and make right. So much damage I've caused that's leaving cracks under each and every footstep I take.

Come to the office.

I stare at the text as Kat flicks on the light switch in the bathroom, the warm yellow hue filtering from under the closed door. She turns on the water as I toss the phone down.

James can go fuck himself.

It's like he knew I'd think that, because the second the phone drops to the nightstand, it goes off again.

It's not about work. You know what it's about.

I was given new information today.

The texts come one after the other in rapid speed and it makes adrenaline slowly pour into my veins, breathing life into me.

The creak of the bathroom door opening and the light switching off forces me to look up at Kat. She slipped on a robe in the bathroom. It's some sort of black and pink kimono from a bachelorette party I think. I've never seen her wear it but it's been hung up by the towels for years. I guess it's all she could find in there to hide herself from me.

She doesn't return my gaze and I can already see that she regrets last night. *Our last night.*

I refuse to let it be true. I refuse to give up. But I'll give her time since that's what she thinks she needs.

"You can come whenever you need to," she says and then pulls a shirt over her head as she lets the robe fall into a puddle around her feet. The sight would make my dick hard as steel if it weren't for the words that hit me at full force. "To get whatever you need. I know you can't take everything all at once."

"You really want me to go?" I question even though I know I need to leave regardless of what she tells me. I need time to sort out my shit and get my life to be one that belongs beside hers.

I wish she'd lie to me. I can see it in her eyes, her posture; I can hear it in her voice that she needs me to go. *Tell me a pretty lie, Kat. Make me believe you still want me.*

"I think it's for the best," she answers as her eyes flicker from me to the door and she pushes her hair out of her face. The dark circles under her eyes are evidence of how worn out she is. She's tired of my bullshit.

"I want to be happy and I feel like we're so used to being something else that it's not going to work."

The argument stirs in my chest, but she's right in a way and I know I can prove to her that we're going to be fine. I just need time. "I'll go now, but I'm coming back when I fix things."

"That's what you do, isn't it? You fix things?" A sarcastic, sad laugh accompanies her comment.

Fixer. That's what they call this job, but really I'm supposed to prevent anything from breaking. There's another small huff of a laugh that leaves her, but it's not the joyous sound I've grown to love so much. It's because of me. I'm the one who broke our marriage.

"I know we grew apart, but we're still together. Even if you want to pretend like we're not for a little while," I tell her. Climbing off the bed, I take a step to go to her, but she shakes her head slightly, crossing her arms and taking a step back.

"It was only one last time, Evan."

My mouth falls open just slightly for me to tell her last night wasn't the last time. I won't let it be. But the words don't come out. There's no conviction in that thought.

My eyes close as the phone in my hand buzzes again and I don't miss how Kat looks at it, a question in her eyes.

"It's James." I answer her unspoken question

She chews the inside of her cheek and doesn't acknowledge me in the least.

"I quit and I've just got to sign some paperwork." The lie slips out so easily. I'm almost ashamed at how easy it's become to hide the truth from her and disguise it as something normal and relatable.

I don't know if she can tell I'm lying, or if she just doesn't care anymore. She leaves me alone with nothing but a small nod in the bedroom we built together.

My blood turns cold and I stare at the open door. The pictures from the hall taunt me. I still hear the laughter. I remember the softness of her skin when they were taken.

The phone goes off again and it pisses me off.

I grit my teeth as I read the messages.

Get here in the next hour.

Out of spite, there's no fucking way I'll be at his office by then. I make sure to hit the message so he knows I read it. He can wait.

chapter 25

Kat

I T'S SUPPOSED TO HURT THIS MUCH. I REMIND MYSELF OF THAT OVER AND over again.

That's what a breakup is. It's pain. It's removing someone you once loved from your life. Erasing them as if they don't exist. As if they've died. And that's the most painful thing one can experience.

That's why it hurts so much. Because I'm supposed to be in agony.

"You look tired," I hear Jules say before she rests her hand on my shoulder, bringing me back into the moment. Standing in my small kitchen, with its clutter and a pile of dirty dishes in the sink, she's so out of place here. "Are you all right?" she asks me softly.

Before I can answer, the sounds of Maddie and Sue laughing over something drift into the room. The wine has been flowing, and half of the only remaining box of pizza is left on the counter. It's what I said I came in here for, another slice, but really I'd just remembered my time with Evan last night and then this morning and I wanted to be alone for a minute.

"You can tell me anything, Kat," Jules says in a voice drenched with empathy. I've always loved the person she is. But never more than now.

"I don't think I'm all right and I don't know if I ever will be," I answer and then arch my neck to stare at the ceiling, keeping my eyes open and trying not to bring this night down any more than I have.

"Is it normal to cry so much?" I ask her. "To be this emotional and this exhausted?"

"When you lose someone you love, yes." She answers easily and calmly, sending a wave of calm through my body, but even that makes me feel that much more exhausted.

"I wish I was past this stage."

"It'll happen before you know it. One day, the reminders won't hurt so badly. The mention of his name won't cut you to shreds. One day it'll feel like it's supposed to be this way."

"But I don't know if it is," I confess to her and then Sue ambles in from the dining room.

Her wineglass clinks on the counter as she sets it down and then she catches a glimpse of me, her expression morphing to one of sympathy. An expression I learned to hate growing up, but right now, while I'm weak and feeling so lost, it's an expression that makes me lean into her when she opens her arms.

"You're all right, babe," she says softly and wraps her arms around me. Sue's arms are filled with warmth and she kisses my cheek too. "It's all right babe, we're here for you."

"Aww," I hear Maddie coo as she makes her way into the room.

"Let it all out," Sue says but I shake my head, my hair ruffling on her shoulder as I sniffle. Sue smells like wine. She sways a little and squeezes me tight. She's definitely more than tipsy.

"I'm sorry, guys. It wasn't supposed to turn into this." I push out the apology, wishing we were having the fun night I promised as I stand up straight and pull my shit together. Sue tries to hold on to me a little longer, but I push her away. I can handle this. At one point in my life I was so good at being alone.

"I'm fine," I tell them, stepping away for a moment and shaking out my hands. "I'm sorry."

It takes a few deep breaths and Sue refilling the empty glasses of wine on the counter for me to get over whatever this breakdown was.

"Don't be sorry. It's a sad time no matter how much you don't want it to be." Maddie's the first to say something and Jules nods.

"It's going to be okay, though," Jules says and then Sue chimes in with, "You've got us, babe. We'll always be here for you, and that's all you need."

"Well, maybe a vibrator too," Sue adds a moment later and a genuine laugh erupts from my lips. It's short and unexpected, and fills the room. But it felt so good to laugh. To smile. To feel anything other than this darkness that's been a constant shadow over me.

"Do you want another?" Sue asks me, nearly spilling the wine from a glass poured too full as she tries to hand it to me. I haven't had a drink all night.

"If I do, I'm going to pass out." Just as I answer, another yawn hits me. "It's been a while since I've been able to sleep through the night."

"I'll take it," Maddie offers and immediately sets it back down on the counter.

"So it's really over?" Sue asks and then takes a sip. For the first time, I see something in her eyes I haven't before. I see sorrow. Genuine pain. As if even Sue was rooting for us. Sue, the valiant heroine against men who cheat and lie.

I nod, ignoring how the emotions swell up again. I haven't told them that he cheated on me back when we first started dating. I can't admit it. I don't want to say the words out loud and make them real. I don't want them to see him as a villain. I love him too much to paint him in that light. Or maybe it's the shame that I still love him even after knowing what he did.

"We're just in two different places and it's better to be apart." I shrug and add, "But we always were, you know? Like this shouldn't be too shocking."

"He doesn't want to change?" Maddie asks. There's always hope in Maddie and I wish I could hold on to that.

"Men don't change," Sue says woefully. "I'm sorry. I'm doing it again," she says, shaking her head. "Sometimes it still hurts, you know? And I don't want you to go through what I did. I promise you, it's the last thing I want for you." Her voice gets a little tight, but she shakes it off quickly.

I love Sue, and I remember how hard her divorce was on her. But I swear this is different. *It has to be.* Her ex was vile and brutal. Evan isn't any of that. He'd never hurt me intentionally. He's just … he's just Evan.

"He said he wants to fix it," I answer as I watch Maddie sip from the glass without picking it up. Instead she crouches down, bringing her lips to the rim to sip. My lips tug into an asymmetrical smile for just a moment at the sight.

"It's not what he says." The hardness in her voice is absent, but there's still a finality in Sue's statement. "It would be hard for him to change, wouldn't it? He's been this way for years."

It's meant to be a rhetorical question, but the answer rings clear in my head. He did something bad. Something that he needed an alibi for. That's enough of a reason to change everything at once.

I stare at the dark red liquid. Sue's voice turns to white noise as she tells a story about something that makes the other girls laugh and I laugh too, when they do. I don't know if it's the first time he's needed an alibi. Or the second or the third. But it's the first time he changed. I knew something was off before the article. Before he told me anything. Before the lies.

I knew something was different.

And I didn't even bother to ask him what he'd done.

Evan

THERE'S A SLOW PRICK OF IRRITATION CRAWLING DOWN MY SPINE AS I sit in the chair across from James. Every limb feels the need to move, like a spider is climbing its way down my back. My fingers dig into the hard wood of the armrests as I stay perfectly still, staring down my former boss. Former friend. Now enemy.

"You aren't the best at listening," he says from across the room as he closes a drawer. The city lights creep in through the window behind him, casting shadows over the large desk.

"I don't follow orders," I grit out from between clenched teeth. My words come out menacing, but I don't mean for them to. One more meeting, and this is over. I'm done with him. He's yet to get that message or to tell me what the hell is going on.

James leans forward, clasping his hands together and his perfectly tailored suit wrinkles beneath his arms, making the fabric look cheap. He's always looked just a bit cheap. Regardless of the brand or how expensive his tastes are. Some assholes will always look like a knockoff.

He taps his fingers on the desk, but my eyes don't leave his. "The reason I called you in here is simple, Evan. The new client we have likes to live on the reckless side, and I'm concerned about drug abuse."

A gruff exhale leaves me from deep down in my chest. "I quit." I ignore the fact that he's hinting around what happened with Tony. My skin tingles and that feeling of a spider crawling on me comes back. I can't help but think he's recording this conversation. Everything in my gut has been telling me there's a setup and that I'm going to take the fall for what happened.

It was my fault, so I should be taking the blame regardless. On my terms, not this prick's and he's responsible for the way it went down. Some of the blame rests on his shoulders.

"I know what you said, but I assumed you'd come to your senses," he says, waving off my curt response. "Like I said, the new client has been known to behave a bit recklessly and I just want to make sure the policy we had in place remains the same."

The policy. I smirk at him, my grip on the arms getting tighter although my fingers are all that move.

The policy where the clients get what they want, but we don't say it out loud to anyone. The one where we're given clean stashes of the best drugs in the rec rooms. That's the policy. Instead of clarifying the policy, I answer, "After what happened with Tony I would think it's more than clear that we should advise our clients against anything too reckless."

James's eyes narrow. He knows I know that he's recording this. I'm not a fool. The only question I have is why. Why record it? More blackmail? Or evidence? What's he after?

I stare him in the eyes as I ask, "What is it you really want? You know you've provided drugs to clients before." I cock my head to the side as I ask, "Are we changing the policy?"

"I've never given anyone anything illegal," he states and I notice how he stiffens slightly but still tries to act casual as he shrugs and adds, "There's no change to the policy."

My wife has this thing she does. It's a smile I hate. A smirk really. I hate it when she gives it to me. It's one that tells me she knows I'm full of shit. While I sit here, staring at this asshole, I can feel the corner of my lips tug up into that sarcastic smirk. It doesn't stay there for long, though.

"Did you know the coke was laced?" James asks me and it takes a moment for the question to register.

The coke I gave Tony.

That doesn't make sense. Our shit is clean and pure and the best there is.

It's also provided to us in the recreation room by the company.

"I wouldn't know a thing about that." It's the only answer I can force out. Keeping a hard stare on my face even as my blood heats hotter and hotter.

Is he serious? It was laced?

I know the laws in and out. I can't admit to any knowledge that could lead back to me. I can accuse him, but not admit to participation or any foresight of drugs being gifted so freely when asked.

I raise my hand as if I'm the one in the wrong. The one who misspoke. "None of it matters anyway. I told you, I quit."

"And I told you, that you—"

"I'm done," I say and my words come out hard as I stand up and tower over the desk. James is quick to get up, tugging at one sleeve and then the other on his suit. "I thought you had something to tell me. Something useful and not some delusion that you could use to blackmail me."

His eyes glint with a darkness at my words. "It's not blackmail. I haven't—"

"Fuck you, James," I say, cutting him off as I turn my back to him to stalk out of the room. It'll be the last time I come here.

"You know what I can do to you," James says the threat to my back.

"I'm calling your bluff," I respond out of anger and instantly regret it, but I don't stop. All the weeks of not knowing if him or Samantha would tell the cops what happened, all the guilt and denial rise up in my chest and cause the next words come out without my consent. "Tell the sm what happened."

Just the thought of the truth getting out lifts a weight off of me.

"Tell them I gave him the coke. Tell them I set him up to get high and came back to him dead. Tell the press. Tell everyone," I say and my heart beats faster and faster as my hands ball into white-knuckled fists. I realize what I've just done. I realize I've said it out loud. But I don't care. It doesn't change anything. None of it matters anymore.

"It's murder, Evan, and you know it," James says as I face the door to leave. Not bothering to acknowledge him in the least.

Yes, it's murder. And it's not the first time something's happened under my watch. But it's the last. I'm done with this shit and this life.

I didn't lace a damn thing. If that stash was messed with, it wasn't me and I'm not going down for a crime I didn't commit. I'll own up to everything else.

I want to pay for my sins and chase what truly matters to me.

A love I took for granted. A love I don't know if I can salvage.

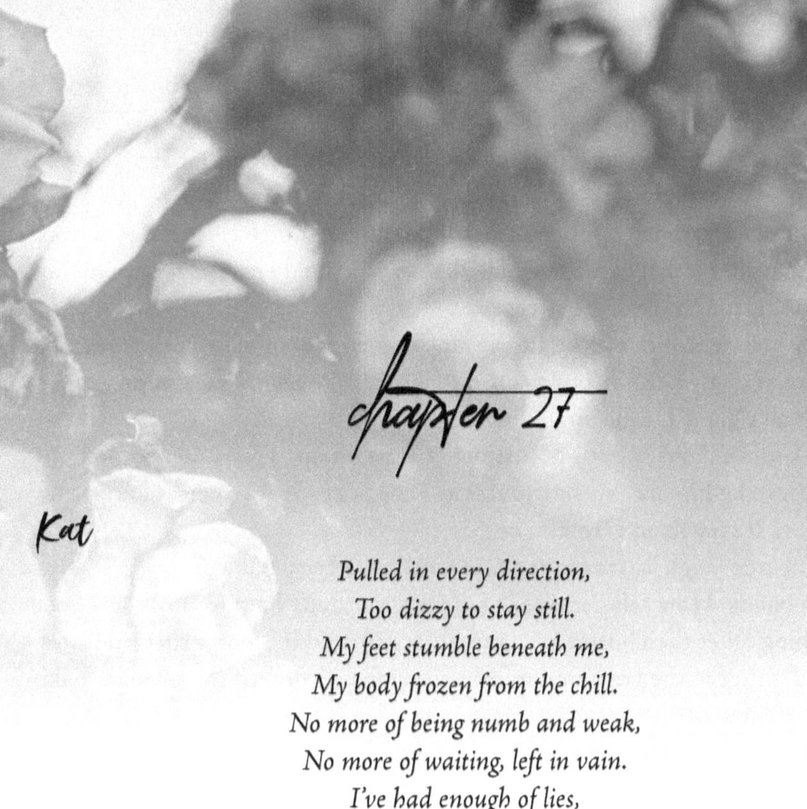

chapter 27

Kat

> *Pulled in every direction,*
> *Too dizzy to stay still.*
> *My feet stumble beneath me,*
> *My body frozen from the chill.*
> *No more of being numb and weak,*
> *No more of waiting, left in vain.*
> *I've had enough of lies,*
> *I've had enough of pain.*

THE BUZZ FROM THE TOWNHOUSE SPEAKER ROUSES ME FROM MY SEAT in the dining room. Buzz. Buzz. It's an annoying high-pitched sound that I can't stand.

My head's already throbbing. It's been like this for hours, ever since I got home and took the test. I can't go back and look at it. It's hard enough to wrap my head around everything that's happening.

And the guilt …

As I walk to the front of the townhouse, hustling down the stairs so I don't have to hear that damn noise again, I realize it's nearly nine and I'm still in my pajamas. At least I have pants on, but the matching light gray cotton shirt has a large spot of coffee on the front and I'm sure my hair's a mess.

"Who is it?" I ask in a voice that sounds more together than I feel as I push the button down and then release it. The only person I can think of is Henry, Evan's father.

"Sorry to bother you, I was just hoping for a quick meeting," a voice says on the other side and it takes me a moment to recognize it.

"Jacob?" I say into the intercom.

"I hope you don't mind. I was in the area and wanted to stop by," he replies and his voice breaks up over the speaker.

I know it's rude to make him wait, it's unkind not to answer him immediately, but this is so unexpected. I don't know how to react or respond.

"I'm not quite dressed for company," I tell him and then close my eyes from embarrassment. He still hasn't signed with the agency and I haven't spoken to him since running into him on the street.

"That's all right with me," he answers easily and I lean into the button, keeping it held down as my head throbs again and my eyes close with frustration.

"Is it all right if I come up?"

"Of course," I answer out of instinct. "Come on up," I tell him and then hit the buzzer to let him up. My heart races as I consider why he's here. I know why, deep down. It's my fault. I led him on.

A sarcastic laugh leaves me as I throw my head back and wipe my tired eyes with my hands. How self-centered and presumptuous I am to think he's here for anything other than business. I ignore the guilt and the worry that riddle my body and glance in the large oval mirror in the foyer as I wait for Jacob to make his way up the stairs.

There are bags under my eyes and a smattering of eyeliner from yesterday still remaining. I wipe carefully under them and pull my hair back, but I still don't look professional. My simple black leggings and a baggy shirt are made somewhat better by slipping on a crocheted sweater. It's better than nothing, laid back at the very best. I find it hard to care that much about my appearance as I open the front door.

I'm caught off guard as he walks up the stairs and comes into view. Of course I look like hell when he looks charming in a relaxed kind of way. His hair is ruffled, but probably gelled to look like it's slightly messy. It's his stubble, though, that gets me. I have a type, and Jacob fits that type to a T. Maybe that's how I know this is going to be trouble.

He gives me a wide smile and doesn't seem to care about my appearance in the least.

"I was just going to call it an early night," I lie, trying to stand with dignity in front of Jacob.

"Oh shit, I'm sorry, Kat." It's odd hearing him call me Kat. Most of my clients don't use my nickname. It's too casual. A type of casual I usually put an end to immediately, but I can't bring myself to correct him.

"What are you doing here, Jacob?" I ask warily. We don't have an appointment, and quite frankly I'm not in a state to be professional.

"It's Jake, remember?" he answers playfully and God help me, but I blush. "I was wondering if I could maybe take you out for coffee? I was hoping for dinner. If not tonight, then …"

"I'm sorry, I don't think that's something," I stammer over my words. "Jacob …" I clear my throat and continue, "Jake, I hope I didn't give you the wrong impression." I suck in a breath and push the stray hairs out of my face.

"It's nothing at all that you did, I just," he pauses to take a deep breath and smiles before letting out a small laugh. "It was stupid of me. I'm sorry, Kat. I just thought maybe there was a little attraction on your side?" he asks although it's a statement.

"Jake, I'm …" I want to say married, taken, in love with another man. The last line would be true. I'll always love Evan, and nothing will ever change that.

"I thought maybe you would like some company," he states, tilting his head as he leans against the wall. The muscles on his shoulders ripple as he does it. "I went through something a bit ago and I know I could use a distraction."

A distraction would be nice. I can't help that the thought makes me more relaxed each second that passes.

His half smile and gentle sigh are what do me in as he shrugs and slips his hands into his pockets. "I thought maybe you needed someone. Or that you'd like the company." He's even more handsome when he looks at me like that. It's a look that makes me feel warmth running through me. Compassion and understanding.

I've never been so tempted in my life. I so desperately need someone. I need someone to pick me up and force me to think about something else, because I'm a hopeless wreck.

"It's very sweet of you and I won't lie," I start to say and then hesitate to finish the thought, but settle on the basic truth. "I wouldn't act on anything because I just can't right now. I would never forgive myself and it wouldn't be fair to you." My words are rushed at the end, trying to defend my decision and assuage me of the guilt I'm feeling.

"Hey," Jacob says with an easy tone that breaks through the anxiety washing over me. His reassuring voice forces me to look into his gentle gaze. It's comforting and relaxing and makes me not trust myself. "How about this? How about you call me if you think you want to hang out or talk, or whatever it is that's on your mind?" he asks in a soothing tone that's almost melodic. It calms me, each word a consoling balm to the hurt that rages through my body.

I want that. More than anything, I want this pain that I feel to stop. I would give anything to make it go away. Jacob could do that, but it would be short-lived. I blink away the haze of lust, the cloud of want and desire leaving me slowly, very slowly. I clear my throat and look him in the eyes as I tell him, "I can't."

"'Cause we're going to work together?" he asks, although the way he tilts his head and strains his words makes it more than obvious that he knows why I can't. My lips form a thin straight line as I shake my head no.

"You love him?"

"I do, but that's not why. I'm just—I'm not okay and I need to figure things out …" I can't finish the thought, but thankfully I don't have to.

"I understand," Jacob says and runs his hand through his thick hair. My eyes are caught in his as I nod in thanks.

"Let's pretend this didn't happen then?"

"I'd rather you remember," he says with a grin that makes me crave him more. "I'll be here when you're ready," he says and then turns to leave. To walk away from me and leave me alone in my misery, just as I asked.

For a second I want to reach out and stop him from leaving; I don't want to go back to what's waiting for me. I don't want to face what I have to do.

But my fingers grip the edge of the foyer doorway as Jacob turns away and heads to the front door.

"I'll talk to you later then?"

I should say no. I should cut off whatever this is. It's dangerous and I can feel myself heading toward an edge where I won't be able to balance. I can see myself falling. And that's why I give him a small smile and nod my head. "Later," I say, the word slipping from my lips like a sin.

chapter 28

Evan

THE RADIO IN THE CAR IS SILENCED AS I TURN OFF THE IGNITION. It's not often I get a parking spot so close to the townhouse. It was a sacrifice we made when we bought the place a few years ago.

My head falls back against the leather headrest and I stare up at the building, at the top two floors on the right side, knowing that Kat's in there. So close, but so damn far away just the same.

My phone pings just as I open the door to get out and drag my sorry ass up to tell her everything. To lay it all out there, beg for her forgiveness, her understanding. But most importantly for her to stay with me. I'll give her space and time. I'll give her everything she asks. All I need is a deadline or something to work toward. I need her.

If she can still love me, after all I put her through and everything ahead of us, then we can get through anything.

I expect it to be Kat who messaged, but it's not her that texted me. It's Samantha.

I heard you quit.

News travels fast, I respond quickly and then debate on how to tell her I won't be responding anymore to her. It's not fair to my wife and now that I've left the company, there's no reason to have any type of relationship with her.

What about what happened?

I stare at the text on my phone as the lights in my car dim, signaling me to leave. She follows up the question with another that makes my stomach churn. *He knows about what happened and you know he won't let it go. He'll hang this over your head until he gets what he wants.*

My brow knits as I read the message. I don't give a shit what he knows or what he wants. For a moment, I think maybe she's messaging the wrong person. I settle on my response.

I have nothing to give him.

He knows about us, Evan.

I stare at the text message, letting it sink in.

You told him? I ask her, my gaze shifting from the phone to the lit townhouse building off the busy city street. The lights are on in her office and the living room. So close. She's so close.

My phone vibrates in my hand and I look back down to see her response. *He's known for years.*

My hand clenches tight as I realize he's been playing me. He's never let on that he knew I fucked his wife.

My first instinct is to blame Sam. *You didn't tell me you told him,* I text and then hate myself for it. I didn't know she was married; we were both high and I wanted any excuse to end things with Kat.

I didn't think he cared.

It was years ago. So now what? I swallow the ball of heat rising in my throat. It doesn't change anything. If he wants to be pissed, he can be pissed.

I don't see him letting this go. Not when he can get back at you. You need to be careful.

A frustrated groan travels up my throat.

Fuck him. He can do what he wants, but I'm not his bitch.

My phone immediately vibrates as I slip it into my pocket, and I cuss as I take it back out. Not to read her response, only to shut it off, silencing it and ignoring all the problems that wait for me. I'm done with both of them. I'm done with it all.

I swallow thickly and step out into the cool night, the city traffic surrounding me as I shut the car door and leave it all behind.

Everything is crumbling around me, but the only thing I care about is losing Kat. I don't see how I can hold on to her when I don't have a plan and I've lost control.

She needs a better man, and I swear I can be one. We'll start over and do it right this time.

I run my hand down my face. Hitting the lock, the car beeps and the bright headlights flash in the dark of the night. The sounds of the city streets are loud as I walk up the sidewalk, past men and women who carry on with their busy lives and don't have a clue how mine is being ripped apart.

I'll confess and then pack a box, and let her know it's only a separation and that even after I'll still love her and want her. That I'll do anything. I'll keep coming back, fighting for her. I'm not saying goodbye, I'm only doing what she asks because I love her and I know she needs time.

The keys jingle in my hand as I make my way home. Every second I'm trying to think of the best way to come clean about everything to Kat. She deserves to know, even if she hates me once she finds out. I have to tell her first.

A heavy breath leaves me as I turn the lock and walk into the building, running a hand over my hair and trying to block the image of her disappointment from my mind.

I can imagine how her deep green eyes will widen, how her lips will part and how she'll think I'm lying at first. I already know how she'll look at me, how she'll question who I am and why or if, she loves me.

My footsteps are heavy as I grip the iron railing and head to the top of the stairwell, to our home we've built together, the one she's kicked me out of. My gut feels heavy, churning with a sickness that rises to my chest as I hear her voice and recall the memory of her telling me to get out. My fingers wrap tighter around the rail, keeping me upright as I force myself to continue. I need to confess and come clean.

I want Kat back and the life we once had. It's all I need to live.

Every thought is lost at the sight in front of me. My blood turns ice cold when I stop at the top of the stairs where Kat's talking to that asshole from the café. Her voice is kind and nurturing and the way she offers him a sad smile … fuck no.

My legs feel like they're trembling; my body's shaking from the sight of him. Jacob, the supposed client Kat said was no one. *No one.* Yet he stands only feet away from the front door.

Anger rises quickly as I watch them. I knew there was something between them. I could tell. I know my wife and I know men like this prick.

"You motherfucker," I sneer the words without thinking twice. The door to my townhouse is still cracked when this dumb fuck looks up at me.

"What are you doing?" Kat calls out with shock as she stands in the doorway.

Kat

I'D RECOGNIZE EVAN'S VOICE ANYWHERE, BUT THE ANGER IS TERRIFYINGLY new. The second I grip the cold handle and open the door, my body freezes and the shock makes my mouth hang open and my eyes go wide. My heart beats in what feels like slow motion.

"Stop it!" I scream at him. My words echo in my head as he slams his fist against Jacob's jaw. It's instantly red and swollen and Evan's already got his other fist up.

Holy shit!

"Evan!" I scream as I run out of the foyer and into the hallway. "Stop it!" I yell and grip onto his arm. I slam both of my hands into Evan's chest, managing to separate the two men as Jacob grabs his jaw.

"You fucked my wife," Evan yells over me, screaming at Jacob and this time I want to smack Evan straight across his face. I don't. I don't give him any reaction except to turn toward Jacob to apologize.

"I'm so sorry," I offer Jacob who keeps a surprised smile on his face, as if it didn't bother him in the least.

"You fucked—"

"Stop it!" I scream again, and this time my voice feels raw and it pains me to scream. My body's hot and shaking, adrenaline coursing through my blood as my heart races.

"Get out of here," I say as I usher Jacob away. His green eyes flash with something, perhaps disbelief.

"You're cheating on me," Evan says it as if it's a question, his nostrils flaring and his hands still clenched into fists.

"You're an idiot," I say, keeping my voice low, apologizing again to Jacob and feeling the heat of embarrassment.

"It was a sucker punch," Jake says loud enough for Evan to hear. "And no, I didn't sleep with Kat." He looks Evan dead in the eye with the last line.

Embarrassment and horror wrap themselves tight around me as Jake leaves.

With my throat tight and arms crossed, I face Evan and say, "I'm not the one keeping secrets, you fucking asshole. He's a client and nothing more." My gaze almost shifts away from him. I know there was something, a chemistry that kindled between Jacob and me. A tension that I wanted to push. But it's only because I was hurting, and I never submitted to the temptation. I couldn't hurt Evan like that. I never would.

"What is wrong with you?" My question is dripping with nothing but disdain. For a moment I think of all the questions on the tip of my tongue, asking him why he's doing it and when he turned into this man. But this is the man I married. I'm the one who's changed. Not him.

Evan takes a step forward and his hand raises to my shoulder. I smack him away, barely feeling his hot skin against mine. "Don't touch me," I yell at him. My hand stings from the impact and I can't stand it.

I can't stand what we've become.

Evan's shoulders rise and fall steadily.

"Kat," he says and his voice cracks, like my name strangles him as he whispers it again. He takes a hesitant step forward, raising his arms and the blood from his torn knuckles is all I can see.

"What were you thinking?" I can barely ask him. Evan's expression falls and he looks past me. It's only then that I turn and see that Jake is gone. "What's wrong with you?"

"What was he doing here?"

"I've never cheated on you, and I wouldn't. Ever. Evan, I can't deal with this. The partying and what you're doing. Punching people for no damn good reason!"

"I quit, Kat. And you sure as hell know what it looked like. If he didn't fuck you, he wanted to."

"What the hell are you doing here?"

"I came to tell you everything," he says and his admission changes the tension in an instant. The evening is seemingly colder in the blink of an eye.

"I might … I might have some things happen." He closes his eyes and moves his hands to his hair. Hands with split knuckles and traces of blood.

Was he always like this? I want to hold and comfort him. But it's no use.

"I was stupid."

"Evan, you've had years to be stupid. Years of me begging you to grow up."

Every word hurts more and more. I know I'm not going to give him what he needs. I can't anymore.

"I wanted you to be my partner." I whisper the words, my voice laced with disappointment.

"I thought that's what we were."

"I need someone who's ready for the next stage of life." I barely get the words out as my throat dries and closes, threatening to suffocate me. But I finish the thought, making my heart split into two as I look deep into Evan's eyes and tell him, "Or no one at all."

"Kat," Evan says, whispering my name as if it's a threat. One against him. Or maybe it's a plea. "I'm sorry, okay?"

My head shakes and the words won't come out.

"I'm sorry I hit him, it looked bad at first. It looked like something else to me, but even then I shouldn't have hit him."

"No, you shouldn't have."

"It was shitty of me. I'm sorry. I'm so sorry," he says and I believe him. But it's not enough. He's still the same Evan.

I wipe the tears from my eyes with the back of my hand as I shake my head. "I can't do this anymore." It's the truth and even though it's the worst pain that I've felt in my entire life, I know it needs to be done. "I will be better on my own."

"Don't say that," Evan pleads, but he stands there not moving, his hands by his sides and his body stiff with disbelief. Or maybe fear. "I can't lose you," he says. I feel like my heart is breaking, but I shake my head.

"Maybe I should just be alone." My eyes burn with more tears as I shake my head again and say, "No, I need to. I need to be alone. I'm sorry," my voice fails me as I whisper the apology. I hate hurting him; I can't stand the pain in his eyes and expression. He doesn't try to hide it in the least, and it shreds me.

But we're just not meant for each other, not with the lives we're leading.

"I love you."

"Love isn't enough!" I yell and hate myself. I truly do. "It's not enough anymore," I say, steadying my voice although it's still low. I cross my arms and try to keep myself together, I try to hold my body upright although it begs me to collapse.

"Is that what you want?"

"I want a divorce," I say the lie in a single breath. The words all come out at once, bunched together and needing to be said, to be heard. To be felt to the very core of who Evan is.

My fingertips dig into my forearms as I slowly raise my eyes to his and the conviction wavers.

He doesn't speak, although his lips part once and then again. He licks them as his brow furrows and he visibly swallows then looks past me at the empty wall.

Again he starts to say something but stops, clasping and unclasping his hands and trying to find some way to tell me what he's thinking.

The worst part is that I want him to say something. I need him to give me something to hold on to him.

I'd go mad waiting to hear him tell me he'll make this right. For him I'd fall again, I know I would. There isn't enough strength in my body to keep me from Evan.

But he doesn't say a word; he never does when I need him to.

It takes a long moment. Each second my heart beats, the steady sound is all I can hear. And then he turns his back to me and walks away without saying another word.

My body is freezing as I slowly turn from the hall and head toward our door. I can't breathe, but somehow I am. I can't manage a thought, but my mind is whirling with the image of what just happened.

The way he spoke my name like he needed me. The way his voice was laced with desperation and his eyes shined with determination, but then failure. The way his expression crumbled when he realized he lost me.

I don't stop walking until I get back to our bedroom, barely glancing at the unmade bed and remembering the last time we shared it and everything about that night. I can still feel his lips on my neck, his hands traveling ever so slowly down my body as he whispered how much he loves me. And I believe the sentiment. No one has ever loved me like Evan, and no one else ever will.

It's just not enough.

For me, I'd go back to him. I'd let him do what he wanted and I'd pay the price. I head into the bathroom.

I pick up the small plastic stick still hanging off the edge of the sink.

My head's been a mess the past month. I didn't realize I'd missed one period, let alone two.

It's the brightest set of pink lines. I may not be the best friend I can be, or the best wife for that matter. But for my child, I'll be the best mother I can be and that starts with saying no to the life I once lived and had with Evan.

My hand splays on my lower belly as I lean my back against the edge of the sink. I have to tell him and I will, but not yet. I need to stop loving him first. I need to move on and focus on what I can change and make better for what's to come.

It's not just me who deserves that anymore.

chapter 30

Evan

> *I promise to love you forever. And that's the easy part.*
> *To honor and cherish you.*
> *To keep your wishes and dreams my own.*
> *To comfort you and keep you safe, always.*
> *Till death do us part.*

MY WEDDING VOWS HAUNT ME. THE PARTS OF THEM I CAN REMEMBER, at least. I can't stop seeing the look of complete devotion on Kat's face on our wedding day, as I read my vows from the scrap of paper where I'd written them.

My heart raced as I spoke each word, my gaze straying from the paper to look back at her. She was so beautiful, with a love that I knew I didn't deserve.

I can still remember the feel of her soft skin as I cupped her cheek in my hand. I can still smell the sweet fragrance that drifted toward me as I leaned closer to her, all of our friends and family clapping and cheering as I took my first kiss from my wife.

I can still taste her lips on mine.

When I said those words, I meant them. I thought they'd be so easy to keep, to be honest, and it never occurred to me that I'd forget.

A large metal door opens at the end of the hall and I look up, my view obstructed by steel bars of the jail cell.

It's been a long damn time since I've been locked up. Years. Almost a dozen years, to be exact. I knew I'd be back soon, though.

It was only a matter of time before they brought me in for questioning. Samantha tried to warn me but it was too late. Soon after I left the townhouse the cops picked me up and brought me in. I sit hunched over, resting my forearms on my thighs as I wait for the attending officer to come get me. With the footsteps echoing down the small corridor, my gaze raises in anticipation, only to drop again to the cement floor. He walks right past me without a glance in my direction and I drop my head, focusing on the cracks in the concrete and recalling every detail of the night that put me here.

My hands sweat as I twist my wedding band around my finger. I can't think about Kat right now or what she'd say. I haven't told her a damn thing about this and we're in the same place we were when I last left.

The worst part about all of this is that I don't have a way out yet. I'm falling into a dark hole, not knowing how I can escape, or if it will ever end. Never in my life has a situation seemed so dire and I'm more than aware that I miss her presence the most. It would make all this hell seem insignificant if only I knew she still loved me.

Someone coughs and I slowly turn my head to the left where it came from a few cells down, but I can't see a damn thing but bars and concrete. I think there's only one other person in holding with me. And he's on the same side so the rest of the cells are empty. I guess Tuesdays are slow days for the station.

My foot tap, tap, taps on the ground as I wait. The cops haven't given me any information to go on yet. Other than the word *murder*. My best guess is that they think I gave Tony the coke and knew it was laced with something deadly.

Even if I didn't know it was tainted, I'd still be held accountable. At least here in the state of New York, I am. If it was deliberately tampered with, though … then someone *wanted* him dead. Although the only two people who knew it was even there were me and James.

My shoulders rise with a heavy breath as the anger gets the best of me. Rage seeps into my blood just thinking his name. The image of him flickers in front of me the second I close my eyes. He smiled as he patted my back, walking out of the room after making sure it'd be ready for our client, Tony.

He's the one who put it there. The only question I have on my mind is whether he's the one who laced it. I can't imagine he did. He wouldn't be that stupid, but I'm not taking the fall for murder. Not to save his skeevy ass. I'm not a rat, but if James plays his cards against me—the proof that I was with Tony before he died, then I'm taking that fucker down.

"Thompson," the cop's voice bellows and echoes off the walls of the small cell.

"That's me," I answer, looking the detective square in his light blue eyes. I don't recognize him as he puts the key in the lock and opens the door wide for me to get out and walk to the interrogation room. Adrenaline pumps hard in my blood. It seems more intense now than it did years ago.

Maybe it's because I don't know how I'll get out of this. I have an alibi, but if James showed them the pictures proving I was with Tony that night, then I'm fucked.

I have to wonder if he would, though. If that's the case, he was deliberately withholding evidence and they'd have to question his intentions and his involvement, as well as the fact that he lied during the first questioning. He could do it anonymously, though, and knowing his character, he'd sure as hell take that route.

My boots smack against the floor and I walk at an easy pace, making sure I don't do anything to piss off the cop. He's a short guy. Probably in his thirties, I guess. Lots of wrinkles around his eyes, though. Maybe from the stress of the job, maybe from the sun.

"After you," he says with a grim look pulling his lips into a thin line as he opens the door. I give him a nod and walk in; he doesn't follow.

I only hesitate to sit down for a moment. There are two men in the room already. A tall cop with broad shoulders and a thin mustache that I want to shave off and Jay McCann, the lawyer from James's PR firm.

"You're fired," I tell Jay the second I sit down. I don't even look at the slick lawyer. He's represented me and plenty of other clients before, but I know he'd break attorney-client privilege and tell James everything. I don't trust him.

"Are you sure?" the cop questions, not hiding his surprise in the least and glancing between the two of us as McCann stumbles over a response. Jay is obviously shocked and I don't blame him.

"Evan," Jay starts, his voice strong although he instinctively reaches to loosen the knot of the dark navy tie that matches his suit, "I highly suggest we talk about this before you—"

"Yes, I'm sure. Sorry, Jay." I turn to face him and wait for a response, but he stands up and straightens his jacket. His clean-shaven jaw clenches as he grabs his briefcase and I can see he wants to say something, but he holds it in.

Probably a good call on his part.

I watch him walk around the table and exit without another word, leaving me alone with the cop.

"I'm Detective Bradshaw, Mr. Thompson."

"I would say it's nice to meet you, but ..." I reply with a smirk and tilt my hands out with my palms up. Detective Bradshaw doesn't laugh or respond to my little joke and that's fine. They never do in here where it's recorded. I know how this works.

"Have you been informed of your rights?"

"I have," I answer him.

"And do you know what you're being charged with?"

"Charged?" I say and although I keep my voice even, my back stiffens slightly as my muscles tense. "I wasn't informed I was being charged with anything." That statement comes out far too casually for the adrenaline racing through me.

"Well, I imagine there's no refuting the charge on your part. You supplied Tony Lewis with the cocaine he overdosed on."

"You want me to admit to handing over the cocaine to him, so you have someone behind bars to take the fall for a hotshot's death?" I ask him sarcastically, seamlessly hiding how my nerves want to crack and how my blood pounds in my ears. I let out an uneasy huff of a laugh and shake my head. Leaning back in my seat, I look him in the eyes with a smile as I say, "That's not happening, Detective."

"Well, someone is going to go down for murder, yes." He sucks his teeth as he stands up and crosses his arms over his chest. "You'd only be sentenced for your part and we're willing to cut you a deal. Whoever laced it with fentanyl intended for it to kill. There's no doubt in the DA's mind that it's murder, Mr. Thompson. I'd take the deal if I were you."

He waits for a reaction, but I use every ounce of energy in me to not give him anything. I won't say a word. Inside, I'm denying it. No fucking way. There's no way James would give a client something that would kill him. They're wrong. If it wasn't James … then who?

"We know it's someone within the firm. It's not the first time one of New York Stride Public Relation's clients have turned up dead." He leans back and adds, "As I'm sure you're aware."

As he talks, he half pushes, half tosses the manila folder that was sitting on his end of the table my way. It lands with a heavy thud in front of me and I open it, feigning disinterest.

"Nothing points to that person being you, but this was intentional. Someone wanted whoever was going to be taking this coke to die. It was laced with enough fentanyl to kill instantly."

I don't say anything as he pauses, opening the manila folder when I don't and pulling out a page with charts and shit I don't know anything about. He points his finger to a graph, then taps it far too hard, turning his knuckles white. "Whoever did it wanted even the smallest dose to kill."

Silence. All I do is stare at the man and then force my gaze back down, to the photos of Tony, dead on the floor of that hotel room.

"If you have any information on how we'd go about finding the killer, that'd be useful, and we'd certainly be grateful for that."

I have to calmly exhale a few times, keeping as still as possible and making sure my expression doesn't change in the least before I can respond. "I really liked Tony and it's a shame what happened to him. It's extremely upsetting to think someone murdered him."

"It is, especially since he didn't have any enemies we can find," the cop answers, his voice tighter now and then he leans forward.

"You know, if we can't find who did it, you'll be taking the full brunt of things."

I let a sarcastic laugh rock my shoulders and then look toward the door to my left. The one that leads to my freedom. "I'm sorry, Detective, everyone I know loved Tony and I didn't give him any drugs." I lean forward, mimicking his posture as I add, "It's illegal."

"If that's the way you want to play it." His jaw is tense as he reaches for the folder and I lean back in my seat again and only watch as he collects the papers.

"Am I free to go now? I'd like to leave."

He stands up abruptly, pushing the chair back a few inches, making the steel chair legs scrape noisily across the floor. "I don't think so. Maybe a night in the cells will help you remember something."

Fucking prick. Not that I'm surprised. It's a game of chess and his side has more pieces and a head start. I stay still and wait, keeping my guard up.

"Be back in a bit, Thompson."

I clench my jaw and crack my knuckles as I watch him leave.

It's only when the door shuts and I'm left alone in the room that I realize the extent of what Detective Bradshaw said.

Someone *wanted* to kill Tony, knowing I'd give the coke to him. Maybe even thinking I'd take it too. I'm known for partying. It's why clients choose me to represent them in the firm. My head spins as I try to recall that night. I don't broadcast that I'm not a cokehead and a glass of whiskey is enough for me. Still, everyone in the scene knows I'm down for whatever they're in the mood for. There's no way anyone else could have gotten in there. James had the master key, and he gave me the only other copy.

I was there to party with the clients and make sure they had a good time, but stayed out of trouble. It was easy enough in the rec room.

For the last ten minutes, I've been thinking that someone was trying to kill Tony. It's what the detective was suggesting.

I'd bet anything that James thought I'd take a hit at least.

Maybe it's paranoia, but as I sit alone in the room, all I can think is that the coke was never intended for Tony.

Someone wanted me dead.

you know I

need you

I married the bad boy from Brooklyn.

The one with the tattoos and the look in his eyes that told me he was bad news.

The kind of look that comes with all sorts of warnings.

I knew what I was doing.

I knew by the way he first held me that he would be my downfall; how he owned me with his forceful touch.

I couldn't say no to him, not that I wanted to. That was then, and it seems like forever ago.

Years later, I've grown up and moved on. But he's still the man I married. Dangerous in ways I don't like to think about and tried to ignore for so long.

I did this to myself. I knew better than to fall for him.

I only wish love were enough to fix this …

You Know I Need You is book 2 of the second duet in the You Are Mine series. Book 1, *You Know I Love You,* must be read first for this duet.

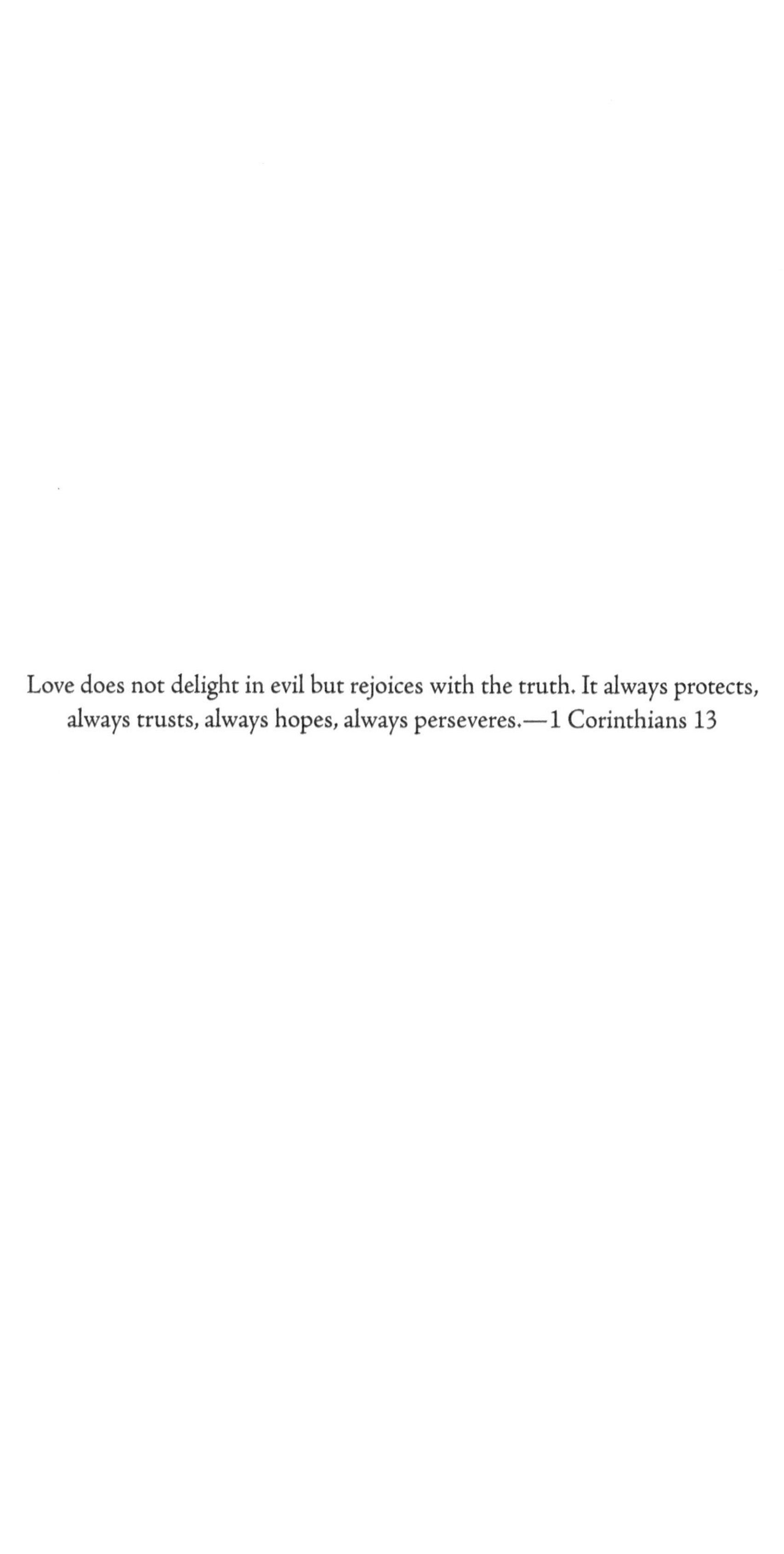

Love does not delight in evil but rejoices with the truth. It always protects, always trusts, always hopes, always perseveres.—1 Corinthians 13

You said you'd love me forever,
But forever was too long.
You said I was your one true love,
But the two of us were wrong.
It's deceit and lies that broke us,
And left me living in pain.
Forever was supposed to be ours,
But forever was said in vain.

IT'S NOT EVERY DAY YOU READ IN THE PAPERS ABOUT YOUR HUSBAND going to jail. That's one way to find out, I guess.

My heels click steadily on the sidewalk as I make my way to the end of the block; just a little farther until I'm home. The plastic bags from the grocery store on the corner dig into my arm, the grooves getting redder with every few steps.

It hurt after a few blocks, but I didn't care. Now I'm just numb to it. I focus on the front door to my townhouse the second it comes into view. Jail. Evan is in jail and the vise squeezed tight around my heart has been unrelenting since I read the article at the corner store.

It doesn't take long before my gaze is drawn from my building to a figure waiting for me.

Standing in front of the building with her arms crossed over her chest, is a cop. She's dressed in dark navy pants and a matching jacket that's not quite baggy enough to hide her curves. She's short, with her blond hair pulled back into a low bun and covered with a cap. My pace slows as I spot her, and I want to break down all over again.

If only I'd stayed holed up in the apartment and didn't have to eat. The thought is bitter as I walk forward. Each step hurts more and more.

I must still love Evan, because knowing he's in trouble twists me up inside.

It was the sign I was looking for, though. The one that drove the nail in the coffin of my marriage. It's really over. He's only in holding, so there's no way for me to get him out of this, but if there was, I'd bail him out and hand over divorce papers the moment we were out of the precinct.

"Mrs. Thompson," the cop says as I traipse up the stone steps.

"Hello," I respond awkwardly, not wanting to look her in the eyes as shame creeps up and makes the cold air feel even colder.

"I'm Detective Nicoli," the woman says and I nod my head, feeling the pinch from the grocery bags digging even deeper into my forearms as I shift on my feet.

"How can I help you, Detective?" I force myself to straighten my shoulders, pretending I have no idea why she's here.

"Could I come in?" she asks me as if I'd let her.

"I'd rather not," I answer, my voice a bit harsh. I struggle with the bags slightly, hearing them crinkle as I let out a low sigh. "It's been a long few days and I don't want company."

"The bags under your eyes could have told me that," she says with no sympathy in her tone.

I huff out a humorless laugh and tell her thanks, the *S* lingering, intending to walk right by her and into the townhouse, but then she adds, "I'm sorry for what you're going through."

With that, I hesitate.

I stand there, taking the sympathy. More than that, I need it. Tears burn my eyes as I look back at her. "What do you want?"

"It might be better for you if I could come in," she suggests, looking pointedly at the bags on my arms.

I shake my head. That's not happening.

The charge will be murder if the papers are telling the truth.

I'm not interested in hearing from anyone other than my husband. He hasn't been formally charged yet, but for it to be in the papers, there's a fifty-fifty chance they have enough to arrest him as far as I can tell, and I'll be damned if I let her inside, and … More shame consumes me at the thought of making sure I don't give them any evidence that could help convict him. As if he really did it. There's no way he did. My husband's not a murderer.

"Ask me whatever you'd like, Detective, but make it quick."

"I know you two are getting a divorce," she says and the article from two days ago flashes in my memory. "I'm sure you've heard he's going to be charged with murder, given your position in the social circles around here."

A deep inhale of the frigid fall air chills my lungs to the point that it's painful. The article was all about how Evan lost his job, his wife, and now he's about to be charged with murder. My heart thuds dully just the same it did when I first read it, as if it's lifeless.

"I wanted to know if you had any information that you'd like to give us," Detective Nicoli says and I shake my head, not trusting myself to speak.

"Look, I know this is hard, but anything at all you can give us would be appreciated."

I stare straight into her eyes and I hope she feels all the hatred in my gaze. He's not a murderer. I don't care what they think.

"I don't have anything I'd like to tell you other than that these bags are heavy."

The detective frowns. "If we have to get a warrant and search your place, it's not going to be pleasant for you." She softens her voice and adds, "I'm just trying to spare you that."

I'm not stupid and her good cop routine isn't going to work on me.

I've had to talk to cops before, years ago. I never said a word. I'm sure as hell not going to now.

"Did you know Tony Lewis?" she asks, and I shake my head. Again, not wanting to speak, but she waits for me to confirm it out loud. The pen in her hand is pressed to the pad as she stands there expectantly.

"Never met him."

"Do you know where your husband would go to acquire cocaine?"

My expression turns hard as I tell her, "My husband doesn't do coke." *Any more* almost slips out. He's done it before. He's done a lot of shit that I'm ashamed of, but that was before me. *Before us.* For a moment, I question it. Just one small moment. But then it passes as quickly as it came.

Detective Nicoli smirks and flips the page over in her notepad then says, "We'll have the warrant for a sample from him soon."

Absently my hand drifts to my stomach to where our baby is growing, as if protecting this little one will protect Evan, but I'm quick to pull it back as one of the heavier bags slips forward on my arm.

She doesn't need to know, but I want to tell her. I want to tell the whole world that the Evan I know could never do what they're saying. But I don't tell her a damn thing and I've given her enough of my time.

"Good for you," I tell her and walk past her. I shove the key into the lock and turn it, but before I can open the door, the cop leans against it and waits for me to look at her.

"Please move out of my way," I say as I seethe, my anger coming through. Anger at Evan, anger at her.

"Someone's going down for Tony Lewis's death."

"Someone should, but my husband is not a murderer," I snap. I grip the door handle tightly, feeling the intricate designs in the hard metal press against my skin. It's freezing and the lack of circulation in my arms hurts. But I can't let go. I don't trust myself.

"I have nothing more to say, so I'm going inside," I tell her, and every word comes out with conviction.

"I'll leave my card," she responds after two long seconds of her hazel eyes drilling into the side of my head. She slips a card into one of the bags dangling from my right arm.

I watch her walk away, biting back the comment on the tip of my tongue for her not to bother.

"What a bitch," I spit out the second I open the door and get inside, then let the bags fall to the floor.

My body feels like ice and my arms and shoulders are killing me. My legs are weak as I lean against the door to shut it and stare absently ahead, my gaze drifting from the empty foyer to the stairs.

I want to cry.

I want to give up.

Mostly I wish I'd been a better wife. I wish I'd kept Evan from whatever the hell he did.

I know him. He didn't do this. I don't know what he did, but he didn't kill anyone.

Evan

EVERY SECOND THAT TICKS ON THAT FUCKING CLOCK MAKES ME WANT to break it.

I haven't felt like this since the first time I was brought into jail. It wasn't here; that place was in a small town, somewhere in the bumfuck boonies outside of Chicago. This restless need to get the fuck out and handle all the hell I created is the exact same feeling I had that first night.

Tick, the clock's minute hand moves again and I peer to my right, staring down the woman at the front desk who's processing the paperwork for my release.

My neck cracks as I stretch out my shoulders. I haven't slept a wink and I'm exhausted, but pure adrenaline is pumping through my veins, keeping me awake and fighting.

I need to get the hell out of here.

I knew something was off from the very beginning. James tried to fuck me over. It had to be him.

The only reason I can think of is because of Samantha, though, and that doesn't make sense. It's been years since we had that affair. Years for her husband to get over it. Shit, all he's been talking about for months is how he wants their divorce to be finalized.

I lean back on the metal bench as I force myself not to look at the desk sergeant, and not to look at the clock either. My eyes focus on the abstract patterns of the cheap linoleum tiles and the sounds of the police station fade into the background as my thoughts take the forefront.

The memory of that night comes back to me.

I flinch as I remember the feel of James's hand on my shoulder, showing me where the new rec room in the renovated hotel was and asking me if I needed anything else. My eyes close when I think about him handing me the key card and looking to his left and right before telling me to make sure I showed Tony a good time.

My lungs still and my vision turns red as my teeth grind against one another while my fists clench.

I can't fucking handle this. If that fucker set me up to die, he's a dead man.

Even if it wasn't him, someone laced that coke with enough fentanyl to kill. I'll be damned if I rest until I know who did it. Whether they were after me or Tony, or it was a mistake, it doesn't matter. They're dead.

"Mr. Thompson." A small voice to my right says my name and breaks my concentration. It takes every effort to raise my head and relax my body as if nothing's wrong. As if I'm not envisioning beating in some unknown man's face with my bare knuckles. I'm quick to get to my feet, eager to leave.

Each step smacks off the floor, the sound drowning out the steady ticking of the clock. My heart beats in rhythm to match my pace.

"Your belongings." A weak smile forms on her thin lips as she hands me a ziplock plastic bag and review the contents one by one, going down the list in her hands.

It's all standard procedure, I tell myself.

I shove my hands into my pockets and rock on my heels as I wait. Each second makes me more and more anxious to get out of here.

"And your keys," she says flatly then finally meets my eyes again.

"Thank you," I answer with a tight smile and grab the bag before she can change her mind. As I slip my black leather wallet into my back pocket, I wonder what James will say. Better yet, I wonder how I can get him to confess.

"Make sure you sign here." I smile as I do what I'm supposed to.

Break his jaw.

"And here," the woman adds, pointing to another line on the release forms.

Bash his knees in with a tire iron.

"You're all set, Mr. Thompson."

Put a gun to his head.

My lips tilt up as if I'm happy to be getting out of here. But my muscles are tightly wound and my stomach's churning.

All because of one question: What if it wasn't him?

No one can know about any of this shit. My heart skips a beat and I hesitate to walk out of the station. *Kat.*

My feet nearly stumble over each other at the thought of someone going after her. They wouldn't. Not when she's through with me. They can't. No one better hurt her. No one touches my wife.

I force myself to move forward. I can't go to the cops, not even to protect her.

All they'll do is go after me. I don't have a shred of evidence other than a testimony that could lead them to convict me. I have nothing but my word. Inside these four walls, my word doesn't mean shit. I'm well aware of that fact.

The sky's gray as I glare through the glass doors, hating this place and what I've done. I have to tell her the truth and make sure she knows I'll keep her safe and not to trust anyone; I shake my head. I'll have to tell her I'm coming home first and with that thought, I take out my phone. Turning it on, I lean against the door waiting to see what I'm up against.

I bet she's heard I'm locked up, but maybe there's a small chance she hasn't.

As the phone comes to life, a series of pings follows the messages popping up.

A couple from Pops, the first asking where I am and if Kat forgave me. The next asking me to call him when I get out of jail. A numbness creeps over my shoulders at the feeling of disappointment that runs through me. He's too old to be dealing with my shit.

My body sags against the door, the chilly temps from the autumn night seeping through the glass.

I scroll through the messages asking all sorts of questions from people who don't really give a shit about me, and vice versa. They don't matter.

The one person who does matter, the only one I want to hear from and the only person I want to run to … hasn't sent a single text.

It takes a second for my throat to loosen enough so I can swallow that realization. I check the missed calls to make sure Kat hasn't tried to contact me, hopelessness runs through my veins before I push the glass doors open with a hard slam of my fists.

I hate that she didn't call me. That she didn't care enough to let me know she heard. If Pops has heard, she's heard.

The bitter cold air whips by my face as I move toward the corner.

I check my messages again, searching for her name like I could've missed it. One catches my eye. Samantha. I pause over her name and read her text. *We need to talk.*

My strides quicken at the thought of meeting with her. She might know something. She could be my way to get what I need from James.

I have to go to Kat first and knowing that, I text Sam back, asking when and where.

Glancing up at the next intersection and seeing the Don't Walk icon flashing, I look over my shoulder to hail a cab. I'm going home, whether Kat likes it or not.

I've kept so many secrets from her.

My head hangs low as a cab pulls up and I step out into the busy streets of New York City. The door slams shut with a loud click, dulling the city noises as I tell the driver our address. It's only after a few minutes of quiet, the rumble of the car almost lulling me to sleep, that I rub my tired eyes and think about what Kat would say. What she'd do if she knew the shit I got myself into.

She's already so close to hating me.

She's close to being over me and what we had.

I can't risk losing her, but right now either choice—to come clean, or to hide it from her—feels like I've already lost her. She needs to know, though … I have to make sure she's safe and she's protecting herself.

chapter 3

Kat

"I WANT TO THANK YOU FOR MEETING ME," JACOB SAYS IN BOTH A charming and professional tone—I'm not sure how that's possible—as my keys clink on the coffee shop table and I take a seat across from him.

It's been three days since Evan came back to the townhouse. And three days since he accused me of cheating on him and punching Jacob. That night I sent Jacob a message apologizing, but then I turned my phone off. Three days of me hiding away in our bedroom and pretending this isn't my life.

At some point, I had to come out. What a fresh hell I walked into.

"I'm so sorry," I tell him again with complete sincerity and my eyes closed tightly as I settle down into the seat. It's a wicker chair with a dark red cushion and the smell of coffee from the café adds to the comfort. This coffee shop has a homey feel to it. Very different from my favorite spot in town, Brew Madison, but I can see why Jacob likes it.

My cheeks are practically frozen from the piercing wind whipping through the West Village, but even still, they burn. "I honestly cannot say—"

"Don't." Jacob stops me from saying more, holding up his hand and waving off my embarrassment.

I can't believe how out of hand things have gotten. As a professional, I'm mortified.

"Please, Jacob." I shake my head slightly then look up at him, staring into his eyes as I refuse to let him downplay everything, especially with a faint bruise hiding behind the five o'clock shadow along his strong jaw. "What happened the other day was ridiculous. Evan had no right to put his hands on you, and I want to thank you for not pressing charges."

"I don't blame him, Kat," Jacob says and waves off my gratitude with an ease that catches me off guard. My heartbeat quickens and it's the only thing I can hear for a brief moment while I take in his words.

"It's fine, really. I mean it, I don't blame him."

I slowly take off my coat as I tell him, "I do. I know it looked a little off." A feeling of confusion clouds my memory of what I'd planned to say.

I was going to thank him for not pressing charges.

Beg him not to hold it against the publishing agency.

And concede that I would not be his point of contact if he did choose to go with us. Obviously, I can't represent him after what happened. I'm prepared for that.

"Evan is in the wrong in every way, and I feel awful."

"It wasn't you who did it." The comfort in his voice makes me slightly uneasy. The next words out of his mouth add to that nervousness. "I'm kinda glad he did."

"Why?" I ask quietly, the nervousness changing to something else. I should stop this. I know that much. It's a slippery slope I'm balancing on.

"You two split, right?"

"Yeah," I answer him, and it makes my throat go dry. My chest feels hollow, with nothing there but the raw emotion I'm trying to ignore. *What am I doing?* I'm feeling something other than the agony that's plagued me for weeks.

"He's not acting like it, judging by the way he talks to you. He's aggressive. He's doing what my ex did to me. And I don't like it."

"I don't know what Evan's thinking right now, but this isn't him. He isn't like this."

"Either way, I don't blame him."

I don't know what to say back. There's a tension between us that's different from what I anticipated.

"I don't like the way I saw him treat you," Jacob states with a softened voice and then raises up his hands as if expecting me to protest. "I know I only saw a small piece." He licks his lower lip and adds, "I just didn't like it. So, if he's going to take it out on me instead, I'll take it."

"It's not like that," I say, attempting to stop what he's insinuating. "Evan doesn't take anything out on me."

"It's just something about what I see between you guys. It gets to me."

"Between us?"

"How you obviously care for him, even though it's killing you," he answers with a sadness in his eyes that could rival mine.

"Either way," he continues, "I'm sorry and you don't have a reason to be, so … let's just agree to let it stay in the past?"

"I didn't anticipate you being the one apologizing today."

Jacob shrugs and it's then I get an even better look at the faint bruise on his jaw. With the rough stubble, it almost blends in, but when I catch sight of it again, I cringe.

Jacob smiles at me and a masculine chuckle makes his T-shirt tighten on his broad shoulders.

"Seriously, Kat," he tells me and moves his hand to the table, turning it so it's palm up. "Don't worry about it. I can see where he's coming from."

Jacob's gaze flickers to his white mug. I glance down at it; it's chai, and a warmth flows through me at the thought of getting myself one.

"So, we're all good?" I ask him.

He shrugs again and takes a sip from his drink. "If you're okay?" he finally answers, and *okay* is not exactly the word I'd use to describe myself right now.

"For you, miss," a woman to my right announces, startling me and catching me by surprise. The barista I barely noticed when I first walked in sets down a mug identical to Jacob's in front of me. The warming aroma of cinnamon mixed with nutmeg hits me immediately and I welcome the scent.

"Thank you," I tell her although my eyes are on Jacob.

"I thought you'd like it," he says, answering the unspoken question with a grin. "I know the shop is new, but I've had their chai almost every day and you have to try it," he tells me like we're good friends. Like we know each other well. After a moment he adds, "Great place to write."

"I can see that." I swallow, feeling a stir of something else in my chest. It pulls at my heart. *Guilt.* I feel like I'm cheating.

Evan and I are separated; I remind myself again. With all the crap Evan's done and put me through, it's over. It has to be.

So this, this little distraction … I refuse to stop it when it makes me feel something other than the turmoil that has been plaguing me.

My hands wrap around the mug and they warm instantly as I take a good long look around the place. The brick walls and picture frames make it cozy and inviting. With the dark wooden tables and wicker furniture, I could see how a writer could make themselves comfy in a corner chair. Using both hands to lift the mug, I take a small sip and then another, much longer one, feeling the warmth flow through my cold chest. And then a third. Even though I feel less consumed with regret about the fight between Jacob and Evan, a different feeling is washing over me.

"So, what do you think?"

I have to blink away my thoughts and try to figure out what he's referring to before a bright blush rushes to my cheeks.

"The chai," he adds comically and nods at my hands.

"It's good," I say with a half-hearted smile and then see the bruise again. "I just …" Why can't I stop apologizing and let it go?

A half-hearted smile graces his lips and it's quiet for a short moment. "Kat, I don't really like your ex."

Ex.

My heart hammers and my blood feels as if it's draining from my body, leaving me cold. "I can see why," I respond easily enough, although I can't look him in the eyes.

"Hey, I didn't mean to upset you." His tone changes to sympathetic and I hate this moment. I hate feeling weak and not knowing what to do or say.

"Please don't worry about me, Jacob." My voice is as strong as I can make it.

"First of all," he says with a gorgeous smile, "it's Jake." I can't help the small laugh that slips out at how serious he is. "And second, I'm not worrying, just being there for someone. That's all."

All my misgivings about him leave me as I look into his kind dark green, hazel eyes. He's the rugged kind of handsome I would have been drawn to back when I was single. I'm honest enough to admit I'm drawn to him now.

He's a good guy, and I can feel that in my bones.

"That's very nice of you, but I think …" I start to say and pause as I try to figure out how to word what I'm thinking without sounding pathetic. *I'm still in love with my ex, pregnant with his child, confused and feeling alone. Even if he's in jail and we're separated, I can't stop worrying about him.* Instead, all I can manage is a mix between a groan and a sigh. I conclude with a simply stated, "I'm just a mess over it all."

"Hey, let's just end it there?" he suggests. "I don't have many friends here and I put my nose where it didn't belong. I'm the one who's sorry."

"You're not in the wrong here."

"I'm not in the right either, am I?"

"What do you mean?" I ask him like I'm oblivious. I know exactly what he means.

"I—" he starts to say but then stops himself and lets out a short laugh before rubbing his eyes. "Sorry, I've been up all night working on this manuscript."

I see the opening to steer the conversation back to work and take it. To keep this relationship just business. "I could bury myself in manuscripts right now."

Jacob lets out a charming laugh and I find myself slipping into the one role I know I'm good at. "Have you thought about who you'd like to be your agent and represent you?" I almost roll my eyes at the question.

"You're shameless," he says with a wicked grin.

"I know," I answer him and smile into my cup. The smile is oddly genuine given my state just a moment ago, but Jacob has a way of making me feel calm and relaxed.

"I'm not ready to talk to any publishers. I still don't know what I want to do with this one yet."

"Want to tell me about it?"

"Well, it's about me. Sort of." He leans back and spreads his legs wider, my eyes drawn to his broad chest as he glances out the picture window at the front of the shop. "My ex, really." He runs his hand through his hair.

I nod my head and reply, "So, it's an emotional book for you. Maybe one to feed your soul, more than your family."

"I have no family to feed, so that'd be an easy one," he jokes. "But yeah. It's more just for me, I think."

"What's the plot about, if you don't mind me asking?" I pry gently as I pick up a sugar packet from the table. I have no intention of adding it to my drink, but I think best when I have something to fidget with. Again, I cling to the chance to talk about work. I'm more than grateful for this distraction. I'd rather talk books all day long than anything else.

"We were high school sweethearts who beat the odds, but we just didn't get that happily ever after, you know?"

I feel a sharp pain in my heart, one that knocks the wind out of me. Another romance story gone south. "Why didn't it work out?"

"She'd been cheating on me for a while. I found out when she got pregnant and the dates didn't add up."

"That'll do it," I say as my mind wanders back to Evan. To his infidelity before we were married but still together. And to my little secret.

"Turns out it was my best friend."

"Oh no." A pout pulls down my smile and I feel gutted for him. "Double betrayal."

"That'd make a good title," he replies and then chews on his lower lip.

A feeling of shame settles on my shoulders. Evan and I are over, and I shouldn't feel like this is wrong. But for the first time in years, I feel *something* for someone else.

There's no way I can justify this feeling right now. Not when I haven't had time to get over Evan. Not when the thought of getting over him cripples me. What's Sue always telling Maddie, though? The best way to get over one man is to get under another. Sitting here right now, I understand the sentiment.

"You think I could sell it?" Jacob asks and holds my gaze as he lifts his cup.

"I'd have to read it first," I answer honestly, even though I know a happily ever after sells better. That doesn't mean there can't be another romance thread added in somewhere. It's not like his story is over. His eyes catch mine and it's as if he knows exactly what I was just thinking … about another romance thread.

"I'm still in the process of writing it. I think the story is going well, though," he says and every inch of my skin catches on fire. It's the way he looks at me. How his stare holds me captive and the tone of his lowered voice makes my blood race. The air crackles between us and with that, I need to get out of here. Quickly, before this conversation turns into something else.

"Send me the first few chapters?" I ask him and then reach for my purse. "Sorry, but I have to get going. I didn't think our meeting would last this long."

He half smiles at me as he says, "Okay then." He says it like he knows I'm lying, but more than that, like it amuses him.

I take out my wallet, but Jacob stops me. "Don't even think about paying."

"Are you sure?"

"You can get the next one if you really want to, but this one is on me."

I give him a tight smile, although I'm grateful. Truly I am. Even if his intentions are less than pure.

I can only nod then make my way out. It's all too much. Separation, pregnancy. Now Evan's in jail. I can't take how quickly my life is unraveling.

"Hey, Kat," Jake says from behind me as I push the door open and the bells ring. I turn to look back at him.

"It's going to be okay," he reassures me and I say thanks, although it's so softly spoken I don't think he could have possibly heard it.

I have to leave. That's the only thing on my mind because I'm so broken that the words *it's going to be okay* are my undoing.

chapter 4

Evan

THE WORST SOUND IN THE WORLD TO ME IS THE MUFFLED SOBS OF MY wife crying.

And the worst sight I could ever imagine is her bundled in a ball on the kitchen floor, whimpering against the cabinets. Her shoulders heave as she lets out another wretched sob and it makes me feel that much worse.

I didn't know it could get any lower than this.

"Kat." Her name is a gentle murmur from my lips, nearly a plea for her to stop. She's crying so hard, lost in the sadness, that she didn't hear me come in. My voice startles her and she jumps back slightly, causing the cabinet door to rattle.

Her lips part slightly, but she doesn't say anything. Instead it appears she's holding her breath.

"What's wrong?" I ask and the second the question is uttered, I hate myself. It's obviously me. I did this. "What can I—"

"Nothing," she answers curtly, cutting me off, more embarrassment and shame present in her tone than the anger I'd anticipated. "I'm fine." She uses the sleeve of her shirt to wipe at her face, leaving her tearstained cheeks bright pink.

"You aren't fine."

"I'll *be* fine," she says, and her tone is harsher this time. "I don't want to cry in front of you," she adds with sincerity. I know the comment isn't intended to hurt me as I walk deeper into the kitchen. Kat's just being honest.

"That's what I'm here for," I tell her and then feel like an asshole. I haven't been here in days. I can see Kat's lips part with some sarcastic response, so I'm quick with my next words. "I know we're going through some shit and I'm not making things any better. But I'm here now."

She doesn't respond as she pushes her hair out of her face and visibly focuses on calming herself down. Glancing up at me only causes her expression to crumple as if she'll start crying again. She rips away her gaze and silence separates us.

I can't help but notice the curve of her shoulders and the way her breasts move as she steadies her breathing. My body is ringing with the need to touch her. The need to make her pain go away. "Whatever it is," I say, "it's going to be okay." I don't know how many nights I've told her that.

And it's always been true. "We'll get through this."

"I'm crying because of you!" she screams at me and angrily brushes away her tears.

"I'm sorry, but I promise, it's not what you think."

She only huffs in disbelief and shakes her head, refusing to look at me. My blood turns cold and I struggle to breathe, but still I walk toward her. Every step is careful and cautious. I just want to hold her. I want to fix this more than anything.

I can't lose her.

"Kat." I say her name as if it's my only prayer, but she doesn't look at me.

As I crouch down next to her, Kat stands just to get away from me and it kills me. She wipes under her eyes then turns from me, giving me nothing but her back. The cup that was on the counter clinks as she places it in the sink.

Her shoulders shudder.

All I can hear is her heavy breathing as she ignores me. Moments pass, my hands clammy and my body hot. I don't know what to say or do, but I stay. I won't leave. I can do that at the very least. So I stand there, waiting and wanting her to tell me anything. I will wait forever for her if that's what she needs.

"They broke in through the window," she states with a shaky voice, followed by a deep inhale, and my blood freezes.

"Who?"

She shrugs her shoulders, turning to look at me with an expression of disbelief and answering sarcastically, "How the fuck should I know?"

"Where?" I follow behind her as she walks into the guest bathroom in the hallway. The second the door opens, I'm hit by the arctic air coming in through the broken window. It's only a half bath and inside the sink are shards of glass.

"They didn't take anything that I can tell."

"What the fuck," I mutter beneath my breath, my hands clenching into fists at my sides. "Were you home?" I should have been here. I should have been protecting her.

She shakes her head no, her hair sweeping along her shoulders as she crosses her arms to protect her from the chill. "I called the cops as soon as I got in. I knew something was off. They went through your drawers, by the way. You may want to check and see if you had anything in there."

Fuck. My heart hammers as I stand there numb.

I don't know who it was or what they were looking for. But if she'd been here … Fear is crippling. It's the resolute tone of her next statement that forces me to move. "Are you going to fix that or should I call someone?" Her voice is flat and completely lacking in any emotion.

"I'll take care of it, but Kat, please," I beg her, forcing my legs to follow her back to the kitchen.

"I don't want to talk about it," she says without even looking at me.

"Kat, I need to know—"

"If you want to talk, then tell me how jail was. How about that?" she spits back.

"Kat, baby, please—"

"Don't 'please' me, don't touch me, don't anything me," she practically hisses, glaring over her shoulders as she opens a cabinet to get a clean glass then slams the door shut. Her eyes are rimmed in red, and she looks paler than usual.

She fills the glass with water and drinks down half of it with her back to me.

I want to reach out and hold her, but I've never seen her like this. Closed off and nothing but worn out and angry.

"Kat, I can explain."

"Oh, thank goodness. I was worried for a minute." Her voice drips with sarcasm, her back still to me as she turns the tap on and refills the glass.

"Please, if you don't mind, you could start with … I don't know," she says then shrugs and turns to face me, the bitterness in her voice never more apparent than now. "How about why I should give a damn about whatever excuse you have?"

My brow furrows as I take in her stance. She slams the glass down so hard I think it may shatter but it doesn't. With her arms crossed again, she waits. Her hair falls in front of her face, hiding part of her tired eyes and she doesn't bother to sweep it away.

"I don't want you to be mad …"

She reaches behind her to grip the counter, her knuckles turning white, agitation showing in every movement she has. I know right then I can't tell her what I think about James. I can't tell her that I think someone was trying to kill me or that I'm bringing more trouble to her.

I have to be the man she *wants* me to be.

I can do that. Just one last lie, once more. To protect her.

I swear it'll be the last. And only so I can hold on to her and keep her safe.

"Kat, I don't know a thing about the coke overdose or James or whatever the hell anyone's told you."

"You said you needed an alibi," Kat states evenly. She blows a few strands of hair away from her face and then folds her arms over her chest once again.

My stomach sinks as I give her just a little bit of the truth. Just enough that she'll stop questioning me. "This is why. I knew Tony was dead, but I wasn't involved." *Lie.* I can barely stand on my own two feet knowing I just lied to her.

"Why an alibi?"

"To save the company's image. We couldn't be associated with it any more than we already were." It's only a thinly veiled lie. What I've said is mostly true.

Kat nods her head, putting a finger to her lips and letting the words sink in as she stares at the floor.

"So, you gave him the coke?" she asks before lifting her head and her eyes flash to mine.

"No," I tell her and my voice is hard. *Lie. Another lie.* I'm digging my own grave deeper. I add in a truth, hoping it sounds believable enough to cover the lies. "I told you I don't do that shit."

"They're going to test you," Kat says like she doesn't believe me.

"I'll have them show you the results if and when they do," I say, and my words come out bitter.

She turns her back to me again as she fills the glass with more water. I stalk closer to her, careful not to piss her off.

"I mean it. I promise you. It was just a job and I barely drank, Kat. I quit for a reason. It didn't used to be like this and it's gotten to me."

She doesn't look at me as I come closer, close enough to touch her, but I don't.

"I did drink with clients, but that's it. I swear to you. I wouldn't touch that shit or anything like it."

She sets the clear glass down and then looks at me as she says, "Tony did." She walks past me, brushing her shoulder against mine.

"I quit for a reason," I tell her again and my tone begs her to listen. To forgive me. "I didn't do anything, and if anyone in the world would believe me, it would be you." My voice croaks on the last word and I have to swallow my plea.

"I believe you," Kat replies instantly, hating that she's causing me pain. This is why she's too good for me, but I'll be damned if I'm not going to do everything I can to keep her.

"No secrets?" she asks and there's a change in her expression.

I shake my head no, although I feel like a fucking coward. "No secrets."

"I have one," she whispers softly.

"What's that?" I ask her, sensing the air changing between us, darkening and chilling.

"I have a doctor's appointment tomorrow," she tells me and her eyes flicker to me, right before darting to the floor. She can't look at me and that makes me more nervous than anything else.

"The doctor's? Are you all right?" I ask her, my voice low, the memories of my mother filtering in. I take one step toward her and wait for her to move back, but she doesn't.

She shrugs and stares at the countertop.

"What's going on, Kat?" I ask her, listening to my heart beat hard then harder still as she makes me wait.

Her forehead scrunches the way it does just before she cries and I chance another step closer to her. I can feel the heat from her body as she sniffles and looks away from me.

"It's okay," I whisper. I reach out to her, praying she lets me hold her, and she does. Her shoulders are stiff at first, but she gives in and I say a silent prayer, thanking God for it. Her soft curves are warm in my embrace and I'm quick to kiss the crown of her head. The smell of her shampoo and every little detail about her is comforting. This is my drug. She's my only addiction.

"Baby, it's okay," I tell her as I pull her small body snugger into my arms. I needed this. I hold her as close as I can, rocking her slightly and loving how she grips me right back.

I hold her like I have for years, and it feels so natural. So right.

"Just tell me what it is, sweetheart," I whisper in her hair as she sobs into my chest. It hurts. Every bit of her sadness shreds me. "I'm sorry," I tell her and pull back to look at her, but she just buries her face back into my chest.

It's a long moment before Kat quietly pulls away.

"I have something you should see," she says and walks off. She wraps her arms around her torso as I follow her toward the stairs.

Anxiousness suffocates me, not knowing what it is she wants to show me.

"Stay here," she tells me, looking over her shoulder as she grips the railing.

I nod and watch her walk upstairs alone. She takes slow steps the entire way. Her bare feet pad softly on the floor as she leaves me.

I wait with bated breath. My body begs me to sit, the exhaustion making me want to give in and fall onto the couch. But I remain standing.

In the silence all I can think about is the shattered window, the fact that someone broke in. If they didn't take anything, maybe they left something behind instead. Whatever it is, a picture of some shit I did, a text or a letter—I don't care what it is that's making her so damn upset. I'll fix it.

I won't let her go, and I'll destroy anyone and everyone who gets between us.

My head lifts when I hear her coming down the stairs, and my feet move of their own accord.

They don't move for long, though. The second my eyes land on the white plastic stick in her hands, my body freezes.

My mouth hangs open slightly as I glance from the pregnancy test to Kat's face.

She stops in front of me, barely looking at me and holds it out. "I'm sorry," she whispers in a cracked voice. As if this is bad. As if she's done something wrong.

"Baby, why are you sorry?" I look between her and the stick. I can't will myself to take it or to even believe it's real. "You're pregnant?" I ask her. She covers her mouth with her hand and nods.

A baby. A little life just like my Kat. Tears prick at the back of my eyes.

It's the best damn thing I could have ever asked for.

And then it hits me. *Jacob Scott.* I looked into him after that … 'meeting' we had. My breathing picks up as my blood heats. I don't have the nerve to ask her, but the words are on the tip of my tongue.

I'll kill him.

"I'm pregnant," Kat says and draws in a steadying breath, taking a few steps backward.

I almost ask her, but I can't do it. Even if the baby isn't mine, I don't care. I'll take care of both Kat and her child.

"A baby?" A swarm of emotions courses through me. "This is why you're going to the doctor's?"

"Yeah, a baby," she says and chances a look up at me. Her long, dark lashes glisten with what's left of the tears before she wipes them away.

"That's wonderful," I tell her and close the distance between us, reaching for her hands. She leans into me and I rub the pads of my thumbs against her knuckles. "Kat, why are you sorry about something so amazing? Don't be sorry; I'm so happy."

I can see her expression fall as she tries to stay strong.

"It doesn't change what's going on, but I just found out and I don't know."

"Don't know what?" A numbness creeps up the back of my legs.

"How we're going to handle all of this," she says and starts to pull away from me.

"Kat, you're mine," I tell her.

"You were just in jail hours ago and we're separated. How are you going to take care of your baby?"

"I'll be the best damn father I can be." *Thump, thump.* My heartbeat slows as what she's saying settles in.

"You said that about being a husband too and—"

"And we're going to be fine," I say, cutting her off. "Better than fine. We're having a baby."

I finally look at her stomach. I wrap one of my hands around her hip while the other splays against Kat's belly.

"I love you, and that's what matters."

"It's not the only thing that matters," she tells me back.

Her emerald eyes swirl with so much emotion, I can't stand it. "I'm telling you right now, Kat. Me loving you is the only thing that matters."

chapter 5

Kat

I DON'T KNOW WHAT TO THINK OR DO.

I don't know what's right and wrong.

But I'm so aware of how I feel.

Every inch of my skin burns with need against Evan's touch. He's got a hold over me that's like a spell. It must be some kind of dark magic because he makes me forget reason. He makes me forget how angry I am at him.

I melt into him as if I was meant to be held by him from the very start.

The worst part is that I don't want him to ever let me go. Because the second he does, I'll remember. Reality will intrude, and the moment will be ruined.

One of these times, I'll let him go and never be held again. I can feel it down in my very soul.

His hot breath tickles my neck as he whispers, "I love you, Kat."

My soul quiets, the pain soothed. For the moment, I grip him just as tightly as he holds me.

My heart clenches in my chest as I swallow the lump in my throat.

"I'm so happy," he murmurs as he brushes his hand against my belly. "We're going to have a baby," he says reverently.

How can I not fall back into his arms when I know he loves me? How can I not cling to him when he talks to me like this?

I'm exhausted and wretchedly weak. Nothing feels better than this.

Every reason this is a bad idea comes to me one by one, the truth too real to ignore. I don't know if the extreme swings of my emotions are from the pregnancy, or from the craziness of Evan's life.

My nails scrape against his shirt as I push away from him. "We need to talk." I push out the words as he reluctantly watches me move away.

"If we do this, we're moving forward together?"

He nods and says, "I promise."

"I just want to be with you, Evan," I speak from the bottom of my heart and I know it's the bottom because it's all I have left.

"I promise," he says again but his eyes are glossy.

"I'm sorry I wasn't the man I should have been for you." He takes my hand and kisses my knuckles one by one before turning it over to kiss my wrist. "I'm sorry I fucked things up so badly." He doesn't meet my gaze and I can't stand the look in his eyes.

"It's okay," I tell him, desperate to take the hurt away from his expression.

"I love you, and that's what matters," he tells me again. "Don't stop loving me. Please. No matter what happens," he begs me.

"You didn't do anything," I tell him, grateful he's finally told me the truth. I get it now; it all makes sense. "Nothing will happen."

He looks me in the eye and says, "Nothing bad will ever happen to you or this baby. I swear, Kat."

"Our baby," I whisper and put his hand on my belly. He lowers his head and I swear I think he's crying, but when he looks up at me, he says, "Nothing bad will ever happen to you or our baby. I'll never put you in harm's way, Kat." He takes a deep breath.

"Just don't stop loving me," he says, almost like a plea.

"Don't stop loving me," I tell him back and he says beneath his breath, "It's all for you. I won't let anyone hurt you."

"Evan," I start to say as I reach for him, feeling the intensity of his words and the chill that comes with it. But as my lips part, a startled yelp comes out. Evan's strong arms wrap around my waist and pull me to his chest as he carries me up the steps to our bedroom.

He sets me down gently on the bed, which is so at odds with how he kisses me. It's ravenous, reckless even. Desire scorches my skin and makes my core unbearably hot.

He groans into my mouth as his hands slip between my thighs and under my panties. He runs his fingers up and down my hard clit.

"So fucking wet," he says, his eyes darkening with lust. "I love how you're always wet for me."

"Always," I say, echoing him, but my head feels dizzy and the need for him to be inside me overrides any sort of logic or reason.

I claw at his shirt, desperate to get it off and it makes him chuckle, a deep, low sound.

I want to scold him for taking so long and leaving me wanting, but the words stick in my throat as I watch him pull his shirt over his shoulders, revealing his tanned, tattooed skin and lean physique.

I lick my lips with the need to kiss him and he grants me exactly that. Bracing one forearm by my head, he leans down to kiss me, pressing his lush lips against mine and tasting me with swift strokes of his tongue as my eyes shut. He traps my bottom lip between his teeth and pulls back as he pushes his jeans down.

It's a short, sharp pain that spikes through my body, directly connected to my clit. When I open my eyes, letting the sweet gasp of longing escape, I'm lost in his gaze. Trapped by his gaze and waiting for him. I'd do anything for him. I swear there's no way I could love him more than in this moment.

"Evan, please," I say, ready to plead with him not to leave me again. Not to make me choose between a life without him or a life without shame, but he cuts me off, mistaking my plea for what my body feels and not my heart.

"Spread your legs for me." He gives me the command and my body obeys before I can even fully register his words.

Every thrust is slow and deep. The air between our lips heats until I arch my neck with a moan, feeling his thick cock push fully inside me, wanting more of me than I can give.

"Evan," I moan, saying his name reverently as my hardened nipples brush against his chest and he groans into my neck, holding himself still inside me.

"I love you," he whispers and then pulls out slowly. My body relaxes thinking he's keeping a slow pace, pulling himself nearly all the way out before pushing back in. But instead he slams himself into me all the way to the hilt and I scream out, my blunt nails digging into his muscular shoulders as pleasure races through me.

"I'll never stop loving you," he says as he pounds into me again, his hips crashing against mine.

"Evan." His name slips from between my lips as my head presses against the pillow and thrashes from side to side. It feels too intense. Way too much for so soon. My breathing picks up as my toes curl and my legs wrap around his hips.

He rocks himself against me, his rough pubic hair brushing against my throbbing clit and I writhe under him, feeling my skin prick slowly with the need for just a little more. I can hardly breathe. "Evan," I moan and again it comes out as a strangled plea.

"Kat," Evan says then nips my earlobe, sending a shudder through my body, "never forget that I would do anything for you. Everything is for you."

Evan

I T FEELS COLDER THAN USUAL AS I MAKE MY WAY DOWN THE SIDEWALK. It's empty and silent, with not a soul in sight. Not even down the alleyways or in the dark shadows. Someone's always there. Always watching and waiting.

But not tonight.

The light snow crunches beneath my booted feet and fog fills my vision with each step I take to get home.

The streetlight outside the townhouse flickers and catches my attention.

Darkness sets in just as I walk up the stairs and open the door.

It's so quiet and my first thought is that I'm grateful she isn't crying anymore. Ever since I told her the truth, Kat hasn't been the same.

She looks at me the way I've always looked at myself. She's always sad now, with red-rimmed eyes and an expression of shame blanketing her beautiful face, and it's all because of me. I ruined her like I knew I would.

I call out to her in the townhouse. It's the same as it's always been, but there's an emptiness to it. A hollow feeling that emanates from the white walls and seeps into my bones.

"Kat!" I call out again, and my voice echoes.

My boots crunch although there's no snow.

My breathing picks up and again fog clouds my vision as I walk toward the kitchen. "Kat." I say her name, but I already know she can't hear me.

The white mist fades and suddenly I see her. Just as she was yesterday, she's balled up on the floor, but she's not crying anymore.

Crimson red has stained her clothes.

"Kat?" Her name slips from me in disbelief as tears flow freely and I run to her.

"No!" I scream as her limp body lies on the floor and her eyes stare back at me, lifeless, but still rimmed in red.

Praying for God to take it back, I cradle her, rocking her and screaming for it not to be true. A note falls and flutters to the floor with an elegance I hate in this moment. I can't let go of Kat; I grip her tighter, reading the words as the ink on the paper appears slowly. The script is feminine and delicate.

You should have let me go. You should have protected me.

It's all your fault.

And then I hear a baby scream.

My eyes shoot open with terror, a cold sweat clinging to every inch of me. My body's stiff and hot as my heart races, pounding in my chest like a war drum. My pulse is heavy, hard, and unforgiving. *It's just a nightmare.*

"Kat," I say just beneath my breath, attempting to hide the fear before moving suddenly, shaking the bed as I put my arm around her.

It's the soft moan from her sleep that keeps me from waking her.

My heart still races in my chest as she breathes easily beside me.

As if nothing's wrong. Like nothing's happened.

My body trembles, refusing to let go of the visions. I blink away the sleep and fright as the early morning light streams into the room. The white noise of city traffic drowns out the gentle and steady sounds of Kat's breathing.

My body's heavy as I lie back in the bed, wiping the sweat from my brow and trying to forget the look on her face as I held her in my arms in the nightmare.

It's hard to swallow, the fear nearly crippling.

It's not real, I whisper. But I know with everything in me it's so much more.

Time ticks by slowly and sleep doesn't come again for me.

I didn't lie just once last night. I lied twice.

The need to be with her made me do it. The need to hold on to her love and let her feel how much I love her. I had to take away her pain. It only makes today that much harder.

There are two truths I know for certain.

1. Someone's trying to kill me and if they can't get me, they'll come for her.
2. But only if they know we're still together. Right now, no one does.

I love Kat too much.

I almost leave a note after going through my dresser drawer. There was nothing in there to take, but I made sure nothing was left behind or planted. The first thing I need to do is have a security system installed. This shit won't happen again and that's how I was going to start the note.

I wanted to write one for Kat saying goodbye and that I'll be back, then leave before she wakes.

She deserves to know why I'm leaving. Only for a little while. Only until I know she's safe.

"The doctor's appointment is at one I think," Kat says sleepily and I turn to face her slowly, my body stiff. My eyes burn from lack of sleep, but I don't care.

I welcome the pain.

"You're finally awake," I answer her and prepare myself for what I have to do. The world thinks we've broken up. And it has to stay that way.

"You've been up long?" she asks and then yawns. There's a slight radiance to her. Her hair forms a messy halo on the pillow and a delicate simper is on her lips.

"Kat." I say her name and swallow my words.

I've been thinking about them all morning, the images of the nightmare feeling more and more real. Every possibility of what could happen has been running on a loop in my mind.

"I have to tell you something." I stare at the dresser across the room. I look in the mirror but I can't see our reflection, only the closed door to the bedroom.

"It's only for a short time, but I have to go do something."

"What do you mean?" she asks, the sweetness she had for me vanishing far too quickly as she sits upright. She reaches out to me, her soft, small hand gripping my shoulder.

"I mean I don't think I can go to the appointment today."

Her expression falls and she visibly retreats, pulling her knees up to her chest and wrapping the comforter tightly around her.

"Why not?" she asks with a little heat in her words. With every second that passes, I can see her getting angrier. "What's more important?"

"I don't think we should be seen in public together," I tell her and swallow the painful lump in my throat. No one knows we're together or that she's pregnant. "This has to stay a secret."

"Are you serious?"

"Kat, I have to take care of some things."

"Bullshit! What about us?" she says and her voice cracks. "What about taking care of us?" She motions between us.

"I am," I tell her and my words come out strangled, shattering the delicate balance that was here only a moment ago.

"If you walk through that door, you're not coming back." Kat's voice shakes as she speaks. Her eyes are wide and the grief I feel is reflected in them. "You can't keep doing this to me. I can't keep …" she trails off and hiccups, on the verge of tears.

"It's only for a short while," I tell her to reassure her.

"I don't understand." Kat shakes her head as if she thinks I'm crazy. As if what I'm saying is incomprehensible and maybe it is, but it's okay. The less she knows, the safer she is. That's the only thing that matters.

"I have something I need to finish."

"You need to stop this, Evan. Please. I'm ready to move forward. We have a baby coming. Our baby. We can do this, but you can't keep going backward."

God, I wish she knew.

I could try to outrun it, but not with her by my side. I'll fight it and come back to her. I just need her to have faith. I know she will. The last thought is what moves me to put space between us.

"Just believe me when I say I love you, but I can't be with you right now."

A silent sob wracks through her body. "Stop it! Stop it, Evan. Please! I don't care what it is, just leave it behind and stay with me. Please, I'm begging you."

"I'm so sorry," I tell her and hate that I'm causing her pain.

"Why are you doing this?" she whispers. "I can't believe … I can't …"

"I love you, Kat, but I can't do this right now." The words come out as if I'm ending it with her, and that's when I realize it's what I have to do.

To protect her and our baby.

"I swear to God, if you walk out of that door, Evan, it's over. I'm done playing games. You're here or you're not." Her words are restrained as she says them, each one sounding more and more painful.

My chest tightens with an unbearable sorrow as I whisper, "I'm sorry, Kat."

chapter 7

Kat

WINTER HAPPENED OVERNIGHT. AND IT'S A BITTER ONE AT THAT. My hands are still freezing as I stare at the fire in Jules's great room. Her home has been painted and decorated since I was here only a week or so ago. Jules didn't waste any time making the space feel cozy and warm. The soft gray walls complement the cream furniture and stone fireplace perfectly. She said it's all in "mineral tones" although many of the accent colors are a dark, luxurious purple.

"I love the color," I tell her in an attempt to cheer myself up and break the awkwardness in the room. Usually when we get together it's nothing but laughter. My face can't hide that I've been a crying mess and so laughs have been hard to come by.

"It's called Mineral Ice," Jules says agreeably from her spot on the chenille rug. Her glass of wine hasn't moved from the coffee table since I walked in. Come to think of it, neither Maddie nor Sue are drinking either.

The only one who seems normal is Maddie, and it's because she's lost her mind. I only just texted them days ago with the news I'm pregnant and she's taken it upon herself to start planning every detail of the next nine months for me. I love her and the distraction, but there's no way I can even think about a baby shower right now. It's all up to her as far as I care.

"I think the grays and yellows will be perfect for a neutral theme," Maddie says. "We could do bees or elephants and it will all match this room perfectly."

Maddie has a few bags next to her on the floor. Each from different party shops with samples of all sorts of baby shower accessories and décor. In the group text earlier she said it was a "few" things to look at. Bless her heart, she's ever the optimist. I only wish I could steal some of her positivity.

It was Maddie's idea to meet up today, and thank God they dragged me here.

I'd rather be looking at tiny yellow clothespins and paper samples for invitations than hysterically crying on the floor in my bedroom. So, I suppose this is a win.

"Thank you for offering to host it, Jules," I say, pushing as much gratitude as I can into the words, but it still sounds lacking.

I'm not happy, and I just can't fake it. There's a hole in my chest and it feels like there's no way it could ever heal.

The father of my baby left me. Not just left me, but left me *again*. All I can think is that it's karma. I slept with him and kicked him out … and then he fucked me and left. This is exactly what I deserve.

I thought we were whole again last night; I felt it. Everything in me felt the love between us. And yet this morning he walked away. I must've been a horrible person in a former life.

"Okay, so menu …" Maddie says, leaning over the laptop that's on the glass coffee table and clicking the keys.

"Is it a little early to start planning all this in so much detail?"

Maddie stops fiddling with her laptop and looks up at me. "I thought maybe it would be a way to cheer you up a bit?" she says before sitting down on her butt right next to Jules. They're closer to the fire, sitting on the rug, and I'm wedged into the corner of the sofa. "If nothing else it's like window-shopping," she offers up.

"I don't think there's anything that's going to cheer me up," I answer her woefully. My hand drifts to my midsection, but there's not even a tiny bump. There's no way I'd know I was pregnant if I wasn't peeing on a stick every other day to prove that it's real.

"Do you … want to …" Maddie trails off as she struggles to suggest something else.

"Do you want to talk about what's going on?" Sue pipes up. "We can listen, you can vent. I could get a pillow and you can hit it?"

"I'm so fucked up right now …" I say and almost swallow the confession, but then I blurt it out, "that I'm actually considering starting to write letters again." I remember how I used to write to my mother when she died. It was what my therapist had suggested. "That's how low I feel," I tell them, emphasizing each word.

"You can tell us, you know?" Sue says and Jules nods in agreement. Maddie's soft gaze loses its ever-present happiness and all that's reflected in her expression is a sad smile.

"I'll probably cry too much to get it out," I respond and huff a sarcastic laugh to keep from completely losing it again. "I just wish someone could explain it. I feel crazy."

"Well, you're pregnant so you're allowed to be crazy," Maddie says as if that's a known fact and it actually makes me laugh. It's just a little bubble of one, but it's something at least.

"So let's have the complete update," Jules says and squares her shoulders as she gives me her full attention.

"It's over." The words come out easier than I thought they would. Maybe I'm just numb to them, I don't know.

"For real, for real?" Maddie asks me.

"Yeah, I'm not," I pause and shake my head then close my eyes. "I'm not doing this back and forth. I know where I want my life to go, I know what I need to do, and Evan just isn't there."

"Did you tell him you're pregnant?" Sue asks me cautiously.

"Yes." The single word nearly strangles me and I swallow down the pain that threatens me. "I told him, and he was so happy." I have to put my hand up to my mouth to keep from getting emotional again.

"I think it's okay if you cry," Sue says gently. "You're going through so much and you can always blame it on hormones."

A soft but genuine laugh sneaks in, shutting down the overwhelming heartache.

"I told him, and he still chose to leave."

"Why?"

"He didn't say," I tell them then correct myself. "No, he said," I try to quote him although I'm not sure if it's exact, "'I have to finish something, but it's only for a short while.'"

"What the heck does that mean?" Maddie asks with her face scrunched up.

"I don't know," I say, raising my voice in exasperation and that's exactly how I feel.

"Maybe he's worried about the stress from everything he's going through getting to you?" Sue suggests and I don't mean to, but I'm well aware that I stare daggers at her. "As if leaving me is any better?" I practically snap.

Her hands fly into the air defensively as she says, "I take it back. He's such an asshole."

"Here's your tea, sweetheart." Jules sits next to me on the plush sofa, holding out a cup for me. The steam itself is comforting. The seat sinks in slowly, dipping as she gets comfortable beside me.

"I'm still so happy you're pregnant," Maddie says, offering up a distraction as she leans forward and reaches for my hand, squeezing it gently. "You're going to be the best mom," she says with such certainty even though she looks so sad.

"Do you want one of us to go with you to your next doctor's appointment?" Sue asks, but I shake my head.

"I'll be fine."

"It's not about being fine, love," Sue says. "I could take pictures or something."

"Of her hoo-ha?" Maddie jokes and Sue rolls her eyes.

"Just to have someone there," Sue says.

"I would love to go with you," Jules says.

"I rescheduled the one I missed yesterday but it's not for a few weeks," I tell them, shrugging it off like it doesn't matter. Like I'm not worried my baby can feel my pain and that every night I cry alone in our bed I'm damaging this tiny life.

Like I'm already a horrible mother and all this shit is going to hurt my baby.

"They couldn't get you in sooner?"

"I told them I wasn't free until the end of the month. I just want to get my life together," I say and take in a calming breath. "I know what I want, and I'm going to go for it whether or not Evan is beside me." Picking at nonexistent fuzz on my sweater I add, "I'm going to need some time before I can … before I can be the kind of happy and grateful I want to be when I first see my baby … even if it is only a little blip on a screen."

"You deserve happiness," Maddie says and the other girls nod.

"Instead of the appointment, I watched a bunch of men I don't know install a security system and fix a window."

"A window?" Maddie asks and Sue tilts her head in confusion that matches Jules's furrowed brow.

Huffing out a breath, I decide not to elaborate on that. "I wish Evan would stop living like he's twenty-one and doing stupid things … like leaving me."

"I can't imagine him walking away when he knows you're pregnant," Sue says although I'm not sure it was intended for me. She stares absently at the roaring fire, the crackling filling the silence that follows her words.

"I think that's what hurts the most. It was so … When I told him, he was just so …" I have to pause and close my eyes. I remember the way he held me and kissed me, and it kills me.

"Hey now," Sue says. "You're going to be fine regardless. He's got a situation he's dealing with."

I roll my eyes at the word "situation."

"The fact that he has any *situation* is the problem." All of my frustration flies out of my mouth. "We should have our lives together. Stability and a family."

It's silent once I've finished. Maddie looks down at the rug and Jules has an expression of sympathy, although neither says anything.

"I agree," Sue responds gently after a moment.

"It's going to be okay," Maddie speaks up although she doesn't look at me, she just picks at the rug. She shrugs and says, "Being pregnant and single is like the new trend anyway."

I let out a little laugh, and it breaks up the tension. Maddie even smiles.

"Well, at least it's fashionable then." My hand moves to my belly subconsciously and a surge of strength eases my pain.

I can do this, and I deserve happiness. I'm worthy of that. If Evan doesn't think so, then he'll have to deal with the consequences.

"Forget him," I tell them. "If he wants to act like he's perpetually twenty-one, then he can do it alone."

I move a throw pillow to my lap and hold on to it.

"You're going to be fine regardless," Sue says, repeating her earlier sentiment.

"And we're going to throw you the best shower ever," Maddie adds, taking over the conversation again. Bringing it to happier topics.

"What theme do you want? The elephants or bees … or whatever else is in that bag?" Jules asks me as if it's all we should be talking about. I suppose it is. I'm done with Evan and this instability.

"I'll have to think about it," I answer and bury myself into the sofa. "Maybe when we know if it's a boy or a girl, then we can decide?" A light feeling seems to lift my shoulders like a weight is gone. Maybe it's the feeling you get when you're truly done with someone. When there's no way they can make it right again and you've come to accept it.

Maddie steers the conversation toward baby shower talk, and her voice is peppy as she says something about a Pinterest board.

My gaze falls on each of the girls in turn, all of them here for me. Jules catches my eye and rests her hand on my thigh, mouthing the words, "It's going to be okay."

For a short moment, maybe a second or two, I feel like it might.

Evan needs time to realize what it means to be the man I need.

Hopefully the time I need to get over him completely and stop falling for his charm is less than that. Because I can't do this again. I can't, and I won't.

Diary Entry One

Mom,

It's been a while.

I miss you guys, but you already know that. I could really use your advice now.

I know Evan loves me. I can feel it when he looks at me, but when he's not with me, I feel like he doesn't. I know I'm insecure, but he's been so weird lately. He's acting crazy and it scares me a little. You wouldn't like it.

I don't even want to tell you. I'm so ashamed.

It's that bad.

I know you never met him, but I swear he's a good guy. I know he is.

But the thing is, he's not doing good things.

The worst part is that he's not stopping.

He knows we're pregnant, and he's not stopping. It doesn't get much worse than that, does it?

I don't know what to do.

He wants me to wait for him and I love him so much.

But I'm scared, Mom.

I cry all the time. That can't be good for our little one.

I remember you crying when I was little and how you held me and sang lullabies to me. I'm trying that late at night. I hold my belly and try to sing lullabies instead of crying. I'm trying so hard, but I'm afraid I'm already failing.

I don't think I can be with someone who isn't willing to stop doing what he knows is wrong. It's not just me anymore.

But it gets worse.

I can't stop loving him. I don't know what's wrong with me, Mom. I could use your lullabies right now.

chapter 8

Evan

> *Threats can make you weak,*
> *To think of what's to come.*
> *To avoid seeing what's here and now,*
> *Living life as if you're numb.*
> *The lies are spinning webs,*
> *To trap and hold you still.*
> *The sinners hiding in plain sight,*
> *Hold your fate against your will.*

NEW YORK CITY IS A SIGHT THAT NEVER FAILS TO IMPRESS. IT'S A mix of things—the nightlife, the skyscrapers, the people themselves. But winter is when it's the most beautiful, I think.

Only the trees are wrapped with Christmas lights this early in November, but soon everything will be covered in white and blue lights. The shop windows in Rockefeller Center will be decorated with luxe details and high-end staging, and people will come from around the world to see it.

It's stunning, but what's best about it, is the crowds. During the winter months, this block is constantly packed. That's exactly what I need right now.

I need to remove one of my gloves to turn on my phone and check the messages. My foot taps on the hard cobblestone beneath my feet as I wait on an iron bench.

The phone goes off in my hand and I stare at the message from my father.

Just a bit overworked because of my dumbass son.

Are you sure you're all right? I ask him and ignore the insult.

I'm fine.

If you went to the hospital, I text him, *it must've been bad.* On the subway here, I got the message from my father that he was being released. He said he felt light-headed in the grocery store and the manager called an ambulance. He said they were just being dramatic, but I know my father. He's stubborn and hates hospitals.

I'm fine. Go make it right with your wife, he tells me, and I have to tear my eyes away from the phone.

I'm trying.

I hesitate to tell him, but the heat flowing through my veins begs me to text my father. *She's pregnant.* I can't help it. I'm so fucking proud. Like I did something amazing for the first time in my life.

His response is immediate.

Thank God. Now she has to forgive you, right? he texts back, and I let a small chuckle escape.

I wish it were that easy. *That's not how it works, Pops.*

He messages back, *It's Pop-Pop now. I'm so happy for you two. You better make it right with her.*

My phone pings again and this time it's not my father, it's the person I've been waiting for. *I'm here.*

A few children shriek with laughter as they run by me and I lift my eyes, watching them chase each other. That's when I see her. Samantha.

I shove the phone in my pocket, stand up and put my glove back on, then shove my hands into my coat pockets as I walk toward her.

"Thank you for meeting me." Sam greets me with bright red cheeks that match the tip of her nose. Her hair's been blown around her face by the wind, even though she has on a white cable knit beanie and a matching scarf. She slips her phone into her fur-trimmed jacket and declares, "I feel like I'm being paranoid."

I don't want to be here any longer than I have to. The only reason I agreed is because I have questions as to who could have broken in and if she has a lead on anything at all. I've got nothing and no one. There's not a soul in the industry I'd trust with this information, sure as hell not with the cops on my ass for murder. "Tell me what's going on."

"James messaged me and said what happened to Tony could happen to me. He told me to lay off the demands for the divorce." Her bottom lip quivers and again she glances over her shoulder.

"As in … an overdose?"

"I don't know." She takes a deep breath and looks to her left and right as her face crumples. "I think … I think he was threatening to kill me."

Anger threads itself through me as the woman in front of me breaks down. "Are you all right?" She shakes her head.

"No," she says and her voice cracks. "He didn't really kill him, did he?"

"The coke was laced with enough fentanyl to kill an elephant and the cops are convinced it was intentional," I tell her.

"I would say I don't think James is capable of that," Sam murmurs with sad eyes. As she speaks, her breath turns to fog. "But he's done things before …"

"Things like what?"

"He's choked me, thrown me against the wall. He's threatened me in the past. But he's never …" Her eyes become glossy as she says, "I didn't think he would ever do it."

"You think he killed Tony? Do you think the threat was a real one?"

She nods her head once, a frown marring her face as she gets choked up. "He said it was for you," she speaks softly, her eyes flicking from me to the cars passing behind us. The chill of the breeze bites down to my bones as her words sink in.

It was James, and the coke was intended to kill me, not his client.

I don't give her a response in the least, hiding the anger as my heart thuds hard in my chest at the confirmation of what I already suspected.

"What did I do?" I ask her.

"It's because of me," she says and her voice cracks.

"You didn't do this."

"You don't understand," she says, gaining more composure and wiping under her eyes as the wind whips between us and forces her hair behind her. "He wants me to give him everything in the divorce. The properties, our investments, the business, he's not budging on any of it."

"I thought it was finalized?"

She shakes her head and says, "I pushed back." Her words come out hard. "He's pushed me around for so long and he thought he could just get rid of me and throw me away like he did his first wife. But I made the company what it is today."

"So why go after me?"

"To prove a point."

"And what point is that?" I ask her.

"That he could eliminate whomever he wants."

Anger narrows my gaze as I tell her, "He missed his shot."

"He'll do it again," she says, "and I'm scared."

"It'll be all right," I tell her although I'm not sure it will be. I'm already trying to figure out how to end this. All roads lead back to James and the only thing I need to know is the fastest and safest way to put that asshole six feet in the ground.

"Please help me, Evan," she begs, and her voice is rife with agony. "I don't know where to go or what to do."

"The police," I tell her and it's the first time in my life I've ever thought of going to them. "You can tell them everything. Tell them he threatened you with that."

"He has them in his back pocket," she says bitterly then adds, "You know that. Did they tell you anything?"

I shake my head and say, "Only that the coke was laced enough to kill. It was made into a murder weapon."

"Oh, God," Samantha says then lets out a gasp and hunches forward slightly. I feel the need to put my arm out to steady her and she clings to me.

A moment passes in the wintry cold, where I think back to a few times we've gotten out of tight spaces. I thought a client here and there would go to trial, but they never did. I didn't think it was because of James, though. I thought they didn't have enough evidence.

"He'll go down for what he did," I assure her as one name and one face come to mind. Mason. Jules's husband. He's gotten off for murder, just last month. There's more corruption in this city than there are tourists. Mason knows it as much as I do and I can trust him.

He killed his father, and everyone knows it. Well, the whispers in certain circles are sure of it.

He's from a different world than me, but I know him from back in the day. Back when both of us were a little too eager to cut loose. I helped him out back then and never called in the favor I'm owed. I haven't spoken to him since I split up a fight a few months ago.

He owes me for that too. And Mason's the type of man who pays his dues.

"What are you going to do?" she asks. Samantha scoots closer to me, almost too close, and I take a step back.

"I know a guy," I tell her and she's quick to nod, but then her face falls.

"Shit," she whispers, her eyes focused on something behind me and I whip my head around to see what she's looking at.

"It was him," she says then covers her mouth. "Shit," she repeats with tears in her eyes.

"He can't hurt you." I turn around and keep an arm behind me to protect her. My eyes search the crowd, but I don't see him.

Her hands tug at my arm, pulling me back to her. Her bright red lips glisten as she licks them and tells me, "He went down to the subway, but he saw us. I know he did. At least I think he did," she says then closes her eyes tightly and takes a step back. "It was definitely him."

"Is he following you?" Her eyes are still on the subway entrance and her body's still as she holds her breath.

"I don't know." Her bright blue gaze flickers to mine as she says, "I'm scared, Evan."

"You should go to the cops, Sam—" I start to tell her she needs to protect herself, and if she doesn't trust the cops she can always hire private security, but she cuts me off.

"It's not me. I'm not worried about me. If he thinks you know, you're not safe."

"I don't care what he thinks. Or what he thinks I know." I stare into her eyes as I tell her, "I'll kill him before he touches either one of us again."

Kat

H

E KNOWS WHAT HE'S DOING.

Jacob Scott.

Coffee? I could use some advice. I reread the message as I sit in a booth at the back of the coffee shop we met at last time.

His place, not mine. The thought makes me huff sarcastically.

My blood rings with guilt and regret. Even as I sit here, looking from my cup of chamomile tea to the entrance of the shop as the bell hanging above the front door rings, granting entry to temptation himself.

I should tell Jacob I'm pregnant. That I'm not at all ready to think about moving on, although I wish I were after the weeks of hell and on-again, off-again hardships Evan and I have been through. I should tell Jacob no. I should tell him sorry for not telling him sooner.

But I don't do any of that.

I give him a small wave and force my smile to stay put as he walks over to me. His shoulders shiver and I can feel the faint chill of the November air flow through the shop.

"I'm so glad you could come," Jacob says, greeting me with a smile, shrugging his jacket off his shoulders. I offer a smile in return as I see the waitress approach, carrying the cup of chai I bought for him.

"You have good timing," I tell him, biting the inside of my cheek and knowing I'm playing with fire. "Now I don't owe you."

A genuine chuckle fills the space between us as he's given his drink.

"Touché, Kat," he says, accepting it and thanking the barista.

I mouth thanks to her as she turns. She's sweet and young, but I don't miss how her gaze trails to my ring finger, then to his. She keeps her smile in place, but it doesn't reach her eyes.

My heart stutters and I wish I'd taken my wedding ring off. I wish I could solidify the separation as easily as Evan walked out on me.

"You okay?" Jake asks and grabs my attention again.

"Yeah." I force a smile to my lips. The singular word was spoken tightly, so I pick up the tea to take a sip.

I clear my throat and try to shake off the unwanted feelings. "Do you want a muffin?" I ask him absently. "Or a cookie?"

I read last night about all the foods you should and shouldn't eat when you're pregnant. Oatmeal seems to be a winner, so the thought of having an oatmeal raisin cookie or two sounds like a win to me.

"A cookie?" Jake smirks and I almost tell him why. But I don't. I gesture to the display cases; I can't be the only one who smells all the baked goods.

"You got the drinks, let me get the snacks."

"Oatmeal raisin?" I ask him and he nods with another smirk before tapping on the table and making his way to the counter.

I stare down at my not-so-big-yet belly and feel slightly guilty. An onlooker may think I look bloated. There's zero evidence I'm pregnant at all. Other than the box of pregnancy tests. I've taken four of them now, just to make sure the pink line turns darker each time.

At least I'm not crying and wallowing in despair. I'm simply crazy with worry. My hand gently rubs my belly.

"At least I have you," I whisper in a sweet, sorrowful voice as I rest my hand on my lower belly. I want a doctor to tell me it's real. That I really do get to have a baby. This little one who will love me, and I can love them back and give them every part of me.

As I take another sip of the tea, watching Jake at the counter, I start to think that maybe it was supposed to be this way. Maybe I don't have enough in me to love both a child and my husband. God must've known it and that's why Evan left me.

I nod my head before pulling the mug back to my lips quickly to hide my face from Jake. There's a reason for everything, isn't there?

He sits down slowly, and I know he saw; I can see it in his eyes.

"Sorry," I say and shrug. "I read this manuscript earlier and it shredded me," I lie.

He hands me my cookie and I feel foolish for a moment, but then he says, "Really?"

I nod like a fool.

"You want to talk about it?" he asks, and I get the impression that I could tell him anything. I think I could tell him the truth right now and he'd know it's exactly that. I could spill my guts to him and say it's all something I read in a book. And he'd let me. He'd give me that bit of kindness.

I'm so grateful for it.

But I'm not ready.

I shake my head, my hair spilling over my shoulders as I do. "Maybe another time."

He nods, peeling back his muffin wrapper enough so he can take a bite. "Good thinking," he says after he swallows. "Very good call on the muffin."

My shoulders rock gently with another small laugh as I take a bite of my cookie, once again feeling the ease that Jake gives me.

"It's okay to not be okay, do you know that?" he asks me.

I snicker and pick at the cookie.

"You can roll your eyes and laugh, but it's true," he says as he peels at the wrapper, exposing more of the treat as he talks.

"If I'm not okay, though, that means I need to talk about it." I point my finger at him and pick off another small piece of the cookie. "And I don't want to," I say smartly and pop the bit into my mouth.

"Nah, you can be not okay, but talk about something else instead. That's a thing, you know?"

"How's that?"

"It's okay to let something bother you, that's all I mean."

"You authors speak in code, do *you* know that?" I use his phrase right back at him.

Now he's the one who laughs. "Well, I guess what I'm saying is that I'm not really okay. I'm sort of running from my own problems. But now I'm okay, 'cause I'm here."

"Here in New York?"

"Just here," he says and gives me a small smile, but I read the real answer in his expression. *Here with you.*

"So, what are you running from?"

"Are we sharing stories?" he asks me in return.

"I'm not sure how much sharing I'm willing to do," I tell him honestly.

"You afraid you'll wind up in a book of mine?" he asks with a sly smile then adds, "One second, before you start I just want to grab my pen and paper."

He acts like he's reaching for an imaginary bag on the floor and I let out a loud laugh, then cover my mouth with both my hands as a lady looks up from her phone at me with a pissed-off expression from across the room.

Jake likes the laugh, though. Enough that he smiles widely as he settles back into his seat.

"You don't have to tell me anything. I just want you to know that you can be not okay around me. I get it. Some days I'm not the best, and it's nice to just go out and get a chai … and a muffin."

"Like today?" I ask him.

"Yeah, like today."

"I have a hard time getting a read on you, Jake," I tell him.

"What do you want to know?" he asks me.

"What do you want from me?" I ask him then immediately regret the blunt question. It's rude and risks losing him and the only distraction I really have.

"Just company, until you want more," he says with his dark green, hazel eyes staring straight into mine as they heat.

"I don't know that I'll want more, though."

"I think you lie, Kat. I think you already know you want more."

"It's only because I'm lonely." The words slip out and I hate that they're true, but a weight is lifted with my confession. I expect Jake to react negatively. Maybe to be angry or offended, but instead, he nods his head.

"Yeah, I know. I am too."

"Sometimes I do stupid, reckless things when I'm lonely."

"Well, if you ever want to be lonely together, I'm free."

I should feel guilty about how Jake makes me feel.

Wanted, appreciated, like he doesn't want to lose me.

It's foolish to entertain what's between us. But I feel so rejected. My husband doesn't want me and yet Jake does. Even if it's only because I'm the only person in the entire state who he knows.

We can be just friends.

At least I can pretend we can, for a little while. Or what did Evan call it? *A short while.*

Diary Entry Two

Hey Mom,

I have a secret to tell you. Do you remember how I told you about Markie in middle school? He's the one who was in Mrs. Schaffer's math class. He had a crush on me and passed me that note. It wasn't important really and I doubt you remember. But I had this feeling back then and I kind of have it now.

It's weird and it's mixed with all sorts of other things.

Obviously, I shouldn't see him, and I shouldn't even be considering talking to this guy, but I've been crying almost every night for so long. I started playing sad movies on the television at night, so I could blame it on that. I know I'm lying, but I'm so tired of crying.

I'm exhausted, Mom, and this guy gives me something else to think about.

It's wrong, isn't it?

I don't even have to ask you to know that it is.

I'm using this man, and I'm still married to Evan. My heart is still waiting for him, even though he's given me every reason to stay away from him for good.

Maybe I'm a bad person. Maybe I deserve all this.

I don't know. Could you tell me, please? You used to give me little signs. I know they were from you. I could use one now.

I don't know what's going to happen and I'm really tired. I'm ready for change and some sanity. The exhaustion is probably from a mix of what's going on with Evan and the pregnancy.

It's wonderful that we're having a baby, isn't it?

See how I changed subjects there? I hope that made you laugh.

I'm so grateful for this baby and I want to feel happy, Mom.

But my life isn't okay and I kind of hate myself right now.

This guy, Jake, changes that. Does that make it better?

Please tell me it does, because I want it all to be okay for the baby. Not the mess that it is.

I know it can't last, but maybe just for a little while?

chapter 10

Evan

"It's been a while," Mason says as I sit down at the booth in the back of the restaurant.

"I saw you just a few weeks ago," I point out to him.

"Not what I meant," he says, correcting me. "It's been a while since the two of us have been up to no good."

That comment pulls my lips up into an asymmetric smile and he follows suit with a wicked grin. "And how do you know that's what I'm here for?" I used to buy some good shit through Mason and vice versa. I came from the poor part of town, and he was from the rich. The only real difference that makes is which drugs you're doing. Pot or snow.

And if you want a taste of the other, all you need to do is make friends with the right people. Long story short, that's how I met Mason and as I moved into his circle, he made a spot for me when I needed one. When he got into trouble, I got him out. It was years ago, but a pact like that never dies.

Mason shrugs at my question. "I'm going to take a guess and say that whatever you want from me, it's something I could go to jail for."

I huff a sarcastic laugh and toss my phone down on the white tablecloth, then glance around casually to make sure I don't recognize anyone. The place is mostly empty, with only a few guys at the bar and a couple in the corner of the diner.

"Are we good if that's the case?" I ask him.

"We're good," Mason answers. "I have to say, considering what's going on, I'm intrigued."

"Intrigued is a word for it, I guess."

The waitress saunters over with a beer, setting it down with a smile and I thank her, although I didn't order it.

"I got you an IPA, seasonal."

"Thanks, man," I tell him gratefully, but I don't touch the tall glass sitting right in front of me. I take off my coat and hang it over the unused chair to my left as the waitress pulls out her notepad and a pen. She's a skinny little thing, which makes her look even younger than she probably is.

"Welcome to Murray's," she says evenly. Her top's unbuttoned a little too much and the way a blush colors her cheeks as she looks at us makes what she's thinking more than obvious.

"Can I get you guys anything?" She bites down on her lip and Mason raises a brow at me.

"Not me," I tell him and lean back in my seat, not looking back at the broad and risking leading her on.

He waves her off politely. "We'll just grab the drinks from the bar," he tells her and her smile falls. She seems to falter, and she clears her throat.

"Sure, if you need anything …" she says and shrugs, "just let me know."

"So, how you been?" I ask him as the pretty little blonde walks off.

"Better now," he tells me.

"I'm sorry to hear about your father."

He readjusts in his seat, making it groan, and looks away as he takes a long swig of his beer.

"I know it's got to suck either way." I choose my words carefully. Word is Mason killed him. Shot him dead. Still, it's his father and I don't know for a fact that Mason really wanted him gone. There was tension between them and rumors they were at odds, but I don't have a firm grasp on the truth when it comes to that situation.

"Yeah," he says without looking me in the eyes. "Thanks, but let's cut the small talk. It's not often I get a call from you."

I nod and crack my knuckles one by one with my thumb as I look out the window, scanning the streets. "I think I need to hire someone," I tell him.

"You're going to need to be a little more specific than that," he replies.

"There's a guy," I say then pause and lean in closer, resting my elbow on the table and moving my hand so that my fingers cover my mouth as I talk. Just in case someone's watching and trying to lip-read.

"He tried to kill me." I blurt out my theory. "Tony wasn't supposed to die. It was meant for me."

"You're still doing coke?" he asks as he eyes me then takes a drink from his glass.

"Not in years, but he didn't know that. It would hurt my reputation if the clients thought I was clean, you know?"

"That's what I thought. I was just asking 'cause that means whoever went for you doesn't really know you."

"I think it's my boss."

"Wouldn't he know?" he questions and for a moment a tinge of insecurity washes over me.

"He never really asked. He doesn't ask any questions so long as the clients are happy."

"All right." He tilts his head slightly and lowers his voice. "So, why does he want you dead?" Mason asks.

"It was years ago," I start to tell him and feel sick to my stomach. "I fucked his wife. Before I married Kat."

Mason's eyes assess me as if he's trying to figure out if I'm lying.

"I've never cheated on her," I say, talking louder than I should and in response to my raised voice, Mason looks to his right.

I lick my lips and calm my racing heart.

"He wants to scare her, so he went after me to prove what he could do to her. That no one's safe from him."

"But you gave Tony the blow?"

I nod my head once, the memory of his dead eyes looking through me flashing in front of me and sending a chill down my spine. "With the stuff James left in the room for me."

"So, your boss, James? You want him dead? You want to prove he did it, frame him, what do you want?"

"You have a fucking menu?" I joke with him to lessen the tension in my body.

An asymmetrical grin forms on his face.

"I don't do anything. I'm not involved in any of the process."

My body feels heavier with his words.

"Doesn't mean I don't still have connections," he adds and I nod. "So, for a friend, what is it that you want?"

"Three things," I tell him. "First, your lawyer."

"That's a given. He's already on retainer in case they take you in again."

"Second, someone to watch Kat. I need her safe."

"Is he after her?"

"He might know that I know, and I can't risk her safety." He merely nods and I add, "I can't lose her. I'll fucking lose it, man."

"The safest place for her is distance. Well, anywhere fucking away from you."

"I know … I know."

"Good thing you're separated, huh?"

"She tell Jules that?" I ask him as dread races through my blood. Before I can tell him we're not, and that there's no way I'm leaving her, he laughs at me.

"Jules tells me everything. I know the papers got it wrong."

"I'm not leaving her; I'm just protecting her. There's a difference."

"If you want the world to think you're broken up," he says, "then you need to treat her like you are."

"I don't know if I can treat her like that. She's pregnant."

"I heard." He lifts his beer in a mock cheers. "Congrats on that, man ... but doesn't that make it even more important not to risk anything happening to her?"

"Don't make me feel worse than I already do." My words are bitter and my heart sinks. "How long's it going to take?" I ask him to get back to the point.

"To dig up dirt, plant evidence, figure out how to kill the guy ... it could be a while."

"I don't have a while," I bite back. "Every day is a day I have to put her through this."

"There are worse things you could do."

"I can't lose her," I tell him and he nods in understanding.

"I'll watch her myself," he offers and a small sense of peace relaxes me, but only a fraction of the way.

I rub my eyes with the back of my hand and finally pick up the beer on the table.

"If anything happens to her ..."

"Nothing's going to happen to her," he reassures me before asking, "What's the third thing?"

I look him in the eye and tell him, "I want him to go to jail for what he did. Whether you get real evidence or have to create some. And if that's not possible, I want James Lapour dead."

<h1 style="text-align:center">chapter 11</h1>

Kat

"I THOUGHT YOU WERE TAKING TIME OFF?"

I didn't even hear Sue come in. I glance at the clock in the upper right of my computer screen. It's already five o'clock and time for our dinner date. The girls are taking turns keeping me occupied. It's almost like they're babysitting me and if it was anyone else, I'd hate it.

But I can never turn down a date with Suzette.

"You of all people should know that working is all I'm good for." My voice comes out flat although I meant it to be funny. God, I'm tired. I'm always tired now even though I'm finally starting to sleep like the dead.

I guess the first trimester of pregnancy will do that to you.

"Oh honey, have you not looked at your shoe collection recently?" she asks, quirking a brow. "You're good for so much more than work."

I stand up slowly, feeling every muscle stretch with a sweet ache as I do and grin at her. "Ha-ha," I say sarcastically, but the smile on my lips is genuine.

"So, what place tonight?" she asks as she turns on a lamp in the corner and settles into the one comfy chair in the room… which isn't even the desk chair.

"Order in takeout, getting pretty and hitting the town?" she suggests then takes her scarf off and looks around the office.

She doesn't even give me a chance to answer her before practically scolding me. "Why the hell haven't you decorated this room?"

I shrug as I follow her gaze. I have a bookshelf in the back, but all the books are still in boxes on the floor.

"Just not a priority," I answer her honestly. "I look at the screen more than anything anyway."

"It's like your décor inspiration was a depressing cubicle."

I snort at her response, but it makes me laugh so hard.

"Maddie should focus on redecorating in here before planning a baby shower."

I don't think the remark was meant to be taken seriously, but I actually love the idea. "I should tell her. I'd like that."

Twisting the scarf around her hand, she crosses her legs. "I'm sure she'd love to."

"Well, actually. I totally forgot to tell you, but I may move in with Jules for a little while so Maddie could really go to town."

Cocking a brow at me, Sue leans forward with her mouth a bit more open than it should be before she says, "You sure you want to be around to hear them when they … enjoy their newlywed activities? I feel like that's the number one concern here."

I roll my eyes. "It was Mason's suggestion, so I'm sure he …" *Ugh.* The thought of them doing it in the room next to me is a thought I'd rather not picture.

"I get it," Sue says, sensing exactly what was on my mind. "You shouldn't be alone, though. Not when you have so many people who love you."

I shut down my computer and give her a tight smile. "That's basically what Jules said."

She adds, "Good. Because you're not alone, and there's no reason you should feel it right now."

Today's been so much better than the last few and Sue's sweetness threatens to change that. "Damn it, Sue, stop it," I admonish her and shake off the unwanted emotions as they creep up on me. "I'm fine."

"I know you are!" she says, pushing herself up from the seat. "And that's why we're going to go out and go somewhere fabulous."

My phone dings on the desk, indicating a text as I start to tell Sue that I don't really think I want to go out.

Holding back a yawn, I cautiously look at the message. I've had four texts today already. Each from a gossip column editor wanting a statement or my reaction to the recent events. Evan's been spotted with Samantha again and the rumor mill is churning with tales of scandal.

They can go screw themselves. I believe that was my response to each of the columnists. Probably not the best quote I've ever given. He promised he wouldn't see her. I guess I got my sign.

"You okay?" Sue asks, and I nod when I see it's a text from Henry this time.

He messages me almost every other day, which makes the fact that Evan hasn't bothered to call me back that much harder to take.

"Just Evan's dad. Wanting to drop by with some lemons."

"Lemons?" she questions.

"He said they helped Marie when she was pregnant and nauseated."

"But you aren't …" Sue trails off with a hint of confusion.

"I know!" I answer jokingly as I text Henry, *Thank you, but I'm fine. Really it's sweet of you but I'm not nauseated.* I wonder if I should ask him how Evan is. Where he is. Or anything at all.

Before I can, he answers that he wants to meet for lunch soon.

"You know, he's really sweet," I tell Sue, feeling guilty and torn about what to do.

"So, that's where his son got his charm from then?" Sue asks sarcastically then mouths she's sorry when she sees I'm not amused.

"I'll just tell him I will, but I can always bail," I reason out loud as if I need her approval.

"Yeah, that's a good way to handle it." She nods with pursed lips then looks me up and down. "You should probably put real clothes on."

"How fancy?" I ask her, setting the phone down as I realize I'm still in sweats and a baggy T-shirt.

"Let's go fancy, fancy." I hope she can see how the thought of getting prettied up makes me perk up. I could really use a night out, feeling beautiful and carefree. I'll just pretend I don't feel like falling asleep at the table.

"Fancy-pantsing it up tonight?" I ask, already feeling better than I did before she got here.

"You know it."

chapter 12

Evan

ALL I CAN FOCUS ON ARE HIS TELLS.

You learn them fast in the line of business that led me to this moment. The sweat on his brow. The way his right foot won't stay still. His dilated pupils and quick breathing.

He's one of two things: high as a fucking kite, or going through withdrawal.

Judging by the look on this prick's face, James Lapour is fiending for his next hit.

I peek over my shoulder. His office is on the first floor. There are apartments above us and plenty of witnesses in case some shit goes down. More importantly, just outside those doors is Mason, sitting in his car and waiting for me in case I need him.

I've got two goals in coming here like this.

1.   Warn him to back the fuck off.
2.   Get any evidence I can.

Seeing as how he's in his office, goal number two will have to wait unless I can get a confession. The tape recorder in my pocket is already running.

It takes everything in me to keep my hate down, but the memory of Kat from my night terrors is all I can see. I can't sleep; I can't do anything without thinking about losing her. It's as if my sanity is steadily eroding. Blinking away the image of her, I prepare to do what I have to. For her. For us. All I want is for this to be done and over with, so I can be with her and be the man meant to stand beside her.

I walk into the office, the wooden floor beneath my oxfords creaking eerily as I do. I've been standing outside the open door watching him for a few minutes. He didn't change the locks and there's no one else here on a late Wednesday night. Just him and me. Well, not quite, there are a few broads in the far back. I can hear them from here. Maybe they're waiting for him with exactly what he needs. I wouldn't be surprised.

"Taking a break from the snow?"

"What the fuck are you doing here?" he sneers at me, ripping his red-rimmed eyes away from the computer screen. With the city lights peeking through the drawn blinds, the room is bathed in a diffuse glow. It's darker than I'd like it to be in here with only the lamp on his desk illuminating the space.

"What I really want to know is, why?" The question leaves me coldly as I stalk closer to him.

"Why what?" he asks me, leaning back in his seat and I can faintly hear him pulling out a drawer, ever so slowly.

Racking the slide on the gun in my hand, I raise it slowly. "Uh, uh, uh," I reprimand him. It's been a long fucking time since I've aimed a gun at someone. I've never wanted to pull the trigger more, though. "I wouldn't do anything stupid if I were you."

He raises his hands slowly, cocking his head and letting out a sick laugh. "So, you here to kill me now? Is that it?"

"I should, shouldn't I?"

"For what, exactly? Spit it out, you coward," he scoffs at me. His eyes appear nearly black with the lack of light.

"I'm the coward?" The ridicule comes complete with an arched brow. I have to be careful with the loaded gun. My anger is putting me on edge, the adrenaline in my veins pumping hard and every second that passes makes my body temperature go up just a little more.

One of the girls from the back room yells out, "You all right in there?" in response to my raised voice.

Before I can respond, James answers her. "Just stay where you are." Good old James, he knows how to talk to the ladies.

"What do you want, Evan?" he questions, slowly placing his hands palm down on the desk.

His arm twitches and I can tell he's fucked up.

"What's going on with you?" I ask in return. "You're not looking so good."

"You look pretty fucked yourself," he spits out without wasting a second and forces a smile to his face.

"We saw you watching," I say, offering him a small piece of the puzzle.

"Watching what?"

"At Rockefeller Center."

"Is that so?" I hate this game. This back-and-forth where no real information is given. "And what exactly was I watching?" he asks with a smirk on his face although I can see in his eyes he's curious.

I shrug and say, "Doesn't matter, does it? What I want to know is what you plan on doing."

He laughs abruptly, deeply and from his gut, but any trace of happiness is immediately replaced with pain. He nearly doubles over and I raise the gun again, my heart beating hard as I prepare for him to come up with a weapon.

He doesn't, though, and when he sees the gun aimed right between his eyes, he forces his hands to the desk again.

"You stop doing coke? I guess Tony told you it was bad for you," I say flatly, swallowing thickly as my hands sweat and the gun feels heavier.

He groans an answer I can't hear then winces again.

"What the fuck is wrong with you? You got the shakes?"

"Fuck you," he manages to get out as his eyes shut.

"You paranoid now? Worried someone's going to do to you what you tried to do to me?"

He opens his eyes slowly, the light shining from the lamp creating shadows on his face. "The fuck are you talking about?"

"The coke you laced. You scared someone's going to do the same to you? Give you what you have coming?"

"It was from my personal stash, you prick."

I almost call him a liar, I almost tell him to shove it and put a bullet in his chest, so I can get back to Kat and end this shit. But the look on his face stops me.

He's always been a damn good liar. I know that much about him. But I'm better with tells.

He adds, "If I wanted you dead … well, I know how to use a gun."

"You want to know what I think?"

"Sure, you can say that I'm intrigued," he retorts.

"I think you're greedy," I tell him as I lower the gun.

"Greedy?" he repeats with a crooked smile.

"I think you wanted to prove a point to your wife." I lay it out there for him. I'm not messing around; I want this prick to know that I'm fully aware of what he's doing.

"That bitch has got nothing to do with this."

There's a skip in my pulse. With a slight cock of my head I ask, "Who does then?"

His mouth parts, but then slams shut a second later. "Fuck you."

"I won't stop until I find out everything. Until every bit of dirt I can get on you is dug up and exposed."

"You know how much shit I've got on you, Thompson?" He seems to find his strength as he leans forward on his desk.

"This is a warning to stay away. From me and Samantha." I almost bring up Kat. I almost say she's pregnant. Every ounce of my being craves to demand that my family's off-limits. But that would only give him that much more of a reason to hurt her. So I keep her name out of the conversation; I keep her safe.

I'll do anything for her. Anything and everything. Fear stirs in my blood at the thought of her being on his radar. It's gone as quickly as it came, eased by his next line of questioning.

"So, it's true then?" he asks with a snort. "You two are together?"

It takes me a moment before I realize he's talking about Samantha and referring to the rumors. "She came to me for help."

"I always knew she'd cross me. I didn't think you'd be the dick she picked to go down with her."

I raise the gun and take a step closer. "Give me one reason I shouldn't kill you right now. You and I both know you deserve it."

He shrugs. "I have the evidence that proves you lied to the cops, for one. I have evidence on both you assholes."

"A dead man can't do shit with evidence."

"The cops will find it, and you know it. You don't want them poking around in here."

"What are you doing back here, baby?" A high-pitched voice rings through the hallway and I look quickly over my shoulder. I hear the door open and James smiles.

"Oh yeah, there are two other reasons. In all the years I've known you, you've never put your hands on a woman. Well, other than Sam, I mean."

"Shut the fuck up," I say, gritting the words through my clenched teeth.

"Come on back, sweet cheeks!" he yells out. He's calling my bluff and I'm quick to lower the gun, hiding it behind my leg.

My heart beats slowly and I can see it all playing out. Killing this fucker and the two girls from the back room screaming, running. I can see the red and blue lights reflecting off the glass.

"Are you ready for us?" A young woman walks in, skinny as a rail with a sharp blond bob. It looks so perfectly straight, my guess is it's a wig.

The smell of perfume floods the room as she enters, swaying her hips and wearing light blue ripped shorts that ride up her ass.

Hookers.

"Let me just finish this conversation really quick," James tells her as the second girl walks in a bit behind the first. The blonde rounds the desk, peeking at me, but stalks toward James to perch on the corner of his desk.

"Whatever you want. I'm not in a rush."

"Hi there," a little brunette says. Her voice is softer, sweeter even, which matches her look. She's got a look that's more innocent, with clothes that actually cover her ass. She might sound sweet, but there's a devil in those baby blues of hers. Her eyes are bloodshot, and she can barely walk straight. She tries to lean against me but I take a step back, and when I do she sees my gun.

Her eyes widen, and she stumbles backward with a gasp. The two girls exchange a look while holding their breath, both on edge and realizing they shouldn't have walked back here.

"I was just on my way out," I reassure them. I tuck the gun back into the waistband of my jeans.

"I want to ask one question before you leave, Thompson," James says to my back as I turn away. "Wives aren't off-limits anymore, are they?" My blood rushes into my ears and I almost do it. I almost kill that fucker, consequences be damned.

"Ah, I see not all the rumors are true. Are they, Evan?"

"Leave her the fuck alone, James." My blood pumps hot as I stare into his beady eyes, but all he does is smile.

chapter 13

Kat

IT'S BEEN THREE DAYS NOW.

Evan hasn't come back or even texted. Just the thought makes my throat tight. My eyes are filled with sadness that I can't shake. A piece of me feels like it's mourning, but not ready to let go of hope.

I've texted and called, remembering how he said he loved me and this was only going to last for a short while. It was pathetic of me.

I'm lonely, emotional, pregnant. I was desperate to believe he still loved me.

The text was simple. *It's really hard without you. I'm sorry; I was wrong to give you an ultimatum. Please forgive me. I miss you and I really need you.* That's what being lonely does to me. It makes me weak and wish he'd just come back to me.

Brushing under my puffy eyes, I stare down at my phone. It's my raw heart and the very last pieces of the shattered thing that bring me down this low. I never heard anything back.

I thought it would get easier, but somehow Evan refusing to talk to me is making it harder. He doesn't return my calls, doesn't text back. Nothing. The only contact I have with him is an excerpt from the Page Six column quoting him as saying that we've split.

I remember how he said it was just for a "short while." Maybe that's how he got me. He left me with hope.

That fucking bastard.

It's like my body doesn't want to hate him and instead, the blame is falling on me.

It's my fault I pushed him away.

My fault I gave him an ultimatum.

Why am I the one hoping he'll forgive me?

Why am I the one praying he'll write me back, leaving voicemails saying he's sorry?

At least at night. And only late at night.

The days are so much easier. Although I know I'm to blame too. I know I contributed. If only I could take it back, I would.

After the unanswered texts, I started packing everything of his to place into storage. Starting with his clothes from a basket of clean laundry. Removing those clothes from my sight didn't make any bit of difference with the sadness. The harsh tears and sobs came when I started ripping the photos off the wall and throwing them into a box.

It was my breaking point, the moment I knew I'd lost it and couldn't stay here, surrounded by pieces of him.

So I moved out and into Jules's guest room.

I don't know if I'm insane, hormonal, or how the hell I'm supposed to react to all this. The only thing I really know is that I'm not the first woman to have a man leave her. I won't be the last, either. It is what it is, and every second that goes by with Evan not saying a word is one more layer added to my armor.

"What about her?" Jules questions and I lift my gaze to her, trying not to show how messed up I am. It's not her fault.

She's cuddled up on the couch, a soft cream and brown striped throw over her legs with the computer in her lap. She turns it toward me so I can check out the profile and résumé she's looking at.

Personal Assistant—Angela Kent

She has experience and an impressive résumé. My gaze scans down the lines on the screen, but it's hard for me to focus. Interviews are a must at this point; I have to hire someone to help me. Or take on less work from the agency. Both are viable options. I only need to pick one. Hopefully sooner, rather than later. I'm drowning in work, but struggling to do any of it.

"Maybe," I tell her and lean back into the sofa. I let my head fall back and wish I had one thing figured out in my life. Just one.

It seems like nothing can go right anymore.

The doubt only lasts seconds and with a deep breath, I find myself glancing back to the screen to read the applicant's résumé again.

"Hey, come on," Jules says, attempting to console me. She places the laptop on the ottoman so she can scoot forward and lean against the armrest of my chair. "It's going to be okay. No matter how dark the night gets, the sun will come up in the morning." She gives me a soft, encouraging smile to cheer me up. It's one of the lines from her first book she gave me as her agent. The memory takes me back to the high point of my life and then it crushes me.

"I'm sorry … It's just that the nights are hard."

"I get that," she says, her kind tone adding extra comfort to the small words. "Do you want me to make you some tea?"

I shake my head. "I think I just need to sleep," I answer her but I really don't know what I need, and that's the problem. There's no solution to this because it's out of my control.

"If he said he's coming back, I guess the real question is: Do you wait for him?"

"I told him it's over." I sniff and absently pick at a snag on the corner of the throw. "I told him if he walked out, I was done."

"I know what you said. But it's obviously not over, not for you."

I mutter softly, "I would be stupid to take him back."

Jules smirks at me as she says, "We've all done stupid things. Haven't we?"

She continues the conversation as she stands, letting the throw fall to the floor so she can stretch her back and adds, "Besides, forgiveness isn't stupid, and neither is love." She speaks so confidently and in a lighthearted tone as if they're so obviously true.

"Can I beat the crap out of him first?" I peek up at her with a half grin, feeling a bit upbeat just from her being with me. She's a damn good friend and I hope one day I have the chance to be as good of a friend back to her as she is to me.

"I think I'll allow it," she responds as her own smile grows.

Mason's footsteps can be heard approaching from down the hall. He's not quiet in the least and part of me wonders if he wants us to know he's coming. "Sweetheart?" he calls out and we both turn to the open doorway before he enters.

"You wanna come to bed?" he asks Jules, bracing his hands on either side of the door jamb before leaning just his upper half into the room. Like he's checking to see if he's welcome.

"I don't know," Jules answers him, but her last word is distorted by a yawn. She's never been a night owl.

"Go to bed, I'll be fine," I tell her, knowing darn well she's only staying up for my sake. I wave her off. "I'm tired too."

"It might be silly," Jules says as Mason strolls toward her and wraps his arm around her waist, "but I'm really happy you're here."

"Thanks," I reply and mean it. Such a simple admission makes my heart swell. That's how badly I need someone right now. "I'm lucky I have you," I tell her. "And I guess you too," I say to Mason, suddenly feeling awkward that he's in the mix of this chick lovefest.

"You staying up?" he asks me.

"Nah, I'm exhausted. I think I'm just going to watch something and pass out."

"I can stay up with you," Jules offers, and her voice is even peppy. She's eager to help me, but she's not the one I need.

"I'm good. Seriously," I tell her easily and for a moment I think I will be when she yields and they say good night. As their footsteps slowly quiet to nothing, the television proves useless as a distraction, because the memories of what happened only nights ago come flooding back. It all haunts me, refusing to let go.

How I opened my heart to Evan, when it was raw and damaged from his doing.

How accepted I felt when he said he was happy we were having a baby. Not just accepted, but complete and whole and like everything was going to be better than okay.

How loved I felt when he held me and kissed me.

How I didn't want to be anything other than *his* when he laid me down in bed.

I think that's the part that hurts the most. I would give up everything to just be his.

And he can't be bothered to text me back. Not even today, and I really could have used his support today. It was hard enough to keep my composure for the full two hours. I didn't say anything the entire time. But on the way back home, I felt a pair of eyes on me. It was like a prickle at the base of my neck, like a sixth sense that told me someone was following me.

I hailed a cab and texted Evan immediately. It was out of habit more than anything else.

I was probably just crazy with paranoia and all the hormones and raging emotions coming with the pregnancy. At least I'm honest with Evan, open and raw. If nothing else, I'm giving him everything I have to offer. He can't even send me a reassuring text.

Absently my hand falls to my belly. It's been doing that. Reminding me that there's another small life in the mix. I focus on taking deep breaths in and out. More than anything, I need to stay calm.

I pick up my phone, intent on texting everything.

He can ignore me all he wants, but I'm going to tell him everything I feel. I deserve that much. To at least be able to tell him what's on my mind. *I'm not the one who keeps secrets. I'm not perfect*, I text him. *I'm slowing down at work. I have to, I'm so tired. I love being pregnant, though. I love knowing we're going to have a baby.*

I'm afraid I'm hurting him by being this way. I don't know how to get better, though.

I delete the last two lines and stare at the ceiling as tears threaten to come.

I used to do this when my parents passed. I used to write to them like I did when I was a kid at camp. After they died, I'd write to them telling them how angry I was. I begged them, pleading with them to come back.

It's not fair that Evan is alive and says he wants me, when a very large piece of my heart feels like I've lost him forever.

Please, Evan. Please come back to me.

Just as I delete all the words, not sending him a single message, my phone rings. It's a number I don't recognize, and I let it ring again in my hand before answering it. "Hello?"

"Hello. This is Dr. Pierce. Is this Katerina Thompson?"

"Yes, can I help you?" The nervousness wracks through my voice at the knowledge that there's an unfamiliar doctor on the line.

"I'm so sorry to call you, but Mr. Thompson's phone has you listed as his daughter. Is that right?"

I'm confused at first, imagining that Evan's in the hospital, but then I realize it's his father, Henry, who the doctor is referring to.

"Is he in the hospital?" The question comes out hurriedly as I sit up straighter, my mind waking up from the fog it was just in. Rather than correcting the doctor and telling him I'm Henry's daughter-in-law and soon-to-be ex-daughter-in-law at that, I rush the next question out without waiting for a response to the first. "Is everything all right?"

The doctor exhales on the other end of the line, but it's not out of exhaustion or boredom. It's the type of sound that accompanies bad news. The kind of sigh that says, *I'm so sorry, I wish I didn't have to tell you.*

No. No, no, no. Denial overwhelms me.

"I would like to first apologize for having to break this news to you over the phone," the doctor says, and I'm taken back to middle school. Sitting down in the principal's office, wondering what I did. I sat there, my legs swinging nervously as he brought in the secretary, then gave me such a sad look before leaving the room. He was so sorry to tell me. They're always so sorry to tell you.

No one wants to be in the room when you learn your parents have died. No one wants to be the person to tell you. I could see it in Mrs. Carsen's eyes.

"Sorry to tell me what?" I ask with caution, but my body is already prepared for it. My heart feels both swollen and hollow, and my head light with denial. I lower myself to the floor, my hand shaking as I hold the phone to my ear.

"Mr. Thompson suffered a blood clot, and unfortunately it traveled to his lungs."

I remember the way the bell rang as I cried and the other students ran through the halls, going about their lives and not knowing my life had changed forever in that moment.

The same agonizing pain rips through me and tears fall freely as I end the call.

He can't be dead. Not Henry. I just talked to him; a voice in my head whispers the reminder.

He was the only dad I had, and I threw him away. He was supposed to be with me tonight. Like he wanted.

If I had met with him, if I hadn't blown him off ... Regret consumes me.

I can hardly breathe as the phone drops next to me and I cover my face. He didn't deserve to die. It's an odd thing to think because it means others do. But Evan's father should still be here. He wasn't supposed to go. Not yet.

My body shudders as I hold back a sob.

I've cried so many tears over the past weeks. So many shed on my pillow, in my hands, soaking into my heated skin.

These tears are different.

It's not from a fear of loss. It's not because I'm disappointed in myself. It's not even because I'm hopeless.

When you shed tears over something that's truly gone, those are the tears that never leave you. They drown your soul and take a piece of your heart. That's what death does.

I have to force myself to text Evan once I've finished speaking with the doctor. *Call me as soon as you can, please. It's urgent, Evan.* I can't help that I add, *I love you.* I'm not conflicted about adding it either, because I do.

I can't tell Evan the news over the phone, though. I want to be there for him. To hold him and ease the pain. Even more, I need him to hold me right now.

I hesitate but then add, *It's about your father.*

The phone shifts out of focus as my eyes blur and my hand shakes, but I hear it ping after only a small moment.

It's not Evan, though, it's Jake. *Hey, you want to grab coffee?*

I have to force myself not to message him. I have to force myself not to tell him that I'm not okay. With how badly I want to be held, I wish I could, but I refuse to use him.

But after an hour going by and a dozen more text messages unanswered by Evan, I cave. I have to tell him, and so I do. I tell him over a text that his father passed away and after crying for hours and seeing that he read it, I still get nothing back.

I text Jake, *I'm not okay.*

chapter 14

Evan

She won't wait for you forever,
There's no way she ever could.
Time changes by the day and life,
Brings both the bad and good.
It creeps into who you are,
Deep down in your soul.
The person that you left behind,
Will never again be whole.

IT'S FITTING IT WOULD SNOW TODAY. I SHUDDER AS I WATCH MEN DIG THE hole my father will be laid in tomorrow. The ground's hard and stubborn. Like my father, in a way.

The frigid air isn't doing a damn thing to aid me in keeping my composure.

All day, all I could think is that it was James who somehow found a way to kill my pops. Mason's the only reason I didn't go back to his office and kill him. Even if he wasn't there, there's no place he could run.

I'm paranoid. I'm desperate. I'm fucking lonely.

I want my wife. I need her. A weak man would go to her and she'd be made a target. Mason assured me she's safe, and this would only help reinforce to James that Kat and I aren't together anymore and she shouldn't be on his radar in the least.

The snow crunches to my right and I turn toward the small parking lot. Mason's early. I didn't even hear him come up behind me until now.

"Thanks for coming, man," I greet him and take his outstretched hand.

"I'm so sorry," Mason tells me as he looks behind me to the gravesite. He found Kat downstairs and I'm still devastated that I wasn't there for her like he was able to be.

Every piece of me is begging to go to her. She can make me feel better—not right, but better.

"You hear anything from your guy?" I ask Mason as I turn from the two men digging my father's grave. I'm desperate for someone to blame this on. It's hard to grasp it's real, let alone just a random occurrence. I'll fucking lose it if he says yes, but that's what I'm praying for. I'm already on edge. Anger is so much easier to handle than despair. If this was because of me, I'll never forgive myself. My heart clenches as Mason stares back at me.

"It was natural causes," he says lowly with more sorrow than I anticipated. I have to turn from him and face the nearly empty parking lot as the wind whips at my face.

I bite back the need to cry and simply nod my head.

Just a blood clot. Just bad luck. There's no one to blame or kill.

That's what hurts the most.

"I'm sorry," Mason says, offering his condolences again. He gives me the space I need as I walk off a few feet closer to the empty plot and I'm grateful for it.

"Your girl," Mason starts and then clears his throat. "You've got to do something for her." His voice is weak like he's begging me.

"You're the one who said I can't," I remind him as I turn back to face him. He told me not to. To not even think about texting her back. James is tracking my phone, just like we're tracking his. He'll know the moment I message her.

"When I asked about her being followed, you said it wasn't your guy," I add.

"This is different," Mason says like it wasn't devastating that someone could've been watching her. If they're watching her, they could be setting her up. If she really felt eyes on her, that is. There's not a hint of activity at our place and we haven't seen anything ourselves.

"She's not doing too well." My blood turns to ice as I wait for him to spit it out. *Not her.* I swallow thickly.

"This morning she said, 'everyone in her life dies,'" Mason tells me with a deep crease in his forehead. "She needs someone."

"You're the one who said she has to believe it too. That we're over with."

"I know, I know," Mason says.

"So, which is it?" I practically scream, the words ripping their way up my throat. Light-headed, freezing and desperate for this all to be over, my world spins around me, too fast for me to keep a level head.

"I'm sorry, I just … it's rough seeing her like this." I can't stand it. This is torture. Maybe it's the punishment I deserve but it's as if I'm dying from a thousand tiny cuts, and I can't stop a single one.

With a chill hammering into my bones, I finally face Mason. My voice is ragged when I ask, "Do I go to her, or not?" If it was up to me, I would. I would hold on to her and lie in bed, denying everything and hiding away with the woman I love. All I can imagine, though, is that the door would be kicked in at some point. He'd come for me, and she'd be right there.

Mason's expression falls and he runs a hand down his face before taking a half step closer. "My mistake, man, I'm sorry. Jules is there. She's not going to leave her. Just … just wait a little longer."

"How much longer?"

"We don't have shit. Lapour's record is clean and there's no evidence of anything. We'll have to plant it. Including tampering with his emails and credit card data."

"How long?" I question again, not bothering to hide the irritation in my voice.

"Only days."

Days … I can wait days. Everything will be right again after that, and I'll make it better. I nod, pacing in a short circle. Just days. The seconds tick by so slowly.

"After what happened in his office …" I voice the concern that's repeating in my head on a loop. "The way he brought her up. Like he was …"

"She's safe. I have her locked away with Jules and she doesn't even know it."

"Locked away?" I ask, stopping in my tracks.

"No one's getting into that house. And Jules knows not to take her out. If Kat wants to go somewhere," Mason says and snaps his fingers, "there's a security detail that'll be on her the second the door is opened."

"So, she's safe?" Knowing she's all right makes not being with her a little easier to swallow. She's protected and that's all that matters. I can't lose her too.

"She's safe and this helps take any heat off her," Mason answers me. "We're tracking his emails and calls, and her name hasn't been mentioned. Yours is, though."

I snort at the idea of James planning a hit on me. "And what's he saying?"

"Wants eyes on you. Wants to know what you're doing and who you're seeing."

My heart sinks at the thought. "Who I'm seeing," I echo, feeling crushed. It's like he wants me to have to stay away from her.

"Yeah," Mason says with a defeated tone. "Could mean his ex, could mean lawyers or cops …" He doesn't finish but I hear the unspoken addition, could mean Kat.

My resolve hardens, but it sends a shooting pain down my chest. I twist the wedding ring on my finger and look back at the grave. I'll be buried with this ring. Either now or years from now. Forever hers.

"Call her from a different phone, just one call?" Mason suggests as I watch the men shoveling piles of dirt. "Not with your phone. From someone else's." I barely register Mason's words.

"If I see her or talk to her," I say, my words coming out as numb as my body feels, "I don't know how I'll walk away again."

"It's a tough call," Mason says faintly.

"She's not at risk now?" I ask him again. It's fucked up, but part of me wants her to already be in the line of fire. Just so I can go to her. To hold her, and take back everything. I hate myself for thinking that for even a second. I'm weak. I need to be stronger for her.

Diary Entry One

Dear Pops,

I've seen Kat do this a few times.

Writing a letter to talk to her parents. It's how I knew back then that she wasn't doing too well. I'd give her extra attention and keep a closer eye on her whenever she took out that journal. I'm not doing too well now, and I need you. Thought I'd give this a try; I don't have anything else.

I miss you already.

If you're with Ma, tell her I miss her too. That I love her and wish you two were here.

God, I do. I need you two.

I'm sorry I wasn't there. I'm sorry I wasn't a better son.

I'm so damn sorry that the last conversation we had was about how disappointed you were in me. I promise I'm trying to do what's right. It's so hard to know, though.

It's too many lies to know what the truth is. Too many secrets to hold on to what's real.

I'm afraid of losing everything. It's like it's all crumbling around me and I can't stop it.

I'm so damn alone, and it's my fault. I'm terrified to be close to anyone right now.

I need you to do me a favor. You gotta look out for Kat.

She misses you and she's not okay.

She used to say that when she'd write, her parents would be there in some way. She said she knew they were watching. She knew they heard. I hope you can hear me now.

Can you go to her? Please?

Give her a sign that you're there and that you love her.

I'm trying, Pops, but it's so hard to know if I'm doing the right thing.

If I lose her too, it's over for me. There's nothing left.

So please, don't watch over me. Stay with her.

I love you forever.

chapter 15

Kat

It's memories that hold me back,
The visions of yesterday.
Back when we were so happy,
And our faith did not yet stray.

"THANKS FOR MEETING ME HERE."

"No problem," Jake responds with a charming smile as he sits down across from me in the booth.

We're back at Brew Madison and not the café closer to Jake's place. It's "my place," but it feels different. Everything feels a bit different now. Nothing feels like it did once; that feeling of being home isn't the same without Evan.

"Tired of the chai?" he asks, and I have to laugh.

"No, it's just that Jules, my friend who I'm staying with for a bit, wanted to meet across the street after we're done, so I asked her driver to bring me here."

"Ah, gotcha. What are you guys going to do?" His question is casual as he looks up at the menu across the wall. It's a large black chalkboard with all their drinks written in elegant flowing script. I'm pretty sure it's not actually handwritten, but I could be wrong.

"The chai is better at your place," I tell him and snag my caffeine-free pumpkin spice coffee from off the small table. Apparently, Maddie's tastes have rubbed off on me. Either that or the baby has ruined my taste buds and given me a temporary sweet tooth.

He chuckles as I take a large gulp then tell him, "I think we're getting dinner at a little Italian place Jules loves. Or maybe heading to the new bar below the hotel a few blocks over." I shrug and add, "She hasn't decided yet, but it's girls' night, so we're doing something."

He lays his coat over the back of his seat as he stands. "I'm going to go with straight black coffee."

"Oh?" I ask him. "Is it one of those days?"

"You tell me," he responds and instantly my smile falls. It's been a week since Henry died and each day is worse than "one of those days." They blur together and time has flown by, but somehow, it's only been a week.

"Give me a sec?" he asks me before leaving, as if he's checking on my well-being, gripping the back of the chair. I nod, not trusting myself to speak.

My fingers play at the edge of my coffee cup. I wore lipstick today and the outline of my lips mars the white rim.

There's a statistic I read once about how lipstick sales and alcohol sales both go up during depressions, while sales for everything else plummet.

The alcohol … well, you drink when you're happy and you drink when you're sad.

The lipstick is because in hard times, we just want to feel special, pretty. We want to feel like we're worth it. As in, if we look pretty and put together, then maybe we can be.

I need to buy more lipstick, I think.

It only takes a moment of me checking my phone before he's back with a brighter spirit and the robust smell of fresh black coffee joining him from the cup in his hand. "So, what's going on?"

"Wow, that was fast," I say to stall a moment longer.

"I'd rate them an A-plus for the service. I'll have to admit that," he answers with a pleasant smile.

I give him a soft one in return, but I can feel it breaking down as I try to formulate an answer to his question.

"Evan's father died." The truth rushes out and my expression crumples regardless of how hard I'm trying to keep it in place.

"Shit," Jake murmurs beneath his breath as I desperately work to maintain my composure. "You all right?"

"I'm fine," I answer in a choked voice, refusing to cry again. "I'm dealing with it. It's not the first time I've lost a family member, but it still hurts."

"What happened?"

"It was sudden. He had a blood clot that traveled to his lungs." As I pick up a napkin from the table and blot under my eyes, I remember the doctor's voice and how calmly he spoke. My lashes graze the napkin as I blink and it comes back black.

"I'm sorry; I'm such a mess," I tell him, flipping the napkin to the other side and being careful not to smudge my makeup too much.

"Don't be." It's only then that I realize how close he is. He's so warm. "Evan," I say, blurting out his name as my tired eyes feel heavy and the need to be held makes my body hot. My fingers itch to lay across Jake's lap. "I tried to call him and got his voicemail."

"About his father?" Jake asks, and I find myself leaning closer to him. Jake doesn't let on that there's any more tension between us than usual. The air between us has shifted. It's something closer and vulnerable. Something I should be wary of, but I need it. God, I need it.

I nod once, twisting the little shreds of the napkin I'm destroying in my lap. "The doctor called me. I was my father-in-law's emergency contact." My throat tightens yet again and my words are choked, thinking about how I was listed as his daughter in Henry's phone.

"And Evan?"

"He didn't answer."

Jake leans back, putting a bit of distance between us and seems to question whether or not he wants to respond. He takes a heavy breath as if he's going to, but sips his coffee instead. I study his face as he stares straight ahead.

"I'm sorry, I shouldn't even be talking about this. I just—"

"Stop saying you're sorry, Kat." Jake turns his head and gazes deep into my eyes as he tells me, "You have nothing to be sorry for, and I don't understand why anyone would make you feel like you do."

My breath comes in shorter bursts, my heart beating faster. But all I can think about is how I wish Evan would say those words to me.

My teeth sink into my bottom lip as I reply, "I am sorry, though." I don't know what else to say. It's just how I feel.

"Well, I'm sorry too. I'm sorry about your father-in-law. And I'm sorry your ex isn't there for you. I'm sure he's going through his own things, but it doesn't seem right that he's ignoring you like that. He's got to know it hurts you."

"He doesn't feel like my ex most of the time," I admit to Jake with my eyes focused on my fingers as I continue to shred the napkin.

I'm anxious for Jake's response. It would lift a weight and burden for someone to understand, and I feel like Jake can. Even if he can't, I don't think he'll judge me. I hope he won't.

"You've been married for years, right?" I nod at his question. "And you only just split?" I nod again to confirm.

"You're going through a lot, and he's not even talking to you. I don't get this guy. I wouldn't throw you away like that."

"I don't think he's throwing me away so much as putting me to the side while he tries to ..." An uneasy sigh slips into the silence when I can't finish my own thought.

"I read in the papers about what he's got going on," Jake says, and I'm forced to look at him, my heart beating slowly as I wait for his judgment. "I don't get how the two of you fit together, honestly."

"We have more in common than you'd think."

"Still have? Or had?" he asks me. Without waiting for a reply, he shakes his head. "Tell me to fuck off if you want," he offers then closes his eyes and takes a quick sip of coffee. "I'm only here if you want to talk. And if I cross a line—"

"You're not crossing any line," I reassure him and find myself reaching out, letting my hand fall on top of his. Mostly for fear of him backing away and leaving me with nothing again. "I don't talk to anyone else really." The plea is unsaid, but Jake hears it. I'm already a burden to my friends. I know I am, even if that's what friends are for. The one thing I know, though, is that they'll remember everything Evan's done, and they'll hate him like I do right now for treating me how he has. Even if they don't say it. So all of this animosity and worry over him and his actions? I can't give it to them. I need someone else. Someone like Jake.

His soothing gaze assesses me and stays on mine as he tells me, "I don't want you to get upset with me because of an opinion I have when I only know a small fraction of the truth. I know the past goes deeper than that."

It's small kindnesses that kill the pain. The tiny bits break down walls, making them crumble all because they hit at just the right spot, at just the right time.

"Just don't hate me for still loving him," I whisper.

"I think you still have feelings for him because you haven't let anyone else in," he says and leans just a bit closer to me.

If Evan would give me just a little, I wouldn't be here. The thought flies through my mind as Jake leans forward a bit more, his gorgeous dark green, hazel eyes focused on my lips.

If Evan would only comfort me or let me comfort him, I wouldn't have even called Jake, I think as I close my eyes and breathe in the masculine scent of Jake's cologne. The deep forest fragrance fills my lungs as he gently presses his lips against mine.

If Evan really wanted me, if he cared about me … the thought is lost when my hands move to Jake's hair, my fingers spearing through it as my lips part and Jake deepens the kiss.

The problem is that when my eyes are closed, I picture Evan. It's his fingers that thread through my hair and cup the back of my head. It's his lips pressed against mine.

The problem is when I open my eyes, it's not Evan. No matter how much I want it to be him.

Diary Entry Three

Dear Mom,

I really could use you today. You had such great advice when I was younger. Evan's father passed away and I don't know what to do. I want to be there for him because I love him even though he's not here for me. But he didn't want me to be there for him. Not even at the funeral. He hardly looked at me.

Mom, I think he blames me in some way. Or there's something I don't know. I don't understand it. You know how you told me to be honest with my emotions? I feel like I'm dying inside. I can't describe how badly it feels to stand near him and be completely ignored because "hurt" doesn't do it justice. It's an emptiness I don't know how to fill.

I love him so much, but I cried alone in the car at the funeral. He didn't hold me. He didn't talk to me. He only hugged me like he hugged everyone else. Like I was no one special.

I thought for a second he would let me cry in his arms. Or that he would cry in my arms like he did when his mom died. But he didn't. He just left.

He didn't need me, Mom. He didn't need me at all and it feels like I need him just to breathe.

There's something else too. Something that you might not like. Or I don't know, maybe you'll like it now that you know what Evan did.

I kissed someone else.

I can't help feeling like I'm cheating on Evan.

But if Evan doesn't want me, it's okay, right? It doesn't feel okay. Separated or divorced, I still love Evan.

This guy, his name's Jake, he treats me like he cares about me. Not that we've done anything really. I don't even know him. I think I want to, though, and that scares me.

My heart belongs to Evan, but there's someone else who wants to take it.

Seeing Evan at the funeral is what broke me.

I don't know what to do.

I tell you that a lot, don't I? That I don't know what to do. But for the first time, I want to do something. I'm ready for something to change. I know you'd know what to do.

I wish you were here. I miss you. I love you.

chapter 16

T HE PILES OF DIRT ARE GROWING LARGER. THE METAL SHOVELS PIERCE *the frozen soil. The sound cuts through my bones, one and then another and another.*

It's been constant as I stand here helplessly. I've never been colder, the bitter wind and blustery snow besieging my body, but I still don't move.

I can't take my eyes from the two graves.

The shovels spill the dirt, the piles mounting as my eyes drift to the tombstones.

The first my father, a man who died before his time. A death of tragedy.

And then to my wife's. My love's. No one believes me. He put her there. James killed her.

My eyes pop open wide when I hear Kat whisper, "It's all your fault."

I wake up gasping for air, my heart pounding and I swear I can feel Kat's hot breath on my neck even though I'm alone. My eyes dart around the room as I slowly lift my body into a sitting position on the bed.

Just a terror. The same as last night.

I'm quick to grab the video monitor for the security system from the nightstand and flick the button on to bring it to life. Mason set it up for me to keep a close eye on her.

It's only when I see Kat in bed that my heart starts to calm, and my heated skin seems to succumb to the chill of reality.

She's okay.

I close my eyes and when I open them, the monitor displays an image of her rolling over in bed. *To my side.* My fingers brush the glass where she is. I'll be there soon. I'll be with her and it'll all be over.

It's that promise to myself that brings me any sleep at all anymore. *It'll be over soon and then I'll be with her.*

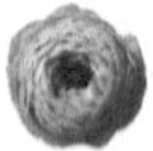

"There's a lot of shit you aren't going to like," Mason states matter-of-factly the second I close the door to his car. He doesn't even wait for my ass to hit the seat. He's situated outside the park and I focus on the people walking by. Moving through their day and carrying on with their lives, while mine's slowly deteriorating into nothing.

I needed this meetup to get the fuck out of this rut and talk to someone. Even if it means hearing something I'm not going to like.

"Let's start with the easiest."

"You have a tail. Hired by Lapour," he says, and his sentences are short, clipped. I nod my head. I figured as much. I've been scoping James out and James is doing the same in return.

"The cops are coming around your place more often too and they've been poking around your family home, looking through the garbage. A few tags on the station's search engine too."

"They're not going to give up, are they?" It's not really a question. The leather of the seat groans as I lay my head back.

"They just need one thing to pin it on you."

"James has the evidence they'd need to do it." The photos come to mind and anxiousness makes my chest tighten. I'm waking up to heart palpitations and I'm constantly exhausted, but not able to sleep. My right leg rocks from side to side as Mason speaks.

"We can wipe them from his computer, but the hard copies will have to wait until tomorrow. My associate will ensure the place is clean, but then he'll know."

"That works. Whatever it costs."

"It takes time to get a batch of drugs that matches," Mason says and I know it's not about the money. It's about the time and executing it correctly.

"It would have been easier if we'd found it on him," I say, stating the obvious.

"Yeah, it would have," he agrees and then it's quiet.

"I'm failing. All this money paying other people to do shit and we're coming up empty."

"You're doing everything you can."

I can't stand the waiting anymore. "I want this over with," I confide in him.

A couple of days turned into a week. And now the weeks are bleeding into one another.

"I'm walking around this city," I tell him, "stalking a man who should be dead. I *need* to do something." It's killing me to wait, driving me fucking crazy. I can practically feel my sanity slipping away.

"You have to be careful when you … take care of someone," he says as if I'm being impatient. "If you're reckless, you get caught.

"Besides, I don't have anything on James. Not a shred of evidence that shows he purchased the fentanyl."

"We need evidence or to set him up if there isn't any. Or we can just murder him and end it all." The thought has been festering in the back of my skull. Picking away at me. I just want to kill the fucker and be done with this.

"You kill him before it's ready, and the cops will be looking for his murderer. Is that what you want?"

I know he's right, and I can't answer. I respond with the only thing that matters. "I need my wife back."

"That's the other thing," he tells me while looking out his window.

"What thing?" I question, a deep groove settling down the center of my brow as I stare at the back of his head, willing him to look at me. "About my wife?"

"She's seeing someone," he answers and it's like white noise.

"You're wrong." Time slows. She isn't. There's no way she's seeing someone.

"She went out yesterday and we kept an eye on her like I promised you we would. My guys saw some things."

That's when a man's face comes back to me. My hands clench into tight fists at my side as I shake my head. Jacob whatever the fuck his last name is. My breathing comes in ragged pants as he says, "Jacob Scott is his name. A potential client of hers."

"Not my wife," I say, biting out the words although I already know it's true. "She's not going to move on so fast."

The worst part is that I don't even blame her. I'm dying inside. Every night I think about how my father should still be here and my wife should be in bed with me. Instead I'm alone, clutching a fucking T-shirt Pops always wore. He gave it to me when he gained a little weight and it didn't fit him any longer. It's just a shirt from a shop he used to work at. The shop's not around anymore.

I didn't give a shit about it back then, it was just a shirt, but all I can see when I hold it now is him. It's funny how the little things that don't matter are the most sentimental when you lose the ones you love.

That's my life. Hiding away and mourning my father alone. Hating myself and not being able to fix it all. I can't fix a damn thing.

"I told you she wasn't doing well," Mason says like I should have known better.

My teeth grind against each other as I seethe. "I can't do both at the same time, lead her on that we're broken up, but also be there for her." Pounding my fist against the window once like a madman, I hold on to the anger. I'll prolong every other emotion I can until I'm forced to deal with it at night when sleep refuses to comfort me. I know I must look like I'm fucking unhinged, but I am. So, I suppose it's fitting. "I can't protect her and have her in my life at the same time. There's no way for me to do it!" Exasperation gets the better of me.

"Well, if you're not there for her, someone else will be."

My heart's in my throat. That's the only explanation for what I feel. It's not in my chest where it's supposed to be. Only pain lingers there.

"I want to kill him. That Jacob fuck."

"Now I know that one isn't serious."

"He's seeing my wife!" I bite down on the inside of my cheek to keep from screaming, but Mason doesn't react.

He's silent as my rage slowly subsides.

"What would you do?" I ask him out of desperation as I imagine her calling him. Alone and desperate for someone to take away her pain.

Mason answers with a shrug, "Kill the asshole."

"You're a real wiseass, you know that?"

"It could be worse," he says.

"How's that?"

"She cried for a while when she got back from dinner with Jules."

I wait for him to continue, not understanding. "Why was she crying?"

"After seeing the guy, she cried all night. She's not moving on. She's not okay, Evan."

"What am I supposed to do? She's everything to me. And all I can see, all I dream about at night is her dying because of me." Mason doesn't answer me.

No one has an answer for me. "If I lose her, I have nothing. There's no reason to live if I don't have her."

"You could always go with the locking her in a room option. She likes her office, right?" Mason jokes and I don't know whether to thank him for lightening the mood, or punch his fucking face in.

"Do you think James would go after her if I took her back?" I ask him. "Tell me honestly."

"If someone wanted to hurt you, the first thing they'd do is go after her." Mason says exactly what I already knew, and I rest my head against the window.

"He still might, but the chance of that seems low. Right now, James is only interested in three people: you, Samantha, and a man named Andrew Jones. Obviously, a cover."

Before I can ask, Mason adds, "We're paying him a visit soon. As soon as we track down his location."

I nod, agreeing with the plan, but all I can think about is that prick with his hands on my wife.

"What if we paid Jacob a visit?"

"You really think that's the way to go? Like Kat won't find out?" he asks me, and I grit my teeth.

"What if she goes home? What if you go home? Just be quiet about it. Rent a hotel room and make sure you're seen there for your tail. But go to her at night and make sure she keeps quiet."

"Kat can't keep a secret for shit."

"She's talking about going back home anyway. You're going to need to be there."

"You think she'd be okay with me just slipping in at night? Maybe if I told her what's going on. But in and out, coming and going as I please? She'd kill me."

"Don't tell her shit. Are you fucking crazy?"

"Lie to her? Kat's always been able to see right through me. Lying is what made all this worse."

"I'm not saying lie to her. I'm just saying this is how it has to be. Right now, she needs comfort … She'll take what you can give her. James thinks you're with Samantha, so be seen with her, then head over to your place."

The very idea of being seen with Samantha makes my stomach coil. "You want my wife to hate me?"

"It's the only real option you have right now," he says and looks me in the eyes to add, "She'll never know."

He's a fool to think that. She'll find out. There's no fucking way I'm going to do that to her. She deserves better than that.

chapter 17

Kat

I HAVE TO TELL EVAN ABOUT JAKE, BUT HE DOESN'T WANT TO TALK TO ME.

He's ignoring me. Intentionally hurting me.

Yet there's still a sense of obligation. As if I owe it to him to let him know that I'm moving on now. I've finally got a grip on my self-respect, but I need him to know it. I roll my eyes at the thought and heave out an aggravated sigh.

I don't care if it's weak or pathetic. He was everything to me.

I nearly trip as I realize what I thought. *Was.*

Is it really over? I struggle to breathe in the cold air as I think maybe a small part of me wants to move on. No, that's not it. It's simply accepting that it's time to move on.

Say something, I'm giving up on you … song lyrics play through my head as my throat dries and I force myself to keep walking up the sidewalk to 82 Brookside. Evan's family home.

The sad lyrics of the soft song are what keep me from knocking on his door at first. I attempt to compose myself because if Evan doesn't open this door, or worse, he does but doesn't hear me out? Then I have no hope left.

I know deep down in my gut, this is my last and final effort.

Say something, I'm giving up on you … and then the melody stops, a feminine voice cutting through. The voice of a woman I recognize. Sadness freezes over, replaced quickly by something … more gruesome.

Samantha.

I hear her laugh and then a muted voice. His voice. She's in there with him. Shock keeps me paralyzed. I listen a moment longer, denying it at first.

The only movement I can make is to hide my hands in my coat pockets as the winter wind brutalizes me. I thought my heart was already broken. Apparently, it was only torn because at this moment, there's no denying my heart's been ripped ruthlessly in half.

I'm numb as I stand in the harsh cold, trying to listen to the faint sounds as I lean my body toward the window to my right. I can barely see her, and I can't see him at all.

There's no way I can make out what they're saying, but I watch her put on her coat.

It's funny how anger can so easily replace sadness. Almost like rock paper scissors. Anger beats sadness, sadness beats … I don't know what, and in this moment, I don't care in the least.

My heartbeat rages; my breathing shallows as I watch that woman I once trusted standing in Evan's parents' home. He can't really be with her.

Time passes, maybe a minute more before I come to terms with it.

What a fucking fool I was.

This is why he left me. Of course. My breathing falters as I take a few steps back from the door, my warm breath turning to fog in front of me. Shoving my hair out of my face, I collect myself before I can fully fall apart.

With my arms wrapped tight around my shoulders, I hug myself as I walk aimlessly down the street. My shoes crunch the thin layer of fallen snow beneath my feet as I get farther and farther away. I let my mind whirl and my emotions stir into a concoction of self-doubt and recklessness.

"He thought I would wait for him while he had one last fling?" I whisper under my breath but then shake my head. "Maybe he's trying to pick which one of us he wants …"

Like a madwoman I talk to myself, ignoring the horns honking and cars speeding along the street next to me. I let out a sarcastic laugh and think, *his choice is made.*

He already left me, and I already told him it was over.

How dumb can I really be?

My hands fumble inside of my jacket as I turn the street corner. I bite down on the fabric of my glove and pull it off so I can unlock my phone.

Evan's cheating on me. I tell Jules first. I've talked to her more than anyone else since she's welcomed me into her house.

No, he can't be! She's quick to respond and I find myself standing still in the middle of the busy sidewalk, texting her back. Everyone walks around me, ignoring me and my mental breakdown.

I'm pregnant with his child and he's cheating on me.

Why would you think that? she texts back as I type my response.

I just saw her.

Saw who? she asks.

Samantha.

And they were kissing??? That bastard!!

I bite the inside of my cheek and hate that I can't say yes. They weren't kissing. I told him to stay away from her and she's inside his house, though. Isn't that enough?

I didn't see them kiss. She's in his house.

What were they doing? she asks, and I find my anger turning on her.

I don't know!

What were you doing, spying??

OMG Jules! YES, of course, I was! I stand there numb, reading the text messages and feeling like I truly am crazy.

What did he say?

About them? I didn't go in, I text her. I'm left with silence for a moment with no response back. The wind seems to pick up and my ears burn from the cold. Or maybe from people talking about me.

I'm going to get proof. I text Jules and spin around on my heels, shoving the phone into my coat pocket and ignoring the dings of her return messages.

I'll confront that bastard and make him pay for the hell he's put me through. All the while I work myself up. Each step back to his house is taken with stronger and stronger resolution.

Until I get there and his car is gone, and just like my gut told me the second I saw the empty spot in front of his house, the door is locked.

"Motherfucker," I scream out as I bang my fists against the door. The chill in the air makes each impact hurt more and more.

I start to text him even though my hands are aching from the freezing cold. One line saying, *I know.* And then I backspace until it's erased. That's not good enough, it's too mysterious. I text him a paragraph about what I saw, but I delete that too, knowing he'll just deny it.

Outside of his parents' house, outside of the house where I fell in love with him, the light dims from the sinking sun and the sudden sheets of gray signal more snow is coming.

Defeated, I slip my phone in my pocket, realizing only now that I've been trembling.

I'm not going to text him or confront him. Nothing. I'll figure out the truth and make sure I have evidence, but I'm giving Evan exactly what he gave me … nothing.

Diary Entry Four

Mom,

I'm worried about the things that I think sometimes.

I'm worried about how angry I get. Did you get like that ever?

I don't know if you would have. I did it to myself by marrying Evan.

I'm filled with anger more than anything anymore. I don't want to be like this, but it's what he's done to me. Maybe that's an excuse. That's probably what you'd tell me, isn't it? I'm responsible for my own actions and no one else's.

I've never been this angry, and I'm afraid of what I'm going to do.

chapter 18

I HAVEN'T BEEN THIS NERVOUS SINCE KAT AND I WENT OUT ON OUR FIRST date.

It was an easy date, a place I knew well. *My* club. I didn't own it; I never got into commercial real estate, although I have thought about it. It was still my club, though. At least that's how I felt. I should've felt in control and powerful to meet her in front of the doors, the music drifting out into the street, but one look at her stepping out of her car had my heart pumping faster and the back of my neck sweating.

Kat's always been able to stun me like that.

As if I don't already know she's beautiful.

It's something else, though, that's got me this nervous.

It's the sense that I can't hold on to her no matter what I do. That's the feeling I had flowing through my veins that night, and that's the feeling flowing through me now as I get ready to step up to the doors of Mason's house in the Berkshires.

I check my phone again to see if I have any more texts from him, but I don't. The last one said she was packing her stuff and planning on moving back to the townhouse.

I rap my knuckles on the hard oak doors, the cold air making it hurt just a bit. My body urges me to do it harder, to embrace the pain and focus on that and not the anxiety of rejection.

I would deserve it, after all.

The door opens in one tug, and the glow from the foyer chandelier carries to the porch. There she is. Holding the door open with her lips parted in shock.

"Evan." She says my name as she stands perfectly still.

A faint dusting of snow settles around me as I take her in. From the white socks on her feet, to the silk pajamas that must be a gift from Jules, because I've never seen them before in my life.

"Hey," I greet her and then swallow the lump in my throat. "I heard you were here."

Her expression hardens instantly as she seems to get over my surprise arrival.

"What do you want?" she asks me, although it sounds like an interrogation. Before I can answer, she takes a half step forward to come outside rather than letting me in, like a fucking lunatic.

"What are you doing?" I ask her with complete disbelief as she tries to shut the door.

"I'm not having this conversation in Jules's house," Kat says as if it's an admonishment, like I'm the one who's lost their mind.

"Baby, get inside, it's freezing out!"

"Don't tell me what to do!" she yells back at me, and her words strike me across the face. I take it, though. I take one step back and watch as she crosses her arms over her chest and her cheeks quickly turn pink from the wind that won't let up, followed by the tip of her nose. "What do you want?"

"Are you sure you don't want to go inside?" I question her as calmly as I can, attempting to be reasonable.

"I went to your house today," she states. The blood drains from my face.

"Is that right?" I somehow manage to reply, knowing what's coming, my body tensing up. All I can hear is my heart pounding as I feel her slipping away from me.

"I don't want anything to do with you, Evan." The cutting words are spoken with a cracked voice. At least there's emotion left. If there's that, then I still have a chance.

"I don't know what you think you saw, but …" I start to tell her and then flinch from her shriek.

"Think?" she yells. "I saw her!" She moves in closer, getting in my face to scream at me. "Samantha. You left me to be with her," she says and seethes, the accusation coming out hard.

"Did you see me touch her?" I ask her, taking a step closer to her. "I know you didn't, because I never would. I'm not seeing her. I didn't even want her there."

"She was with you," she says the words then breathes out with nothing but pain and agony.

"Yeah, she was. A few times in the last week," I confess. I don't want her to find out any other way. "I'm trying to fix things and she's—"

"I want you to go," she says, cutting me off.

"I won't until you tell me you believe me." I look her in the eyes, silently begging her, and wait for it.

"I told you not to. Just go!"

"Never. I would never stray from you." As I say the words, it's crippling. Because I know she did what she's accusing me of. She's the one who's seeing someone else, but I gave her the space to do it. I left her side.

It's all fucked.

She doesn't answer me, merely shivers in the cold as her bottom lip starts to turn a purplish blue.

"Let's go inside," I urge her, but she doesn't respond. "I want to talk."

"I thought the funeral might be a good time to talk," she finally says with tears in her eyes. "Guess you didn't?

Her words slice through me, down to my core. "It meant a lot to me that you were there," I manage to say, but I can't look her in the eyes. The tips of my fingers turn numb and the feeling flows through every inch of my body.

"Didn't seem like it," she replies, although she's lost a bit of strength in her voice.

"I'm having a difficult time handling it," I tell her, scrambling for an excuse, but there's so much truth in those words.

James was there at the funeral. He even shook my hand, the fucking bastard. The reason is right there on the tip of my tongue. I wanted to go to her, to hold her. To go home with her and get lost in her love. More than anything.

"You think it was easy for me?" she asks me after a moment of silence.

"You think it was easy for me?" I shoot right back and the memories of the grave, the service hit me. I have to pinch the bridge of my nose and close my eyes as I see the visions of the nightmares mixing with the memories. *I shouldn't even be here.* Regret flows through my veins. What am I doing?

"I'm sorry," she whispers, and her breath turns to fog. The wind blows, and her hair falls in front of her face as I tell her, "I'm sorry too." I get a little choked up, but I manage to tell her, "He loved you so much."

He really did. His voice telling me to make it right keeps playing in my head and it kills my strength.

"I told you I just needed time." I try to make the words come out strong, but instead, it's a plea. I don't know what to do anymore.

All I want to do is protect her. *Maybe that means losing her forever.*

She shakes her head. "What part of us moving on with our lives didn't you understand? I don't have time for games or whatever trouble you've gotten into."

"I'm fixing the trouble." I refuse to give up. "I just need more time."

"And how much longer is that going to be? How much longer do I have to sit on the back burner and wait for you to love me again?"

"I still love you," I say.

"You don't act like it."

"There's a reason for everything, I promise." I have to blink away the scenes of the funeral, of the night terrors.

"I don't want to hear your excuses anymore," she says and wipes under her eyes. Her voice is drenched with defeat. "You're supposed to be here for me."

I question everything in that moment. I'm so afraid of losing her, but the image of her dead on the ground makes me harden my resolve. I hesitate and immediately regret it.

"I need you to go, Evan. For good."

"It's because of Jacob, isn't it?" I can't help but blurt it out. I want someone else to blame. Someone else to hate other than me. "You're moving on with him?"

I can't help but point out that she's the one who wants someone else. I only want her. I won't lose her. I'll fuck her so good when all this is over, she'll forget any other man exists.

"You think I need a man? You think I need someone?" Her voice is coated with an anger I haven't seen from her before. "I never needed anyone! You're the only one I ever let in. You were the only one I let get close and I'll be fine, living the rest of my life alone."

"You want him more than me?" My jealousy gets the best of me.

"Get away from me!" she spits out as she opens the door to head into the house.

"I'm coming back for you," I tell her, and I mean it.

"Well I won't be here, and I'm changing the locks on the townhouse. So good fucking luck with that."

Kat

IT'S A HEAVY, SINKING FEELING IN THE PIT OF YOUR STOMACH. IT ROCKS back and forth, making you queasy and your body can't sit still. That's what it feels like when you know you're about to hurt someone.

At least that's how it feels right now.

I don't need anyone at all and I don't want anyone either. Maybe I'm proving it to myself, or maybe to Evan. I don't care which.

My pulse quickens, and I try to swallow the spiked ball in my throat when I hear the bell at the front of the café.

Jacob smiles sweetly with genuine happiness as he strolls over to the table, letting his jacket slip off his shoulders. I'm going to miss that charming grin he has. I'll miss the comfort his presence brings more.

"One more nice day before winter comes in," he says easily. It's felt like winter for weeks now to me, but he's from farther up north, so I suppose it hasn't been as brutal to him as it's seemed to me.

"One more nice day," I repeat, nodding my head at the ceramic mug on the table. I have to force the smile to stay on my face, but it doesn't fool Jacob.

"What's wrong?" he asks me, not touching the mug of chai already waiting for him.

I hate that I get choked up. It's stupid really. Childish and I'm far too grown for little kid games.

It was just friends, then just a kiss.

But it never should have been anything.

"Nothing," I answer and shake my head slightly then pick up the mug. Jake's face falls, but he still tries to cheer me up.

"So, I never got your answer about the movies tomorrow night." He's quick to change the topic, gracing me with that ever-present kind smile. "I heard it's going to be good."

My mug clinks on the small saucer as he adds, "I love coffee shops and all, but it'd be nice to do something more."

More.

It would be. I can see it. I can feel it. If my heart didn't belong to someone else, I could see Jacob being so much more. Well, not only that. I'm going to be a mother. My priorities have nothing to do with dating or starting anything new that doesn't involve the little life I'm carrying.

"I have to tell you something." I get the words out before I change my mind and swallow them. Before I give in to getting over Evan by getting under another man.

Jacob visibly winces then scratches the side of his neck as he looks to the right. "That doesn't sound so good."

"I kind of lied to you," I confess, feeling a viselike grip on my heart.

"You're not separated?" he says.

"No, we are. But I don't want to be."

"You still love him. I know you do."

"There's more," I continue, not daring to look him in the eyes, and hesitate.

"Just tell me," he urges me as if this is going to be easy, moving his hand to mine, and I stare down at where his skin touches mine. It's gentle, kind. It's the comfort I desperately need. But I can't be expected to always have someone to lean on. More than that, I want to stand on my own.

"I'm pregnant," I tell him and the only reaction I get is that his brow raises just slightly. It's comical really, and the small movement forces the corners of my lips up. I'd laugh if my heart didn't hurt as much as it does.

"*That*, I didn't see coming," he responds, keeping a small bit of humor in his voice. Slowly, he pulls his hand away but keeps it on the tabletop. I notice the absence of his touch instantly, though.

"Not far along?" I shake my head no at his question, feeling the end of my ponytail swish around my shoulders. "How long have you known?"

"A while," I answer honestly.

"So that's the lie?"

"Yeah … I'm sorry. I never should have kept that from you."

"Don't be," he tells me and waves it off, as if it's no big deal.

"I knew better. It was just …" I trail off and swallow my words, staring at a stain on the table. One that will never go away.

"It was nice being *okay* with someone. Right?"

I chance a peek up into his eyes. There's nothing but understanding there. "Yeah," I answer him and chew on my bottom lip. "I wanted to pretend to be okay for a little bit."

"Well it's not pretend," he continues and adjusts in his seat. "You can be okay if you want to." It's hard to hold his gaze as he brings his hand back to mine.

"Does he know?" I answer his question with a nod, my throat too tight to speak.

"And he …?" he starts to ask, but doesn't finish the obvious question.

"Says he's happy but he's still not with me. He's not committing and carrying on like he was. I want him, but I need him with me and he's not …" I'm ashamed of the answer.

It's quiet for a short moment. The ceramic mug in my hand slides against the wooden table and it's the only noise to be heard. The itch in my throat matches the prick behind my eyes. I've cried enough over all this. It's been weeks and this is simply how it is. With a sip of my peppermint tea, I accept it.

"So, do you want to go to the movies?" Jacob asks then picks up his mug. "I'd still like to go if you would."

My heart does this little flutter, a quick flicker of warmth that lets me know it's still there. It's gratitude and I think that's all I could give anyone else. It's all I'm willing to do.

I shake my head, once again, and give him a sad smile.

"I had to ask. I think it would've been good," he tells me, forcing a smile then covering his disappointment by taking a large sip of the chai.

"You going to be okay?"

I shrug, honestly unsure of whether I'll ever be okay. "Some people are meant to be alone." *Or waiting for a love that may never come back.*

"You sound like me," he comments with a huff of humor that doesn't reach his eyes and then he takes a deep, heavy breath. "Gets tiresome, though."

"A story for another time perhaps?"

"I think it's the same story mostly, with only one big difference."

"What's that?"

"I think Evan may love you back, just like you love him. Whether or not he deserves it … well, that's a matter of opinion, I guess." I can't respond and instead, I let my gaze wander back to the stain on the table. "It wasn't the same for me. It was very much one sided."

"I'm so sorry, Jake." It's all I can respond and I genuinely am.

"Don't be," he says easily. "Fate puts people in our life for a reason." He takes a steadying breath before saying, "And now I know it's possible."

"What's possible?" For a moment I worry that he thinks the two of us being together is still an option when it's not at all for me.

"Not this like you and me," he says, rushing out the words as if hearing my unspoken thought. "Trust me, I wish it were. But I meant … just that there could be someone else for me."

"You could always write the story. Although I doubt you'd want me to be your agent, huh?"

"No … I don't think that would work really," he says with the same sad smile on his face that I've been giving him.

"Maybe we could still be friends?"

"I don't think that's for the best, Kat. I can't just be friends with you."

My hair tickles my shoulders as I nod and reach for my coat to leave. My movements are sluggish; I don't want this to be the last goodbye. But it is. I know it. I barely touched my drink and didn't have anything to eat, but that's okay. I knew I wouldn't anyway. Morning sickness has been rough this week so it's not like I'd be able to keep it down anyway.

"How about this," Jacob offers as I pull my wool coat tight around my shoulders. "You call me if you're ever not okay and want more. But I won't call you or text you again. It's in your hands."

"I'm sorry, Jake." I say the words, but they don't even make a dent in expressing what I feel.

"Stop being sorry. Do that one thing for me, will you?" he questions, his dark green, hazel eyes shining back just like they did the first moment I met him, and I merely nod and say my goodbye.

Every step back to my townhouse, I want to go back.

Every breath, I wish I could tell him that what he did for me, I can never repay, and I'll be forever thankful for that.

But neither of those things happen. I walk back to my townhouse alone and the first thing I do when I get home is delete his emails and his number.

I don't want to have the option to run back to him.

Jacob is a good man, but he's not for me. I don't need someone else to love me. I need to learn to love being alone again. So I can be whole for my child. So I can be a good mother.

Diary Entry Five

Dear Mom,

It's not so bad being alone. I'm not really alone, alone. Not with this baby growing, but I can't feel him or her yet. I still talk to him, though. I think it's a boy, but I won't know for weeks.

Like I said, though, I think it's going to be all right being alone for now. I remember having that same thought for a while after you guys left me. I know it's not your fault.

I just can't stand to think of needing someone. Not when it hurts so freaking bad when they leave you. Did you see what Evan did? I gave him that power and that's my fault. I won't do it again.

I should have known better.

If you could just remind me, maybe? The next time he comes around and says he wants me and that he loves me, can you give me a sign? Something that will remind me that he's just going to leave me again and how much that will hurt?

People don't change, and some people are meant to be alone.

I promise I'll be okay from now on, Mom.

I just forgot that I'm one of those people. But I remember now. I won't forget again.

chapter 20

Evan

I'M USED TO SNEAKING AROUND. I'VE DONE IT ALL MY LIFE. I'M A professional at it, after all.

The door to the townhouse opens and I turn to look over my shoulder at the cold, barren street. No one knows I'm here and I need to keep it that way.

The pictures of my wife and me stare back at me as I slowly close the door. Feeling the warmth and familiarity of the home I built with Kat makes the ache deep in my chest twist and turn to a sickening degree. She took down several of our photographs, leaving dark rectangles on the wall where they used to hang and the sunlight failed to lighten and fade the paint behind them.

The large clock on the back wall ticks loudly as I move through the place we made together. It's nearly 3:00 a.m., but still, I make sure I wasn't followed. With bated breath, I check the surveillance system … again.

The life I led destroyed the only thing I ever had that I wanted to keep. My marriage.

The knowledge pushes me forward, each step bringing me closer to her. Closer to the bed we once shared, and closer to her warmth under the covers. As I push the door open, my heart beats slowly. With every second that passes my skin burns hotter and the worry threatens to consume me.

But the sight of her steady breathing and the faint movements of her body as Kat stirs in her sleep put all my worries behind me. She's safe, and that's what matters.

Her eyes flutter open and I stand as still as possible, terrified she'll see me, but she merely rolls over in bed, moaning slightly, pulling the thin white sheet with her.

The moonlight filters in through the curtains and leaves a trail of shadows that accentuate her curves as they fall across the bed. She's still as gorgeous as ever. Even in her sleep with no makeup on and her bare skin kissed by the faint light of the early morning, she holds a beauty that, for me, surpasses all others.

How many nights have passed with me failing to see that? How much time have I wasted?

I can't let a soul know I still love her. They'll use her to get back at me.

My eyes widen and my grip tightens on the door as I hear my name slip through her lips. "Evan." It sounded like a prayer, or maybe a plea. A soft moan escapes her as I take a hesitant step forward, wondering if she saw me or if I'm only with her in her dreams.

I start to question if she even said it, but then she says it again. The sweet sound of her soft cadence whispering my name is everything I need to keep going.

I swallow thickly, hating myself for what I've done and what I've put her through.

I dare to whisper the only thing that helps lure me to sleep at night, hoping it'll soothe her too, "I'll make it right, Kat. I promise, I'll make it right."

Kat

MY EYES POP OPEN AT THE FAMILIAR CREAK FROM THE STAIRS. My heart races faster and faster as I lie as still as I can, not daring to move a muscle. My body's hot and the covers are making me even hotter, but I don't move. I try not to even breathe as I wait for another sound. But nothing comes.

It's just my nerves. Maybe a nightmare.

Slowly, my breath comes back, but I'm still too scared to move. Nearly paralyzed still, I blink away the sleep and tilt my head just enough to look at the clock on my nightstand. 04:14 AM stares back at me in bright red digital numbers.

The sounds of the city streets filter in and my quickened heartbeat fades. It was nothing, I whisper and reach for my glass of water, downing it then wishing there was more.

Get up.

I will my body to move. I wince and crack my back, letting my bare feet hit the cold hardwood floor. Sleeping alone has never been a favorite of mine. Until Evan, I spent years with poor sleep patterns, both in falling and staying asleep. Even more than that, I don't like how Evan's side of the bed doesn't have the faint smell of him anymore. I can feel the solemn expression on my face as I glance at where he used to sleep, but it only pushes me to stand up straighter and wipe the sleep from my eyes.

The floor protests as I walk, and I let the feeling that someone was in here leave me. I have the security system … but I think I'd like a dog. *A big dog.*

The corners of my lips tip up into a smile as I walk down the stairs.

Pushing back the hair from my face, I slink down to the kitchen and turn on the light. It's early, but I'm starving. To sleep, or not to sleep becomes the question.

It only takes a glass of water, two Twinkies and a couple handfuls of grapes before I don't feel so hungry anymore and sleep is calling me upstairs again.

Passing through the dining room, I check over my shoulder just to make sure there's no one here. That eerie feeling still clings to me.

I think I'll name the dog Brutus. My lips purse as I wonder how dogs do with infants ... I make a mental note to look that up first thing tomorrow.

I think I'm starting to really *feel* pregnant. It's beyond being exhausted. It's something else, something that makes me rub my belly and talk to him or her as if they're already here. Some type of knowing and it makes me smile.

Before I can head back upstairs, my eyes catch sight of the flowers on the table. The flowers Jacob sent me when Henry died are already wilted. Bright yellow sunflowers. They're large and the stems are thick. They'll eventually die and by the look of them, that time is coming soon. What a shame ... that's what flowers do, though. They die.

Next to the vase is my laptop and I absently pull it toward the edge of the table then take a seat. My body aches, my hips especially, and sitting up feels better than lying down. I might as well get a little work in before I try to sleep again.

A yawn leaves me as the dim light of the computer brightens.

Studying the flowers again, I think about how twisted it is that I turned down a man who could have been perfect for me. A shrink might have something to say about that decision. My fingertips brush gently along the petals. I'll never know if we could have been more, but right now I'm content with that decision.

It's time I took control of my life.

My to-do list is already set. First step: I need a new place. Somewhere near the Manhattan Bridge, I think. It's far more family friendly. Dog friendly too.

I check my messages and emails, simply out of habit. A few of the candidates I picked to interview to be my personal assistant emailed me back. There are two of them I really like. I might actually hire both of them. Maybe that's really the first step. And then finding the perfect place will be step two. A smile plays across my lips and I nod to myself in approval of my "early morning can't sleep, aha" moment.

Those two tasks are momentous and huge leaps for me. Delegating work and settling down somewhere my child can have deep roots. Resting my hand on my belly, I promise I'll make it happen. I may have failed to be there for Evan, but for this baby, I'll do anything. I'll have it all fixed and ready before this one gets here. He or she will never know this place or all the hell that went on here.

My gaze drifts across the room and the night that started it all plays out in front of my eyes. Suddenly, it hurts. That numbing prick comes back. It's been happening like that. I'm so sure, so ready to move on ... and then I remember. The visions of myself sitting there in the dining room chair like a ghost, drinking wine and wanting to deny it, and at the same time hating Evan because I knew he was lying.

A dreadful breath leaves me, and a sadness weighs down on my chest, but there's conviction there too.

A new place, a new way of life. My fingers drift to my belly button and then lower. A new life entirely.

Diary Entry Six

Hey Mom, can I take back what I said? I don't think I want to be alone.

I don't think alone is the right word. Alone hurts my heart a lot. It hurts more than I want to admit. Mom, it feels like the worst thing in the world sometimes. Now that I know what it's like to not be alone, I'm not sure that's really what I want.

I think that's why I clung to Jake. I just didn't want to be alone. You probably knew that, didn't you?

More than that, I want to be loved by someone who can love me the way I need and I can admit that.

How did you know Dad loved you the way you needed? I just laughed a little writing this. I'm sure he made it obvious. He didn't hurt you like Evan does to me.

I hope what Evan did doesn't make you mad. I don't think he means it. I think he doesn't know any better and I knew that when I married him.

Everything has settled now, and I know I want more, Mom. I really want someone to love me.

I want them to love me like Evan used to love me.

I don't know if it's possible.

I'm going to find someone one day. There's a lot to do between now and then, but I promise I won't settle for being alone.

Maybe not now. I don't know when. I'm not going to use them or compare them to Evan. It'll take time, but I think eventually I'll be able to do this.

This baby makes me feel loved and I know I love him or her.

I promise I'll give him every bit of love I have. A little extra too, lots of kisses from you. I know you'd love to hold him. I'll hold him extra tight for you. And for Henry. Henry would have loved this baby too.

chapter 22

Evan

SHE TOOK OFF HER WEDDING RING TODAY.

I watched on a tiny-ass security monitor as she slipped it off and held it between her fingers. Miles away with the sins of the city between us, all I could do was watch her stare at it, as if wishing it would answer some unspoken question for her.

I hold my breath as I quietly open the door.

Kat didn't change the locks like she threatened to do, but that wouldn't have stopped me anyway.

This is the point that I've truly gone crazy and I know it. She's set boundaries and I don't give a shit about them. It's the first time in my life that's happened, but losing the woman you love will do that to a man. Watching her walk away when you know she loves you and you love her; it's a torture that's immeasurable and the destruction it leaves is irrefutable.

One slow step in, and not the faintest of sounds. The front door to the townhouse closes behind me softly. She'll forgive me one day. I'll hate myself forever if I stayed away.

Maybe I should have called, maybe I should have announced myself, but it's my home. She's my wife and this is where I belong.

I can accept that now. If I can keep secrets, so can Kat. I swallow thickly, closing my eyes and hating myself as I lock the front door. *She better be able to.*

I'm a desperate man. If anything happens to her, I'll end it. I already know that. But I'm so fucking weak that I'm risking it. If only she can keep a secret, we'll be all right.

My head whips around to the sound of the microwave beeping in the kitchen.

Beep, beep, beep followed by the click of the microwave being opened and a soft hum of satisfaction.

Kat. My love.

She's only a room away, and knowing what I'm about to do makes my heart race as I find it hard to swallow.

My body doesn't wait for me. My feet move on their own, pushing me closer to her. I need to see her, even if she doesn't see me. I can't explain why it needs to be in person.

The only light in the townhouse that's on is the kitchen light. It's early morning and I wasn't planning on her being awake.

Maybe the fact she's awake is a sign. A sign that I can't be a coward any longer.

That's what a man who waits in the shadows is. That's what a man who hurts his wife is. A fucking coward.

Stalking into the kitchen, I expect her to see me, but her back is turned as she stirs something in a bowl then slips it into the microwave, still humming something. It takes me a moment to realize it's a lullaby.

In nothing but a thin cotton sleep shirt, she tempts me.

Fuck, I've missed this view. When she raises her arms, the T-shirt she has on slips up past her thighs and gives me the smallest peek of her cheeks.

I almost groan from primal deprivation. It feels like forever since I've held her, laid her in bed and enjoyed her in every way possible.

"Kat." I say her name softly as the microwave starts and she whips around, backing into the cabinets with her hand on her chest.

"Sorry," I say and there's not a single second of hesitation when I apologize. "I know you said not to come ... I just ..."

I can see the outline of her breasts through the shirt and with her dark brunette hair a mess from sleep, she's never looked more beautiful. More fuckable. More *mine*.

"You scared the shit out of me," Kat whispers after a second, breathless.

"I'm sorry," I repeat. "I didn't mean to." I take a chance to move closer but stop at the kitchen counter. Boundaries. I've already broken so many of them. It's hard to keep my distance, but I'll wait.

"What are you doing here?" The microwave beeps and she rips the door open without taking the bowl out then slams it shut. Merely silencing it before crossing her arms over her chest.

I cock a brow at her anger, but she doesn't react.

"I brought these." Slipping my hand into my jacket pocket, I pull out the pair of baby shoes I got from home. They're the same pair I wore when I was little. Smooth leather and simple, but before me, they were my father's. I found them in a box in Pops's basement. Ma put them there. It's her handwriting.

Kat pinches the bridge of her nose and turns her shoulder to me, hiding her expression, but I saw it. The sweep of sadness cuts me to my core.

"Baby?" I whisper softly, cautiously even. "I—"

"What are you doing?" she says, cutting me off as she stares daggers in my direction.

"I know you're angry." My tone is placating, but it does nothing to soothe her.

"Angry doesn't even begin to cover it."

A second passes, followed by another as I struggle to form the right words. "I have faith you'll forgive me," I tell her with feigned confidence.

"Fuck off," she spits out.

"Because you love me. And you know I love you."

"You love me?" she questions with a deep scowl. Storming toward me, she sticks her finger in my chest as she yells. "This is what love is?" She shoves me back and I take it, loving the fight in her. But it doesn't last long.

"Your father died, and I had to be alone." She murmurs the truth I already know and takes a step back. "You chose to be alone," she whispers. She tries turning from me again, but I grip her waist.

"I didn't want it to be like that. I swear to you." Bringing up my pops hits me hard. I keep forgetting and that's how I want it to be. I keep thinking he'll call or text. I keep thinking when all this is over, we'll have dinner together on Sundays again. I hate it when I remember he's not here anymore. I can't handle losing them both at once.

"I'm not all right." I whisper the truth to her as something pricks at the back of my eyes. "I'm sorry." Sincerity is there, but I don't know that she can hear it anymore. The feeling of worthlessness washes over me.

"Sorry doesn't cut it." She takes in a deep breath meant to steady her, but it seems to do the opposite.

"You know what loving you means?" I ask her, raising my voice. "It means protecting you."

"You can take all those words and—"

"They're in my vows," I say, heaving out the words as I interrupt her, my emotions rising and the thought of losing Kat forever becoming more and more real. "Protecting you is in my vows."

"Don't talk to me about vows." I've never seen her so angry. The look in her eyes is pure hate mixed with mourning.

"Come here," I tell her and her eyes narrow.

She tilts her head to the side and looks at me as if I've lost my mind. My heart feels like it does a somersault, a painful flip in my chest as she says, "Don't tell me what to do."

"The only reason I've been gone is that being seen with you would put you in danger." I hate myself the moment the confession slips out. Weak. I'm so fuck-ing weak. I need to be a better man for her, but I've never been good enough and we both know that.

Kat's silent, but her expression is unchanged.

With a hesitant step forward and my hands held out to her, I add, "I had to do it."

"You don't have to do a damn thing but breathe," she finally responds, her voice hollow, the devastation I've caused ringing out clearly.

"I was only trying to keep you safe." I say the words quietly as the sight of Kat in front of me becomes more of a reality than my fear ever was.

She hates me. I've made my wife hate me. Pain ricochets through every piece of me.

"Well, thank you for that," she answers sarcastically with tears in her eyes as she shakes her head.

"I swear." I feel tears prick my eyes as I fall to my knees in front of her. I'm not in control anymore. I'm not in control of a damn thing and purely at her mercy. "I'm here right now because I can't stay away any longer." My heart crumples at the words that I choke on.

Kat takes a small step back, brushing against the counter as she does, and I wish I still had a grip on her.

I murmur my apology. "I didn't know it would take this long. I'm sorry. I fucked up. Repeatedly and I'm trying, but I'm failing."

"Didn't know what would take this long?" she asks, crossing her arms and re-fusing to look into my eyes, but she's full of emotion and on edge waiting for me to open up to her. I know her, and I know that's exactly what this is. That's what made her fall in love with me. I swallow the thick lump in my throat and pray I'm not making a mistake.

"I'm …" I can hardly breathe as the words *threatening, investigating, framing* get caught in my throat.

"Tell me, Evan." Kat licks her lower lip and stares down at me with tired eyes. "I've had enough and I'm over the secrets and the lies. I'm over this," she says and gestures between us although as she does, her expression morphs into pain. "What was so important that it had to be done to protect me?"

"It's going to sound crazy," I warn her, staring up at her from where I am as the dawn slips in through the windows, playing with the shadows on her gorgeous face.

"It already does."

"James is the one who's responsible for Tony's death." I confess still on my knees, although I let go of her. I hate myself for telling her and bringing her into this, and I almost don't say another word.

"He was trying to kill me, not Tony." My throat is dry and scratchy as the words slowly leave me and I rise to stand, feeling the weight of it all rain down on me. "And he knows I know."

Denial forces Kat to shake her head, a crease settling between her brow. It's a small motion of disbelief, but she doesn't speak as she drops her arms, listening.

"It's because of his divorce. He wants Samantha scared and he wanted to prove he'd do anything. So he tried to kill me, thinking I'd do a line of it. It backfired."

Her mouth opens and closes, but she still says nothing. A lightness carries me forward, knowing she's listening. At the very least, she's listening.

Please believe me. "I've been tracking his schedule and routines, breaking into his house and office looking for evidence or something that can prove it."

A huff of disbelief so faint I almost think I imagine it leaves Kat's lips as she turns from me, facing the sink and putting her fingers to her lips.

"Talk to me, please," I beg her and a trace of anger flashes in her eyes.

"You could have gone to the cops," she finally says. "Like a normal human being."

"I couldn't go to the cops with nothing on him. James has proof I was with Tony. It's his word against mine, and he has photos. I listened to him that night. I went along with the alibi and lied to the cops. I fucked up and he tried to blackmail me, but I called his bluff."

"Jesus Christ," Kat says then exhales.

"You see why I didn't tell you? It's too much and you're pregnant. If he's after me and he knows I love you, he'd go after you too." My biggest fear slips from me and I can't control how my eyes glaze over as the terrors I've dealt with every night for weeks linger between us. I've pictured her here on the floor, just by my feet, dead almost every night.

Yet I'm here. I've told her. And there's a chance I just brought that reality to life.

"You could have messaged me; you didn't have to hurt me."

Swallowing thickly, I gather my composure, refusing to let the fear win although everything else has failed. "He's tracking my texts, babe, he's following my every step. Just to get here, I had to make sure to lose the guy he paid to follow me around."

"This is insane, Evan. You know that, don't you?"

"I know, and I'm sorry. I have someone working on it and we're trying."

"Who?" she asks and when I don't answer she adds, "No more secrets, and no more lies. I want all of it."

"Mason," I confide in her, and it takes a moment to register.

"Does Jules know?" she asks, worry riddled in her downturned expression.

"I doubt it."

"So, because you think I could have been in potential danger, you left me alone, treated me like I was … like I was nothing?"

"He would have killed you," I tell her, stressing the truth of the situation.

"You don't know that."

"I met him, and he brought you up." My throat goes dry at the memory. "He would have gone for you, Kat."

She shakes her head in disbelief.

"If I lose you, I have nothing!" The words are ripped from my throat, desperate for her to see what I've been seeing. To feel what I've been feeling, complete and utter loss. I calm my voice and take a step closer to her then say, "If he killed you, I would have nothing to live for."

She stares into my eyes with a look I can't quite read and whispers, "I'd rather die beside you than live without you."

"I would kill myself if anyone hurt you because of me. I don't know how you can't see that." She appraises me for a moment, her shoulders rising and falling with soft breaths. "I promise it's almost over. I promise you Kat, I wouldn't do this if I didn't have to."

"You should have known better than to keep it from me. What if you had died?" she asks me, and I can't answer right away. I'd never considered it. "What if he killed you? I would have never known."

"My only thought was to keep you safe; I wasn't concerned with anything else.

"If you do what I say, we can still be together," I tell her and the reaction I get is nothing like what I'd planned. She's not at all moved by my confession. She can't tell a soul or let on that we're together. "If we're together," I say then stop midsentence, afraid that we're not. Afraid that it's too late.

"You don't control me anymore." Although her words are spoken easily, and she seems to understand everything, her walls are still high, guarding her from me.

"Kat, I love you, but I will lock you in a fucking room to keep you safe. If you don't listen to me, then you leave me with no choice. I swear to God I will."

Smack!

My face burns with a stinging sensation as the sound rings in the air. My lungs halt as my eyes widen, taking in the vision of a pissed-off Kat in front of me with her hand still raised. My hand slowly rises to my jaw.

I've never seen Kat strike a person in my life. She's not a violent person by nature.

But I guess I had it coming to me.

"Don't you dare tell me that you love me."

I don't fucking hesitate to respond, "I love you more than anything, and I'll never deny it. I'll tell you every single day for the rest of my life." Even with my jaw stinging from the impact.

"I can keep a secret too. You could have told me. You didn't have to put me through this with everything else I'm dealing with."

"One slip is all it will take. If anyone even thinks we're back together … that's all it would take."

"Well, you told me now," she states with finality and I take her hand in mine, forcing it up so she can see.

"Because you took off your ring," I tell her, not holding back the pain it caused. "Because you kissed someone else." Her fight vanishes, not all at once, but slowly as both of us breathe heavily, the air between us growing hotter. "Because I thought I was losing you forever."

"You left me with no choice," she says although a look of regret flashes in her eyes.

"I didn't have one either. You have to believe me."

"You really love me?"

"I do. You must know it's true. I know you do."

"You want to be with me? You want to keep me yours?" she asks, completely serious as if there's any other option for me.

"Yes, it's all I want. And to keep you safe."

"Evan." She utters my name softly but as it rings through the air, I hear the threat that comes with it. Her eyes pierce through me as she stares back at me.

"You'll come back to me, every night. Every fucking night. You'll message me back every time I text you."

"I can't text you back from my phone." Her eyes narrow and I'm quick to come up with a solution as I offer, "But I can get another."

"Damn right you will," she answers me and I find the corners of my lips kick up in amusement. I love my wife and she loves me. *Thank fuck.*

Just as that truth begins to comfort me, she adds, "I don't like you doing this."

"I promise it's almost over."

"Evan, you better never do this to me again."

"I promise, baby. I promise never again. Everything's going to change from here on out. I promise."

"We can get through anything, but never this again," she whispers, and I know I have her. I have her back and I'll be damned if I ever let her feel lonely again.

chapter 25

"TALK TO ME," EVAN SAYS AGAIN, AND I WANT TO. GOD, I DO, BUT there's so much to say.

"You want to hear what I've been wanting to tell you for weeks?" I ask and even to my own ears, I sound like I've lost it.

"Kat, you—"

I don't care what he has to say, I'm going to lay it all out there for him and he can decide what he wants to do with it. I have a plan, I have needs. Either he's in, or he's out. I'll accept either; I'm willing to give it a chance. There's only so much that's left of me, though, and he needs to be very aware of that.

"I'm exasperated. Just because you said sorry doesn't take away everything. It doesn't make it all just fine and back to normal. I'm still … *feeling*." The spiraling that's come over me day in and day out threatens to take me over now, and I let it happen. "I feel like someone's run over my body with a truck and then backed up. My hips and back hurt. I can't sleep. And that's just the pregnancy." With a deep inhale, I continue before he can interrupt me.

"You know, the baby you put in me? That's still happening and by the way, pregnancy doesn't just pause because things have been insane. So, I'm dealing with hormones, and I cry way too much for no reason. I feel sick and I can't sleep. I'm paranoid and I'm so damn alone that I've truly been scared. I feel crazy and I don't even know what part of this is normal and what part isn't." The words leave me in a fluid mix of emotions. Like a purge of everything I've been feeling, piling up until it drowned me. With a shuddering breath, I attempt to calm myself, not knowing how he'll take any of it and very much aware I'm an absolute mess.

After a moment, he speaks. "I want to hold you," is all he says. I'm caught, shaken and uncertain as I stand in front of him in nothing but a T-shirt in our kitchen. My God do I want him, but murder? People trying to kill him? I can barely handle normal life. "I want to make all the pain go away; I'll take it from you. I promise," he says in a deep cadence that washes a sense of calm over it all. Evan slips closer to me, wrapping a hand around my waist and I can feel myself falling back into the same trap. Because he does that to me. He makes the pain go away and he makes it so easy to give in.

"Stop," I say, pleading with him. "It's like history repeating itself." My body and my thoughts are at war with each other. I'm brought back to every kiss we've had, every time he's held my hand, every heated moment that's left me consumed. The world is nothing without him in it and I know it, mind, body and soul.

"It's not," Evan says matter-of-factly to me, his voice begging me and my body persuading me to once again fall into his arms. Which is right where I want to be. The very thought tugs at every string wrapped around my battered heart.

"We have a baby coming and I can't put this baby through what we've been going through, Evan," I say, admitting my fears to him. If only he knew how much it hurt. "I'm afraid every time I cry the baby can feel it. I terrified I'm hurting him already." As I say the words, tears prick my eyes.

"Him?" Evan asks. "You think we're having a boy?" The shine in his eyes is of pure devotion. That's how he breaks me down. By truly loving me.

"Don't change the subject," I warn him although it warms my heart and I can't help but feel it resonate. "I want you, Evan. But I want you here with me, and committed to me and this baby."

"I know," he says. "I love you, Kat. I love you with everything in me and I won't stop proving that to you every day for the rest of our lives."

Even though he's saying all the right things and I love it, I have to be honest. "I swear I can't take it anymore."

"Never again. I can't stand not being with you," he tells me, and my body succumbs to a warmth that's been there all along, waiting just beneath the surface.

He pulls me into his arms and I let him. Even more, I grip onto his shirt as he wraps his muscular arms around me and I breathe in his scent of fresh forest after rain. This is home. This is what feeling complete feels like. I'm so very aware of everything he said only moments ago. The threats and danger are legitimate, but it all comes with him. I can keep a secret. I'll do whatever I have to if it means I get to have Evan completely.

My eyes shut tight, willing the unwanted thoughts away as Evan whispers just beneath the shell of my ear, "I want to make it all better." He's so close that my hair tickles my neck as it moves gently with his breath.

He says the right words. He's always been good at that.

He lowers his lips to the sensitive part of my neck. "I only want to love you, and have you love me back."

My poor heart has barely survived all this time without him, but it rages now, pounding against my rib cage. I suppose it's only beating still because it hasn't belonged to me in years. *It's always been his.*

I nod my head and look down at his chest, inhaling his scent I've missed for so long, feeling his touch I've been craving.

"You're still wearing your jacket," I comment softly as I run the tips of my fingers down the zipper. I lift my gaze to his dark eyes, swirling with desire. "Take it off."

I bite my lower lip then take half a step back as he keeps his eyes on mine and slips his jacket down his arms.

"Your shirt," I say in a breathy voice and in an instant, he tugs it over his head then carelessly drops it to the floor. The fabric puddles at his feet. He closes the space between us as desire spikes in my blood. Like the first night I saw him, knowing he was trouble, yet I can't resist.

"What now?" Evan asks, moving his pointer finger to the bottom of the cotton T-shirt and slipping it upward, tugging ever so gently until he reaches the peaks of my breasts. He closes his fingers around my nipples with a slight pinch and then tugs. Gasping, I let my head fall back. The sensation is directly linked to my clit and it forces me to part my lips with a soft moan. "What now, baby?"

"Mmm," I manage, and that's all I can offer as lust clouds my judgment. I missed this. I missed him. Such a small touch and yet it feels all-consuming.

"How about this?" Evan suggests and then he unbuckles his belt. The sound of his pants being unzipped fills the small kitchen and my body aches to reach out to him.

His pants fall to the floor and he pushes his boxers down with them, stepping out of them and exposing his already hard cock. Every nerve ending in my body lights just seeing him bared to me. Knowing how much pleasure he can and will give to me.

A rough chuckle distracts me from focusing on his erection and I look into his eyes.

"You still want me?" he asks and it's only then that my cheeks warm with a blush. My body sways slightly. I murmur my answer. "Always."

Evan runs the same pointer finger along my upper thigh past my panties and traces the center seam of the cotton, brushing my throbbing clit and sending sparks of heated pleasure through my body. My body leans forward, my hands gripping onto his corded forearms.

"I will never risk making you unhappy again. I promise," he says. My head is so dizzy with desire, I can only moan in response.

"Tell me," he says as he slides his fingers under the thin fabric and runs them along my hot core. He pushes against my clit with just the right amount of pressure then nearly slips into me as he runs his fingers back down. My hands fly up to his chest, gripping onto him for balance as my toes curl and my body begs me to ride his fingers.

"Tell me," he repeats then stops. My heavy-lidded eyes open, and I pull back to object. "Tell me you still want me."

"I still want you," I whisper without hesitation; the words rush out of my lips with need and desperation. Before the last word is even spoken, Evan splays his hand on my lower back and pulls me closer to him, forcing my chest against his.

"Fuck, you're so wet," he groans in the crook of my neck as he forces two fingers deep inside of me. I cry out in pleasure, clinging to him as the sensation nearly topples me.

"Evan." I moan out his name, but he doesn't answer as the pleasure builds. It's been so long but I don't remember it ever being like this.

It's so intense, so overwhelming that I know I can't remain standing for this.

"Evan," I plead for him to understand, but my head flies back and strangled moans fill the air, both from him and from me as I find my release on his fingers.

My body buckles and shakes as the orgasm rocks through me. I'm paralyzed as Evan moves me to the counter. It's cold and hard, and I lean against it for balance as slow waves mercilessly continue to flow through my body.

"And your shirt?" Evan asks me as if I didn't just experience the strongest orgasm of my life.

I grip the counter tightly while I catch my breath, staring at him.

"I want it off," he commands and with my back to his chest, he tugs the shirt off me. My body sways easily, caving to his every whim. "And these," he tells me, pushing his hand back down my panties. I'm trapped with my back to his front and his strong arm pinning me to him, his other hand on my hip, keeping me still.

My fingers clutch at his wrist and my blunt nails dig into his flesh as he strums my sensitive clit.

"Evan." His name is a plea as my body falls forward, and I struggle to take more.

He's not gentle with his strokes in the least. And I love it. My nipples pebble and my body goes weak with a numbing, blinding intensity.

The pleasure stirs deep in my belly, but like a flame it grows hotter and hotter, warming me and threatening just the same.

It's only when I come again that Evan slowly pulls my panties from me, leaving them by my feet. I'm not blind to the fact that they're damp with my desire.

Evan moves his hard erection between my thighs and I widen my stance slightly. He kisses my ear as he runs the head of his dick up and down my folds. A shiver runs through my body. Every inch is covered with a heated pleasure so sensitive to touch, that I shudder from just his hot breath on my neck.

"I love you, Kat," Evan whispers as he pushes himself deep inside of me. Slowly, stretching my walls. My head falls back onto his shoulder as he wraps his arm in front of me, holding me to him. He reaches up and grabs my throat.

Buried deep inside of me, he whispers, "Tell me you love me."

"Always," I say and the word slips out easily, my eyes still closed. I slowly open them to see Evan's expression. I'm struck by the intensity of his gaze. The need, the desire, the possession. "Say the words," he commands.

"I'll always love you," I tell him softly, the words barely audible.

He crushes his lips against mine as he bucks his hips. The sudden spike of near pain makes me push my head back and scratch along his forearm. He doesn't stop pounding into me, letting the pleasure build.

He pistons his hips relentlessly, each thrust forcing a pleasured groan from me. I try not to make too much noise, I try to be quiet, but I can't.

I come again and again, each climax feeling more intense than the last. Evan's ravenous as he kisses me. He doesn't stop his hands roaming over my body. He doesn't stop until I have nothing left, and only then does he bury himself in me to the hilt and find his own release.

Diary Entry Seven

Mom,

I think I've lost my mind.

Evan's like a tornado in my life.

That's not news to you, but I think that's how I want it. Crazy and reckless, but deeply rooted and unstoppable.

I'm ready to fight for him, Mom. For us. I'm eager to, even.

I love him. I love what he does to me when he's with me.

Mom, I'm afraid you'd be ashamed of me if you were still here. That's the only part that hurts.

But believe me when I tell you that I love him and in all his fucked-upness, he loves me.

That hole I was telling you about before? It's the one that came when you left, but it's not there when Evan's with me.

I think he has a hole in his heart too, Mom.

And I think I'm the only one that can fill it.

I told you I've gone crazy, didn't I?

Maybe it's not the worst thing in the world, though. I don't know. I don't think I care about it much anymore. So long as I keep Evan close to me.

I hope I make you proud. And if not, I'm sorry, Mom. I didn't choose this, but I choose him. I want to see it through.

Evan

THE PAPER RUSTLES IN MY HAND. IT'S A LIST POPS LEFT ON THE COUNTER. He didn't tell me about it, but I'm sure it was for us.

Bottles.

Pacifiers.

Bibs.

Onesies.

It goes on for a bit, but it's everything I need to buy. I'm not sure if he was going to give it to me, or if he was going to get this all himself. A pain radiates in my chest, right where that beating organ is. I miss him. I've never needed to talk to him as much as I do now.

You have to do it. I read the text that buzzes through and then put both my phone and the list in my pocket. I already know what Mason is getting at.

He's convinced I need to be seen in public. To make sure the tail James has on me sees me keeping my distance, moving on. He wants them to back off and that means I need to look like I'm backing off too. No more of this tit for tat. The plan is to let them think I've moved on from looking into James. That I've given up or simply decided it wasn't worth it. It doesn't matter which.

I stare down the aisle as a kid runs past, holding up a plane in the air and making swooshing noises. It's crazy that one day, I'm going to have one of them. A kid. A baby first. And before that, a pregnant wife.

It's fucking terrifying.

This particular setting isn't what he had in mind and I made sure no one followed me here. Family first, though, and then I'll take care of the mess. Bars and old hangouts. Then back to the apartment every night before I sneak out to go home. She's a saint for putting up with me and all of this.

"Hey," I call out as a young guy in a blue Kiddie Korner T-shirt walks by with a clipboard in his hand. He has to push his glasses up the bridge of his nose when he looks at me. "Can I help you, sir?"

"Yeah, I was looking for simple baby things. Like bottles and tiny clothes. Things like that," I tell him. "I can't find them anywhere in here."

"We don't have infant merchandise. You'll have to go to Little Treasures," he responds and starts walking to the center of the store to point. "Two blocks down and make a right. It's a bit of a walk, but it's right there on your left."

"Thanks."

I rub my tired eyes and walk out of the shop, hearing the ding of bells above my head and I'm instantly accosted by the bitter cold.

Just as I'm shoving my hands into my pockets, I catch sight of Detective Bradshaw.

"It's one of those days," I mutter under my breath as he kicks off the wall. Guess the prick was waiting for me.

"Mr. Thompson," he says, greeting me without a hint of emotion as he closes the distance between us.

I take a few steps forward as a couple of kids run behind me and into the store. Meeting him halfway, I answer him, "Detective Bradshaw, nice to see you again." *Not fucking really.*

He huffs a laugh like he heard my thought and says, "I'm glad I found you here."

"A bit odd that we just happened to run into each other." Holding his gaze, I let him know that I know he must've been following me. "Not my usual hangout."

"Yeah, I noticed. Your schedule's a bit different now?"

"A bit."

"For the best, I hope?" he asks and a prickle runs down my neck. I don't like it.

"Yeah," I answer, and my word comes out hard. My back's stiff and my muscles are wound tight. "You taking me in?"

I wait as he assesses me, enjoying the suspense.

"Should I?"

"I can't think of any reason off the top of my head." He doesn't think my answer's funny in the least. My lips quirk up into a smirk at his hard-assed expression. "I'm good to go then?"

"You got any new information for me?" he asks, getting to the point of this meeting.

"I got nothing to say."

"Why are you doing this to yourself? Protecting someone who wants to issue harassment charges?" he asks me, and I can't help that my forehead creases with both confusion and anger.

"Oh," Detective Bradshaw says, finally showing a little joy. "You didn't hear?" He rocks on his feet like he's happy to deliver the news. "James Lapour wants us to keep you away from him. He filed for a restraining order and all."

"That's why you're here?" I ask, not sure what to make of James's move. He went to the cops and maybe I grew up different, but that's something you just don't do when you're neck-deep in criminal shit.

"He said you were snooping around, making him uncomfortable and issuing threats."

"Threats?" I echo, getting more pissed off by the second.

"Nothing solid we could work with, so I thought I'd give you a shadow."

"Ah, and thus this wonderful meeting." I don't talk to cops. Never have, never will. Half the city's cops are in someone's back pocket. *Someone's* like Mason and James; the rich *someone's*. Not *someone's* like me and the kids I grew up with.

"I'm sorry to say I couldn't really give two shits about James Lapour so if you want me to stay away, I'm happy to keep my distance."

Detective Bradshaw's less than pleased with my statement. "Just thought you'd like to know."

"Thanks, Detective, am I good to go now?"

"Have a good day," he mutters as he walks past me, brushing my shoulder as he goes.

I finally bring my hands out of my pocket and open my clenched fist only to see the scrap of paper balled up. My breathing comes in shorter and my blood heats.

This shit has to stop. Right fucking now.

Diary Entry Two

Dear Pops,

I'm ashamed. I feel like I've lost complete control and I know it's hurt Kat.

Help me to be a better husband and take the nightmares away. Please. Just get them out of my head.

It's just getting worse every night, and it's scaring my wife.

What kind of a man am I? Dreams are tearing my life apart.

I can't sleep without seeing you. Don't get me wrong, I love and miss you so damn much, but you always die in my dreams. You're gone. All of the memories of our life together are changing. I don't want them to, but I don't know how to stop it.

I have them with Kat too, and it's killing me.

I yelled in my sleep last night, and it woke me up. Kat was crying next to me, Pops. She said she'd been trying to wake me up and that's when I started screaming.

She's worried, and I feel like less of a man and husband because I can't stop it.

Please, Pops, if you're there and you're able to, please help me.

I miss you. I can't stand this.

Please just take it all back.

chapter 25

Kat

AT WHAT POINT DID THIS BECOME MY LIFE?

I've been asking myself that question all morning. I've showered, I've eaten and cleaned most of the townhouse. But my mind is fuzzy with disbelief.

A sigh leaves me at the thought as I hail a taxi just outside our townhouse. The winter weather has lightened up some, and I almost feel like I could wear a light jacket and not this heavy wool coat. Maybe I've just gotten used to the cold.

It doesn't take long for a yellow and black cab to pull to a stop in front of me. Ushering myself in, my mind still fails to grasp all the details of everything that's happened in only months.

If an author submitted my story to me as a manuscript, I'd tell them it's too unbelievable. What's that quote from Mark Twain? Something about how truth is stranger than fiction because fiction needs to make sense.

"Where to, miss?" the cabby asks me as I get in the back seat and close the door.

"Saks on Fifth, please," I answer confidently, although my nerves creep up. Evan would kill me if he knew what I was doing, but it's not going to stop me. I need this.

There are only two things I'm certain of.

1.   I can't afford to let Evan leave me again or else I'll truly lose my mind.

2.   I'm not going to stay out of this like Evan wants.

The car moves forward, taking me away from the empty townhouse. He's gone off to meet with Mason and tell him what we agreed on. He's staying with me, committing to me and our baby. And he promised to move past this. I'll listen to what he tells me to do, but every night he comes back to me and sleeps with me in our bed. No more secrets and hiding. I have to help him, not let the fear of what might happen ruin what we have in the present.

I'm still pissed that Mason knew when I didn't. It's the second knife in my back, but I let it slide simply because it's not his ring on my finger.

Instead, I focus on the real target here. Samantha Lapour. I'm not over her being with him when we were separated. The hate and jealousy are still there.

She loves Fifth Avenue. What rich New York socialite doesn't?

I remember her bragging about her apartment above Saks when I first met her. She was so happy to keep it even though she and her husband were happily married. It wasn't so much a humblebrag as it was just bragging.

That should've been my first clue we were never destined to become friends, but her smile was charming and her stories were alluring. I'll admit, I was dazzled.

The cabby stops before I'm ready, my nerves getting the best of me, and it's only then that the weight of what I'm doing makes my stomach churn.

I pay the cabby, slipping out and onto the curb to avoid the traffic.

My pulse races faster and faster, adrenaline surging as I make my way through the throngs of people and into the apartment foyer, disappearing from the crowd and readying myself to knock on her door on the fourteenth floor.

I don't know the exact address, though. There are only so many up here, so if at first I don't succeed, I'll simply try again.

My legs are shaky as I climb the stairs; I should have taken the elevator. Some small part of me is quite aware that the decision was made to eat up time.

"Good evening," a feminine voice says, and I have to raise my gaze to watch an older woman with a stylish white bob and a small Pomeranian in her arms close the door to 1401. There are only two other apartments on this floor, the one I'm sure Samantha told me about.

But that was years ago …

"How are you?" I greet the woman as if I'm supposed to be here, as if I'm visiting a friend and not a woman I have every intention of warning to stay the hell away from me and my family. In an effort to be convincing, I open my clutch, keeping my eyes on her with a simper plastered on my face. I'm sure it looks like I'm getting out a key or maybe my phone to call a friend.

The woman simply smiles tightly and nods then carries on her way, not answering the question. I hesitate, glancing between the remaining two doors and wondering which one I should knock on first.

This is crazy.

My heart races and a mix of adrenaline and anxiousness make me question why I'm even here.

The real answer, the absolute truth, hisses in the back of my head.

She was with him. In his family house.

Two confident strides and I knock, one, two, three times on 1402. I don't breathe until I take a small step back and wait.

Silence. No response. The confidence threatens to leave with every second that passes, but the moment I take a step to the right, to knock on the only other option, the door opens.

In red silk pajamas and her hair in curlers, Samantha looks so different from any other time I've seen her. She wasn't expecting company, that's for sure.

Her expression is nothing but irritation at first, and then she recognizes me.

"Oh, hello," she says, greeting me somewhat easily but with her lips pressed in a thin straight line as she stands up straighter. "Kat."

I have to clear my throat before I can answer her. "Samantha," I respond in the same stiff way. "I apologize for dropping by with no notice. I was hoping I could talk to you." Clutching my purse with both hands in front of me, I add, "It's about Evan."

She crosses her arms, instantly on the defensive and I'm quick to add, putting on a bit of a show, "I'm worried about him. About the loss of his father and how he's handling it." The words are the truth and the emotion that comes with them is genuine. But I just want an in so I can get a better grip on exactly who this woman is … and maybe details on her estranged husband.

"I'm so sorry for your loss," she responds tightly, still looking me up and down as she considers what to do with me.

"I know you've spent a little time with him and I was just hoping you could tell me how he is."

She nearly flinches then has to take a moment before she can answer. As if she has no idea how he's doing. Or maybe she's shocked that I know she's seen him, but it's all over the papers, so why wouldn't I?

Evan's told me one side of this story, but there are always three sides … sometimes even more. In this case I'll stay away from James, for Evan's sanity, but I'm sure Samantha will have a thing or two to gossip about.

"Did you guys talk at all?" I ask her. My throat tightens as I add, "He doesn't talk to me at all anymore."

"Oh, God," Samantha says, sounding exasperated and then tells me, "We didn't talk about his father. I'm sorry." She struggles to gather a response. "I'm sure it's difficult and I understand you two are going through something, but I assure you that I'd like to stay out of it."

With the creak of the heavy door, she attempts to close it, but I'm quicker.

My palm smacks against the door and I plead with her, "I just need someone to talk to. Please! If you could just let me in."

My blood rushes in my ears as I wait, the door remaining right where it is, only slightly cracked. She opens it again cautiously, pursing her lips and appearing more irked than anything else. As she lets go of the door, it opens with my weight and she nods her head, letting me in.

"What is it that you want?" she questions as she walks with her back to me inside of the apartment. I close the front door myself and take the place in.

It's a barren disaster.

I nearly ask her if she was robbed, but looking to my left at a cluttered kitchen I can easily spot a potential cause of the state of her place. Three small bags of white powder and a line wait for her. Right next to them is a colorful bag of pills. A mix of what could be Adderall and pain meds.

She turns with a smirk on her lips. "Like the place?" she asks sarcastically. "My prick of an ex made sure to sell all my belongings when I went out of town."

"Oh my God," I say, the words coming out in a whisper of disbelief and pity, neither of which truly resonate with me. There's only a sofa in the living room, a sleek gray contemporary sectional. I imagine it would look beautiful if the living room itself wasn't devoid of any other piece of furniture. She settles down onto one end and I take the other.

Glancing up at the chandelier I tell her, "I'm so sorry. I'm sure it was beautiful …" my voice trails off and she doesn't say anything.

"You could go to the cops," I offer her, and she laughs with ridicule. If she weren't so arrogant, I'd feel sorry for her. With her cheeks sunken in and the silk pajamas baggy on her slim frame, she appears far less beautiful and enviable than I remember her.

"He's got them all on payroll, sweetheart. I'm barely surviving."

"I am so sorry," I say, at a loss for words and feeling so much more uncomfortable than I anticipated. I even feel bad for her to some degree.

"Divorce isn't always a bad thing, love," she says and then takes in my expression. "I'm sorry for you two, though, I really am."

It's hard to judge her tone, so I'm not sure how to take it.

"I actually had something to ask you about your husband." I shift on the sofa, preparing to question her. Samantha reaches for a pack of cigarettes and slips one out.

She lights it then asks, "What's that?"

There's a glint in her eyes and her back stiffens slightly.

"Evan doesn't like him much anymore," I offer her, gauging her reaction and she lets out a small laugh that's accompanied by smoke.

"I don't much like the asshole either."

"Can't blame you," I say, keeping my tone agreeable as I set my purse down beside me and feign a casualness I don't feel.

"He told me weeks ago he thinks James is trying to hurt him." I hold her gaze as I say, "I think he's paranoid, but he's worried about his reputation since leaving the company."

Samantha takes a long drag of her cigarette, ignoring the question until I tell her.

"I was hoping that if I talked to you, you could tell me the truth. Evan's just being crazy, isn't he?"

Every nerve is on edge in my body. There's something about how she looks at me. It's as if she's wondering what to do with me.

I don't trust the look, and I don't trust her.

"Evan told you what, exactly?"

"Evan told me that James tried to kill him, thinking he'd do coke left out for him."

"Did he?" she asks condescendingly. "I'm surprised because from what he told me, he didn't want you to know."

I hate her in this moment. I hate the expression of disinterest.

I hate that Evan was with her when he should have been with me.

I hate that she knew he was keeping secrets.

More than that, I despise that she has any hold over my emotions at all. How could this woman affect me so much? My inner voice hisses, *because you let her.*

"It was a mistake on his part," I lie to her, my fingers tensing as I grip my purse harder. "He got drunk one night a few weeks ago and lashed out at me. It's the last time we spoke." Her expression changes slightly, but only slightly, with a raised brow and the hint of a smirk. Amusement. I fucking hate her.

"Maybe it was a mistake to come here. I thought you'd know or maybe get a sense of how Evan's doing since you were with him."

"I have no idea what you're talking about." Leaning forward, she puts out the cigarette in a mug that's sitting on her furnace. It's then that I know she's not going to tell me a damn thing. She's far too stiff and closed off.

"My apologies for coming then," I say, shrugging it off. There's some piece of me that wants to confront her about the affair years ago. A part of me that wants to tell her I know.

She's a liar, though. It's so very clear. There isn't anything I need from this woman.

"It was a mistake on my part," I say then offer her a sad smile, taking in the room once again. "I hope you get everything you want from the divorce." I leave her with that false sincerity. The only thing I hope is that I don't have a reason to ever think of her again. She's nothing more than a waste of time and breath. Every second I've wasted on her is one I'll never get back and this woman isn't worth my time.

chapter 26

"**W**HAT'D YOU DO TODAY?" KAT ASKS AS I TURN ON THE STOVE, listening to the clicks before the gas lights.

"Not much," I answer her as I look over my shoulder. *Just hunting down the identity of a drug dealer.*

"What do you think you want to do?" Kat asks me as I pour olive oil into a pan. Chicken marsala for dinner. My throat goes dry as I remember how Pops taught me how to cook it; it was one of his favorites.

"Like do for work?" I ask to clarify and put the chicken in the pan. The sizzle is perfect.

She shrugs and hops up on the counter, setting her ass down and letting her feet dangle. "I know you have some investments."

"'Some' is putting it lightly. If you're worried about money, don't be. We'll be fine." I haven't checked in a week or two on some of the stocks, but the savings account is more than enough. We've been here so long, both of us working and not doing much of anything else, the money piled up. "I promise we'll be fine, baby. You don't have to worry about that."

"I'm not really worried about money, it's more about what you're going to do with yourself." She's kept her distance in an odd way I haven't experienced before. She's careful with me. Every question seems planned, every touch cautious. It's obvious that she's still scared.

I flip the breasts over and pick up the pan, making sure to spread the oil before setting it back down. Just like how Pops used to do.

"We have a baby coming and you want to move," I answer her and stride over, my bare feet padding on the floor as I go. Standing between her legs with my hands resting lightly on her hips, I tell her, "That's all I've been thinking about for now."

There's a small hesitation before she speaks and a tension that flashes between us. *That and James.* His name is always on the tip of my tongue for any conversation we have. The threat of him lingers, even though we pretend it doesn't.

"The baby won't be here for a while," she finally says and threads her fingers through my hair. I love it when she does this. When she loves on me. I missed this. "I'm worried about you," she adds and I back away slightly, but she keeps me there, tightening her legs around me.

"Don't be upset," she says and her tone begs me to listen.

"I'm fine," I respond stiffly and even I know it's a lie.

"You just lost your father, and …"

"Stop worrying about me."

"You scared me last night with the night terror. And the ones you've had before," she adds.

"It'll be over soon," I reassure her and get back to cooking. "I have sleeping pills and that's going to help." It's quiet for a moment, but that doesn't last long. Kat's not the best at giving up on what she wants.

"What about seeing someone?" she asks.

"What, like a shrink?"

"They aren't called shrinks," she says, reprimanding me. Some days I think she thinks it's all in my head. Like maybe I'm crazy.

"I'll see one. I promise." It's on my to-do list. It's just at the very bottom of it for now.

The tension clears as I reach for the Italian mix of spices. With just a pinch of cayenne.

"Thank you," she whispers and before I can respond, she asks again, "So what do you *want* to do?" At least she moved on from talking about Pops, the nightmares, and seeing a professional about all the shit going on in my head.

Peering back at her and wiping my hands with a kitchen towel, I note the devotion in her gaze. It'd bother me, if I didn't know how damn much she loves and needs me.

"I'm not worried about keeping myself busy."

She purses her lips and nods, but she doesn't seem convinced.

"I'm going to be fine," I say and stir the sauce before layering it onto the cooked chicken.

She murmurs in that sweet voice of hers, "You better be."

"You know what I'm going to do?" I ask her as I continue cooking and ignore the sick feeling in the pit of my stomach about everything *currently* going on. "I'm going to move us out of here and into our forever home. I promise," I say, and she rolls her eyes.

"For the love of God, hire a moving company this time," she states with exasperation and I give her the laugh she's after. The move here was … something for the books.

"I'm going to find a house you love and help you make it ours." I tap the tongs on the side of the pan as I pull it off the burner and then walk back to her. "I'm going to set up our baby's room and make it perfect with all the little details."

She likes that. Kat sways on the counter like she's giddy at the thought and a genuine smile lifts up her lips. Making them that much more kissable.

"I'm going to make sure the two of you have nothing to worry about and that the three of us are happy and healthy, and all that good stuff they write about in fairytales."

She lets out a small laugh and wraps her arms around my shoulders. That's what I'm after. That's all I'm after.

"I love you, babe," I tell her, and she leans in for a small kiss.

"I love you too … I just hate seeing you anything other than happy."

"I'll be better when this is over with," I say, bringing up the one thing I don't want to speak about. She kisses me soft and sweet, and it feels right. She's a balm to my soul, but it doesn't take the pain away.

She doesn't release me like I think she will. Instead she holds on tighter.

"I'm worried about you," she whispers against my lips.

I brush my nose against hers. "It's not supposed to work that way."

Her green eyes peek up at me through her thick lashes and she says, "Yeah it is. It works both ways. Don't you know that by now?"

Kat

"**I** THOUGHT WE WERE JUST GOING TO ORDER OUT,**" EVAN SAYS FROM** across the table. The silverware clinks in his hand as he picks up the white cloth napkin and lays it on his lap.

The Savinga Grill has always been one of my favorite restaurants since I first discovered it years ago. With exposed dark red brick, raw wood beams, and high ceilings, it's rustic, it's cozy, and it's only a cab ride away.

That's what I told Evan to get him here when he asked where I wanted to go. *Just a cab ride away.*

I shrug and say, "I wanted to go out."

"It makes me nervous," he tells me. I know it does. I realize this is a risk and one he didn't want to take, but time is not on our side and I've waited long enough.

I lay my hand on the table, palm up, and wait for him to take it. "Mason said you need to be seen."

"Me, not *us*." He emphasizes the word "us."

"It's part of us moving forward together." The smile on my lips is small but it's still there. "I won't let someone keep me from you or us from our lives."

His lips twitch with a response, but he doesn't say anything. Two weeks have passed since I told him we were pregnant. Two weeks came and went, and I'm officially in our second trimester now.

"We tried this your way, now we try it mine," I tell him, and my words come out hard.

"And your way is to go out and risk being seen?"

"I want us to go out, yes … like we used to." My answer is blunt as I pull my napkin across my lap. "I'm not going to hide away in some dark room and let my fear cripple me." My voice is stern but also sympathetic. "If someone wants to know if we're together, let them know." He woke up last night with sweat pouring down his face. He was screaming in his sleep. I refuse to play this psychological game. I'm going to be there for my husband. I'm going to do everything I can to make him better. And that means not hiding and not being scared.

I'll be strong for him. I'll be strong for us both. At this point I don't know what to think of his ex-boss or how Tony died. I know my husband is letting his fear kill him, though. It's shoved itself between us and I can't let that happen anymore. He refuses to go to the cops. He's not ready to see a psychologist. I'm okay with that, but I'm not okay with nothing changing for the better.

"I won't let a single person keep us from moving on with our lives. That means being together and going to my favorite restaurant to celebrate."

I flash him a smile as the waiter walks over to us. Like this conversation doesn't put me on edge.

It's quiet while the water is being poured, and stays that way except for the waiter informing us of the specials and handing us a pair of menus.

It's only when he leaves us that I continue what I was saying.

"Yes, I want us to be seen. I also want to celebrate being pregnant. I want to buy a new house, a bigger one closer to the park." My fingertips play along the stem of the water goblet and I rest my elbow on the table as I talk while reading the menu, even though I already know what I want. "I want to slow down with work and I want the world to know it all. I want to move forward, Evan. I want everything that happened to stay in the past."

He only responds with a tight smile.

"I'm not going to let this change us and who we are."

"I don't want you to be in danger," he answers me, leaning back in his seat and casually glancing to his left and right. I recognize a man sitting alone a few tables away. Occasionally he glances up at us. It was Evan's concession and I allow it.

"Too late, baby," I say and my smile falters.

"I feel uncomfortable being here," he says and guilt digs its claws into me at his admission. I'm trying to do what's right. That's all I want to do.

"I feel like"—taking a deep inhale, I steady myself to continue, meeting his concerned gaze—"like you're perpetuating your fears by hiding away and only focusing on them. Not just focusing, but allowing them to dictate everything." My voice cracks with the confession. I have to take another sip of water to calm myself down. "I hate that you're constantly on edge when we leave the house."

"You don't understand," he tells me with a frustrated sigh that pisses me off.

"It felt like you'd died when you left me," I say. "So, I think I do understand." I take another drink of water and ask, "What if the cops stop looking into what happened? They have no leads." I stress the basic truth. "What if James gets away with it all? What then? Will you carry on like this?"

He doesn't answer, although I can see his will to fight me has left.

"I just want us back," I say. "That's really what it comes down to."

This time it's Evan who puts his hand on the table and I'm more than happy to reach for him. He kisses my knuckles then my wrist. "I'm sorry," he whispers against my racing pulse.

"I know you are, but what am I?" I give him a joking response to lighten the mood and it works somewhat.

As Evan's lips pull into a smile and he relaxes his posture, he takes my hand in his.

"You know I miss this side of you?" he tells me.

"What side?"

"The playful side," he answers and squeezes my hand … kind of like how my heart squeezes. This is the version of my husband I want all the time. The man I know and love.

"Can I tell you a secret?" I whisper just before the waiter walks up to us. "I miss it too."

"Are you two ready to order?" the waiter asks, looking between us and clasping his hands in front of him.

"You first," Evan says and gestures at me.

"The lasagna please, with a house salad." I almost order a glass of cabernet but then I stop myself. Every time I remember we're having a baby, it's a gift in itself.

"I'll have the same," Evan says, and it surprises me.

When the waiter leaves, I comment with a questioning smirk, "You never have lasagna."

He shrugs and says, "I guess I want to try it your way."

"We have the next doctor's appointment coming up and since you're no longer working, I assume you're coming with me?"

"Of course," Evan says then nods and leans forward, lowering his voice and adding a huskiness to it that makes every inch of my body tingle. "You know you look beautiful, right?"

I can't help the smile and blush that spread across my face at his compliment. "Stop," I say, brushing him off.

"Never," he answers playfully, his handsome asymmetric smile toying with my emotions.

That warm cheery feeling in my chest slowly drifts away as I remember my own little secret. Not so little, really.

"I have something to tell you," I say, uttering the words even at the risk of upsetting Evan. I guess I waited intentionally for us to be out in public before I could tell him. "I did something that I don't think you're going to like."

"What's that?" he asks easily, although I notice his shoulders stiffen.

"I was curious about something and I think it's something only I would know how to ask appropriately ..."

I don't know how to word this, and I find myself staring at the ice in the glass of water.

"You can tell me. Whatever it is."

"I went to see Samantha a couple days ago. At her place on Fifth Avenue," I tell him, confessing before I can stop myself. The air instantly changes as Evan doesn't respond. He seems uncomfortable if anything.

"I had to know for myself."

"What did you have to know?" He shifts in his seat

"I had to know if she was your type. What she was like. So I know how to react when her name comes up."

Evan runs his hand down the back of his head as he looks away from me. "Her name isn't going to come up ..."

"You don't understand—" I start to explain but he cuts me off.

"There's no one else for me, Kat," he tells me bluntly, his hands hitting the table and rattling the small plates. The couple a table down from us glances in our direction and Evan grimaces. Sometimes he doesn't realize his own strength.

"I knew you would be upset—" I begin my apology and again he cuts me off.

"But you did it anyway." His cocked brow adds some humor although I still feel guilty over it all.

I nod my head once. "I did. And it's over."

The tension between us lifts a bit as I look him in the eyes and say, "It's over. There's nothing there and I'm fine now, but I had to tell you."

"You're fine?"

"Yes," I answer and I am. "There's no way she's your type."

My response gets a short laugh from Evan. A genuine smile even. "You know you're crazy?" he asks me.

"I do. And you made me this way."

"Fair enough," he says but then his expression gets serious.

"I know, don't do it again," I say before he can tell me.

"I'm serious," he says, and I nod.

I glance to Evan's right, toward the front of the restaurant as another couple walks in. "I was surprised that Samantha does pills," I say absently. More to gossip than anything else. Well, maybe to throw her under the bus a little. I can admit that I'm not a big enough woman not to.

"What?" Evan asks.

"There was coke on her kitchen table, lying out in the open." He looks back at me with an expression that's not quite disbelief, but something else.

"Coke?" he echoes. "Sam doesn't do drugs."

I ignore the fact that he called her Sam and nod my head once while I add, "And a bag of pills. She had a variety pack, Adderall and a mix of things. It was like a grab bag. I would never have guessed she does drugs." I wait for him to say something.

"Speed?" he asks me again although it's not quite spoken like a question.

"I didn't say speed," I reply.

"Adderall is speed," he tells me with a concerned expression.

"Oh, I didn't know. I don't know what they were. I just know what I saw and I was shocked. I'm just guessing it's Adderall." I swallow thickly, wishing I'd just kept my mouth shut and saved the gossip for the girls.

I watch as Evan's forehead pinches, but there's something else in his expression that catches me off guard. It's hard and unforgiving. Something that sends a chill down my spine. Even his hands clench into fists on top of the table. I glance at them and then his eyes, but movement behind him at the front of the restaurant catches my attention.

"Is that Suzette?" Even with the shock of seeing her stride in just now, I don't think I've ever been happier for a change of subject. I wish I could snatch the last two minutes of our conversation from the air and shove them back into my petty mouth.

"It's definitely Sue," I say, holding up Evan's end of this conversation since he's still silent. I'd know that blunt bob anywhere. She walks slowly as she digs in her purse, looking for something at the front of the restaurant.

I'm pushing my chair out from the table when my mouth drops open at the sight of a man coming up from behind her.

He's much taller than she is even in her heels. I don't recognize him; he's facing away from me. In a black suit, he stalks up behind her, moving his hand to her waist and pulling her close to him.

"Who is that?" I say beneath my breath, but when I look to Evan and try to get his attention, he's busy on his phone.

"Babe," I say, not so quietly trying to get his attention. It's not every day you see one of your good friends being felt up by someone you don't know. I much prefer this conversation. It's easy and Evan always has something to say about whoever Sue is "dating."

I have to turn my head when I look back up to keep my eyes on them and try to follow them down the hall. But they're gone before I even get the chance to stand.

I swear it was her and I go to reach for my phone to send her a message, but glancing at Evan, he stops me in mid reach.

"What's wrong?" I ask him as he stares at his phone.

"We have to go." His response is hard and nonnegotiable.

"We just got here," I object, but that doesn't stop him from standing up abruptly as the waiter returns to our table.

"I'm so sorry, we have to go," Evan tells the waiter. "Please cancel the order."

"Are you serious?" I hiss as the couple from before looks at us again.

"I'm sorry, but something just came up," he tells me and there's a look in his eyes that's begging me not to push him.

"Please, Kat," he says, ushering me away. "We need to leave. Now."

chapter 28

Evan

"THIS ALLEY SMELLS LIKE PISS," MASON SAYS AS WE STOP BETWEEN a Chinese restaurant and a shoe store. I met up with him on Prince Street and we walked our way here. Just me and him ... and business to take care of.

I take a whiff and immediately regret it. "This is where he's going, though, right?"

"Should already be there," he answers.

"That's what it said on his profile. 'Getting ready for the party,'" he elaborates beneath his breath and shoves his hands in his pockets.

It's bitterly cold and the city streets are packed with people shopping and moving about like normal.

"I don't believe in coincidences," I tell Mason and bring it up again.

His eyes flicker to me and then back across the street.

"There's no way she happens to do speed," I tell him. I've known Samantha for a long damn time. "Her husband dabbles in all sorts of drugs recreationally. But she doesn't touch it. She never has."

"It's possible she does it on the down low," he suggests. "You'd be surprised how many people do coke nowadays."

I shake my head. "There has to be a connection between her and the dealer."

"We're gonna find out, aren't we?" he asks me, although it's a rhetorical question.

"What's the plan?"

"All we need is an address."

"Just follow him, then?" I ask with disbelief.

"Only for a bit, then we switch off so we aren't seen."

"Switch off to who?"

"I got some guys," Mason says, and frustration gets the best of me.

"I want to be the one—" I start, but he's quick to cut me off.

"You want to keep her safe? Getting into this shit isn't what you need. That's not what the man who deserves to be at Kat's side would do."

That shuts me up, but I fucking hate it. He's been edging me out of this. Giving me less and less.

"So, we just wait?" I ask him again.

"Yeah," he answers, and his breath turns to fog, "just wait."

Almost an hour passes before I think about going back to Kat. She has no idea what this could mean. I'm sure she'll be pissed I took off in addition to cutting our date short. Sirens wail in the distance and the busy city night reminds me of how things used to be.

"Fuck me," I say out loud and run my hands down my face.

"Sorry, you're not my type," Mason says so matter-of-factly from his spot next to me, I grunt a short laugh despite myself. "I feel so fucking trapped."

"I know the feeling," Mason tells me, and I give him a sidelong glance. His stare only hardens. "I know what it's like to be in a lose-lose situation where the stakes are high." He looks forward, staring at the opposite brick wall in the thin alley. "Too high," he mutters under his breath.

"So, what do you do?" I say and get his attention again. "How do you win?" I ask him with complete sincerity as if he has an answer that will put an end to this hell.

He shakes his head as he looks down at the ground and replies, "Sometimes there's not a way to win, only a way to survive."

I have to tear my eyes away from him, knowing he's right and when I do, I spot something. My arm reaches out and I smack him in the chest.

"Visual." The single word is barely spoken from me, and Mason doesn't hesitate to take out his phone and call the tail. "He's here," he speaks into the phone as both of us watch the perp, chatting with some guy in an open doorway on Twentieth and Broadway. Even from his profile, I know it's him.

Every muscle in my body coils, ready to fight. It's been weeks of holding back and not being able to do anything. And just across the street is the last piece to this puzzle of fucking misery.

Dark black hair slicked back and tanned skin with a tattoo scrolling up his neck. It's definitely him. We got this prick.

The second he's walking down the stone steps, we're moving out of the alley and following from across the street. I keep my eyes on him, walking through the thick crowd with my jaw clenched.

"Johnny, we got him." Mason talks into his cell phone as we walk. I try not to make it obvious that we're following the fucker. At the same time, I'm holding back every desire to chase the dealer down and beat the shit out of him to get every bit of information from him.

Mason says we should bribe him. It's not exactly my style, though.

"Heading down Twenty-second," I hear Mason say and instinctively I glance up to look at the street sign before turning left to follow him.

My blood's pumping hard and with every step it gets harder and harder not to pick up speed.

Right as we get to the end of the block and the crosswalk sign turns to a red hand, the fucker walks out, ignoring the oncoming cars and nearly getting hit, but he keeps going, yelling out, "Hey, watch it!" at the drivers as if it's their fault. I move to do the same. We can't risk losing him, but Mason puts his arm out in front of my chest to stop me.

"He's got him," he tells me, his eyes glued to the dealer's back as he vanishes into the thick crowd. "Johnny's on him."

My shoulders rise and fall with my heavy breaths. I'm calm on the outside, but inside I'm pacing. The nerves eat away at me. "I need to do something," I tell him, ignoring how the woman to my right turns back to look at me as if I've lost it. Maybe I have.

"Then go home," Mason says and turns halfway around to walk right back up the way we came.

His leather jacket bunches in my fist as I pull him back to me. "I can't sit around and do nothing," I say, pleading with him to understand.

"The best thing for you to do is go home to your pregnant wife and stay right the fuck there," Mason tells me. That's it? That's all I can do when this is the prick that laced that coke? When he's the one who sold the tainted version and he's the only one who can tell us who he sold it to.

I swallow thickly, feeling guilt settle in my stomach. "She needs you to be there," Mason asserts, with caution thick in every word. I wonder if he's just saying that to make me listen to his order, or if he really means it.

"You told her you were done with this shit. Be done with it. You saw him, you know we got the guy. It's just a matter of time now."

chapter 29

Kat

EVAN IS ... NOT HIMSELF IN THE LEAST. HIS SHOULDERS ARE HUNCHED, and he keeps checking his phone like he's waiting for something.

Ever since we left dinner last night, he's been closed off. I wish I'd never brought up Samantha. It was a mistake.

Evan checks his phone again as an explosion on the television booms through the living room. He doesn't flinch or react. He's numb.

I scroll through the list I've added to the baby registry. Maddie sent me a check-off chart and it's so, so long. All the clothes in miniature and every odd and end, from pacifier holders to little mittens, should be enjoyable to add, but there's a nagging feeling that claws at my chest.

I peek up at him again, scooting closer into the cushion and pulling the throw tighter around me. "Why do you keep checking your phone?"

"It's nothing," he answers.

I'm slow and deliberate as I arrange myself into a cross-legged position across from my husband on the sofa.

The expression on his face is one I've seen before, the "what is she doing?" look.

He sets his phone down beside him, and I don't take my eyes off his, but I notice how he tries to hide it.

"No secrets," I remind him. "You promised."

Another loud boom from the television distracts me and I reach for the remote without hesitation, bending over Evan to grab it from where it sits right next to his phone. As soon as the television screen goes black, I toss the remote behind me.

Giving him my full attention I tell him, "I feel like maybe you have something to tell me." I hold his gaze and his expression gives me nothing.

I'm so close to snatching his phone out of his hands just to prove him wrong, but before I pull the trigger on that idea he says, "I don't want to bother you with these things."

"You're my husband. You're supposed to bother me." I say it with a little humor, but again, he doesn't react.

"Tell me, Evan. I *want* to know." I scoot closer to him, just a bit so my leg touches his and I rest a hand on his thigh.

"It's something you said. About Samantha having drugs." Dread washes over me. I never should have gone to see her, confront her or spoken her name. I regret it all. He glances away from me at the far wall in the room. "It's something bad," he adds.

"Her having drugs is … what? I don't understand." I hate that an inkling of jealousy creeps up on me, but it's quickly followed by a darker realization. The coldness that came with the dread sinks down deeper, coating every inch of my skin.

"The coke that killed Tony was laced with another drug. High amounts, enough to kill." He looks me in the eye and slowly the pieces come together, one by one.

A chill sinks into the marrow of my bones. Samantha. Not James. "Did you tell Mason?"

He nods and then adds, "He thinks he has something concrete."

"What?" I ask him, eager for more. I can't lie. There's a part of me that's afraid, but a bigger part that needs to know. Ever since Evan told me his theory, I've questioned it. I've questioned his sanity even. I started to think it was all in his head.

"He can't tell me over the phone," Evan says as if that's the end of the discussion.

"Is it good or bad?" I ask him, guilt and stupidity both weighing down my words.

"Good, I think." He hesitates, but then adds, "He said it's done and to come see him. I'm just waiting for the time and place."

"It's done?" I question, feeling my eyes widen with hope. My lungs stay perfectly still until Evan nods his head once.

"Just waiting for the time and place." He turns his attention back to the television and then glances at the remote.

There's an eerie feeling that settles between us, a darkness I can't seem to grasp.

"You know I love you, right?" he asks as he brushes the hair out of my face.

My eyes flicker from his chest to his eyes as I say, "I do."

His lips twitch into a smile and he leans forward to kiss me. It's chaste and quick, but he rests his forehead against mine, his hand still on my jaw.

"I don't like this," he whispers.

I can't respond. The words are caught in my throat and I have nothing to say other than, "I love you too. I'll wait with you."

chapter 30

Evan

I STARE DOWN AT THE PAPER AND THEN LOOK BACK TO MASON. I'VE known since Kat told me. Samantha's the reason that coke was laced, and it wasn't meant for me at all. It was James she wanted dead. I'm a fucking fool.

Anger rolls through me like a low tide. Slowly rising and each wave threatening to take more and more of me away.

"She was fucking him," Mason says.

"Fucking who?" Kat asks, still clinging to my side. With my arm around her, I pull her in closer. She insisted on coming and at first, I didn't want her here. I didn't want to involve her in this more than I already had.

Now though, knowing she went to Samantha, that she spoke to her, and was inside her apartment, so close to a woman capable of murder, I need her here with me.

She's not allowed to leave my side until this is finished.

I rub soothing circles along her hip as I look past Mason and out through the picture window in his sitting room. I need to feel her. I need to know she's still here, alive and by my side. Away from any danger.

"Samantha was fucking Andrew, the dealer. They planned to kill James and it went sideways. He was supposed to do the coke, not give it to Evan to share with Tony."

"Do you have evidence?" Kat asks, and I look down at her. She's standing there as if she just asked for a receipt for an item she wants to return to Nordstrom, not at all affected in the least.

"Enough of it," Mason answers and I look back at him when I can feel his eyes on me. "Shots of her with Andrew taken from his own surveillance feed.

You can't tell it's him, since it's his back and he's wearing a hoodie. More importantly, my guy was able to grab a sample."

We can plant the tainted coke. That's easy enough. Send the picture anonymously to Detective Bradshaw, plant the coke and boom, there's the evidence they've been after. There's the matter of what she'll say when they come for her, though. Who she'll blame and throw under the bus.

The details still need to be decided, but the truth is there. Now we know what happened.

"She wanted James dead because the divorce wasn't going to leave her with anything?" Kat asks Mason and he's quick to respond.

"She's the one who cheated and according to their prenup, if we go by the gossip columns, a divorce would leave her without a penny to her name."

"Better to kill him than to finalize the divorce," Kat comments under her breath and steps away from me, walking to the far side of the room to pick up the cup of hot tea she left on the side table.

"What about James?" I ask him. "He really had nothing to do with this?"

Mason shrugs. "Still a prick, and now he's onto his wife because of the nudge we gave him, but I don't have shit on him."

I break eye contact and wipe a hand down my face. I feel like a fool. Guilt and regret swirl together, and the mix of emotions makes me numb. I have to remind myself that all I need right now is Kat, just my wife.

"You were wrong," Kat says from across the room.

"I wanted to kill him … I would have," I admit to them, and it hurts to do it. The past few nights I've lain awake, thinking about all the ways I considered murdering him. As I stood outside of his house, I knew it'd be easy. I craved to see his body lifeless on the floor.

"It's because of her," Kat speaks lowly, but her breathing picks up as anger gets the best of her.

"It's not hard to focus on revenge," Mason says as if reading my mind. "It's not your fault for wanting this over so you could protect your wife."

The clink of ceramic on glass gets my attention as Kat sets down her mug and makes her way back to me.

"So, what do we do now?" Kat asks then leans her back against my front.

Mason smirks at her and looks between the two of us. "See, this I love," he says, tapping the folder in his hands.

"We came up with a plan. The cops have to find out. James and Samantha need to be focused on each other and forget about me."

"So … what's the plan? Leak it to them somehow?" Kat questions.

Mason steps in and says, "James is going to post about how Samantha's fucking a drug dealer. He's going to write all about how he found coke and a grab bag of pills in her office and that's why they've split."

"How do you know that?"

"Because my guy has access to his email account. And he drugged him about two hours ago. James is going to wake up with a hangover and unleash hell when he realizes he emailed his contact at the *News Journal*, who's eager to post anything at all about this case.

"The cops are itching for something and they know they have nothing. This city talks, and Derek at the *News Journal* will foam at the mouth to have the inside scoop before anyone else," Mason answers Kat.

I hope it's enough to satisfy her. She can't know the last piece. Just one more secret. One final release.

"James will be relieved more than anything else," I add, trying to ease her worry. "He's a time bomb of paranoia waiting to go off." Mason backs up, leaning against the back of a sitting chair as he adds, "And Samantha will be behind bars by morning."

"She can't deny the pictures of the evidence," Kat murmurs, grasping the plan, but quickly licks her lower lip and shakes her head, seemingly finding a gap in the details. "She'll make bail."

"With the cops James has in his back pocket?" Mason looks at her with disbelief. "No way. She's done." He's good at convincing her this will work, even though I'm still not convinced. If anything, I know nothing is bulletproof.

A moment passes and I let my hand slip to the small of her back. It takes everything in me to assure her, "It's done. This will work and it's done." There's a nagging feeling in the pit of my stomach, knowing either one of them could mention my name. I could go down too. But it's a risk I have to take for all this to be over. I can't outrun it and I'm willing to take a deal, I'm willing to do anything to put an end to it all.

"Good," Kat says with finality.

"Do you need me to do anything?" I ask Mason as Kat cradles her body against mine.

"I can take it from here, but I'd stay inside and keep a low profile until there's word about the arrest."

I give him a tight smile then lean down to kiss Kat's hair, savoring every moment. I'm doing it for her. With my throat tight and everything inside me ringing, I whisper, "Let's go home, baby."

One week later

"Is he in there?" I ask Mason as we sit in the car.

Andrew Jones, also known as Mathew Staller, is about to meet his maker. The man who sold Samantha the drugs, helped her plan a murder, and got off with nothing has to pay for what he's done.

He didn't get a single charge that stuck to him. Not a damn thing. Samantha protected him and pled guilty when it came down on her. So did James, accepting the weaker charges that were merely slaps on the wrists. I slipped under the radar, although I'm certain Mason had something to do with that.

Andrew got off completely. Until now.

"Yeah, this is his address," Mason answers as he unbuckles his seatbelt. The click is loud in the still night air.

I watch the light at the end of the street turn green, but there's not a single car down the road where Andrew's house is. Not a person in sight, in fact.

It's only him and us.

I guess he liked being out here for his privacy, away from the city in a Podunk area … maybe it's where he cooks up the drugs. Or maybe he's lying low since it all went down only days ago.

I don't know, and I don't give a fuck. All I want is for every person responsible to pay the price.

As I step out of the car, the chill of the evening creeping into my bones, I tell Mason, "You better never tell Kat."

He grins at me and says, "It's our secret."

The doors to the car close softly, although they cause a gentle thud to resonate in the bitter cold. I keep my gaze on the warm yellow light coming from the upstairs of the two-story house.

"Sticking to the plan?"

I nod at Mason's question, not stopping my pace, and not taking my eyes off the light upstairs. Duct tape and rope are in the trunk.

I crack my knuckles one by one, all the pent-up anger and fear from the past couple of weeks raging through my blood, begging for revenge.

I came so close to losing everything because of this fucker. My wife would have been a pregnant widow. And it's because of this asshole.

"Yeah, stick to the plan," I answer Mason.

He grins at me. "I'll get the front, you get the back."

Just as we break, the man of the hour walks right out the front door, hoodie on and straight out onto the sidewalk, only feet from the car.

"I don't do meets here, get the fuck out," he informs us with a threatening tone that only heats the rage coursing in my blood.

"Not here?" Mason questions as if we're here to buy or sell or whatever the hell Andrew thinks we're here for.

"Yeah, like I said, I don't do meets here," Andrew repeats and then opens his coat, flashing a gun tucked in his waistband. "So get the fuck out."

Dumb prick should have had the gun in his hand.

The rage turns my vision red.

Before I know what I'm doing, I go for the first punch, slamming my fist right in his jaw. It's reckless, but it's a damn good release of all the tension I've been carrying. My blood rushes in my ear as he and Mason both fumble for the gun. Mason grabs it from him as a bullet goes off, flying through the air and ricocheting off the car. Crouching down, I get in another punch, stunning the dealer. It's cold and the freezing air bites into my white-knuckled fist. Over and over I feel my muscles tighten, gripping onto his collar, then letting the rage pour out of me, blow by blow. My teeth grind against one another as I don't hold back a damn thing.

Crack! The prick's jaw snaps and I feel the bones crunch under the weight of my fist. I see the images that haunted me for weeks.

Andrew pulls back his arm and lands a single solid punch to my cheek. It'll bruise, but it barely affects me. Nothing can pull me from this haze of vengeance. My head snaps to the side as another punch lands on my chin. I throw all my weight forward, pushing him to the ground and feeling my body fall on top of his, slamming hard onto the concrete sidewalk.

"Fuck!" he screams out just as I pin him under me and throw punch after punch. His nose cracks under one of them; I don't know how many I get in. I can't stop.

"Evan!" Mason cries out, his fingers prying into my shoulders then my chest, desperately pulling me backward, but I get one more hit in that snaps Andrew's head to the side and for a moment, I think he's dead. He lies there nearly lifeless. Blood's covering his face and soaking into my knuckles. Red lays in streaks everywhere.

Andrew spits blood onto the street next to him and coughs it up as I attempt to rein in my heaving breaths.

"Snap out of it. It's not the plan." Mason repeats, "It's not the plan. This isn't the plan." There's a ringing in my ears that won't quit. One that balances out my tunnel vision and the stinging pain that shoots from the split knuckles on my hand.

When I finally catch my breath, Mason is on top of him on the ground, pinning him down. Andrew knees Mason in the stomach, desperately trying to win a losing fight. But I'm too quick, grabbing his own gun and shooting him once in his thigh.

I don't want to kill him. That's not my job to do.

He's not for me. But I'll be damned if I didn't love beating the piss out of him.

Andrew screams out in agony and Mason, still wincing and holding his gut, socks him right in the mouth.

Mason catches his breath as he slowly stands up and Andrew stares up at us, begging for mercy.

"Are you Andrew Jones?" I ask him and he hesitates to answer, so I fire a shot off right next to him.

"Yes!" he screams. "Fuck! Yes!"

I crouch down in front of him, gun still in my hand. "The same Andrew Jones that left those messages for Samantha? The ones convincing her to murder her husband?" The blood drains from his face as I talk. I'm not some dealer looking to get more turf. I'm not a cop. True fear permeates the air as the fool shakes his head. "The same Andrew Jones that gave her tainted coke so she could end his life and pay you half of what the insurance company was going to give her?"

"I don't know any Samantha …" he tries to lie, and I shoot off the gun again, feeling the shockwaves run up my arm. It's closer to him this time and Andrew screams out.

"He pissed himself," Mason comments and when I look, sure enough, his sweats have a dark wet ring around him. He's pathetic.

"That Andrew Jones?" I ask him.

"She wanted him dead!" he yells. "She was going to do it whether I helped her or not."

"You can tell her husband that; I'm sure he'll understand," Mason says and then tosses handcuffs at his feet. "Put those on. First your feet, then your hands."

"Please," he begs. But there's no mercy for what he's done.

It takes a good fifteen minutes to tie him up. The gagging was the hardest part.

The trunk slams shut, and the dark night seems so empty. Empty is what I needed, though. It's done and over.

Mason turns the car on, the keys jingling in the ignition before it roars to life and we leave in silence, listening to the fucker in the back. It's already starting to snow. They're calling for ten inches and that will wash away any evidence of us being here. Not that anyone will come looking for a while. Like he told us, he doesn't do meets here.

My heartbeat slows, and the end feels so fucking close. Every loose end is finally being resolved.

"Thanks for doing this," I tell Mason, ignoring Andrew's muted thumps in the trunk as we go over a speed bump and then another.

"No problem." His nonchalant response is as if I've only thanked him for picking up milk on the way home.

"I just needed to do something about it all." I feel the need to explain. We could have let Mason's guy take care of him. I needed some kind of part in seeing this through, even if I promised Kat I'd stay out of it. It's the last secret and I'm done. One last deal to see through.

"It's not like he doesn't have it coming to him."

I nod at Mason's comment and listen to Andrew's muffled screams.

"You sure he's going to be here?" Mason asks me as we pull up to a vacant lot.

Even as the car slows, I can see James inside, moving aside a curtain in the bedroom.

"Yeah, I'm sure," I tell him.

I know James is here. He's waiting for sentencing and not going anywhere near the city. *He's hiding.*

I know what that's like.

"You ready?" Mason asks me, and I nod once again. "Let's do this."

We'll leave Andrew bound and gagged on James's porch. And the hard copy photos James kept of me are already in my possession.

It's a truce of sorts. I give him his final piece, he gives me mine.

More than likely he won't see a day in jail and half his charges were already dismissed. His wife is sentenced to prison for life, his worries behind him. All but the drug dealer. He was foaming at the mouth to get him.

It was an easy call to make.

Andrew's slamming every which way, but it's 4:00 a.m. in the suburbs. There isn't another house for nearly half a mile. Even if I took the gag out of his lying mouth, there's no one here but us and James.

James is right there in the doorway, rifle ready.

"Just leave him here," I tell Mason and we let Andrew drop to the ground with a muffled scream piercing the air. "James will take him from here."

With the cold air blowing in my face and the city skyline lighting up the dark night, I finally relax into the leather seat. The bite of pain that hovers over every cracked knuckle is all that's left of what happened. It'll heal and my life will go on.

I'm done now. It's all done.

It's just me and Kat now. Just the two of us.

No. The three of us.

chapter 31

Kat

"**D**O YOU THINK HE TOLD THE COPS ANYTHING TO TRY TO GET A lighter sentence?" I ask Evan as the newspaper in my hand rustles. Samantha pled guilty to multiple attempted murder charges and got life in prison.

James pleaded guilty to his charges as well, but his sentence is nothing compared to hers even though they found him complicit in his client's death. It's rumored that he gave up information to cut a deal. He'll be out of jail in a year or less according to what the rumor mills are saying. The dealer got off scot-free and now people are saying he skipped town in case more evidence comes in.

"Told them what exactly?" He doesn't look back at me. Instead he lifts a picture frame off the wall of his parents' dining room. He considers it for a moment before wrapping a handful of bubble wrap around it like he has the others.

The moving company is going to be here tomorrow, but Evan wanted to box up the pictures and a few other things himself. The *valuable things* is what he told me when we left this morning. All he's packed up so far are pictures and I wish I could steal the pain away that reflects back in the glass as I catch his gaze.

"That you were there," I say, whispering the words quietly as if it's a dark secret no one can ever know. "With Tony," I add. A part of me thinks it's just too easy. I can't shake it just yet. I can't quite grasp that I get to have my happily ever after with Evan.

He shrugs a heavy shoulder and then looks me in the eyes, gauging my reaction as he lowers the wrapped picture into the box. "He doesn't have a reason to say anything. He wanted Samantha to go down, and we made that happen." His lips are pressed into a thin line as he makes his way around the table to pull out the chair next to mine.

"You really want to talk about this?" he asks me.

I glance at the article and him, swallowing my words and not knowing how to feel. The entire situation makes me uncomfortable. Worse than that … dreadful. "I want to know it's going to be okay." I offer him the truth. "I want to make sure *you're* going to be okay."

Evan smirks at me then leans forward, kissing the tip of my nose, which makes me close my eyes. "You're cute, you know that?"

I love how at ease he is. It feels like I have my husband back. Truly. Yet I'm still waiting for the other shoe to drop.

Reaching up, I quickly grab his hand and keep him close to me. "I'm serious," I say as I look him in the eyes. "I want to know you're okay."

"Baby, I told you there's nothing to worry about." He brushes his hand against my cheek, forcing me to let go. Evan pinches my chin between his thumb and forefinger, and stares into my eyes. There's a look there that makes me all warm and fuzzy. He's always been able to do that, and I love him for it.

"You promise?" I ask him softly and he pecks my lips once, then goes in for a deeper one before answering me.

"Well, we do have a baby coming," he says, still staring at my lips. "So, I'm sure we've got some things to be worried about, but that mess is over."

The stir of desire drifts away, dissolving instantly when I peek back down at the article. The picture they chose is one of Samantha giving James a death stare as she was arrested. The papers paint her as the villain she is.

"And you got that package too," Evan comments, bringing my attention back to him. My heart flickers once, then twice as I bite my lip and shrug.

"It was really nice of him," Evan says, and I feel the need to smack his arm playfully as he stands up to keep packing.

I place a hand on my belly and tell him, "It was a goodbye and good luck gift from a friend."

"A friend you kissed," Evan reminds me.

"A friend who was there for me when you weren't," I point out.

His shoulders stiffen a little as he stops midway from taking another photo off the wall. "I know," he says beneath his breath.

"It was a nice gift, though, wasn't it?" I ask him. Evan looks at me with an eyebrow raised and I have to laugh. "He doesn't have our new address anyway and he didn't put his on the package either."

"Yeah, yeah, yeah," Evan says.

"I really like it." I shrug my shoulders and remember the gift box Jake sent. Inside was a baby book called *I'll Love You Forever*. I can't read it without crying. All the note said was that he gave a copy to all his friends who were expecting and he didn't feel right not giving me one. One last kindness.

"It was nice of him, but it better be the last of him," Evan warns me jokingly. I love the trace of a smile on his lips. He knows I'm all his.

I lean back in the chair, and a yawn escapes before I can stop it. I'm halfway to telling him off in some way or another, but the words are stopped.

"You ready to go home?" he asks me and I nod my head, but add, "Only if you're all done."

He takes a look around the half-packed house and shakes his head. I have to admit watching him cleaning up his father's place makes my heart ache for him. I know I can't take the pain away. It'll always be there.

"You know our baby is going to be tough, right?" he comments just as the emotions start to get the best of me.

I rub my swollen bump in smooth circles as I pray our baby is okay in there and doesn't know how sad I am in this moment. I only want love for him or her.

"I hope so," I whisper as Evan comes back over to me. He wraps his arms around my shoulders and pulls me into his chest. I'm more than grateful as I wrap my arms around him and my cheek presses against his shirt.

"It's true. When a mom goes through hell during pregnancy and handles it as well as you have, the baby can handle anything, you know?"

I let out a sad but genuine laugh into his shirt and try to calm myself down as he rubs my back.

I peek up at him and smile as his lips touch mine.

"Everything's behind us," he adds.

I feel the need to remind him, "There's good behind us too, isn't there?"

"So much good," he says and then kisses me again before splaying his hand on my belly. "And so much more to come."

Epilogue

Kat

SEEING THAT LITTLE BLIP MAKES IT REAL. "I CAN SEE HIS HEARTBEAT."

"You're still convinced it's a boy?" Evan says although he doesn't take his eyes off the monitor. A trace of a smile is on his lips and it only grows when the little one moves.

"We'll find out soon," I tell him with a little more glee in my voice.

"Soon as in right now," the doctor comments, breaking up our little moment. With Evan to my right, I hold his hand as I lie back on the white paper, hearing it rustle under me. Dr. Harmony holds the wand right above my belly button. My belly is covered in clear gel and there's more than a little bump now that I'm twenty weeks along.

I'm quiet as the sound of a steady heartbeat comes through the speaker. *Lub-dub, lub-dub, lub-dub.* The only thing that distracts me for a moment is Evan placing his second hand over our joined one.

"Our little baby," he whispers in awe.

"Your little *boy*," the doctor corrects him, pointing to the screen. She keeps the wand there for a moment, tapping on the keyboard to take photos before removing the wand and the soft, rhythmic heartbeats are gone. But I heard them, I heard that steady heartbeat and that sound will stay with me forever.

"He's healthy?" Evan questions and my heart swells.

"Perfectly healthy," Dr. Harmony says as she wipes down the equipment and tosses the paper towels into the trash.

"I'll be back in just a bit with some pictures for you two." The young blond doctor has a pretty smile; it's one that reaches her eyes.

"Thank you," Evan and I say in unison.

"A boy," I murmur to him before he cuts me off with a kiss.

"We're going to have a son," Evan says, running a hand down his face. "It's real."

"Does it feel real to you now?"

Evan takes my hand again and kisses my knuckles before nodding his head.

My gaze moves from Evan to the screen. The little heart is beating in a perfect rhythm.

"I have a feeling it's going to be really, really good," I tell him and get a little choked up.

"It is," Evan says and kisses my hand once more. "I know it is."

Evan

The morning brings a bright light,
Hope and laughter too.
And with time comes a new love,
Faded dreams become anew.
Just remember to hold tight,
And fight for what you love.
For our lost ones will watch over,
And keep us safe from up above.

"We should name him Henry," Kat suggests as we walk into the house. The homes near the Manhattan Bridge are an expensive area to live, but the park is close, and this school district is where Kat wants to live for our little one, so how could I say no?

She tosses the keys onto the side table, walking past a row of cardboard boxes and a stack of dishes I brought back from the old place last night. "I've thought a lot about it. And I think we should."

"Henry." I say my father's name and a swell of unexpected emotion catches me off guard. I slip the jacket off my shoulders and move to busy myself, opening the window in the dining room and ignoring the look Kat gives me.

"I know it hasn't been a long time since he passed," Kat says. "It feels like it was yesterday."

She holds her swollen abdomen and drags out the head chair in the dining room. At least this room is mostly put together. Kat's nesting has her up all hours and doing shit she shouldn't do. Like carrying heavy boxes and climbing on the furniture to hang curtains. She's ever the stubborn one.

"I wish he were here with us," she murmurs and gets teary eyed; she's been crying a lot more recently, probably due to the third trimester pregnancy hormones. "But we can give him this, you know?"

Her voice is tight with emotion and I nod my head, understanding what she's saying but not wanting to voice it.

The wind blows through the house. It's warm for late March. The breeze gently moves the napkins on the table so I'm quick to tuck them into the holder and attempt to form a response. I miss my father. More than I ever could have imagined.

"He'd have loved to help us move down here." I say the thought out loud to offer her something.

"At least this time you hired movers," Kat says with a bit of humor, but her voice is solemn.

She winces with pain and grabs ahold of her belly, her eyes closed tight and my heart races.

"Babe?" She ignores me, just like she's been doing. For some unknown reason, I continue to think she'll respond during these Braxton-Hicks contractions.

Hovering over her, I eye her carefully then walk slowly to her and wait, afraid to do anything wrong.

I may have made mistakes while learning to be a good husband, but Pops showed me how to be a good father and I won't let him down.

"Oh my gosh, that was a long one." Kat finally breathes out as her body visibly relaxes.

"Do you want to go in?" My nerves are all on edge. I'm terrified, but I won't tell Kat. I've never even held a child, let alone having one depend on me to live.

Kat rolls her eyes at me. "For one contraction? I think not."

She reaches into the bag at her feet and pulls out a water bottle. "Besides, I read a baby comes when you're ready and relaxed, and we have four more rooms to set up and get settled in before I'll be anywhere near relaxed. And another two weeks until our due date."

A huff of humor leaves me and I move the top box off the nearest stack, ripping the tape back to expose what's inside.

"So, what do you think?" she asks me.

"About what?"

"About naming him Henry?" She tilts her head to the side and her long hair falls over her shoulder.

"I think Pops would have loved that," I say, getting out the answer before my throat goes tight and take in a deep breath. "I think he'd be proud."

Lowering myself to the floor in front of her, I let my hands rest on her thighs and bring my forehead down to rest on her belly. "What do you think?" I ask our son and Kat's belly shakes as she laughs.

"You think it's funny, but he's going to know my voice." Kat doesn't hesitate to lean down and kiss me. The first one is a peck on my cheek, but then she moves her hand to my jaw and keeps me still for a longer one, a deeper one.

It's slow and sensual and makes my blood heat.

"I know he will, and I love you for it."

I take her small hand in mine and look deep into her eyes. She's seen so much of me. All of my bad along with the little bit of good I have in me, and she still loves me. There's no way I could doubt that. "I know this past year has been rough, but I'm going to do everything I can to make our lives easy for … forever."

A small smile seems to tickle Kat's lips, still a darker hue from our kiss, and she moves her fingers to them.

"I mean it, Kat. I love you and this baby more than anything." Tears come to my eyes and I only pray she knows that I love her just as much as she loves me.

After a moment, she nods. "I know you do, and I know you will."

Moving my hand to her belly, I feel our little one kick just beneath the small bit of pressure. It still gets me every time.

"He knows too," Kat says with a smile that lights her eyes.

"So, Henry?" I question, feeling a swell of pride in my chest.

She nods her head, her eyes getting glossy as she puts a hand on her belly. "Henry."

Diary Entry Three

Hey Pops,

I wanted you to know, every day I think about what I should do to make you proud. Even the days I mess up. I guess those days especially. Your voice is always there, telling me to make it right.

Lately, I've been doing good. I think you'd agree. Sometimes I make mistakes. Like when little Henry peed through his diaper last week at four in the morning. I changed his diaper but didn't change the onesie. Kat let me have it for that one.

Common sense and all that goes out the window when it comes to him. She didn't tell me to change the onesie too. I should have known, but I'm just so careful around him. She's teaching me, though, and we're learning together. You'd love it. We miss you so much.

He's so small, Pops, I can hold him in one hand. I'm scared I'm gonna break him some days. Kat tells me I'm fine, and that I look good holding him. But I'm terrified I'm going to mess up.

I guess I'm just nervous to ruin it, so I keep waiting for her to tell me what to do.

She's taking good care of me. Especially in that department.

She's not going to mess up and that's the only thing that makes me think it's all going to be all right.

Kat's not gonna let me get away with anything anymore.

The best part about that is that I love it.

I wish I'd listened to you sooner, Pops. I want you to know, I'm trying to make sure my marriage is like yours and Ma's.

I've got to go. I just really wanted to talk to you tonight. Some nights are harder than others and I'm not sure it'll ever get too easy. Even if it does, I'll be thinking of you and wanting your advice.

I love you. We all do.

tell me you
want me

From *USA Today* best-selling author, Willow Winters, comes a sexy office romance with a brooding hero you can't help but fall head over heels for … in and out of the boardroom.

I didn't get to where I am by being nice.

I'm the boss, the CEO, the owner of whatever I want. Right now, that includes every person in this building of the company I just bought.

I stop at nothing once I've decided I'm taking something.

And then she showed up … full of spitfire just for me, the man she's decided is her worst enemy.

Like I said, I stop at nothing once I've decided I'm taking something. This pretty little thing just moved to the top of my "must acquire" list.

Adrian

"CAN YOU BELIEVE HOW WE STARTED?" SUZETTE QUESTIONS, HER voice barely above a murmur. I've gotten used to her whispers this late at night. It's nearly midnight now. I've gotten used to far too much because of her. This room, on the top floor of the most coveted skyscraper facing Bryant Park, has been hell every morning when the partners arrive. When they leave, and most of the lights turn off, and Suzette hesitantly knocks on the large walnut door to my office … it's been nothing but heaven.

As if I would ever turn her away. As if I could possibly deny myself, let alone her.

"Can I believe how we started?" The low timbre of my voice carries an echo of her question, a chill flowing along my shoulders as the air conditioner switches on. My gaze slips to the dark wood flooring barely lit by a single lamp in the corner of the office. Then it falls to my silk tie atop the puddle of Sue's cashmere blouse, both items thrown carelessly on the floor. She's still naked, completely bared to me, although I've pulled up my slacks. I relax into the high-back chair, my bare skin against the leather, and watch Sue reach for the bottle of scotch. The glasses clink together when she grabs them next. Her pale rose nipples are soft now that she's sated and the sight of them persuades me to run my thumb along the pad of my pointer, desperate to toy with her and bring them back to hardened peaks for me to suck and pluck, forcing more of those delightful sounds from her cherry-red lips.

As she turns slightly from where she's lying across my desk, the dim lights of the city shine through the large paned glass windows and cast shadows along her tempting curves. She is my safety, my temple of solitude, my everything. At this moment, I'm far too aware of what she means to me.

"Yes," she speaks confidently, raising her voice as the amber liquid is poured into the first glass. "I was just thinking that I never would have imagined we'd have …" she pauses, her chest rising and falling with a single breath before carefully placing herself in front of me. The bottle sits to the left of her, and both glasses are to the right. "This," she finishes. With Suzette seated on my desk, her bare feet planted on my chair between my spread legs, her ass balanced on the edge and her breasts directly at my eye level, I have to tilt my chin up to meet her gaze.

The little vixen smirks. She knows what she does to me. I didn't even realize I'd fallen for her until it was too late.

It was nothing more than a game at first. I don't know when it all changed and turned into "this," as she put it. I don't know when it became what it is, but now that I have it, I don't want to lose it.

Can I believe how we started? Did I know it would turn into this?

"No," I say, giving her the answer I know she wants to hear. Her simper and huff of a laugh warm the coldest depths of me, but they're quick to freeze the moment she hands me the cut crystal tumbler of whisky.

I sip it regardless, because she wants me to and because as I do she indulges herself, relaxing and confiding in me. It's all I want, for as long as I can have it.

She has no idea that everything is going to change only hours from now. I'm the only one suffering of the two of us. I can only imagine the betrayal she'll feel tomorrow when the headlines reveal the truth in black and white.

With the soft hum of a satisfied woman, Suzette leans forward, lowering her lips and positioning them right there for the taking. The glass landing with a hollow *thunk* on the maple desk is the only sound in the room besides the raging of my blood pounding in my veins. A moment passes, the heat blistering in her gorgeous gaze as if she can see through me. My stomach sinks and a sick feeling takes over in only a split second as her head tilts and an unasked question seems to linger at her lips.

I act before I let on that anything is wrong. My kiss is nothing shy of ruthless. I don't hold back a damn thing. I take exactly what I want from her because I know, in the depths of my soul, it will be our last time together. Tomorrow, she'll want nothing to do with me. Nipping her bottom lip, I take advantage of that sweet mouth of hers when her lips part with a provocative moan.

"I want you again," I confess to her in a low groan that rumbles up my chest. Both her hands have gripped my shoulders so it's no surprise when her nails dig into my skin and she calls out in surprise as I grab her ass off the edge, pushing her back flat against the desk so I can take her again as I have a dozen times or more.

I have to have her at least once more. One more time where she's mine. Where we have *this* … before I lose it all when the sun rises.

chapter 1

Adrian

Several weeks earlier

Y POLISHED OXFORDS SMACK ON THE SLEEK MARBLE TILE. THE floors are the only thing that look expensive in the foyer of this building. It's old and dated just like their business practices. But that's all about to change now that I'm in charge.

Although I keep my expression neutral, maybe cold, as I make my way to the elevator and then to the top floor where the conference room is located, I smirk to myself as I hear the soft whispers and see the secretaries huddling together.

They know who I am. Everyone who's *anyone* does.

Asshole. Prick. Hell, I've even been called a villain. And I couldn't care less.

I pull at the sleeves to my suit and fix my cufflinks before opening the glass door. A dozen people instantly still as I walk into the room, one swivel chair squeaking as everyone goes silent. The conference room smells like the lemon polish the cleaners use on the large oval mahogany table.

That'll be the first thing to replace. The table needs to be glass so I can monitor their body language with every meeting. My father says I was blessed with two gifts: reading people and placing bets. As a gambling man with a head for stocks and companies, I know damn well he was right. And I've left a sea of people who hate me for it in my wake.

I didn't get to where I am by being nice.

I'm the boss, the CEO, the owner of whatever I want. And right now, that includes every person in this building. Straightening my tie, I remind myself I'll have to cull the herd sooner, rather than later. For the sake of both profits and efficiency. The numbers never lie; people always do, though.

"Good afternoon," I say, greeting them as Mr. Holt stands from his spot just to the right of the head of the table, which is empty. No one's seated there because it's reserved for me.

"Mr. Bradford, it's nice to see you again," Jonathan Holt says as he shakes my hand. He's the former owner and now a wealthy man.

A nondisclosure agreement was signed. No one knew I've been the acting CEO for the last quarter. Every email, every camera feed, every contract and meeting was passed through my team. They had a quarter to prove to me this company is worth salvaging.

Not that Holt gave a fuck. He was getting paid regardless. With a tailored gray suit and fresh shave, he's already a lighter, wealthier man than he was when I first met him six months ago to negotiate this deal.

As my eyes skim across each of the members I've invited for this meeting, half likely to stay, half likely to leave, a gorgeous woman catches my interest. She's in a skintight, bloodred dress that matches her perfectly manicured nails. I've seen her wear it before, if I'm not mistaken. Twice, and this makes the third. The third time is the charm.

I already know who she is before she dares to stare back at me with an openly hateful look.

Suzette Parks. Passionate. Dedicated. And hot as hell. I can't help the smirk that slips into place when she meets my gaze directly, daring me to call her out. I've witnessed her lose her patience, all alone in her office, on the brink of losing it. Entertaining isn't enough of a description. I wanted nothing more than to push her against the wall and fuck the frustration out of her. My cock stirs just thinking about how her nails would dig into my back. She's wound tight but not easily shaken. No matter what happens to this company, I'll be damn sure to keep stock of my little vixen.

She's the first to back down and break eye contact. At the same time, the door closes behind me thanks to Mr. Holt, and it signals the beginning of the meeting.

My smile widens and I cover it with my fist, clearing my throat and getting a grip. I knew she'd distract me, I knew she'd get under my skin but I wasn't prepared to be this … off-balance.

I begin, still standing, and Mr. Holt follows suit. He nearly takes his seat but stands upright when I speak. "I'll make this short. Last quarter was unimpressive and changes will be drastic. That will include layoffs and budget cuts, but is not limited to other necessities. I will rely on each of you selected from your teams for this advertising management firm." I meet all eleven of them eye to eye as I speak. Noting which ones nod, and which ones tense up. I'm not surprised in the least until I get to Ms. Parks, who doesn't bother to peer up. As I speak, her attention is on the pen in her hand. It's an ink pen with a sleek silver body and it silently taps against her leatherbound book. No notes are being taken.

My voice is harder when I state, "I don't believe in failure. Even mistakes are lessons." The quote I've heard her say a dozen times in the last month rewards me with her icy blue gaze. That's better.

I hold her there, pinning her down as I let a second pass and then another. I can practically feel the temperature rise in the room as she struggles not to squirm. The fucking table should have been replaced already.

"Unless you have anything you'd like to say, Mr. Holt," I say and gesture toward the man. He shakes his head, his thin lips pressed in a straight line. "I don't have anything to add," he states and glances across the room.

I don't miss Ms. Parks's hardened expression toward him as well. Good. I'm not the only one she blames.

"Meeting adjourned." I remain where I am, standing tall and watching them disperse while what I was supposed to say comes back to me. I have every name memorized and anger rises inside of me that I didn't make it clear to them I know every detail and statistic that matters. My jaw clenches and with that, they move faster, nodding and giving short waves as they leave.

The annoyance morphs into something else as I peer back at Ms. Parks, the pen tapping harder. She hasn't budged.

"Did you want to say something?" I question her lowly. The last two men in the room pause where they are beside Mr. Holt. Jeffries and Woods. Both were seated farthest away, both paused to my left. Woods knows what he's doing but he's far too casual with clients. I'll be surprised if the threat of a severance package turns his performance around.

In her silence, I add, "You look like you have something to say."

"Adrian Bradford," she states, looking me in the eyes and giving me a tight smile, "we all know why you're here."

For the first time today, I let my emotion come through, simply raising a brow in curiosity. "Is that so?" I ask her.

"You want the company," she says matter-of-factly and then sits back. It's a confident move on her part as if she knows my cards.

"You're very astute," I say clearly condescendingly, and I love how she raises a brow back.

"To rip apart," she adds and then pushes her chair back, standing up and letting me finally see her curves in person. The short red dress rides up just a bit too high on her left thigh, exposing more of her skin and teasing me. I'm usually able to keep my focus, but for her, I let my gaze slip.

She yanks it down.

"Leave my department alone. I won't let anyone ruin it," she warns. Warns me. Like this is a tit for tat. Like she has any authority at all in this game we're playing.

"If I want to ruin something …" I pause to adjust my stance slightly as I take another long look at this woman.

"You can try all you'd like, Adrian." The faint smile on her face when my expression hardens upon hearing her use my first name only adds to the insult.

"Suzette Parks, correct?"

Suzette. I taste her name on my tongue. I love everything about it, from the way it rolls off my lips to the manner in which it lingers there, tempting and taunting me.

She offers a nod and that's all, swallowing down her spite and leaving the room.

"Is she typically so … combative?" I ask Mr. Holt as the glass door slams shut so hard that I wouldn't have been surprised if it had shattered. I haven't been on the receiving end of her wrath, but damn if it doesn't make me harder than steel for her.

Jonathan clears his throat, obviously uncomfortable as he shifts his weight where he stands, gripping the back of the chair. "I apologize, sir," he tells me, but that's not the answer to the question I asked.

"Not a worry at all," I comment, not bothering to look back at him as he rambles on. Instead I watch her go, loving that she can't get away from me. Loving that I'll be seeing more of her any damn time I please.

chapter 2

Suzette

HOW FUCKING DARE HE.

How dare this man who doesn't know a single thing about me get to me the way he did? The way his piercing gaze seemed to see through me made my entire body heat. He pinned me where I stood. I felt the intensity of his hunger ignite through every nerve ending in my body, rendering me paralyzed.

I couldn't even speak, let alone look at him. It was embarrassing. Every little thing I did in that room was horribly embarrassing. I'll apologize, only because it's the professional thing to do, but I'm not backing down. My team is worth saving, worth keeping. *If he dares to fuck with me …* I swallow thickly, knowing there's not much I can do to stop him, but he's going to hear every reason why he needs to back down before he ruins what I've spent a decade building.

I've heard rumors about him. All he does is rip apart things that aren't profitable, selling them off or merging what's worth salvaging with other companies. Adrian Bradford is a death sentence. He's my worst enemy come to life and I despise Holt for leaving me in this man's hands.

Steadying my breath, I raise my hand and form a fist at his door. One breath in, and I can't even knock. My knuckles graze the wood and I can't bring myself to do it. "Fucking hell," I mutter beneath my breath.

How has he gotten under my skin the way he has? I'm a strong woman. I pride myself on it. And yet here I am, cowering in front of a closed door.

It makes me hate him all the more.

It's not just the way he looks at me. Shaking off the anxiousness, the pent-up anger, and the desperate need to get out the rage boiling inside of me, I try yet again.

I'll blame the hell I went through last night for being so shaken.

If I wasn't so shocked, if I wasn't so sleep deprived, if I wasn't so passionate about everything that has to do with this job, storming into his office would be easy.

I know every nook and cranny of this business. When I got here, I knew nothing and quickly discovered the upper-level executives knew even less. Holt was a trust fund baby in over his head. I climbed a steep learning curve and brought my team with me.

How dare he come in here and think that he can take everything away from me? Everything that I've worked for. Everything that *we've* earned.

With an audible exhale, I nod. That's right; that's what I need to be focused on.

With another deep breath, I straighten my spine.

The image of him standing at the head of the conference table is burned into my memory. The hint of a five-o'clock shadow showing already. His dark gray, perfectly tailored suit and sharp jaw. He's like the devil—charming and wicked; threatening yet thrilling. There's a power beneath him that's undeniable. A thought creeps into my mind. Even if he was stripped bare of every expensive fabric that graced his lean but muscular frame, even then, I imagine that man would look expensive as hell. It's not wealth, it's something else. Something entirely different than what I'm used to.

All of these men can walk around in whatever designer suit they'd like but they'd still look cheap. They wouldn't know their dicks from the pens they use to sign away their inheritances. And yet here's a man, the first one I've seen in a long damn time since my divorce has been settled, who makes all of those bastards who have hit on me, who have expected things from me simply because of their bank accounts, look like the arrogant pricks they are.

Every man I've ever laid eyes on in all of New York City pales in comparison to Adrian Bradford. And I was safely surrounded by others, in the light of day, for a total of less than ten minutes.

Here I stand, outside his door, daring to get closer to him and all alone, after hours … this door will remain wide open so long as I'm here. That's for damn sure. There's not a soul on this level and truth be told, I'm not even sure he's in this room. It's Holt's former office and the top floor was reserved for him and meetings only. So … even if this door was open, we'd still be alone.

With my blood heating and my nerves running high, no matter how much I'd like them not to, I imagine what he'll do. I imagine Adrian saying the kind of things that have been said to me in the past by men who have held power over me, like my husband used to, and it has a completely different effect on me today than it ever has before. The very idea of it turns workplace harassment from a lawsuit waiting to happen, into late-night thoughts in bed I share with my vibrator.

Knock, knock, knock.

My hand trembles at my side, but I hold my ground.

Raising my voice, I call out, "Adrian, I'd like—" The door opens far too quickly. I'm left with my mouth hanging open, my words spoken far too loudly and the rest of whatever I was going to say jumbled at the back of my throat.

My heart races as I realize just how close to this man I am. It's no longer a thought, it's reality. He's a man who intimidates me. Not only because of his power, of him merely being in this building and what that means. But also because of what he does to me simply by existing. It's sinful, it's wrong. I fucking hate it.

"Ms. Parks."

Fuck.

My name sounds positively sinful in the rumble of his baritone voice. His steely gaze never leaves mine as I stand there, once again paralyzed. Taking one step back, barely giving me enough room to come in, he motions with his right hand, his left hand holding the doorframe. I break the hold he has me under, shifting my attention to the wall of windows behind his desk.

They're paned windows running from floor to ceiling, and the city is vibrant behind them. I know from experience it's loud as hell far down from this high-rise. But right now, this sight could be a painting, a beautiful masterpiece of a deep blue sky turning a dusky gray with silver buildings that creep into the clouds, the yellow squares of illuminated office windows slowly bringing light to the incoming night.

I've never stepped foot in this office before. I've never been invited here by Holt, I only knew it was his office. From here on out he'll be known as the asshole who took a hefty paycheck instead of giving this company what it truly needed. Essentially, he got a get-out-of-jail-free card and we got … Adrian Bradford.

The room is sparsely furnished. A hardwood maple desk carved with intricate detail catches my eye first. From the smell of lemon in the air, it's been freshly polished. A dark auburn leather wingback chair sits at its head, with two high-back lounge chairs across from it.

Other than that, the vast room is empty, with blank walls that have been freshly painted as if it were brand new. In other words, on the market for the new buyer.

Anger simmers inside of me.

It's only when the door shuts behind me that I remember exactly what I'm doing here. Although the city will never cease to amaze me. I shudder at the click behind me, turning quickly to find Adrian between myself and the door. Tapping the face of his watch, Adrian tells me, "It's nearly six, Suzette."

"Suzette?" is all I can manage. There's tension between us, thick and hot.

His full lips slip into a smirk. "That's what I said." He's calm and so damn sure of himself. Everything I normally am.

"Oh, I'm Suzette now?" Even to my own ears the indignation sounds feigned. My voice quavers as I add, "Only a moment ago I was Ms. Parks."

With a single step forward, Adrian adjusts the expensive silk tie around his neck and his expansive, barren office ignites in an instant.

For a moment, a very quick moment, his icy blue gaze drops to my lips but then they reach my eyes again before I can object to wherever his thoughts have gone. "I said it's nearly six," he murmurs. "Well, after five."

My fingers busy themselves with the hems of my sleeves. I haven't felt so nervous in ages, not since I first stepped foot in this city. All of the anxiousness that comes with starting over, starting something new that pushes you out of your comfort zone is not unfamiliar to me, although it's been a long damn time since I last felt this way. Not since my divorce was finalized.

"Is that a way to tell me to hurry up, Mr. Bradford?"

"No. Not at all. After six I have other business to discuss with you."

"After six?"

"Once work is over." He swallows and my treacherous mind focuses on the cords of his neck. The curves of it, the strength there and that masculine scent, fresh and clean with a hint of sandalwood.

"I beg your pardon, but I'm here on business."

"Yes … other business than what we discussed this afternoon." My pulse races as he locks his gaze with mine. I can't help but to feel like the prey, already caught by a much too powerful hunter. One who wants to play with his dinner before devouring it whole.

"Other business?" Again my voice falters. I make the next statement firm. "What could I possibly want to discuss with you? Other than the threat of you simply stepping into this building." I add with indignation, "My building."

With the little courage I can muster, I lift up my chin. Feeling what I felt hours ago in that boardroom creep back into the forefront of my mind, I try to shove it down. He's no longer a sex god reducing me to a puddle of want. He's the man who threatens my very career. And for what? For statistics on the balance sheet? For the likelihood of an easy payout rather than doing the hard work?

Just as the thought hits me, Adrian checks his watch again. "It's six now, Ms. Parks."

His domineering stature abates as if he's slightly more relaxed. He reaches up to loosen his tie. The act does horrible things to my conviction.

"You're in need," he states beneath his breath. I can barely focus on his lips as his deft fingers work to undo the top button of his shirt. In one step, he's far too close and the smell of his cologne turns heavenly.

"Excuse me?" I whisper, not as confidently as I'd intended. It's darker than it was, as if the night fell around us, granting much-needed privacy.

Leaning down so his lips grace the shell of my ear, he whispers, "All you have to say is that you left something outside of this office." Shivers run down my shoulder, then lower. My nipples are already hard and I curse the fact that I haven't been touched in months for how much I want this man to do horrible things to me right now.

With my lips parted I can barely comprehend what he said. As he takes a single step back, giving me more room to think, he removes his tie completely. The silk whispers in the air as it slides against his collar. It's the only sound I can hear other than the beating of my heart. He doesn't turn around fully and he doesn't take his eyes from mine. He locks the door with one hand and tosses the tie on the floor.

"You very much have the wrong impression of me," he says and I breathe out although I don't know how. My chest rises and falls with every heavy breath I take.

"I was praying you would walk through that door," he tells me. Adrian takes a step forward with his right hand undoing the buttons of his white dress shirt one by one, starting at the top. My gaze slips down his torso, following the line of buttons to the bulge in his pants.

My God. The temperature in the room erupts.

"I was hoping you'd come see me to work out our … differences. I was prepared to spend all fucking day listening to you rant, taking every insult with stride. I was ready to let you get it all out." For every step forward he takes, I take one step back until my ass hits the edge of the desk.

"I would be very surprised if I had the wrong impression, Ms. Parks. But I'd like to get one thing clear." With both of my hands gripping the edge of the desk, I peer up at him, bracing myself. He reaches out and brushes against my jaw with his thumb.

His touch is as commanding as his tone, his stare, every detail about him. I'm left paralyzed. Caught in a trance.

"After six o'clock, all of that shit ends and what's between us is between us." I stare into his eyes, barely breathing as he continues. "I'll say it again; all you have to do is say you've left something outside of this office." His eyes search mine and I believe him. If I were to say it, he'd back away. He'd let me leave. And then what? Would this tension be gone? Would he pretend it didn't exist?

The reality of what's happening and the consequences of the decision I'm about to make are far too real in these few seconds.

With his eyes on my lips, his thumb moves there, parting them slowly so that just the tip of his thumb presses down, enticing me to suck it. He's far too close, far too intoxicating, far too tempting.

"Have you left something outside?" he questions. That deep voice rolls through me again. I know what's appropriate in this situation. I should jerk my head back from his touch and tell him that I did leave something outside. Mention the HR complaint I'm filing against him. That's what you're supposed to do when an asshole like Adrian backs you up against his desk.

It's what I should do. I know it. And yet … I know damn well that I want him. I want this.

The aching need between my thighs reassures me that I fucking *need* this.

Instead of answering, I move my mouth just enough to bite down on his thumb, my teeth sinking into the tip of it. The deep groan at the back of his throat is stifled and with that little movement, I force this rather dominating man to shift in front of me. "I'll need you to answer me, Ms. Parks. Because if you haven't left anything outside, I'm going to fuck you against this desk like I wanted to the second I laid eyes on you."

It's a heady feeling to bring a man like him to the point of desperation. The desire ignites in his eyes and I push him just a little further, flicking my tongue against his thumb.

His eyes close and he speaks without opening them. "Have you left something outside?"

It seems simple, in a way. He was right when he said I was in need. And letting this man do whatever he wants to me would soothe an ache I've had for days. A pent-up need that's been dying to be sated. It would be everything I've needed since I gave my ex the finger and fell down the black hole of an endless to-do list.

Of course it would. Look at him, in his expensive suit with his thumb still tracing a path on my lip and his eyes shut. He's hot. He's more than hot. He's everything I could possibly want in a man. Physically, at least. It doesn't matter that he's an arrogant asshole. I can still hate him as much as I did when I first stormed in here, but right now … I'm worked up and hot for him.

When his eyes finally open and he stares back at me with an intensity that burns inside of me just the same, I barely speak, "I didn't leave anything outside."

Before the last word is spoken, his lips are on mine, devouring them. Both hands cup my face, pulling me in and my hands splay against his broad chest. He's all man beneath the suit. Strong muscles bulge and tense.

The layers of fabric between us are in the way and I do my part to help strip them off. Adrian isn't hesitant about a damn thing. His hands roam, his lips mold against mine and with every small movement I make, he meets it tenfold. I don't think a man like him is capable of being timid about anything. He puts his tongue in my mouth, glides it against mine, and seems to taste me more deeply than any man ever has before. Wanting more and forcing small sounds from me as his hands roam and the zipper is pulled down my back. The chill of the air greets my bare skin and I have to break the kiss, breathing in the cool air as I arch my neck and throw my head back. Adrian doesn't stop, doesn't pause for anything. His nimble fingers work my dress, sending goosebumps down my skin where his fingertips leave traces of his heated touch.

As I stare up at the ceiling, he leaves a trail of openmouthed kisses down my neck. Hot and greedy, it's enough to pull me back to him.

To rid myself of any thoughts other than those drenched in lust.

Scorching desire prickles over my skin and I find myself kissing him back, maybe a little desperately. Shamefully so. I've always wanted to be kissed like this. It's every girl's dream to be kissed like the other person can't get enough of you. It's only fair if I kiss him back just as hard and make him think I want this. Adrian can think whatever he wants about me. He can think I hate him. He can think I'm melting for him.

If I'm going to do this, I'm going to take as much as I give.

All I care about is the way it's going to feel when he takes control of all the heat between my legs. Will he kiss me there too? Will he be just as ravenous as he is now?

He kisses me harder, demanding more with a rumble from deep in his chest when he puts his hand on one of my legs and slides it slowly up under my dress. There's no hesitation at all with this movement. He got all he wanted from me when I told him I wasn't leaving. Now I'm his to take.

He pauses there before breaking our kiss and letting me breathe, his hand gripping my upper thigh. It's only then that I feel his cock pressed against my leg. He's hard and I wasn't mistaken earlier … no wonder he's so fucking arrogant.

I shiver when he reaches my panties. They're not full coverage ones, because those don't sit well underneath my work clothes, but they're not a thong, either. His fingertips play at the band. Then he cups me through the cotton fabric and I moan into the kiss.

"You're hot for me," he says into my mouth. "I knew you would be the second you started to mouth off to me." Adrian strokes against the fabric and when his knuckles brush against my clit I'm all too aware of how sensitive I am for him. My head lolls to the side and I sink my teeth into the fabric of his shirt. My hands fist his dress shirt, pulling it from his suit pants with a desperate need for it to be ripped from him so we can get on with it.

"Good girl. Such a good little slut for me." My back arches and I rock myself into his hand. "Fuck you," I mutter but even as I do, the pleasure builds and Adrian chuckles. He's playing me like a toy.

The words make me hot even though I know they shouldn't. I roll my hips against his hand and he groans a deep rough sound, wrapping his other hand around the nape of my neck to pull me in close.

"Do you want to be my whore or my good girl?" he asks me.

I can only gasp as his fingers slip past the band and his thumb rubs ruthless circles against my clit. Moaning, I don't answer him.

"Degradation or praise?" he presses further.

I have both hands on his chest, slid under the expensive fabric of his shirt. "Whatever you want. I just need you inside of me." The plea is desperate, and I don't give a fuck.

He doesn't say a word as he smiles down at me like he's won. For a half second, I worry he'll leave me like this, wanting and admitting it so boldly. The fear is gone just as quickly as it came. His hands go under my ass and he roughly lifts me onto the surface of his desk. Adrian uses one hand to push my legs apart and I balance myself on the desk while he shoves the hem of my dress up to my hips. The fabric rolls up in an awkward bunch and remains there. This dress isn't meant to be treated like that, but he doesn't care. He's busy pulling my panties off and down over my shoes, which fall to the floor with dull thuds. Finally, his fingertips meet my bare, wet center.

It turns me into a woman I don't know. A woman who five minutes ago was coming in here to tell him to keep his hands off my department. Now I'm so hungry for his touch that I practically throw myself into it. Adrian doesn't allow it. He takes what he wants, and he pushes me away from him, one hand splayed across my chest while reaching for his belt buckle with the other. His cock springs out with a flash of lust in his eyes. "Spread wide, Suzette."

I obey and he pulls my hips closer to the edge.

His eyes sweep down to my spread legs and he groans, his hand working at his cock. He wants the same thing from me that I want from him. He wants to work off some of the tension from endless meetings and boardrooms and constantly working, constantly holding everything in.

With a hand on the back of my head, he bends low to kiss me as he nudges the tip right where I need him. Adrian isn't taking time to make sure I'm ready and he doesn't have to. I'm more than ready for him. He pumps his hips and I hang on to the desk to stay on it.

Fuck! He fills me with a single hard thrust, his hand coming down to brace my ass so he can fuck me deeper. My hands fly to his shoulders, needing to hold on to something more solid. My body's hot all at once and tense. My heels dig into his ass.

"Fuck," I moan. Not slowing down in the least, Adrian's lips find mine again. "Fucking perfect," he groans. I bury my head into his chest, my eyes closing and my teeth biting down on my lip as he fucks me like he owns me. He whispers, "Take it like a good girl."

A cold sweat covers my forehead as I pull away, stifling my moans as best I can.

It's dirty to do this and so wrong. It's against every rule of office life to spread your legs on a man's desk … especially when he's your boss. And certainly when he's your boss's boss. My body doesn't care. It clenches around him, making him grunt, and his lips capture my screams of pleasure. My release builds and rises like the tides on the shore until it's crashing down on me. The only option I'm left with is to hang on for dear life.

chapter 3

Adrian

NO MATTER HOW MUCH SHE TRIES TO HIDE IT, I CAN STILL HEAR HER catching her breath.

Fuck, it's hard enough to keep steady myself. My muscles are still coiled with adrenaline rushing through my veins. That was exactly what I needed.

With a hushed moan slipping through her lips as I button up my shirt, I amend the thought: *She* is exactly what I needed.

With my back turned to her, a satisfied smile creeps to my lips and I bend down to pick up my tie. "Do you have plans for dinner?" I ask, balling up the silk and pocketing it rather than attempting a professional appearance in the least.

The unmistakable sound of a zipper replaces the silence in the room, as do the muffled sounds of her attempting to slip her heels back on. I turn to see her peering up at me.

Fuck.

There are so many questions that dance in her gorgeous light blue eyes. The vulnerability is unexpected. Her red dress is still open in the back; her attempt to zip it up only moved it partway.

Distrust riddles itself in every small movement she makes. It's so damn obvious as she stares back at me like she's afraid to even breathe.

"Turn around," I command her, not liking wherever her pretty little head has taken her. "Let me help you with that."

She only hesitates a moment, still not having answered my question. I take my time, using the backs of my fingers to brush her brunette locks to the side. My hand brushes against her bare back before I zip up her dress to the top. I don't miss that she uses her right hand to brace herself on the desk and she stares down at it rather than looking back at me. The obvious insecurity has my dick hardening already. If she thinks I only wanted her once or that this was some kind of manipulation tactic, my little vixen is dead wrong.

"I have reservations for dinner. Come with me."

She's silent still as she comes back to reality. Her cheeks are still flushed, her lips still swollen from my bruising kiss. With her hair disheveled, she looks well and thoroughly fucked.

Stepping to her right so as not to be trapped between myself and the desk I've just fucked her on, she leaves me wanting.

"I should go," is all she says.

Panic is something I didn't expect to feel. Certainly not with a woman like her, confident and transparent. If she leaves right now, I'm fucked. We barely spoke. There's no chance in hell she'll let me near her again.

This is not at all the way it was supposed to go.

"We have reservations and we're going to be late."

"We? *We* have reservations?" she says and finally looks me in the eye. That's better. Wherever her head is, whoever screwed her over to the point of not trusting another man, it's in the past.

"I don't want to go alone. So yes. We have reservations at the Waldorf."

"I'm not dressed for that," she responds far too quickly.

I make a point of letting my eyes undress her from head to toe. "The hell you aren't. You look utterly delectable."

"I would never wear something like this to the Waldorf."

Watching as she smooths her hair, her gaze dancing between me and the door, I offer her a simple solution. "We can stop on the way."

She rolls her eyes and my cock answers in response, hardening and wanting so desperately to punish her. "I have plenty of money if I—"

"I could buy you a thousand times over." My voice is harder than I'd like but I'm through with this little back-and-forth. "If I say we can stop to buy you whatever the hell I want, it's not because I wish to spoil you or show off. It's to save time and for your comfort."

My statement must have come off harsh, because her jaw clenches. I add, "I couldn't care less what you wear."

"I wouldn't want to be seen with someone like you, showing off your recent conquest." The bitterness to her tone might as well slap me across my face.

Is that what she thinks this is? Is that who she thinks I am?

Invading her space, I tower over her and say, "When did I give you the impression you were something to conquer? I want you because I want you, and I couldn't care less what anyone else thinks of that."

All that anger, all that resentment—it all vanishes the second I exert any dominance over her. It's addictive. It's heaven and hell, a concoction I'd gladly get drunk on every second for the rest of my life.

"I am one thing in the boardroom. I'm another outside of that. If you can't compartmentalize, tell me now."

"I'm sorry," she says and her doe eyes fall to my chest. She's on the verge of running and that's the last thing I want.

"I don't want you to apologize," I say, gentling my voice, tipping up her chin so she'll finally look at me. See me. "I want you to come to dinner with me."

chapter 4

WHAT THE FUCK JUST HAPPENED? I'm not certain how I made it downstairs from his office with his hand splayed across my lower back, in front of anyone who dared to look. My legs are weak and there's an odd mix of satisfaction and nervousness that has my head clouded.

Adrian Bradford just fucked me across his desk like I was his personal toy. The feel of him between my legs is all I can focus on. How effortlessly he destroyed every wall I've built and fucked me like he had every right in the world to ruin me.

I'm barely with it as he helps me to his car until he speaks to his driver, who politely greets me before opening the back door. Adrian says something to him that I don't quite make out because I'm still catching my breath from the sex.

The cool spring air brings me back to the present as I thank his driver. He's an older gentleman with a lean frame and silver hair. His wire-rimmed glasses and black suit complete his polished look.

"Thank you," I say, barely getting out the words before I'm left alone in the back of the car, until Adrian climbs in on his side.

It's a Mercedes, one of the new ones from this year, and it smells like he just drove it off the lot. Adrian's driver rolls up the divider that separates the spacious back seat from the front the moment he gets in.

Adrian sprawls out on the seat next to me as the driver navigates the city streets. He's on his phone like nothing happened and I try to act like nothing happened too. I'm having a bit of trouble with that. He seems casual, swiping at the screen and no doubt answering emails, but there's tension crackling between us. No matter how hard he tries to make this into nothing, it's anything but.

Gaining a semblance of balance and sanity, I peer up at him and say, as clearly as I can, "I'm not a toy to be played with."

He glances at me, then slips his phone into his back pocket. "You seemed to enjoy it quite a bit."

My face reddens. "I did. But that doesn't mean it can continue or that my job …" my voice trails off and I can barely swallow. *What the fuck did I just do?*

He studies me with his pale blue gaze. "Would you like it, though?" There's far too much space between us in the back seat of his car. Adrian's taking care not to touch me. It feels deliberate. He doesn't move his body toward me or reach for me, but I can still feel his hands on me from just a moment ago. I can feel where he gripped my ass and held me close for a kiss by my neck, and where he stroked between my legs. "Would you like it if I toyed with you again?" he asks, his voice low and his words sinful.

The rest of my body feels as hot as my face. Now that we're out of the office and away from the moment, I can't believe it happened. What was I thinking? I can't answer him, because I'm not sure of myself enough to speak. It's all too much and far too fast. Suffocating.

"I'd like an answer, Suzette," he says and his murmur is laced with something different. Concern.

Swallowing thickly, I admit, "I enjoyed it very much, but now—"

"I enjoyed it immensely and I intend to toy with you, to fuck you until you're as limp as a little ragdoll, and to walk back into the office tomorrow knowing full damn well you may give me hell."

The leather groans in protest as he leans back, moving farther away as he studies me. "Nothing that just happened will interfere with our work," he reassures me.

With a jostle of the vehicle, the driver pulls the car to the curb, and I blink at the scenery outside my window. The Waldorf, another public arena for his games … and a far too expensive one at that. I murmur, "You should take me home."

He's silent for a moment, just watching me. "If that's what you'd like. I believe I owe you more than just a drink, though, Suzette."

Hearing my name from his lips like that … like every syllable rolls off his tongue as if he was the first to utter them, turns me even hotter. It also makes me speechless, which isn't like me at all. None of this is like me at all. I don't get swept up into anything.

Adrian holds me in place with his piercing gaze. "I'd very much like to play with you, Suzette. I'd like to kiss you. I'd like to fuck you. And not just because you're a pretty little thing who stormed into my office making demands you have no authority to make."

With every word, he inches closer to me until he's close enough to kiss me. The proximity is comforting in a way I don't care to admit. Adrian actually leans down and does it. He kisses me full on the mouth, his lips steady and confident. When he pulls back I have to keep my hands in my lap from grabbing his shirt.

"It was a brutal day, and the only thing that kept me grounded and kept me looking forward to tonight was the very idea that you were coming to my office to do exactly what you did." His admission shocks me.

"Adrian …"

"You may see me as ruthless and heartless, and you may not like what I do, but I'd like to see you again. In and out of the office."

It's strange for him to admit this to me. Most men won't ever acknowledge they're aware of other people's feelings. Men like Adrian aren't supposed to care what anyone else thinks. It's possible he doesn't care, but at least he's aware of it. It causes a shift in the way I see him. The hatred softens and becomes something else.

"When the workday is over, there are other things we must do. And then there are things that we *want* to do." He leans in closer, whispering at the shell of my ear, "I want you."

His hand comes down on my knee and without hesitation he pushes it up between my legs, forcing my skirt up as his fingers brush against my slit. It's the softest of touches and my eyes close, my lips parted and my head falling back. Adrian lets out a groan, the tip of his nose running along my neck, teasing me. "You didn't put your panties back on."

I shake my head, unable to speak. I didn't. I tucked them into my purse, not liking their condition after … well, after what he did to me. Adrian dips his head again, close enough to kiss, and I want it so much that tears come to my eyes. I'm not even sure what they mean. Adrian seems to know.

"You," he says, "are exactly what I want."

He takes a deep breath and then exhales, the warmth of it lingering as he pulls away slightly. Trapped in his car, every sensation feels heightened, knowing how easy it is for him to admit his desire. I become aware of his hands. One holds the seat behind me, just above my head, and the one that was between my legs is now braced against the door, like he must hold on to something to keep him from touching me. From doing whatever it is he so desperately craves to do. Adrian's eyes close for a moment and when he opens them, he seems steadier than before. "If you'd like to go home, I'll take you home. I'll have my driver take you wherever you need. Though I'd very much like to take you to dinner."

"I'm not dressed for this place."

"We could go somewhere else."

"You have reservations," I say and my pulse races, not wanting me to deny him … or myself.

"That's a weak excuse, Suzette." Disappointment flashes across his face, and surprise grips my heart. I'm surprised I care about his disappointment and I'm even more shocked that I *want* to go to dinner with him. He feels dangerous, like he could crush me if he wanted. Yet I find myself wanting to be under his thumb, wondering what he'll do to me.

I don't know where I'm supposed to draw the line, though. This is … this is something that could certainly destroy me, and then what would I have left?

I imagine how it will feel to have the car pull away from the curb and drop me at my place. And then I imagine what it would be like to let him help me out of the car and take me inside this restaurant. Both options leave me wanting, but only one feels safe.

"Is it a business dinner?" I ask, keeping my voice low and even.

A grin tugs the corners of his mouth upward. "No. It's after six."

"If someone asks?" A bit of desperation creeps into my tone, and I can't stop it. "Could it be a business dinner if someone were to see us?"

"You'd like to be discreet?"

I have to be discreet. I don't even know what this is. A hate fuck turned into a dinner date? There's no telling what I might want to keep hidden later.

"Yes," I answer. "Please. It would make me feel better."

He seems to consider it, searching my expression as we sit in the back of the parked car. "Would you like to see me again after tonight?"

There's a pressure in my chest, like a balloon getting filled up with helium. It reminds me of the excitement I felt when I was young and dumb and dating. Before I got married and everything went to shit. There was a period in my life when it seemed like anything could happen. That woman would revel in this moment. But that woman got her heart ripped out long ago. She's long dead and buried.

"It depends," I finally make myself say. "On how our discreet dinner goes."

Adrian smirks, charming and seductive, making him all the more handsome. It sends a shiver of desire down my spine. I already want him again. Even at this point there's so much heat between us and it seems impossible to turn it down. Above all, I want to see him smile at me with approval. I've never been a people pleaser. I've always been about making change, and change is often uncomfortable for others. Part of me still wants to *please* him. *I want to hear him call me his good girl again.*

"So you'll come to dinner with me and then decide? That's a fair deal."

Adrian stares at me across the table of our rather private curved booth. His gaze is fire; everything about him is possessive, but in a manner that's effortless. Every little thing, including the way his touch never left me when he escorted me into the Waldorf, is dominating yet in a way that's gentle. I could have walked faster or simply pulled away from him, but there was never a moment where I considered such a betrayal. Both to what he obviously desires, as well as my own.

Tucked away in the corner of the restaurant, with fine leather upholstery covering the padded wooden frame, it's easy enough to peek out at the other guests, although they feel miles away. It feels like they're all staring at us, though they're not. I shift in my seat. If they're looking over here, they'll notice I'm underdressed.

"I love seeing you squirm," says Adrian in a low voice.

"About the meeting today …" I begin.

"We're off the clock," he says simply, ending the conversation without breaking my gaze.

I bite my lip and try to keep from bringing up work again. It would be so easy to fall into that.

The tension is still there, and I do my best to not so nervously lay the napkin across my lap as the waiter presents the menu to us.

I let the menu fall as Adrian orders for me. He's quick and confident, as if we already know each other.

"Would that be all right?" he asks and inclines his head toward me before the waiter can leave. Nodding, I give my seal of approval.

I wait until the waiter has stepped out of earshot before I speak to him. "You're lucky you chose what you did."

"I guessed right? Or are you just saying that?" His eyes on mine seem to see right through my dress, as if he's remembering earlier at the office.

"You did guess right." My fingers slip along the stem of my water goblet.

"If it's not to your liking, I'll have them bring you something else," he says, and I feel myself blushing with a sudden shyness I haven't felt in years. Not since I was a girl. There's no place for shyness in a business career like mine. Adrian puts a hand to my face and runs his thumb over my cheek.

"You get to me, Adrian."

"That seems fair, since you get to me as well." Butterflies stir and I can't help it. "Are you always like this?" I question but all I'm rewarded with is a charming, knowing smirk before we're interrupted.

The waiter reappears, and there's distance between us again. In his starched black uniform, the waiter sets out a wineglass. Then he shows Adrian the bottle, and at Adrian's nod he opens it and pours a sip or two. Adrian tastes it. The waiter watches him the same way I'm watching him. Probably too closely. He lets the wine linger on his tongue before swallowing it and giving the waiter a nod.

He fills my glass and places it in front of me, murmuring his replies to our thank-yous, and Adrian curls his fist around his own glass. Whiskey, on the rocks.

I watch him take the first sip and notice the way his shoulders relax.

"Is this how you are with all your employees?" I ask.

Adrian raises an eyebrow. "I haven't slept with an employee ever, actually."

"Why do I find that hard to believe?" I arch an eyebrow, leaning in, trying to flirt with him.

He answers me in an utterly serious tone. "Because you don't trust me and seem to hold a rather low opinion of me."

I jerk back a few inches, shock settling in. Is he really offended by this? We just had sex on his desk, in his office, at work. The only boundary was that it was slightly after 6:00 p.m. "I didn't mean to imply that I think poorly of you. And for the record, it's because you exude sex appeal so I imagine you could sleep with anyone you wanted."

Adrian chuckles, his rough short laugh a baritone rumble in his chest, and it breaks up the tension. "You do seem very hesitant around me. Is there something I can do to ease that?" His words fall slowly, drifting to the pressed and starched linen tablecloth as his eyes drop to my breasts. "To break the ice, perhaps?"

"You have a reputation, Adrian."

"Everyone does, Suzette. It doesn't mean that's who we are. One person could tell you I'm loyal to a fault, another that I'm a miserable asshole. Both could very well be honest impressions of me. So, believe them both."

Before I can even respond, we're interrupted yet again.

"Excuse me, sir." The waiter steps to the side of the table and passes a folded note to Adrian.

With Adrian's nod we're alone again, although I might as well not exist.

He reads it, tucks the thick white note card into his pocket, and checks his phone.

My stomach drops. "Is everything all right?"

His phone goes back into his pocket. "As all right as it always is."

My teeth sink into my bottom lip as I gather my courage for the next question, which I should have asked before I fucked him. "There isn't another woman, is there?"

"No." The answer comes quickly and decisively, and I believe him. "I haven't had a sexual partner for the better part of a year."

The handle of my fork rests in my fingertips, but I drop it back down to the empty small plate again. "No other man?" he questions in turn.

"No." It's a relief to hear that. A bigger relief than I would have thought.

"And we're to be discreet?" Adrian finishes.

"Yes," I say.

"Work during the day, and play at night?"

"Yes," I answer.

His eyes narrow. "I like when you answer me like that, a single word rushing out of your perfect, parted lips." His gaze burns. "I'd like to see those lips when I—"

Adrian gets another text and curses under his breath. He's not the only one. My phone buzzes too.

It's from Maddie: *Hey! Are you coming?*

"Oh … I'm so sorry." I push my hair back from my face and brace myself with both hands on the table. "I'm supposed to meet a friend tonight. I completely forgot."

Of the three women I'm closest to, Maddie is like my little sister. She's also going through a breakup and relying heavily on company to keep her from texting the asshole when she feels lonely.

"I can't believe I forgot."

"No time to eat?" he questions, not pressuring me in the least. His phone buzzes yet again before I can even answer, and he closes his eyes, visibly annoyed.

"I'm sorry, I really have to go. She's a good friend of mine and I don't know how it could have possibly slipped my mind that we had plans." I swallow down the horrible feeling of failing her, knowing exactly how I came to forget about anything other than the man seated in front of me. "I'm going to take a cab."

"If you insist."

"I'm afraid I do, Mr. Bradford." As I speak, I stand and he mirrors the motion.

"No longer Adrian?"

He holds his hand out to me and it takes me a minute to understand what he wants. "I'll walk you out."

It's almost unreal what a gentleman this man is after hours. "Will you be so kind to me tomorrow?" I question as if it's banter, but the truth is obviously buried there.

It only takes one motion from Adrian for the doorman to bring around a taxi for me. The night has fallen dark and the chill brings me closer to Adrian as the car pulls up.

"Phone." He says the one word and I hand him my phone without question. Adrian frowns down at the screen while he types something. It's his number. His fingers fly across the screen. I'll probably find out he's sent a text to himself with my number.

"I'll see you tomorrow," he says, handing it back to me. "Perhaps you'll give me the opportunity to play with you once the clock strikes six."

chapter 5

Adrian

I T TAKES GREAT EFFORT NOT TO LET ON THAT MY PANTS ARE TIGHT FROM my little vixen's text messages. I'm certain Wyatt wouldn't appreciate that fact. With that being said, it's my office. My meeting.

And if I want to read the filthy things she's messaging, I'll damn well do as I please.

I'll have to scold her when I see her. Not now, while she's working, when I'm not buried deep inside her and she has nowhere to go.

Scrolling through the last messages she sent, I have to readjust in my seat.

Suzette Parks has a very dirty mouth and I want to do very dirty things to it.

It's work hours, though, so I don't respond to the three she's sent me.

This morning was one thing, and technically I started the "sexting games" as she called it.

No panties today. I want to fuck you without having to rip them off.

Yes, sir.

That's my good girl.

You say that now but if you tell me to crawl under your desk, that will be a firm no from me.

Why do I think you're lying?

I remember when I sent the last message, I watched both the clock and the security monitors that kept track of her entering the elevator. It was nearly 9:00 a.m.

Tell me what you would do then, if I wanted you to keep me company in my office.

Did I set her up? Fucking right I did. Am I going to fuck her hard and rough to punish her for the unprofessional behavior she's displayed? Hell yes I am. And we're both going to enjoy it.

It's all talk from her. I know it is. So, scolding her will have to wait.

"I don't know, man," Wyatt says, nudging the container of lo mein closer to me. Piling the bit of it left on his plate onto a white plastic fork he tells me, "I prefer the place on Fifth."

"Shing Kwong?"

He nods, still shoveling the Chinese food into his mouth. Wyatt is tall, lean, and three years younger than me although it feels like there's a decade between us. He's naive, positive about far too much and riskier than he should be.

I didn't come from money. We were slightly well-off, but not like the Pattons, Wyatt's family. It shows. He makes deals like there will always be a safety net beneath him. I'd be lying if I said I wasn't resentful of it at one time in my life. As the end of a noodle slaps his chin, sauce dripping down his amber skin, the corners of my lips turn up.

Wyatt is a puppy dog in the elite groups I run in, but he's damn loyal.

"Yeah."

"Well, you're welcome to bring your own takeout next time you decide to swing by then, rather than having Andrea order it."

"So I'll have that contract for you in just a little bit."

My brow arches at the very sudden change in topics. "I knew you'd bring it up."

He smirks, not looking back at me, and says, "I can't help it; I'm excited."

"I haven't said I'll sign, and I'm still waiting on my lawyer to look over the clauses."

"It's been a year in the making," he comments, finally putting down his plate.

"I'm not sure it's the right time right now."

It's silent for a moment and Wyatt finally looks up at me, running his hand over his curly, jet-black hair. It's cropped close to his scalp with a slight fade on the sides. "Cause of this," he says and motions behind him with his thumb.

Because of the eight-figure company I just bought? Yes. That would be why. Although I'd never admit it out loud. My funds aren't typically tied up in so many holdings. The timing was right for Holt & Hanover, though. He was desperate and I had the last bit of cash flow I could manage.

"You know I don't go into these things lightly."

One thick black brow raises as he leans back in the chair, pointing a finger at me. "You know this is a good deal."

"It *could* be a good deal," I respond, correcting him and before he can say any more, I tell him, "Let the lawyers talk out the details."

"They're minor," he presses, his insecurity showing as he grips the armrest of the lounge chair. "The merger is going to be a hit and I know you want in on it."

I mirror his posture, leaning back in my seat as I ball up my napkin and toss it onto my empty paper plate that's stained from lunch. "A number of events need to go accordingly." In this business, there are ebbs and flows. Some people can't handle the wild swings. Some don't prepare for the crashes.

"You sound like my father," Wyatt quips.

I merely grunt, checking my phone again and see she hasn't messaged any more. I'm tempted to send another text regardless. My thumb taps on the desk, my attention very much focused on the last line she sent an hour ago.

"Who is she?" he asks and I stare back at him blankly.

"Of all the—" Just as a grin stretches across his face, ready to lay into me, there's a knock at the door.

"Come in." I'm grateful for the interruption.

"Mr. Bradford," Andrea says, stepping into the room. If it weren't for the faint wrinkles around her eyes and the corners of her mouth, she'd look two decades younger than she is.

"Andrea could look it over?" Wyatt suggests and then huffs a laugh.

"She looks over all my contracts," I'm quick to tell him. She may only hold the title of secretary, and she looks the part, but Andrea Anderson is sharp and has a legal background that could rival the best. Times were different back then and instead of a firm, or the head of an academic department, Andrea left law altogether and I was lucky enough to meet her before someone else got ahold of her.

"Sir." Andrea folds her hands in front of her pencil skirt. "Your one o'clock is seated in the conference room."

All traces of humor are gone and dread seeps in.

"Thank you, Andrea." As I stand, Wyatt watches me button my jacket and take a mint.

Everything feels stiff and uncomfortable.

The moment the door closes gently, Andrea disappearing behind it, Wyatt comments, "Uh-oh. I'm guessing someone is about to get a harsh scolding from their new CEO."

I huff a humorless laugh, striding around him and tossing what's left of lunch into the trash.

"Can you clean up on your way out?"

"Yeah, you all right?" he questions as I open the door and glance through to the conference room. There's a reason there's only one office up here and then that room.

I get a glimpse of some of the employees seated around a table, my hand still on the doorknob. My hand is clenched so tight, my knuckles have gone white.

"You going to fire someone?" Wyatt makes another guess and this time he's right. I look over my shoulder to inform him, "An entire department. A very inefficient, very much *unneeded* department." I feel sick to my stomach just saying it. Knowing how in a single meeting I'll change their lives forever. But it's the right decision. The company is bleeding money with these cookie-cutter executives. Their pay increased while tasks were delegated and as the company grew, their roles diminished as new employees took on tasks that came with new demands. A dozen men and women walked into this building today overlooking tasks they barely comprehend.

"Shit," Wyatt says and he doesn't hold back on the misery. "I know if you're doing it, it must be done." His large brown eyes look sympathetic.

"Tell that to them."

ADRIAN IS MOST OF THE REASON I COULDN'T SLEEP. THOSE DREAMS were too hot to forget and they made me twist and turn in the sheets until morning. There was plenty to keep my mind occupied between replaying what happened on his office desk and the way he treated me after. The man himself is a whirlwind and I can barely hold on. There's an ache between my thighs still, even though it's been hours and hours.

The tall macchiato does nothing to help the bags under my eyes, but with a deep breath in, I prepare to make my way to my office like nothing happened.

Stepping foot inside feels illicit in a way it never did before. I've always come in with my chin up, ready to do battle for another day. Today that kick-ass persona is nowhere to be found. It's somewhere between a childish puppy dog love and the feelings that accompany the walk of shame.

In all those hours of tossing and turning, I came to one conclusion: I have, what feels like, a crush. Back in high school I used to get this fluttering-heart feeling for some of the guys in my class … that ended less than well. Pining after men in college led to my ex-husband. So all of these feelings can fuck off. It's against everything I stand for to have that kind of feeling for Adrian. It's forbidden to have sex with your boss on his desk. It's wrong to daydream about it so much you lose focus on your work.

It's a no go. A hard pass. But I'll be damned if I didn't text him the second he messaged me. Those giddy little feelings are my kryptonite. I suppose there's always an exception to every rule and Adrian Bradford is just that: exempt from every boundary I've spent years defining. Even as I sit at my desk, the tapping of keys and hushed chatter around me, I can barely keep from looking toward the elevator. All I want to know is if he's up there. I want to know if he can't stop thinking about what happened on his desk either.

Hours pass slowly through the day until I get a text message from him at four. His name on my phone makes the temperature of my body kick up a notch. I swallow hard, trying to subdue it all.

Adrian: *Meet me at the elevator at six.*

The hours went by slowly before but now they drag on and on, each tick of the clock taking forever. I stare at my computer screen, rereading every email twice. Triple-checking my responses to clients and sending back nearly every design I'm given from the graphics department. Not because they need changing or that they don't fit the branding for said clients. But simply because I can't focus and there's no way in hell I'm approving anything when all I keep imagining is my boss's expression when he calls me good girl.

At four fifteen there's a meeting in one of the smaller conference rooms downstairs. It's all I can do not to stare at Adrian through the large paned windows. In the glances I do steal, he appears less than thrilled. Every expression is dour as they leave one by one, Adrian leaving last and not looking back.

At ten to five, half a dozen executive assistants and senior executive assistants, some of whom I know but most I don't, move through the office in a clump. It's a relief that something has happened to break up the routine of the day.

"Fired," Gail whispers to me. I nearly spill my coffee when she does. I didn't realize she was standing so close, also spying.

"What?" I question. I've known Gail for years now. She's a damn good resource for client retention, but also the lead watercooler gossip. "Did you say fired? Are you sure?"

Nodding, she sweeps her curly dark brown hair back over one shoulder and then holds her coffee cup with both hands. In heels and leaning against the wall, the modelesque Latina in her late twenties towers over me. "I bet there will be an email going out soon."

All of them? Fired? She leaves me with a sick feeling stirring in the pit of my stomach as she bids her farewell. "It's what he does. No one should be surprised."

I know he has a reputation, but how the hell can a company run if every executive is severed?

Not long after that, an assistant director, Daniel Prath, who I spotted in the conference room earlier, has a screaming fit at the elevators with another man I don't know. Including the phrases, "this company would have gone under without me" and "good luck staying in business."

They must be fired, then.

Although the whispers that spread, in part largely to Gail, include fears of the company running with so many leads laid off at once, most don't mind seeing them leave. I'm certain a few who were under the executive assistant in finance will cheer in celebration to that prick's departure. All I ever heard about him were complaints.

It doesn't take more than an hour to pass before there's a conclusion among the majority of whispers: Those men encompass all that is wrong with the corporate world. They let people go rather than compensating them in the manner they should have been paid. They hired new employees and paid them less, pushing more onto everyone else's plate. They demanded more and more from all of us, wanting everyone to take one for the team while increasing their bonuses every year.

It's not good for a business to run that way, and it's not good for people to live that way. The management here uses up employees until they break, then fires them and starts over. They've never acknowledged or paid their respects to the employees who made the company what it is.

And now they're walking out the door.

Five o'clock comes and nearly everyone is gone already. Most taking the day off to "readjust" to new procedures from their higher-ups. I stay, like I always do. The last hour, when everyone's left and it's quiet, when the emails stop and calls go to voicemail, are my most productive. Judging by Adrian's statement yesterday, and his message from today, six is when the clock strikes midnight for him as well.

Somehow, that makes those giddy, girly feelings all the headier.

It's six on the dot when I press the silver button with the arrow icon pointing downward for the elevator. I don't know how I'm able to stand upright, with the nervousness that runs through me.

It isn't like me, none of this is. But I'd be lying if I said it wasn't thrilling.

When the doors open, my heart races at the sight in front of me. Adrian is already there waiting for me. Forcing myself to move slowly so he doesn't see my anxiousness, I move to his side and turn to face the doors. "I expect there will be a company-wide email shortly," I say to him as if it's casual conversation. We both stare straight ahead, the doors still open, making each second pass by at an achingly slow rate.

"Why is that?" He moves to press the button for the foyer and I note the way his bespoke suit wraps around his broad shoulders. And the way he fills the not-so-small cabin with his presence alone.

"I hear heads will be rolling."

As the elevator door closes, he smirks at me, a devilish look that brings an overwhelming heat to my cheeks. The elevator begins its descent and he asks, "Is that the talk at the watercooler?"

"More like the profanity Prath screamed on his way out."

He chuckles, then reaches for the button again. One strong knuckle pushes in the emergency stop button.

Tick, tick, tick, my heart rages in my chest. Desire fills me, moving over my skin and pinning me in place. I should know better than to do this but I don't. He's a fantasy come to life and I won't deny myself. How could a lowly sinner say no when the devil himself tempts her?

Confined in a small space together with no way out unless he decides and presses that button … all I feel is want and desire.

With one decisive stride, Adrian towers over me and personal space is nonexistent. My heel slips back half a step before I think better of it. He was calm and collected when I stepped onto the elevator, but now his eyes burn with a hunger I know all too well. With my next breath, the scent of his cologne fills my lungs.

"I've had a rather difficult day," he rasps. "And it's well after six p.m."

He pushes me against the wall all at once and it's just like when he put me on top of his desk. Reasoning becomes impossible and pushing him away is even more unlikely. Adrian slides my dress up, his hands hot and his touch sending every nerve ending beneath it into flames.

His hands roam in every place I've thought of him touching, of him claiming, since I left him last night. He's rough and commanding, gripping my curves and devouring my neck with openmouthed kisses. Every sensation is ignited and all I can do is hold on. With my arms around his shoulders, I can barely breathe, the heat suffocating me.

I don't doubt he's missed this as much as I have. Maybe he did spend his day like I did, obsessed with the idea of continuing what we started yesterday.

With ease he spreads my legs, standing between them and undoes his buckle. My back is pressed against the hard metal. I hook my knee around his hip and drop my head back against the elevator wall. "Suzette," he growls against my neck. It's even hotter now in the small space, because of how much I want him and because of the need in his voice.

He strokes his fingers between my legs, teasing me and I can barely stand it. "You were hot and bothered all night, weren't you?" he says, his piercing gaze staring deep into mine. He smirks while he asks the question, confident that he's right.

"No, I barely thought of you."

He chuckles at my response and then calls me a liar as two of his thick fingers push inside of me. "Tell me how much you want me."

"I want you," I moan, and rock as much as I can to feel more of him inside of me.

When he tsks, stilling his motions, I open my eyes. "Uh, uh, uh. If you're going to move your hips like that, it won't be for anything but me."

He takes his cock in his fist and lines it up with my wet slit, then thrusts in. The movement is so hard and controlling that it takes my breath away. I gasp at the size of him and he pauses, buried deep inside of me, as I adjust to his girth.

"That's my good girl," he says in a breathy voice against my neck. It doesn't take long for him to move again, and I meet him with every thrust, my heels digging into his ass.

"Yes," he coaxes. "You have no fucking idea how hot you are," he groans, pulling a strap of my dress down and kissing, nipping down my shoulder to my breast.

My voice deserts me and I can't reply other than to angle my hips to take him deeper. My nails scratch at his jacket, in an effort to hold on to him.

It's fast. It's dirty. And I want to remember every last detail.

The elevator door dings. I'm still trying to get my breathing to a normal rate, but at least my hair doesn't give anything away. My dress is as smooth as it can be, but there's no doubt that I'm a hue pinker than I ought to be given that the city has a chill in the air this late in April.

As I walk with him, keeping pace, I remind myself there are no obligations. This is nothing but a fling, or an office fuck buddy. Given that I haven't dated in the better part of a decade other than the one-night stands I had to celebrate leaving my piece of shit ex, I have no idea what we are.

But I want more of it.

The thought of whatever we are is both exciting and terrifying. Adrian makes me feel things, but I'm smart enough not to fall for him. I have to be, or this could end very badly. Hands to my hair, I smooth it down one more time and prepare to tell him a quick good night. My heels click on the marble floor of the lobby and I note that the place is nearly vacant. But not entirely. No one looks our way, though. I thank my lucky stars for that.

As we get to the large glass doors that lead to the bustling streets, I start what I think will be an acceptable farewell, "That was—"

"Come with me tonight." He's firm, businesslike as he stands toe to toe with me, waiting for an answer. His words reverberate through me, cutting off the farewell in addition to my thoughts.

"You don't need to buy me dinner."

"Do you eat?" he questions and there's not a trace of humor.

"Yes."

"Good." His eyes glint. "I want to feed you. Besides, we have things to discuss and we have—"

"You've made decisions regarding my department?" I question him, the sight from this afternoon putting me on edge instantly. "The only thing I've received from your team is a request for the client list."

That list is as good as gold. Everything they wanted in that email was essentially preparing paperwork so that another person could take over if need be. I'm not stupid, but I am under contract and not the only one with the list.

"We won't be discussing work at dinner."

"I can damn well discuss what I'd like."

"Watch that mouth of yours." His mouth quirks but he doesn't quite smile. More of a smirk. "It's after six," he whispers, and with the look he gives me, I glance over my shoulder to be sure no one is watching.

Adrian fixes his cuffs, readjusting his sleeves. "I have a late meeting with an associate. His wife wanted to do a tour of New York on a private ship. You could accompany me. The meeting will be short, and they're good company. I've heard the chef they hired for tonight is excellent as well."

The heat from the elevator is back, and all of it is on my face. "I thought we were just—"

"I want more than sex, Suzette. Although I enjoy that immensely."

"What exactly do you want, Mr. Bradford?"

"To get to know you," he says simply.

It throws me off. What we were doing in his office and the elevator is so forbidden that I'd assumed we would have strong boundaries and never cross them. Getting to know each other is definitely crossing them. "Well … the first thing I typically tell someone is I'm divorced and I hate the male species."

The lift of his brow is telling: *I wasn't acting like I hated him in the elevator.* "Surely there is more to you than your dating status."

I hesitate. "I'm not looking for anything serious."

"Having dinner after sex is serious?"

"Hanging on your arm as a date to an after-hours event? Being seen together … that's not discreet."

"I assure you, my evenings are discreet. Nearly everyone I speak to has signed an NDA with me at some point or another and it's all business."

"If you think you need to woo me or somehow …" I can't finish. I don't know how to say what I'm thinking.

"Or what?"

I decide to be blunt. "I don't mind just being a fuck toy," I admit to him, my voice low. "In fact, I enjoy it."

He groans as if I said it just to torture him. "Your fucking mouth, Suzette."

He must know how hot he is when he does that. When he speaks to me like that. It's not fair in the least. I have to bite down on my lip to keep from grinning. A genuine smile, different from the one I use in meetings or when I pass people in the hall at work.

He straightens and runs a hand over his mouth. "I'll make this very simple for you. I'm attracted to you. I'd like you to come with me tonight. Now say yes."

I try to read his expression. Unsettled and hot, I search for the meaning behind his words and the meaning behind his intentions. More importantly, what they'll do to me.

"Don't make me beg, Suzette," he states as if he really would. "Come. Say yes."

I answer without thinking, "Yes."

chapter 7

Adrian

SUZETTE'S PHONE RINGS THE MOMENT SHE GETS INTO THE CAR AND she chooses not to answer it, texting instead.

With a cocked brow, I glance at her phone and she shakes her head, her expression not hiding the humor. She holds up her phone and says, "My friend Maddie."

The texts read as follows:

Sorry, can't take the call, everything okay?
Fine. Any word on what Lucifer is planning to do?

Nothing yet.

Well come over and drink with me, we'll do a binge watch of Grey's or something.

I have to work.

Booooo. Well don't let Lucifer get you down.

"Lucifer?" I question, feeling the corners of my lips pull into a knowing smirk.

She clears her throat, crossing her legs in an attempt to look dignified. "When I heard Holt sold the company to some asshole with a reputation … We nicknamed him Lucifer."

My smile grows. "Hmm, sounds like a prick."

She has the decency to appear nervous under my gaze.

"Why is she asking about the company?"

"I outsource to her at times. And I've been … nervous and venting to her."

"You overthink things."

"I think them through as much as I need to, thank you for your concern, though," she responds with every ounce of the defiance I covet.

"Your smart mouth reminds me of something." My cock hardens as I pull out my phone and read her messages aloud.

"I'd like the wall first, fucking me midday so everyone could hear what you do to me." My tone is even as I read but when I pause, I make my desire obvious, readjusting in my seat. With a devilish grin I peek over at Suzette, finding her cheeks to be a scarlet red. A gruff chuckle escapes me as her lips part and her eyes widen.

"Adrian." The admonishment is hushed and it's only when her gaze darts to the front of the car that I understand why.

"Noah, would you put the divider up please," I call up to him and within seconds the dark partition is in place, granting us more privacy.

"You're blushing as badly as I am," she teases, joy clearly peppered in the statement. I can feel the heat in my cheeks.

"I'm sure he didn't hear anything," I tell her, although … I have no fucking clue. "He's signed a nondisclosure agreement," I add for good measure.

Before she can distract from the conversation anymore, I read the second text. "At night, I'd love for you to fuck me against the window, so I could feel the city beneath us and know every single one of them would trade places with us in a heartbeat." My words are spoken lowly, carefully but not in a whisper.

With her hands spearing through her hair that sits on her shoulders, she pulls the loose strands back as if she needs to feel the cool air against the back of her neck. "What?" she says and shrugs, her expression the picture-perfect resemblance of a minx.

"We have a work relationship during those hours, Ms Parks. I'm going to have to punish you for such … foul language and indiscretion."

Her brow arches, although she plays along with me. "Should I not respond to you then from nine to six?"

"It depends," I answer, "do you want me to play with you in the car on the way to dinner or not?"

Her simper grows wider. "That depends. What exactly do you have in mind for my punishment?"

Her chest rises with a heavy breath and her skin flushes as I unzip my pants and pull my cock through. At the sight of a bead of precum, Suzette licks her lower lip. I pat my lap. "Lay your head here and put your ass up on the seat so I can reach you."

Lying across the seat, her buckle still in place, she eagerly takes the head of my dick in her mouth, moaning and sending soft vibrations of lust to run through me.

I stifle the groan and press the intercom button for Noah. "Go round the block if we get there before I call up."

"Yes, sir," he answers back just in time for my little vixen to pull herself off my dick with a little pop. She works my length as she looks up at me, a perfect view of her breasts on full display.

"Back down, take your punishment like a good girl."

She asks breathlessly, her lips already reddened and slightly swollen, "This is my punishment?"

Smirking down at her, I take my time, pulling up her dress and feeling her bare pussy already wet. "My cock is to keep you quiet."

She eases herself back down my length and I palm one globe of her ass before squeezing it and then the other, warming her ass up.

"You're going to take my cock as far down your throat as you can," I tell her, lowering my lips to be closer to her ear. "And I'm going to toy with you, spank you, and bring you to the edge."

Her gorgeous blue eyes look up at me through her thick lashes and I swear it's the most beautiful sight I've ever seen. "Don't you dare bite me," I warn her before slapping my hand against her ass. It's enough that my palm stings, her mouth opens wider and my cock drives deeper into the back of her throat.

She doesn't choke, but she sputters. The sensation of my cock being pressed against the back of her throat feels like heaven.

My middle finger drops lower, playing between her folds as I wait for her to readjust. With my toes curled, and her mouth already bringing me close, I spank her ass again and again. Two quick strikes and she cries out, whimpering and pulling off my cock.

Thank fuck.

Barely containing myself, I tsk her as if she isn't doing everything perfectly. Everything is just as I want.

"Adrian," she pleads, but doesn't object, taking a moment to readjust, the leather groaning beneath us.

"You're doing well," I say and comfort her, rubbing soothing circles against her heated skin. With her lips putting pressure on the head of my cock, she works her way down again and I'm quick to decide on the punishment in my head. There's no fucking way I can get through ten of these. "Two more," I barely get out, the pleasure building.

I make them harder than the first two, and the slaps resonate in the small cabin.

She groans, her cheeks hollowing and her brow pinched until I massage the sensitized skin and then lean over more. With one hand splayed across her back, keeping her down, the other is in the perfect position to play with her pussy.

She jerks on my cock as I dip my middle finger inside her, curling it and finding that sweet spot. I know the moment I hit it because she writhes for me, unable to stay still.

Thank fuck. "I want to feel you come on my hand," I tell her and she mewls. She fucking mewls for me and then she moans my name as if she's already on edge.

I'm merciless as I finger fuck her, desperate for her to come before I do. She loses her composure, pulling off my cock and opting to pump me with her hand so she can breathe in short pants.

"Adrian." She says my name as if she's begging.

"Come for me. You're such a good fucking slut for me, taking whatever I give you."

"Oh my fuck," she says as her hands grip my thigh, her back arches and she cries out her pleasure into my suit pants, burying her head there and leaving my cock aching with need.

When she spasms around my fingers, I swear it takes all of me not to come undone with her.

"Good girl." The praise comes with deeper, calming breaths and she pushes herself up with chaotic ones of her own.

She glances down at my erection as I pull out a tissue to clean up after her release. I save my fingers for last.

The moment it looks like she's going to attend to me, I tell her to wait. "When we stop, I want my cock buried inside of you." Surprise lights her eyes. With her lips still parted, I run my thumb along her bottom lip. "As good as your mouth is, I think I'd rather bring you to the edge again."

And that's exactly what I do. I fuck her hard enough to rock the car in the dock's parking lot after asking Noah to take a walk so we could have a moment. I have her bite down on the leather to keep her as quiet as she can be.

It's much darker with the short hour it's taken to get to the dock, and cooler by the Hudson River. As I open the car door for Suzette, silently thanking Noah for parking in a rather private area of the lot, the breeze sweeps by us.

"I don't think I've ever taken a tour of New York at night on a cruise ship," Suzette comments softly as she steps out, her hand in mine. Her heels click on the pavement and she looks out toward the harbor.

I can barely focus on what she's said as the chill hits us. "Do you have a jacket?"

"I wasn't expecting to come out tonight."

"I'll have Noah deliver one." The moment I've shut the door, I slip off my jacket that's far too large for her and wrap it around her shoulders.

"You don't have to," she says as she shakes her head, her locks falling down her shoulders as she does. She smiles up at me with a sweet, sated look on her face. "But I appreciate it."

With my arm wrapped around her back, I hum in response and search the dock for Trent's ship.

From where we're standing, I'm not sure which ship is his and where we should start.

"And they say chivalry is dead," she teases.

Without thinking much of it, I murmur, "If I'm going to fuck you in the back of my car, I can at least make sure you're comfortable after."

"And to think I just called you a gentleman."

"Mr. Bradford," Noah says behind me, clearing his throat.

If I could experience shame, I'm certain I'd feel it at this moment. "Noah," I say and turn to face him, not missing the glee that shines in her devilish eyes. "I was just about to message you.

"If you could see to it, Ms. Parks doesn't have a jacket this evening. Very much my fault."

"Say no more, sir."

"Thank you."

"Thank you so much," Suzette speaks up, "but truly—"

"Truly you will be cold once we set off, and as much as I adore you in my jacket, I'm not sure it's the look you'll be going for."

There's a pause where Suzette stares back at me, and I wonder if my little vixen is going to fight me on something so simple.

"Mr. Weston is near the northern end, I believe," Noah speaks before she can object. "His wife Laura is hard to miss tonight. And I'll see to it that there's a jacket on your shoulders that's more suitable, Ms. Parks." With a nod, he's off before Suzette can object. I make a mental note to give Noah a bonus for his discretion.

"You don't have to buy me things."

"It's a jacket," I state as if it's nothing.

"Come, the Brooklyn Bridge and the Manhattan skyline are waiting for us."

"It's why I love the city," she says and there's an awe in her tone that draws me closer. With my hand on the small of her back, she leans in closer. I fucking love it. Those walls of hers are crumbling down.

"The skyline?"

"How bright it is at night. How beautiful and lively."

"It is the city that never sleeps." Walking toward the railing, we take a moment to appreciate the towering steel lit with shades of blue and yellow lights. "It's gorgeous, isn't it?"

"Mm-hmm," I hum in agreement, watching her take in the view as the water crashes beneath us.

"I've never taken a tour of the city via cruise either. If you weren't here, I wouldn't."

Peeking up at me, Suzette questions, "You wouldn't have come?"

"I would have, and I would have made the deal before the ship left. It's the same with the galas and charity balls and all of these … social gatherings. I stay at the bar, I meet and greet who I must and then I leave."

"All work and no play," she comments, her eyes locked on mine. There's a softness tonight I only got glimpses of before.

"Would you like to wait here for your jacket, or meet the hosts for the evening?"

"I think we should get on with it," she answers, shedding my jacket from her shoulders.

"That's not going to happen." I scold her lightly, slipping the jacket into place. "I wouldn't be caught dead wearing a jacket while you shiver."

"I won't shiver." The wind rushes by in that moment, as if to prove she's a liar.

A rough chuckle leaves me and I give her the option again. "We can wait here if you'd like or if you don't mind wearing my jacket for a moment, we can start the night."

"I think I don't mind either way," she says softly, staring up at me like she was before, although her gaze is ripped away the moment I hear my name in the distance.

"There you are!" Trent calls out.

"Well," Suzette whispers, "I suppose your jacket will do for now."

chapter 8

Suzette

THE BOAT CUTS THROUGH THE RIVER BELOW US AS THE SKYLINE RISES above. The bright lights twinkle against the black sky. Up close, it's intimidating but there's still something elegant about those tall buildings. The air at the bow of the boat is crisp and clean. With both of my hands holding the railing, I breathe in deep, grateful for a moment alone after the last hour of socializing. My cheeks hurt from the constant smiling. I laugh when it's appropriate and keep everything light. This isn't my first time at a gathering that's … out of my league.

I'm sure it's obvious that I don't quite fit in, but it's gone well as far as I can tell. Champagne flutes clinked as we worked through the crowd, and the small gathering of women mostly gossiped about social circles I'm not privy to.

Most notably, the view is stunning.

I grew up in New York, but not in the city. I knew the dream of it, breathed in the hope of what NYC offers. I believe in this city. It will never cease to amaze me.

New York City is freeing in the same way my divorce was liberating.

Admittedly, that freedom came from the fact that I had security in my job. I could make it on my own and live the dream I've had since I was a little girl without fear. That was then. My hands twist against the cold, smooth metal. This is now.

Apprehension spreads through my gut. I can't deny the fear that my job might be on the line now. I've slept with Adrian and he's sending emails about gathering client lists like he wants to rearrange everything at the office. Or rather his "team" is. If I don't have that security anymore, then everything is at risk.

"You've been out here a while." The deep rumble from behind me is startling.

Adrian appears at my side by the railing, looking out with me. "I was spending time with my thoughts." Smiling at him, I step a bit closer. "Is your meeting done?"

"Yes."

"Did you seal the deal?" I ask him as he breathes in deep, looking over my shoulder to gaze at the skyline. He peers down at me, a charming smile at his lips. "Always, my little vixen."

With the heat in his eyes, I let out a nervous huff of a laugh and pull away.

"Dinner's about to start. Let me get you a drink."

It gives me a bit of relief that he's not pressing me about what's on my mind. I'm not sure how to talk about it with him yet. Adrian leads me back inside the cabin, the mood seeming a little more somber as more thoughts race through my mind. Thoughts of anxiety and anticipation about what's going to happen at work.

Adrian takes me by the elbow to guide me through the tables, stopping at the bar for a glass of wine. The ship is massive and spacious. It's obvious they spared no expense for this evening's outing. The group of women I was chatting with earlier are seated with their companions, dining on caviar as they overlook the river.

All the tables have been set with linen tablecloths and beautiful dishes. This is how the other half lives. It's elegance and convenience that will only ever be a dream for most.

"We're toward the stern ... for more privacy."

We reach our table, nestled in a corner with lit candles and the perfect view of the ship splitting the water that reflects the bright lights of the city. I stop at the edge, bracing myself, suddenly uncomfortable. With a firm hand he tilts up my chin. "What's wrong?"

"Just worried." The knot in my stomach ties tighter.

"About what?"

It takes great effort to keep my expression neutral, in case anyone may see when I say, "My job."

Light dances in his eyes. "It's after six."

"Unlike you, I can't just turn it off. I can't stop worrying about my responsibilities and wondering what's going to happen to my income ... and what might happen between us."

There's a pause, a tension that gathers between us before Adrian pulls out my chair and tells me, "We can discuss it later, but I'm telling you, I don't want you to worry."

"As if I can just stop."

"You can. And you will."

"It's just hard to believe right now."

"Let me help you with that." His gentle smile is as confident as his touch. "You need to eat. Sit." He takes my wineglass from my hand, only a few sips gone, and helps me to my seat.

It's a bit chillier now than it was earlier and even with the beautiful double collar Mackage jacket Noah was gracious enough to have rush delivered before the boat set sail, it's brisk.

"May I?" Adrian asks, still standing as I take my seat. He moves the remaining chair around the table, dragging it to sit beside me.

"You'd rather sit next to me?"

"I'd rather have my arm around you."

There's comfort that's unexpected, in the way he simply wants to be with me. Next to me, with me, touching me. I crave it without realizing it.

The waiter comes by with appetizers: oysters on ice, bruschetta, and marinated olives with feta. Where we're seated, the chatter is muted and drowned out by the water, the breeze is comforting and it feels like the city has stayed awake just for us.

We're finished with our appetizers when Adrian orders two glasses of ice water.

"I'm all right with the wine," I tell him.

"I thought we could play a game," is his reply. "To keep your mind off work."

"What kind of game?" My cheeks are instantly flushed and hot, though no one seems to be paying attention to us, tucked away back here. "Would it be … discreet?"

"Very," he says and his gorgeous pale blue eyes rest on mine as he smirks, "as long as you can keep quiet."

"I have no problem with that." The suggestive game is enticing, and there's no doubt I would much rather get lost in this man's touch than ruminate on matters I cannot control.

Just as I rest my hand on Adrian's thigh, the waiter returns and a hot blush creeps to my cheeks realizing I'm the one caught. The waiter only offers a polite smile, not saying a word as he sets down the goblets of ice water and then uncovers dinner: filet mignon and lobster tail with mashed potatoes and asparagus, all neatly arranged in a tasteful way.

My mouth waters instantly.

Adrian's quiet and commanding as he tells me, "Pick up your fork and make sure you appear to be eating, no matter what I do."

"Appear to be eating or actually eat?" My fork hovers over the plate.

"You should eat," he decides. "I'll try to be fair and give you time to chew and swallow."

Adrian looks down at his own plate and says, "Enjoy dinner. That's all you need to do."

Small talk ensues. About the city, the ever-changing neighborhoods and real estate. Nothing heavy, yet it chips away at who each of us is and what we want.

"Why am I not surprised that you live in Tribeca," I comment offhandedly knowing how damn expensive it is. Yet another checkbox on tonight's elite list that I could never fulfill.

That's when I feel his hand on my thigh underneath the table, pushing my dress up. My fork scrapes against the porcelain, giving away my surprise until I can steady myself. His touch goes up and up until his knuckles brush against my clit through my panties.

Cold shocks me so suddenly, I gasp.

"With a sound like that escaping those lips of yours," Adrian scolds, his tone teasing, "people will wonder if something happened to you."

He doesn't let up with the pressure against my clit and I struggle to perfect my expression.

"Keep your thighs apart," he murmurs. "That's the only way to play this game."

Circular motions of his knuckles make me hotter, increasing the heat until all at once he removes his hand.

My initial reaction is to object, but that's quickly silenced as he plucks a piece of ice from his glass and, with his eyes on mine, his hand disappears under the table. My lips part with a hiss as the cold hits my inner thigh first. He doesn't stop, slowly trailing it up.

I let out a breathy laugh. "That's freezing," I admit. "It's so, so cold."

"Sensitizing, isn't it?" he says quietly and casually spears a stalk of asparagus with one hand, while his other slips the ice up and down my slit until slowly he presses it inside of me. Goosebumps dance along my skin as I focus on my breathing and simply staying still.

Adrian repeats this process, bringing me to the edge and then stopping me with the freeze of an ice cube. Abruptly, he stops.

"You're going to give us away," he warns lowly, his lips at the shell of my ear and his warm breath tickling my neck.

That's when I realize my fork is fisted in my hand and my eyes were closed tight.

"I know you can do it. My little slut knows how to hide it. Don't you?"

My breathing is rushed when another piece of ice slips along my skin, and my hand trembles. Adrian watches this with curiosity burning in his eyes.

"Oh my," I whisper and breathe, my eyes half-lidded.

"I want you to come for me."

"I don't think—" With two fingers he enters me, his fingers deft and knowing. As if he's memorized just how to get me off.

"I know you can. If you must, lay your head down on the table." The moment he suggests it, I obey, pushing the plate away and resting my head down.

He doesn't let up, not even when the waiter questions if I'm all right and he orders Dramamine for me.

The second his footsteps disappear, Adrian's touch becomes merciless and he whispers at my ear, "If you don't come for me right now, I swear to God I'll throw you over this table and fuck you until all of Manhattan hears you crying out my name. I couldn't care less about this deal if I can't even get my little whore to come on my hand."

My lips part, my warm breath heating my face still resting against the table and hidden by my arms. That's what does it. It's what brings me to the edge. I clench around him thinking of what he's just described.

The moment I'm granted my release, he removes his hand and it's only a moment after that his hand rests on my shoulder while rubbing soothing circles. Adrian informs the waiter that I will be fine.

"Take these, sweetheart," he says clear as day, without a trace of anything that's just happened in his voice.

"If she needs anything at all, let us know," the waiter says and I don't dare lift my head just yet. I'm flushed and shamelessly sated.

It's only once he's gone that I dare to peek up.

"Bad girl," Adrian admonishes me. "You'll do better for me next time, won't you?" he teases and I only blush harder.

Setting two small pills down on the napkin, he brings my plate back, placing it in front of me.

"The appetizers were … delicious," he comments.

"You're shameless," I counter, still breathless and gather my fork once again.

"I'm hard is what I am," he tells me, cutting into his steak.

"Do you want me—"

"No. No, not here." He considers me for a moment. "I want to make sure you know what you do to me. Watching you come undone for me … that's all I wanted."

I don't know what to make of him. He's ruthless. Confident. On the side of being arrogant. But the things he does to me make me forget everyone and everything else.

"You look like you want to say something," he comments, taking another bite. His food is quickly disappearing and mine's barely been touched.

"I thought you would be different."

"My reputation is not kind. I'm aware."

"They say you're an asshole and I thought it would be easy to hate you." It's the truth. And it slips out without censorship. Adrian smirks. "I've heard you're merciless."

"I am."

I guide my fork over my plate and lift a bite to my mouth. "Are you an asshole or are you merciless?"

"Both. I can be vicious." Adrian says this with a casual tone that makes me think he's telling the truth. Of course, I already know this about him. There's a reason the entire office is in a furor with him simply being in the building.

"I don't know what to make of you."

His eyes meet mine and his gaze lingers as if he's waiting for me to elaborate. My heart pounds with curiosity and fear that this will go badly and I won't have an office to go back to.

"There are people who earn big paychecks and then there are the people who write them," Adrian begins. "I wasn't born into wealth, but I watched my father work his way up to being one of those people who earned his paycheck. And then it was taken away from him after one wrong deal."

My body goes as cold as the ice he used to play with me earlier.

"I've looked into it since then," continues Adrian, "and it was a bad deal. He made a mistake. But that was after years of making the right decisions over and over, after working his way up only to be knocked down the second something went wrong. Not because it was deserved, but because he made too much and it would be too easy to give his tasks to someone else. Then the person who wrote the big check could simply make back that money by letting him go."

This is by far the most Adrian has ever shared with me, and my curiosity is piqued again. I don't know anything about his father, only what I've read about him, which is simple. He buys companies, breaks them apart, moves some departments around and eliminates others. He's the man writing the checks and doing the firing now.

"That company went under within two years," Adrian says quietly. Judging from his tone, this is important to him. The measured cadence of his words and the look in his eyes as he speaks.

"Without your father?" I manage to ask.

"Partially because of that. Partially because I bought the competitor. I hired my father. As the stock grew, I invested in other companies, including two crucial to my father's former employer ... And I dismantled them."

Adrian uses a cool, almost bored tone to tell me this, and I'm even more afraid for my job now. He could do anything he wanted with the company. "Vindictive much?" I say, to cover the nervous pulse in my throat.

"He treated certain things, certain people, as if they were disposable. I showed him exactly what that meant. There are highs and lows in this business. Harsh decisions must be made. But the reasoning behind it is what matters. Is it for efficiency? For the bottom line? For power plays?"

"Why do you do it?"

Adrian's eyes flash. "Because if there isn't passion behind it, it shouldn't exist. It's a waste of time for everyone involved. It will fail, and the only ones who will benefit are the ones who are willing to sacrifice the purpose of it all." His deep voice is filled with conviction. Adrian believes what he's saying, and I imagine it's why he fired so many of the executives today and sent them all packing. He has a passion for this business, not simply an investment.

"I learned a hard lesson early on: if you can't beat them with morals and ethics, cut their throats and say that it's business."

A chill flows over my skin and numerous questions rest on the tip of my tongue. "I didn't buy Holt and Hanover to cut anyone's throat," he states before I can ask. "The numbers are still being run with slight changes." His tone is one of comfort, but the conversation is anything but. "When I know anything, you will as well. Do not worry."

I can only nod as a shiver runs down my shoulders and I realize we're back at the dock. The water is quieter and the chatter from the others much louder.

The waiter returns to check on me just then and he's relieved to hear I'm feeling better. If my head wasn't clouded with current topics, I would have blushed violently.

"Are you finished?" Adrian asks after time passes with easy silence, with a patient tone that says I could sit here for another hour, if I wanted.

Once again, I tell him the truth. "Yes." I put my napkin on the table next to my plate.

"Good. When we get to the car I want you on your knees," he mutters beneath his breath, standing up at the same time I do. A shiver returns, but this one is heated and causes flutters in places I shouldn't be concerned with in public.

"So demanding."

Adrian's smile seems to light up the dining area. "Are you just now learning that, Ms. Parks?"

chapter 9

Adrian

THE CITY BLURS BY, A STREAK OF GRAYS WITH SPLASHES OF COLORS as Noah speeds up down the avenue. It's late, far too late given I have an early morning meeting with the executives of a company based overseas. There's no doubt in my mind that rescheduling it would not go over well.

Leaning forward, I spread my knees, resting my elbows there and stretch my back, feeling the pull of it in my spine. Without thinking, I stare at the empty seat beside me, where Suzette was yesterday. The corners of my lips pull up, remembering how she squirmed, how easily she gave in. How she melts for me. And how much she loved it.

Today was hell. Meeting after meeting and when she texted that she had plans tonight, I can't deny I felt loss. With her, I want every moment I can get. This evening held precisely none of them.

"Mr. Bradford?" Noah calls back, peering at me in the rearview although he doesn't use the intercom.

"Yes?" I answer him and then lean back in the seat, resting my head and meeting his gaze in the mirror.

"Shall I make it a habit of keeping the divider up between us when Ms. Parks joins you?"

The hum of the night surrounds us as I consider his question. There's no judgment; it's honest professionalism.

Something I've lacked today.

"I think it would serve us all well if you did, and I apologize if anything made you uncomfortable recently."

"Nothing at all, sir, just thinking of your lady."

Your lady. My brow rises, but my phone buzzes in my hand, interrupting my thoughts. There are only a few numbers I allow this late at night.

My father: *Did Wyatt send you the contract?*

My eyes roll back in my head as I inhale long and steady. My father is friends with his, and that's how we became acquainted nearly a decade ago.

My phone buzzes again: *Dale's here and we were wondering.*

Dale is Wyatt's father, rather protective but a supportive man.

I text him back quickly: *The lawyers have it atm.*

It occurs to me then that Suzette has yet to message. I'm quick to type a message but then I delete it. I try another that's less … domineering.

I prefer for that role to be played in person. Just as I finish typing her a message asking if she's home, a message comes through from my father, followed by one from her.

Suzette: *Just laying down for bed and thinking of you. Thank you again for last night.*

I ignore my father for a moment, choosing to message her: *The pleasure was all mine.*

She doesn't waste time replying: *You lie, Mr. Bradford. I enjoyed it immensely.*

With a satisfied hum, I sit back and see my father's messaged twice.

The lawyers will be fine with it.

Are you working this late? Please tell me you've cut back.

He's been on me for years now to work less. With the team in place and fewer projects, although they're costlier and more rides on their success, I've been able to slow down, little by little. Small steps toward a more "sustainable lifestyle," as my father refers to it.

Just got back from a date actually. I text him the white lie. It's not exactly truthful, but it will make him smile.

"Is that her?" Noah questions from the front. Again not using the intercom, and it takes me a moment to understand he means Suzette.

"Ms. Parks?"

"You have a smile for her. I can tell it's her. I have one that was just for my wife."

"Oh, calm down with that talk now, Noah," I joke with him. "We've only just met—"

"I told you Ann and I … it was two weeks and then forever." His voice holds a hint of reverie.

"Yes, I know the story well." Noah's worked for me for the better part of a decade now. As my driver and at times my assistant when needed. "One day … one day I'll have that," I say and then run my hand through my hair, thinking that *one day* seems to get farther and farther away as the years go by. "Ms. Parks is … we are only getting to know each other."

"Is that what you kids call it nowadays?"

Letting out a brutish laugh, I turn my attention back to my phone.

There are emails and calendar notifications. My father messaged me about details of some buildings Wyatt is hoping to acquire, but he needs the capital first. My capital. As well as some questions about my date and whether it's serious.

Another message comes through, this time my mother, wanting to know about the date.

I debate on answering them, but I let my phone sit in my lap, thinking of Suzette at the dock yesterday and how easy it was. I haven't had that before. No one has ever fit so well, even if she fights me along the way.

As if she knows I'm thinking of her, a message comes through: *I need to sleep.*

Then you should sleep, my little minx.

I watch the phone with anticipation, knowing she's typing something, but then deletes it. A moment passes and she starts again. My phone buzzes, with the messenger open: *I like being your little minx, I think.*

I like it too.

The moment I send my response, it doesn't feel good enough. It doesn't carry the weight of just how much I enjoy her simply being there. I follow up with:

When you sleep, I want you to dream of me.

Yes, sir.

chapter 10

ADRIAN FILLS MY MIND EVERY HOUR THAT I'M AWAKE, AND MOST OF the ones where I'm sleeping. His text messages make my pulse quicken with excitement.

I can hear how he would speak the words when I read them. It feels like falling. In only a week's time, I feel like I'm falling for him.

No one else at the office is fawning over him.

I'm often worked up and overheated, carefully avoiding him and the topic of him because everyone calls him the devil.

They complain about not knowing what's going to happen and how they think every task is in preparation for someone else to take over. Then there's me. I can't stop thinking of how he put that ice between my legs, and the soft groans that he makes when he fucks me on his desk. Purposefully avoiding the obvious and doing everything I can not to worry. Because he told me not to, even though all signs point to the company being sold off.

It's all ridiculous and overwhelming. If I wasn't fucking him, I might have quit already … well, not if I couldn't take the clients with me. Maybe. I don't know. Like I said, it's all too overwhelming, so I choose to believe him. I'm doing everything I can to listen and not worry.

With my fingers tapping aimlessly on the keys, I have to snap myself out of it. Not that it matters; we're on a freeze with clients this week. I could lose my shit and it wouldn't make a difference in productivity. The only work that's getting done is paperwork and severance packages. I could be a nervous wreck like the rest of the office, or I can fantasize about the clock turning six.

Every day, I rock back and forth between the two of them.

A light knock at my door takes me out of my thoughts. A young brunette in joggers and a flowy tank stands in my doorway.

"Maddie," I say, greeting my friend for lunch. "I was wondering when you were going to get here." My chair rolls to the left as I push my keyboard to the side to make room for takeout.

Passing me a brown paper bag she sighs and says, "Sorry. Traffic was hell."

She's gorgeous, as she always is, but there's a sad curve to her mouth. "You okay?"

She takes the seat across the desk from me and opens her bag in her lap, waving me off with the other hand. "I think I need a man or a really good vibrator."

"I vote vibrator," I joke with a short laugh, unrolling the top of the bag without taking my eyes off Maddie. She's young, naive, and a romantic. A.k.a. the prime suspect for assholes. She barely cracks a smile. "Is that dipshit Daniel still on your mind?"

Maddie groans. "He's always on my mind, and I can't get him off of it. It's not fair. Why did such a shitty person have to get so far into my head?"

"That's how it always seems to be. The worse the person is for you, the more you think about them."

"Let's go out and go man shopping tonight. There's a new club down on Madison Avenue. It's like my grandmom always said, get over one by getting under another." She takes a bite out of her turkey club and guilt washes over me.

I haven't told Maddie about Adrian yet, and it seems like a betrayal of our friendship, almost. Suddenly I have no appetite. The chicken caesar wrap stays at the bottom of the bag.

I'm not sure what I would tell her. Being discreet means not blabbing your business to anyone who'd listen. I wince at the thought. Maddie's not just a random person. She's my friend, one of very few, and she's been my friend for far longer than I've known Adrian.

"I've looked up Lucifer," I joke. "He's hot as hell."

"Why don't you cuddle up to him?" Maddie half teases although her tone is dull. Her large doe eyes twinkle as she grins, pausing between bites to say, "Get a little action. Save the day. You'd be the office hero."

"The office needs a hero," I comment, keeping my tone light. "Everyone's nervous about their jobs now that entire divisions have been laid off."

My department has kept the same workload, but four people have been taken for interviews. Not by Adrian himself, but by some team he hired.

"Speaking of heroes," Maddie says, and then she talks about the new TV show she's been watching on HBO for the rest of the time we're eating. I'm grateful for the change in subject and somehow I've gotten out of going to the club with her this weekend. It's pleasant conversation and a much-needed break in the day. The wrap was decent too although I barely tasted it.

All I could think is that I should tell her. Maddie would keep my secrets and maybe she would smack some sense into me.

I know part of the reason I don't is because of that very fact: She would give her opinion, and what if it's to stop seeing him? What if she says it's wrong and it's going to end in failure and heartbreak? She's the romantic of the group, and yet I don't even have faith she would approve.

When she's gone, there's a small fire under my ass. A need to prove there's nothing at all wrong with it. We work during the day, play at night. I haven't changed who I am and there's nothing wrong with it.

This feeling that everything's up in the air isn't good for my productivity or anyone else's, and the only way to know what's going to happen is to ask him directly. And it's not six yet, so business is business.

Every single time I gather the courage to demand answers or terms, to know what the hell is going on so I have something I can tell everyone who needs answers, there are people in his office.

Adrian's secretary furrows her brow whenever I pass close to her desk. On my third trip, I decide to ask her what she knows. I imagine she's got to know something, given how close she works to Adrian. And any little piece of info I can bring back would be a win. "Hi there," I say, greeting her with a smile. Laying on the charm. "I'm Suzette. You're new to the company." My hip rests against her desk.

"That's right," she says with a tight smile. "Not new to Mr. Bradford, though. I'm Andrea."

There's a tinge that runs through me. It's a feeling I don't like. My gaze slips to this woman's hand, a woman who could be my mother, and I find a wedding ring back there. Jealousy is unbecoming and I can't believe I felt it for a second. In her white flowy blouse and pencil skirt, Andrea most certainly takes care of herself.

"How long have you been his secretary?"

"Oh, years and years. You know how it is with a good job. You stick with it."

"I do know about that." My stomach turns over. That's exactly why I'm here—to talk to Adrian about the future. This job saved me after my divorce and made it possible to have the freedom I gained, but if I'm let go, I'll be in an even worse position. "Sticking with it is usually for the best. I've heard he can be …" I deliberately let my voice trail, waiting for Andrea to pick up where I left off.

She gives me nothing, tilting her head with her perfectly plucked brow raised and her hands folded in her lap. Touché. I finish it myself. "A bit … ruthless."

"I would agree with that at times."

She nods and I do as well … neither of us giving the other anything.

"If you've worked for him for that many years, you must have seen him take over a number of companies like this."

Her eyes widen. "Oh, yes. It can be unsettling for the people who have been there the longest. Adrian insists on changing things where they need to be changed instead of sticking with the status quo. It means a lot of shuffling around at the beginning."

I wince. "That's what I've heard … the shuffling, though, that's—"

"Ruthless." Now she finishes it.

Hearing about a powerful man like Adrian shuffling people around doesn't soothe me when it comes to my own job. He's merciless when we have sex, and he must be the same way when it comes to business. He won't keep me on if it's not the right thing for the company. My throat tightens at the thought of being let go by him. Stomach turning, I breathe deeply to keep myself in check. I've had to do this many times over the years, working with men who didn't know how to listen to a woman.

Oddly, the thought of being fired from my job isn't the only thing at the forefront of my mind. Adrian is there as well. If I'm let go from this position, there will be no more meeting up at six for discreet activities. So his secretary's words aren't very reassuring. I hadn't considered how I might lose my job and Adrian at the same time. Though it's a bit presumptuous to think there's such a thing as losing Adrian when what we have is a fuck-buddy agreement.

"You work till six," she comments and now it's my turn for my expression to pinch.

"I do."

"I only noticed because of the submissions."

I pause, nodding but not contributing; it's her turn to show her cards.

"Mr. Bradford seems to have changed his habits," she says and leans back in her chair. "He never used to stay late. Once it was five o'clock, he went home. But it seems his preference, for this company only, is now six."

"Oh?" The back of my neck tingles.

"Mm-hmm," she hums.

"Well, that's something." Does she know? It's all I can think as she stares up at me. She's older, wiser maybe. I don't know. But everything in me is screaming that she knows.

"I'm sure he won't let you go," the secretary says, her expression innocent. "Seems to me you've been doing quite a bit for this company."

"I've done a lot of work," is my distracted reply. She might not let me in to see him, but that doesn't mean I'm any less hungry for information. I'm not sure how to phrase it, though.

"Can I tell you something?" she asks.

"Of course," I reply and my nervous voice betrays me.

"He seems to be distracted lately."

"Oh? I'm sure I wouldn't know anything about that."

She takes in my red cheeks. "Hmm. I think you might. I'm good friends with his driver."

I blush deeper. "I see."

Reaching for her glasses, she barely contains her cat-ate-the-canary grin. "If it were up to me, I'd let you in there, love, but I can't."

"Oh, I'm not—I don't do this kind of thing." A numbness creeps through me. How long have I worked here, only to potentially have my reputation ruined by the rumor mill? I have no idea if I can trust this woman in the least, although she seems friendly. I did just lie to her face, though.

Restlessly, I shift my weight from one foot to the next. I stop as soon as the secretary notices. "I really don't do this," I say again.

"Neither does he," she says, leaning in, her tone friendly still. It eases something in me. "I mean it. I've worked with him for over a decade now. Mr. Bradford ... he doesn't behave like this. He's strict with his regimen and occasionally a woman has come in to speak with him. But it's never ... like this."

chapter 11

Adrian

"Y ou know how I know you want to push me today and not in a good way?" I question the vixen at my side. Her cherry-red heels clip on the pavement as I open the door, waving toward Noah that I've got it. The spring day is a cloudy one, with gray skies and the threat of rain clouds.

"How's that?" she asks, gripping the door frame, one shoe inside the car, the other firmly planted on the curb. She stares at me from over her shoulders, the wool coat perfectly hugging her frame.

"Because you're eager to get me alone in this car. I didn't have to fight you."

Her smile is wicked, her rose petal lips trying all they can to stay pursed, but they fail. "Inside," I command her and she obeys, properly and politely as I shut her door for her, knowing damn well she's going to try to get information out of me. While I sat through meeting after meeting, she came looking for me. Andrea let me know. She suggested I order flowers, of all things.

I'm not sure what exactly she thought Suzette was coming to see me for, but if I had to guess, with the cars buzzing by us and the nightlife of the city turning vibrant, it's about her department and the upcoming meetings.

With a steadying inhale, I climb into the back seat and shut the door.

"I tried to speak to you all day." She doesn't waste a second. She peeled her coat off, laying it across her lap and at first glance, I'm given a damn good look of her breasts. Whatever contraption she's wearing has pushed them to the top of her blouse which hangs low, I presume to display cleavage.

Not fair.

Reaching for my seat belt, I prepare myself.

"I had roundtables with my team." The belt clicks into place and the tick of the blinker is barely heard as Noah rolls up the partition, allowing us privacy.

"Your team who's talking to *my* team," Suzette stresses and I can't help but to let out a chuckle.

Leaning my head back, I turn to face her.

"I don't find it funny," she tells me and there's a hint of hurt there.

"Because you aren't in control," I tell her honestly.

With her hands in her lap, she fidgets with her fingers and tells me, "I just need to know what your plans are."

"It's after six, Suzette." I'm soft with the reminder.

"I don't like this." She's equally soft with her disappointment. It's unsettling. Not anger; she's genuinely upset.

"It's okay to be uncomfortable. That's how progress is made," I tell her, in an attempt to ease her mind.

"I suppose I could leave you uncomfortable then?" It's not quite a tease or a threat, but some combination of the two.

My response is firm. "Don't tempt me to punish that mouth of yours before we've had dinner." She swallows, the threat coming through as it should. To remind her that she loves what I do to her, that right now the office is behind us and we're to get lost in each other.

Her posture remains stiff, though, and her gaze guarded.

In an attempt at a truce, I rest my hand on hers, and she reciprocates by turning her small hand to hold mine. "Thank you," I murmur and then run my thumb along her soft skin.

"Please, answer me one thing," she presses and I close my eyes to respond with a short nod.

"What are you going to do with it?"

"With what?"

"The company?"

I remain silent. As if it were so simple to have a one-sentence answer, or to even know what would be best so early on.

"A split-up? Go public for shares? I looked into the other companies under your LLC, so I doubt you have a merger in mind."

When I finally open my eyes and look back at her, fear lingers in every nuance.

I debate on confiding in her, knowing how quick office rumors are to spread and the chaos that little bits of information can create. But then she utters a single word, staring back at me like I could make every little worry she has vanish. "Please."

"The plan is a split-up and the merger of the new entity and another company I have in mind … if possible."

She doesn't hesitate to question, "And what about the other? The original entity? The departments that aren't useful for the merger?"

I'm silent, half wondering if she's playing me. If all of this was a setup and she's pumping me for information. "There are inefficiencies that cannot be overlooked."

"Where does my department—"

My tone is harsher than I'd like as I interrupt her. "Not everything has been decided." Gentling it, I add, "You don't need to worry."

"As your lover or as your employee?"

"When I tell you that you don't need to worry, I need you to believe it. I need you to trust me."

She's silent, and every second that passes feels as if another weight has been added to my chest. It's obvious I haven't eased her concerns in the least. She wants a definitive answer and I can't give her one. I can't say anything with certainty.

"No more. It's after six and I promise, I will make time for you at work. As your boss. Right now I only want to be your lover, as you put it."

It seems for a moment that she'll say something; her lips part and she inhales, but then her gaze falls and she merely nods. Not looking back at me.

"Thank you for respecting the boundary."

"I don't like it," she whispers, at first looking out the window but then she meets my gaze.

"You look gorgeous squirming, though." I pick up her hand and kiss the back of it, our fingers laced together. "It would please me if you wouldn't worry."

In a breath she laughs, as if it's the most ridiculous thing she's heard. "Is that all you need, for me to just not worry?"

Softly, I repeat the reassurance, "You will be all right."

She's quick to tell me, "It's not just me." She shakes her head. "I'm sorry. I'm done. I'm done for right now. I won't bring it up again."

"I want you to confide in me, I do. I wish I had the answers for you, but I don't."

"When you do, will you tell me?" There's hesitancy in her tone, but also hope.

"The second I know, I will tell you everything."

Her shoulders drop slightly and she sinks deeper into the seat, not responding other than a nod and a soft, "Thank you."

A moment passes, and the tension lessens.

"I had a hard day today," I confide in her, our fingers still intertwined.

"I did too," she speaks softly. "Fridays are long days, but at least we have the weekend." Just when I think that's all she'll say, she offers, "Can I do anything?"

"Do anything?"

"To make anything better."

"Not with work—"

"No, with you. Can I …" she trails off and tosses her hand in the air, the one I was holding. "Can I yell at someone, or massage your shoulders? I could …" she pauses and rolls her eyes. "I don't know, write an angry email or order us takeout for dinner." In my silence, her tone is laced with exasperation when she says, "I could … I don't know. What would make it better?"

"You could kiss me."

"Would that make it better?" she questions, the hint of a smile on her lips.

"Yes. If you kissed me, it would."

She doesn't waste a moment, and when she kisses me, her hands wrapped around my face, I can feel her smile.

THE NEW YORK SKYLINE IS MUCH DIFFERENT FROM THE WINDOWS of Adrian's penthouse. I'm used to feeling as if it's towering over me, but in his living room we're a part of it. In the heart of Tribeca surrounded by historic industrial buildings and new construction that's all steel and glass.

It's the epitome of New York.

It almost seems like a movie backdrop is wrapped around the entire room. Floor-to-ceiling windows that, with a touch of a button, darken for privacy surround us. Every other day, Adrian introduces me to more wealth than I've experienced in the years I've planted roots in this city.

Behind me, he busies himself in the foyer answering a call. The design is open concept but so far away, I feel lost in the view. Even his furniture seems to play a part in the city.

It's the perfect layout for a home with so much luxury. Hardwood floors shine under my feet and the neutral color scheme is fresh and strong. He has high ceilings and windows that kiss those ceilings, and beneath is a living room with sumptuous leather furniture that looks like it cost a mint.

Nothing in his home is out of place. There's not a single ounce of clutter, which adds to the masculine energy. It even smells like wealth, if ever there was a scent, one so clean it makes me a little jealous. I can imagine the people it would take to make a home look like this. A housekeeper at least, and others to make sure the walls and furniture stay perfect. The view alone is worth millions.

I can hardly keep my mouth closed as he gives me the tour, passing quickly by his bedroom and ending up back in the living room. "I didn't realize just how wealthy you are." I swallow thickly, my fingers playing at the hems of my silk sleeves.

The last time I felt awe like this was when I was flying into New York City for the first time. I couldn't believe I was finally going to live here, in a place I'd dreamed about for so long.

Adrian grins, slipping his arm around my waist. "I'm certainly not the richest man in New York."

"How very modest of you," I teasingly respond although my normal bite is lost.

There's a deep rumble from his chest, a short hum. I've noticed him do it a few times now and with it, his hand drops lower, to the side of my hip and his thumb rubs soothing circles there.

It causes a tension, a nervousness inside of me. It's more *serious*. Because I crave it. I want more of that masculine hum of satisfaction.

Being in his personal space and seeing his things and furniture is way beyond what I ever thought I'd do with him. I'm nervous to get it right and keep my cool, but I'm a strange mixture of giddy and hot. The more I learn about Adrian, the harder it will be when things end between us. I'm not sure I want things to end between us. Which only adds more to the feeling of not having the upper hand.

I certainly don't want them to end here, in his beautiful penthouse with all his fancy furniture and Adrian in his suit from the office. Despite working all day it's still crisp. I'd like for him to take it off, or to play the game we always play … but in his home, we don't have to rush.

"Are you all right?" he asks, his voice low.

"I'm fine."

"Do you want a drink?"

I nod. A drink would be good. Something to hold in my hands and busy myself with.

"Let's step into the kitchen, then." In Adrian's kitchen, which is an elegant, masculine space with dark marble countertops and tall reclaimed wood shelves, he takes down two cut glass tumblers. Light bends through them, refracting as he cradles them in his large palms. Even his tumblers reek of wealth. "What would you like?" he asks.

"You choose," I offer, not knowing what's in his kitchen.

"Whiskey?" he questions. "I have a favorite you may not have tried before."

"I don't mind whiskey."

"Chocolate cream cold brew whiskey," he speaks clearly, opening cabinets and leaving me alone by the kitchen island, standing quite alone in the expansive space.

Once he has what he needs, the bottles lined up and large spherical ice cubes taking up space in the tumblers, he strips off his jacket so he's just in his shirt from the office. Like his suit, his dress shirt is still pristine after a day of sitting in meetings and restructuring the company. My mouth waters at the thought of what's hidden under the belt around his waist and the white shirt above.

How did we come to be here? How did I find myself in this penthouse, with a man like him?

"If you don't care for it, I'll happily drink both and get you something else," he offers and I nod a thanks, deciding I should take that seat at the island after all.

He's capable in the kitchen, mixing this drink like he's made it a thousand times before. I have another flash of jealousy. Maybe he has, for some other woman, though it's none of my business who he brings here or who he makes drinks for. It comes and goes, leaving me questioning how much he's gotten to me. We've both been with other partners. And this, whatever is between us, is mutual.

Evening light glows around him as he tells me, "Let me know what you think."

"Thank you," I tell him as he hands me the heavy glass. The first sip goes down smooth. "Wow." I never would have guessed chocolate and whiskey would be a combination so easy and delectable. He's made it better than any bartender could have. It overwhelms me, how good it is.

"You like?" he questions, standing and leaning against the island.

"I do."

"Now that you've seen mine, I'm wondering about yours," he says, sipping his whiskey.

"My place is nothing like this," I comment, a bit worried, but also blunt. I'm sure he's aware. I don't come from *this* kind of money and my position certainly doesn't pay a salary where I could afford anything close to this in my lifetime.

Adrian sips his own whiskey, which he takes straight.

"I imagine you bring work home?" he asks.

"I prefer to stay at the office, but yes. My apartment is small. When I split with my ex, I sold off everything and bought a place in the West Village that I'd wanted for so long."

"Hell's Kitchen is fitting for you." I nearly tell him I'm barely there anymore, although I still love the neighborhood, but then I realize what he's revealed and discussing my apartment location seems unimportant.

"How did you know where I live?" I question and then answer for myself. "Did you snoop in the company files?"

"Of course I did. When I saw you that first day staring at me across the con-ference table, I already had your number."

"Well, that's not fair," I say with a pout, although it comes out a lust-filled whisper.

"I don't play fair."

"So you liked me while I hated the thought of you?"

He nods. "It's easy to hate the devil. So no offense taken."

I laugh, the nervousness dissipating. The drink Adrian made for me is help-ing. His expression intensifies, though, and he takes another sip of whiskey. "If it makes you feel any better, I don't think you're the devil anymore." Without thinking much of it, I raise my drink and confide in him, "That name is solely reserved for my ex-husband now."

His next question is casual: "What happened between you and your ex?"

Immediately I regret bringing Carl up in conversation at all. His name is the equivalent to an ice water bath.

I'm over that man, and I'll never want him again, but it still causes an old pain in my heart to talk about it. Luckily, the pang of betrayal is over quickly, and I can answer Adrian honestly. "He cheated … with the company secretary."

Anger darkens his features. "So he was a fucking idiot. Got it."

"No. Not an idiot. He was a manipulative bastard and damn good at it." My throat is tight as I correct him, once again feeling like a fool. "It wasn't just once, either. He had an affair for over two years. He used her to get details he shouldn't have been privy to."

Adrian takes a step closer and puts a hand on my shoulder. "I'm sorry," he says, his voice rumbling through me. "I'm sorry he hurt you and took advantage of you." He seems to make a decision. "My last ex was somewhat similar when it came to dishonesty."

Setting the glass down I admit to him, "I googled your name and love interest."

"You tried to look up my dating history?" He grins at me as if it's comical. "Did you find anything?"

"No," I state and he chuckles at my pursed lips.

There's almost no information online about Adrian's love life, as if it's been purposefully kept offline or scrubbed from the internet. There are companies that will do that for a person, and Adrian has enough money to hire them. Though most people don't care so much about erasing their exes from history.

"What happened with your ex?"

He drains his glass and pours another, taking in a deep breath. Just then, the intercom at his door rings, stealing his attention.

"One moment," he tells me and Adrian goes to answer.

"Food's here, Mr. Bradford."

"Bring it up."

It's quiet as he pours his whiskey, and I attempt a bit of small talk thanking him for dinner.

A doorman appears a minute later, in gray slacks with a shiny black name tag on his crisp white shirt, and two bags in hand. I cling to the tumbler, feeling out of place once again.

Adrian takes the bags out to the living room, where there's a massive sofa and a coffee table large enough to dine on.

As I slip off the stool, he opens the bags and lays out the containers on the table.

"The view is better in here," he tells me and when I reach the sofa, my hand on the soft leather, he peeks up at me to add, "and touching you will be far easier here."

A blush creeps up into my cheeks and I take the seat next to him. The savory smells of basil and marinara waft toward me.

"Italian?"

"Have you had Scalini Fedeli before?"

I shake my head gently, glass still in hand. "I haven't."

There's that hum again, that satisfied hum coming just before he balls up the paper bags. Rising from his seat, he tells me I'm going to love it.

As he plates the food, capellini with prosecco, porcini ravioli and arugula and buffalo mozzarella salad, my mouth waters. I do however notice that the conversation from the kitchen has stopped altogether.

Maybe he's not going to tell me. It's obviously a painful subject if he's just going to move on from it. Curiosity flares again, but I don't want to ask the question. I'd rather sit with him, enjoy this meal and wait for more of those deep rumbles from him.

"She never loved me," Adrian says, breaking the silence after the food is plated. "She never even wanted to be with me. She was with someone else the entire time."

"Oh my God." My heart breaks for him. I know this feeling so well. I wish I didn't, because it means my ex was a horrible person who wasted my time, but I know the betrayal that's coursing through his veins. It makes you feel so sick and stupid. Like you should have known all along what was happening, but you didn't.

"He told her to sleep with me because he wanted her to persuade me into certain deals."

"That is …" Horrible. Worse than horrible. Devastating. It would make it hard to continue trusting people in business after that. Almost impossible. No wonder Adrian rearranges companies to such an extent. He doesn't truly trust anyone to be what they say they are.

"We were together for nearly six months before I realized."

"I'm sorry." I set the tumbler into my lap, both hands cradled around it. His focus is on his plate. His fork twirls the pasta around but he doesn't eat.

His eyes find mine and he offers me a smile that doesn't reach his eyes when he says, "Maybe it's not polite dinner conversation."

"It's fine. I want to know more about you."

He gestures at the food on the coffee table. "You must be hungry," he says, and I know this part of the conversation is over.

My appetite has vanished, though, apart from small bites, which are delicious. We eat in relative silence. I'm sick on his behalf, and on mine. I never thought

Adrian Bradford and I would have something like this in common—such complete betrayal by an ex. I guess betrayal doesn't care if you're rich. It can find you anywhere.

"What do you think?" he questions.

"About what?"

He huffs a small laugh, taking another bite before glancing at my half-eaten plate.

"Oh, it's delicious. I—You were right. It's delicious."

He's barely touched his plate as well. "I'm not as hungry for dinner as I thought I'd be."

"Me either."

A moment passes as he leans back, the sofa groaning under his weight. The plates stay where they are on the table, the empty tumblers of whiskey next to them.

"I'll never do that to you," he murmurs, his gaze drifting to my lips.

I turn onto my side, lifting my knees up and letting my heels fall to the floor so I can rest my legs on the edge of the sofa. "I won't either. Cheating and lying are—"

"For assholes who can live with their misery," he says, finishing the statement for me.

I rest my cheek on the back of the sofa, and my hand slips into his. "Yeah."

As if he senses my thoughts, he says, "I want to get lost in you."

I don't have a chance to respond, only to part my lips as he crashes against them.

As soon as he touches me it's like we're back in the office, frantic for each other. He strips off my clothes with brutal efficiency. A gasp leaves me as he lifts me, forcing my legs to wrap around his hips.

I think he might take the floor, but instead he takes me to the windows looking out over the city. He's still fully clothed, save for the top buttons undone from my efforts a moment ago.

My stomach drops at the height of the building but Adrian murmurs in my ear, "You're safe here, safe from everything except being my fuck toy. Isn't that what you said you wanted?"

I wonder if they can see me. There's no other building this tall, but it would only take someone craning their neck to see me bared to the powerful man behind me.

My answer is a moan. He puts both my hands on the cool glass. "Keep your hands up," he commands me. "And spread your legs." My breasts press against the glass as my hips are pulled against his crotch. His erection pushes against my ass.

His hand dips down between my thighs and teases up until he's stroking my clit, alternating it with pushing his fingers inside me until I whimper for more. Then he focuses relentlessly on my clit until I come on his fingers with a cry, shaking against the windowpane. My legs nearly give out and I cling to Adrian as best I can, holding on to him to keep my balance. His lips trail down my neck as he toys with me, bringing me closer and hotter to yet another release. It's hot and my pulse races, for the sheer force of my orgasm and from the view. The chill of the glass is at odds with how my body hums. He plays me like he knows every inch of me, and I fucking love it. I love what he does to me.

He tells me, "I think I'll fuck you here." His fingers slip lower, to a place I've only experimented with once. My eyes widen slowly and my lips part in an O. "Have you had anal before?"

I swallow thickly before answering, "Not in a long while."

"Did you enjoy it?" he questions and I rest my head back, staring down at the city. "It was … different. We didn't get far," I admit. A college fling once tried … we were drunk and lube was scarce. "It was a no go for lack of … preparation."

A deep rumble of consideration comes from his chest as he seems to consider what I've told him. "Are you curious?" he asks.

"Yes," I admit, my heart racing.

"And you would you trust me to do my due diligence?" he questions and I can feel his smile against my neck. His fingers play at my clit again and my "yes" becomes a moan of approval. The thought instantly makes me nervous, but I would let Adrian do anything. I trust him.

"Lie down for me over here," he says, picking me up and taking me to his sofa. At first I yelp in surprise, clinging to him, but it quickly turns into a short laugh, smiling into the crook of his neck.

He's gentle as he sets me down on the soft leather cushion. "Wait here."

He comes back a moment later and puts me into position on his couch, on my belly, knees bent slightly. I'm quick to grab a pillow, laying my cheek against it and wondering what he'll feel like … *there.*

Adrian kneels behind me and spreads me wide, his fingers playing at that place, cool and slick with lube. He pushes one finger inside, then two. It's an odd pressure and it makes me tense slightly before relaxing. The simple act heats my entire body and with it, my head thrashes and I moan gently into the pillow.

"How does it feel?" he questions.

"Good," I respond in a groan as his other hand finds my clit, his fingers still in my ass. "Fuck," I moan into the pillow.

"Tell me if anything feels uncomfortable," he tells me. "This shouldn't hurt, Suzette. It should feel good." All I can do is nod with my eyes closed. The sensation is all consuming, tingling every inch of me. With a whimper, I swear it's more sensitive and more illicit to be fucked like this.

He shifts us to the floor, which gives me a sensation of stability that the couch didn't, and I feel the head of him against me. I take in a quick breath.

"Push back," he orders, and I do. My body goes hot as he presses inside. My hands fist the pillows and he tells me to relax.

"I want you to enjoy this," he whispers at the shell of my ear, his warm breath and gentle kisses adding to the overwhelming sensation.

With my eyes half-lidded, my lips part and I push back. Strangled moans pour from me. "That's my good girl," he urges me on, slowly pulling out and then pushing back in. Adrian murmurs things behind me but doesn't rush. It's very slow, and it makes me all the hotter. The full sensation turns to something else, something needy and undeniably pleasurable. Inch by inch I push myself back on him until he's fully inside me.

It's that last thrust that seems to shock my system. My eyes go wide and it feels too much, too hot, too full. Just too much.

"Oh," I gasp. Biting down on my lip, I utter a small grievance. "Stop, no. I don't know." It happened too fast, out of nowhere. He stops at once, stilling and my hand grabs the top of his.

"It's all right. How do you feel?" he questions. Fuck, it's just so much. I want it, I want him. *I want this.* It's a sweet mix of pleasure and pain.

"Scared," I admit to him, remembering how much it hurt before. It was nothing like this. Not at all, but with a cold sweat on the back of my neck, I swallow down the unwanted memory.

"Just breathe," he says softly. "Give me a word that means stop."

"Whiskey," I say, the first thing that comes to mind.

"I'm going to move, Suzette."

He does, and it feels overwhelming to the point of paralyzing. There's not an ounce of control left for me; all I can do is hold on. I've never been taken in such a forbidden way before. Adrian is slow at first, then faster and deeper. I clutch a blanket he's thrown on the floor beneath us. With one hand on my clit, he takes full advantage of pushing me to the edge.

His thrusts get harder and deeper still and if it weren't for his lips on my neck that beg me to kiss him, I would be writhing beneath him.

"What's your word, Suzette?"

"Whiskey," I whisper, feeling the pleasure build and build.

"Good. I need you to remember that."

I almost ask him why, but he doesn't give me enough time. Adrian holds me down and fucks me ruthlessly. With deep strokes, he takes me like I'm his fuck toy.

I come instantly, his name on my lips and pleasure like I've never felt before rocking through me.

Adrian

Exhaustion lays heavy against me, in the best of ways. The city lights creep through the edge of the curtain and cast a soft glow in the bedroom. The bed is warm and Suzette's body is molded to mine under the sheets. Her back to my front, my hand over hers. She makes this little humming sound every time I kiss her just beneath her ear. It's addictive. And when I sleep, I pray I hear it. The contentment, the satisfaction. I could see myself devoted to that soft sound.

"Did you enjoy it?" I question in a whisper at the shell of her ear.

Her response is a hum, a sated one cloaked in sated fatigue. My cock twitches at the memory.

"You'll tell me if it hurts," I whisper, bringing my hand to her hip as she presses her ass against me.

"Mm-hmm," she murmurs. She's quick to take my hand back, slipping her fingers through mine. Her eyes stay closed. She's well and thoroughly fucked, and after the night we've had, sleep should come easy.

All I can think is that I didn't ask to fall for her. It wasn't a part of any plan.

Every detail in the beginning was something I had planned. But she was unexpected, and *this* is entirely unexpected. Falling for her feels like it changes everything. I don't know what exactly changed, but everything feels different.

"I'll dream of you," she says.

"As you should," is what I reply. I bite my tongue before I let slip, *I'll dream of you too.*

If you're reading this, put your phone down and listen to your father.

My mother's text shows on the screen as I pick up my BlackBerry. I can't help but huff out a humorless laugh before setting it back down and tending to the pan on the stove.

The smell of bacon fills the kitchen as I flip the pancake one last time before slipping it off the skillet and onto the pile of six on the plate.

The fresh fruit was already sliced and prepared. All I had to do was pour the mix of cantaloupe, berries, and watermelon into the small bowl.

I'm not a chef by any means, but I can manage a simple breakfast.

The stack of pancakes joins the table next to the syrup and butter. Deeming it acceptable, I glance behind me toward the stairs deciding to wait until Suzette is up so she can join me. My BlackBerry buzzes again and I'm not certain if it's my father, telling me I need to take the weekend off, or my mother, agreeing with him. It could also be a work email, calendar notification or someone else who needs something from me.

With a black coffee in hand, I stalk to the adjacent living room and peer out of the windows overlooking the early morning in the city. It's already bustling beneath us.

This city never sleeps and, if you want to keep up with it, you can't either. The only thing that stops me from heading to my office is the knock on my door.

"Come in," I call out, knowing exactly who it is.

"Mr. Bradford," Noah greets me, carrying a variety of large department store bags in different colors, half of them with tissue paper peeking out. "This should do, I hope."

"Have you got everything?" I question, very much focused on the details beneath Suzette's clothing.

The older man nods, professional but with a knowing look as he sets the bags down. "Ann selected the delicates." His sport coat and dark jeans are evidence that he has plans, more than likely with his wife.

"I appreciate it. Please let her know I am grateful."

"Is there anything else, sir?"

"Not at the moment."

"I'll be off then," he says and waves a short goodbye before glancing around the room, I imagine to spot the lady these clothes are intended for.

Much to my gratitude, the front door closes before Suzette quietly makes her way into the room. Her bare feet padding softly on the hardwood floor give her away. With her hair a messy halo, and dressed only in one of my undershirts, she could not possibly look more fuckable.

My grip on the mug in my hands tightens as I suppress a groan.

"Good morning," she offers, brushing her hair from her face. As her arms fold in front of her she gets reacquainted with my penthouse, glancing around before stopping in front of the set table.

"Good morning. Your clothes arrived." I motion toward the bags with the mug. "Coffee's on as well. Should I make you a cup?"

With surprise lightening her gaze, it dances between the bags and myself. "I'm sorry, did you say clothes arrived?"

"I think you could use some caffeine," I state rather than answering her. As I make my way to the kitchen, the tissue paper crinkles behind me.

"You ordered these for me?"

I pour her a cup, listening to the sounds of her opening each bag. "You needed something to wear home. Cream and sugar?"

"Please." Tentatively, I take in her posture. She's not unfamiliar with wealth, but I imagine it can be difficult for a woman like Suzette to readily accept.

"I should pay you back," she murmurs. I imagine she's attempting to tally the total.

"It's a gift."

"You didn't have to," she tells me, still holding an crimson silk shift dress with both of her hands.

"You keep saying that and I'll keep reminding you, it's because I want to." Setting her coffee on the table, I add, "Besides, I will very much enjoy seeing you in that dress." It's that deep red shade she seems to love so much. "I just hope it fits you."

"You're too much," she tells me, and I catch her gaze. "Thank you."

Good. That's all she needs to say.

"And breakfast?" She finally sets the dress back into the shopping bag, careful with the fabric, and gives me a simper. "You made breakfast?" She selects a small chunk of fruit.

"I thought you might have an appetite this morning.

"You would be right. I'm famished."

"I was thinking breakfast and then a shower?"

"As much as I like the smell of you and your body wash, I don't have anything to shower with."

"Everything you need should be in one of those." I motion toward the bags.

"Toiletries?" Again she seems surprised. Nodding, I take the seat across from her, making my plate of bacon and pancakes.

She seems shy as she speaks. "Thank you for letting me stay overnight … and for all of this."

What kind of men has she been with? Did she think I'd fuck her and then send her home in a taxi?

Her apprehension fades as we eat.

"What are your plans for the day?"

"I'm behind on a contract for—" she starts, picking up a slice of bacon and then pauses. "What are the rules for the weekend?"

A short chuckle leaves me and I smirk at her. "We can negotiate those terms, Ms. Parks."

There it is. Her gorgeous smile and lightheartedness.

"I would like to spend the day with you, but I'm a bit behind with work." She sighs dreamily and adds, "A man has been distracting me."

I hum in agreement. "I know what you mean. There's an exceptionally beautiful and stubborn woman who's been distracting me as well."

Her simper widens and she rocks slightly in her seat.

"You look gorgeous, by the way." She blushes, as if she's a shy little thing. Does she know how all of these facets of her have me more and more addicted?

I offer, "We could plan on working and fucking, fucking and working. Occasionally we must eat, though."

The smile dims as she lays her arms on the table, slightly more serious. "As much as that sounds exactly like the productive weekend I'd enjoy, I'm a little sore and I think I'd like to work from home."

I can't help that the corner of my lips tips up in an asymmetric smile. "Sore?"

She blushes again. "I think I may need to rest for the day, if you don't mind."

Before I can feel any kind of disappointment she questions, "What are your plans for tonight?"

"Wide open, Ms. Parks."

"Would you like to go on a date with me?"

"You're asking me out?"

"Officially. Yes. I think the weekends … maybe we could date on the weekends?"

My smile matches hers. "I think I'd like that."

chapter 14

Suzette

I T'S DIFFICULT, AND UNLADYLIKE, TO EAT YOGURT AND TALK AT THE SAME time, but I'm managing it. Gail shovels a handful of almonds and raisins into her mouth as well, completely unfazed. We're both rushing through lunch and it's not uncommon in the least. Today is different, though. It feels as if everything is riding on this one task delegated from the "team."

Projected profits and client referrals based on previous numbers. A.k.a., how profitable is our division on its own? I'm more than certain we'll impress. Perhaps it's cocky or arrogant, but I know we're damn good at what we do and, as Gail so eloquently put it, it's time to whip our dicks out.

Lunch break be damned.

Maddie sits on one end of my desk, watching the conversation as she eats her caesar salad, and another of our coworkers is at her side. His name is Dale and Dale is … well, he's Dale. He's got a sharp eye for marketing but his social skills are subpar. So he stays in his cubicle avoiding us as much as he can.

Today, I wish he'd done just that. There's an uneasiness about him and it puts a damper on the atmosphere that would otherwise be motivating.

"No, listen," I say to Dale. "I have an idea I want to pitch to you before we part ways again and you leave us to the figures."

"I'm not sure you should be pitching any ideas." He gives me a look that definitely means something and my face goes hot.

"What do you mean? I always pitch you ideas. It's no different for me to do it right now."

He arches an eyebrow. "Even with all the rumors flying around the office?" At once, my ears turn red hot. Gail pauses mid-chew, her dark brown eyes going wide and Maddie peeks up from her salad.

My heart drops in nervousness. "What rumors?"

"People have seen you with a certain someone," Dale says, his gaze darting toward the elevator.

"Who?" Maddie asks. *Fuck. Fuck, fuck, fuck.* With numb fingers I drop the mostly eaten yogurt to the small trash can.

As I do, I shoot her a look that gives her all the information she needs to know. Betrayal doesn't pair well with the sweet yogurt. It tastes far too sour.

Her mouth drops open. Two weeks of seeing Adrian nearly every day, and it was bound to happen. Shakily, I sip my water and take a few deep breaths to calm down, not responding at all to Dale.

"You're seeing him, aren't you?" Gail questions to my left. All eyes are on me and I fucking hate it. I knew this would happen. Office trysts *always* get out. I just wish it wasn't today of all freaking days.

Dale watches me carefully, as if he's not sure he can trust me anymore. I don't like that feeling. It's a sensation of being accused of something, though he is right that I'm seeing Adrian.

I nod in confirmation. The corners of Dale's mouth turn down. "So he sleeps with you on the weekend and then fires your coworkers on Monday."

A chill runs through me at his bluntness, but my back straightens.

Sighing, I put the bottle of water down on my desk. "That's pretty much how it is." My tone is bitchy yet stern as I meet his gaze head-on.

"And none of that has anything to do with the last decade of work I've put into this client list. So," I say and glance over my shoulder at Gail, "back to putting together this presentation because as much as I wish fucking Adrian would save our asses, we both made it very clear that lines would not blur." I pause, waiting for Dale to say anything at all. For Maddie or Gail to pipe up.

A long moment passes with a heat tingling at the back of my neck.

"What if you tried blow jobs too?" Maddie says, then shrugs and Dale shakes his head although there's a hint of his smile showing.

Gail is less than impressed. "I need a moment," is all she says before walking out, leaving that pit in my stomach to weigh heavier.

That particular feeling only grows as the day progresses. Each time, it grows and grows until I feel like I could throw up.

The rumor is confirmed within minutes. It's easy to tell when each of them know.

Dale was correct that Adrian does the firing, and not me, but it's me who my coworkers come to for answers when it's done. All of them are upset, and nothing I can say offers them any comfort.

It's as if my office becomes the place to vent. The place for them to safely unleash their anger. Unfortunately for me, it also appears to be the day the graphics department is getting culled.

So one after the other pass snide looks my way before heading to their office with empty boxes to clear out their things.

They just lost their jobs. I feel compassion for them, even the ones I didn't get along with very well. Frustration mounts and I'm more upset than ever toward the end of the day.

A woman who's just been let go comes into my office at three. "What the hell, Suzette?" Her face is almost white, and her voice shakes from how upset she is. "Half of the department was just let go."

"He's rearranging things," I say helplessly. "I'm so sorry."

"Let me guess, there's nothing you can do."

"I'm sorry," is my only reply. I can't give her anything else. I'm not the owner of the company; Adrian is, and I'm not even the second step down in the company. "I have no input or authority."

"Wonderful," she says sarcastically. "Goodbye, Suzette."

A few minutes later, another person who has been fired storms across the hall. He turns his head and stares at me on his way past, but doesn't say a word.

It's not until Gail comes back, taking her seat and appearing on the verge of tears. "If you knew something, you would tell me, right?" We've worked together for years and I've never seen her like this. Her tan skin is flushed. "If I'm going to lose my job, I just need to know so—" her voice cracks and I can't take it.

"The second I know anything—"

"Could you ask him?" She stresses, "Please?" Her dark brown eyes are rimmed in red and I know she's a mess witnessing so many layoffs so quickly and with whispers of a merger, where our jobs would no doubt overlap with others and thus, more layoffs.

"Please," she begs me. With a nod, and a tight swallow, I agree.

"I can ask him," I tell her and then I firm up my response. "I'll ask him today."

Sitting here and waiting for an answer isn't enough, not for me and not for the team members I have left. I've worked far too hard for this company to let it all go to shit like this. If we lose Gail, the report we put together today is irrelevant. Clients stay with us because of the team. We can't break down like this.

I won't let it happen.

At five forty-five, I knock on the door to Adrian's office. Shaking out my hands, I prepare myself. Not the version of me he sees after six. But the version who existed before that man dared to walk through the doors to this building. The badass businesswoman who doesn't take any shit.

It's a small blessing that his secretary is gone for the day and her desk is empty now. Most of the building is cleared out, but not everyone. And I have fifteen minutes. He can offer me fifteen minutes if it means saving the most profitable department in this company.

"Come in," Adrian calls from inside the office.

Steeling myself, I open the door and go in, then close it behind me. The move is fast and I say a silent *thank you* that his door was unlocked.

Before he can say a word, I approach his desk. It seems to take forever and the scent of people's fear as they got fired today hangs in the air. His large, spacious office must have seemed like an awful joke to the people who lost their jobs. I could be one of them, and Adrian is the only one who can confirm my fear or dismiss it. That's why I'm here. This conversation is needed, because I can't sit at my desk for another day with nothing to say to the people I've worked with for years as they file out past me. I handpicked my department. They should be able to rely on me.

"My department is essential to what our company does," I begin, without waiting for his permission. I don't need it outside of the games we play. "If you want to keep the company going, you'll need to keep the core team intact. Every single one of them is essential, and I can vouch for them and their work."

Adrian shifts in his seat, his dark suit crisp, his expression inscrutable. As he leans back, his hands relaxed on the armrests, I wait for any reaction at all, but I'm given nothing.

"Almost everyone I could part with is already gone, and my team won't be able to keep functioning if we lose any more people. We've brought in the most revenue of any other department over the last few years, and you can expect more of the same over the next five years. We're projected to triple our profits by then."

Adrenaline rages through me at the very fact that we will triple in only five years. There's not a damn word I've said that's exaggerated. My heart hammers in my chest as I stare back at Adrian's cool gaze. Again, he doesn't react other than to gesture to continue.

"I'm damn good at my job, and I have good people, and we're going to keep striving for excellence."

"Are you done?" he questions.

"There's no one who can do what we do and keep those clients. No one has the relationships we do. No one has the word of mouth that we do. Replacing any of us would be a mistake."

I swallow so hard, it's audible and still, I'm given nothing.

"Adrian." I whisper his name, on the verge of breaking. Anger simmers but also a hurt I can't describe.

"We're on the clock, Suzette," he warns, the first sign of compassion noted in my name on his lips.

"If you're going to lay them off," I say and swallow, "I need to be able to tell them. I need to know what's going on."

"That's what you came here for? To figure out who's getting fired next?" His tone is unimpressed.

"I want you to keep in mind that we're a team. We work efficiently and our plan is solid; our performance speaks for itself."

He eyes me from across his desk, lips pursed. "You'll have an answer when the team is ready."

Frustrated, I look him in the eye. "You could at least say you'll consider it. You can at least tell me you'll let me know if anyone is in danger."

"I won't. It doesn't matter, Suzette. The team is running the numbers. The numbers are what guide my decision, not emotions. Not a plan, but what has been done and what is comparable. You're aware you have a list of clients, but they aren't the only clients and even that list is sellable."

Heat spreads over the back of my neck. I'm burning with frustration and anger, tears stinging the corners of my eyes. "You're heartless. You know what this means."

"And you know I bought this company for profit, and it's been bleeding money for far too long."

I'm left speechless, staring at him with nothing but resentment.

He won't give in, and somehow it shocks me. I should have known this about Adrian Bradford. He takes what he wants and does what he wants.

I knew that all too well when he fucked me on this desk the very first day we met. My heart hurts and I put my hand up to cover it, but it's too late. The damage is already done. "I can't believe you won't even give me the respect of letting me know if my team is at risk of losing their livelihoods. If you're just going to sell off the list, you could tell me that. I'm not fucking stupid. You would know if you already had a buyer."

Adrian folds his arms over his chest. "I listen because it means something to you. Do you think I would have let anyone else barge in here without a meeting?"

That same sickness from earlier stirs and I say nothing, knowing he's the one who's caused it.

"There needs to be a ... separation for us."

"How the hell am I supposed to separate this?" is all I can respond, my voice shaky.

"I want you to be happy," Adrian says simply, unfolding his arms and pushing the chair out from his desk slightly. "I want you to know I care for you."

There's a pause, and my frustration grows again. He cares for me? But can't answer a simple question? "They need to know as soon as possible so they can prepare," I press further and Adrian doesn't budge, his lips pressing into a thin line.

"Would you really sleep with me one night and then fire me in the morning?" I question with my voice tight.

"Suzette," he says, his voice carrying a note of warning. He doesn't say no.

Betrayal seems to push out every other feeling I have, making my face hot and my chest hurt. I know a losing argument when I see one and I know Adrian won't be convinced right now, but I can't help myself. "The company—"

"It's after six, Suzette," he replies, cutting me off. "You'll have your answer when the team has consolidated numbers and risks."

"Oh," I say with a bitter tone. "You can't tell me now because you're off the clock. Because it's six, so now I'm just a lowly fuck toy for you to come in?" Even as the words escape my mouth, I know they cross the line.

"You know that's not why." His statement is a string of carefully restrained anger, his grip tightening on the armrests, turning his knuckles white. Good. I hope he's pissed off. I hope he's upset like I am.

"I would never speak to you like that," he continues. "I would never treat you like you didn't matter. You know that," he tells me, his tone softening, his pale blue gaze pinning me. "And I don't like you talking about yourself like that."

"How am I supposed to—"

"You told me you could separate the two—" I cut him off before he can finish.

"I'm trying to compartmentalize," I argue back. He's gripping the desk, obviously upset now. "I'm sorry. I need a moment and I think—" Just as I turn my back to him, ready to get the hell out of here so I can lose it alone in a bathroom stall, he speaks up.

"No. We need to get out of here. We have dinner plans."

How am I supposed to sit through dinner like this with my stomach in knots and my face burning? I don't think I can do it. "Maybe we shouldn't tonight."

All my emotions tumble over me, filling my body and seeming to spill over into the room. Tears fill my eyes, but I don't want to cry in front of Adrian. I don't want to cry here in the office, where we've done so many things and where he keeps chipping away at my department and the company I've worked so hard to build.

"Maybe we shouldn't," I say again weakly, and start to leave.

His voice comes immediately, so deep and commanding that it stops me in my tracks. "Don't you dare walk out that door."

chapter 15

Adrian

I'M MORE THAN AWARE THAT THERE ARE EMPLOYEES STILL IN THE building. A few might be close enough to hear as Suzette bites out, "What the hell did you just say to me?"

She's visibly upset and spiraling. I've seen it before. A hundred times at least. Crying, cursing, screaming at me. I've been struck more than once.

My skin blazes with both indignation and embarrassment. I don't do squabbles in the office, I don't have shouting matches with employees. Then again, I've never slept with anyone at the office before either. This is why. This is exactly why it was a mistake.

With daggers in her eyes, Suzette stares back at me and says, "Did you just say, 'don't you dare?'" Her voice is deathly low and her gaze narrowed.

Her breasts rise and fall, peeking through her blouse as she breathes in deeply, stalking back toward me.

"I'd like you to calm down," I say, keeping my tone gentle. The last thing I need is publicity or a lawsuit.

Her eyes widen. "Calm down?" Outrage coats the two words. *Fuck.* I can't do anything right by her. This is a lose-lose situation and she sure as hell knew it when she walked in those doors.

I take in a steadying breath, standing from my seat, my dick hard, needing to fuck the anger out of both of us.

"Suzette." I speak her name as she stalks toward me.

"I am struggling today." Her words are frantic. "Watching coworkers pack up their offices, while others didn't even come in. Do you know how many people have given their notice?"

"Fourteen so far," I answer without hesitation. "Change is difficult, uncertainty is difficult, doing *my fucking job* is difficult," I stress, feeling the frustration rise.

"What am I supposed to tell them, Adrian? Rumors are going around about us and they're coming to me like I'm the one who did this," she starts and before she can continue, I stop her in her tracks. Toe to toe I stand apart from her.

"I am doing my best. If my best isn't good enough, then they can go find better." My words are stern and she acts as if they've struck her. Gripping her hips in both of my hands, I lower my lips to hers to say, "And if any of them have a problem with the two of us, tell them I want you more than anything. More than this company. More than profit, more than any fucking thing. I want you."

She's silent, her wide blue eyes brimming with a mix of emotions. Her hands on my chest put distance between us, so I take them in my own.

"I want you," I repeat, my voice strained and the words raw. "I want you," I tell her a third time, letting it sink in. "This will all be over soon, and when it is, I will still want you."

"Adrian," she says and my name is a plea on her lips, like I'm begging her for something she can't give me. Panic sets in, something I haven't felt in a long damn time.

She knew this was a possibility. I will vouch for her if something happens, but her résumé is impeccable. She will survive. I'll make sure of it. But I cannot guarantee an entire department. I can't promise her the things she's asking for.

"Tell me you want me."

"Adrian," she whispers and her voice is pained. It's unexpected and feels as if she's struck me. I can't remember a time when I've given her a command and she hasn't obeyed.

Moving my hands to hold her, one spearing through her hair and the other on the small of her back, I whisper in her hair before kissing her temple. "Tell me that you want me and I'll make sure you get everything you need."

All I can hear is the sound of her swallowing. I can't lose her over something like this. Something so insignificant. *It's significant to her, though.*

"It's after six," I remind her. "Come here, let me fuck the memory of that prick boss out of that pretty head of yours."

"Don't," she warns me and uncertainty clouds my judgment. Every inch of my skin is hot, anxiousness quickening my pulse.

"Let it rest for one more night. I promise your department will be the priority tomorrow." I shouldn't have said that. The second the words are out of my mouth, I know I shouldn't have spoken them.

"You promise?"

And still, I double down at the thought that it's what she needed to hear. "I promise."

She pulls back, staring into my eyes. "You promise? Because I don't think I can take much more of what happened today and as much as—"

"I told you, you have my word." With my pulse hammering, I bend to kiss her, deeply and desperately. I've lost the upper hand and I couldn't care less. Her lips mold to mine, but she's quick to break them.

"I'm sorry," she whispers between us. Picking her ass up, I move her to the desk, her legs spread as I stand between them.

She repeats, "I'm sorry, I shouldn't have come in when I was—"

"Stop," I say and then kiss her again.

"No." She pushes me back, breaking my hold on her and heaving in a breath. "I'm sorry I didn't tell you that I want you too. I do. I do, Adrian, and I'm sor—"

With my finger pressed against her lips, I give her the command, "I said quiet." Heat dances along my skin. Both of us pent up, both of us suffering from the way we came to be.

Working the knot of my tie, I order her, "Lie back, with your hands by my chair."

She doesn't hesitate, eager to make it up to me.

My mind whirls with the implications of what's happened in the last hour, but I can barely focus on anything other than taking back control.

"You'll be quiet," I tell her in a whisper, steadying my breath as I use my tie to form a handcuff knot and stalk around to the other side of the desk. Slipping both of her hands through, I tighten them and then order, "Above your head."

She doesn't object and although the loose end is short, I'm able to tie it to the drawer handle. Lying flat on her back across the desk, her hands above her head, she has to bend her knees so her heels balance on the edge of the desk.

"What am I going to do to you?" I round the desk, loving how she looks.

This is better. This is how she should be.

With a hand on each of her hips, I drag her so her ass is at the edge of the desk. Her gasp fuels me further. Reaching up her skirt, I bunch it and drag her panties down her ass until they're free from her and a pile of lace on the floor.

"Spread your legs," I command and she obeys.

I position her heels how I want them, her legs spread as wide as she can. Fucking gorgeous. Her cunt is right there for the taking. Standing between her thighs, I unbutton her blouse one button at a time, exposing her blush-colored bra. I wish I'd taken it off before I thought to have her lie down. Her breathy pants are additive.

"This is how I want you in this office after hours."

Dipping the cups down, I free each breast, plucking and pinching her nipples and taking my time to play with them.

"My plaything, mewling for me."

"Adrian—"

"You'll be silent or I'll gag you, my little vixen. Do you understand?"

She starts to answer and thinking better of it, she swallows thickly and nods. The cords around her neck tighten, and I lean down, trailing kisses there as my hand slips to her slit.

"So fucking wet already," I murmur against her neck. "My greedy little whore … let's see how much you can take." With my lips on hers, I keep her quiet as I slip two fingers inside of her, curling them and quickly finding the bundle of nerves that has her sucking in a breath and arching her neck. My thumb moves to her clit and I'm ruthless as I force the first orgasm from her. It doesn't take long at all, her heels slipping from the edge of the desk, her muted cries of pleasure silenced as I devour her mouth with my own.

When she clenches around me, I only pause for a moment, wetting a third finger with her arousal before doing it all again. I don't kiss her this time, I stare down at her as she closes her and her head thrashes.

"Adrian." My name is hardly recognizable as it mixes with a tortured cry of pleasure.

Pulling my hand from her I smack her pussy, my middle finger landing directly on her clit.

Her arms pull back, the tie keeping her restrained, and her back bows as she cries out a beautiful sound of desperation.

"Quiet now, my little vixen," I tell her and her darkened gaze finds mine. Once she's regained her composure, I do it again, fucking her with three fingers until she comes undone.

My cock is hard watching her skin flush. When I finally thrust inside of her, I'm not merciful in the least. The desk allows me to fuck her deeply and roughly. Punishingly so.

She thought she was sore two days ago … she won't be able to walk out of here when I'm done with her.

chapter 16

Suzette

T HE ONLY THING ALLOWING ME TO CALM DOWN LAST NIGHT WAS, ironically, Adrian. If he hadn't taken me in his office, I don't think I would have been able to sleep. After being taken so thoroughly all I could think about was a hot bath, pajamas, and a glass of wine. My worries couldn't keep me awake long after that and I took my well-fucked body to bed.

A part of me is convinced he only said those things to pacify me. That he told me tomorrow he would give me a straight answer so I would calm down. The other part of me knows he hasn't given me a reason to think he'd lie to me. He's many things, but he hasn't lied to me. All of me, though, every single part of me is embarrassed for losing it on him. It wasn't professional and it crossed the lines we agreed upon.

With all of those thoughts fighting for the center stage of my insecurity, sleep wasn't as restful as I'd hoped it would be. My light dreams were far too real. Coworkers glared at me from outside my office door. No one would tell me what was happening, though. They wouldn't give a reason why they were so angry. "We're transitioning," I said, and I knew it didn't make any difference. Eventually, the dreams stopped and I fell into a deep sleep for all of a handful of hours.

I think it's safe to say the reality of my position at work is catching up to me.

My outfit for today was a decisive choice. It consists of a pencil skirt and blouse that is the epitome of attire for head bitches in charge. Selecting my accessories carefully, I went with classic pearl studs and paired them with a triple strand of pearls.

Giving myself a once-over, I nod. My outfit is perfect, and I'm calm enough from last night to face whatever Adrian says this morning. Although I'm exhausted with bags under my eyes, I'm a professional and I'll act accordingly.

None of it explains how my hands go numb and my stomach turns over every time I think of Adrian, though. This is exactly why they say not to fuck your boss. Every instinct I have tells me that today is our last day and potentially my last day at work as well.

He's taken over my mind and my emotions. How the hell did I let that happen?

I can lie to myself all I want as I smooth my skirt down, but he's still lingering behind every one of my thoughts.

I reassure myself on the trip into the office that I'll be professional and that whatever happens, I will survive. And that these emotions are warranted. It's perfectly normal to experience insecurities around something as intimate as sex, and something as forbidden as sex with the man who holds your future in his hands. Not just your future, either, but that of everyone you work with.

The thoughts marinate all throughout my morning routine. From paying for my morning coffee at the stand on the corner, to nodding at colleagues on my way to the elevator. These feelings and thoughts don't leave me. Dwelling on it all won't help. All I want to do is rip the fucking bandage off.

My thoughts will only get more complicated, and what can simplify them is answers. The email went out this morning, and four people have already texted me. The only one I replied to was Gail, who's waiting for me so we can head to the conference room together. Three departments are meeting at once this morning. The last three. Just the thought sends unease washing through me again.

"You ready?" Gail asks me, a notebook tucked under her arm as she pulls the hem of her dress down. It's a dark red number with three-quarter sleeves, and it hugs her curves all the way down to her thighs.

Red is a confident color. Nodding, I lift my coffee to her. "Let's do this."

It's quiet as we take the elevator up. "At least we'll know," Gail murmurs and I nod, choosing not to say anything at all. Her nervousness is as obvious as mine.

I hate this. I hate every bit of it and that's all I can think as we settle into the room, all twenty chairs filled and three men standing in the back corner.

The conversation swells from soft murmurs and gossip to one man speaking far too loudly in the room and then all at once stops.

Adrian strides to the head of the table to address everyone. If I hadn't spent so much time with him, knowing the curve of his jaw, the strength in his stance, I might not notice the subtle darkness under his eyes, as if he hasn't slept either.

His suit is crisp, though, custom fitted no doubt, and his shoulders set back, the air seeming to bend around him.

"Good morning," he says, and my body instantly heats. He has all the power to turn our lives upside down, but I still crave the sound of his voice. "I'm not going to waste any time. As part of this company's restructuring, some departments will be dissolved."

Sucking in a breath, I prepare myself.

"Your applications will be suggested to a competitor who will need to hire a number of positions after a merger." His eyes meet mine. "The only department that stays is brand positioning and marketing. It will stay in its entirety."

Mutters fill the room instantly, but Adrian cuts them off with a gesture.

"Did he say our department?" Gail whispers. And I nod without thinking. It's what he said, isn't it? He said brand positioning and marketing?

Gail lets out a not-so-subtle sigh and grabs my hand, squeezing so tight that my knuckles hurt. My department is safe. I can barely breathe, let alone sit here and absorb everything else he said.

There will be a merger.

He said there will be a merger.

We are safe, but what are the details of the merger? What exactly is happening? A split-up? He continues, fielding questions and a few men file out without a single word. They're pissed, dealing with the gravity of the situation. Everything seems to happen around me in a whirl. I have a million questions for Adrian. If the other sectors are being merged, what does that mean for my department? I rely on finance and purchasing and production to do what I do. Our department is all about ideas and relationships, but bringing those ideas to life relies on others. Does this mean I'll have to outsource? To the new company, even?

It's not long before I feel lingering stares on the back of my neck, and my ears go hot. They're all stealing glances at me, one by one. The corners of their mouths are turned down in disapproving frowns.

They know. This looks bad. So fucking bad. And yet, it's what I asked for. The reality of their assumptions hits me.

Everyone here knows I've been sleeping with Adrian, and they think he's keeping my department because I couldn't keep my legs closed. It will never matter to them that I took my own power in being fucked by him. All they see is a woman who went behind everyone's back to sleep with the boss and guarantee her department would stay intact.

That sickening feeling takes over again. Every part of me is on edge and Gail seems to catch on, squeezing my hand again and whispering, "Fuck them."

Frustration clenches my jaw. For so many years, I've thrown myself into this work and made tough calls and spoken my mind to my superiors even though I knew it would be risky to do it. I've been the one on the line many times, all in service of building this company into something worthwhile. Now everyone in the room thinks I slept my way to the top. Not even to the top. They think I slept my way to keeping my job.

My discomfort grows with the silence. I'm not sure what Adrian is waiting for, but no one does anything. No one pretends to have another meeting or rushes out with their cell phone to their ear.

It hits me then, that he's reading the room the same as I am. He knows exactly what they think and why they're all looking at me. Not Gail or anyone else from my department. Only at me. His gaze slips to mine and the back of my eyes prick. I can take it. I'll deal with the fallout and whatever damage is done to my reputation.

Adrian is handsome and stone faced at the front of the room. He's a defensive, arrogant asshole, that's what he is. Adrian has a strong jaw and an even better smile, but the expression he wears now is hardly encouraging.

"Not one of you came to pitch to me," he says finally in a deadly tone, and the room holds its breath. They've been waiting for the release of finally knowing what's going to happen, and now Adrian's dragging it out. "Not a single one of you but the lead for brand positioning and marketing. One of you came to me with a plan, and I may be a heartless prick, but if there is value and a potential profit ..." He's looking deeply into my eyes now, in front of all my colleagues. Every eye in the room is on us. "I do consider it."

chapter 17

Adrian

TODAY WAS LESS THAN IDEAL. I'VE NEVER FELT SO CONFLICTED WHEN it comes to business.

Because she's a factor now. The moment the meeting ended, I left first and I'm ashamed to admit, I closed the door to my office to avoid it all. Especially Suzette and all the questions written in her expression in that conference room.

There's not a doubt in my mind word will get out.

Wyatt clears his throat across from me, and I wish I'd canceled this meeting, but in truth, I'd forgotten about it until he walked through the door.

"Whatever's going on, just tell me," he comments from across my desk. A stack of papers, or more specifically, the contract he wants me to sign sits in front of him. To-go bags from a sushi place are in the other lounge chair beside him.

"We don't have to discuss business," he offers. He's dressed in his lucky dove gray suit. He's worn it to every wedding and every business meeting I've accompanied him to. He told me once that it's his lucky charm. But as he fiddles with the thin pale pink tie, he leans forward, and his eyes search mine. "Whatever it is, you can tell me."

"You didn't come here to be my therapist."

"No, but I'm always your friend. Business aside, you look wrecked." He leans back, his tie wrapped up in one fist that lays on his chest. His brow's pinched as he speaks with concern. "Like, is it a chick, is it your parents? What's going on with you?"

"A chick," I utter before I can stop myself and then I hate it. I hate the description. "She's not just some woman."

"Oh shit." Wyatt elongates the words, pushing the contract out of the way to make room for the sushi.

"I'm not hungry," I tell him and he only pauses to tell me, "Look, I need to eat. You pour your heart out, I'll stuff my face. Whatever's left you can have later." The plastic bag crinkles as he digs out his carton of choice. "So, what'd she do?"

"Nothing that I shouldn't have known was coming." It was written on the walls. Before I even stepped foot in this building, without even looking at the security footage to detail employees, I knew Suzette Parks was going to fight me. It was written on the fucking walls.

"You're going to have to elaborate," he states, opening up a small container of soy sauce. "She cheat on you?"

"No. No. She wouldn't do that."

"Do we hate her? Want to date her? You haven't given me anything at all, so I'm going to need you to fill me in."

I stare across the desk at Wyatt. He's young, a player, never held on to a woman for more than a few weeks. There isn't shit he could tell me that would help in the least.

"You can vent to me," he assures me, separating a pair of disposable chopsticks and giving me an exasperated look. "Whoever she is, she's gotten to you. You were distracted last time I was here; you're obsessed to—"

"I have feelings for her," I admit to him rather than listen to him continue. "I like her … a lot and because of that, I compromised a business."

The California roll stops midair. "What business?"

Tapping my two fingers on the desk, I point to the door. "This one."

"What do you mean? You okay moneywise? You need help or something? You know my father—"

"I don't—No. No. It's fine moneywise. It's just …."

"Oh thank God," he mutters, far more relaxed as he leans back with the container in one hand and the chopsticks in the other.

"It's just, I'm taking a risk I wouldn't, if it weren't for her."

"It's not so bad," he says after an exaggerated swallow. "You've done it before," he reminds me.

"And I nearly lost it all before."

"Passion outweighs statistics." He tells me something I've told him years ago. Pointing the chopsticks at me he adds, "You know that."

I can only nod, feeling the anxiousness of this morning come back to me. "She knows what she's doing and I think this would be best for her," I tell him.

"But not for you?" he guesses.

"… It would be much easier to merge, which means she could lose her job, her entire department even. It would mean uncertainty for her."

"So what, you're keeping her out of it?"

"I'm forming a business for her and her department alone. Allowing her to keep the clients while the remainder of the business is merged with another company."

He arches a brow, surprised. "One of your other companies?"

I shake my head. "I'll profit quickly and be done as far as the merger goes. The investment goes into her business, though."

"Does she know that it's her business?"

"She'll find out soon enough."

"Is she ready for that? That's kind of," he says and repositions himself, more serious now. "It's kind of a lot."

"It was that or the alternative, giving her passion to someone else to control."

Wyatt shakes his head, his brow still raised as if it's stuck there now. "Well okay, so … now I see why your mind is occupied." He aims for another piece of sushi but stops before picking it up. "Wait, you're screwing someone here?" he questions. "Like you're sleeping with the head of a department and because of that, you're forming a company for her to protect her from the obviously correct business decision?"

My stomach drops as I nod. "More or less."

"How long have you been with her? It's got to be serious."

"Less than a month, but yes. I'm serious when it comes to her."

If I thought his brow couldn't raise any higher, I thought wrong. It's quiet a moment, and the weight of my decision settles against my chest, uncomfortable and heavy.

"So, you're telling me," Wyatt pipes up, chopsticks once again aimed at me, "all I have to do to get you to sign these papers is sleep with you?"

The laughter is unexpected and if there was anything on my desk, I'd toss it at him. It's the first time I've smiled all day. "You're an ass, you know that?"

"I'm an ass who's happy you're in love," he comments and everything stops. "Men in love do stupid things but, if she's worth it, she's worth it."

"She's worth it," I tell him quickly. Ignoring the cold sweat that slips down the back of my neck at the thought of being in love with her.

"Good, maybe marry her or something. In case the company takes off."

"Marriage is not a business deal."

Wyatt shrugs. "It could be."

The knock at my office door is discreet and Andrea reveals herself. "Mr. Bradford, I just wanted to let you know the next meeting is seating now."

"Thank you, Andrea."

"All right, I'll get going then." Wyatt stands to leave. He takes in a deep breath and pushes the contract my way. "While you're a little puppy dog in love, could you take a look at that and sign it, please?"

Picking up the contract, I tell him, "You got it." I decide then and there that I'll sign it tonight.

Andrea watches our exchange from the threshold of the door.

"Give me five, and then can you scan this in for me?"

"Of course," she says warily and I look up at her.

"Everything all right?"

"Just checking on you. I know things are a bit tense at the moment."

"It's nothing I haven't dealt with before."

She stares back, her glasses slipping slightly from the bridge of her nose and her brow rises just as Wyatt's did. "Is there something else? Something you want to say?"

She shakes her head softly, the corners of her lips turning down. "No, sir."

"You can tell me," I say. "If there's something on your mind, speak freely."

"If Ms. Parks asks to meet with you, would you like me to let her up still?"

"Of course," I'm quick to answer.

"Good, good." Relief colors her face.

"Why would you ask?"

"She seemed upset yesterday, and so did you this morning. I just … I'm glad to hear that, is all."

chapter 18

Suzette

GUILT AND NERVOUSNESS AND GRATEFULNESS SPIN THROUGH MY mind for the rest of the day at work. All I can do is count down the minutes until 6:00 p.m. when I know Adrian will step into that elevator and I can be raw with him and let everything out. It's a gray area regarding the boundaries we set, but I have to get it out of me.

It's a mix of every emotion, so intense I have trouble concentrating on anything at all. My office door stays closed and I ignore every text and email and knock. I rescheduled several meetings and give myself the day to gather my composure.

This is what I wanted. It's exactly what I was hoping he would tell me was going to happen when I stormed into his office yesterday. Keeping my department whole is security and yet I feel nothing but insecure.

It all feels wrong. Just then my inbox pings with a new email notification and the subject line encompasses exactly what plays on repeat in my mind: *If you weren't sleeping with him, you'd have to fight for your job like the rest of us after the merger.*

There's a sinking feeling in my chest and when I click on the email header, the address is one I don't recognize. More than likely it's a throwaway account.

"Fuck you," I mutter and click delete although I can't say that they're wrong.

For the last hour, I do what I can, making plans for reassuring our clients and reaching out to other department heads to ensure we have what we need to continue.

If we don't, we will. I won't let us miss a beat. It's critical for our clients to know we're stable and there won't be any delays.

If Adrian is keeping our entire department, I have to make sure we have something to show for it. We have to be the best, now that he's singled us out.

I feel guilty that my department is staying because of what Adrian and I have done together … but not guilty enough to stop doing it.

I'm nervous that he'll change his mind and even more nervous that he'd be right to do it. And I'm grateful to him for announcing in front of everyone that he would be keeping our department. It saves me an untold amount of time trying to reply to questions when I don't have any firm answers.

I shake off the nervousness as best I can when it's finally time to get into the elevator. The office has been emptying out for a while now, and there's no one to see me step in. Adrian is already there waiting, occupied with his phone. When he glances up at me, my heart races. All the jitters rev up and I forget everything I was going to say.

"I can't do dinner tonight. I have a number of things that have piled up and arrangements that need to be finalized." My heels click as I step into the elevator, pretending like that's all right. Like it doesn't feel as if he's struck me and confirmed that everything is wrong and off between us.

"Okay," I say softly, staring straight ahead as the doors close.

"I can drop you off at your place if you'd like," he says briskly. It's cold and I stand a little further away from him as the elevator moves. He puts his phone in his pocket and presses the button for the first floor.

"Are we okay?" Now what I'm feeling is all nerves. It's tense between us, and different. There's none of the hot playfulness that's been part of every meeting we've had, and I can't help but wonder if it's because of what he did earlier. I know Adrian made that choice because of me. Guilt comes roaring back.

Adrian lets out a sharp breath and punches the emergency stop button on the elevator. "I need us to be—" he begins, and then he grabs me, pulling me commandingly across the space and into his arms. He lifts my face to his and kisses me hard and passionately, his tongue seeking entry into my mouth, and I part my lips for him with a moan. Heat blazes between us in an instant. It's unexpected but oh so needed.

Relief and desperation stir inside of me as I cling to him. My back hits the wall of the elevator and everything else slips away, fading to black and blurring into nothing.

My breathing is chaotic and my eyes stay closed as Adrian pulls back. His plea is what forces my eyes open. "What do you need from me to prove to you that you matter to me? That I want you happy and I want you mine and I couldn't give two shits about anything else?"

Gripping his collar, my fingers grazing against his stubble, I selfishly pull him in for another kiss, soft, slow and deliberate. He tastes minty and every bit of the man I know him to be. I could live here in this elevator if it meant kissing him forever.

Staring back into his pale blue gaze, I stop myself from the response that begs to be heard. The words are on the tip of my tongue. *I love you, Adrian.* Instead, I kiss him again, needing the stability of his body, until he pulls back to catch his breath. "Will you text me tonight when you're done?" I attempt to make it sound casual, but I'm not sure if it works. "I'm sorry I'm so needy right now."

He takes my face in his hands and looks me in the eye. "Stop saying you're sorry. I will text you." Adrian leans down and presses a kiss to my cheek. "Do you want Noah to take you home?"

I shake my head. "I can spend the evening with Maddie."

Adrian reaches for another button on the elevator's panel, and then we're moving down again. He kisses me all the way to the bottom. "I'll text you," he promises again. One more kiss and the elevator doors open. Adrian is completely self-possessed and put together by the time he steps out of those silver doors and disappears into the lobby.

If only I could be the same.

Maddie's apartment is a cute, small place in SoHo. By small, I mean teeny tiny. It's a one bedroom with a decent-sized living room. A crocheted blanket from her grandmother rests on the back of her sofa and our takeout containers are spread out on the coffee table. The comparison of her place to Adrian's is unavoidable. They are complete contrasts. From the view to the flooring, even the light fixtures. All Maddie has is a single lamp in the corner and ceiling lights in the kitchen. Maddie's fridge hums in the little kitchen off the living room and every so often the radiator makes a clicking sound. Even if it is small, it's comforting to be here. It reminds me of when I first moved here. Before my ex, before this job. Over a decade ago now.

Curled up on the other side of the couch, Maddie works her way through the Chinese I picked up on the way here and groans about her latest hellish dating experience.

"He wanted me to pay for everything, including his dinner, after he was such a dick because, quote unquote, 'If you don't want to see me again, that's on you and you wasted my time,'" she says. Her eyes widen just as mine do, with disbelief. "I shit you not."

"That is … exceptionally … like, I don't even have words."

"I would have been happy to split the bill, but are you kidding me? I'm not going to pay a fee for not liking the guy."

"That sounds awful," I say, commiserating. "It's bullshit that you even have to put up with guys like that."

"I don't," Maddie tells me and laughs. "I left him in that restaurant. I just wish there were more good guys on this freaking app, you know? It's so exhausting to have to search through all of them. Like I'm obviously not good at picking, could someone else do it for me?" A titter leaves her, but I know she's less than happy and there's truth to the statement.

"I haven't looked at a dating app in a long time now." Stirring the lo mein with my fork, I add, "Not for … months now?" I surmise, "Not since those first few weeks of the separation."

Chewing my inner cheek, I keep my next thoughts to myself. I never would have found a man like Adrian on an app. My throat is tight with how much I miss him, and how I want things to be normal between us. It's been a long damn time since I've missed someone. Truly missed them, and that realization toys with me as well as Adrian himself does.

"Men are trash," Maddie says and sighs, and that's what does it.

I break down crying over my Chinese food. What the hell is wrong with me? "I swear I better be getting my period or something because I am nothing but an emotional wreck today." I create the excuse, pushing it out the moment I lose it. The small napkins from the restaurant make for perfect tissues.

"Oh my God." Maddie places her container onto the coffee table and scoots over next to me, slinging an arm around my shoulders. "What happened? It's okay to cry," she tells me. Of course she would say that. She's the emotional one. I'm not. This isn't me. It's not who I am.

"You know about Adrian," I barely manage to get out. "You heard the gossip at lunch, and you know what those rumors say and you know it's true but … it's not just sex."

Maddie's eyes are wide. She keeps giving me little nods, like she's following along, but when the pause comes her mouth drops open. She cracks a bright smile. "It's not just sex? Is it—"

"No," I cut her off. "It's more than that." Another sob wracks me and it only frustrates me more. "I think I'm falling for him."

chapter 19

Adrian

SITTING IN THE OFFICE, OVERLOOKING THE CITY, I COME TO ONE conclusion. There's only one reason I would negotiate everything like I have the past three days. Every meeting, the marketing department and client list was mentioned. Every deal, the number went up, with the condition it was included in the acquisition of the company … and I turned all of them down. Settling for less. Barely breaking even on a deal I spent months pursuing.

It was all to her and compromising every other deal.

Of course they took what I offered, though. Everyone who needed to sign, did so. Ending the majority of their competition was a worthwhile deal for them. Even if the coveted list remains with Suzette. Her job is secure. It will be unsteady for a while I imagine as she adjusts. She will, though, she will survive and she will thrive. There's no doubt in my mind, even from the numbers' side, and the team agrees. It's not cost-effective and it's a risk to float the company, but for her, knowing that there's not a chance in hell her position will be in jeopardy, it's worth it.

And there's only one conclusion I can make of that. It would have been a quick few million, freeing up my cash flow, ending one project and moving on to the next. Instead, I'll be supporting a company who may lose clients, whose stock will plummet once the split is finalized. A company that will have to prove themselves … a company run by her.

I think I love her.
I think I want to propose to her.

My phone rests in my lap and I stare down at the messages I typed out. I delete the two texts. It's insanity. Running my hand through my hair, I groan at the ridiculousness of it all.

I haven't a clue how Suzette will even react once reality hits her. I've gifted her a company. Technically the board will meet and vote on the positions needed to be filled to move forward. She will be nominated and everything she worked for, will come to fruition.

Heat tingles along my skin, not knowing how she will take it.

The meeting is set for next week and my instinct screams to secure her before then. To propose, to woo her, so that when the time comes and it dawns on her, she'll already be mine.

All of that doubt and insecurity will be worthless if she's already wearing my ring.

It's one thing for a man infatuated to shower a lover with wealth, a lover with trust issues and one that seems to be ready to run any minute. It's another for a future husband to secure his fiancée's livelihood.

The only question that remains is whether or not she'll say yes. Whether she wants me like I want her.

I'm infatuated. I've lost my fucking mind over her.

I think I'll propose to her. I type it out to Wyatt and wait a moment, debating on whether I should do it without telling anyone. I could take her to any jewelry store she wanted, let her choose the ring she wants most and do it then and there.

My thumb hovers over the message.

I already know Wyatt is going to try to talk me out of it. That's what I would do, if he texted me out of nowhere that he wanted to propose to a woman he just met last month.

A woman who's gotten into his head and clouded everything.

But isn't that what love is?

I don't have a moment to send it. Wyatt and my father message me at once.

Wyatt's message asks if he can see me.

He adds: *It's important. As soon as you can, I need to see you.*

An anxiousness comes with my father's message: *You didn't sign that contract, did you?*

My gut drops and Wyatt messages: *Where are you? I'll come to you now. I fucked up. It's all fucked up.*

There's a prick at the back of my neck, a numbness that flows through my veins.

I respond to them both immediately. To my father: *I signed it.*

To Wyatt: *At the office.*

My father: *Fuck. Call me now.*

Wyatt texts back at the same time that my father calls. Clearing my throat,

I glance at the closed office door and then turn my back to it, facing the office windows.

"Adrian." My father greets me and before I can do the same he says, "Tell me you didn't sign it."

"I already told you I did."

The tone in his voice is unsettling, enough so that my entire body tenses. There's desperation I can't help but to feel pulling at me through the line.

"Whatever he's gotten himself into, I'll help him out."

"It's not just him," my father grits out between his teeth. "Did your lawyers not change the fucking clause? You're on the hook for his investment in the building."

"What?" My pulse races and I'm quick to open up the drawer, pulling out an unsigned copy, a previous version Wyatt had given me. Andrea has the signed copy. Signed, sealed, delivered.

"He made the purchase this weekend for the real estate not two days before the city announced the fucking highway would be built across the street."

Wyatt's deal, his big idea, was high-end residential builds. It's what his father made his name doing. They're builders and damn good. "A highway?" I can't fucking believe it. "How did he not know?"

"The more important question is, how the fuck does he sell it now and how the hell do you get out of this contract? If not, you're going to have to sell as much as you can. It's to the tune of twenty million."

"Twenty million," I repeat, bracing myself on the desk. The numbers run in my mind, all of the companies, all of the holdings and deals I could maneuver just to cover a short like that.

"Twenty fucking million." Every way I look at it, one company stands out above the rest. Worth eight million for a single client list.

I could fucking throw up.

"You'll sell if you have to, hold on to the best investments only. I'll help where I can, but I don't see a way out. You're going to have to shift money and hold out for the right timing."

"I need at least a hundred grand a month for a different investment." All the numbers for payroll and transitions tally in my mind. The company will earn it back, but not in the first quarter. Probably not for the first year. It has to float.

"For what?" My father's tone is exasperated. "You'll be lucky if you have enough for your personal expenses."

"I'll leave those numbers to my financial manager," I bite out, irritated but also fucking terrified. I saw what happened to my family years ago when my father lost it all.

As if reading my mind he states clearly, "You might be fucked, but you'll survive this. You're going to have to sacrifice a number of things, but I'm calling the lawyers, I'm calling everyone. I will do everything I can, but I'm not sure there's much we can do but sell. Take the hit. Reinvest when there's time. At least it's only twenty million lost."

I can barely swallow, my eyes closed as I realize what I would do if things were different. A quick eight million is right there.

"Fuck," I say and breathe out. I promised her. I promised her she didn't have to worry.

"I can't fucking believe I signed."

"I can't believe he was that fucking stupid."

"It's his first on his own."

"Even still, he should have fucking known to talk. He could have made fucking sure there weren't whispers and deals in the making. If he'd told his father, at the very least, he could have been given a heads-up."

Investors talk. Politicians are paid. Deals are made. It's how this business is run. But only those in certain circles are privy to high-level information. Wyatt's father would have known. He would have stopped him from buying property whose value was days away from plummeting.

"If the sellers knew—"

"Do you know how long litigation would take? And that's if you can prove it." I swallow thickly. There's a reason they say the business world is run by crooks.

He got fucked over. And I signed the dotted line to come along for the ride.

Just then, the office door opens, Andrea calling out behind Wyatt.

With my phone pressed to my ear, my father cursing and repeating lines of the contract. Wyatt stares back at me, his eyes rimmed in red and looking like hell. His light tan skin is blotchy like he's barely keeping it together.

"I fucked up. It's a lot of fucking money."

"Sir," Andrea starts, a nervous energy around her.

"It's fine, Andrea." I wave her away as Wyatt takes hesitant steps inside the barren office, his hand running down his face. "I'll call you back," is all I say to my father without taking my eyes off my good friend, who just made a horrific deal … one for the both of us.

chapter 20

Suzette

I KNOCK SOFTLY AT ADRIAN'S DOOR AND GO IN. IT'S THE LATEST I'VE EVER visited him, but he's been busy all day and evening. As it stands I've barely seen him the last two days, and when I do, he's reserved with me and soft in a way he hasn't been before. I nearly left, thinking maybe he just needed space and wasn't telling me, but I thought better of it.

I messaged: *I have work I can do too, do you mind if I stop by later tonight?*

His response told me everything I needed to know: *I'd love it if you did.*

So with all these nerves still wreaking havoc inside of me, and the realization that I'm head over heels for a man and I think he may be head over heels for me too, I crack open the door to his office.

"Adrian," I call out, saying his name as if to gauge whether or not he's done even though he told me if I came up at nine he should be finished.

Sitting at his desk, Adrian runs his hands over his hair. "Suzette," he responds, my name a murmur on his lips. His stress is apparent even from the door.

"Come have a drink with me," he offers and I instantly relax.

I go around his desk and fold my arms around him from behind, resting my chin on his shoulder. He leans into me for a kiss on the cheek and I feel like I could burst with all the things that threaten to spill out of me. There are so many things that I can't decide what to say first. That I love him? That I'm in love with him? It feels almost childish, raw and vulnerable. It doesn't escape me that I'm insecure and he hasn't given me a reason not to be. I'm holding back and he hasn't as far as I know. This is the part of the relationship where it doesn't feel even.

He may be my boss, the devil in a suit, rich and powerful and I'm lowly compared to him on the surface of it all, but I've never felt inferior. Not until now.

Not until I've realized how I feel and that I'm terrified to admit it, just in case he doesn't feel the same.

Adrian turns his face to mine and stands up, pushing his chair out of the way before I can speak. I can taste alcohol on him. He's been drinking, no doubt to get rid of the stresses of the day, though it's a good stress. At least I thought it was. The numbers are good and I'm excited for our meeting next week. I'm not sure what it will entail but I already have a business plan laid out. It'll be wonderful, I can reassure him of that.

"I need you," he whispers against the crook of my neck and the warmth of his breath forces my head to fall back and desire spreads through me like wildfire.

He's almost frantic at my clothes, pushing my skirt up and lifting me onto the desk. A gasp leaves me and it's all too welcomed. Maybe he needs this as much as I do. Adrian strips off my panties with an efficient movement as he looks me in the eyes, his emotions running through them too fast for me to name them all. He undoes his belt and zipper and pushes into me with the same ferocity he used that first day. He's not shy about putting his hands on my body wherever he wants them. He touches me everywhere he can reach, with a firm grip on my thighs and my hips. Adrian fucks me in the way I love him to, with possessive strokes. Pleasure pools between my legs at how close he is and how intimate it is to be used like this.

My nails dig into his shoulder as I moan his name. His thrusts are merciless and the pleasure builds and builds without warning.

We're in danger of knocking things off the desk now and it's so hot to see him unraveling like this.

All too soon, I come first and then he follows. It's only when he leaves me, both of us still catching our breath that I realize he's fully clothed.

"Would you want me still if I couldn't afford it?" His question came out of nowhere.

"What?" My head is cloudy with lust and my legs still tremble as I try to gather what he's said. "Afford what?"

"To support the split. To fund the company during the changes."

I pull back so I can look into his eyes, following his movements as he undoes his tie and then reaches into his desk for tissues, no doubt to clean up. I'm surprised that he's talking business after six, let alone the second he finished inside of me. Of all the things I want to respond, I want to tease him about it, to lighten it and allay any worries he has.

Before any words can leave me, his gaze pins me. It's one of a wounded man. The same vulnerability that plagued me all day stares back at me.

"I couldn't give two shits if you have money. I don't care." The last couple of days play through my mind. "Is that what's been bothering you?" I ask. "Is it because of my department? I mean it, Adrian." I lick my lips, rushing my words out and praying he understands just how much I mean it. "If you don't want to save the department, if it has to go … I would still want you."

His pace has slowed, but it's as if he can't bring himself to end this conversation. Adrian looks down and I swallow hard.

"Adrian. I swear to you. If you need to tell me something, it's okay." Reaching for the box of tissues and taking it from him, I attempt to convince him. "If you need to tell me something, you can." There's an ache that starts in my chest, but it works its way outward. "I'll still want you."

His pale blue eyes come back to mine again. "Suzette."

"Jobs come and go." I get a lump in my throat from unshed tears and my love for him. *How did this even happen?* I've never wanted to cover myself more, but I'm on his desk and my clothes are on the floor. "Just like clients. I love my job. I love what I do, and I believe in it. But if something were to happen …" Feeling his eyes on my naked body like this makes me even more emotional. Adrian is so connected to this job for me. I met him here, even though he came to change everything. I don't know whether I'm just clinging to those memories or if I'm genuinely afraid to lose my job. "If funding fell through …" He doesn't react at all, other than to pull my hips to the edge of the desk and rest his forehead against mine. "If it all fell to shit and was taken away …"

"Hush."

I do hush, because I can tell what he wants right now is to lose ourselves in the pleasure of this moment.

"I need you again," he whispers and I'm shocked as he pushes me back. Still hard, still demanding and as rough as he was earlier.

"I want you and I'll always want you," he tells me between thrusts, his voice thick with emotion. My lips crash against his and a wave of emotion spreads through me.

I want to tell him, "That's all that matters." But words fail me and strangled moans are all I can offer him.

He groans, "I need more of you."

I spread my legs wide for him and brace my hands on the desk so he can fuck me as hard as he likes. "Come for me," he whispers in my ear, and heat explodes between my thighs in clenching pulses that make him groan and pulse. When he's finished he pulls me off the desk and into his chair. I'm straddling him now, his hands on my waist, and I try to catch my breath so I can continue our conversation.

Even if he doesn't want to. Even if it means being too open, too raw, too needy. I just need him to know exactly how I feel.

"Listen to me." I take his hand and put it to my chest. "I would survive. I could start my company from scratch. I might not be able to keep the clients, but I would find more. I don't want you because you can support me, if that's what you're worried about. I want you for you. God knows I hated the idea of you when I first saw you but I—" I swallow, and chicken out, backing away from the truth I'm too scared to voice. "I want you." It's all that I can say.

It's true. If I learned one thing from my divorce, it's that I'll always be able to find a way to support myself. I might worry about it but if the occasion arises, I'll handle it. That's what it means to be a woman in the world. You always have to be able to find a way.

I put both my hands on the sides of his face. "Are you all right?"

He strokes my cheek. "It was only a question. I didn't mean to make you worry."

"If I should worry, you would tell me, wouldn't you?"

He looks deep into my eyes and pulls me in for another kiss. This one is deep and slow and it's like he wants to memorize every part of me. "You don't have to worry," Adrian whispers against my lips. "I want you."

"I want you too." I pull his lip between my teeth and add a little pressure so he can feel it. His deep groan is everything I needed to hear.

Adrian's already hard beneath me again, so it takes nothing to lift myself up and ease back down on his thick length. It's a sweeter connection this time, though he's just as possessive with me. I lean down and kiss him while we move together. Adrian can't help but take control, making his thrusts deeper and harder, and it feels so good that it brings on another orgasm. It moves through my body and makes me tip my head back with the kind of ecstasy I've been looking for all this time for so long. I never thought I'd find it again and I found it here in Adrian. Here in this most forbidden of arrangements.

When it's over I open my eyes and look into his. He's watching me with heat in his expression and love too. "I love you," I tell him.

He groans and pulls me down onto his cock, fucking me as deep as he ever has. He holds on tightly, as if he never wants to let me go, but he doesn't say it back.

chapter 21

Adrian

"The penthouse in Tribeca is five million," I speak clearly, standing in the office and imagining how this office in the high-rise could easily double for temporary housing. I'll take the meetings in the conference room. "I'll sell the furniture with it, that should bring it up another million."

"Business shouldn't affect your personal—"

"We tallied the numbers with the other assets," I repeat to my father. My financial advisor is on the phone as well. He's seen the contract, he knows what deals went down. More importantly, he has a tally of every investment I have. I simply can't lose the majority of them. If I sell now, I'll lose so much more than the current value. There is only so much that can give. "I'll find somewhere cheaper, and that's far better than losing investments or paying the interest."

My financial manager, Sean, speaks through the line, "I agree and there are plenty of other markets on the upswing. It could be beneficial in the long run."

"There's no reason not to sell the list and dissolve the—" My father attempts to chime in. If I didn't respect him as much as I do, I'd tell him to fuck off. To get off the line. To get out of my business. But as it stands, he's my father. He's just as involved in this deal as he has been in the others. He's my mentor and I know he means well. That list and Suzette's departments are nonnegotiable.

I told her I would protect her. And I meant it.

"Yes, there is."

"I saw the deals, Adrian. Why the hell are you doing this? I didn't raise you to—"

"Because she'll hate me," I bite out, forming a fist as my muscles coil. "This is a business call. If you cannot remain professional, I will take the call alone as I would have preferred to do."

"Who is she?"

"It's personal. I'm keeping that investment and I want you to respect that."

"It's worth you losing your home?"

"It's worth me losing everything." The amount of rage is equal to my desperation. Chaos swarms in my blood. "I cannot lose her."

There's silence on the line before an awkward cough from my advisor. Sean states the numbers we've gone over a hundred times in the last six hours.

"If she would hate you for it, then she's not the one for you." My father's tone is somber and before I can say anything else, there's a click on the line.

"Adrian?" Sean questions, "Are you still there?"

"Yes, it was my father who left." There's a hollowness in my chest that fills with a mix of emotions. "Where were we?" I say and then sit back down in the chair.

The money, the power—none of it means anything if I can't have her.

Keeping Sean on speaker, I text my father: *She doesn't know any of this and I don't want her to. I love her and you will too when you meet her.*

I know it's the right thing to do by her. I can make this work. I can have it all.

I text him again before he responds. *Maybe hate was strong. She would be upset, but she wouldn't hate me. I want to do everything I can for her. You need to trust me on this.*

All she needs is this chance. I believe in her and I'll make the money back. I'll be a man worthy of a woman like her.

I just don't know how to tell her or if I even should.

"If we could touch base about the article today," my advisor starts, "it does not seem to be as telling as we were led to believe." I was given a heads-up yesterday that Wyatt's dealing would make headlines. It's a scandal in the making given how the property deal went down.

"I was able to pull some strings," I tell him.

"Have you gotten any pushback from investors? Any concerned calls?"

"A few." My brow pinches at remembering the early calls and emails this morning, wanting to know whether or not the deals would still be going through. "As far as I know, everyone is satisfied."

"Excellent. I know this isn't ideal, but this is manageable. I do, however, recommend not signing any contracts of that magnitude until the lawyers have approved. I spoke with Carly and she told me she had not finished negotiations."

I can only nod, remembering how light I felt, signing that contract … with Suzette on my mind. With Wyatt's approval, about her. Coming to terms with how I'd fallen for her.

"I was distracted," I admit to him.

"Whatever it was, see to it that this doesn't happen again. There's only so much we can do and next time it may not be salvageable."

The knock at my door is hesitant and then Andrea opens it without waiting for a response. It comes at the same time that a text comes through.

"Not now," I tell Andrea who nods and closes the door softly.

I thought it would be my father, but it's Suzette.

I want you. I love you for you. I don't need your money, and I wouldn't think less of you if you weren't in the position you're in.

As if this day could get any harder. I know she loves me. And I'm going to prove to her that I love her back. Words aren't enough.

"It will be tight for a few months unless something breaks. We can file for a few extensions. It will get you through and we can keep it discreet, but you do not have leverage to spend for the time being."

"I understand." A heat tingles the back of my neck. This position I'm in is less than ideal. I can't blame Wyatt. The blame squarely falls on my shoulders.

Sean twists the knife even more. "For all intents and purposes, you are broke."

"I know, Sean. I know what it means."

There's another knock on my door, more forceful than before.

"Mr. Bradford," Andrea speaks up and her tone makes it evident that whatever it is, it needs to be said now.

"I'll call you back shortly," I tell Sean and hang up before he can respond as Andrea walks in. The door closes behind her. Dressed in loose gray pants and a billowy white top, she's nothing but professional.

"What is it?" I question.

"I made a mistake," she tells me, not taking the seat she stands behind.

"We all do," I say, attempting to ease any worries she has, but her expression doesn't appear to reflect that. There's not a worry line in sight.

"The error in the contract with Mr. Wyatt Patton's—" she starts.

I still, my blood going cold. "What about it? What error?"

"I sent in half of the contract signed, but the second half ... Somehow," she says and gestures in the air, a shrug rolling from her shoulders, "I faxed it over unsigned." Her lips quirk up at the end. As if she knows.

Of course she does.

"Andrea." My head falls into my hands for only a moment, the relief waning as if this isn't real. "Could you repeat that, please?" I swallow thickly, praying that what I heard her say is exactly what she did say.

"From what I can tell," she tells me, now taking the seat slowly, "I must have had some questions and somehow I mixed up the paperwork."

"I have to call my lawyer," I tell her, still in a state of disbelief, my hands nearly trembling. If she's serious, if she didn't send it … It's twenty million that she saved me.

"I thought you might say that." She pats the desk before standing. "She distracts you, but like I've always told you, I've got your back."

"I could kiss you—"

"Please don't," she says jokingly.

"I don't know how to repay you," I tell her softly before she can leave, still not truly believing. Not until I see it myself and not until it's confirmed.

chapter 22

Suzette

I DON'T THINK I'VE EVER BEEN SO NERVOUS FOR A DINNER DATE. THIS man has fucked every part of me, he's seen me break down and punished me in ways a younger me wouldn't understand.

He knows me and every inch of me. And that's what scares me. He could crush me so very easily and it would take far more than a bottle of rosé at Maddie's to get over him.

In the back of his car, with Adrian's driver taking me through the city, I sit alone. According to Noah, he's to take me to dinner and Adrian is meeting me there.

I play it off as if I'm not nervous at all. As if tonight doesn't feel different. As if that's a perfectly normal thing to happen. It's a perfect New York City evening. The sunset is a watercolor painting above the buildings, slowly growing darker as the few stars we can see appear high above us.

I'm in love with him, and no matter what he says, I think he loves me too. My heart beats faster with every minute that passes on the drive, and I can't concentrate on my phone. Finally, I put it in my purse and ignore it completely. All the emails I need to send can wait.

I don't miss Noah's eyes peeking back at me and the third time I meet them, I cave.

"Is he going to break up with me?" I question, my voice squeakier than I'd have liked, though I know he's not the person I should be asking.

His head tilts a bit and if I'm not mistaken, the wrinkles that form around his eyes indicate that he's smiling although I can't see that part of his face. "I didn't think you were dating, Ms. Parks."

I laugh, feeling a little less nervous. "Very funny." My fingers fidget among themselves.

He laughs back at me. "He would be a fool to do such a thing. And Mr. Bradford isn't a fool." I can only nod in agreement although I don't feel entirely reassured.

"Besides, we're here so it's a little too late to run."

Peeking out through the tinted window, my gaze focuses on a tempting man in a suit. Heat flows through me seeing Adrian's waiting for me on the sidewalk. He pulls the door open for me before I know what's happening. I step out, slipping my hand into his to keep my balance.

"I'll take it from here," he tells Noah, and that's when I see we're at the Waldorf again. Glancing down at my office attire, I give Adrian a look and he only smirks back.

"If you'd like to go shopping first," he offers although I'm certain it's more for comic relief than anything else.

"You are a devilish man," I comment, and move to stand beside him, his hand still holding mine.

His rough chuckle is a soothing balm. "You look gorgeous," he reassures me.

With every step, the nervousness lingers but it's different now that I'm with him. Maybe it's the way he holds me, or the way he peers down at me. The way his hand splays against my back as we walk in or how he helps me into the booth. I'm not sure what it is, but I want it all.

I would give him everything I have today, for him to simply want me tomorrow.

Adrian

"Sir, another?" the waiter asks, politely gathering my attention. If I recall correctly, he's the same waiter we had our first night at the Waldorf, our dinner that never came to be.

The same tucked away booth as well.

I shake my head once. "Thank you, though."

"And for you?" he asks Suzette.

"I'd like dessert I think," she says and gazes back at me as if asking if I'd like to join her.

I only smile back, feeling the nerves heat.

"Maybe the dark chocolate tart?" the waiter suggests and I pray I don't show my reaction in the least.

When the plate comes out, her diamond will be on it. My composure threatens to break when she agrees.

I've gone over every response she could have.

If she says it's too soon, I'll respond, if not now, then when?

If she thinks I've gone crazy, I'll agree, I am losing it because of her.

It doesn't matter what she thinks of it, so long as she says yes. So long as she's mine to have and to hold, to be with me forever. For fuck's sake, if she thinks it has to do with work, I'll tell her how I signed a damn contract I shouldn't have because I couldn't get her off my mind. That alone should convince a businesswoman like her that she should say yes before I go broke drowning in thoughts of her all day.

"Are you all right?" Suzette questions and it's only when I look up to see her glancing at the cocktail napkin in my hand that I realize I've twisted and pulled and creased it to death.

"Fine," I answer her and in my periphery I see the waiter slipping the plate down in front of her.

My heart races and I tell her that I'm perfectly fine and wait.

Her gaze doesn't leave mine. Even when I motion to her dessert, spotting the four-carat diamond sparking from where it sits in the red velvet box.

"I just—" Suzette starts and then licks her lips. "I know I'm … I know that I—" she hesitates. This gorgeous, intelligent, strong-willed woman hesitates, because of me.

Because I didn't say *I love you* back. I know damn well that's why.

"I want you to marry me," I murmur, unable to hold it back any longer.

Her kissable lips part and her light blue eyes widen. "Adrian."

I motion to the ring on her plate and she gasps, a loud yelp of a gasp, covering her mouth and jumping back slightly.

She stares at it, as if I'm not waiting, unable to breathe and desperate for her to answer me.

"Marry me," I tell her, a command this time and that gets her attention. Her hands lower, although she still stares at me as if she's in shock.

"For the love of all things holy, if you don't say yes right now, I swear to God I'll throw you over this table."

When she smiles, this beautiful smile that reaches all the way up to her eyes, I know it'll be all right.

"I love you," she tells me, her cadence soothing.

"That isn't a yes and I'm going to need you to say—"

"Yes," she says in a breathy voice and it takes everything in me not to topple the table as I rush to her.

To kiss her. To hold her. "I love you too," I tell her the moment she breaks our kiss. "I love you and I need you with me."

Her eyes shine back with every emotion I feel stirring inside of me.

"I love you and I want you, and I need you too."

Epilogue

THE CITY NEVER SLEEPS. IT PROVIDES A CONSTANT LIGHT AS IT SLIPS into the office. Even at nearly 1:00 a.m.

With a deep breath in, I lie back, nestling beside Adrian on the pullout sofa. His smell surrounds me, fresh and clean with a hint of sandalwood, and so do his arms as he wraps them around me, planting a kiss on my forehead.

This is how we've slept for the last two weeks nearly. He stays with me, working and taking calls, while I do the same.

The numbers are promising, but not guaranteed.

"Was it a good day?" he asks me, his chest rumbling as his hand runs down my back.

"A great day. Gail secured the final client."

"That makes me happy to hear," he comments and although exhaustion coats his tone, I know he truly is happy. It was shaky at first. A number of clients debated on leaving, and they all wanted to renegotiate. Gail took the brunt of it.

"Me too," I say and then ask him, "And what about you? Any updates from Wyatt?"

His friend got into a bad deal. I'm not certain of the details but I know it's been rough on him and it involves politicians and a lawsuit and some other developer.

I was nervous at first that it might involve my friend's husband, Mason. He's a developer and I've heard whispers about the depths of corruption that surround him and his family.

He loves Jules, though, and she swears he's one of the good ones. Thankfully, he wasn't involved.

"He'll be all right, but the next few years will be difficult for him. The loan I gave him will help, but he's in for a hellish year if not longer."

"And what about the contract?" Again, the details are murky, but I know at some point, Adrian had signed on to some piece of this shit show.

"It's null and void. Even if I'd signed, he said it was his mistake, we'd never discussed it and he would deal with the fallout."

"He's a good friend."

"He's a good man. Not everyone survives the lows, but he will."

"You still seem down," I comment.

"Just a long day," he says and settles higher up on the bed, "and my little whore has been ignoring me at work."

"It's after six, we're not supposed to talk about work," I tease him, sitting up slightly to nip his bottom lip. He gives me a gruff groan and I love it.

"Hey," I whisper and nudge my nose against his, "I want you."

He hums, that sound I crave before giving me the command, "Roll over."

Heat rushes to my cheeks and I do as he says, laying on my stomach and watching him pull the white T-shirt over his head. This sexy powerful man who comes undone just for me. It's heady, and I'll never get enough of it.

My eyes close when he kisses my neck with the same passion we had the first day.

"Be a good little slut for me, and get on your knees."

I fuck my boss every night in his office.

And I love it.

I love him.

sealed with a kiss

USA TODAY BESTSELLING AUTHORS

Willow Winters
& Amelia Wilde

We made a deal … one I thought I'd never make.

I'm trying not to judge myself but it's a bit shameful.

Rent was due and I simply didn't have it. I love the big city and I've
done everything I could to make it. But after a rough few years, a
breakup that nearly destroyed me, and a personal issue that I just can't
talk about…I'm broke and hit rock bottom.

Then there's Graham.

Richer than most could ever imagine, devilishly handsome with a charming
smile, and a sparkle in his eyes that I swear is just for me.

He owns the building, and now once a month when the rent is due, he gets a
piece of me I can't believe I agreed to give. His lips on mine are addictive, and
the way he groans my name in pleasure is scorched into my memory.

We sealed it with a kiss, and I'm all too aware that the next rock bottom for me
will lead to nothing but despair and a broken heart.

Prologue

Maddie

SOME NIGHTS ARE MEANT TO BE PERFECT, AND THIS IS ONE OF THEM. My fingers are thread through my fiancé's, Kevin's, hand as we step into the elevator in our building, my shiny new engagement ring glinting on my left hand. After a year together getting engaged is the natural—perfect—progression. We met on a blind date, moved in together three months later, and tonight he popped the question on our one-year anniversary at one of New York's most exclusive, expensive restaurants.

It could have been a scene out of a movie. Our table, with its pristine table-cloth, candles, and fine china, was completely surrounded by people who *beamed* at us, like our romance is one for the ages.

Because it *is* one for the ages. Even the waiters and waitresses clapped for us, looking genuinely happy, and I felt a little buzzed on the complimentary cham-pagne and cake and the *happiness*.

This is bliss. I've always been called a hopeless romantic and a decade in this city has put me through the ringer. It was all worth it though. I always knew I'd find my happily ever after.

Kevin pushes the button for our floor, his bicep flexing under my hand. A simper slips into place, and I feel the hint of a blush in my chest. I love the way he feels. The way he smells, the way he does everything.

Tonight makes the last few years feel like they've come to a close. Like I'm ready for my new chapter. I hesitate to call them bad, because that's a negative way to spin things when everything in my life has brought me to this moment.

No, they weren't bad years, but they were…challenging.

Yes. That's the right word. They were *challenging*. I went through a nasty breakup and needed a lot of late-night texting with Suzette, who's like a big sister to me. The whole situation made me feel young and naive, which in a way, I was.

Maybe I still am.

But I don't feel young and naive. I feel like a woman who's finally got her life figured out. I rose from the ashes of that boyfriend and found a man who loves me enough to marry me. I've upgraded my apartment from a teeny, tiny one-bedroom with secondhand furniture to a luxury apartment where everything's brand new and as perfect as my recent engagement. The only sign of my former life is the crocheted blanket from my grandmother, which the cleaning staff takes special care to smooth over the back of the couch every week.

The elevator lifts off with smooth acceleration.

That's probably why my stomach drops a little. It's just the elevator, not my nerves or any subconscious feeling that life can't be this good.

The future is going to be as perfect as the present. Our reflection stares back at us from the silver elevator doors. Kevin bought my wine-red dress and paid for the hair appointment that turned my dark brunette hair into gorgeous, shining waves. It feels too good to be true.

As we wait for the ding of our level, I go over my to-do list in my head, rubbing my thumb in soothing circles on his forearm. Next week, I'll refocus on my charity work. None of the positions Kevin's gotten me are paid, but they don't have to be. He told me he makes enough money that I don't have to work.

It's perfect, I remind myself again, leaning against his arm just slightly.

He doesn't lean closer to me. He's watching our reflection with a frown, like his mind is miles away. That nervous feeling comes over me again and I peer up at him, waiting for him to look back down. He doesn't.

The elevator slows, and Kevin lets out a harsh sigh. We live on the eighth floor and this is only the fourth.

"You okay?" I squeeze his arm, feeling the brand-new weight of the engagement ring on my finger.

"I just want to get home."

It takes effort for my expression to stay even and not show my shock and slight disappointment. Kevin's tone doesn't reflect a newly engaged man. I'd expected… passion, maybe. That he'd want to push me up against the wall of the elevator and kiss me until we got upstairs. I feel all these bundles of desire and want, but it's obvious he doesn't feel the same.

Kevin just sounds tired.

He seemed happy enough at the restaurant, though, so…

Maybe he *is* tired. Maybe he's desperate to get to our bedroom so he can get out of his suit and spread me out on the covers. Maybe he's as excited to continue the next phase of our perfect life as I am, he just needs a minute to collect himself.

It's good. This is good. My life is just the way I wanted it when I was living in that one-bedroom apartment, my heart aching from the breakup and my head spinning from how confused and angry I felt at my ex.

This is supposed to be the reward for coming this far. For healing my heart finding a new man and accepting everything life had to offer. This is the prize at the end of the race. I love New York City, and I love my life in it, and I've loved it hard enough to convince it to love me back.

The elevator comes to a stop on the fourth floor, and the doors slide open to reveal a man in a suit that looks more expensive than Kevin's. It's crisp and tailored perfectly. He moves into the elevator with confident strides and takes his place next to me, then leans forward to press the button for the sixth floor. The air fills with the masculine scent of his cologne and all it takes is one inhale.

One single breath and I'm drawn to him. I can't help stealing a glance in the reflection. He's tall, with dark hair and carved features. As he straightens from pushing the button, his eyes catch mine. They're so blue—*so* blue that my breath catches.

I look away, my pulse racing. This isn't how a woman is supposed to feel about a man who isn't her fiancé. I'm not falling in love with him. It's not one of those fairy-tale scenarios. I'm past believing in those.

But I can't bring myself to look away. My eyes keep finding him in the reflection.

The elevator glides upward again. My heart races and I chide myself for feeling anything in the slightest.

We only have a few moments together. The elevators in this building are fast, and he's only going up two floors. I try to make it seem like I'm not staring, but I am, and that's how I notice when he looks at me.

His eyes linger on my body in the reflection, trailing down the dress Kevin bought for me.

Any thoughts of him are a mistake. I shut them down quickly, holding onto Kevin's arm with both hands.

Because the moment I tear my eyes off the stranger, I become aware of Kevin watching both of us with a clenched jaw. Kevin dislodges my hold on his arm and puts his hand on the small of my back.

His possessiveness takes me by surprise but I lean into it. Staring straight ahead as if the man isn't even here.

I do not want any part of being kissed or touched by a stranger in a nice suit who happens to have one of the most gorgeous faces I've ever seen.

My face gets hot at my imagined fantasy of this stranger kissing me in the way I wish Kevin would. That's all it is—a fantasy. A short, unasked-for fantasy that's only happening because of the champagne and the excitement of the evening.

That's all. I clear my throat and shake the odd thoughts off, ignoring the prying eyes I swear I can still feel on me.

The elevator stops, and the man next to me shifts his weight to leave.

His elbow brushes against mine.

The fabric of his suit brushes against my bare elbow and it feels as sensual as a kiss, almost as intimate as one. He didn't have to touch me—there's room in the elevator for him to get in and out with zero contact—but he did, and it's electric.

What's going on with me? Electricity over a man's suit?

He turns his head as he reaches the doors. "Good night."

His voice matches his impeccable suit and his gorgeous face. It's low and rich and somehow, deep in my bones, sounds familiar.

"Good night," Kevin snaps.

The other man doesn't seem to notice the bite in Kevin's tone. As the doors begin to close, he turns to go down the hall and looks back in at me. His eyes are still locked on mine when the doors shut completely, cutting me off from him.

He was an attractive man, and I couldn't help but notice. He doesn't have anything to do with me and Kevin.

He doesn't.

"What a prick," Kevin mumbles under his breath.

I actually don't think we can fault the man for using the same elevator, but I don't say that. I slip my hand into Kevin's instead.

"Don't worry about him." I smile up at my new fiancé. "Think about us. This is our big night."

"You're right about that." He turns my hand in his and runs the pad of his thumb over my ring. "You're mine now."

"Now?" I joke. "Wasn't I yours before? Or does it only count once we've made vows?"

Kevin frowns, not even giving me a courtesy laugh.

The elevator takes us up the remaining floors, and I step close to him and try to communicate that everything is normal. Better than normal. It's the start of our forever.

There's always a comedown when you do something special, right? The adrenaline fades. Soon we'll be in bed together, and the guy in the elevator won't matter at all.

I'm not going to think about him again.

I don't think about him when the elevator doors open, or when Kevin takes us inside the apartment. I don't think about him while I slip into the lingerie I put on Kevin's card earlier this morning. I don't think about him when Kevin takes me to bed and we have fast, perfunctory sex that unfortunately doesn't do the trick.

I don't think about him when I'm lying on the pillows afterward, Kevin already breathing deeply beside me.

I really don't think about him. Not his blue eyes, not the way his suit fit on his body, and not the way he brushed his arm against my elbow like he just had to touch me, even if it was through his clothes.

I don't think about him at all when I lift up my hand in the dark and watch the diamond catch the tiniest glimmers of light.

I don't think about him when I find the texts on Kevin's phone a week later.

I don't think about him when the woman comes to confront me a few days after that.

I don't think about him when my world falls apart and I'm left feeling foolish and naive and alone again.

All I think about is how well and truly fucked I am and how my happily ever after turned into a nightmare.

chapter 1

Graham

SOMETIMES, WHEN I'M ON MY WAY BACK FROM A BUSINESS MEETING, I stop across the street from the luxury apartments I own and take it all in. It's a modern building. Clean. A wrought-iron fence surrounds a narrow lawn out front with a bricked-in path leading to the doors adding old city charm. All of it is tended by a team of landscapers who maintain the property daily. I'm not the person who built it from the ground up, but I bought it and made it mine.

On afternoons like this one, the building represents the epitome of my success. It would have been a dream come true for my parents to see how far I've come. They didn't grow up with money and when I first saw this place it reminded me of a make-believe house my mother used to say we would have one day. My father worked too hard for too little and died too young to enjoy it. My mom couldn't bear to live without him. Once I was alone in the world, I swore I wouldn't have that kind of life.

I wouldn't settle for just getting by.

The apartments should be proof that I've more than reached those goals. Everything about them is meant to remind people that they're home, and that home is somewhere important. That's why the front facade is pristine and white. That's why the windows shine in the sun. That's why plants rise above the rooftop.

It means everything to me.

Or at least it should.

But sometimes, when I'm coming back from a business meeting, I look at the building and think I have a hell of a long way to go before I'll feel like I've made it.

Today's one of those days.

A lunch meeting about a property I'm hoping to acquire ran long. I don't have a good feeling about how things are going, which only makes me more determined to see it through. It's twice as large as the luxury apartment building that's been my personal pet project for the last five years, and it will mean leveling up.

Though some part of me wonders what's next *after* that. Some part of me is already looking ahead to even bigger things. There's never enough. There's never a stopping point.

Right now, I'm separated from the building—technically, my home—by two lanes of traffic. The cars move past in a steady stream. For a moment, I could be anyone at all. A stranger in New York City. I could be the man I was ten years ago, staring at buildings like this and swearing I'd get there someday. I'd own a penthouse here.

Now I own more than one building, but something's still missing.

There's an emptiness no amount of money can fill, and it's more and more apparent every passing day.

With my gaze moving to the yellow light, I wait for the traffic to stop before I cross. The sidewalk in front of my building is busy. A couple passes by me, focused on each other, and I look away.

My mind wanders back to the woman in the elevator.

I haven't stepped into an elevator in six months without thinking of her.

The woman. Dark hair. Dark eyes. A look in her eyes that I haven't forgotten. A red dress that clung to every curve on her body like it was made just for her. For all I know, it was.

She was standing in the elevator with another man, which should have been enough to make me forget her instantly. Immediately. I don't fuck with women who are already involved with someone else, certainly none who have a ring on their finger.

Lucky for me, remembering a person isn't the same as getting involved with them.

It would be convenient if I could stop thinking about her, though. If I could stop thinking of the way her eyes met mine in the reflection of the gleaming door. I felt something just from her dark eyes on mine. Sensed something in the air. Her perfume had been all around her, and it made me want to do something crazy. Something like…lean in and kiss the side of her neck even while she had her hand on another man's arm.

He was nothing compared to her. Even the way her breath hitched was fascinating.

I've thought about the way her breasts rose and fell underneath her dress every damn day for six months. Like whatever had come over me was felt by her as well.

Attempting to rid her of my mind and ignoring the fact that I have to ride that damn elevator again, that it may have hints of her perfume if she's ridden it today, I stride into my building.

I head into the lobby, scanning to make sure everything's as it should be. Custom tiled flooring is polished and shining. Custom sconces on the walls have every bulb burning. The doormen behind the desk are properly uniformed and both of them nod to me as I go by.

It's the weekend, but I'm headed back to my office, not to the penthouse. I don't want to stand in the elevator and think about her. Beyond that, my personal space is as luxurious as the rest of the building. Obviously—I wouldn't settle when it came to that, either.

Sometimes, despite all the high-end furnishings and the professional kitchen and the miles of extra space, it still feels empty.

I could have my pick of dates and outings, but after a meeting like that one, I'm not in the mood.

My office space on the fifth floor is lit from the outside. I'm not planning to turn on any lights. I'm barely past my secretary's desk when my phone buzzes in my pocket.

The number on the screen is an unfamiliar one. It could be one of the people from the meeting, wanting to continue the conversation, and my pulse pumps harder at the thought. I could tackle some of this bullshit today. Find my footing as far as the deal goes.

I accept the call. "Graham Maxwell."

"Hi," a woman says. She wasn't at the meeting. Her voice heats something low in my torso. "I mean—hello, Mr. Maxwell. My name is Madelyn Cunnigham. I live on the eighth floor of your West Grove apartments."

I stare out my office windows, hardly seeing the cityscape outside. "I think you're looking for the building manager, Ms. Cunnigham."

"No. No. I was looking for you."

"Were you?" I entertain the conversation for no other reason than because *that* woman lived on the eighth floor. I allow myself to imagine it's her, although I'm careful with my thoughts. I'm more giving than I should be.

"Yes. I was hoping to have a conversation." My gaze drops as her tone turns with slight desperation. "The building manager sent me your way as…I'm having a difficulty I am hoping you could help me with. If you had a few minutes. I wouldn't take up much of your time, I promise."

"Something wrong with your apartment? A broken appliance? Because I can direct you to the weekend maintenance team."

"All the appliances are fine, but there's a slight emergency."

I move closer to my desk in case this woman with the beautiful voice has panicked and called *me* instead of the fire department.

"Fire? Flood?"

"Neither of those," she says quickly. "Nothing's on fire. I just wanted a conversation. I need to have a conversation with you." I like the way *need to have a conversation with you* sounds. "I could meet you in your office or…or anywhere, really. I'm right upstairs. I can be ready on a moment's notice."

"How about this? I'll come to you." I have no idea what's happening here, but I intend to find out. "Which unit are you in?"

"Unit 8A."

"All right." I pull the chair out from behind my desk. "Are you sure you don't need the fire department?" I attempt to add a touch of humor to ease her concerns.

"I'm completely sure," she promises.

"Give me five minutes."

"Okay. Thank you so…thank you. I'll be here."

The call disconnects, and I tap my password into my computer. I'm not going up to the eighth floor without some basic information in my back pocket.

I have the lease agreement in a few clicks. Not much here. There's Madelyn's name listed underneath a guy named Kevin. My stomach sinks, but I ignore that. I don't have any reason to be disappointed. I liked the sound of her voice. That's all. The odds that she's the woman in the red dress are low I tell myself. There are thirty-some apartments on that level.

Now I have no choice but to think about the woman in the elevator. She's a welcome distraction from thinking about this woman on the phone.

I go out and push the call button.

There're plenty of other things to occupy my mind. I own properties all over New York City. None compare to this building, which is my pride and joy, but they all add to the considerable balances in my bank accounts.

I'm richer by the second. Money piles up even as I step into the elevator and hit the button for the eighth floor.

The doors close and I can almost see her there in that dress, with those hooded eyes. If she stood just behind me, most of her body would be hidden by mine. If I turned around to touch her…

I'm not thinking about this. I'm not thinking about some mystery woman, who lives in this building that I own, with whoever the hell was in the elevator with her that night.

The elevator stops at the eighth floor and the doors open. One of the doormen is waiting in the hall and he steps back with a deferential nod. "Mr. Maxwell."

"Tom."

He waits for me to exit, then takes my place in the elevator.

I'm alone in the hall. Compared to how loud the city is, even a space like this—a hallway meant to take people from place to place and not much more— feels luxurious. I made sure it was that way. I insisted on plush carpeting, crown molding, and neutral paint colors with a hint of warmth. This place isn't institutional. This is a home for people who need an escape. An oasis.

The only person it's not an escape for is me.

I own the building. I headquarter my business here. I live in the penthouse. There's not a square inch of this building that's meant for anything but making money, and that's what I intend to do. Double it. Triple it. Become so unfathomably rich that I can forget about my past entirely and never have worries or burdens like the ones I grew up with, the ones that put my father into an early grave.

And this…this isn't an errand that will make me any money.

I don't pay house calls. I have people for that.

Today, I'm making an exception.

That's her door. 8A.

I raise my hand and knock, not expecting to see her there. Staring wide-eyed at me in a simple yet elegant red dress like we're back in that elevator.

Fuck me.

Maddie

THIS IS IT.

This is *it*.

I move quickly through the apartment and call out, "I'm coming," in what I hope is a calm, confident voice. I'm definitely not calm or confident. That means faking it is my only option.

I take a deep breath and open the door, not prepared for a wave of air to be pulled from my lungs.

Graham Maxwell is gorgeous. That's the first thought that comes to mind. He's tall and dark haired with the kind of face that belongs in the movies. Blue eyes that look me up and down with a kind of heated curiosity. The sight of him makes my heart race and my palms sweaty.

"Oh!" I blurt out, because…oh my God. It's him—the man from the elevator. I'm reminded of that night all over again. And then the pain that happened afterward. "We've met before. Or…I saw you in an elevator before."

He flashes me a smile that's all charm. He is a million times more confident than I am when he offers me his hand to shake. "Graham Maxwell."

I take it, immediately overwhelmed by how solid and strong it feels. His touch is hot and I have to pull my hand away sooner than I'd like. I slip my hand out of his, concentrating hard on keeping my breathing steady. "Maddie."

"Maddie," he murmurs my name, like he's testing it out. The way he says it is nearly sinful.

That buzz between us is still there. I can *feel* it, just like I felt it for those thirty seconds in the elevator six months ago.

"Please. Come in. Can I offer you anything to drink?" I swallow thickly, attempting to calm myself down. I keep telling myself it'll be okay even if this doesn't work out, but I know it's a lie. I need him to help me, or the downward spiral of my life is going to get even worse.

"I think we'd better cut to the chase." His voice makes it hard to think. "On the phone, you said you had an…urgent problem to discuss."

My face gets hot. I knew what I was asking for when I made that phone call. Actually having him in my apartment is overwhelming. "Let's sit down. Is that okay?"

He hesitates; his hands find their way into his suit pockets. I watch his Adam's apple as he swallows, and I admire the way the cords in his neck tighten. Every inch of him could be cut from marble. "Lead the way."

I take him to the living room and tuck myself into a loveseat. Mr. Maxwell takes the armchair across from me. His scent fills the room—the same hint of expensive cologne as before. I remember it.

"The emergency," he prompts.

I square my shoulders. "Right. Yes. First, I wanted to apologize for the inconvenience. I know you're very busy."

"It's nothing. Tell me what's wrong."

My face gets even hotter. "I'd like to speak to you about the rent."

"The rent for this apartment?"

"I'm sure, in a place like this…" Why didn't I plan this speech out before I called him? "I know you're probably not the one people come to about problems like this, but it's the weekend. I was up all night." Anxiousness sweeps a heat over my entire body. I can barely breathe knowing the weight of this conversation.

He studies me. "What's the problem with the rent?"

"I can't pay it." I'm quick to correct myself. "I can't pay all of it." *Deep breaths, Maddie.* "This is my home, it's the only thing I have right now, and I can't quite cover the rent for this month."

"Your husband can't cover it?" he asks, and it's like a knife to the chest.

I twist my hands together out of habit, and his eyes drop to my fingers then snap back to my face.

"He wasn't my husband, actually," I tell him. "He was my fiancé, but he's not anymore. We're over. He left."

"Without leaving enough money to cover the rent?" He lets out a disbelieving laugh. "The kind of people who live in this building have second homes in Europe."

"He was that kind of person. He was going to be, anyway, but I'm not." Okay. Here it comes. "I hope you know that this isn't a long-term problem. I have a plan to fix it, I just need more time because I wasn't prepared for this. If I go to him, I'm sure he'll simply end the lease, and there's nothing around here that I can afford and that's available. I've been off the market for a couple of years, so it's taking me longer than I thought to find a job that can pay enough. I've gone through my savings, and I've sold most everything I could."

"Off the market?"

"Out of the job market. My ex thought it would be better for his career if I focused on philanthropy instead of building my own career, so that's what I did. And I don't regret it. I helped a lot of people, but I'm at a loss at the moment. I paid everything but the five hundred and everyone said that I needed to talk to you."

His blue eyes are absolutely captivating. "What's the exact situation with the rent, Maddie? You can't afford any of it?"

"No, I can afford most of it. I'm five hundred dollars short. And I'll give you anything you want to cover it."

I'm shocked at the words that have just come out of my mouth, but I mean it. I'm solving this problem. I don't care what it takes. I've sold almost all my jewelry in the past months to make it work. I can't even afford to break this lease now. I don't know what else to do.

"*Anything*," I insist. My heart races.

Graham Maxwell looks at me across my living room, his eyes going dark. "We can come to an arrangement."

Relief hits me like a gust of fresh air. "Oh, thank you. Thank you so much. What kind of arrangement?"

"I have an idea," he says as his eyes drop to my breasts, and I have to admit, I want it. If that's what he wants, I wanted it anyway. Before I can stop myself, I agree to what he's suggesting.

"If you want me, you can have me however you'd like."

He pauses, almost as if he's stopped breathing and embarrassment lights my cheeks aflame. But that look in his eyes lights a different part of me ablaze.

"What exactly is it that you have in mind?"

"I think…I'm not sure. I haven't…"

A moment passes and then he asks, "A quick fuck then?"

I gasp in spite of myself. I've been nervous about what he might say, but I never expected him to say it like *this*.

Although, if I'm being truthful, I love the tension between us. I love the way it felt to meet his eyes in the elevator. And if this is what it takes, if I get to experience a fantasy I had…I'm more than willing.

"You really want me?" I whisper the question and wonder if I'm merely daydreaming.

"From the moment I saw you in that elevator."

"Oh my God."

"You wanted me, too," he guesses as he spreads his legs a bit wider, and my gaze drops to the bulge in his pants. I'm instantly hot.

I bring my hands up to cover my face, then comb my fingers through my hair and look back up at him. "Yes," I admit. "I did."

"Then take your clothes off, and you can stop worrying about the rent."

My heart races. "I…," I did say *anything*.

"You don't have much time," he adds. He looks hungry now. Almost desperate. "No doubt you've spent all weekend trying to collect the money with no success. So let's do this instead." I stare wide-eyed back at him, knowing this is my only chance to back out and if I do… well I don't know what I'll do. "I've wanted you for months, Madelyn. I'll make it good for you. I'll make sure you enjoy yourself."

I close my eyes. My heart beats and beats a steady *thud*.

Then I open them and get to my feet.

My shirt is the first thing to go. Then the bodysuit I'm wearing underneath.

"Stop," he says.

I freeze. Graham Maxwell gets up from his seat and comes around the table to me, his eyes raking over every inch of my skin covered only by my bra and panty set. His breath turns heavier as he unbuttons his shirt.

Then his hands are on my waist, gentle but firm.

"Fucking gorgeous," he murmurs.

"You're gorgeous yourself," I say, feeling drunk on how close he is with his palms on my waist. His touch is electrifying and it's in this moment I know I'm going to remember this forever.

"Birth control?" he asks, and I nod. "Have you been tested since—"

"Yes. You?" He nods. "Good."

He lets out a groan and peels off my panties and bra in quick movements. Then his mouth is on the side of my neck, and I—

I can't think about anything but how good his lips feel.

I tilt my head back to give him better access, and he takes full advantage, leaving opened mouthed kisses that force me to moan from the instant pleasure.

And then—it's like he reaches some breaking point. Mr. Maxwell maneuvers me over to the arm of the sofa, the pad of his thumb brushing over one of my nipples. I let out a soft sound. It feels so damn good to be touched. To be wanted. I wish I could live in this moment. After the hell of what I've been through, I need this.

With firm guidance, he turns me around and bends me over, forcing a gasp from me.

"Fuck. Your thighs are perfect." His voice is low and rough. He slides a hand between my legs and nudges them apart, then finds my wet slit with his fingertips. When he finds my clit, I can't help the moan that comes out of my mouth.

Graham curses again, his fingers working faster on my clit. I hear the sounds of his zipper and of fabric moving, and then he's working me harder while the tip of his cock nudges against my opening.

"Yes," I tell him. "Fuck me. Please fuck me."

It's filthy to beg a man this way, but Graham likes it. He makes another primal sound from deep in his chest and pushes himself inside me.

His cock fills me and pushes me to the brink of pain, and it forces another gasp out of me. He's so fucking big. He stops, buried inside of me, and lets me adjust. It takes a moment, while I hold my breath, for the sting of being stretched to be eased by the pleasure. I spread my thighs a little wider and rock back against him, lost in the feeling of being completely filled by a man for the first time in months.

Graham doesn't hesitate. The second I move against him, he fucks into me hard, then harder. Between his fingers and his body, I'm drowning in pleasure.

"Oh," I gasp. "Oh, oh—"

"Come on my cock," he orders in a breathy tone at the shell of my ear. "That's what I want for the rent."

That statement alone nearly makes me come undone. I think about how I'm a little whore for him. How the perverse act is a fantasy come to life.

I let out another moan and come undone. My fingernails scrape against the couch cushions as I try to brace myself.

"That's a good girl," he praises me as he rides through my orgasm.

With one broad hand on my lower back, he comes inside of me. I can feel every bit of his heat pulsing inside me. Everywhere. Holy shit. My eyes widen as I'm brought back down from the highest of highs.

His thrusts slow, but it's a long minute before he pulls out and helps me up.

As he offers me his hand when my legs take a moment to stabilize, I can hardly believe it's done. He kept his word. It was a quick fuck. A damn good quick fuck that left me wanting more.

"That was," I start to tell him and have to catch my breath as he hands me my shirt. "That was really good."

My eyes meet his and I catch his smirk. "You were incredible," he tells me, and I have to look away as I dress myself. A mix of emotions swarms over me.

"Do you need anything?" he asks, and I only shake my head.

He puts himself back together, faster than I could have imagined. His eyes burn over my body, and I wonder for an instant what he's hiding behind them. "Don't worry about the five hundred dollars. We're even."

Graham Maxwell sees himself out of my apartment but not before turning and telling me that if I need anything at all not to hesitate to ask.

Technically, it's *his* apartment. He's the man who owns this building and has the power to kick me out if I don't pay rent, and he's also the man I've just had sex with to cover the shortfall.

Oh my God. I've just had sex with the owner of the building to pay the rent.

Did I...like that?

Did I *love* it?

I still feel buzzed from the way he fucked me, his strokes deep and possessive. It's been a long time since I was with a man who took me like that. He took me like he owned me and fucked the shit out of me. That's exactly what Graham did. I don't think it *ever* happened that way with Kevin, or any of my other exes for that matter.

My heart races. Graham isn't even in the room anymore, and I'm still feeling the effects.

I sweep up the clothes from the living room floor and walk on shaky legs to the bathroom where I toss them into the hamper. I turn on the shower without thinking, wait for the water to get hot, and climb in.

"I just paid the rent with sex," I say out loud, just to test it out.

My whole body feels like it's blushing, but I don't feel ashamed.

Should I feel ashamed?

No, right? I didn't do anything wrong. Two consenting adults. A business arrangement sort of...for rent.

"Oh, God, I *loved* it," I admit to the empty shower.

They're really two separate things. I needed to come up with five hundred dollars for this month's rent, and I needed to get over Kevin. I've spent months in a panic, trying to find a job and failing, waking up all night freaking out about the future.

I wondered if I could have done something else to make us work. But it wasn't *me* in the end. It was him. He found someone else, cheated for months, and left once I found out. He wanted to have his cake and eat it too. I'm still not over the heartache entirely, mostly because it proves just how naive I am.

It's hard to feel hung up on past mistakes after the way Graham touched me though.

Mr. Maxwell?

I don't know what to call him, but that's okay. This won't happen again. I'll find a job and fix my life, and I won't have to have sex with anyone to pay the rent ever again. I was acting out a fantasy. One that paid well. But I will never do that again.

Even if I did like it.

Even if I did come *hard* while he was inside me. I came on his cock like he told me to. I've never been talked to like that. Not once. And I loved it.

That didn't happen with Kevin. I never came that hard. I'm more ashamed of the fact that I used to wait until he fell asleep and get myself off under the covers so I didn't hurt his feelings. How did I ever accept that as my normal life when something so much better was out there?

I take a deep breath of hot steam, pushing the wet hair from my face, and let it out.

He seemed stable and kind. That's why I was with Kevin. He was so nice…so nice that I didn't see through the lies and the cheating. I've been through bad break-ups before, and I thought my relationship with him was the next step in my life. I thought I was leaving behind all those unpredictable men and finally growing up.

I'm not going to blame myself for that.

I'm not going to downplay the memories of Graham, either.

I shake my head under the hot water, unable to stop imagining what just happened. That felt *good*. It felt *amazing*. Maybe it shouldn't have. Maybe I should have demanded that he buy me dinner and roses before we had sex. Kevin did all those things for me. He bought bouquets of roses and took me out to dinner and asked me to marry him…and he left.

But I didn't want those things in the moment. I wanted a quickie with the guy from the elevator with fuck-me eyes.

I'm *not* going to get hung up on either Kevin or Graham. That's not what I'm going to do.

I focus back on the shower. I'm not in any hurry to get the scent of his cologne off my skin. I mostly came here as a matter of habit, but I regret it a little as I'm soaping up my skin. I can still feel the places he touched me. He wasn't rough. He was firm, though. Like he already knew me. Like I already belonged to him.

Except this was never about belonging to anybody. It was just to pay the rent.

I keep convincing myself of that as I get out of the shower and get dressed. I feel like I've just woken up from a deep, refreshing sleep, and my mind is clear for the first time since my ex left.

Is that what happens when you're with a person who understands you? Because it felt like Graham understood me.

I might not know much about the man, but I understood what he needed from me in that moment. *Needed.* That was right there in his eyes. I pause, the towel wrapped around me, in front of the mirror that's edged with steam. Hopeless romantics get their hearts broken. Suzette told me that just last week over red wine and another hard cry.

I need to stop these thoughts. I need to focus on the task at hand.

I shut down all thoughts as I get ready and get back to emails and resumés intent on finding a job and writing Graham off as a one-time divulgence.

That's the plan, anyway, until my phone buzzes on the kitchen counter. I hear the soft hum from my walk-in closet and dash out through the apartment in bare feet. It's too big a place for one person with two bedrooms, two bathrooms, an office, and a breakfast nook. But I've done the math on getting a new place on short notice. I was five hundred dollars short on this rent. I don't have enough to cover a deposit on another place, either, unless I have roommate.

I reach the phone and snatch it up from the countertop without looking at the screen.

"Hello?"

"Maddie, it's me."

"Kenzie! How are you?" My heart speeds up again at the sound of my cousin's voice. I love Kenzie to death, but her life is even more precarious than mine was before I met Kevin. "Everything okay?"

"Not really," she says with a sigh. "I need help."

"Oh, Kenzie," I can't hide the strain in my voice. My stomach sinks. I want to be in a position to help my cousin any time she calls, but I'm not. I used to be, and I will be again, but right now? I can't even help myself.

I'm hoping all she needs is to talk things over.

"I didn't want to have to call you," she continues. "But I don't have any other choice."

"What's due?" I ask, pacing out of the kitchen and back to the big picture windows in the living room.

"My student loans."

My cousin never made it to graduation. She had a hard time the first two years of college. It wasn't easy for her to settle on a major. She went through three student advisers, and all suggested she get a different degree. Now she's part way through two separate majors and three minors and hasn't taken classes in a year. The student loan companies won't let her off the hook. She's young and in severe debt.

"When?" I ask automatically.

"The fifteenth."

"Then you still have two weeks to work it out, right?"

"I'm not going to get there." I can hear the panic in her voice, though she tries to hide it. "I'm behind on other bills, too. Had to cover those with my savings so the electricity didn't get turned off."

I hate the sound of that. I don't want my cousin—my family—to be in a position where she can't afford basic necessities. She already works two jobs. Waitressing doesn't always make ends meet. Today is a perfect example of that.

"Kenzie." I try to sound as calm and reasonable as I can. "Are you sure you don't want to—"

"Don't say I should move in with you, Maddie. I don't have the cash for that, either. It's just too far."

This is the worst part about Kevin leaving. Looking back, it's obvious that I wasn't happy with him. He wasn't going to be in love with me no matter how hard

I tried. That's a tough lesson to keep learning from men, and I'm determined not to have to learn it again.

But at least when we were together, money was no object. I could send Kenzie what she needed to get by and hope that it would be enough to get her where she needed to go.

Ugh. I wish I'd ignored him about quitting my job. My grandmother was right when she told me to keep a separate savings account and build it up as much as I could. If I'd followed her advice, I wouldn't need help covering the rent.

Then again, Graham Maxwell never would have come to my apartment. My thighs tighten and I have to close my eyes and shut down the memory.

"Kenz, I really, really want to be the person you can count on," I begin.

She huffs a sigh, and I know it's out of disappointment and desperation. I know that *exact* feeling because that's how I felt when I woke up this morning. It's probably a pipe dream to think that I'll ever live a worry-free life.

"I just can't cover this month. I'm sorry. I barely made the rent."

"I don't get it." Traffic goes by in the background, making her voice sound even shakier than it is. My heart hurts for her. I know what it's like to be on your own with your life constantly on the brink. "What went so wrong with Kevin?"

"He cheated on me. You know that's what happened."

"Couldn't you have—"

"Couldn't I have done *what?*" This day has been a rollercoaster, and now I'm heading up another high hill, frustrated as all get out. I'm guilty of blaming myself for Kevin leaving but hearing it from another person reminds me that it's bullshit. "Convinced him not to cheat? Been better somehow? I did everything he asked me to do."

"I know, I know," she says, softening. "I'm sorry. I didn't mean to accuse you of anything, I just—"

"It's fine. It'll be okay," I tell Kenzie. "All of this will work out. We just have to—"

"Keep trying?" My cousin lets out a bitter laugh. "I knew you'd say that. I gotta go. I'm almost at work."

"Okay, but—"

She hangs up before I can finish my sentence and the guilt weighs heavy in my chest.

"I'll always be here for you," I shout at the phone. "That's what I was going to say. I'll be here for you, I just don't have the *money* you need." Tears sting the corner of my eyes and my throat goes dry.

I whirl away from the window, frustrated beyond belief, and as I do, the phone flies out of my hand.

It tumbles through the air in slow motion and hits the window much harder than I thought it would.

It hits the window so hard that it cracks. All the blood drains from my face and my hands go cold.

"No!" I shout, and rush to the window. The phone's landed on the floor with only a minor scuff on the case, but the window has a crack in it.

A crack. In the giant picture window. *Shit.*

Shit, shit, shit.

How the hell am I going to pay for this?

chapter 3

Graham

ANOTHER DAY, ANOTHER MEETING.

More stress.

All the while, my mind wandered.

The man I've been meeting with, Harland Porter, is throwing up roadblock after roadblock to the sale. Concern after concern. Question after question. I don't know why he put the damned property up on the market if he's so obsessed with it.

I'm not obsessed with any property like that.

Although, my mind drifting once again, I'm a bit concerned I may be becoming obsessed with Madelyn.

Obsession has no place in a deal like that.

I can't stop thinking about her. It was one fuck, so it shouldn't mean anything. I'm the one who was in charge of the situation. I could've offered anything and I offered that deal, and she *wanted* it. I run my hand over the back of my neck as Harland drones on and my business associates answer.

It takes great effort to keep my expression stern and unmoving as my thumb runs over the tip of my pointer and I imagine her soft skin and delectable moans.

Years ago, I thought that being filthy rich would solve all my problems. It hasn't. It solved some of them, that's for sure. I won't ever have to worry about losing my house or being on the street. I won't ever be in the position of begging someone for rent money.

Those concerns are far behind me, and the ones that are ahead have much higher stakes. People work for me now. People depend on me. Which means it's not just me I have to think about when it comes to making these deals.

It might be easier if I had something to take the edge off. Something real and constant in my life other than my penthouse apartment. What my apartment has going for it is that it's predictable. It's expensive and luxurious, decorated exactly to my taste, and nobody else ever interferes. It offers me privacy and an escape. But it's hollow and far too quiet.

For the second time this week, I catch myself thinking about what it would be like to come home to *someone,* not just *some place.*

Not a wife. I can't imagine marriage. And not a girlfriend…I'm not interested in complications and emotions.

All that is a distraction. I know what happens to men who fall too deep into finding that missing someone. Statistics on love and marriage are far too telling. The majority of people never find 'the one' and end up alone. Half of those who do take the leap into love end up unhappy and broke after divorce.

"Let's take five?" Harland questions and the associates agree. The computer screen shows them all nodding, and I agree to the short break. Once the camera is off, I rub a hand over my face and lean back in my chair. I click over the tabs to another long email chain. We've been going back and forth for an hour. Part of me wants to cut my losses and stop spending time trying to acquire a property that's not truly available.

What would it say about me if I invested all this time and walked away with nothing? It would say that I wasn't up to the challenge. It would say I could be deterred by a few annoying emails.

Nobody's ever going to be able to say that about me. If they say anything, they'll say that I was too determined. That I wouldn't stop at anything to get what I wanted. If this business has taught me one thing it's that patience is immeasurable.

I respond to Porter's latest email and click over to the app for the building's security system. A window showing twelve small rectangles, each with the view from a separate camera, pops up on the screen. This, unlike working on the acquisition, gives me a sense of peace. I can see that everything is how it should be in the parking area. A delivery man taps away at his tablet at the back entrance, then jogs back to his truck, climbs in, and drives away. In the lobby, an older tenant chats with the doorman, who looks like he's explaining something to her, his hands flying.

This is the place I've made through my money and my effort and my force of will.

I've built something to be proud of, something that runs smoothly and provides for others, but that doesn't mean there's nothing else I want in my life. It doesn't mean I don't have other goals. My heart speeds up, stress spreading across my shoulders and back. What I want is something physical—a trip to the gym or a run, something to let my muscles work.

What I want is Maddie.

How does she fit in to a life like mine? I can't be the man who never gives up on anything if I want her and don't go after her. I can't be the man who goes after her and keeps his eyes on the prize at the same time.

It's like she hears my thoughts, or the universe does, because the instant her name enters my mind, a woman walks into view of one of the security cameras.

It's her, crossing the street to the building. She tucks a lock of dark hair behind her ear and waits for traffic to stop. Then she strolls into the sidewalk, looking gorgeous and elegant in heels and a dress that hugs her hips and shows off her collarbone with a square neckline that makes me want to stick my hand underneath it just to feel the softness of her skin.

Maddie is completely put together as she moves across the white painted lines on the road. She flashes the drivers in the cars a perfect smile and gives them a little wave to thank them for stopping.

I'm hard just looking at her. Out there, in public, she looks lovely and demure. She *is* lovely and demure. But I know how she sounds when she's bent over a piece of furniture and moaning for my cock. I know how wet it makes her to come to filthy secret agreements with a man with money—very, very wet. And *fuck*, it's hot. That damned voice in my mind tries to remind me that there's so much more than raw sexual desire. There's so much more I could give her beyond a few hundred dollars and a quickie.

I'm not going to go there right now. I take a deep breath and adjust myself in my pants. A more decent guy would turn off the security app, but I'm not exactly interested in being a decent man when it comes to this situation.

Maddie strides into the building, smiles at the doorman, and says something to him. My brow creases as a touch of possessiveness overwhelms me. It's unexpected and my finger hovers on the key to turn the camera off. Tom is a trustworthy man, otherwise I wouldn't have hired him, but another man's eyes on her makes my stomach knot with jealousy.

I can't even *be* jealous. She's not mine.

She's just beautiful and holds a spark I haven't felt from anyone else.

If there was a woman waiting for me in my apartment at the end of every day, I'd want her to be Maddie.

Fuck. I can't think like that. What we have isn't anything long-term or deep, no matter how much I think I want that.

I dig my fingernails into the arm of my office chair to keep myself in the damn seat. Maddie has every right to walk into the lobby of my building, where *she* lives, and talk to the doorman. She has every right to talk to whoever she wants. She doesn't belong to me.

Just when I've finally fucking lost it and started to get up from the chair, Maddie turns away from the reception desk. For a split second, I can see her face before she heads for the elevators. The kind smile that she wore into the lobby drops away into a worried frown.

I pause. Concern spreading through my veins.

What's that about?

My computer pings with a message that the meeting has ended. I click over to the meeting tab. Harland apologizes but something has come up and he'll email once he's available again. Irritation spreads through me but I remind myself: patience.

I click both windows closed, get up from my seat, and go to the floor-to-ceiling window. My only thoughts are of Madelyn and how to approach her again. It was expression on her face. There's no way I can tell her I was watching her on the cameras—that would be an invasion of privacy, and she'd never want to fuck me again.

Which isn't the only thing I'm worried about.

I'm worried about *her*. I'm worried that some serious problem worries her. I don't care for it.

As I stare down at the bustling streets, I debate on how to handle her. I can go knock on her door and make sure everything's fine. Maddie came to me with a problem. It would be a gentlemanly thing to do to check in.

There's a quiet knock at the door. "Mr. Maxwell?"

"Yes?"

It's my secretary, Miss Dawning. Her expression is slightly hesitant, the wrinkles around her eyes even deeper than normal.

"There's someone here to see you. She doesn't have an appointment, but I told her I'd see if—"

"Who is it?"

"Madelyn Cunnigham."

"Of course. Send her in."

"Oh!" My secretary blinks. No doubt surprised. I typically hate unscheduled meetings and simply decline. "Of course, Mr. Maxwell. Right away." As she closes my office door, she holds the lone pearl dangling from her gold necklace over her white blouse, an amused look on her face.

A moment later, my secretary leads Maddie into my office. Maddie flashes her that same bright smile she used when she was crossing the street, then looks at me. The smile gets smaller…and hotter. Pink spreads across her cheeks. Her doe eyes take on a sensual heat.

This isn't how she looked at the doorman.

I can't help the pull of an asymmetrical grin at the sight of her reaction.

"Hello, Maddie." The scent of her perfume has already spread lightly across the office. "I'm surprised to see you here during business hours." The camera didn't do her justice. She's even more beautiful in person. My grip tightens on the desk as she makes her way in.

She laughs, a little nervously. "I just finished some errands, and you're my next stop. Do you have a few minutes?"

I gesture to the chair across from my desk. "For you?" I pause, allowing a moment to pass while our eyes lock. "Of course I have time."

Maddie blushes a deeper red and moves across the office. The modern lines of my office furniture are hard and sharp, there's a coldness in its simplicity, and then there's her. Warmth and beauty and femininity. I settle back into my chair and she takes her seat, balancing her purse neatly on her lap. I don't know which I like more—Maddie in a bodysuit or Maddie in this classic dress.

She smiles hesitantly across the desk at me. "So…I have some bad news."

My blood runs cold and I despise the worrying tone she has. If she were mine, she wouldn't have to worry about a damn thing. "What kind of bad news?" I keep my voice calm, but I'm anything but. I don't want to hear that she has bad news—if someone's done something to her, like her ex-fiancé, it needs to be fixed immediately. My palms itch and it takes great effort not to let on every scenario that runs through the back of my mind.

"I may have…well, I *did* break a window in the apartment. Yesterday." The corners of Maddie's mouth turns down. "It was an accident. My phone completely slipped out of my hand, and I never expected…" She takes a deep and steadying inhale. "I know repairs like that get added to the rent, so I've visited two different places to see if I could figure out a way to afford it, but—"

"Let me guess. It was the picture window?"

Maddie bites her lip and gives me an embarrassed nod. Fuck, my cock is so hard precum leaks from the seam. If I could have created a storyline for us to play, this would be fucking perfect.

"None of the companies would agree to work on a project like that. Too complicated with the large sheet of glass. Not worth the trouble," I tell her. There's no way in hell she's going to find someone to come and fix that window. I have my contacts though; it's not a problem in the least.

"That's exactly what I found out." Maddie leans forward, her lips parted, clearly trying to decide what to say next. "I didn't want to…I don't want you to think I'm making any assumptions about—"

"What kind of man I am?"

Her eyes snap to mine. "I don't see anything wrong with…with making more deals, if it's two consenting adults, and I…"

She pauses for so long that I lean in, too. If it wasn't for the desk between us, I'd have her in my lap already.

"You were thinking about the last deal we made, weren't you?"

"I was," she admits in a soft voice. "I was thinking about it. I…I liked it."

"I told you I'd make it good for you."

"And you did." She looks down and away, collecting herself. "So I wondered if you'd be willing to make another arrangement with me." The vulnerability in her tone is a temptress herself.

I know what I should say to her. I know that I should keep my focus where it belongs—on the deals I'm trying to make and the goals I'm trying to reach. I shouldn't take advantage of her situation.

I just can't do that. I can't be that man. I want her too much.

"I'd be happy to do that, if it's what you would like to do."

Her eyes widen, the heat in her gaze simmering. "You would?"

"I wanted you the first time we came to an agreement," I say, hoping to hell I don't sound as if I'm completely smitten with her. "I still do."

"Okay." Maddie glances over my desk. "Is this—"

"Not here. I'll come up to your apartment when I'm finished for the day." As soon as the words are out of my mouth, I regret them. Why the hell *not* here? I'd like to fuck her on my desk. Fucking hell, I can only imagine how hot she'd look. I'd like to see her all spread out over my paperwork. But that would be a decision based on my cock, and I didn't get where I am by constantly leading with my dick.

She nods in agreement and asks politely, "Is there anything I can do in the meantime?"

"I'll make the calls and the repair crew should be here within the next hour or two. The company I work with never makes me wait more than an hour, so they should be done by the time I wrap up for the day."

"Wow." Maddie looks me up and down. "I thought it would take at least a week or…I don't know, even longer."

"And leave you with a broken window?" I shake my head. "Next time there's anything broken, call me as soon as it happens. Don't let it sit overnight."

"I didn't cut myself or anything," Maddie says. "It's more like a spiderweb."

"As soon as it happens," I insist, lowering my voice.

A sexy shiver runs through her and it's addictive. "Okay," she whispers, then clears her throat. "Okay, Mr. Maxwell. I'll do that."

I get up from my chair and help her out of hers, ignoring the intense urge to slide my hand up under her dress to see how wet she is. I already know how much this turns her on.

It'll be torture for me and probably for her, too, but I need to reinforce my self-control.

I guide Maddie to the door with my hand on the small of her back. She looks up at me and murmurs a quick *thank you*, and then I watch her walk away, ignoring the prying look from Miss Dawning.

chapter 4

Maddie

IT HAPPENED UNBELIEVABLY FAST—THE WINDOW'S FIXED AND THE CREW is already gone. They were the most efficient team I could have imagined. I barely had time to go through two applications in that time they were here.

They weren't like the repair places I visited earlier. In those places, the men behind the counter shook their heads even as I was telling them the problem. I could already tell they wouldn't take the job.

This crew came in as a team, moved fast, and had the big pane of glass out of the frame and replaced in less than an hour.

For them it was a quick fix.

For me it was the longest day of my life. I made a compromise and it's one I'm trying not to think about as I pace behind my sofa and stare at the blue door to my apartment. Waiting for the knock. Waiting for the payment to be made. I close my eyes, take a deep breath in, and breathe out slowly.

All I want is for Graham to get here.

I realize that a second deal with him is past the point where I can explain it away through sheer desperation, but he smelled too damn good. Afterall, damages are probably covered by renters' insurance…maybe? I'm sure there could have been another way. I didn't want it any other way, though. He looked at me with those gorgeous blue eyes, and I wanted to feel his hands on me again. I wanted to give him something, too.

I hadn't actually meant to make another arrangement with him, though. What I'd meant to do was go to his office, confess what had happened, then ask him for the name of someone who could fix the window. I'd have called myself and asked about a payment plan, something to make it affordable. Or given the information to insurance. I'm sure there is some other way to handle an accident like that. I'm almost one hundred percent certain.

And then he'd been there, sitting behind his desk, so handsome and charming and a little bit, what felt like, protective and flirtatious. I couldn't help myself.

The clock behind me in the kitchen ticks.

I can hear it in the quiet of the apartment. I'm standing in a spacious entryway, which happens to be the first—no, *second*—place I ever saw Graham. An open archway leads into the kitchen. The entryway leads into the wide living room with the big windows I've loved since I moved in. My bedroom and bathroom are off to the left. My ex's office is to the right of the living room. I wanted to make it a guest bedroom, but now it's just…empty. Empty and luxurious, with crown molding and a calming paint job and enough room for my cousin, *if* she'd agree to live with me.

Graham's going to be here any minute. Standing right where he was before.

I take deep breaths and pretend to be calm about it. There's nothing out of place in the entire apartment. I've already cleaned everything there is to clean. I've prepared myself as best as I can as well.

A text pops up on my phone and I'm more than grateful for the distraction. It's from Kenzie.

> **Kenzie: Hey, Maddie, I'm sorry about the phone call the other day**
>
> **Maddie: It's okay! Are things any better?**
>
> **Kenzie: Not really, but I don't want to fight with you or take out my frustrations on you. I love you.**
>
> **Maddie: I love you too and we're not fighting. Call me later if you want?**
>
> **Kenzie: I will.**

I don't think she will call. Her texts make me believe she might be in a worse financial situation than before, and she feels like she needs to be on good terms with me just in case.

If only she knew the bad luck I've been having. A broken window doesn't help anybody who's short on cash.

I'll be all right. I'll get back on my feet. Until then…I glance back at the door, willing there to be a knock on the other side.

The only thing that worries me is how much I've been thinking about Graham, what we did together, and the way I feel when he's touching me.

After my last two exes, I don't need to fall head over heels with a man, especially one with so much more than what I have. More power and an imbalance… it's exactly what got me into this problem in the first place. I fell in love with a man who was far more wealthy and powerful than me. I did everything he wanted to feel safe and because I loved him. I'm not saying I'm in love with Graham, but I am saying it's something I need to be aware of.

Nothing has felt as new and exciting as being near Graham, but how can I trust that feeling when it's led me to disaster more than once?

I have to be careful. The romantic in me needs to die. This is just sex. It's practically business…an arrangement sealed with a kiss.

Shaking off the hesitation, I go to the bedroom and plug my phone in on the side table, doing my best to keep thoughts of Kenzie and my job search and my past out of my head. Today is about the present. Today is about giving Graham what I owe for the broken window.

Another wave of desire runs through me, and I wonder if I should wait for him naked on the sofa or if he would want me to strip for him again. He seemed to really like that. The memory brings a heat through my chest.

That probably shouldn't be so hot to think about, but I already have to press my thighs together to keep myself from stripping out of my clothes and having some private time in the bedroom. Graham seemed to like my dress when he saw it earlier, so I decide to keep it on.

I peek down at the phone to make sure it's charging and that's when I notice the time: five o'clock.

It's officially the end of the workday.

I hover in the living room, waiting. I want to stand right next to the door and pull it open the second I hear footsteps, but that would make me look…

I don't know how it would make me look. Too eager? Too into him? I've never been very good at playing. I've always worn my heart on my sleeve, and no amount of forbidden sex with the man who owns my building is going to change something that's right at the center of my personality.

Sometimes I wish I could be cool and collected and keep my cards close to my chest, but that's never been me.

The knock at the door is loud and confident, and I know before I get to the peephole that it's him. Graham stands on the other side of the glass. Even with this strange fisheye view, he's the most handsome man I've ever seen. His suit is sharp, his tie undone and laying over his collar. It's sexy as fuck.

I square my shoulders, lift my chin, and open the door.

The man who stands in the hall is every bit as tall and beautiful as he was before, but not as reserved. He has a darker look in his eyes. Before, he didn't let me see the hunger in them until he was sitting down with me. Now it's apparent, as if he's not even trying to hide it.

"Madelyn," he says, his voice low, a certain strain in it like he's been holding in how much he wants this all day. Maybe even all week.

"Graham," I respond, opening the door wider and waving him in.

713

As soon as the door closes behind him, he takes my chin in his hand, tilts my face up to his, and looks into my eyes.

"Did any of the repairmen bother you?"

"Bother me?" I let out a giggle. "No, of course not. They were perfectly professional."

"Good. Is the window fixed?"

"It's in one piece again. They were very fast about it. You would've been impressed."

"I doubt anything could impress me as much as you in this dress." His eyes drop down over my body, and I'm *so* glad I didn't change. "I think that's what you owe me for the window."

"My dress?" His hand on my face is gentle, but I can feel the strength behind it. "You want me to give you my dress?"

"I want you to give me your body in that dress," he says, then leans in and kisses me.

It's a hard kiss, harder than I thought it would be, and Graham lets out a relieved sound like the most frustrating part of his day is that he wasn't already here to kiss me and fuck me and…whatever else he has planned.

When he pulls back, I'm short of breath from the intensity of the kiss. "I can give that to you. Just…just tell me where."

With a sexy grin, Graham guides me into the kitchen. It's bright and spacious and clean. I'd expected him to take me to the bedroom, but instead he lifts me up and puts me on the countertop I wiped down three times today. With his hands on my waist, he leans down to drag his teeth over the side of my neck. Shivers run down my body and my nipples harden. Graham inhales deeply, and his lips brush over the same spot before his hands slide down and he spreads my thighs.

It makes my dress hitch up and he pushes it higher, almost to my waist, exposing the matching fabric of my panties. I give myself to him without hesitation. I want this more than he could possibly know.

"Did you wear these for me?" He asks in a low tone, gliding a finger underneath the lace waistband and dragging it away from my skin. Graham lets the panties fall back into place, then pulls them away again, letting cool air come into contact with the dampness between my thighs.

"Yes," I answer, dizzy from the way he touches me ever so slightly with his knuckle.

"How hard did you try to get the window fixed?" he muses, pulling the panties a little farther out from my skin and letting his fingers move toward my clit. I spread my thighs a little more. "Or did you plan to come to me the whole time?"

His fingers dip down, his knuckles making faint contact with my clit, and I moan out loud.

"No, I tried," I tell him, my face hot, the space between my thighs even hotter.

His fingertips stroke fully against my clit. "I could've told you that you'd never find anyone to fix this window. And then you walked into my office and made an offer. You knew I'd take you up on it, didn't you?" he questions, and there's an edge to his tone.

"I hoped you would," I answer honestly, my eyes caught in his gaze like a hunter to the prey.

"You should *know* I want you," he says as if it's a command. I almost tell him yes Sir. So close to being weak for him and putty in his hands.

"I want you, too." I tell him, although it's barely spoken under my chaotic breath.

"Are you in need Madelyn?" he questions, and my cheeks go hot.

I need his fingertips on me more than life.

"I want more from you this time," he says in a gravelly voice before I can answer. "I don't just want to make it good. I want to see how good it is by the expression on your face. Look at me."

I look into his pale blue eyes, overwhelmed by his hand moving under the lace of my panties. He stops, and I freeze. "Did I do something wrong?"

His eyes glint. "No, kitten, you didn't. I just need to get these out of the way."

He strips my panties off slowly, bringing them gently over my thighs, and crushes them into a ball in his fist. The rip of the lace tearing is audible, and it makes my bottom lip drop.

"You wanted this, didn't you? Your panties are already wet."

I spread my legs a little more for him, feeling reckless at the way he called me *needy*.

Yes. I want to be your little whore, I think, but I don't tell him that. I'm too afraid to.

"That's it." His fingers return to my core, and he pushes two of them inside me, letting out a hiss when they sink in easily.

"I want to watch you come for me," he says as my pleasure climbs with every thrust of his fingers. He moves his thumb in relentless little circles over my clit, the pleasure building and building, his blue eyes locked on mine. There's nothing to do but keep my thighs open for him and come, clenching on his fingers. My toes curl as my body heats and I get closer and closer.

"Fuck, Graham," I call out his name as I reach my climax all too easily.

His face is flushed, his eyes dark, and he leans between my legs and unzips his pants.

This is the sight I didn't get to see before. He was bent over me from behind, and I didn't get to see how he looks when he wants from me this badly.

When he wants *me* this badly. It's a heady feeling, to know a man like him wants me.

I feel like I might lose my mind from wanting him, so I wrap my legs around his waist as he lines himself up and pushes in. He's much thicker than his fingers and I gasp at the stretch. My head falls back in pure bliss, but his hand cradles the back of my head and instantly his lips are on mine.

Graham isn't rough, but he doesn't hold back, either. He moves against me with smooth, powerful thrusts, his hands bracing me where he wants me.

"Fuck," he says. His voice is low, and it does nothing but make me hotter for him.

Graham kisses me with passion, his hands roam my body, and the sensations are all too much at once, and yet at the same time, not enough. He takes control of my mouth completely, tasting me deeply, and I taste him back as his hips work faster and deeper, pushing in until he bottoms out. Desire screams through my veins with a scorching heat and I can't get enough. He tenses, his body going still, and then he wraps his hands around my ass and grinds me against him while he comes. My orgasm hits right before his, turning my mind to sheer pleasure.

I'm not sure exactly what happens. He says something to me, but none of the words make much sense. He lifts me into his arms and takes me through the apartment to my bedroom.

He leaves me for the bathroom, and I catch my breath and slip on a nightie. The faucet runs in the bathroom, and I attempt to figure out what to say, but my mind is blank.

I have to say something about the window. I have to thank him…and maybe tell him I like our arrangement more than I thought I would. But I don't want it to seem like I want money from him. The words stay scrambled in my mind as he comes back out, gorgeous muscles on full display. It's then that a phone goes off from the living room.

"Wait here a moment," he tells me before giving me a searing kiss. I lie down under the sheets sated and exhausted, just barely able to hear him answer the phone. I try to think about what to say and how to handle this in a way where he knows I could be interested in more.

He comes into the room, a hand over his phone and tells me he'll be right back. But he's gone before I can answer. The apartment door opens and closes, and I'm left in bed alone.

It doesn't take long for me to rest my eyes and somehow, I drift into sleep.

When I wake up in the morning, it's quiet in my apartment. Thoughts that the night before was only a dream come to mind, but the soreness between my thighs shuts that down immediately. The only sound is the heating and cooling system and its whisper of air. If I lie very still, I can just make out the hum of the fridge in the kitchen. Eight stories below, the city is already awake. Cars honk in the traffic. Breaks squeal. I'll be out there soon, looking for a job.

For now, I roll over onto my back and stretch. I feel good. Well rested. Well fucked, if I'm being honest. I slept deeply all night and didn't wake up worried about anything.

Sunlight streams through the window, and it's like Graham was never there.

I swallow thickly, realizing he never came back. I force myself to shut down all emotion that creeps in and instead concern myself with the task of getting a job so I never have to approach Graham for another arrangement again.

chapter 5

Graham

USUALLY, WHEN I GET TOGETHER WITH ONE OF MY FRIENDS—*IF* I HAVE time to get together with a friend—it's business that distracts me. There's never a moment there isn't something to do. Someone is always waiting, the emails never stop. There are fires and problems everywhere and every day.

I know I shouldn't let my work life get in the way of relationships, but if I don't do it, no one else will. And more importantly, everything I've spent years working my ass off for could unravel.

My friend Brian, with short brownish red hair and a five o'clock shadow, sits across from me at a sports bar that rides the line between upscale and pretentious. The TVs boast the football game and I know Brian has a couple hundred riding on it.

On the next run, when Brian settles into our booth with his hand curled around his beer and his eyes focused on the play, I take out my phone. I tap the screen and scroll through the emails that have come through. But I'm also checking for something else.

Any messages from Maddie.

She hasn't sent one, but I have half a message typed out.

No pressure, but I was thinking…

It's a ridiculous way to start a text. I delete it and try again.

The apartment building is nice, but there are other places we could go, if you were interested in…

That's a smooth way to ask a woman out. By reminding her that other places exist. I delete it all again with frustration that Brian picks up on. His gaze drops to my phone and then back to the flat screen TV. I'm sure he assumes it's just business. Heat scorches the back of my neck. In a way, that's what it is. *But I want more.*

I clear my throat and take a swig of my beer.

I want to ask her out. That's the whole point of writing and rewriting the text. I just don't know how, given the way things started between us.

I'm willing to accept responsibility for that. I just don't know how to fucking fix it.

"Always the emails, right?" Brian smiles at me, his eyes crinkling. He's the same way. We keep tabs on our money at all hours of the day. "They never stop."

I swipe into my email app just so I'm not a total liar. "Yeah. That's how it goes." He must sense something off because his eyes narrow, and even though the next play starts, he doesn't give the TV his attention.

"What's new with you?"

"More acquisitions," I tell him, that burning feeling at the back of my neck comes back at the thought of my most recent *acquisition*. "Getting into stocks and hedge funds as well."

"Sounds boring," he states and then takes a large gulp of beer.

I laugh at that—can't help it. Brian works on Wall Street, like he always planned to. He came from money, but not the kind the two of us are making now. He always wanted to get to that next level, and Brian's done it without leaving a single thing behind, unlike me.

I guess I haven't left Brian behind, which is saying something. We've been friends since grade school. His parents are proud of him. They've said they're proud of me, too, and they've always been kind, but I don't see them as family.

Brian and I watch the game until a commercial break comes on. He orders chips and salsa, then looks at me across the table.

"You should come to the Berkshires with us this winter," he suggests.

I've been there before. They have a nice place, but it's a little too family-oriented for my liking. It makes sense for Brian to want to go, though. He's married, and before too long, they'll only want places that are family-oriented.

I tend to my drink and ignore how that makes me feel cold.

Not the Berkshires in the winter, but Brian and his wife—all my friends and their wives—becoming *families*, with me on the outside.

I've never wanted a family or a *replacement* family. Not since my parents died. Families are a limited-time thing. They always fall apart and it fucking hurts when they do.

The waitress comes back and puts the chips and salsa between us. Brian dips a chip into the salsa and looks at me, eyebrows raised.

"We'll see," I hedge.

Brian scoffs. "What else are you going to do? Sit in your fancy penthouse alone?"

I've never thought much about being alone in my penthouse on Christmas. It's another day. There's nowhere to go on Christmas, and the more my friends pair off, the less I feel welcome going to their places on holidays. Who wants a lonely third wheel on Christmas morning? I won't be someone's burden.

Thoughts of what Maddie will do this winter come to mind and I find myself curious.

My life hasn't been empty. It's been full of goals to meet and money to make and projects to close. Then Maddie came into it, and now I can't see anything *but* how empty all of it is. A great big penthouse. Me on my phone. Snow falling outside. Christmas, and no one to open presents in the light of the tree.

I glance back at my phone and think about texting her.

I could…offer to tend to her needs. Take care of her. If she wants.

I still don't know how to say it though. How to present the offer in an acceptable manner. Especially given it will be in writing.

Half of what I want to say should never be written in black and white.

Even if I want her in my penthouse on Christmas. Fuck I could just imagine unwrapping her lingerie as if she's my personal gift.

I glance down at the black text and my thumb taps aimlessly.

I don't want to sound like I'm offering money for her company, or anything of that manner. Like I'm paying her for companionship.

Although if money is what she would want, I'd give it to her. A *Pretty Woman*-esque arrangement.

"What's going on with you?" Brian asks, his tone careful. "You're quiet."

I watch the game on the TV, purposely not looking at my phone, and try to figure out what the hell to tell my oldest friend in the world. If I told him it was nothing and to drop it, Brian probably would. But then I'd be exactly where I was when I came into this bar.

"I'm thinking about asking a woman out." I blurt it out without looking at him.

Brian lets out a low whistle. "Look at you. This girl must really be something for you to keep checking your phone like that and looking like a nervous school kid."

Normally, I'd deny the hell out of it. I *always* check my phone. That's not new. And if I look nervous, that's because I have other things to be nervous about.

But this is Brian and he's asking, and for once it seems important to tell the truth. Because I am all too aware I need help. Afterall, he landed a wife. He has to know something about this arena that I don't.

"It's just…someone. I met under odd circumstances."

"What kind of—"

"Don't ask about the circumstances." I cut him off, a little harsher than intended and hold his gaze a moment too long.

"Okay?" He raises his eyebrows. "And you want to ask her on a date?"

"I would like to, yes. And maybe more. I don't know."

"More?"

Frustration gets the best of me as I run my hand through my hair. "I'm telling you, it's ridiculous. I can't stop thinking about her."

"I'm not asking about the circumstances," Brian says after a minute. "But…is that what's making it tough for you to ask her out?"

"Yeah. You could say that."

"Maybe you just have to forget about the circumstances, then."

I can't. A huff of a sarcastic laugh leaves me. There's no way in hell I could forget what happened…it's burned into my memory.

"Things can always change." Brian eats another chip with salsa. He pushes the basket toward me. "I think it's best if you take matters into your own hands. Just let her know what you want. It's like an offer," he suggests and motions with his hand as if I should know how to make an offer.

It takes great effort to breathe evenly and consider a response other than *I've done that. I literally took Maddie into my own hands, and now there's always going to be some kind of tension between us.*

"And if I already have…made an offer, that is? If it's too late to change the way she sees me?"

I don't even know *how* she sees me. All this is based on my own assumptions and the unwanted anxious emotions I can't seem to shake off.

"What kind of an offer?" he questions, and I shake my head once. He readjusts in his seat. "You made an ass out of yourself or something?"

"Don't ask."

"You're not giving me much here," he mutters, and then a foul is made on the screen and the corner of the bar erupts with outrage that distracts us both for a moment.

It settles quickly enough.

He finally says, "Just talk to her. What's the worst that could happen?"

That I lose her, obviously. The chance to have her fill this emptiness that's been glaringly apparent slips through my fingers.

When the chips are gone and the game is over, I haven't decided what to send in a text. All I've decided is to wait until the next time rent is due.

chapter 6

Maddie

M Y FRIEND SUZETTE BREEZES INTO THE CAFÉ WITH A WIDE, BRIGHT smile on her face. It's the kind that says she has good news, and God, I hope she does.

Even if it means I won't have to go to Graham and ask for help anymore. Thoughts of him make my thighs tighten and a shiver of want runs down my shoulders. He has a little spell on me. I'm certain it's because of my broken heart and hopeless ways with men. I need to shake it off. I need to shake *him* off.

I ignore the sharp feeling of regret at that thought. After Kevin, I've learned my lesson. But I can't help it if I loved having Graham in my kitchen. It felt forbidden but familiar at the same time, like something we both needed. Almost like the broken window didn't matter at all.

I loved every second of it, but it can only be a moment of my life. And now it's time for me to move on.

Pushing those thoughts from my head, I stand up and wave at Suzette, returning her smile with the biggest one I can. "Hi! How are you?"

With wide steps that cause her red-soled heels to click on the floor, she comes over and gives me a quick hug, smelling like the fresh air outside and her hairspray. "How are *you*? You look like you're doing so much better!" Her jet-black hair with a blunt bob and bangs pairs perfectly with her sharply cut dress that hugs her curves. She looks expensive, mostly because everything she touches is expensive. Her hug is nothing but warmth and compassion. Just like always. I might have bad luck with men, but with my friend group, it's always been wonderful. All of them are married and they don't have quite as much time as they used to, but still, I'm grateful I have good friends in my life.

We take our seats at the table and the barista brings us our coffees as we make small talk. It's easy and Suzette updates me on her new place and what Julia and Kat have been up to. Suzette sips her coffee with an appreciative grin. The café is bustling at this hour of the morning, and the sound of other people chatting does something great for my nerves. At the counter, a guy is flirting with the barista, and she's flirting back. Maybe I should've spent more time meeting men in cafés instead of…well in dire circumstances.

But then I wouldn't be where I am now. Granted, being jobless and late on rent isn't great. I can't argue with the other parts of my life having abundance, though, and I'm grateful for that.

"Have you find your dream job yet?" Suzette asks when a moment of quiet passes.

"Not exactly, but soon." I hold up crossed fingers. "I've been applying for jobs like my life depends on it."

I'm not kidding. I must've applied for forty jobs since Graham left my kitchen last week. I've written and rewritten my resume twice as many times, trying to frame my charity board experience in the best light possible. It's really too bad I can't figure out a way to fit in *problem-solving by getting the hot rich man who owns my building to float me the rent*, because that feels like a real achievement as well.

"Like your life depends on it," Suzette shakes her head as she repeats what I've said, raising her eyebrows. "Doesn't money always feel like that? I really think you should have called me sooner."

I make a face at her. "I didn't want to." In truth, my friends are much better off in life than I am. But I'd never want to burden them. Even venting to Suzette felt wrong. I didn't want her to take it the wrong way. A bottle of pinot will really open me up though.

"Why not?"

"Because I was such a mess before Kevin, and you had to…you know. You were there for all of that."

"I was *glad* to be there for all of that," she says firmly. "That's what being friends is for. Being there for one another even when things get shitty."

I can feel it, all over again, how heartbroken, confused, and angry I was. That was a breakup that seemed to last forever. I would wake up in the morning and swear I was over it, and by evening I'd be calling Suzette again to vent just so I could hold back tears.

I hadn't wanted to tell her what happened with Kevin, too, because in some ways it felt like *my* failure.

I don't think that anymore.

It doesn't make it easier to let other people see me when I'm down…again.

So I'm not going to be down. Not about this, even if what was supposed to be a simple transaction is turning out to be more complicated than I thought, at least in the feelings department. I remind myself again that I can't make assumptions about what Graham feels—I *won't* make assumptions. That'll get you into trouble faster than your fiancé can say *I'm leaving*.

"You're right." I take a drink of my hot coffee, savoring the warmth and the flavor. That's a good reminder that no matter how hard things get, there are still parts of life that are *wonderful*. Like coffee with hazelnut flavoring. "But we're here now."

"Next time, just call me," she insists in a serious voice, but cracks a smile. "Because I have good news."

"What kind of news?"

"Good news for you, silly." She twists in her seat and looks through her purse, then pulls out a business card. Suzette slides it across the table like it's worth a million bucks.

I take the card and turn it over. It's the classy kind of business card—thick paper, smooth ink. This isn't the cheap kind you can get at any office supply store.

The name on the front reads Michael Davies, CEO.

"What is this? I mean, *who* is this?"

Suzette smiles, pleased with herself. "I asked around, and it turns out a friend of a friend has a close friend whose company consults with nonprofits."

I tip the card one way, then another, watching the light move on the embossed letters. "Consultation?"

"It's right up your alley, Maddie."

The name seems to ring a bell and then I read the website on the back and the tagline. "Wait, I applied for this place." I nearly gasp as I the realization dawns of me. The company name looks familiar when it didn't only moments before. "Only I applied to work in filing, not as anyone's assistant or consultant."

"Well, the CEO needs an assistant with a consultation background, and you have tons of experience."

"I don't, though. I've never worked as a consultant."

"On the other side, I meant. You were on all those boards. And it's not like that's all you've ever done. You had jobs on boards before and always made it work. You know the ins and outs, and you have recent insight into costs and strategy. Don't sell yourself short."

I stare at her across the table. "You spun my board experience into a lead?" My heart pounds; I was on boards but it's not like I was making the executive decisions. I have insight yes, but I wasn't in charge of any major decisions.

"You can lean in this direction. Don't undersell yourself."

"I just don't want to oversell myself," I tell her.

A knot in my chest releases. I hadn't known how much stress I was actually under until Suzette handed me this card.

"That's impossible to do, Maddie. You have so much worth to provide. And they need it. Truly, this will be a match made in heaven."

I let her words sink in and think back to all the strategy meetings. I did have a lot of success in that department, and more than that, I loved doing it. "It's good to hear you say that, because I've felt like a total fraud lately."

"Don't." She waves a hand in the air. "The last thing you are is a fraud. And if Michael thought so, he wouldn't have given me a card. All you need to do is call and set up the interview."

"You have no idea how good that sounds."

"It's not going to be good, it's going to be *great*." Suzette beams at me. "And, honestly, I don't think you'd be an assistant very long. Once he sees how good you are at fundraising, he'll have no choice but to put you in charge of a team."

"A *team?*"

"They have a whole department just for gifts and philanthropy. You'll get your foot in the door, and it'll be like that." She snaps her fingers.

"Oh, wow." I take a few deep breaths, feeling lighter and hopeful once again. "That's…thank you. I was starting to lose hope a bit on the job front. Having a rich fiancé isn't impressive on a résumé."

"Well…" Suzette gives me a meaningful look. "You don't have a rich fiancé now." She glances around the café as if we might be overheard. "You know what? Michael's building isn't far from here. Why don't we walk over and see it?"

We take our coffees and go. I'm equally nervous and excited. Suzette's confident enough for the both of us about this new job. I fall for her enthusiasm hook, line, and sinker. It only takes a block or two for excitement to win.

"So." Suzette tosses her empty cup into a garbage bin. "What had you so excited before I gave you the best job lead ever?"

"Oh, it's probably not…it's nothing, really."

"Did you meet someone?" she guesses. Suzette is sharp as a whip.

My face gets hot. The truth is that part of me wants to tell everybody I meet about Graham, but the other part wants to keep him a secret. That way, what we have together only belongs to me. Well that and the fact that I exchanged sex for rent also stays a secret.

"Maddie!" Suzette nudges my elbow with hers, and for a second I fear she can read my mind. "I can see you blushing. Did you meet a guy? No, no…tell me *where* you met a guy. I can tell you have a crush."

I swallow thickly, holding onto my paper coffee cup with both hands. "You can't say anything."

Her eyebrows go up. "A secret boyfriend?" I can tell she wants to laugh, and I let out a long breath.

"He's not my *boyfriend*." I glance around us, but there's nobody even close to recognizable on the street. The city block looks vibrant in the sun. "He's just… someone I met."

"Blind date?"

"Actually…" I steel myself to tell her the truth; my heart beats faster. "I met him in an elevator"—she eyes me, waiting for more details—"and I first saw him when I was still with Kevin."

Her mouth drops open. "*Madelyn*." She whispers my name, and it takes everything in me not to respond *yes, Mother*.

"I didn't find out until after Kevin left that he owns the building."

"And you're *dating?*" she drags out the word as if it's unbelievable. Which it is because we are not dating.

"Shh!" I look around again, but the only people in sight don't seem to have noticed. "And no. We're not dating."

"What *is* going on, then? I know you, and I know something is going on. I have to know!"

My heart beats hard as I question whether or not to tell her. With my nerves racing and her wide eyes boring into me with desperation, I know I have to tell her. Besides, Suzette would never judge me. She's been married, divorced, and involved in an office scandal with her boss. All the while, I've been there for her. I swallow down my fears knowing out of all the people in the world, she might get what I'm feeling. The good and the bad.

"I needed some help with the rent." Now that the moment is here, I don't know how to describe it in a way that's not going to make it seem…immoral. "So I asked, and he offered me an…arrangement."

Her eyes brighten. Her cheeks turn a bright pink and her voice raises in octave. "Like…a sexy arrangement?"

"You wouldn't believe how sexy it is."

Suzette tips her head back and stares at the sky in disbelief. Then she picks it back up and looks at me. "Maddie, that's—"

"Wrong. I know. I shouldn't sleep with anyone to pay the rent, much less—"

"That's *hot*." She corrects, stopping in her tracks and waiting for me to look her in the eyes.

"—a man who happens to…what?" It takes me a moment to realize what she's said.

"That's hot. And adventurous. I don't think I'd have been brave enough to take him up on it. Was it in his office?"

"My place."

"So now your rent's covered for the year?"

"The month," I say quickly. "It's not supposed to be anything long-term. A one-time deal…that turned into a two-time thing." I start to explain but then slam my lips shut.

Suzette immediately looks skeptical. "Yeah, right. I bet he fell for you already. There will be a third time," she states matter of factly, taking a sip of her coffee. We continue walking down the sidewalks of Manhattan.

I think of Graham standing at the door of my apartment, his eyes dark, desire clear on his face. At the time, I wouldn't have said it was love, and I probably still wouldn't, because…

Because that would be getting my hopes up for nothing. What I have with Graham was never meant to be about a relationship. If he'd wanted that, I'm sure he would've said as much.

And I'm not falling for him, either. Fantasizing about different excuses to get him to my apartment again doesn't mean love, it means that he's so sexy I can't breathe, I like the feel of his hands on my body, and I want to know more about him.

Not that I'm in *love*.

"I'd put money down that there's going to be a third arrangement." She mocks the way I said it and I can't help but blush.

"I don't think so." I hold my head high. "It was just a…business deal."

"Then why do you have that look on your face?" she asks me softly and I wish I wasn't so easy to read.

Suzette's known me long enough to know that I love falling in love. Sex and love are hard for me to separate. I think. I don't know. It's just the way I am. I love the rush at the beginning and the giddy feelings whenever you get to see the other person and how it seems impossible to spend even five minutes apart.

She *also* knows how devastating it can be when it all falls apart. She was there through the last major breakup I had before I met Kevin, and she stuck by me through the ups and downs without ever saying *I told you so.*

"It's just about having fun?" she questions softly.

"It's about paying the rent." I glance over at her, and the corners of her mouth are turned up. "And…yes. It's fun."

"As long as you're happy."

"I am happy enough to leave that behind. And now that I have this lead, I'm sure I'll be *very* happy."

We reach the building where Michael Davies' company is housed. It's a sky-high, gleaming tower that says *this is a business doing important things in the world.*

It reminds me of my apartment building. Graham's building isn't quite as tall as this one, but it has a vibe to it that says *important people live here, and they love it. You would love to live here, too.*

I try to blink away the thoughts of him as Suzette rambles on about the company.

"The company's housed on the tenth floor, so you'll have a view when you're at work." Suzette counts the floors with a fingertip in the air, then points. "That'll be nice, right?"

"Really nice." Even if all I can think about is the view from my very own apartment. Every time I look at the windows, I think of Graham, and the way he feels when he's inside me. I wonder if I'll think of him the same way if I get this job and head to the office every morning. I wonder if I could even stay in that apartment…or if I should.

Suzette and I stare up at the building together, taking it all in. She's right. This is going to be it. This is going to be the job that puts me on the path to a life I want.

She would know. I watched Suzette accidentally fall into love, too. It was a sizzling scandal and I freaking loved that for her. Miss prim and proper and all business, doing the deed in her boss' office…apparently against the skyscraper window too. She knows a thing or two about unorthodox relations. Years later, it's easy to see how happy she is. Everything turned out just the way it was supposed to for her.

And it's going to turn out that way for me, too.

Hope warms itself in my chest. I've been called naïve plenty of times in my life. People want me to be more cynical about the world. For some reason, it bothers them that I want to be optimistic. And yes, sometimes I'm not. Sometimes, in the middle of the night, I forget that worrying doesn't help anything.

Action helps. Doing things helps. Meeting handsome men and asking them for help with the rent helps.

There I go again.

A soft laugh from Suzette pulls my attention away from the building and back to her.

"What's so funny?"

"You," she says gently. "I can tell you're thinking about him."

I blush violently and then blatantly lie. "I'm not. I was thinking about how this job could help me get my life back on track. And after *that*, I'm never letting it get off track again."

"That's my girl," Suzette says, and loops her arm through mine. "Call this afternoon to set up an interview. He's waiting for the call."

"Call? Shouldn't I submit a separate application? Send some emails or something?"

She shakes her head. "I told you, I asked around. They're going to be ready for you. Just call, and I'd bet anything you'll be headed in to work on Monday."

Suzette lets out a satisfied sigh. "In the meantime, I want to hear all about this man you're having a torrid affair with."

"A *torrid affair?*" I squeak. "It's not an affair *at all*, Suzette. We're both very, very single, and I—"

"You needed help with the rent," she says simply.

I needed help with the rent. I nod, and then that unsettling feeling sets in again. "Which is in the past and the whole thing is over," I assure her.

She gives me a skeptical look and I shake my head. "It's done. No more. One-time deal."

She corrects me. "I thought you said it was twice." She peers at me from the corner of her eyes with a smirk.

"Twice and done."

She laughs. "Said no one ever."

chapter 7

Graham

Days go by, and I don't hear from Maddie.

I suppose I didn't expect to hear from her. There's a possibility that by the end of the month she may be in need of another…deal. But likely she'll have found work and given our encounters, she may avoid me.

It's unsettling how much that bothers me and how often I think of her and wonder if when the clock strikes midnight, she'll call. The one thing I'm sure of is that she hasn't moved out. Not that I'm stalking her, but I am aware of her comings and goings from the security cameras.

I check them throughout the day as it stands, so I'm not doing anything out of the ordinary. I'm making sure my residents and my building are both safe and protected.

The third time I check this morning, I find her. I lean back in my seat, holding the cup of black coffee and watch her gorgeous curves sway as she walks. She's so fucking beautiful. How I wasn't obsessed with her for the entirety of her residence here is beyond me.

She heads out of the building at a quarter after eight, wearing a skirt suit that makes me instantly hard at my desk. Maddie leaves with her hair swept back into a bun and her head held high, looking confident and beautiful.

She also carries a powder blue work tote that appears to be large enough for a laptop. The uneasiness that settles at the thought of Madelyn acquiring a job is once again unsettling. It's certainly good for her for a number of reasons to be busy with work and to have an income.

Yet…I find myself at a loss.

I'm far too aware that I don't know what job she got, where she's going, or who she's working for. Clearing my throat, I rock back in my seat, contemplating the possibilities.

I ignore the urge to station myself in the lobby of the building just for the chance to run into her. The things I want to say aren't appropriate for the arrangement we have.

The arrangement we *had*. I don't think, if my instincts are correct and she's now employed, that Maddie needs anything else from me. Look at her, with every single strand of her hair in place, her perfect, pert body, and the spring in her step that says she's got everything under control.

Once she's gone, I turn the monitor off and go back to the tasks at hand, attempting to ignore thoughts of her throughout the day. Coffee comes and goes as do emails. The clock ticks by seemingly slower than it should. Every so often, I imagine Maddie on my desk, her legs spread as they were in her kitchen, and I groan with frustration and have a hardened cock that aches to be inside her again. It's impossible for the hours to tick by without thoughts of her.

Right around five, she comes back from the office the same way, only a little more satisfied, like she made the day hers.

That's what she did. I'm sure of it. I should be glad for her and that's what I tell myself, that I'm glad she has found a way out of the trouble she was in.

A week passes, and then another, and I don't get any other calls about broken windows or being short on rent money that's due any day. I try not to look for her on the cameras, but my little seductress has a routine now. She leaves for work at the same time every day, and most days, she comes home at the same time, unless she goes out with friends. On the weekend, she goes to a yoga class with a slightly older woman who has a ring on her finger and smiles at Maddie like they're close friends.

I hate that I can't let go of thoughts of her unless I'm buried in work. I hate that I feel compelled to initiate a new arrangement with her, but I'm unsure of what exactly it would entail and whether or not she would be interested. I need to ensure the proposal is tempting for her. As tempting as she is to me.

I watch her leave on the screen and then I focus on the business deal sitting in my email, instead of occupying more time with thoughts of a woman who doesn't appear to be thinking of me.

Immediately, I'm agitated and turn from my computer to face the office windows, watching the cars stories below drive past.

Harland Porter is a pain in my ass. He wants to talk about different details every day in no pattern that I can figure out. Every conversation we have makes it tempting as hell to walk away, which only makes me dig my heels in deeper. I can outlast a nervous asshole like Harland Porter. I can grow my empire by one more building. I can have anything I want.

Except Maddie.

To hell with dwelling on her. I'm not going to lose my mind over the fact that she hasn't called, even if it's getting harder to sleep at night. When I do sleep, I dream about her—the way she bent over the furniture, the way she wrapped her legs around me in the kitchen, the way her mouth felt.

The dreams aren't as good as the real thing.

I'm thinking about the real thing *again* near the end of the month, my cock hard and my teeth gritted, when there's a knock at my office door.

Annoyance grows. I'm not to be disturbed and the office is aware.

Before I can turn around, a feminine and soothing voice says, "Hi, Graham."

It's her.

Adrenaline courses through me and I do everything I can not to show a change in demeanor. As I turn and catch sight of her, I'm forced to slightly readjust myself. A cream-colored lace dress that appears youthful and springish, but also luxurious and even bridal, clings to her as she stands in the threshold. She could be a bride getting married at city hall in one of those ceremonies they feature in the Lifestyle section.

The sight does something to my lungs. I suck the air from them as a stray strand of hair falls in front of her face, and I'm forced to meet her gorgeous gaze.

"Madelyn," I greet her and with her name on my lips, my cock twitches.

She bites her lip, glancing over the office and breaking our heated gaze. "Your secretary wasn't here, so I showed myself in. I hope that's okay."

"Of course. Come in." I gesture to the seat across my desk and take my seat. "Is this about another arrangement?" I ask her and her wide eyes look back at me. I've never felt more on edge as she nods slowly.

"Close the door and lock it." I answer and she obeys. Fuck, I'm harder than I could imagine. It's almost like a game…or like a dream.

Maddie closes the door behind her, her hand hesitates, and then flips the lock. The sound is sinful, and it elicits a raw and desperate need stirring inside of me. Almost like a hunter to a prey, but this prey is coming to me. Fuck, I wish she'd crawl to me.

I almost request it, but I don't want to push my luck.

"Have a seat," I offer and I'm surprised by her response.

She shakes her head, then crosses the room to me in graceful, confident steps. Within seconds she's close enough that I could wrap her in my arms if I wanted. My heart pounds at the doe eyes staring down at me, her heart-shaped lips, and her body in that dress.

"What's this about, Madelyn?" I cross my arms over my chest to keep from touching her. I won't touch her unless she asks. Maybe not until she begs. "It's time to pay the rent again," I state the obvious.

"It is," she murmurs softly. I can practically hear her heart pounding and for a moment I'm taken aback. Speechless. That's not what I thought she'd say at all. Not given she's employed, but perhaps she isn't.

"And you need…an extension? Or…what exactly?"

"I don't want to use you for money," she says and her voice wavers. She swallows thickly and the tension between us heats. "But I liked what we did," she whispers as if it's a confession.

"We can keep doing what we've been doing," I offer, and I love the very thought of it.

"I thought maybe…it could be…" She swallows thickly, barely able to keep my gaze. "It doesn't have to be about the money," she suggests, and lifts a hand to trace one of the buttons on my shirt.

"I don't want your money, I want you available to me," I tell her, and I've never felt more needy—more greedy—in my fucking life. I want her on her knees sucking my cock. I can already envision those hollowed cheeks. I want her spread on my desk so I can toy with her pretty pink pussy. I want to go home after a long day and fuck her on the edge of her sofa until she screams my name and comes on my cock. "Available whenever I like, and you can have whatever you'd like," I offer, although I second guess how exactly I've presented the deal. I bite my tongue, thinking perhaps a contract should be drawn up. I don't want to get ahead of myself.

"That seems like it could end badly for me." Her doe eyes shine with nothing but vulnerability.

"It could for myself as well," I counter. It could be a disaster, if everything goes to shit because I can't keep my mind off her…and my hands.

And I can't. It's been too long, and I can't stop myself from touching her. I work my fingers through her hair and tip her face up. Maddie blinks like she's on the edge of pleasure already.

"Why did you come here?" I ask her bluntly. As she attempts to take a half step back, I wrap my hand around her thigh, worried my tone may have been too blunt. "I'm glad you did."

"I just needed a one-week extension, but also…I missed you." I love the way she says she missed me. I have her where I want her, but my head is fogged with nothing but desire. I can barely think straight.

Fuck, my cock aches for her.

"An extension for rent? Because you got a job?"

"Yes. I just need a—"

"I don't care about an extension. I don't want your money Madelyn. I want you to be my little…" I almost say whore. I almost say it, but luckily, she does it for me.

"Your whore?" she questions, and I don't know how she feels about the word.

"My seductress. My…whatever you want to call it. You can be my little whore…if that turns you on." I'm careful with my words, and whatever I'm saying, she seems just as intoxicated by it as I am.

She takes a step forward and I wrap my other hand around her other thigh and turn my chair to face her.

"I'm scared," she admits in a whisper, and I know it's true. It's so fucking obvious.

"We could use a safe word," I suggest quickly and then take a deep steadying breath. "If either of us want to stop."

I take the moment, pulling her toward me and she straddles me like the good girl she is. Her scent is intoxicating, and her breasts rise and fall with each breath she takes. Maddie tips her head back, making the line of her neck irresistible.

I press a kiss there, then lick over it. "And when it's like this, then a safe word is a good idea."

"Like what?" she questions.

"Intense like this."

She lets out a soft sound when I suck at her neck.

I whisper at the shell of her ear. "When two people who…who like to make deals with each other. When I want to call you my little whore and tell you to crawl to me. When you want me to spoil you. Which, my little seductress, I desperately want to do."

"Like a sugar daddy?" she questions, humor on her lips but her brow is pinched.

"I don't love the name of it. I'd prefer for you to simply be my…my toy, my plaything, my whore—as you suggested. Do you like any of them?"

"I love all of them," she admits, and I press a kiss to her lips. Slow. Savoring every pounding heartbeat between us.

"You could break me so easily and I…I know…" Her eyes beseech me and I know this is what's holding her back. This is what's kept her from me.

"There's a power imbalance I will admit, but a safe word will be helpful. Especially if we are playing this game with boundaries neither of us have pushed before," I suggest. "I've never told anyone to crawl to me," I tell her as I unbuckle my belt. "I've never called anyone a little whore," I admit and sweep my thumb over her bottom lip. "I've never done anything with anyone else like I've done with you."

"I haven't either," she tells me, and I believe her.

"So we need a safe word," I tell her. "That way, we're both safe. We know when to get closer and when to"—I brush a kiss over the curve of her jaw—"and when to back off."

"Mmm. That's a good idea. I agree." She says as her hands find the back of my neck and she lets her head fall back, moving her breasts to my lips. Fuck, I'm hit with a wave of her perfume. My little seductress could be playing me and I wouldn't even fucking care. I'll get everything I want from her and she'll get everything she wants from me.

"Do you really think it's a good idea?"

"Yes. But what word?" she asks in return.

She'll have to take the lead on that one, because I've thought of plenty of things I'd like to say to her, and none of them mean *stop*. They all mean come live in my penthouse. Stop going places where I can't see you. Let me possess you, and I swear I'll take care of everything.

"I intend to fulfill my desires with this arrangement," I tell her. "So I suggest you choose a word you will remember, and one you'll use if you aren't interested in my suggestions."

The tension is thick and hot, and I can see the wheels turning as she thinks of a word. All the while I kiss over the line of her shoulder. The neckline of this dress is demure, office-appropriate, but there's enough skin showing to make me hot as hell. It's like she's inviting me to imagine her body underneath.

Luckily, I don't have to guess. I know. I knead her ass as I wait, and she gasps the sweetest sound.

Gorgeous. Perfect.

I get lost in thinking about what her tits look like and forget she's choosing a safe word for both of us.

"Maybe something like…"

I go back to kissing her neck, and Maddie's entire body responds. She writhes against me, begging to be fucked.

"Think, my little temptress. I need to know that word."

"Temptress," she says and her eyes light with mischievousness. "I like that."

I nuzzle into her neck, commanding her to come up with a word. "What word is going to tell me to stop?" *My temptress.*

"Red," she says.

"Red?" I kiss her just to see if I can taste the word on her lips. I can't. She's much sweeter.

"Red." She breathes. "It's simple and easy."

"Before we start, is there anything you don't want? Anything I've said that you aren't interested in. Crawling, being available anytime…anything?"

"Only when I'm here?" she says although it's a question. "Like I'm available when I'm here, but if I'm out with my friends—"

"When you're here or at preplanned times," I counter.

"If I'm here…in the building…at any time."

"Your pussy is available for me to fuck, as is your ass and your lips."

"My ass…I haven't…I haven't done that before."

"I can go slow. Or is that a 'red' situation?"

She thinks a moment and once again that spark shines in her eyes. "I think I want to try it."

"And if you change your mind, you say red."

She nods. "Right. I can do that."

"I know you can," I tell her and rock my hips, rubbing my cock against her cunt.

"I've never done this before," she tells me again.

"I haven't either but we can take it slow and find the arrangement that works. Right now though, I am more than ready for you to show me how much you want this."

She wastes no time, her hands fly over the buttons of my shirt, popping them open one by one. I don't take the dress off. I want to fuck her in it. She spreads her thighs over mine. I can't get my cock out fast enough, and the second I do, Maddie sinks down on it with a sigh. I keep my hands in her hair and let her work her silk-covered pussy over my shaft.

"Don't fucking tease me." I groan and her eyes spark. "Give me what I want."

"Yes, Sir," she says, and it ignites a deep pleasure inside of me.

This is everything I want. She is *everything* I've been missing.

Fuck, her cunt is heaven. She rides me with her hands gripped to my shoulders and nothing but pleasure written on her face. Her lips find mine and she moans, and it's everything I need.

She's slow at first and I can tell there's something she's holding back.

Maddie murmurs as she rides me. "I've thought about you every day that I've been in the office. I tried…I don't know." I thrust up and she gasps. "I tried to stay away, thinking it would be better somehow. It's not right to have sex for rent money." Her face is an even deeper red. "I shouldn't have asked you in the first place. But I want it."

"There's not a damn thing wrong with this," I tell her and pump my hips again, forcing a beautiful, tortured sound from her lips. Her dress rides up her hips, showing her bare skin.

She grinds down on me and her eyes go half lidded as her clit rubs against me.

With one hand on her neck and the other on her hip, I help her fuck me harder and deeper. Her blunt nails dig into my shoulders as the pleasure gets the best of her.

She sinks down again and again on my cock, her pussy clenching until I reach between us and give her some contact on her clit. She throws her head back and lets out a soft, sexy moan, her dress hitching up higher on her waist as she comes undone.

I let her ride me, using me to get her off until my own release is too much to hold back. Maddie moves her hips in small circles while I fill her with my own release. My head is full of ways that I could mark her.

Every little sordid thing we can do. And the things I can give her that would tempt her to stay for as long as I want.

I kiss her before my mouth can run away with me. Maddie kisses me back, her body still hot around me. I kiss her slower until her breathing slows down, too, but Maddie stays where she is instead of getting up.

She runs her fingers through my hair. It's a soft touch, intimate like we're actually together, and I let myself indulge in the fantasy for a minute. This is the perfect arrangement.

It doesn't take long for her climb off, and I help her steady herself.

Her eyes find mine and a question lingers there.

"Tell me," I say easily. I'm sure she has questions. Fuck, even I have questions racing in the back of my mind.

"When you say all the time…" she asks. "That I'm available *all* the time."

Yes. All the time. Every second. Every minute. She should be in my office, under my desk, all day until it's time to go back to the penthouse.

"What about it?"

"There will be times when I just want to be alone or I…"

Her hesitation is clear and the one thing I'm not going to do is lose her before it's even begun. "Once a week at least." It's so much less than I want, but it's the only thing I can say to her right now. If I told Maddie the truth, it would go badly. It would be too much for her, and she'd run. Or she'd like it too much, and when it crashed and burned we'd both be taken down with it. "And…if you're in need, I'm the one you'll come to."

"If I'm in need," she repeats quietly.

"If you need to be touched, you call me." I take a hand off her waist and stroke her hair. "If you need to be fucked, you call me. If you wake up in the middle of the night and can't sleep, call me, and I'll make you come until you can."

"What about…" She tilts her head to the side, thinking. "If another window breaks?"

"Don't break your windows on purpose."

"I didn't do it on purpose last time."

"I don't care if it's a broken window or a needy pussy. You call me. Only me. Nobody else."

Her eyes come back to mine and her lips part. I can tell she wants to ask me whether this goes both ways. She'll want to know if I'm fucking anyone else, and if I'm allowed to call in other women whenever *I* need.

"And you will be the only one I see for my needs as well," I tell her to ease any worries and then kiss her. I keep my eyes open and watch as she closes hers. Good girl.

I don't want any other woman. I don't want my hands on anyone else. I don't want to be inside anyone else. "And if you need anything else. A dress, a dinner out…anything. You'll let me know."

Maddie closes her lips, a smile curving the corners of them. I trace her bottom lip with the pad of my thumb. It sends another throb to my cock, though I've just fucked her.

That's how much I want her.

"We have a deal," she says.

"I like it when you call me Sir," I tell her.

Her lips form a tempting smile as she looks up at me with a devilish and playful spark in her eyes. "We have a deal, Sir."

chapter 8

Maddie

SMILING, A CUP OF COFFEE IN ONE HAND AND THE BREEZE FROM THE bustling city blowing my hair back, I wait at the cross walk and think back on this past week. Showing up at Graham's office was even better than the 'good idea' Suzette suggested, and so was the safe word.

When I walked in, he looked like he'd been starving. Butterflies bat away in my chest at the memory, and my smile widens. There's no denying it, he's into me. And I'm into him. It's hot and I don't care what anyone else would think… not that I'm shouting it from the rooftops or down the streets of New York City.

It still feels a little scandalous. A little forbidden. I never thought I'd trade my body for rent money. I also never thought I'd like it so much—this power-play thing that's happening. I freaking love it.

I never thought I'd get addicted to the feeling.

I clear my throat and bury the thoughts away as a work text comes through. I have to pause on the street to answer it.

Even with what's going on between Graham and me, I've been bringing my best to my job as Michael Davies' new assistant.

Suzette made it sound like he just needed one secretary, but it turns out the company is large enough that the CEO has one lead secretary and three assistants. I'm one of the three, and I'm going to stand out if it's the last thing I do. With the text sent, I take a sip of much needed caffeine and continue on, my heels clicking and my confidence rising higher and higher.

It's easier not to think of Graham when I'm actively taking notes, making copies, and answering emails, but every time my mind wanders…

There he is.

I'd be lying if I said I didn't struggle with it at first. The arrangement we made where he took care of my rent had been illicit, something people only do in secret, and I knew I shouldn't go running back once I could handle the rent on my own.

But I wanted him.

I wanted more of him. More of that naughty, illicit feeling. I wanted to do something dirty. I won't lie, the idea of crawling to him makes me hotter than I thought it ever would. Yet, there's another side that has me questioning if this is wise. It was *more*, and sweeter, and when he'd admitted he wanted me to be there for him—*just* for him and nobody else—my heart almost flew out of my chest. I wonder if he knows how needy he looked at that moment.

I'm not going to tell him. Graham is handsome and charming and rich, and he doesn't want people to know he needs anything. But there's a piece of him that's missing something, and I know I can be that. And I am enjoying every second of it…I'm just a little nervous that I'm the one who's going to fall head over heels and I'm the one who's going to get my heart broken again.

At that thought, I catch him outside walking like he's coming back from a coffee shop, a to-go cup in his hand.

"Isn't it late for coffee?" I call from the crosswalk, a smirk on my face as I toss my own cup into the metal trash can.

Graham looks over at me, not seeming very surprised that we're running into each other. After all, the past few days we have and I'm starting to think it's because he knows my schedule and he's waiting for me. His handsome eyes rake down my dress and my body heats. As they lift to mine, he smirks and responds, "Needed a pick-me-up."

"You're going to be up all night," I tease, twining my fingers together to keep from playing with his tie. It's a dark navy silk number and it suits him well in his crisp gray suit.

He raises his eyebrows. "What's wrong with staying up all night?" His voice is low, throaty, and I love it.

"A man with as much work to do as you have needs his beauty sleep."

"Hmm." He looks down at me just as the wind takes a lock of hair out of the clip I've had it in. He catches it with his finger and tucks it back behind my ear. His touch is like fire and I lean into it. "What are your plans for the evening? Maybe you could help me take the edge off."

"I don't have any," I tell him, my heart fluttering. "Did you have more work to do?"

"I do. A few things need tending to, but I take my work upstairs for the evening," he says. "Care to come up?" The tension between us grows with every passing second we walk to the building. As we step into the elevator I have high hopes… unfortunately it's occupied by an elderly woman so I keep my distance and so does Graham, although our eyes catch in the reflection. With every second, my heart beats a little harder and a little faster, but he doesn't put his hands on me, not even as the woman steps out with a little hum and nod, and the two of us make our way to the penthouse.

It's not lost on me that the first time I ever saw him was in this elevator. I catch him looking at our reflection as it whisks us up, and I bet he's thinking the same thing.

Even as he steps out of the elevator with me following, he still hasn't touched me. My steps halt before I make it even three steps in.

The view from his living room windows takes my breath away.

"This is stunning," I breathe, unable to help myself as I look out over the city.

Graham comes up behind me and puts his hand on my lower back. My eyes close from the simple contact. I crave his touch like I didn't know I could. "It's the same view you have, my little temptress."

That nickname, with the warmth of his hand on my back, sends pleasant shivers all over my body and I'm all too aware my nipples harden. "It's different up here," I tell him, meeting his gorgeous eyes. A spark ignites and I sink my teeth down into my lower lip.

"Have you ever considered that it's different because you're here?"

"No." I huff the smallest of laughs. "I'm sure it doesn't matter where I am."

"Yes, it does." Graham looks down at me with intensity in his blue eyes. "It matters more than you think."

I'm ready to crawl into his bed and never come out again, but I shake myself out of it. "Did you say you had work to do?"

Regret crosses his face, but he steels himself. "A few things before I'm done for the night."

Graham's penthouse is massive compared to mine. No surprise, since his takes up the entire top floor and mine is only a small section floors below. A large living room in the middle *reminds* me of mine, only it's wider, with more understated furniture and built-in shelves underneath the floor to ceiling windows. A small office is off to one side, and a hall leading into another section of the penthouse. I can see through to his kitchen and peek into a dining room from here. He waves his hand toward the right. "My bedroom is down that way."

I resist asking him to take me there right now. If I had an hour alone in here, I'd have to explore, because there's so much space and soft, tempting lighting, and I bet he has a private gym and a library, too.

Graham sits at a large, rounded sofa in his living room, his laptop on his lap. At first, I try to sit primly next to him, my feet on the floor and my dress, a simple cream pleated number smoothed over my legs. I kick my heels off and ready myself to tuck my legs under me.

But…

"Is it all right if I put my feet on the sofa?" I ask. I imagine it's far more expensive than anything I've ever owned, and his entire place looks spotless. "This couch is too comfortable."

"That's why I bought it," he says, a smile quirking his mouth. "Put your feet wherever you want."

I tuck my feet up under me and find a blanket spread over the back of the couch. It's lightweight and luxuriously soft, and it feels good to cover my legs.

"What has you working late?"

"Building my empire," he says simply, then taps away at his keyboard for another few minutes. "But I want you here while I work," he murmurs and then looks at me, "so I can have you after as a little reward."

A blush heats my cheeks and I have to look away a moment. When I finally come to my senses I ask him, "A real-estate empire?"

"That's the type." Graham seems to hesitate, his typing getting slower. "I'm working on acquiring a property from a man who doesn't want to sell it to me."

"Why doesn't he want to sell it to you?"

He laughs, the sound a quiet huff. "I don't think he wants to sell it at all, but I can't back down now."

"Why not?"

"Because I've already spent weeks going back and forth in emails and lunch meetings and phone calls. I'm not willing to let it go now that I've made an investment."

My face gets hot. I wonder if he thinks about me the same way—if I'm an investment that he's made, and now wants to get his money's worth. It's as forbidden a thought as fucking him for rent money.

And...hot.

In a way. I shift on the sofa and he notices.

"You're not an investment," Graham says.

I startle next to him. "I didn't...I would never say that...what?"

"Your cheeks got all pink." He lifts a hand from his keyboard and brushes a knuckle over my cheekbone. "I took a guess that you were thinking of yourself as an investment."

"Fine," I admit. "I was...a little bit."

"And what did you think about that?" he questions, his focus entirely on me.

I think...I'd like to be one of his investments. Sought after and taking his attention and focus. Even if it is just to be a reward at the end of a long workday. I think I'd love it.

"I think the idea of being acquired by you is sexy." It takes everything in me to admit, but once it's out, it's more freeing than I thought the admission could be.

"Sexier than paying the rent?" Graham's hand finds its way lower, under the blanket, and to the soft part of my inner thigh. I spread my legs just a little more for him.

"Oh, I don't know." I can barely say the word. My breath is coming too fast. "We could try both."

"What's your safe word, my naive temptress?"

"Red," I say in a heated breath.

"Good girl," he says before kissing me, and in a single moment I'm swept away in his touch. My head is fuzzy with lust. His hands are everywhere at once, his lips never stopping. He consumes every inch of my neck and lips. I'm barely cognizant as he strips me down to nothing and he fucks me over the edge of the sofa, facing the big picture windows, sliding inside me with hard, fast strokes. Graham makes me come that way, too, with his hand wrapping around and stroking over my belly until his fingertips find their way lower to circle my clit. He has to hold me in this position because my knees are weak and shaky. With every hard stroke I climb higher and higher until pleasure wraps itself around both of us at the same time. I'm breathless and stunned, really, by the time he's planting small kisses on my neck and settling everything back into place. When it's over he pulls me back into his lap and folds his arms around me. He plants a kiss and then another. It's silent as he leaves me on the couch, zips up his pants, and hands me what I need to get dressed again.

He sits next to me as he was before, although his arm is around me this time. I'm cuddled up to his side and he reaches for his laptop, reminding me that he has work to do.

"I thought…do you want me to stay?" I gather up the courage to ask him as the moment seems to come to a close.

"Yes." His answer is simple, and I start to feel out of place. "If you're available and don't mind that I'll be working," he adds.

I settle myself into his side, enjoying the warmth and comfort and simply nod.

The evening is easy. I have a few messages I answer on my phone and for the most part, I'm able to lay into him in comfortable silence, his laptop ticking away as he occasionally asks me questions. Sometimes he asks if I need anything, like the champagne he brings me. Sometimes he asks questions like whether I prefer tea or coffee and what restaurants I like in the city.

As the night gets later, his touches become more focused on my curves and he lingers longer. Two glasses of champagne down and his laptop closes. He pushes it back on the coffee table and then murmurs something about 'earning this' before his lips press to mine and his body covers mine. When we fuck this time, he's on top of me with my legs spread around his hips. The climax is higher and heavier than the last, and he groans my name into my neck just as I cry out his with the blinding pleasure.

I'm breathless and the most at ease I've ever been as I lie down on the sofa with my back to his front and the blanket wrapped around us. An old movie is playing on the TV; the New York skyline surrounds us.

"What do you think?" I ask after a while. "Worth the investment?" A small smile tugs at my lips.

"Every single penny," he says, and kisses the back of my neck. The simple kiss feels like heaven.

Time passes easily. The two of us finding out little pieces of each other, and each night falling into a steady rhythm.

We don't only have sex, which is what I imagined originally, though I'm sure that given a week without any obligations, we probably could. I can't get enough of him and the same seems to be true of him.

Graham takes me to get coffee in the mornings. And if he isn't there, I find a text on my phone telling me to have a good day and that there's a coffee waiting at the front desk for me.

Although the mornings have been the same, tonight is a little different.

He texts me before I leave the office and asks me if I want to meet for dinner. I expect someplace too fancy for my work clothes, but he takes me to an Italian place I told him once that I loved. "You really haven't been here?" I tease over our entrées.

It's not high-end, but it's authentic and the atmosphere is amazing. He simply shakes his head, folding the cloth napkin in his lap. With the candles lit on the table and the soft din of conversation around us, I can't help but think how romantic it feels.

"I usually come with my family. My aunt loves pasta and we're very close," I tell him casually and have a sip of the cabernet he ordered. "You should bring your parents." It's divine, so delicious that I almost miss his reaction.

Graham glances at me, his eyes guarded. "I see..." He trails off and doesn't say anything for a few minutes. For the first time, insecurity sweeps through me. It's sudden, but enough that I feel it in the tips of my fingers. I set the glass down and swallow thickly.

"I'm sorry if I said something out of line."

"You didn't." He twirls his fork over his plate, seeming to decide what to say. "I was close to my parents as well."

There's a *but* at the end of that sentence that Graham doesn't say.

"My dad died young, and my mother couldn't live without him. They're both gone."

"Oh, Graham." I reach for his hand across the table and squeeze it. "I'm so sorry. I didn't know."

He opens his mouth like he might reassure me and say it was a long time ago, but instead he says a quiet *thank you.*

We sit for a minute. Silverware clinks against plates at the tables around us. Faint noises from the kitchen float out to our table. I wish I could think of something to say but all I can think of is, "I'm happy to be here with you."

He offers me a smile but doesn't say anything else. I take another sip of wine, attempting to start any conversation.

"I feel awful," I admit to him and he tells me not to.

"According to a good friend of mine, it's why I work as much as I do. I wanted to make sure that never happened to me," Graham continues. "I wanted to make sure I had my life under control. Nobody would be able to run me into the ground."

He clears his throat and then says, "He says I work too much. I tell him he's just mad I make more than him." He attempts to joke, and I smile back at him, letting this admission sink in.

I run my thumb over his knuckles, considering my next words. This arrangement doesn't mean that we have the kind of relationship where I can comment on his choices. But I've seen how he works. I know he pushes himself beyond the regular working hours.

"Do you ever go on vacation?"

He laughs, his blue eyes crinkling. "I live in a penthouse in one of the most beautiful buildings in Manhattan. I'm always on vacation compared to the life my parents had."

I laugh along with him, but…I understand the sentiment. I get what it's like to struggle and not have enough money and always worry about making ends meet.

I also know that fixing it is hard work, and it's the kind of work you can't keep doing forever. Everybody needs a break sometimes, even if your father's life was objectively harder.

"Would you ever consider going on a vacation? A real one, I mean."

I keep my voice casual and take a sip of wine, watching Graham's face like this is just a getting-to-know-you conversation.

He watches me back, his eyes hot.

"Up until a few weeks ago, I probably wouldn't have. I don't see the point of being out of the office when I'm just going to take my work to another location."

The pause between us suddenly feels charged and even hotter than it did before. I can feel the flush coming to my face. Hopefully, Graham doesn't notice how often I blush around him. It's not because we're falling in love or anything, it's just because he's incredibly attractive and everything that comes out of his mouth turns me on.

Which might mean we're falling in love.

Or at least I'm falling in…*something* with him. Want, maybe. I'm falling into a much deeper want than the beginning, when all I could think about was not getting kicked out of my apartment.

"What about now?"

"Now…" He wets his bottom lip with the tip of his tongue. "Now, I might consider it, if the right offer came along."

"The right offer?" I question as my brows knit. My pulse feels like it's going too fast to actually pump blood, and I'm getting lightheaded. If I wanted to know for sure how Graham felt about me, I'd say…*if I asked?*

But I'm not sure I'm ready to know.

"If the right man asked me if I wanted to go somewhere with him, I'd think about going on a vacation…somewhere," I offer instead.

Something flickers across his face. "What kinds of places do you like to vacation to? Would you rather ski or lie on the beach?"

I answer with a smile and with the tips of my fingers slipping around the stem of the glass. "Anywhere I can wear a bikini."

"I like the sound of that. You can't wear one when you're skiing, though, so I guess Vail is out."

"That's where you're wrong. They have a *lot* of hot tubs there. I could spend practically the whole time in a bikini or at the spa while you…play in the snow?" I guess and he laughs, a deep husky laugh that soothes whatever part of me was concerned.

"I enjoy skiing and I do believe there is a spa I could leave you while I 'play in the snow.'"

The night carried on easily and when it was time to take me home, he did so like a gentleman, leaving me with a kiss and something else that made me feel like we took a small step forward in a direction I didn't know we would go.

The next week, Graham texts me when I'm in for the evening and I can't help but to smile.

Graham: Looking at some vacation spots. Can I get your opinion?

Maddie: Of course.

Graham: Come upstairs

Diligently, I take the elevator upstairs to the penthouse. Graham gave me a keycard that lets me onto the top floor, and when I get there, he's on his comfortable couch where he's already fucked me half a dozen times, his computer on the coffee table, and he's looking up places to vacation.

I cuddle in next to him, as I'm getting far too comfortable doing, and he angles his laptop toward me.

"The Virgin Islands," he says, and scrolls past gorgeous photos of cabanas next to a sparkling blue ocean. "Or there are some places closer that could be fun, and we could spend a week or two enjoying each other."

My heart does a little twist in my chest, that insecurity very much riding through me again. "A weekend getaway is probably all I could manage right now with my job."

He glances at me, reading my expression and then nods as if it's an easy answer.

"A weekend it is then." Graham scrolls through a few more resort listings. "In this hypothetical vacation, I think we should lie in the sun and enjoy drinks and the sound of the ocean."

We echoes in my head and makes me hot all over.

"Oh yeah? Is that what we should do?"

"For now…" He closes the laptop, sets it aside, and kisses me. "I think we should relax."

"Did you realize you were tired?" I ask him and he leaves me a moment, only laughing at my question as he goes to the kitchen. I watch as he opens a bottle of champagne and pours us each a glass.

It's only after he's back next to me, each of us sipping the bubbly, that he admits, "I do think I could use a moment to sleep in, and"—he lowers his voice, planting a small kiss on the crook of my neck before whispering in the shell of my ear—"enjoy my investments."

As I inhale his masculine scent, his eyes reach mine and the kiss we share in that moment is perfect. Everything is perfect with him. It's almost too good to be true and I find myself hushing that voice in the back of my head.

I anticipate him taking me again, but instead we lie down and relax into each other.

We relax so much that he ends up sprawled on the couch, his arms around me. I let my head rest on his chest and listen to his heartbeat for so long that Graham falls asleep.

He looks younger when he's sleeping, and it tugs at my heart.

I want to pull the throw blanket over both of us and stay all night, but thoughts race in my mind.

The way he talked about his parents and getting more from his life makes me hesitate. There's a decent chance he doesn't want anything serious because of this, and I don't want to be the one to get in his way.

And…I don't want to be the one who falls in love too fast.

That little voice in my head says it's already too late.

I slip out of his arms anyway, tuck the blanket around him, and go back down to the eighth floor. Back down to reality where I can't sleep because I'm almost certain I'm way in over my head, over my heels, and all the way back around again.

A T THE END OF THE MONTH, NEARLY FIVE WEEKS OF SEEING EACH other, if you can call it that, Graham whisks me away on vacation. I know from experience that there are plenty of beautiful sunny places to visit on the coast, but it hardly feels like five minutes on the private plane before we're touching down.

I spent most of the ride with his mouth on mine or sipping champagne and enjoying the little touches so that helped pass the time.

The beach house he rented for the weekend is so close to the water that I hear every wave that rolls in. It's minimalist, with everything nearly white so the view holds even more impact. Palm trees bend in the breeze. The air smells like ocean salt, and Graham strips off his dress shirt almost immediately and takes me into a massive bedroom overlooking the sea.

There are three lingerie sets on the bed already: one pink, one red, one black. "Your choice, temptress."

A blush rises through me and I can't help but think this is a fantasy I never dared dream before. One a girl like me couldn't have even imagined.

Graham stands with his hands on my waist while I look them over, pulling me into him. I can already feel how hard he is and how hard he has been since we were on the plane. My whole body is hot with how much he obviously wants me.

"Black."

He lifts the lacy lingerie off the bed and puts it into my hands. "Go change," he says. "Then come back to me."

My heart races as I ready myself and slip on the lingerie. It's beautiful and expensive, and when I'm wearing it, I really do look like a temptress.

I feel like one, too.

The sun is on an angle in the sky when I pad back out into the bathroom, completely enamored by everything about the present moment. Graham sits on the edge of the bed, in a suit that makes him look all the more powerful, his knees spread and his hands clasped between them. His eyes darken at the sight of me in the things he bought.

"Fuck," he says softly, his gaze wandering down my body as if he's undressing me with the simple action. "Strip for me."

I work my fingers under the straps and peel the lace away from my skin. I just put it on a few minutes ago, but it already feels like it's part of me. Graham bites his lip when the lace comes away from my nipple. They tighten in the cool of the air conditioning, and he motions for me to turn around while I work the panties over my hips and down to the floor.

"Bend," he says.

The cool air touches a soft, wet part of me, and Graham groans.

"Come here, temptress. Bring the lingerie."

It feels strangely small in my hands as I cross the room and step between his knees. All the while I can barely control my breathing. All I want is him to take me. Graham's hands find my hair, and he pulls my face to his and kisses me. It starts out hot and gets hotter, his tongue exploring my mouth and my body going into overdrive. It always makes me want more, but Graham only deepens the kiss, teasing me, taking his time while his hands roam over my waist and my nipples and the curves of my ass.

I'm out of breath when he finally takes the lingerie out of my hands and wraps the larger piece around my eyes.

With the lace folded over so many times, I can't see anything. It only adds to the tension that rolls through my body. *I need him.* I almost tell him but instead I swallow the confession.

His knuckles brushing over my ribs come as a welcome surprise, goosebumps spread all down the front of my body. His lips press against my collarbone. He works his way up the side of my neck, and then he shifts, pushing me onto the bed. He puts me on my hands and knees, my ass in the air, and gently slips a pillow under my stomach to prop me up.

"What—"

I don't get a chance to ask the rest of my question before his hands are on my hips and his mouth is between my legs. I've never been eaten out from this position and it's intoxicating and new and mind-blowing. My inner thighs shake. Heat concentrates between my legs, where his tongue is running over every inch of me and licking inside me. His hands stay firm on my hips until he uses them to spread me open a little farther. Every nerve ending across every inch of my skin is on high alert as the pleasure builds and builds.

I'm collapsed onto the bed, my head in my arms, and don't realize at first that his tongue is moving *up*.

It brushes against my hole and I tense, but Graham doesn't let me move. "Stay how you are, temptress. I want all of you."

"Okay."

"Good girl."

My mind is already overwhelmed by his mouth, and the feeling only intensifies as he licks my hole. I'm a mess, trying to push my hips back into his face, and it takes me a few seconds to realize he's pulled away.

A bottle clicks.

Something cool lands between my spread cheeks, and then Graham's circling my hole with his fingertips.

"Good girl," he murmurs in a deep tone coated with lust, though I haven't done anything but remained still. I'm trembling over a pillow, caught between wanting to come and wanting to stay in this hot, liquid feeling forever. "I'm going to put my fingers inside you. Get you ready. Have you ever taken like this before?"

"No," I gasp with my heart pounding.

He makes a pleased sound. "Don't worry, temptress. I'll help you. What's your safe word?"

"Red," I answer him, and he tells me what a good girl I am for him and how good it's going to feel. My nails dig into the comforter with anticipation.

He slides one finger into me slow, coaxing me to keep breathing. It burns a little, and when I make a noise, he adds more lube and keeps fucking me with that finger. His other hand slides between my legs. It feels so *full* and so *hot* and the pleasure builds inside of me like I've never felt before.

The second his fingers meet my clit, my inhibitions fall away. I can't concentrate on two things at once and my head thrashes. Graham circles my clit slowly, patiently, reminding me to stay where he put me, and it's all I can do not to try and fuck his hand. I get used to the finger in my asshole and moan, wanting more, wanting to come.

He adds another finger.

I don't mean to ride them, but it happens anyway. I want sensation any way I can get it. His fingers on my clit and inside me. It feels shockingly sinful, when he's rubbing like that, keeping my desire at a steady level.

The third finger is still hard to take.

"Please," I beg. "Let me come."

"When I'm all the way inside you," he says, voice soothing. "You can do that for me, can't you?"

"Yes." I rock my hips back toward him. "Graham. Fuck me. I can't wait any longer."

"You can," he murmurs.

He makes me wait.

He keeps fucking me with three fingers. They're thick, stretching me, and I bury my face in my arms and pant. I didn't realize it would be so much, but I never want to stop.

"What's your safe word, temptress?"

It takes a lot of effort to think of words at a time like this. "Red."

"Remember," he warns. "I'm going to fuck your ass. Stay relaxed for me."

He pulls his fingers out of my ass, and my heart climbs up into my throat. It's quiet for a moment and then the bed groans as he positions himself. I've never done this before. I'm not totally convinced that I *can*. But then his hands stroke down my hips, spreading me, and the head of his cock nudges against my lubed hole.

"Push back," he says softly.

I do it, my breath stuttering at how impossibly big he feels.

Graham fucks into me slowly, with as much patience as he used to kiss me, and when he finally slides inside I gasp at the stretch and my entire body lights on fire.

"I'll let you adjust," he says as my heart pounds. I struggle to take him and his hand trails back down between my legs, finding my clit.

The pleasure and the stretch are both so intense that I grab for anything I can reach. The only thing to hold is the blankets, so I curl my fingers around them and hold on, trying to breathe. I don't know what I want to do. Rock back against him, I think, but I don't know if I can take anymore.

His fingers on my clit make the decision for me.

I want to move with them so much that I tilt my hips forward, and when I move them back, another inch of Graham enters me.

"You're beautiful like this," he says, his voice strained, and I don't know if I believe him but I can't do a thing about it. All I can do is breathe into the covers. His fingers speed up on my clit and I rock back harder, taking more of him.

I get lost in the movement, surrendering to the stretch and the effort, and Graham grunts. "There," he says. "That's all of me, good girl."

I grind back on him, begging for more contact with his fingers. They work me faster as he pulls out and thrusts back in.

Over and over, steadily increasing in pace.

Everything goes hazy with pleasure beyond control.

My orgasm builds and builds until it explodes and every single inch of me clenches down on Graham.

"That's it temptress," he murmurs at the shell of my ear as I shake out my orgasm. He feels even bigger inside me, too big, and I brace myself on the bed as he pushes in as deep as he can and comes with the sexiest groan I've ever heard in my life.

It's hot inside me, and he feels so big I almost can't stand it, and every part of me shakes and shakes and shakes.

A short time later, Graham pulls out. I let him go with a hiss. He unties the blindfold with gentle hands, takes me in his arms, and then we're moving. Toward the bathroom, hopefully. Toward a really long bath. I need it for my wrung-out muscles.

He kisses my forehead. "You were so good."

So were you, I think about saying, but can't make it happen.

I barely remember dinner when I wake up the next morning. Graham strokes my hair and gives me new outfits to choose from and checks emails while I take a shower almost as long as the bath then dry my hair until it shines and put on the brand-new sundress he gave me.

Then we go out into the sunny resort town and stroll the sidewalks.

It's a dream vacation, really. The main street is quaint and busy with people coming in and out of shops, a lot of them obviously enjoying some time away from home.

My only problem is the soreness.

I hold Graham's hand as we walk past stores and restaurants, my thighs aching and my ass even more.

"That's nice," he says, nodding his head toward some art in a gallery window. "What do you think?"

"I think I need to slow down," I whisper.

He takes my chin in his hand and tilts my face toward his, his gaze intense and concerned. "What's wrong?"

"I'm sore," I admit with a laugh. "From last night."

Graham takes us to the edge of the sidewalk so we won't be in anyone's way and puts his hands on my waist. "You know that you can use your safe word without consequence, don't you?"

"Of course I do."

"How sore are you?"

I've been trying to ignore the pain, but…it's more than I thought it would be. "A lot," I tell him. "It was my first time, so maybe…"

"There are things we can do about that." He steers me to the nearest cafe and orders me an iced tea, sitting me firmly on one of the padded outdoor seats. "I'll be right back," Graham says. "Don't move."

When he comes back five minutes later, there's a packet of ibuprofen in his hand. He opens it with his teeth and watches while I swallow down two of the pills.

"We'll sit here until it starts to kick in," he says, then takes the seat next to me and holds my hand.

"I'm really okay," I promise, but he shakes his head, still worried about me.

That makes me feel as warm and loved as I did last night.

Loved. I shouldn't be thinking that word. I swallow it down and focus on feeling better.

I finish my iced tea, and when we step back onto the sidewalk, I can't help tipping my face up to kiss him. I feel a thousand times better with the painkiller, and it's wonderful to be out in the sun without anything to think about but relaxing together.

The kiss turns hot, Graham's hand coming up to grip my chin, and someone nearby shouts. "Cute couple!"

Graham picks his head up, his eyes narrow, a smile curving his lips only slightly. "Thank you." All the while my heart races and my body heats. *Couple.*

I watch him with emotions storming through my chest. I shouldn't want him to agree this badly. Maybe I just wanted to hear what it sounds like for him to say *yes, she's mine* in public.

Graham looks back down at me, his expression softening. "Ready to shop?" he asks.

"I'm ready," I tell him.

I don't tell him I'm ready for much more.

chapter 10

Graham

Brian: Come on, we want to meet her.

I STARE AT THE TEXT. BRIAN'S MESSAGE SITS IN MY PHONE UNANSWERED.
Brian: Just do it.

The sigh that leaves me as I stare out the window from my penthouse is filled with both agitation and apprehension. I shouldn't have fucking told Brian anything. He badgered me for an update and now this. I watch the cars move below me before deciding to text her.

It seems to me that it could be woven into the verbal contract that she would accompany me to social gatherings. After all, I do enjoy her company. The small sighs she makes when something romantic happens on the television and the way she bites down on her bottom lip, her brow scrunched, when she gets an email from work that something didn't go well. It's…noticeable and quite distracting in a good way. I find myself enjoying her and it's quite possible she'll fill a need within my friend group as well.

Graham: You have plans tonight?

Maddie: Tonight?

Graham: I need a date.

Maddie: Ooh, a date for what?

I can practically hear her response. The touch of excitement. It warms something inside of me and I bite the bullet. Why shouldn't I after all? She's mine when I desire and if it's something she doesn't prefer, we'll make that accommodation.

Graham: I'm getting together with my friends. Three of us. Small group, but they're bringing their wives.

Three dots bounce on the screen while she types his answer.

Maddie: You can't be the only one there by yourself.

Graham: That's what I thought.

Graham: Will you join me?

Maddie: Of course I will. What time?

Graham: I'll stop by your place at seven.

Maddie: See you then.

The moment she agrees, there's a relief that's unreliable, but it's quickly followed by unwanted nerves. I shake them off and do the best I can to focus, but for the rest of the day all I'm able to think about is whether or not she'll enjoy herself tonight and what Brian and the others will think of her. It's unsettling and given that I've never brought a date or had a girlfriend I've been interested in long enough to introduce to my friends, I'm not quite sure how to get rid of the anxiousness or what to do with it. I remind myself she's not my girlfriend, this is different. Even if it all goes to hell, I can simply keep them separate.

It's not until I knock on her door, wearing a suit and tie with no jacket, and she opens it that all apprehension falls away.

Her little black dress and kitten heels are both casual and yet elegant.

"Is this all right?" she questions, and I murmur that she's perfect. She's stunning. Once again I find myself wrapped up in Madelyn Cunnigham. It's odd how everything slips into place when she's with me. How the uncertainty fades away. She puts her arm through mine, and I guide her to the elevator and then into my private car. I find myself thinking I would feel even more at ease and these little hiccups like earlier wouldn't occur if she would move in with me.

I recall her stipulation about time apart initially but that was weeks ago, and I'm almost certain she'd agree things have been easy between us and that we are spending more and more time together. With the streets dark and the city lights surrounding us, I take glances at Madelyn the entire drive to the restaurant, wondering what she would say if I offered.

Maddie

All the nervousness in my belly keeps me relatively quiet, although I have a million questions on my mind.

Graham lays his hand palm up in the middle of the seats and I slip my hand into place. I can't help but smile as he rubs soothing circles on my wrists as if he can sense I'm nervous.

"So. Tell me about your friends. Have you known them a long time?" My heart pounds as he nods.

I almost ask him, 'this isn't like a test or anything right?' but then my lips slam shut. *A test of what?* We enjoy what we're doing and that's all there is to it, I lie to myself, knowing damn well this is different but not wanting to jinx it.

Graham answers more thoroughly, "I've known Scott and Drew since college and Brian since grade school. We've never lost touch. I don't have siblings, so they're the closest thing I have to brothers."

My throat gets tight at the subtle emotion in his voice. "That's really nice, Graham. My friend Suzette is like that. Basically a sister to me."

"Suzette?"

"Maybe you could meet her sometime," I offer. "I owe her a drink since she helped me get my new job."

He hesitates, then says, "I'd like that."

"I would, too." I scramble around for another question before the conversation can get too deep. "Do you get together with these friends often?" The car hums as we move through traffic.

"A few times a year." Graham says and then confides in me a little more and the small talk is more than helpful.

My nerves settle as he tells me more about his friends, the classes they took in college, and the things they got up to on the weekends. The driver pulls us into a curved drive that takes us off the city street and close to the door as we arrive at the restaurant.

It's on the first floor of a skyscraper with manicured plants in the front and lights glowing above the windows. A pristine awning covers a door made from dark wood that shines like it's been polished. Uniformed valets wait to park cars for people, and everything I can see looks freshly painted and lovingly maintained.

"Wow," I breathe. "This is a *nice* place." I nervously look down at my dress and wonder if I should have opted for something more…delicate or detailed or higher heels. I've been to a number of high-end banquets for charities and exquisite dinners and events with my ex, but this is…*more.*

"You look beautiful," Graham says, and offers me his arm. "Stunning even," he adds with a charming smirk that eases my mind.

He holds my hand in his as the hostess takes us through the restaurant. We walk past people at candlelit tables to a private room in the back. Graham's friends sit at a long table with their wives. When we step inside, all of them get up from the table to shake Graham's hand, slap his back, and sneak in hugs. The atmosphere is easy and friendly. They're more than welcoming.

"Graham, who's this?" one of his friends asks, barely concealed excitement in his eyes. "You've never brought a date before."

A blush heats my cheeks and I do everything I can to not let my nerves show as I give a little wave.

Graham rolls his eyes. "I told you I was bringing someone. Everyone, this is Maddie. Maddie, this is everybody." He goes around, telling me his friends' names and the names of their partners. The man who asked the question is Scott. He's tall and has dark hair like Graham. Drew has lighter hair and a quick smile. Brian's a redhead with a big laugh.

I know I'm supposed to play a part—to fill the space so Graham doesn't have to be the only single one here—but as soon as we sit down at the table, it all starts to feel…*real.*

All Graham's friends are married, and all the wives are friendly, open, and funny, and they include me in their group without hesitation. It's easy to imagine how it would be if I was Graham's wife and not just his stand-in date.

Too easy.

I remind myself throughout the night that this is fake. They call me his girlfriend and I swallow down the lie as I answer their questions.

Graham brushes his knuckles over the back of my neck as everyone's chatting between dinner and dessert. It's an affectionate gesture. It's casual and intimate, and I *like* it.

"You okay?" he asks in a low voice as the appetizers are passed around the table and dinner menus are swept away. "Having a good time?"

"The best time," I answer honestly, trying not to think too much. Doing my best to simply play my part and not let my heart make my head think this is something it isn't.

"Really? Because we could duck out early, if you're not."

"Your friends are great." On an impulse, I lean in and kiss his cheek. It's a risk I can't help but take. As he smiles down at me, a friend at the end of the table tells him to get a room and I blush violently. The table laughs and I laugh along too, and as the night goes on, with every small kiss and touch from Graham, I feel less and less like a fraud.

chapter 11

Maddie

NEARLY TWO MONTHS OF THIS ARRANGEMENT HAVE PASSED AND everything seems just perfect. It's like a dream I didn't dare to dream before. Without the cost of rent, my job is more than enough to keep me afloat and contribute back to my savings. I don't have a worry in the world, other than how so much of this new world of mine is reliant on Graham. Just like it used to be with my ex.

I swallow down that thought as often as it comes up and focus on the positives.

Meeting Graham's friends has definitely either taken us to the next level or given me mixed signals. That combined with little trips on private jets for weekend vacations in the sun…life is very much too good to be true.

I've been added to a group chat with Julie, Bee, and Whitney, and they're just as lovely, welcoming, and funny as they were at the dinner. They're very interested in Graham and me, but I keep it light and vague. Although for the most part, I don't have to hide anything. Like when they ask how long we've been together or how we met. Eight weeks and in an elevator in his building. Oh how they thought that was scandalous…if only they really knew.

Between time with Suzette after work, an after-hours meeting to schedule a charity function, and Graham leaving town twice for meetings, before I know it, the week has gone by and I haven't seen him.

He's busy and I'm busy, and even though the ache I feel when I think about being with him doesn't go away, I get lost in my life for the first time in a long time. Lost in a good way, this time. Not the way I was lost with Kevin, when the days started to blur together and the only thing that broke it up was getting engaged. Which obviously ended worse than it began.

It feels like a century ago that I was worried about the rent and made that frantic call to Graham. It almost feels like a new life, even though I'm living in the same apartment.

I want it to stay like this, all new and exciting, for as long as possible.

I want things to stay okay. I think, this time, it might stick.

Since I haven't heard from Kenzie, my needy cousin, in about a week and a half, my aunt tells me she's doing much better. Some small part of me thinks that it might not be a good thing that my cousin hasn't messaged, but I can't bring myself to worry about it when I'm finally in a decent place.

Worrying never helps anyone, anyway. One of the best parts of all this is that my optimism doesn't feel so hard, now that I have a job and Graham and a group chat with another group of women who I can really see myself being friends with.

Friday after work, I come home from the office at the end of the day and find a paper taped to the door of my apartment.

My heart jumps into my throat and my blood goes cold. In my experience, sheets of paper taped to your apartment door never mean anything good, but as soon as I swallow down my knee-jerk reaction, I realize it's too small to be an official notice. The paper is too nice, too.

Actually, it's a note from Graham on a page torn from the pad on his desk. It's thick, heavy paper with his monogram on the top.

I want to see you. Come up when you get this. I've missed you.

That's all it says.

I peel the paper off the door, dislodging the tape he used to keep it there, and run my fingertips over the words. This feels different. He could've just texted me, or called, and told me he wanted to see me. Leaving a note in his handwriting, though…

It means he wrote the note and came up here, thinking of me. It means he pressed the tape to the top of the paper and looked it over before he left. He stood here in the hall, wondering when I'd be home to see it.

It means he knew that anyone could walk by and see this.

No, he didn't sign his name, but they'd see that someone with bold, clean handwriting wanted someone else enough to tape a note to their door.

That probably shouldn't make me as giddy as it does. It probably doesn't mean as much as I think it does. But still, I remind myself, I'm allowed to be a hopeless romantic, even in a not-so-romantic arrangement like this, so long as I protect my heart.

I rush inside, tuck the note on my bedside table, and change out of my work clothes. I think Graham likes my work clothes—his eyes go dark every time he sees me coming through the lobby or meets me for drinks after—but it's Friday, and I've been in those outfits all week. I choose a flowy dress instead and a beautiful pair of emerald earrings Graham bought me while we were on vacation and take the elevator up to the penthouse. It's my first time wearing them, they stay in a trinket tray on my bedside safe and sound so I don't lose them. But today feels like a special day and for that, I choose the beautiful earrings that feel just as special.

The elevator lets me directly into the wide, spacious entryway, which looks over his kitchen and the big living room with the stunning view of the city. I've been here several times, and I know it shouldn't be anything special considering I live in the building, but it is. Everything about this space is just what I would have imagined for a man like Graham. It's clean and beautiful and classy, and the best part of it is him.

Or it would be if I could see him.

I pause, closing the door quietly behind me, and listen. He said he wanted to see me and to come up, so I know he's in here.

After a second, I hear his voice floating in from one of the other rooms. I kick off my heels, leaving them at the entryway, and follow the low rumble past the spacious kitchen with Graham's shiny, expensive espresso machine that I know how to use now; past the sitting room with the *very* comfortable sofa that costs more than furniture should and the TV that rises out of a hidden compartment so it doesn't block the view; and past the original art framed on the wall that Graham got at an auction after he bought his first New York property.

These things mean more than they did the first time I was here. He's told me enough to know that he doesn't choose things without a reason, another fact about him that gives me butterflies.

He thinks about me even more carefully.

Graham doesn't have to say that for me to know it. He's always considerate when we go out, despite the dirty deal he offered me to pay the rent.

Could that have been fake, somehow? Not the deal itself—that definitely wasn't fake given I'm the one who technically offered it. The more Graham and I spend time with each other, the less I think he's the kind of guy who'd ever do it again. He's said in passing it was reckless for us and I agree. And Graham isn't a reckless kind of man.

I swallow down nervousness. I don't know if these feelings will ever go away. I'm not concerned that he'll end things between us when I don't see it coming. I'm more nervous about impressing him and living up to his expectations. I want him to enjoy this in the same way I do.

I *really* want to impress him, because…

I don't want this to end.

It doesn't escape me that when this ends, he'll be the one doing it. And I don't think I'll see it coming. I take a deep breath and promise myself not to think about *any* of this ending. Setting a timeline hasn't been what this is about. That's why we have a safe word, and why he seemed so relieved to see me in his office for the second rent payment. That memory goes a long way to soothe my nerves every time they creep up.

We can do this for as long as we want.

Graham is in a smaller, cozier den at one side of the penthouse. He sits on what I now know is his favorite working chair, an elbow propped on the arm, the phone to his ear. It's a worn brown leather that fits the masculine natural tones of the room.

"Go into more detail about that," he says. "I'm not sure I know enough to give you an answer you'll be satisfied with."

His tone is confident and commanding on the phone. The cadence of his voice sends a shiver down my spine. Nobody I've met before makes me feel like they could take charge of just about anything in the world and make it better than it was before.

Nobody would look as hot as Graham doing it, either. The natural light from the large, paned windows accentuates his perfect features and the way his clothes fit his body like they were made for him.

Which they were.

I pad quietly in through the door and he turns his head. His blue eyes brighten when he sees me, then immediately get darker as his pupils expand.

Then it's just like the first time I saw him in the elevator. My heart goes a little crazy over how attractive he is. Something electric about the air around him makes my chest get hot, and it feels like I've gotten an intense crush on this man in the space of seconds. It's been longer than that, obviously, but stepping into any room he's in makes it all feel new again.

I give him a little wave and mouth *I can go if you're busy.*

He shakes his head and readjusts in his seat, spreading his legs wider all the while staring at me. "That's something I considered, but only in the context of— yes, that's right."

I can almost feel him undressing me. Imagine his hands pulling my dress over my head. Feel his fingertips drag when he does it. This man hasn't even touched me and yet my body can already feel what he'll do to me. That's the power he has over me and I freaking love it.

I take two steps toward him, and Graham holds up a hand. I freeze in place, my face hot. He mouths the command, *strip.*

Every nerve ending in my body lights ablaze. I do as he commands, slowly, like I know he likes. Letting the dress fall to a puddle of cloth on the floor. He stops me before I can unsnap my bra and slip off my panties. They're a matching nude lace duo. Apparently he wants me to keep them on.

He slowly holds up one finger, then points at the floor.

I put my hand over my mouth to cover my gasp.

Crawl, he mouths, still pointing at the floor. He looks down, like he needs to emphasize the point, then looks back up at me, his eyes moving slowly over my nearly naked body.

"Right," he says, his voice shocking me into action. "My plan is to recoup the investment through a series of targeted improvements. I'm not talking about razing the place to the ground. That would be a waste."

I sink slowly to my knees, feeling the pattern of the rug press against my skin, then lower my hands to the floor.

This is so hot, on the verge of degrading or maybe submission, that I have to stop and take a few deep breaths.

Graham snaps his fingers.

It's one small sound and it draws my whole attention to him. His blue eyes are intense on mine as I begin to crawl across the rug.

He never looks away from me, even as he continues his conversation. It sounds to me like he's talking about the deal he's been working on—the one that's been keeping him up at night, the one he can't let go of even when it annoys the hell out of him—and it makes crawling across the floor even sexier. If he wants me to know about this conversation, he'll tell me about it later.

What he wants more is to watch me crawl to him.

I take my time, making each movement as slow and languid as I can. I'm a foot away from him, maybe less, when Graham spreads his knees and unzips his pants.

My mouth waters and my breathing quickens as I settle between his feet.

Graham takes his cock out and runs his fist over it, biting his hip. "That's fine," he says, voice terse. "I'm switching over to my people now. Email me with anything else you need."

He pauses, watching me, his hand still moving on his cock. He's thick and long, and I'm far too eager to give him everything he wants.

"I'm off the call," he says, and then he rattles off a list of details. I don't really hear any of them. I'm too busy watching his hand. On the next downstroke, I lean in and lick his tip. The slit already has a bead of precum, and I lick it away before hollowing my cheeks and taking his head into my mouth. He's smooth and already hard as iron. I cover my teeth with my lips and take more of him in.

Graham chokes back a groan. "Whatever you think. Just get it done."

He hangs up and tosses his phone to the side. It bounces off the chair and falls to the carpet. Then his hands are in my hair and he guides me down his cock.

He's so hard that he must've been thinking about this all day. If I'd known that note was on my door, I'd have thought about it all day, too. Graham's hips thrust up as I take him deeper, my throat fluttering around him.

"Fuck," he says, his voice strained. "Your mouth feels so fucking good."

I continue, and his hands work through my hair and gather it away from my face so it doesn't get in the way. I lick every inch of him that I can reach. I wrap one hand around his base and stroke. It's wet and messy and I know damn well my lips will be swollen, my lipstick ruined. But to hear that groan and the way his breath hitches, *I fucking love it.*

My eyes sting and water as I take more of him down, eager to get him off.

Graham groans again and tells me to be a good girl and take it.

It doesn't take much effort to stop my movements, not when he starts pumping into my mouth, holding my head gently while he does it.

After a minute he stops, pulling my head away. His abs bunch up below the waistband of his pants. His shirt is an untucked mess. Graham closes his eyes and breathes.

When he opens them again, all I can see his how much he wants me.

"Maddie," he says, running the pad of his thumb over my cheekbone.

"Hi," I breathe, not knowing what else to say and not caring.

He growls, and the next thing I know I'm being lifted off the floor and arranged on the chair on my knees, gripping the back of the chair. He rips the lace of my underwear at my entrance as he kisses my neck and tells me he's wanted me all day. The fabric of Graham's pants brushes against the backs of my thighs, and then he's pushing into me, his fingers stroking my clit.

"You're so fucking wet." His first stroke is deep and hard and takes my breath away. "Did you think of me when you were at that office?" He questions between kisses down my neck and then shoulders.

"All day," I tell him because it's true. Every time I finished a task or started a new one or got a drink or ate my lunch or stapled some documents, I thought of him. He rakes his teeth over my shoulder, and I admit in a rushed breath, "I missed you."

"You should have told me," he scolds, and fucks into me harder. With a hand on my hip and the other gripping the back of my neck, he pounds into me.

I dig my fingers into the leather and nearly bite down on the back of it to stifle my moans. His fingers are taking me right to the edge. I can feel my orgasm gathering, centered over my clit and deep inside me. "Would you have come to the office and taken me?" I question, although I'm nearly breathless.

"I should have done it already," he says, his voice low and dangerous.

"Yes," I gasp, and the orgasm comes on fast and hot. I move my hips back against Graham until he holds me still, filling me while he curses.

"Do you have any idea how fucking hot you are?" He leans over me, covering me with his body. "Do you have any idea how bad I want you?"

I can't answer because I'm holding on for dear life.

Graham pushes in so deep he bottoms out and lets out a low grunt, and then he's finding his release as well.

He pulls out with a reluctant sigh, then gathers me onto his lap.

He tips his head back to rest on the chair. I kiss down the line of his neck to his collar and he makes a satisfied noise.

We stay like that for a long time, and then Graham offers me a shower and some clothes to borrow.

"Borrow?" I tease. "You want me to spend the night?"

"I don't want you going downstairs," he says, and guides me into the shower. "I didn't have you all week, stay with me tonight."

Graham

I've never thought much about lying around in the bath before. Baths don't make money, and lying around doesn't, either.

But you couldn't pay me to get out of the bath with Maddie. It's fucking heaven.

Her wet hair drips onto my chest, and she curls her whole body up onto mine, and *fuck*. I don't care if I lose everything so long as I can hold on to this.

The air is filled with the scent of her shampoo and her body wash and the clean, warm smell of her skin, and part of me wants to save this memory somehow so I have it forever.

Maddie sighs, turning to kiss my collarbone.

"What's on your mind?" I ask, running my fingers through her hair. It's slippery from her conditioner and doesn't snag at all.

"Oh, it's nothing."

"Tell me anyway."

"I was just thinking about how content I am." She lifts her hand from the water and the sound is soothing. I take her hand in mine, enjoying the warmth as she settles into me.

I murmur and kiss the side of her neck, loving how her body reacts. "Is that right?"

"Yes. And…" She makes another soft sound. She's careful with her words. "I don't know how to feel about it. I always thought it would take more of a fight. That's what I was used to, before."

"Before?"

"When I was younger."

"You're young now."

Maddie presses her sweet body against mine, and that's almost the end of the conversation. "I mean before I met you. I always felt like I was fighting for something. I felt like…if I *wasn't* fighting and going after my goals, then it would definitely turn out wrong. And it did, with my ex. I stopped fighting, and everything went to shit."

I stiffen at the mere mention of men who had her before me.

We're both quiet for a minute.

"It's different with you," she admits. "I don't feel like I have to fight for everything."

I don't want her to fight for a damn thing. Not when she's mine. Tension builds in my shoulders and I bite back so much of what I want to say.

Instead, I lean down and kiss her, my heart aching. Because I want to be the person who gives her the world. I want to tell her that.

But something's stopping me.

Something says I shouldn't go that far, and shouldn't offer her that, because maybe I'm not the man she needs. And one day this is going to end. It's merely an arrangement. A negotiation that has an undefined timeline. She knows it. I know it. But neither of us says it out loud.

chapter 12

Maddie

I T WAS TOO GOOD TO BE TRUE.

It's all I can think, and I nearly tell Suzette just that when she texts me and asks how it's going.

I should have known that the minute I started to settle into what I thought was a fresh start, it was too good to be true. But I wanted to see the best in it. Looking on the bright side is what got me through hard times.

Now it all feels like a joke.

The next Monday after Graham leaves me a note, everything goes wrong at work. The weekend was amazing. Easy and carefree. Sleeping in, having lazy morning sex, and then enjoying the benefits of the penthouse while Graham worked. But it came and went far too quickly.

First thing in the morning, dressed in a prim and proper skirt suit, I show up at the office ready to tackle the day, but the CEO is in a terrible mood. I've worked for men like Michael Davies before. When they're irritable, everyone walks on eggshells. It's not a comfortable feeling.

Some of the work we were doing at the assistant level was misfiled or submitted to the wrong person, and when he calls the three of us in for a meeting with his secretary, I know it isn't going to go well.

And it doesn't.

I didn't cause any of the trouble—my work was fine and that's determined—but the CEO isn't happy to let the other assistant's mistake go. My jaw drops. I've been here almost three months and other than a few moments where small comments were made here and there, it's been fine. It's been great even connecting the company to charities and sharing successful strategies. I don't work directly with the CEO though. And now I know there's no way I ever could. I sit through about three minutes of him *yelling* at her—actually yelling—before I can't stand it anymore.

Someone had to defend the poor girl. And then he's yelling at me. As it turns out, I'm the one who's leaving, because the CEO fires me on the spot. I leave the office with shaking hands and angry tears in my eyes and call Suzette.

"I'm really sorry," I tell her, the second the call connects. "It didn't work out."

"Maddie, what?" There's a rustling sound like she's moving the phone to her other hand. "What didn't work out?"

"The job. I just got fired for being unable to handle the pressure." I tell her the story, getting angrier with every word that comes out of my mouth. "I couldn't sit by and let it happen, so I'm done. I left the office. It's over."

"Okay. Maddie, this is fine. It's a setback, obviously, but it's not the end—"

"Maybe it should be." I toss my hand in the air, frustrated beyond belief. "Maybe I should get real with myself and stop pretending that a positive attitude can fix every situation. I was kidding myself when I thought I could stay in this apartment."

"I don't think—"

"And I was kidding myself if I thought that I could get involved with a man and keep it casual." Emotions sweep through me and every small negative thought I've had for the past two months tangle with themselves at the back of my throat.

Suzette doesn't say anything. I get to an intersection by a flower shop and look away from all the pastel blooms in the window. They look like flowers for a celebration, and there's nothing to celebrate today.

"Did something happen with Graham?" Suzette asks carefully.

"He took me to meet his friends."

"I thought that went well. You said it did."

"Well, no, it didn't, because now they all know me, and I don't understand why he'd want that. He didn't want to show up alone, and they were *too nice*, like he's actually interested in anything beyond being fuck buddies."

"I thought that's what you wanted."

"I did, at the beginning," I burst out. "It seemed like fun, at the beginning. But every time we're together, I just get more confused. He seems like he wants something real with me, but he never says so."

"And you want to be with him."

"I can't be with him. I shouldn't even be in that building."

"Because of the cost?"

"Because of the rent, and because…" I don't want him to notice that I got *fired*. Tears leak into the corner of my eyes. It's then I realize, I'm so embarrassed. I don't want him to start thinking of me as the woman who couldn't handle her own life. We'd turned it into a sexy game, and now, in the space of a day, it's not a game anymore. I don't understand why everything feels like it's crumbling all at once. "I just can't."

Suzette says all the right things a friend would, but I don't hear any of it. All I can think about is how I'm going to have to explain to a man like Graham, someone who works their ass off day in and night out, that I got fired because I couldn't keep my mouth shut. I confess to Suzette as I try to calm myself down. "I would have willingly quit if he hadn't fired me. After all of these years, I don't have a job." My breath catches and I try to pull myself together, I try to get my emotions to make sense. I don't have a passion like he does. The voice in the back of my head tells the truth. *I'm just not good enough for a man like him, for an apartment like that, for a life like this. I'm a fraud.* My phone beeps. Another call is coming in.

"I have to go," I tell Suzette.

"Call me later," she says, just before I answer the next call.

"Hello?"

"It's me." Kenzie's voice wobbles, like she's been crying, and my stomach sinks. I close my eyes, pressing my back to a building as the city passes me by. This is the worst timing. I can barely exhale as she continues. "Listen. I know you just started a new job, but I need help. The loan company said they're going to start taking money from my paychecks, and I need all of it for the rent, so I need—"

"You'll have to move here, then. You'll have to just…I don't know, Kenzie. You'll have to come here, and we can figure something out."

"I can't do that. You *know* that. My whole life is in Chicago, and it's not like I can just rent a car—"

"I don't know what else to tell you!" I try my best not to raise my voice at my cousin, but my throat feels like I swallowed a rock and my eyes were burning *before* and there's just nothing I can do. "I got fired today, Kenzie! I got fired. I don't have any extra money. I have to take drastic measures myself, so the only way I can—"

"Mom's sick," Kenzie says, her voice cold.

"What?"

"My mom is sick. That's why I haven't asked her. That's why I'm always asking *you*. Do you even care?"

"Kenzie." I lean against a lamppost, taking deep breaths. "What do you mean she's sick?"

"She has cancer," she tells me, and my entire body goes cold.

"Oh my God. I'm so sorry."

"I am too," she says, and she's choked up.

"Why didn't you tell me this before?"

"Because she said not to tell anyone. It's treatable, just expensive. She's going to be okay. She will…but also because I wanted to handle it," she tells me. "I wanted to figure out a way to solve it on my own. And I couldn't, obviously, or I wouldn't be calling. But it's not like I can call *her* because she's dealing with so many medical bills that she might lose her house, too."

"I'm sorry," I say. A driver in traffic cuts across to the opposite lane, almost hitting another car, and horns blare. "I'm sorry, Kenzie."

It's not enough, just to apologize. I'm stick to my stomach at the thought that my aunt has been sick…and nobody told me.

They probably didn't tell me because I got a whole new life with Kevin and disappeared into it and thought my cousin needed to get *her* head together.

I guess she's not the only one.

"None of this is your fault," Kenzie says in a voice that tells me it *is* my fault, at least a little. "I know how hard you worked to get where you are. I just thought…" She lets out an angry sigh. "I thought you'd understand, because of that."

"Kenzie." I rub at my forehead with the back of my hand, blinking back tears. "I just need some time. I'll figure something out, I swear, I just can't do it right this minute. I haven't even gotten home from the office yet."

"No." She takes a deep breath, and I can almost see her straightening her back. "I'll figure this out. You deal with your stuff. I'll deal with mine."

"Kenzie, please—"

My cousin hangs up.

I don't blame her for how she feels. I couldn't possibly blame her for that when I've felt the same way so many times. But this, on top of getting fired, on top of thinking that I'd avoided disaster…

It's too much. I'm quick to text my aunt that I love her and miss her. I almost tell her I know but I don't. Instead I just let the tears out.

She answers back with a text telling me she misses me, and she hopes I'm living my big-city-life dreams and maybe one day she can come down to see me. I have to read it all through glassy eyes. We've never been a super close family, but I that doesn't mean I don't love them all.

I get back to my building and go through the lobby as fast as I can, my head down. If Graham is in here today, I don't want to see him. My phone buzzes with a text, but I don't look at it. I throw myself into the elevator.

It's empty and I shove myself into the corner of it.

The hall on the eighth floor is empty too, so nobody sees the tears start to fall as I fumble to get my key in the door.

I slam it behind me and kick off my shoes, drop my purse, and go for my clothes. I don't want to be in the skirt suit for another second.

"Don't feel sorry for yourself," I say out loud. "*Don't.*"

But I do. I feel sorry for myself, for my cousin, for my aunt. I feel sorry for my family that they have me to deal with.

My chest aches, my head hurts, and it's all gone wrong. *Again.*

In the bedroom, I fall on the bed and cry. The sheets and blankets Kevin and I picked out together feel awful, but they're the ones I have. At least they shelter me a little while I cry into the pillow.

It almost feels like the world got together and decided to put me in my place. Let's be honest, it's what I deserve. For so long, I wanted to believe that the world was on my side. It seemed too sad to think that we live in a universe that doesn't care what happens to us.

It's true, though. The universe doesn't care what happens to us. It doesn't care about anything, and no amount of finding the silver lining will change that.

My phone buzzes three more times, and finally I push it off the bed. It lands on the floor, muffled by the carpet. What does anybody want from me? They don't want to sit on the other end of the phone and listen to me cry about the mistakes I've made in my life, and they *don't* want to come over.

I don't want Graham to see me like this.

I don't want anybody to see me like this.

I don't even want to see myself like this.

Every time I think I've cried all of the feelings out, more tears come. It starts to seem like one long pattern. Everything went wrong before Kevin. It went wrong when I got cocky about my abilities in life. It went wrong when I thought I could come back from any breakup, any setback. It went wrong when I just kept pushing ahead into the next thing instead of taking stock of how I was causing all the trouble *myself*.

I don't know how long it's been when someone knocks at the door.

Shit. I didn't lock it. I closed it, but I didn't lock it, and now anybody could walk in.

Only I know that it's not going to be *anybody*. It's going to be Graham, coming to see me at my most pathetic. My stomach turns. He could fix all of this, but I'm done asking to be bailed out. I'm not going to sit up on the edge of the bed and tell him he can fuck me in exchange for fixing…

I don't know. All of it. Kenzie's situation, my situation, my aunt, the apartment.

And that might mean I can't enjoy *him* anymore. So it's not just all this bad news in one day, it's him, too.

He keeps knocking, and I don't say anything. My throat feels too rough to answer him. My body feels too heavy to get up and answer the door, much less push the covers off, so I just lie there.

He's going to leave, eventually. That's what always happens in the end. People want you for one thing, and the second you don't give them exactly that, they're gone.

I don't even blame him.

I'm the one who pushed for all this. I'm the one who thought it would be okay.

I keep waiting for Graham to leave and for the knocking to stop. Instead, after a while, I hear the door to my apartment open, then close.

It's quiet for a while longer, and then soft footsteps come toward the bedroom. He's passing the sitting area where we fucked the first time. I wonder if he thinks about it.

I hope I can stop thinking about it.

The bedroom door creaks a little on its hinges. Even the door is a sign that things aren't going how they should. Doors in an apartment like this shouldn't creak, which means I should have called maintenance to make sure the hinges were oiled or whatever, and I haven't done that.

It's a tiny failure, barely even a mistake, but it makes more tears leak out of my eyes. I try to wipe them away.

It doesn't do anything.

Graham steps into the bedroom and hovers near the door, his mouth a thin line. His shoulders are tense. He's obviously uncomfortable, and I didn't expect anything else. He didn't sign up for me crying in my bed because I got fired. He signed up for hot sex in exchange for the rent.

I sniffle into my pillow and try to get myself under control.

It doesn't work.

"Madelyn…" Graham says carefully. "Are you okay?"

There are lots of things I want to say to him, like, *please get into the bed with me*. Like, *could you explain how everything keeps going to shit when I try so hard*. Like, *what is it about me that makes it so impossible to keep anything good? Why aren't I just better? Why can't I just go along with what life wants from me?*

"No."

There's an even longer silence. I wait for him to leave without saying anything else, but Graham just stands there, watching.

"Should I come back another time?" he asks.

The answer is no. He shouldn't come back. He should go on with his life and forget the game we've been playing. Both of us should, because games like this only end in heartache, even if they're not the final cause of it.

But my heart hurts for how much I want to be touching him. If I were the strong woman I pretend to be, I could tell him the real truth—that it was a mistake to get involved with each other and the best thing we can do now is walk away gracefully.

I don't feel very strong at the moment. I feel weaker than I've ever felt, and I just can't give him up.

Not right now. What the hell am I supposed to do? Tell him I got fired, I failed my cousin, and my aunt is sick? No. No, I cannot and will not burden him with that when I don't even deserve him.

"Yes." I tell him. "Red." I tell him because I don't know what else to say. I just want him to know I'm not okay.

Graham takes a breath, and I can't tell if it's a disappointed noise or a relieved one. His hands come out of his pockets, and then he puts them back in.

"I'll leave you alone, then."

I nod, mostly into the pillow. My bedroom door opens again, and then it shuts. My heart breaks.

It's more painful than being fired, more painful than my conversation with Kenzie, more painful than anything else. I can't breathe because it hurts too much.

I was hoping he would come to me. I was hoping he would see what a wreck I was and just make this feeling go away.

I was hoping he'd fallen in love with me, because I've fallen for him, even if I haven't been willing to admit it.

Graham is the only person I want comfort from right now, and I sent him away, and he just *went*.

That's the proof I needed and it hurts. I need to leave. I should have left when Kevin did and made my way somewhere else. I could've figured it out; I know that now. But leaving felt like giving up.

Well, sometimes it's better to give up. That's obviously a lesson I've learned too late. Somehow, I thought that if I had the apartment, I'd at least have *something* to prove myself, but I don't.

I have nothing.

I turn over and sob into the pillow until I fall asleep.

chapter 13

Graham

This is why I don't do relationships. Because what the fuck was that?

She's not well. I know she's not well. But she sends me away and…I fucking had to because of a goddamn word? I pace the entrance to my penthouse, staring at the security camera in her hall. *What the fuck even was that?*

I've never felt so inadequate.

I text her to tell me when she's available to talk and I get no response.

I text Brian to tell him what happened and ask what to do and all he can say is that sometimes women are emotional and to give her space.

That doesn't feel right. None of this feels right. But I have no experience in these matters. I don't know what the fuck happened, let alone what to do.

It keeps me awake all night. I can't sleep. I can't even lie down. I just keep staring at my phone, typing out messages and deleting them.

I've been a fool. I took her to meet my friends, but the problem is that I don't know any of *her* friends. There's nobody I can call to find out what happened. If I did, it would be overstepping a boundary. She already safeworded me. Legally I probably committed a crime entering her house like that. Maddie's never introduced me to any of her friends, she's only talked about a few people in passing. If she wanted me to meet them, she would have made that happen. I have to remind myself that what we have is an arrangement, and it's one she needs so she'll come back. She'll answer me when she's in better spirits and she'll tell me what happened. She has to, doesn't she?

Uncertainty washes through me and I feel like an even bigger prick assuming money will keep her coming back to me. *Fuck!*

All through the evening and then the next day she never texts me and never calls.

The only person who *does* call is Harland Porter.

He calls at one in the fucking morning, and when my phone rings, everything in me lights up. It's her. It's *her*.

But it's Harland goddamn Porter.

"What is it?" I snap, not caring if he doesn't like my tone.

"I've been up, just going through some things in my head, and I wanted to run them—"

"Harland, if you want to sell me the building, then sell the damn thing to me. If you don't want to, then stop stringing me along. I've had enough of this. You know where I stand. Make up your mind by tomorrow at five, or I'm pulling out."

That shocks him into silence. "Graham, I—"

"Tomorrow at five," I repeat, and hang up the call.

My entire body trembles as I sit back down and stare at the security cameras. I text Brian to ask how bad it may get if I were to go back down there. And foolishly I text Maddie again and she texts back that she needs to sleep.

Graham: what happened?

Maddie: I need to get back to sleep.

Graham: you told me that but I need to know what happened.

Maddie: I can't right now. I just...I'm sorry.

It's then that Brian texts me as well.

Brian: Seriously. Just give her some time.

I drop my phone, hating every fucking minute of this. Sometime after dawn I doze off on the couch in my living room and wake up again with a jolt at ten to nine.

Fuck me.

I'm usually in the office by now, but I feel wrecked from the night awake. Every single one of my muscles hurts like I've run a marathon. I stomp into my shower and let the hot water do its work. The steam surrounds me and my head races with every thought imaginable. The only conclusion I come to is that she's leaving. Something happened to pull her away. Was it her fucking ex? I don't know what I'll do if she's actually leaving me.

There are no messages from Harland Porter on my phone when I get out, but I don't care.

I don't *care*. What the hell was so important about this property? What was I trying to prove by sticking things out with a man who doesn't know what he wants? The only things that matter are Maddie and the fact that she didn't message me.

I shave at the sink, barely looking at myself. This is a horrible feeling. It's the feeling I've been resisting for years. I didn't want anything to be more important than making sure I had the right life, and I was wrong.

I was just wrong.

I tap the razor too hard on the edge of the sink and get a grip on myself.

I didn't know what to do for her because I've spent all this time worrying about buildings instead of people. I lost my parents, so I thought that was it. There was nothing else for me to concern myself with but building a legacy that surpassed them.

I'm the one who did this to myself, and now to Maddie.

Getting dressed feels worthless. None of this shit matters, either. None of the custom suits or tailored shirts or expensive watches. What the fuck are they worth? When it comes down to it, I'll be alone because I don't know how to love anyone anymore. I don't let them close so they don't let me close.

And I've never wanted anything more in my life than to wipe her tears away and to make whatever it was that hurt Maddie vanish.

I was focused on the wrong damn things in the first place.

Once I've got my shirt buttoned up, I put my head in my hands and force myself to breathe.

No. This is not how I wanted things to go. If she's going to push me away, I need her to know that I don't want her to. I need her to know that I…that I…*fuck!*

I don't know what to do for the rest of the day. I pace around my apartment, waiting to see if she'll call.

Eventually, I'm ready to admit that I'm the one who has to choose what I'm going to do. I can't keep waiting. So I make the decision to go down to the lobby and check in with the doormen.

I need to reset my view of the property, of Maddie, and of my entire life.

The ground floor is the best place to start.

I dress, double check to make sure I have my phone and wallet, and head for the door. My penthouse feels empty without Maddie. It's always been too much space for one person, but I ignored that feeling because it was a status symbol. A man like me is *supposed* to have a penthouse. It's what's best. It's the crowning jewel. But what the fuck good is a king without his queen?

In reality, a man like me is supposed to know better. He should understand that he can't just waste away by himself, alone in his penthouse, counting piles of money that do fuck all to fill the gaping hole in his chest.

He should've known from the beginning that all the money would never be enough.

In the elevator, I lean against the wall and tell myself over and over again that it's not too late.

I don't even know what it's not too late for.

My phone rings as I'm stepping out of the elevator, and my heart pounds thinking it's her.

It isn't.

"Hey, Scott," I say into the phone, trying to hide my disappointment. "I'm on my way to the office."

"Oh, please. You can spare a couple minutes for me."

"Yeah."

"We need to get together again. What are your plans on Thursday? All my wife talks about is seeing you two again."

You two.

I go the opposite way from the lobby, following the hall without looking where I'm going until I find an alcove with a bench.

"I'm not sure I can make that happen."

"What?" Scott laughs, like I've made a hilarious joke. "We all want to see her again, and we're sick of seeing you twice a year."

"You see me twice a year because I'm busy."

"We're all busy," he argues, still laughing. "We can't let you slip away, man. That's how you lose people."

"I…" What am I supposed to say to that? Not having dinner together isn't how you *lose* people. They work themselves to death and die. That's how you lose them. And I don't think eating at fancy restaurants will do anything to stop that.

Except…he's right. I felt miserable last night because there was nobody to call. Nobody I wanted to talk to except Maddie. Because I've pulled myself away from all of them. "I know that."

"You okay?" His voice gets softer, and I can tell Scott's catching on to the fact that he got me at a bad time.

I almost lie out of habit. That's what I've done all this time. There's no reason to burden anyone else.

Then I think of Maddie, crying in her bed.

"I don't know." Unwanted emotions surface and I pinch the bridge of my nose.

"What happened?" There's a *creak* in the background of the call, like he's sat down behind his desk. A door closes somewhere nearby. Scott didn't call me to listen to me complain about my own foolish mistakes, but somewhere in the city, he's sitting down, ready to listen.

"I don't know." I feel sick from how little I know. From how little I asked. From how unwilling she was to confide in me. "Something's going on with Maddie."

"Oh," he says, thoughtful. "And she didn't tell you what it was?"

"No." I don't know how much to tell him. It's not really my business, what's happening in Maddie's life, only…it *is* my fucking business. I care about her, and

I'm not going to stop because something happened that I wasn't there to prevent. "I went up to see her last night, and she was crying. Told me she wanted me to leave."

"And have you talked today?"

"No."

"This was last night?"

"Yeah."

"Jesus, Graham. Go knock on her door."

"I don't think she wants that."

"You're her boyfriend. I'm sure she wants that. Even if she doesn't want to lean on you, she wants to lean on you. Trust me."

This is the worst possible time to admit that I lied about all the details I gave my friends. "We didn't meet at the bar. We met at the building."

Scott lets out a surprised laugh. "At your building, you mean?"

"She lives here. And she fell behind on the rent, so..."

"So you swooped in to be her hero?"

God I love his version so much better. Her hero. I roll my eyes and know damn well I took advantage. If only he knew how much I wanted to tell him that story. If only he knew how much I wanted it to be true.

"In a way."

"Um...what *kind* of way?"

"The kind where she told me she'd do anything if I could help her out with the rent, and I agreed."

He doesn't say anything.

I check my phone.

Call's still connected.

"Scott?"

"You made a deal with her for sex?"

"It sounds terrible when you say it like that."

"I'm not judging." I think he might not be. Scott's always been the most level-headed of us all. I can hear him drumming his fingertips on the desk in a slow rhythm. "She was into it, I'm assuming, since—"

"Yes, she was *into* it," I snap. "I wouldn't have done it otherwise. You know that."

"I do," he says quickly. "I do. Then what happened? You decided to date her?"

"The arrangement continued in a way where we became closer and there are feelings...at least on my end."

"Okay," he says slowly and appears to be more agreeable with the situation. "But...it's nothing formal."

"We're not boyfriend and girlfriend," I say, hating how cynical it sounds and how petulant the statement is.

"You might want to have a conversation about that, if...things are happening."

"Yeah."

A minute passes. It starts to seem like a good idea. To tell her that I'm her boyfriend now and that she can confide in me for more emotional things. I shift where I stand, thinking it's not going to work, but if she's going to leave me, it's an offer. I don't know what it's worth, but it may be worth something.

Scott just waits on the other end of the line.

"Graham."

"Yeah?"

"Go talk to her. You're not going to fuck up your life by telling someone you love them."

"I didn't say that."

"You didn't have to," he answers, and I let that sink in. "Go talk to her. Text me tomorrow. We're all going to come to your office and drag you out kicking and screaming if that's what we have to do."

"Don't or I'll send building security after you," I attempt to joke although it doesn't make me feel any better.

"I can take your security," he says comically and hangs up.

I'm left standing there in the alcove next to the bench, wondering if Scott's right or if I'm right or if nobody's going to be able to tell until I find Maddie and talk to her.

Although doubt creeps in, I'm almost certain she feels for me a hint of what I feel for her.

Before I can head back up, the lobby doors open and a gust of air comes through, as does Madelyn, the woman who's tempted me to want more in this life.

When the hell did she leave? The question answers itself as I remember I dozed off earlier. I swallow thickly, feeling even less than worthy.

The sight of her is like a punch to the chest. She's wearing a gorgeous pink dress that looks like a dream and large sunglasses, probably meant to hide how long she spent crying yesterday. Maddie stops when she sees me, hesitates, then continues on toward the elevator.

I don't say a word, instead I step out to meet her in the middle of the floor. Maddie lets out a breath and we continue walking. I settle in beside her and we go toward the elevators.

Privacy will be good for this. My hands go numb as she doesn't make a move to touch me, to kiss me. I think she's really going to fucking end it with me and the thought won't leave me alone.

She can't. The only thing I know is that if she plans to leave, I have to tell her I love her. I can't let her leave me without knowing that she means more to me than our arrangement.

She takes one look at the silver doors and keeps going past, finally stopping at the same alcove I just took that call in. Maddie turns to face me. One more deep breath, and she pushes the sunglasses up to the top of her head.

I was right. Her eyes are all red, her cheeks are blotchy, and she looks like she needs a hug.

"Hi," she says.

"Madelyn."

At the sound of my voice, she closes her eyes. After a beat, she opens them again. "I'm glad I saw you down here, because I…I wanted to give my notice."

Fuck, no. "Your notice?"

"I wanted to ask you if I could end my lease early. I know that's technically not what's in the contract, but I've considered all my options, and I need to move somewhere that's…within my means."

What the hell is she talking about? We have an arrangement. She could live here for the rest of her life and still be well within her rent budget.

"I can take on whatever bills you need," I offer her. "Credit cards or whatever it may be. Simply give them to me."

"No," she says, and her chest rises with a stutter.

"Why?" I'm not proud of how I sound in the moment, and I can't help stepping closer, my chest aching. "Should I have stayed last night?"

Maddie looks down and away, slowly dragging her eyes back to mine. "It's not that."

I can't let her do this. I can't let her disappear out of my life. I can't spend from now until I die thinking about her.

"I should have stayed last night," I tell her, taking charge of the conversation. At least *my* part of the conversation. "That was a bad move, to leave you alone like that. I could have stayed in the living room, given you space, but been there." I think out loud, attempting to learn from my mistake. "I am not well versed in…" I swallow, not knowing what to call what we have given the circumstances. "Let me make it up to you."

"Graham, I don't—"

"Come to dinner. Have something to eat, and we can talk." My voice is even, my suggestion strong yet gentle. So at odds with the chaos and loss that run like wildfire through my blood.

She presses her lips together, and I'd give just about anything to kiss her.

Red. The word hasn't been said in this moment, but it was before and it lingers between us. "It'll be all right," I tell her. "Whatever it is, whatever you need," I remind her, "I will take care of you."

But she's on edge, tensing up, and I don't want to push her until we've had a chance to lay everything out on the table.

"Are you hungry?" I ask.

Maddie runs a hand through her hair, almost knocking her glasses off in the process. "I haven't eaten much," she admits. "Yes. I'm hungry."

"Then come to dinner. Or just…come upstairs. I can have dinner brought to us."

She hesitates one more time, and I offer her my arm.

"It's not far," I tell her, keeping my voice light. "Only an elevator ride away." At this moment I remember the first time I laid eyes on her. I can't lose her. I did once before, and I don't know what will come of me now that I know every little bit about her that I do. "I don't want to lose you," I confess to her, and her eyes meet mine with surprise and maybe hope.

"Okay," she says softly, and takes my arm.

Thank fuck. I at least have a chance.

chapter 14

Maddie

I HAVE A SLIGHT HEADACHE FROM CRYING MOST OF THE NIGHT, AND I DON'T feel like I look my best, but Graham doesn't say a word about it as he whisks me upstairs to the penthouse.

The first thing he does is put me on the couch in the living room and hand me a bottle of water. I take sips from it while he moves around the apartment.

He's tense and I feel awful for all of this. I don't know how it got to this point. I was living a fairy tale that wasn't meant for me. I'm so sorry I dragged him into this.

"Are you drawing a bath?" That's definitely the sound of running water.

Graham doesn't answer. He returns a few minutes later with a stack of clothes in hand. A robe—new and silky—along with a comfortable outfit that could easily be pajamas or the classier version of loungewear.

"You had these laying around?" I ask as he hands me the folded bundle.

"Maybe," he says. "Why don't you get changed? If we're not going out, then you're allowed to be comfortable."

"Get changed or have a bath?"

"Either. Both. Whatever will get you to talk to me."

When we get to the main bathroom, the tub is filled, a candle flickers on the edge, and there's a small glass of wine balanced on a tray that stretches over the water.

It's far too romantic for what I feel like I deserve. I've messed this up. Just like I messed everything else up.

"Are those *rose petals?*" I can't help a soft smile of disbelief at the crimson petals floating on the surface. "Did you put rose petals in the bathwater?"

"I told you I'd make it up to you."

Graham bustles toward the door. "The remote on the tray connects to the sound system. It'll play whatever you want, just scroll through the screen for the options."

He's drawn a *bath* for me.

"If you don't want to talk, we can listen to music."

I put the clothes on the towel shelf and look down at the steaming hot water. It looks like heaven although I may fall asleep in it, I'm so damn tired.

"Where did you get rose petals?" I whisper, and then decide to take him up on it.

The wine's sweet and chilled, the water's hot and soothing, and the music brings it all together. I expect him to follow me in, but when I sink fully in, he isn't there.

The music is quiet enough that I can hear him moving around in the penthouse. A door opens and shuts. Low voices talk to one another. I watch the rose petals float across the surface of the tub. I feel awful for last night.

It's all on the tip of my tongue. I didn't really want him to go. I just didn't know what else to say. I just wanted it all to stop.

With both hands, I splash the water on my face and attempt to just calm down. Suzette's advice echoes in my head: calm down. Tell him when you're calm.

She said it will be okay, but I don't see how any of this is going to be okay.

I sip the wine until it's gone and let the heat of the water take some of the ache out of my muscles. Whew. A girl really shouldn't cry that hard if she doesn't want to feel like crap all day.

When I've soaked up all the relaxation I can, he still isn't in the tub.

I get out and dry off with one of Graham's ridiculously fluffy towels. His initials are monogrammed on them in dark blue, like his stationery, and that makes me feel lighter for some reason. I think I just like the sight of his initials.

There's an arrangement of glass dispensers on the counter with lotion that has the light scent of aloe, and I spend some time rubbing it into my skin, waiting for him, before I change into the clothes he's brought.

He *must* have had them here. But I don't think he bought them today.

Did he have them here for me all along?

Did he want to ask me to stay and make it clear that he has everything I need?

I look much better in the mirror when I'm finished with the lotion. Last night was rough, and it showed on my face, but now my cheeks are pink from the bath and my eyes aren't as red as they were. You can hardly tell I was crying.

I slip the robe over my shoulders, tie the belt in front, and go back out into the main penthouse, quietly, but not without calling out his name.

He doesn't answer so I call out louder, "Graham?"

There's music playing in the living room, and someone has set up a table with a white tablecloth in front of the floor-to-ceiling windows. Graham's lighting a candle in the center as I pad up behind him.

I have to blink away the disbelief.

"You shouldn't have done all this," I say, more heat flooding my face. "After last night—"

"Yes, I should because I want to." He finishes lighting the candle and smiles at me. "And because I want *you*." It's a shy, vulnerable smile, and he leans forward to kiss my forehead before he pulls out my chair and helps me into it.

Graham has unbuttoned the top two buttons of his shirt and rolled the sleeves up to his elbows, so I'm not the only one who's made themselves more comfortable.

My mouth waters, looking at his forearms. There's a deep need and a deep ache at the thought of lying in his arms.

It's all I want. He pulls the chair out for me and I thank him, once again taken aback.

I have a feeling though that he really wants to talk, and I know I have a lot of explaining to do.

I focus on the table instead. He's put two flowers in a vase near the edge of the table and they're lovely. I was *not* in a good place when I saw that flower shop yesterday. I love flowers, and I happen to believe that beautiful flowers can make any bad situation at least a little better.

I almost start to admit how foolish I feel. How I'm just emotional because of my cousin, because of my aunt, and because of money and this situation and all of my uncertainty. I nearly let all the words tumble out, but when I look up, Graham has an expression I can't place, and I keep my lips firmly shut.

Graham steps away from the table, returning a minute later with the bottle of wine. He hesitates over my glass. "Did you like it?"

"I loved it." I give him a smile I know doesn't reach my eyes, and he smiles back. He's a striking man, and his charming look sends heat all through me.

Graham pours us both a glass, then leaves again.

It's quiet but for the gentle classic music. With steadying breaths I prepare to just come clean and tell him I'm in over my head in more ways than one.

He comes back with plates that go on top of the fancy china at our places, then leaves one more time. By the time he's done bringing the food, we have a basket of hot, fluffy rolls, a silver dish of mashed potatoes that look like they're to die for, two more sides, a plate of seared scallops and lobster tails, and a plate of very tender beef that almost looks like stew. All I know is that it smells like heaven, and I hadn't realized how hungry I was.

Graham takes his place across from me and scans the table. "Is there anything else I can get for you?"

You, I want to say but instead opt for gratitude. "No. This looks amazing. Thank you."

We eat for a few minutes. I was right. The mashed potatoes *are* to die for. Everything is swimming in butter and just the right amount of salty goodness. Graham looks even more handsome with the candlelight on his face.

We eat, although I eat slowly. I'm certain I know what comes next and I'm not ready.

It's still too silent and I know it is when he clears his throat. "I wanted to talk to you about last night," he says tentatively.

"Are you sure we should…now?" I nearly chicken out.

"I think we should. I'm sorry I didn't stay to talk longer." Graham looks me in the eye, his regret clear. "I mean it, Maddie."

"I'm sorry I said that word."

His silverware stops in midair. "I'm sorry I listened to it," he tells me. "I know that's wrong but leaving you because you safeworded me isn't what—"

"I didn't want you to leave. I just wanted it to stop."

He stops and I apologize for interrupting.

"Did you not think I'd leave?"

"I thought you wouldn't push for what was wrong," I tell him.

He drops his silverware. "Did you want me to stay?" he asks.

"I wouldn't have pushed you away if you'd come to bed." I almost tell him I'd rather he have taken me to his bed though.

His jaw clenches and he drops his silverware to his plate for a drink of wine.

"I only left because I thought that's what you wanted," he tells me when he puts the glass down. "No, not what you wanted. I left because when you say red, it means it stops, which means I leave."

"No. You didn't have to leave." I'm quick to correct him.

He pauses, his eyes boring into mine. "Don't use that word again unless it's because of something sex related Madelyn. Even if you want me to leave." He's deathly serious and I nod and tell him I won't use it if it's not about something in the bedroom.

He's more tense and starts to say something but then stops.

"I'm sorry. I didn't know you would think I meant for you to leave. I just didn't know what to say, I didn't want to say what I was thinking, but I didn't want to be alone."

"Are you all right?" he asks me when tears prick my eyes.

I swallow, thinking about how badly I've messed this up, about how I lost my job, thinking about my cousin and how she can't rely on me, and about my aunt. "I don't think so."

"I'd like to know what made you so upset, if you're willing to share it."

"I don't know where to start," I admit.

"Start from the beginning."

"I got bad news yesterday. A lot of it actually."

"What kind of bad news?" he asks, his elbows on the table, his hands folded under his chin, entirely focused on me.

I want to tell him. I want him to know everything. I don't care if he fixes it or not, I just want him to know. I don't know what's going to happen between us, but I do know that if I don't tell him, I'll wonder what he would have said. I'll wonder what would have happened after this moment.

"Well. It turns out that my boss is an asshole. *Was* an asshole, I mean." I dab the corner of my eyes.

His forehead furrows. "Was?"

"I mean…" I wave my wine glass at him. "He didn't die. He's just not my boss anymore. I got fired because I told him to stop yelling at one of the other assistants. It was…" It hits me, maybe for the first time, how silly that whole thing was. Why would I have wanted to work there, anyway? I'd have come to that conclusion sooner or later, and I'd have had to find another job. "It was just not a good situation. But I worked so hard to get the job in the first place that it felt like a total disaster."

"Anyone would be upset about that."

"That's not all." I let out a sigh and a frown deepens in my expression. "My cousin called on the way home with more bad news."

Graham stays quiet and patient.

"She's struggled with student loans for a long time. I love her so much, and I've always done all I can to help her, but when my ex left, I couldn't help and it really screwed her over. She can't afford it on her own and I told her I'd be there for her. I promised her because I thought…well because I didn't know my fiancé was cheating on me. I thought that if I could get a job, I'd be in a position to make things easier. But she called yesterday, just after I'd been let go, and I snapped at her. I told her to figure it out for herself."

"I'm sure, given time…she can't blame you for that."

"Well, she also told me that my aunt is sick." This is the part that feels the worst to talk, or think, about. "I called her today. Complications from cancer treatment. I spent the night texting her and then my aunt. It's treatable but…they can't afford it. She can't get the medicine she needs because she has so much medical debt already, and insurance is a nightmare, and…"

He looks across the table at me, nothing but concern in his face. My first thought it that I hope he doesn't think I'm lying. That I'm trying to use him. "I want you to know that I don't expect anything from you. This isn't…" Tears blur my eyes at the thought of him thinking I would lie to him. That I would use him for money. "This is exactly why I couldn't…" I start to say and his chair groans against the floor as he pushes it out to come to me. He sits closer, his arm around me and telling me it's all right. All the while I'm falling to rubbish all over again.

"I know I couldn't have fixed all of it, but yesterday, it felt like I couldn't fix anything. And I wanted to. That's why I was so upset. Then, when you came to my apartment, I was…"

Graham presses his lips together, like he's stopping himself from interrupting.

"I was ashamed," I finally manage. "I was ashamed to let you see me like that. Because in the beginning of all this, I felt like our deal was giving me a little control over my life."

"I understand."

"Do you? And I was ashamed because I already feel like I'm using you."

"How could you possibly be using me?" he asks.

"For the money…like degrading myself for—"

"Do you find being with me degrading?" he cuts me off to ask.

My face gets twice as hot. "No. I don't. I liked what we did together, and even more than that, I liked spending time with you. Your friends…I was so happy to meet your friends. That meant a lot to me."

"But?"

"But when I got fired, all I could think is that you're going to think less of me. That…" I can't even get the words out because they all scream in my head telling me to shut up and that I'm making it worse. And that I'm going to lose him.

"I don't want you to think I'm coming to you because I'm desperate and need money."

Graham's quiet for a minute, looking down at his plate. Then he looks back up at me.

"What I spend my money on is my choice. And if I want to give it all to you, that is for me to concern myself with, not you."

"It doesn't change that I was scared you'd think a certain way or that…" It takes me a minute to find my voice. "I thought I was losing you, too. I just thought that you wouldn't want to keep doing that when it was clear I didn't have another option and that I was hard on money."

"Did you have another option when we started?" He asks in his logical sensical way.

"No," I say slowly. "But my feelings weren't as complicated."

He nods as if he understands, and my heart pounds.

"Okay." Graham takes out his phone. "First off, I'm going to take care of these problems."

"Which problems?" I feel sick. I don't want him to think for one second that I only want his money.

"All of them."

"Graham, I don't want your—"

"I would like it if you would allow me to do what makes me happy, my little temptress." He holds my gaze and then gives me an asymmetrical smile. "Let me do this simply because I want to."

"I want you because I want you," I tell him and hope he believes it.

"And I want you because I want you," he responds, and I do believe it. I believe him. This time when tears prick they're for a different reason, but I push the emotions down.

"And as for your job—"

"You can't get me my job back."

"You don't want that job back," he says simply, and he's right. "But if you want to search for one, I will help however I can. And if you don't want one and want to go back to charity work, I will help however I can there as well."

"You're too good to me," I whisper and there's a voice so loud begging me to tell him that I love him. That this is more to me than what we said it was.

"I'm fixing it," he says, steel in his eyes. "Tell me about the loan companies. Do you have the information, or is there someone I need to call to get it?"

"I…I have all the information. I've been helping Kenzie with these for years." I manage to get up out of my seat and get my phone, then scroll through my inbox until I've found the ones with the account numbers.

Graham is still seated next to me and he sees. He takes his own phone out rather than taking mine. He doesn't dial the number of the service department at the student loan servicer. He calls the president of the company, at home, after business hours. He tells me to eat, kissing my forehead before disappearing into the back office.

How could I possibly eat? I push the food around on the plate praying, all the while hoping, I can text my cousin that she doesn't have to worry any longer. She only moved out there because I convinced her to follow her dreams. I set her up for failure like I did myself. If Graham can fix this, I will owe him more than just a blow job or anal.

Kenzie's loans are gone in less than twenty minutes, vanished into thin air.

Then he moves on to my aunt's medical bills. That takes closer to thirty minutes, because some of the bills have gone into collections.

Those are gone before I can finish my glass of wine. I'm practically dizzy with disbelief. I know he's wealthy. Wealthier than my ex and wealthier than most. But I didn't realize just how much money he had.

I can't stop thanking him and I don't even know how to tell Kenzie or my aunt.

"I told you this would be easy for me to do and that I wanted to do it."

Finally, Graham puts his phone face down on the table, and I put mine down, too. It's like the weight of the world has been lifted off my shoulders. I've been worrying about my cousin for so long that I can't remember what it's like *not* to worry about her.

"Graham, I don't know how I could ever repay you."

"I'm not asking you to," he tells me, and my gaze drops to my plate. I'm grateful but I also feel so inadequate.

"I wish there was something I could do," I finally manage.

"I will settle for you telling me that you will spend this week with me in this apartment and you will keep me company."

"For just this week?"

"For this week, in my penthouse. Not going to your apartment," he adds as if that stipulation would make the deal somehow harder to accept.

"Just be with you…for the week?" I ask him.

"Just be with me," he answers, and I take a steadying inhale.

"I would stay with you regardless."

"And I would pay those bills regardless as well. So we can call it even."

My bottom lip drops slightly and I remind myself that this is real life. That this man I have fallen for is better than any dream. He is more than any picture-perfect catalog man I could have sold my soul to Satan for.

"You know you're my hero don't you?" I whisper, my fingers playing with the stem of the glass.

"You don't know how happy that makes me to hear. Madelyn, I am fairly certain I…"

My shoulders straighten at his hesitation, "You what?"

"That I…have caught feelings for you."

"I don't know what you mean," I whisper not because I don't, but because I don't believe he's saying it. Is he says he loves me?

"Yes, you do." His face has never looked so open. "It was never just sex for me. I don't care about your rent money. I don't care about any problem you could ever have with money. I don't care how much you need, or how much you want."

He pauses, and my heart beats faster. "What do you care about, then?"

"I care about being with you," he says. "So be with me. Stay with me. That's all I want."

"Do you love me, Graham?" I ask him cautiously, my heart beating wildly.

"I think I've loved you since the first moment I saw you, my little temptress."

The world moves slower as if something perfect has just slipped into place and all I can do is look him in the eyes and tell him the truth. "I love you too."

chapter 15

Graham

One month later

I MADE SURE TO BOOK DINNER AT THE SAME RESTAURANT WE WENT TO before. Afterall, last time went wonderfully and I know it impressed my Madelyn. Only this time my friends have reserved a larger table.

We have more two guests this time.

I flew in Maddie's aunt and cousin, and they stood in the airport lobby and hugged her and cried for almost ten minutes straight. It was the most touching thing I've ever seen, although incredibly uncomfortable to be surrounded by three crying women.

It was the least I could do given everything I've been told.

It's easy to see the family resemblance in all their faces. Some of that resemblance is down to relief, I think. From what Maddie explained, they've been going through a hard time for years.

It makes my chest ache to see them sitting at the table, eyes bright and smiling, because I never got to do this for my parents. Paying it forward to Maddie's family is the next best thing. There's no point in everything I've worked for and everything I've built if there's no one to share it with. It's all I can think as they chat away, sharing stories and telling me all about Madelyn as a little girl. The drive is easy, and I imagine the weekend is going to go exactly as I planned.

"We couldn't get you to bring a date ever and then you bring one and now three," Brian jokes as we walk in. Hugs are given all around and the four of us sit at the far end of the table.

After introductions, appetizers, and small talk, the conversation turns to us. To Madelyn and me.

Kenzie asks, her eyes shining as she looks at her cousin. "Did you know he was going to fall in love with you when you first kissed him?"

Maddie hesitates, her nose wrinkling with an adorable grin. I know she's going to say *no*. She couldn't have known anything. And that first kiss, that first night… it was a one-time reckless thing that could have ruined everything.

"You know what?" The table has fallen silent, and all my friends—my family—are waiting for her answer. "I think I might have felt that. But that was the first time I saw him, not when we…" She lets the sentence remain unfinished.

"What?" Julie says, truly curious. "The first time you saw him? When was that?"

"In an elevator." Maddie leans farther into my arm with a little shake of her head. "I was coming home from a dinner with my…well, with my ex-fiancé. He had proposed, and it was supposed to be one of the happiest days of my life."

Scott looks at me with wide eyes from his side of the table.

I mouth *shut up* at him.

"And I was happy." Maddie sounds thoughtful, like it was decades ago that I first saw her in that elevator. "I was excited, but…something was off about it. I was trying to convince myself that both of us were tired from the evening, and that's why he…I don't know. I just knew something wasn't right."

"He was such a fucking dick," Kenzie says quietly and her mother scolds her, smacking her gently with the cloth napkin.

"He wasn't the best," Maddie agrees. "So we were going up to the eighth floor, and the elevator stopped and then the doors opened, and Graham got on."

"Oooh," Julie says, then covers her mouth with her hands. "This is getting scandalous." I clear my throat and ignore her innocence.

"I just…" Maddie wriggles her shoulders a little. "I felt it. I felt *something*, looking at him, and I was barely even looking. I was mostly looking at him in the reflection on the doors. It probably seems crazy, but when his elbow touched mine, I—"

"Fell head over heels for him?" Scott asks.

"Yeah sure, something like that," Maddie says shrugging it off, and everybody at the table laughs.

"That's a fairy tale," Julie says, her fingers linked under her chin. "That's true love at first sight."

Maddie's eyes shine. "Yeah, I think it might have been."

I thought about Maddie for six long months after that single elevator ride. I'm not the kind of man who puts a lot of stock in fate and destiny, but when she opened the door to her apartment—when it was *her* and not some random woman I'd never seen before—I knew that was my chance. You don't get many second chances in life.

I couldn't admit it to myself at the time, but I'd have gone for her, fiancé or not. I might have tried to put it off and deny what I felt, but it wouldn't have lasted.

There was something in that moment, trapped in that elevator with her, that changed me. Some piece of her fit perfectly with some piece of me, and I would have forever felt I was missing something if I hadn't found her again.

Dinner is served and the conversation at the table moves on to Kenzie's new classes. I set her up with an academic counselor in Chicago who was able to piece together her unfinished degrees and come up with a plan to finish both of them in two semesters. She talks about her projects and the inspiration she feels when she attends classes and how she's already made strong connections with several professors, which will come in handy when she goes job hunting. Just listening to her talk about all of her plans and how optimistic she is and how ready to take on the world she is…I know every penny was worth it.

Her aunt is doing very well, too. The medical bills had been a crushing weight on her, making it hard to recover from her treatments. Now that they're gone, Maddie says she's doing better than ever. She gets teary whenever she gets good news from her aunt.

And, just to make sure there are no more nasty surprises when it comes to hospitals, I've gone behind the scenes and made sure Maddie's aunt will never be turned away from any specialist she needs. She's not to see a single bill.

It's almost hard to imagine this table without Maddie. Her cousin fits here. Her aunt fits here. It's like they've always belonged here. I just didn't know anyone was missing.

It's tempting to bask in it for the rest of the evening. It wouldn't be so bad if we all just enjoyed ourselves without a big surprise event.

But what's the fun in that, if you have the most important question of your life to ask?

The conversation flows easily, with lots of laughter and inside jokes and explanations so that nobody's left out.

"Graham," Julie asks. "I was going to ask you. Did you close on that property?"

"Of course I closed on the property." I flash a smile across the table at her. "Did you think I gave up?"

"I heard things got a little dicey at the end."

"Harlan just needed some…strong encouragement."

He'd signed the contract to sell me the property while I was taking care of Kenzie's medical bills. The signed document showed up in my email, and he's been a delight to work with ever since.

I tell them, already looking forward to the new penthouse my little temptress is helping design, "Renovations on the building start next week, and it's going to be incredible when it's done." Turns out she has a passion for interior design and spending my money. Both of which are suiting her well and I'm enjoying it just as much as she is.

It's only when the night is coming to a close that I feel the nerves pick up. The waiters come in to take the dinner dishes away in preparation for coffee and dessert, and the conversation naturally lulls as they lean in, stacking plates and silverware and whisking it all away.

When they straighten up again, I pick up my drink and stand.

With a steadying breath, then another, I take in my friends who exchange meaningful looks with each other. I want to tell them all to cool it, to *relax*, but I can't say anything. Maddie looks up at me, her doe eyes bright with anticipation. She glances over at my friends with raised eyebrows, like they might give her some clue about what's going to happen, but they just look back at her with equally excited expressions.

"Madelyn," I start and stare into her eyes even as her mouth drops open. "From the first moment I saw you, I couldn't get you out of my head." Both of her hands cover her mouth and her eyes turn glassy.

Kenzie squeals, and Madelyn's aunt shushes her. Out of the corner of my eye, I can see them gripping each other's hands.

"I thought about you every day for six months after I got out of that elevator. The second I stepped out, I regretted doing it. I wanted to know more about you, and somewhere deep down, I knew there was something there I needed in my life."

Maddie's eyes shine with tears.

"I have to be completely honest with you. I've never been happier that someone couldn't pay the rent."

Affectionate laughter goes up around the table.

"I've told you this before, and I'll tell the entire world. There has never been anyone who made me feel what I feel for you. I wanted to be near you anyway I could. I still want to be with you in any way that I can."

Maddie keeps her eyes on me, and I want to remember her like this forever. She's pleased and content and in love, and I can't believe it took me so much of my life to look for this.

Then again, maybe it took me so long because she had to be in the right place at the right time.

Fine. Maybe I am the kind of man who believes in fate and destiny. I'll believe in anything that brought Maddie to me. My only wish is that my parents were here to see that I found someone like her. Someone to share my life with. Someone to help me through the dark times. Someone I can help through the dark times. I think somewhere, somehow, they know.

"I love you," I say and bend down on one knee, pulling the ring out of my pocket and presenting the diamond to her. "I want to spend the rest of our lives together so I can take care of you, make you happy, and be your husband. Will you marry me?"

She stands up out of her seat, tears running down her cheeks, throws her arms around my neck, and kisses me.

We're instantly surrounded by cheers. Her lips on mine is everything I need.

"Is that a yes, then?" Kenzie shouts and only then does she pull back from the kiss and looks me in the eyes.

Technically, she hasn't said *yes* yet. Not with her words. Technically, these are the last moments she'll spend as my girlfriend instead of my fiancée.

They're absolutely beautiful.

And what's to come is going to be *stunning*. I can't wait for all of it. Marrying her. Loving her forever. Being by her side for as long as I can.

I couldn't have earned a better deal than that if I worked every single minute for the rest of my life. I can only accept her for the gift that she is.

My Madelyn leans in, her lips close to mine, gives me a light kiss that feels like a promise, and whispers. "Yes."

Graham

Five months ago…after a frantic call.

THE DOOR OPENS AND IT'S HER. THE WOMAN FROM THE ELEVATOR. Same dark hair. Same dark eyes.

And now I know that it's her voice I like.

My head turns foggy with all the thoughts I've had of her for the last two months as she invites me into her apartment.

The scent of her in the air is the same, if a bit more subtle, and for a few seconds she's all I can see.

My gaze instantly flies to the rest of the room. Expecting to see the man on the lease. Expecting to see the man she was with in the elevator.

The door closes and the place is silent. She's all by herself, petite and gorgeous. And seemingly nervous.

The way she spoke on the phone says she needs something, and it's likely on her boyfriend's behalf, too.

Her husband's.

Whoever he is.

The flush in her cheeks and her wide eyes are all the confirmation I need that she recognizes me, too. Her breathing quickens.

It takes great effort to keep my gaze on her eyes and not lower it. That's…not a thought I should ever have about a woman who lives here with someone else. A woman who hasn't been thinking about me as I have her, I'm sure.

I have the thought anyway. What the hell can anybody expect me to do? She's gorgeous, and she needs *something*.

And, from the look on her face, she's glad to see me.

She shakes her head, recovering. "Oh! We've met before. Or…I saw you in the elevator before."

I flash her an even and professional smile, and she smiles back in response, looking even lovelier than she did before. Then I offer her my hand. "Graham Maxwell."

She takes it, her hand feeling small and delicate in mine, but her touch is electric. It's exactly as it was when I brushed against her in the elevator. I shouldn't have felt anything.

"Maddie." She looks down at our hands and swallows, then drops her hand. "Please. Come in. Can I offer you anything to drink?"

"I think we'd better cut to the chase." Because if I have to stand here with her, looking at her, drinking her in, I'm going to do something foolish. "On the phone, you said you had an…urgent problem to discuss."

Her blush gets deeper and that color on her…fate is tempting me to be a lesser man. "Let's sit down. Is that okay?"

She could ask me for anything right now, and fiancé or not, husband or not, I'd give it to her. I can't explain why. I just know that it would feel absolutely right. "Lead the way."

She takes me through the apartment. It's done in understated neutrals with pops of color in the furniture and throw pillows. Maddie gestures toward a sitting area by the picture window in the living room. From here, we can see a long stretch of the city. It's an expensive view, and it's worth every penny. She lowers herself gracefully into a loveseat. I take an armchair across from her.

Maddie watches me.

"The emergency," I prompt.

She sits up straight, her chin coming up like she's about to go into battle. "Right. Yes. First, I wanted to apologize for the inconvenience. I know you're very busy."

"It's nothing. Tell me what's wrong."

Tell me what's wrong so I can fix it. There's no reason I should feel this drawn to a woman who's already taken. I need to get the hell out of here as quickly as I can. She's nothing but a temptress.

"I'd like to speak to you about the rent."

That's…not what I expected her to say.

"The rent for this apartment?"

"I'm sure, in a place like this…" She bites at her lip, fumbling for her next words. "I know you're probably not the one people come to about problems like this, but it's the weekend. I was up all night."

She sure as hell doesn't look like she was up all night. Maddie Cunnigham looks like she floated down from a cloud in heaven after a perfect night's sleep. The only sign that anything's wrong is the worry in her eyes.

"What's the problem with the rent?" I ask.

"I can't pay it. I can't pay all of it. This is my home, it's the only thing I have right now, and I can't quite cover the rent for this month."

Her breath comes shorter, and it all makes sense, how urgent she was on the phone.

"Your husband can't cover it?"

She twists her hands together, and I let mine curl into loose fists. I'm not going to touch her. I swear, I'm not going to touch her.

"He wasn't my husband, actually," she says. "He was my fiancé, but he's not anymore. We're over. He left."

Is that right?

"Without leaving enough money to cover the rent? The kind of people who live in this building have second homes in Europe."

Maddie looks at me, her eyes painfully hopeful. "He was that kind of person. He was going to be, anyway, but I'm not. I hope you know that this isn't a long-term problem. I have a plan to fix it, I just need more time because I wasn't prepared for this. If I go to him, I'm sure he'll simply end the lease, and there's nothing around here that I can afford and that's available. I've been off the market for a couple of years, so it's taking me longer than I thought to find a job."

"Off the market?" Fuck my cock hardens in an instant. *The fuck is wrong with me?*

"Out of the job market. My ex thought it would be better for his career if I focused on philanthropy instead of building my own career, so that's what I did. And I don't regret it. I helped a lot of people, but I'm at a loss at the moment. I paid everything but the five hundred and everyone said that I needed to talk to you."

"What's the exact situation with the rent, Maddie? You can't afford any of it?"

"No, I can afford most of it. I'm five hundred dollars short. And I'll give you anything you want to cover it."

I have to get up and walk out. Her words are a wet dream, and I'd take them in a heartbeat.

She has no idea about the thoughts coming through my head.

"*Anything*," she insists.

So I look her in the eye. "We can come to an arrangement."

"Oh, thank you. Thank you so much. What kind of arrangement?"

"I have an idea," I say, intent on extending the payment date or halving her rent. I can barely think though, with the thoughts of her telling me "anything" as if I could simply have anything from her.

My gaze drops to her breasts and I have to admit, I would take whatever she offered.

"If you want me, you can have me however you'd like."

Fuck, this is not something I ever thought I'd do, but the way she's looking at me and the way she makes me feel… Before I can stop myself, I agree to what she's suggesting.

"What exactly is it that you have in mind?"

"I think…I'm not sure. I haven't…"

A moment passes and then I offer in desperation, "A quick fuck then?"

Instantly I regret it. *Quick?* What the fuck was I thinking? And just once?

"You really want me?" she questions, and I can't believe I have any ability to hide it.

"From the moment I saw you in that elevator."

Thank you so much for reading my romances. I'm just a stay at home mom and avid reader turned author and I couldn't be happier.

I hope you love my books as much as I do!

More by Willow Winters
WWW.WILLOWWINTERSWRITES.COM/BOOKS